'**Magnificent** . . . chronicle of small-town America, and the battle between good and evil. **Classic King, and clearly written with joy** . . . He is **one of the best writers on childhood and teenagers**'

Richard Osman, *The Sunday Times*

'**King's delight in the world he has created is infectious** . . . there's much to revel in here'

Daily Telegraph

'Stephen King is **the world's greatest storyteller**. *Fairy Tale* had me enchanted from page one. I remain in total awe at his genius'

David Walliams

'**A blazing flash of creativity** . . . King's best book in over a decade'

Esquire

'A trip to **a magical, terrifying land where wonders and horrors are one**. But also a trip

he into

he King'

PRAISE FOR FAIRY TALE

'Because it's Stephen King's, it's a Once-Upon-A-Time tale like no other' – *Daily Mail*

'A page-turner driven by memorably strange encounters and well-rendered, often thrilling action' – *New York Times Book Review*

'A spellbinding tale that bursts with imagination' – *Woman's Own*

'Brilliantly written escapism . . . King at his finest' – *Evening Standard*

'Wickedly haunting' – *i*

PRAISE FOR FAIRY TALE

'*Fairy Tale* is vintage, timeless King, a transporting, terrifying treat born from multiple lockdowns which, in true King style, puts its finger right on that tender point which is the threshold between childhood and growing up' – *Guardian*

'A dark, dazzlingly inventive fantasy novel' – *Daily Mirror*

'The book bursts with creativity . . . A profound story of good vs. evil that's timeless and timely . . . life-affirming . . . After turning that last page, you'll feel a little stronger in spirit, yearn for another story and, dare we say, maybe even live happily ever after' – *USA Today*

'Scary, original and thrilling, King never disappoints' – *Sun*

THE INSPIRATION for *Fairy Tale* came from a question King asked himself at the beginning of the pandemic: what could he write that would make him happy?

'As if my imagination had been waiting for the question to be asked,' he says, 'I saw a vast deserted city – deserted but alive. I saw the empty streets, the haunted buildings, a gargoyle head lying overturned in the street. I saw smashed statues (of what I didn't know, but I eventually found out). I saw a huge, sprawling palace with glass towers so high their tips pierced the clouds. Those images released the story I wanted to tell.'

ABOUT THE AUTHOR

Photograph copyright © Shane Leonard

STEPHEN KING is the author of more than seventy books, all of them worldwide bestsellers, including *The Institute*, *Sleeping Beauties* (co-written with Owen King) and *The Dark Tower* series.

Many of his titles are the basis for major motion pictures, TV series and streamed events, including *IT*, *Stand By Me* (adapted from *The Body*) and *The Shawshank Redemption*, which is IMDb's top-rated movie of all time.

King is the recipient of *The Sunday Times* Award for Literary Excellence 2022, the 2020 Audio Publishers Association Lifetime Achievement Award, the 2018 PEN America Literary Service Award, the 2014 National Medal of Arts, and the 2003 National Book Foundation Medal for Distinguished Contribution to American Letters. He lives in Maine, with his wife, novelist Tabitha King.

By Stephen King and published by Hodder & Stoughton

NOVELS:

Carrie
'Salem's Lot
The Shining
The Stand
The Dead Zone
Firestarter
Cujo
Cycle of the Werewolf
Christine
Pet Sematary
IT
The Eyes of the Dragon
Misery
The Tommyknockers
The Dark Half
Needful Things
Gerald's Game
Dolores Claiborne
Insomnia
Rose Madder
Desperation
Bag of Bones
The Girl Who Loved Tom Gordon
Dreamcatcher
From a Buick 8
Cell
Lisey's Story
Duma Key
Under the Dome
11.22.63
Doctor Sleep
Mr Mercedes
Revival
Finders Keepers
End of Watch
Sleeping Beauties (with Owen King)
The Outsider
Elevation
The Institute
Billy Summers
Fairy Tale
The Dark Tower I: The Gunslinger
The Dark Tower II: The Drawing of the Three
The Dark Tower III: The Waste Lands
The Dark Tower IV: Wizard and Glass
The Dark Tower V: Wolves of the Calla
The Dark Tower VI: Song of Susannah
The Dark Tower VII: The Dark Tower
The Wind through the Keyhole: A Dark Tower Novel

As Richard Bachman

Thinner
The Running Man
The Bachman Books
The Regulators
Blaze

STORY COLLECTIONS:

Night Shift
Different Seasons
Skeleton Crew
Four Past Midnight
Nightmares and Dreamscapes
Hearts in Atlantis
Everything's Eventual
Just After Sunset
Stephen King Goes to the Movies
Full Dark, No Stars
The Bazaar of Bad Dreams
If It Bleeds

NON-FICTION:

Danse Macabre
On Writing (A Memoir of the Craft)

STEPHEN KING

FAIRY TALE

A NOVEL

HODDER

First published in Great Britain in 2022 by Hodder & Stoughton
An Hachette UK company

This paperback edition published in 2023

A Hodder Paperback

1

Illustrations by Gabriel Rodriguez (odd number chapters and epilogue) and Nicolas Delort (even number chapters)

A CIP catalogue record for this title is available from the British Library

A format ISBN 978 1 399 71777 9
B format ISBN 978 1 399 70545 5
eBook ISBN 978 1 399 70543 1

Typeset in Bembo by Palimpsest Book Production Limited, Falkirk, Stirlingshire

Printed and bound in Great Britain by
Clays Ltd, Elcograf S.p.A.

Hodder & Stoughton policy is to use papers that are natural, renewable and recyclable products and made from wood grown in sustainable forests. The logging and manufacturing processes are expected to conform to the environmental regulations of the country of origin.

Hodder & Stoughton Ltd
Carmelite House
50 Victoria Embankment
London EC4Y 0DZ

www.hodder.co.uk

Thinking of REH, ERB, and, of course, HPL

'And always let your conscience be your guide.'
– Blue Fairy

CHAPTER ONE

The Goddam Bridge.

The Miracle. The Howling.

1

I'm sure I can tell this story. I'm also sure no one will believe it. That's fine with me. Telling it will be enough. My problem – and I'm sure many writers have it, not just newbies like me – is deciding where to start.

My first thought was with the shed, because that's where my adventures really began, but then I realized I would have to tell about Mr Bowditch first, and how we became close. Only that never would have happened except for the miracle that happened to my father. A very ordinary miracle you could say, one that's happened to many thousands of men and women since 1935, but it seemed like a miracle to a kid.

Only that isn't the right place, either, because I don't think my father would have needed a miracle if it hadn't been for that goddamned bridge. So that's where I need to start, with the goddamned Sycamore Street Bridge. And now, thinking of those things, I see a clear thread leading up through the years to Mr Bowditch and the padlocked shed behind his ramshackle old Victorian.

But a thread is easy to break. So not a thread but a chain. A strong one. And I was the kid with the shackle clamped around his wrist.

2

The Little Rumple River runs through the north end of Sentry's Rest (known to the locals as Sentry), and until the year 1996, the year I was born, it was spanned by a wooden bridge. That was the year the state inspectors from the Department of Highway Transportation looked it over and deemed it unsafe. People in our part of Sentry had known that since '82, my father said. The bridge was posted for ten thousand pounds, but townies with a fully loaded pickup truck mostly steered clear of it, opting for the turnpike extension, which was an annoying and time-consuming detour. My dad said you could feel the planks shiver and shake and rumble under you even in a car. It was dangerous, the state inspectors were right about that, but here's the irony: if the old wooden bridge had never been replaced by one made of steel, my mother might still be alive.

The Little Rumple really is little, and putting up the new bridge didn't take long. The wooden span was demolished and the new one was opened to traffic in April of 1997.

'The mayor cut a ribbon, Father Coughlin blessed the goddam thing, and that was that,' my father said one night. He was pretty drunk at the time. 'Wasn't much of a blessing for us, Charlie, was it?'

It was named the Frank Ellsworth Bridge, after a hometown hero who died in Vietnam, but the locals just called it the Sycamore Street Bridge. Sycamore Street was paved nice and smooth on both sides, but the bridge deck – one hundred and forty-two feet long – was steel grating that made a humming sound when cars went over it and a rumble when trucks used it – which they could do, because the bridge was now rated at sixty thousand pounds. Not big enough for a loaded semi, but long-haulers never used Sycamore Street, anyway.

There was talk every year in the town council about paving the deck and adding at least one sidewalk, but every year it seemed like there were other places where the money was needed more urgently. I don't think a sidewalk would have saved my mother, but paving might have. There's no way to know, is there?

That goddam bridge.

3

We lived halfway up the long length of Sycamore Street Hill, about a quarter of a mile from the bridge. There was a little gas-and-convenience store on the other side called Zip Mart. It sold all the usual stuff, from motor oil to Wonder Bread to Little Debbie cakes, but it also sold fried chicken made by the proprietor, Mr Eliades (known to the neighborhood as Mr Zippy). That chicken was exactly what the sign in the window said: THE BEST IN THE LAND. I can still remember how tasty it was, but I never ate a single piece after my mom died. I would have gagged it up if I tried.

One Saturday in November of 2003 – the town council still discussing paving the bridge and still deciding it could wait another year – my mother told us she was going to walk down to the Zippy and get us fried chicken for dinner. My father and I were watching a college football game.

'You should take the car,' Dad said. 'It's going to rain.'

'I need the exercise,' Mom said, 'but I'll wear my Little Red Riding Hood raincoat.'

And that's what she was wearing the last time I saw her. The hood wasn't up because it wasn't raining yet, so her hair was spilling over her shoulders. I was seven years old, and thought my mother had the world's most beautiful red hair. She saw me looking at her through the window and waved. I waved back, then turned my attention to the TV, where LSU was driving. I wish I had looked longer, but I don't blame myself. You never know where the trapdoors are in your life, do you?

It wasn't my fault, and it wasn't Dad's fault, although I know he blamed himself, thought *if only I'd gotten up off my dead ass and given her a ride to the damn store*. It probably wasn't the fault of the man in the plumbing truck, either. The cops said he was sober, and he swore he was keeping to the speed limit, which was 25 in our residential zone. Dad said that even if that were true, the man must have taken his eyes off the road, if only for a few seconds. Dad was probably right about that. He was an insurance claims adjuster, and he told me once that the only pure accident he ever heard of was a man in Arizona who was killed when a meteor hit him in the head.

'There's always someone at fault,' Dad said. 'Which is not the same as blame.'

'Do you blame the man who hit Mom?' I asked.

He thought about it. Raised his glass to his lips and drank. This was six or eight months after Mom died, and he'd pretty much given up on beer. By then he was strictly a Gilbey's man.

'I try not to. And mostly I can do that unless I wake up at two in the morning with nobody in the bed but me. Then I blame him.'

4

Mom walked down the hill. There was a sign where the sidewalk ended. She walked past the sign and crossed the bridge. By then it was getting dark and starting to drizzle. She went into the store, and Irina Eliades (of course known as Mrs Zippy) told her more chicken was coming out in three minutes, five at the most. Somewhere on Pine Street, not far from our house, the plumber had just finished his last job of that Saturday and was putting his toolbox in the back of his panel van.

The chicken came out, hot and crispy and golden. Mrs Zippy boxed up an eight-piece and gave Mom an extra wing to eat on her walk home. Mom thanked her, paid, and stopped to look at the magazine rack. If she hadn't done that, she might have made it all the way across the bridge – who knows? The plumber's van must have been turning onto Sycamore Street and starting down the mile-long hill while Mom was checking out the latest issue of *People*.

She put it back, opened the door, and spoke to Mrs Zippy over her shoulder: 'Have a nice night.' She might have cried out when she saw the van was going to hit her, and God knows what she might have been thinking, but those were the last words she ever spoke. She went out. The rain was coming down cold and steady by then, silvery lines in the glow of the one streetlight on the Zip Mart side of the bridge.

Munching on her chicken wing, my mother walked onto the steel deck. Headlights picked her out and threw her shadow long behind her. The plumber passed the sign on the other side, the one that reads BRIDGE SURFACE FREEZES BEFORE ROAD! PLEASE USE

CAUTION! Was he looking in his rearview mirror? Maybe checking for messages on his phone? He said no to both, but when I think of what happened to her that night, I always think of my dad saying the only pure accident he ever heard of was the man who took a meteor to the head.

There was plenty of room; the steel bridge was quite a bit wider than the wooden version had been. The problem was that steel grating. He saw my mother halfway across the bridge and hit the brake, not because he was speeding (or so he said) but out of pure instinct. The steel surface had started to freeze. The panel truck skidded and slued, starting to come sideways. My mother shrank against the bridge rail, dropping her little piece of chicken. The panel truck slued further, struck her, and sent her spinning along the rail like a top. I don't want to think about the parts of her that were torn off in that death-spin, but I'm helpless not to sometimes. All I know is that the nose of the panel truck finally drove her into a bridge stanchion near the Zip Mart side of the bridge. Part of her went into the Little Rumple. Most of her stayed on the bridge.

I carry a picture of us in my wallet. I was maybe three when it was taken. She's got me on her hip. One of my hands is in her hair. She had beautiful hair.

5

Shitty Christmas that year. You better believe it.

I remember the reception after the funeral. It was at our house. My father was there, greeting people and accepting condolences, and then he was gone. I asked his brother, my Uncle Bob, where he was. 'He had to lie down,' Uncle Bob said. 'He was really worn out, Charlie. Why don't you go outside and play?'

I had never felt less like playing in my life, but I went outside. I passed a bunch of grownups who had come outside to smoke and I heard one of them say *poor guy, drunk as a skunk*. Even then, deep in grief for my mother, I knew who they were talking about.

Before Mom died, my father was what I'd call 'a regular drinker.' I was just a little kid in the second grade, so I suppose you have to take that with a grain of salt, but I stand by it. I never heard him slurring, he didn't stumble around the place, he didn't go out to bars, and he never laid a hand on me or my mother. He would come home with his briefcase and Mom would give him a drink, usually a martini. She'd have one, too. In the evening, while we were watching TV, he might have a couple of beers. That was it.

All that changed after the goddam bridge. He was drunk after the funeral (*as a skunk*), drunk on Christmas, and drunk on New Year's Eve (which, I found out later, people like him call Amateur Night). In the weeks and months after we lost her, he was drunk most of the time. Mostly at home. He still didn't go out to bars at night ('Too many assholes like me,' he said once), and he still never laid a hand on me, but the booze was out of control. I know that now; then I just accepted it. Kids do that. Dogs, too.

I found myself getting my own breakfast two mornings a week, then four, then almost all the time. I'd eat Alpha-Bits or Apple Jacks in the kitchen and hear him snoring in the bedroom – great big motorboat snores. Sometimes he forgot to shave before leaving for work. After dinner (more and more that was take-out), I'd hide his car keys. If he needed a fresh bottle, he could walk down to the Zippy and get one. Sometimes I worried about him meeting a car on the goddam bridge, but not too much. I was sure (*pretty* sure, at least) that both of my parents couldn't possibly get wiped out in the same place. My dad worked in insurance, and I knew what actuarial tables were: figuring the odds.

He was good at his job, my dad, and he skated along for over three years in spite of his boozing. Did he get warnings at work? I don't know, but probably. Was he pulled over for driving erratically, once the drinking started in the afternoon? If he was, maybe he was let off with a warning. Make that probably, because he knew all the cops in town. Dealing with cops was part of his job.

There was a rhythm to our lives during those three years. Maybe not a good rhythm, not the sort you'd want to dance to, but one I could count on. I'd get home from school around three. My father would roll in around five, with a few drinks already under his belt and on his breath (he didn't go out to the bars at night, but I found out later he was a regular at Duffy's Tavern on his way home from the office). He'd bring a pizza, or tacos, or Chinese from Joy Fun.

Some nights he'd forget and we'd order out . . . or rather, I would. And after dinner the real drinking would start. Mostly gin. Other stuff if the gin was gone. Some nights he fell asleep in front of the TV. Some nights he'd stumble into the bedroom, leaving his shoes and rumpled suitcoat for me to put away. Once in awhile I'd wake up and hear him crying. It's pretty awful to hear that in the middle of the night.

The crash came in 2006. It was summer vacation. I had a Shrimp League game at ten in the morning – hit two home runs and made an awesome catch. I came home just after noon and found my father already there, sitting in his chair and staring at the TV, where old-time movie stars were having a duel on some castle stairs. He was in his undershorts and sipping a white drink that smelled to me like straight Gilbey's. I asked him what he was doing home.

Still looking at the swordfight and hardly slurring at all, he said: 'I seem to have lost my job, Charlie. Or, if I can quote Bobcat Goldthwait, I know where it is, but someone else is doing it. Or soon will be.'

I thought I didn't know what to say, but words came out of my mouth anyway. 'Because of your drinking.'

'I'm going to stop,' he said.

I just pointed at the glass. Then I went into my bedroom and shut the door and started to cry.

He knocked on my door. 'Can I come in?'

I didn't answer. I didn't want him to hear me blubbing.

'Come on, Charlie. I poured it down the sink.'

Like I didn't know the rest of the bottle would be on the kitchen counter. And another one in the liquor cabinet. Or two. Or three.

'Come on, Charlie, what do you say?' *Shay*. I hated the slur in his voice.

'Fuck you, Dad.'

I'd never said such a thing to him in my life, and I sort of wanted him to come in and give me a slap. Or a hug. Something, anyway. Instead I heard him shuffle into the kitchen, where the bottle of Gilbey's would be waiting.

He was asleep on the couch when I finally came out. The TV was still on, but muted. It was some other black-and-white movie, this one featuring old cars racing around what was obviously a movie set.

Dad always watched TCM when he was drinking, unless I was home and insisted on something else. The bottle was on the coffee table, mostly empty. I poured what was left down the sink. I opened the liquor cabinet and thought about pouring away everything else, but looking at the gin, the whiskey, the vodka nips, the coffee brandy – that just made me tired. You wouldn't think a ten-year-old could be tired like that, but I was.

I put a Stouffer's frozen dinner in the microwave for supper – Grandma's Chicken Bake, our favorite – and shook him awake while it was cooking. He sat up, looked around like he didn't know where he was, then started to make these horrible chugging sounds I'd never heard before. He weaved his way to the bathroom with his hands over his mouth and I heard him puking. It seemed to me like it would never stop, but eventually it did. The microwave binged. I got the Chicken Bake out, using the oven mitts that said GOOD COOKIN' on the left and GOOD EATIN' on the right – you forget to use those mitts once while you're taking something hot out of the zapper and you never forget again. I blopped some on our plates and then went into the living room, where Dad was sitting on the couch with his head down and his hands laced together on the back of his neck.

'Can you eat?'

He looked up. 'Maybe. If you bring me a couple of aspirin.'

The bathroom stank of gin and something else, maybe bean dip, but at least he'd gotten all of it in the bowl and flushed it away. I sprayed some Glade around, then brought him the aspirin bottle and a glass of water. He took three and put the glass where the bottle of Gilbey's had been. He looked up at me with an expression I'd never seen before, even after Mom died. I hate to say this, but I'm going to because it's what I thought then: it was the expression of a dog that has taken a shit on the floor.

'I could eat if you gave me a hug.'

I hugged him and said I was sorry for what I said.

'It's okay. Probably I deserved it.'

We went into the kitchen and ate as much of Grandma's Chicken Bake as we could manage, which wasn't very much. As he scraped our plates into the sink, he told me he was going to stop drinking, and that weekend he did. He told me that on Monday he was going to start looking for a job, but he didn't. He stayed home, watched old movies on TCM, and when I came home from baseball practice and noon swim at the Y, he was pretty much blotto.

He saw me looking at him and just shook his head. 'Tomorrow. Tomorrow. I absolutely promise.'

'I call bullshit,' I said, and went into my room.

6

That was the worst summer of my childhood. *Was it worse than after your mother died?* you could ask, and I'd say yes, because he was the only parent I had left and because it all seemed to be happening in slow motion.

He did make a halfhearted effort at job hunting the insurance biz, but nothing came of it, even when he shaved and bathed and dressed for success. Word gets around, I guess.

The bills came in and piled up on the table in the front hall, unopened. By him, at least. I was the one who opened them when the stack got too high. I put them in front of him and he wrote checks to cover them. I didn't know when those checks would start to bounce back marked INSUFFICIENT FUNDS, and didn't want to know. It was like standing on a bridge and imagining an out-of-control truck was skidding toward you. Wondering what your last thoughts would be before it squashed you to death.

He got a part-time job at the Jiffy Car Wash out by the turnpike extension. That lasted a week, then he either quit or got fired. He didn't tell me which and I didn't ask.

I made the All-Star Shrimp League team, but we got knocked out in the first two games of a double-elimination tournament. During the regular season I'd hit sixteen home runs, I was Star Market's best power hitter, but in those two games I struck out seven times, once at a ball in the dirt and once sucking for a pitch so far over my head I would have needed an elevator to make contact. Coach asked what was wrong with me and I said nothing, nothing, just leave me alone. I was doing bad shit, too – some with a friend, some on my own.

And not sleeping very well. I wasn't having nightmares like I did after my mother died, I just couldn't get to sleep, sometimes not until midnight or one in the morning. I started turning my clock around so I wouldn't have to look at the numbers.

I didn't exactly hate my father (although I'm sure I would have come to in time), but I felt contempt for him. *Weak, weak*, I'd think, lying in bed and listening to him snore. And of course I'd wonder what was going to happen to us. The car was paid for, which was good, but the house wasn't and the size of those payments was horrifying to me. How long before he couldn't make the monthly nut? That time would surely come, because the mortgage had another nine years to run, and there was no way the money would hold out that long.

Homeless, I thought. *The bank will take the house, like in* The Grapes of Wrath, *and we'll be homeless.*

I had seen homeless people downtown, plenty of them, and when I couldn't sleep my mind turned to them. I thought about those urban wanderers a lot. Wearing old clothes that bagged on their skinny bods or stretched on their corpulent ones. Sneakers held together with duct tape. Crooked glasses. Long hair. Crazy eyes. Boozy breath. I thought about us sleeping in our car down by the old trainyards or in the Walmart parking lot among the RVs. I thought of my father pushing a shopping cart full of all we had left. I always saw my bedside alarm clock in that basket. I don't know why that horrified me, but it did.

Pretty soon I'd be going back to school, homeless or not. Some of the kids on my team would probably start calling me Strike-Out Charlie. Which would be better than Juicer's Kid Charlie, but how long before that got into the mix? People on our street already knew that George Reade didn't go to work anymore, and they almost certainly knew why. I didn't kid myself about that.

We were never a churchgoing family, or religious at all in any conventional sense. Once I asked my mom why we didn't go to church – was it because she didn't believe in God? She told me that she did, but she didn't need a minister (or a priest, or a rabbi) to tell her how to believe in Him. She said she only needed to open her eyes and look around to do that. Dad said he was brought up a Baptist but quit going when his church got more interested in politics than the Sermon on the Mount.

But one night about a week before school was scheduled to start again, it came into my mind to pray. The urge was so strong it was really a compulsion. I got down on my knees beside my bed, folded my hands, squeezed my eyes shut, and prayed that my father would quit drinking. 'If you do that for me, whoever you are, I'll do something for you,' I said. 'Promise and hope to die if I don't keep it. You just show me what you want and I'll do it. I swear.'

Then I got back into bed, and that night, at least, I slept through until morning.

7

Before he was fired, Dad worked for Overland National Insurance. It's a big company. You've probably seen their ads, the ones with Bill and Jill, the talking camels. Very funny stuff. Dad used to say, 'All the insurance companies use ha-ha ads to get eyeballs, but the laughing stops once the insured files a claim. That's where I come in. I'm a claims *adjuster*, which means – nobody says it out loud – that I'm supposed to knock the contractual amount down. Sometimes I do, but here's a secret – I always start out on the claimant's side. Unless I find reasons not to be, that is.'

Overland's Midwest headquarters is on the outskirts of Chicago, in what Dad called Insurance Alley. In his commuting days it was just a forty-minute drive from Sentry, an hour if the traffic was heavy. There were at least a hundred claims adjusters working out of that one office, and on a day in September of '08 one of the agents he used to work with came to see him. Lindsey Franklin was his name. Dad called him Lindy. It was in the late afternoon, and I was at the kitchen table, doing my homework.

That day had gotten off to a memorably shitty start. The house still smelled faintly of smoke even though I'd sprayed around the Glade. Dad had decided to make omelets for breakfast. God knows why he was up at six A.M., or why he decided I needed an omelet, but he wandered away to use the bathroom or turn on the TV and forgot about what was on the stove. Still half-loaded from the night before, no doubt. I woke up to the bray of the smoke detector, ran into the kitchen in my underwear, and found smoke billowing up in a cloud. The thing in the frypan looked like a charred log.

I scraped it down the garbage disposer and ate Apple Jacks. Dad was still wearing an apron, which looked stupid. He tried to apologize and I mumbled something just to get him to shut up. What I remember about those weeks and months is that he was always trying to apologize and it drove me bugfuck.

But it was also a memorably good day, one of the best days, because of what happened that afternoon. You're probably way ahead of me on this, but I'll tell you anyway, because I never stopped loving my dad, even when I didn't like him, and this part of the story makes me happy.

Lindy Franklin worked for Overland. He was also a recovering alcoholic. He wasn't one of the claims agents who was particularly close to my father, probably because Lindy never stopped at Duffy's Tavern after work with the other guys. But he knew why my dad had lost his job, and he decided to do something about it. To give it a try, at least. He made what I later learned is called a Twelfth Step visit. He had a bunch of claims appointments in our town, and once he finished with those, he decided on the spur of the moment to stop by our place. He later said he almost changed his mind because he didn't have backup (recovering alcoholics usually make Twelfth Step visits with a partner, sort of like Mormons), but then he said what the hell and looked up our address on his phone. I don't like to think what might have happened to us if he'd decided not to. I never would have been inside Mr Bowditch's shed, that's for sure.

Mr Franklin was wearing a suit and tie. He had a sharp haircut. Dad – unshaven, shirt untucked, barefoot – introduced us. Mr Franklin shook my hand, said it was very nice to meet me, then asked if I minded going outside so he could speak to my father alone. I went willingly enough, but the windows were still open from the breakfast disaster and I heard quite a bit of what Mr Franklin said. I remember two things especially. Dad said the drinking was because he still missed Janey so much. And Mr Franklin said, 'If booze would bring her back, I'd say fine. But it won't, and how would she feel if she saw how you and your boy are living now?'

The other thing he said was, 'Aren't you sick and tired of being sick and tired?' That was when my father started to cry. Usually I hated it when he did that (*weak, weak*), but I thought maybe this crying was different.

8

You knew all that was coming, and probably you know the rest of the story as well. I'm sure you do if you're in recovery yourself or know someone who is. Lindy Franklin took Dad to an AA meeting that night. When they got back, Mr Franklin called his wife and said he was staying over with a friend. He slept on our pull-out couch and the next morning he took Dad to a seven A.M. meeting called Sober Sunrise. That became Dad's regular meeting and it was where he got his first-year AA medallion. I skipped school so I could give it to him, and that time I was the one who did some blubbing. No one seemed to mind; there's a lot of blubbing at those meetings. Dad gave me a hug afterward, and so did Lindy. By then I was calling him by his first name, because he was around a lot. He was my dad's sponsor in the program.

That was the miracle. I know a lot about AA now, and know it happens to men and women all over the world, but it still seemed like a miracle to me. Dad didn't get his first medallion exactly a year after Lindy's Twelfth Step call, because he had a couple of slips, but he owned up to them and the AA people said what they always say, keep coming back, and he did, and the last slip – a single beer from a sixpack he poured down the sink – was just before Halloween of 2009. When Lindy spoke at Dad's first anniversary, he said that lots of people get offered the program but never *get* the program. He said Dad was one of the lucky ones. Maybe that was true, maybe my prayer was just a coincidence, but I chose to believe it wasn't. In AA, you can choose to believe what you want. It's in what recovering alkies call the Big Book.

And I had a promise to keep.

9

The only meetings I went to were Dad's anniversary meetings, but as I say, Lindy was around a lot and I picked up most of the slogans AA people are always spouting. I liked *you can't turn a pickle back into a cucumber*, and *God don't make junk*, but the one that stuck with me – and does to this day – is something I heard Lindy tell Dad one night.

when Dad was talking about all the unpaid bills and how he was afraid of losing the house. Lindy said my father getting sober was a miracle. Then he added, 'But miracles ain't magic.'

Six months after sobering up, Dad reapplied at Overland, and with Lindy Franklin and some others backing him up – including his old boss, the one who pink-slipped him – he got his job back, but he was on probation and knew it. That made him work twice as hard. Then, in the fall of 2011 (two years sober), he had a discussion with Lindy that lasted so long that Lindy ended up sleeping on the pull-out couch again. Dad said he wanted to go independent, but he wouldn't do it without Lindy's blessing. After making sure that Dad wouldn't start drinking again if his new business failed – as sure as he could be, anyway; recovery ain't rocket science, either – Lindy told him to go ahead and take a shot.

Dad sat me down and explained what that meant: working without a net. 'So what do you think?'

'I think you should say adios to those talking camels,' I told him, and that made him laugh. Then I said what I had to. 'But if you start drinking again, you'll screw it up.'

Two weeks later he gave Overland his notice, and in February of 2012 he hung out his shingle in a tiny office on Main Street: George Reade Investigator and Independent Claims Adjuster.

He didn't spend much time in that hole-in-the-wall; mostly he was out pounding the pavement. He talked to cops, he talked to bail bondsmen ('Always good for leads,' he said), but mostly he talked to lawyers. A lot of them knew him from his work at Overland, and knew he was on the square. They gave him jobs – the tough ones, where the big companies were either drastically reducing the amount they were willing to pay or denying the claim altogether. He worked long, long hours. Most nights I came home to an empty house and cooked my own dinner. I didn't mind. At first when my dad finally did come in, I hugged him so I could surreptitiously smell his breath for the unforgettable aroma of Gilbey's Gin. After awhile, though, I just hugged him. And he rarely missed a Sober Sunrise meeting.

Sometimes Lindy would come to lunch on Sundays, usually bringing take-out, and the three of us would watch the Bears on TV, or the White Sox if it was baseball season. On one of those afternoons, my father said business was picking up every month. 'It would go faster if I got on the claimant's side more often in slip-and-fall cases, but so many of them smell bad.'

'Tell me about it,' Lindy said. 'You could make short-term gains, but in the end that work would bite you on the ass.'

Just before the start of my junior year at Hillview High, Dad said we had to have a serious talk. I braced myself for a lecture about underage drinking, or a discussion about some of the crap I and my friend Bertie Bird had gotten up to during (and – for awhile – after) his drinking years, but neither of those were what he had in mind. It was school he wanted to talk about. He told me I had to do well if I wanted to get into a good college. *Really* well.

'My business is going to work. It was scary at first, there was that time when I had to reach out to my brother for a loan, but that's almost paid back and I think I'll be on solid ground before long. The phone rings a lot. When it comes to college, though . . .' He shook his head. 'I don't think I'm going to be able to help you much, at least to start with. We're damn lucky to be solvent at all. Which is my fault. I'm doing everything I can to remedy the situation—'

'I know.'

'—but you need to help yourself. You need to *work*. You need to score high on the SATs when you take them.'

I planned to take the Scholastic Aptitude in December, but didn't say so. Dad was on a roll.

'You also need to think about loans, but only as a last resort – those loans'll haunt you for a long time. Think scholarships. And play your sports, that's also a road to scholarships, but mostly it's grades. Grades, grades, grades. I don't need to see you graduate valedictorian, but I need to see you in the top ten. Understand?'

'Yes, Father,' I said, and he gave me a playful swat.

10

I studied hard and made my grades. I played football in the fall and baseball in the spring. I made varsity in both sports as a sophomore. Coach Harkness wanted me to play basketball as well, but I told him no. I said I needed at least three months a year to do other things.

Coach went away shaking his head at the sad state of youth in this degenerate age.

I went to some dances. I kissed some girls. I made some good friends, most of them jocks but not all. I discovered some metal bands I liked and played them loud. My dad never protested, but he got me EarPods for Christmas. There were terrible things in my future – I'll tell you about them eventually – but none of the terrible things I had lain awake imagining ever came to pass. It was still our house and my key still unlocked the front door. That was good. If you've ever imagined you might wind up spending cold winter nights in a car or a homeless shelter, you know what I'm talking about.

And I never forgot the deal I made with God. *If you do that for me, I'll do something for you*, I'd said. On my knees I said it. *You just show me what you want and I'll do it. I swear.* It had been a child's prayer, so much magical thinking, but part of me (most of me) didn't believe that. Doesn't now. I thought my prayer had been answered, just like in one of those corny Lifetime movies they show between Thanksgiving and Christmas. Which meant I had my end of the bargain to hold up. I felt that if I didn't, God would take back the miracle and my dad would start drinking again. You have to keep in mind that high school kids – no matter how big the boys, no matter how beautiful the girls – are still mostly children inside.

I tried. In spite of days not just crammed with school and after-school activities but bulging with them, I did my best to pay back what I owed.

I joined a Key Club Adopt-A-Highway commitment. We got two miles of Highway 226, which is basically a wasteland of fast food joints, motels, and gas stations. I must have picked up a bazillion Big Mac boxes, two bazillion beer cans, and at least a dozen pairs of castoff undies. One Halloween I put on a stupid orange jumper and went around collecting for UNICEF. In the summer of 2012, I sat at a voter registration table downtown, although I was still a year and a half from being old enough to vote myself. I also helped out at my dad's office on Fridays after practice, filing papers and doing computer input stuff – your basic scutwork – as it grew dark outside and we ate pizza from Giovanni's straight out of the box.

Dad said all that stuff would look great on my college apps, and I agreed without telling him that wasn't why I was doing it. I didn't want God deciding I wasn't holding up my end, but sometimes I thought I could hear a heavenly whisper of disapproval: *Not good enough, Charlie. Do you really think picking up roadside trash is payback for the good life you and your father are living now?*

Which brings me – finally – to April of 2013, the year I was seventeen. And Mr Bowditch.

11

Good old Hillview High! Seems like a long time ago to me now. In the winter I rode the bus, sitting at the back with Andy Chen, a friend of mine since elementary. Andy was a jock who went on to play basketball for Hofstra. Bertie was gone by then, moved away. Which was kind of a relief. There is such a thing as a good friend who is also a bad friend. In truth, Bertie and I were bad for each other.

In the fall and spring, I rode my bike because we live in a hilly town and biking was a good way to build up muscle strength in my legs and backside. It also gave me time to think and be alone, which I liked. Heading home from HHS it was Plain Street to Goff Avenue, then Willow Street to Pine. Pine Street intersected with Sycamore at the top of the hill that led down to the goddam bridge. And on the corner of Pine and Sycamore was the Psycho House, so named by Bertie Bird when we were only ten or eleven.

It was actually the Bowditch house, the name was right on the mailbox, faded but still legible, if you squinted. Still, Bertie had a point. We had all seen that movie (along with such other required eleven-year-old viewing as *The Exorcist* and *The Thing*), and it did look sort of like the house where Norman Bates lived with his stuffed mother. It wasn't like any of the other neat little duplexes and ranchers on Sycamore and in the rest of our neighborhood. The Psycho House was a rambling slump-roofed Victorian, once probably white but now faded to a shade I'd call Feral Barncat Gray. There was an ancient picket fence running the length of the property, leaning forward in places and sagging back in others. A rusty waist-high gate barred the broken paving of the walk. The grass was mostly weeds that had run rampant. The porch looked like it was slowly coming detached from the house to which it belonged. All the shades were drawn, which Andy Chen said was pointless, since the windows were too dirty to see through, anyway. Half-buried in the tall grass was a NO TRESPASSING sign. On the gate was a bigger sign reading BEWARE OF DOG.

Andy had a story about that dog, a German Shepherd named Radar, like the guy in the *M*A*S*H* TV show. We'd all heard him (not knowing this Radar was actually a her), and had gotten the occasional glimpse, but Andy was the only one who'd seen the dog up close. He said he stopped on his bike one day because Mr Bowditch's mailbox was open and stuffed so full of junk mail that some of it had fallen to the sidewalk and was blowing around.

'I picked up the litter and crammed it back in with the rest of the crap,' Andy said. 'I was just trying to do him a favor, for crying out loud. Then I hear this growling and a barking that was like *YABBA-YABBA-ROW-ROW*, and I look up and here comes this fucking monster dog, must have weighed a hundred and twenty pounds *at least*, and he's all teeth with slobber flying back and his eyes are fucking *red*.'

'Sure,' Bertie said. 'Monster dog. Like Cujo in that movie. Riii-ight.'

'It *was*,' Andy said. 'Swear to God. If it hadn't been for the old guy yelling at him, he would have gone right through that gate. Which is so old it needs Medicure.'

'Medi*care*,' I said.

'Whatever, dude. But the old guy came out on the porch and he yells, "Radar, *down*!" and the dog dropped right down on its belly. Only it never stopped looking at me and it never stopped growling. Then the guy goes, he goes "What are you doing there, boy? Are you stealing my mail?" So I go "No sir, it was blowing around and I was picking it up. Your mailbox is awful full, sir." And he goes, then he goes "I'll worry about my mailbox, you just get out of here." Which I did.' Andy shook his head. 'That dog would have torn my throat out. I know it.'

I was sure Andy was exaggerating, he had a habit of doing that, but I asked Dad about Mr Bowditch that night. Dad said he didn't know much about him, just that he was a lifelong bachelor who'd been living in that wreck of a house for longer than Dad had been living on Sycamore Street, which was going on twenty-five years.

'Your friend Andy isn't the only kid he's yelled at,' Dad said. 'Bowditch is famous for his foul temper and his equally foul-tempered German Shepherd. The town council would love for him to die so they can tear that place down, but so far he's hanging in there. I speak to him when I see him – which is rarely – and he seems civil enough, but I'm an adult. Some elderly guys have an allergy to kids. Steer clear of him would be my advice, Charlie.'

Which was no problem until that day in April of '13. Which I will now tell you about.

12

I stopped at the corner of Pine and Sycamore on my way home from baseball practice to unpeel my left hand from the handlebars of my bike and give it a shake. It was still red and throbbing from that afternoon's drills in the gym (the field was still too muddy to be playable). Coach Harkness – who coached baseball as well as hoops – had me on first while a number of guys trying out for pitcher practiced pickoff throws. Some of those guys threw really hard. I won't say Coach was getting back at me for refusing to play basketball – where the Hedgehogs had gone 5–20 the previous season – but I won't say he wasn't, either.

Mr Bowditch's slumped and rambling old Victorian was on my right, and from that angle it looked more like the Psycho House than ever. I was wrapping my hand around the left grip of my bike, ready to get going again, when I heard a dog let out a howl. It came from behind the house. I thought of the monster dog Andy had described, all big teeth and red eyes above its slavering jaws, but this was no *YABBA-YABBA-ROW-ROW* of a vicious attack animal; it sounded sad and scared. Maybe even desolate. I have thought back on that, wondering if it's only hindsight, and have decided it wasn't. Because it came again. And a third time, but low and kind of unwinding, as if the animal making it was thinking *what's the use*.

Then, much lower than that last unwinding howl: 'Help.'

If not for those howls, I would have coasted down the hill to my house and had a glass of milk and half a box of Pepperidge Farm Milanos, happy as a clam. Which could have been bad for Mr Bowditch. It was getting late, the shadows drawing long toward evening, and that was a damn cold April. Mr Bowditch could have lain there all night.

I got the credit for saving him – another gold star for my college applications, should I throw modesty to the winds as my father suggested and attach the newspaper article that was published a week later – but it wasn't me, not really.

It was Radar that saved him, with those desolate howls.

CHAPTER TWO

Mr Bowditch. Radar.

Night in the Psycho House.

1

I pedaled around the corner to the gate on Sycamore Street and leaned my bike against the sagging picket fence. The gate – short, hardly up to my waist – wouldn't open. I peered over it and saw a big bolt, as rusty as the gate it was barring. I yanked on it, but it was frozen solid. The dog howled again. I slipped out of my backpack, which was loaded with books, and used it for a step. I clambered over the gate, banging my knee on the BEWARE OF DOG sign and going to the other knee on the far side when one of my sneakers caught at the top. I wondered if I could broad-jump it back to the sidewalk if the dog decided to come after me the way it had at Andy. I remembered the old cliché about fear giving somebody wings and hoped I wouldn't have to find out if that was true. I was football and baseball. I left high-jumping to the trackies.

I ran around to the back, the high grass whickering against my pants. I don't think I saw the shed, not then, because I was mostly looking for the dog. It was on the back porch. Andy Chen said it must have gone a hundred and twenty pounds, and maybe it did when we were just little kids with high school far in our future, but the dog I was looking at couldn't have weighed more than sixty or seventy. It was skinny, with patchy fur and a bedraggled tail and a muzzle that was mostly white. It saw me, started down the rickety steps, and almost fell avoiding the man who was sprawled on them. It came at me, but this was no full-out charge, just a limping, arthritic run.

'Radar, *down*,' I said. Not really expecting it to obey me, but it went to its belly in the weeds and began to whine. I gave it a wide berth on my way to the back porch, just the same.

Mr Bowditch was on his left side. There was a knot pushing out his khaki pants above his right knee. You didn't need to be a doctor to know the leg was broken, and based on that bulge, the break had to be pretty bad. I couldn't tell how old Mr Bowditch was, but pretty old. His hair was mostly white, although he must have been a real carrot-top when he was younger, because there were still streaks of red in it. They made it look like his hair was rusting. The lines on his cheeks and around his mouth were so deep they were grooves. It was cold, but his forehead was beaded with sweat.

'Need some help,' he said. 'Fell off the fucking ladder.' He tried to point. That made him shift a little on the steps and he groaned.

'Have you called 911?' I asked.

He looked at me as if I was stupid. 'The phone's in the *house*, boy. I'm *out here*.'

I didn't understand that until later. Mr Bowditch had no cell phone. Had never seen the need to get one, hardly knew what they were.

He tried to move again and bared his teeth. '*Jesus*, this hurts.'

'Then you better stay still,' I said.

I called 911 and told them I needed an ambulance at the corner of Pine and Sycamore, because Mr Bowditch took a fall and broke his leg. I said it looked like a bad break. I could see the bone poking out the leg of his pants and his knee looked swollen, too. The dispatcher asked me for the house number, so I asked Mr Bowditch.

He gave me that was-you-born-stupid look again and said, 'Number 1.'

I told the lady that and she said they'd send an ambulance right away. She said I should stay with him and keep him warm.

'He's sweating already,' I said.

'If the break is as bad as you say, sir, that's probably shock.'

'Um, okay.'

Radar limped back, ears flattened, growling.

'Stop it, girl,' Bowditch said. 'Get low.'

Radar – *she*, not *it* – went on her belly at the foot of the steps with what looked like relief and started to pant.

I took off my letter jacket and started to spread it over Mr Bowditch.

'What the hell are you doing?'

'I'm supposed to keep you warm.'

'I *am* warm.'

But I saw that he really wasn't, because he'd started to shiver. He lowered his chin to look at my jacket.

'High school kid, are you?'

'Yes, sir.'

'Red and gold. So. Hillview.'

'Yes.'

'Play sports?'

'Football and baseball.'

'The Hedgehogs. What—' He tried to move and gave a cry. Radar pricked up her ears and looked at him anxiously. 'What a silly name *that* is.'

I couldn't disagree. 'You better try not to move, Mr Bowditch.'

'Steps are digging into me everywhere. I should have stayed on the ground, but I thought I could make it to the porch. Then inside. Had to try. Going to be fucking cold out here before long.'

I thought it was pretty fucking cold already.

'Glad you came. Guess you heard the old girl howling.'

'Her first, then you calling,' I said. I looked up at the porch. I could see the door, but I don't think he would have been able to reach the knob without getting up on his good knee. Which I doubted he'd have been able to do.

Mr Bowditch followed my gaze. 'Dog door,' he said. 'Thought maybe I could crawl through.' He grimaced. 'I don't suppose you have any painkillers, do you? Aspirin or something stronger? Playing sports and all?'

I shook my head. Faint, very faint, I could hear a siren. 'What about you? Do you have any?'

He hesitated, then nodded. 'Inside. Go straight down the hall.

There's a little bathroom off the kitchen. I think there's a bottle of Empirin in the medicine cabinet. Don't touch anything else.'

'I won't.' I knew he was old and in pain, but I was still a little cheesed off by the implication.

He reached out and grabbed my shirt. 'Don't snoop.'

I pulled away. 'I said I won't.'

I went up the steps. Mr Bowditch said, 'Radar! Go with!'

Radar limped up the steps and waited for me to open the door rather than using the hinged flap cut in the bottom panel. She followed me down the hall, which was dim and sort of amazing. One side was stacked with old magazines done up in bundles that were tied with hayrope. I knew of some, like *Life* and *Newsweek*, but there were others – *Collier's, Dig, Confidential*, and *All Man* – that I'd never heard of. The other side was stacked with books, most of them old and with that smell that old books have. Probably not everyone likes that smell, but I do. It's musty, but good must.

The kitchen was full of old appliances, the stove a Hotpoint, the sink porcelain with rust-rings from our hard water, the faucets with those old-timey spoke handles, the floor linoleum so worn I couldn't tell what the pattern was. But the place was neat as a pin. There was one plate and one cup and one set of silverware – knife, fork, spoon – in the dish drainer. That made me feel sad. There was a clean dish on the floor with RADAR printed around the rim, and that made me feel sad, too.

I went into the bathroom, which was not much bigger than a closet – nothing but a toilet with the lid up and more rust rings around the bowl, plus a basin with a mirror over it. I swung the mirror back and saw a bunch of dusty patent medicines that looked like they came over on the Ark. A bottle on the middle shelf said Empirin. When I grabbed it, I saw a little pellet behind it. I thought it was a BB.

Radar waited in the kitchen, because there really wasn't room enough for both of us in the bathroom. I took the cup from the dish drainer and filled it from the kitchen tap, then walked back down the Hall of Old Reading Matter with Radar padding right behind me. Outside, the siren was louder and closer. Mr Bowditch was lying with his head down on one forearm.

'You okay?' I asked.

He raised his head so I could see his sweaty face and haggard, dark-ringed eyes. 'Do I look okay?'

'Not really, but I'm not sure you should be taking these pills. The bottle says they expired in August of 2004.'

'Give me three.'

'Jeez, Mr Bowditch, maybe you should wait for the ambulance, they'll give you—'

'Just give them to me. Whatever does not kill me makes me stronger. Don't suppose you know who said that, do you? They teach you nothing these days.'

'Nietzsche,' I said. '*Twilight of the Idols*. I'm taking World History this quarter.'

'Bully for you.' He fumbled in his pants pocket, which made him groan, but he didn't stop until he brought out a heavy ring of keys. 'Lock that door for me, boy. It's the silver key with the square head. The front one's locked already. Then give them back to me.'

I worked the silver key off the keyring, then gave the ring back. He got it into his pocket, groaning some more as he did it. The siren was close now. I hoped they'd have better luck with the rusty bolt than I'd had. Otherwise they'd have to knock the gate off the hinges. I started to get up, then looked at the dog. Her head was on the ground between her paws. She never took her eyes off Mr Bowditch.

'What about Radar?'

He gave me that was-you-born-stupid look again. 'She can go inside through the dog door and out when she needs to do her business.'

A kid or small adult who wanted to have a look around and steal something could also use it, I thought. 'Yeah, but who's going to feed her?'

I probably don't need to tell you that my first impression of Mr Bowditch wasn't good. I thought he was a bad-tempered grouch, and it was no wonder he was living alone; a wife would have killed him or left. But when he looked at the aging German Shepherd, I saw something else: love and dismay. You know that saying about being at your wits' end? Mr Bowditch's face said he was there. He must have been in excruciating pain, but right then all he could think about – all that he cared about – was his dog.

'Shit. Shit, shit, *shit*. I can't leave her. I'll have to take her to the goddam hospital.'

The siren arrived out front and unwound. Doors slammed.

'They won't let you,' I said. 'You must know that.'

His lips tightened. 'Then I'm not going.'

Oh yes you are, I thought. And then I thought something else, only it didn't seem like my thought at all. I'm sure it was, but it didn't seem that way. *We had a deal. Never mind picking up litter on the highway, this is where you hold up your end of it.*

'Hello?' someone shouted. 'EMTs here, is there someone who can open the gate?'

'Let me keep the key,' I said. 'I'll feed her. Just tell me how much and—'

'Hello? Someone answer or we're coming in!'

'—and how often.'

He was sweating heavily now, and the rings under his eyes were darker, like bruises. 'Let them in before they break down the goddam gate.' He let out a harsh, ragged sigh. 'What a fucking mess.'

2

The man and woman on the sidewalk were wearing jackets that said Arcadia County Hospital Ambulance Service. They had a gurney with a shitload of equipment piled on it. They had moved aside my backpack and the man was trying his best to yank the bolt. He was having no more luck than I did.

'He's around back,' I said. 'I heard him calling for help.'

'Great, but I can't get this thing. Take hold, kid. Maybe with both of us.'

I took hold and we pulled. The bolt finally shot back, pinching my thumb. In the heat of the moment I hardly noticed, but by that night most of the nail had turned black.

They went alongside the house, the gurney bumping its way through the high grass, the equipment piled on top of it jittering and jiving. Radar came limping around the corner, growling and trying to sound fearsome. She was giving it her best shot, but after all the excitement I could see she didn't have much left.

'Down, Radar,' I said, and on her belly she went, looking grateful. The EMTs still gave her a wide berth.

They saw Mr Bowditch sprawled on the porch steps and got busy unloading their gear. The woman made soothing comments about how it didn't look that bad and they'd give him something to make him more comfortable.

'He already had something,' I said, and took the Empirin bottle out of my pocket. The male EMT looked at it and said, 'Jesus, these are *ancient*. Any pop they had is long gone. CeeCee, Demerol. Twenty should do it.'

Radar was back. She gave CeeCee a token growl, then went to her master, whining. Bowditch stroked the top of her head with a cupped hand, and when he took it away, the dog huddled on the steps next to him.

'That dog saved your life, sir,' I said. 'She can't go to the hospital and she can't go hungry.'

I was holding the silver backdoor key. He looked at it while CeeCee gave him a shot that he didn't even seem to register. He gave another harsh sigh. 'All right, what fucking choice do I have? Her food is in a big plastic bucket in the pantry. Behind the door. She gets a cup at six, and one at six in the morning if they keep me overnight.' He looked at the male EMT. 'Will they?'

'Don't know, sir. That's above my pay grade.' He was unwrapping a blood pressure cuff. CeeCee gave me a look that said yeah, they'd be keeping him overnight, and that was just for starters.

'Cup at six tonight, six tomorrow. Got it.'

'I don't know how much food is left in that bucket.' His eyes were starting to get glazey. 'If you need to buy more, go to Pet Pantry. She eats Orijen Regional Red. No meat and no snacks. A boy who knows who Nietzsche was can probably remember that.'

'I'll remember.'

The male EMT had pumped up the blood pressure cuff and whatever he was seeing, he didn't like it. 'We're going to get you on the gurney, sir. I'm Craig and this is CeeCee.'

'I'm Charlie Reade,' I said. 'He's Mr Bowditch. I don't know his first name.'

'Howard,' Mr Bowditch said. They made to lift him, but he told them to wait. He held Radar by the sides of her face and looked into her eyes. 'You be a good girl. I'll see you very soon.'

She whined and licked him. A tear ran down one of his cheeks. Maybe it was pain, but I don't think so.

'There's money in the flour cannister in the kitchen,' he said. Then his eyes cleared for a moment and his mouth tightened. 'Belay that. Flour cannister's empty. I forgot. If you—'

'Sir,' CeeCee said, 'we really need to get you into the—'

He glanced at her and told her to hush a minute. Then he looked back to me. 'If you need to buy another bag of food, pay for it yourself. I'll pay you back. Understand?'

'Yes.' I understood something else. Even with some prime dope doing a number on him, Mr Bowditch knew he wouldn't be back tonight or tomorrow night.

'All right, then. Take care of her. She's all I've got.' He gave Radar a final stroke, ruffling her ears, then nodded to the EMTs. He gave a cry through his clamped teeth when they lifted him, and Radar barked.

'Boy?'

'Yes?'

'Don't *snoop*.'

I didn't dignify that with an answer. Craig and CeeCee more or less lifted the gurney around the side of the house, so as not to joggle him too much. I went over and looked at the extension ladder in the grass, then up at the roof. I guessed he'd been cleaning out the gutters. Or trying to.

I went back to the steps and sat down. Out front the siren started up again, loud at first and then diminishing as it headed down the hill to the goddam bridge. Radar looked toward the sound, her ears pricking up. I tried stroking her. When she didn't bite or even growl, I did it again.

'Looks like it's just you and me, girl,' I said.

Radar put her muzzle on my shoe.

'He didn't even say thank you,' I told her. 'What a snot.'

But I wasn't really mad, because it didn't matter. I didn't need to be thanked. This was payback.

3

I called Dad and filled him in as I walked around the house, hoping no one had stolen my backpack. Not only was it still there, one of the EMTs had taken a moment to drop it over the gate. Dad asked me if there was anything he could do. I told him no, I'd stay where I was and do some studying until it was time to feed Radar at six, then come home. He said he'd pick up some Chinese and see me when I got there. I told him I loved him and he said right back atcha.

I fished the bike lock out of my pack, thought about lifting the Schwinn over to the house side, then said screw it and just locked it to the gate. I took a step back and almost tripped over Radar. She yelped and scrambled away.

'Sorry, girl, sorry.' I knelt and held out my hand. After a moment or two she came to it, sniffed, and gave it a little lick. So much for Cujo the Terrible.

I went around back with her right behind me, and that's when I noticed the outbuilding. I figured it for a toolshed; no way was it big enough for a car. I thought about putting the downed ladder inside and decided not to bother, since it didn't look like rain. As I discovered later, I would have toted it the forty yards or so to no avail, because there was a huge padlock on the door, and Mr Bowditch had taken the rest of his keys.

I let us in, found an old-fashioned light switch, the kind that turns, and walked down the Hall of Old Reading Matter to the kitchen. The light there was provided by an overhead frosted glass fixture that looked like part of the set dressing in one of those old TCM movies Dad liked. The kitchen table was covered with checked oilcloth, faded but clean. I decided *everything* in the kitchen looked like set dressing from an old movie. I could almost imagine Mr Chips strolling in, wearing his gown and mortarboard. Or maybe Barbara Stanwyck telling Dick Powell he was just in time for a drink. I sat down at the table. Radar went under it and settled with a small ladylike grunt. I told her she was a good girl and she thumped her tail.

'Don't worry, he'll be back soon.' *Maybe*, I thought.

I spread out my books, did some math problems, then put in my EarPods and played the next day's French assignment, a pop song called 'Rien Qu'une Fois,' which means something like 'Just Once.' Not exactly my cup of tea, I'm more of a classic rock guy, but it was one of those songs you like more every time you hear it. Until it turns into an earworm, that is, and then you hate it. I played it through three times, then sang along, as we'd be required to do in class:

'Je suis sûr que tu es celle que j'ai toujours attendue . . .'

One verse in I happened to look under the table and saw Radar looking at me with her ears laid back and an expression that looked suspiciously like pity. It made me laugh. 'Better not quit my day job, right?'

A thump of the tail.

'Don't blame me, it's an assignment. Want to hear it one more time? No? Me either.'

I spied four matching cannisters set up in a line on the counter to the left of the stove, marked SUGAR, FLOUR, COFFEE, and COOKIES. I was pretty damn hungry. At home I would have checked the fridge and gobbled half the contents, but of course I wasn't at home and wouldn't be for – I checked my watch – another hour. I decided to investigate the cookie jar, which surely wouldn't count as snooping. It was filled to the top with a mixture of pecan sandies and those chocolate-covered marshmallow jobbies. I decided that since I was dog-sitting, Mr Bowditch wouldn't miss one. Or two. Even four. I made myself stop there, but it was hard. Those sandies were certainly delicious.

I looked at the flour cannister and thought of Mr Bowditch saying there was money in there. Then his eyes had changed – sharpened. *Belay that. Flour cannister's empty. I forgot.* I almost peeked, and there was a time not so long ago when I would have, but those days were gone. I sat back down and opened my World History book.

I plowed through some heavy stuff about the Treaty of Versailles and German reparations, and when I looked at my watch again (there was a clock over the sink but it was stopped), I saw it was quarter to six. I decided that was close enough for government work and decided to feed Radar.

I figured the door next to the fridge had to be the pantry, and I figured right. It had that good pantry smell. I pulled down the dangling cord to turn on the light and for a moment forgot all about feeding Radar. The little room was canned goods and dry goods from top to bottom and side to side. There was Spam and baked beans and sardines and Saltines and Campbell's Soup; pasta and pasta sauce, bottles of grape and cranberry juice, jars of jelly and jam, cans of veggies by the dozens and maybe hundreds. Mr Bowditch was all set for the apocalypse.

Radar gave a *don't forget the dog* whine. I looked behind the door and there was her plastic food cannister. It had to hold ten or twelve gallons full, but the bottom was barely covered. If Bowditch was in the hospital for a few days – or even a week – I would have to buy more.

The cup measure was in the cannister. I filled it and poured the kibble into the dish with her name on it. Radar went at it with a will, tail wagging slowly from side to side. She was old but still happy to eat. I guessed that was good.

'You take it easy now,' I said, pulling on my jacket. 'Be a good girl and I'll see you in the morning.'

Only it wasn't that long.

4

Dad and I pigged on Chinese food and I gave him the expanded version of my afternoon adventure, starting with Bowditch on the steps, progressing to the Hall of Old Reading Matter, and finishing with the Doomsday Pantry.

'Hoarder,' Dad said. 'Seen my share of it, usually after the hoarder in question dies. But the place is clean, you say?'

I nodded. 'The kitchen, at least. A place for everything and everything in its place. There was some dust on the old medicine bottles in the little bathroom, but I didn't see any anywhere else.'

'No car.'

'Nope. And not room for one in his toolshed.'

'He must have his groceries delivered. And of course there's always Amazon, which by 2040 will be the world government the right-wingers are so afraid of. I wonder where his money comes from, and how much is left.'

I'd wondered that, too. I think that kind of curiosity is pretty normal in people who've come within a whisker of going broke.

Dad got up. 'I bought and carried. Now I need to clear some paperwork. You clean up.'

I cleaned up, then practiced some blues tunes on my guitar. (I could play almost anything, just as long as it was in the key of E.) Usually I could get into the music until my fingers hurt, but not that night.

I put my Yamaha back in the corner and told Dad I was going up to Mr Bowditch's house to check on Radar. I kept thinking of her being there all by herself. Maybe dogs didn't care about such things, but maybe they did.

'Fine, as long as you don't decide to bring it back.'

'Her.'

'Okay, but not interested in listening to a lonely dog howl at three in the morning, no matter what sex it happens to be.'

'I won't bring her back.' He didn't need to know that the idea had at least crossed my mind.

'And don't let Norman Bates get you.'

I looked at him, surprised.

'What? You think I didn't know?' He was grinning. 'People were calling it the Psycho House long before you and your friends were born, little hero.'

5

That made me smile, but it was harder to see the humor when I got to the corner of Pine and Sycamore. The house seemed to hulk on its hill, blotting out the stars. I remembered Norman Bates saying *Mother! So much blood!* and wished I'd never seen the damn movie.

The gate bolt was easier to pull, at least. I used my phone's flashlight to walk around the house. I ran my flash over the side of it once and wished I hadn't. The windows were dusty, all the shades pulled. Those windows looked like blind eyes that were somehow still seeing me and not liking my intrusion. I rounded the corner and as I started toward the back porch there was a thump. It startled me and I dropped my phone. As it fell, I saw a moving shadow. I didn't cry out, but I felt my balls crawl and pull up tight against my scrote. I froze as that shadow rippled toward me, and then, before I could turn and run, Radar was whining and nosing at the leg of my pants and trying to jump up on me. Because of her bad back and hips, all she could do was make a series of abortive lunges. The thump must have been the dog door swinging shut.

I dropped to my knees and grabbed her, one hand stroking her head while the other scratched her ruff under the collar. She licked my face and crammed against me so tight that she almost tipped me over.

'It's okay,' I said. 'Were you scared to be alone? I bet you were.' And when was the last time she *had* been alone, if Mr Bowditch didn't have a car and all his groceries were delivered? Maybe not for a long time. 'That's okay. All good. Come on.'

I picked up my phone, gave my balls a second to settle back into their proper place, then went to the back door with her walking so close beside me that her head kept bumping my knee. Once upon a time Andy Chen had encountered a monster dog in the front yard of this place, or so he said. But that was years ago. This was just a scared old lady who'd heard me coming and bolted out through her dog door to meet me.

We went up the back porch steps. I unlocked the door and used the turn-switch to light the Hall of Old Reading Matter. I checked the dog door and saw there were three small bolts, one on each side and another on top. I reminded myself to run them before I left so Radar wouldn't go wandering. The backyard was probably fenced like the front one, but I didn't know that for sure and for the time being she was my responsibility.

In the kitchen I knelt in front of Radar and stroked the sides of her face. She looked at me attentively, ears pricked. 'I can't stay, but I'm going to leave a light on and I'll come back tomorrow morning and feed you. Okay?'

She whined, licked my hand, and then went to her dish. It was empty, but she gave it a few licks and then looked at me. The message was pretty clear. 'No more until morning,' I said.

She lay down and put her muzzle on her paw, never taking her eyes off me.

'Well . . .'

I went to the cannister marked COOKIES. Mr Bowditch had said no meat and no snacks, and I decided he could have meant no meat snacks. Semantics are wonderful, aren't they? I vaguely remembered hearing or reading somewhere that dogs are allergic to chocolate, so I took one of the pecan sandies and broke off a piece. I offered it. She sniffed, then took it delicately from my fingers.

I sat down at the table where I'd done my studying, thinking I should just go. She was a dog, for Christ's sake, not a child. She might not like being alone, but it wasn't like she was going to get into the cabinet under the sink and drink bleach.

My phone buzzed. It was Dad. 'Everything okay there?'

'Fine, but it's good I came. I left the dog door open. She came out when she heard me.' No need to tell him that when I saw that moving shadow I'd had a single flash of Janet Leigh in the shower, screaming and trying to avoid the knife.

'Not your fault. You can't think of everything. Coming back?'

'Pretty soon.' I looked at Radar looking at me. 'Dad, maybe I should—'

'Bad idea, Charlie. You've got school tomorrow. She's a grownup dog. She'll be fine overnight.'

'Sure, I know.'

Radar got up, a process that was a little painful to watch. When she got her hindquarters under her, she walked off into the dark of what was probably the living room.

'I'll just stay a few minutes. She's a nice dog.'

'Okay.'

I ended the call and heard a low squeaking sound. Radar came back with a toy in her mouth. I thought maybe it was a monkey, but it was so chewed it was hard to tell. I still had my phone in my hand, so I took a picture. She brought me the toy and dropped it by my chair. Her eyes told me what I was supposed to do.

I gave it a soft lob across the room. Radar limped after it, picked it up, made it squeak a few times to show it who was boss, and brought it back. She plunked it down beside my chair. I could imagine her as a young dog, heavier and much more agile, going after that poor old monkey (or its predecessor) at a full-tilt run. The way Andy said she'd run at him that day. Now her running days were over, but she was giving it her best shot. I could imagine her thinking, *see how good I am at this? Stick around, I can do it all night!*

Only she couldn't, and I couldn't stay. Dad wanted me home, and I doubted if I'd sleep much anyway if I stayed here. Too many mysterious creaks and groans, too many rooms where anything might be lurking . . . and creeping toward me once the lights were out.

Radar brought the squeaky monkey back. 'No more,' I said. 'Rest up, girl.'

I started for the back hall, then had an idea. I went to the darkened room where Radar had found her toy and groped around for a switch, hoping nothing (Norman Bates's wrinkled mummy of a mother, for instance) would grab my hand. The switch made a clacking sound when I found it and flipped it.

Like the kitchen, Mr Bowditch's living room was old-timey but neat. There was a couch upholstered in dark brown fabric. It looked to me as if it hadn't had much use. Most of the sitting appeared to have been done in an easy chair plonked down in the middle of an old-fashioned rag rug. I could see the divot made by Mr Bowditch's skinny shanks. A blue chambray shirt was tossed over the back. The chair faced a TV that looked prehistoric. There was an antenna thing on top of it. I took a picture of it with my phone. I didn't know if a TV that ancient could possibly work, but judging by the books stacked on either side of it, many marked with Post-it notes, it probably didn't get much use even if it did work. In the far corner of the room was a wicker basket piled high with dog toys, and that said all anyone would need to know about how much Mr Bowditch loved his dog. Radar padded across the room and grabbed a stuffed rabbit. She brought it to me, looking hopeful.

'Can't,' I said. 'But you can have this. It probably smells like your guy.'

I grabbed the shirt off the back of the chair and spread it on the kitchen floor beside her dish. She smelled it, then lay down on it. 'Atta girl,' I said. 'See you in the morning.'

I started for the back door, thought again, and brought her the stuffed monkey. She gave it a chew or two, maybe just to please me. I backed off a few steps and took another picture with my phone. Then I left, not forgetting to bolt the dog door. If she messed inside, I would just have to clean it up.

As I walked back home, I thought about gutters no doubt plugged with leaves. The unmowed lawn. The place badly needed a paintjob and that was beyond me, but I could do something about those dirty windows, not to mention the sagging picket fence. If I had time, that was, and given the upcoming baseball season, I didn't. Plus there was Radar. That was love at first sight. For her as well as for me, maybe. If the idea strikes you as weird, or corny, or both, all I can say is deal with it. As I said to my father, she was a nice dog.

When I went to bed that night, I set my alarm for five A.M. Then I texted Mr Neville, my English teacher, and told him I wouldn't be there period one, and to tell Ms Friedlander that I might miss period two as well. I said I had to visit a guy in the hospital.

CHAPTER THREE

A Hospital Visit.

Quitters Never Win. The Shed.

1

The Psycho House looked less psycho by the dawn's early light, although the mist rising from all that high grass did give it a gothic air. Radar must have been waiting, because she began thudding against the bolted dog door as soon as she heard me on the steps. Which were loose and spongy, another accident waiting to happen and another chore waiting for someone to do it.

'Easy, girl,' I said, putting the key in the lock. 'You'll sprain something.'

She was all over me as soon as the door was open, jumping up and putting her front paws on my leg, arthritis be damned. She followed me into the kitchen and watched, tail wagging, as I scraped one last full cup from her diminishing food supply. While she ate, I texted Dad and asked if he would stop at a place called Pet Pantry on his lunch hour or after work and pick up a bag of dog food: Orijen Regional Red. Then I sent another, saying I'd pay him back and Mr Bowditch would pay me. I considered and sent a third one: **Better get a big bag**.

It didn't take me long, but Radar was already done. She brought me the monkey and dropped it beside my chair. Then burped.

'Excuse you,' I said, and soft-tossed the monkey. She pounced and brought it back. I tossed it again, and while she was going after it my phone binged. It was Dad. **No problem**.

I gave her another toss, but instead of going after it, she limp-trotted down the Hall of Old Reading Matter and outside. Not knowing if there was a leash, I broke off another piece of pecan sandy to coax her back in if needed. I was pretty sure it would do the job; Radar was the original chow hound.

Getting her in didn't turn out to be a problem. She squatted in one place to do her number one and in another to do her number two. She came back, looked at the steps the way a mountaineer might look at a tough climb, then made her way halfway up. She sat for a moment, then managed the rest. I wasn't sure how long she'd be able to do that without help.

'Gotta go,' I said. 'See ya later, gator.'

We'd never had a dog, so I didn't know how expressive their eyes could be, especially up close and personal. Hers told me not to go. I would have been happy to stay, but as that poem says, I had promises to keep. I stroked her a few times and told her to be good. I remembered reading somewhere that a dog ages seven years for each one of ours. Just a rule of thumb, surely, but at least a way to figure, and what did that mean to a dog, time-wise? If I came back at six to feed her, that would be about twelve hours of my time. Would that be eighty-four hours for hers? Three and a half days? If so, no wonder she was so happy to see me. Plus she had to be missing Mr Bowditch.

I locked the door, went down the steps, and looked toward the place where she'd done her business. Policing the backyard was another chore that could use doing. Unless Mr Bowditch had done it himself. With all that high grass it was impossible to tell. If he hadn't, somebody should.

You're somebody, I thought as I went back to my bike. Which was true, but as it happened, I was a busy somebody. In addition to baseball, I was thinking of trying out for the end-of-year play: *High School Musical*. I had fantasies of singing 'Breaking Free' with Gina Pascarelli, who was a senior and gorgeous.

A woman bundled up in a tartan coat was standing by my bike. I thought she was Mrs Ragland. Or maybe it was Reagan. 'Are you the one who called the ambulance?' she asked.

'Yes, ma'am,' I said.

'How bad is he? Bowditch?'

'I don't really know. He broke his leg for sure.'

'Well, that was your good deed for the day. Maybe for the year. He's not much of a neighbor, keeps mostly to himself, but I've got nothing against him. Except for the house, which is an eyesore. You're George Reade's son, aren't you?'

'That's right.'

She held out her hand. 'Althea Richland.'

I shook with her. 'Pleased to meet you.'

'What about the mutt? That's a scary dog, a German Shepherd. He used to walk him early mornings and sometimes after dark. When the kids were inside.' She pointed to the sadly sagging picket fence. '*That* certainly wouldn't hold him.'

'It's a her and I'm taking care of her.'

'That's very good of you. I hope you won't get bitten.'

'She's pretty old now, and not mean.'

'To *you*, maybe,' Mrs Richland said. 'My father had a saying, "An old dog will bite twice as hard." A reporter from that rag of a weekly came by and asked me what happened. I think he's the one who does the call-outs. Police, fire, ambulance, that kind of thing.' She sniffed. 'He looked about your age.'

'I'll keep that in mind,' I said, not knowing why I should. 'I better get going, Mrs Richland. I want to visit Mr Bowditch before school.'

She laughed. 'If it's Arcadia, visiting hours don't start until nine. They'll never let you in this early.'

2

They did, though. Explaining that I had school and baseball practice after didn't quite convince the lady at the front desk, but when I told her I was the one who called the ambulance, she told me I could go up. 'Room 322. Elevators are on your right.'

Halfway down the third-floor hall, a nurse asked me if I was here to see Howard Bowditch. I said I was and asked how he was doing.

'He's had one operation and he's going to need another. Then he'll be facing a fairly long period of convalescence, and he'll need a lot of physical therapy. Melissa Wilcox will probably be the one to take that on. The leg-break was a particularly bad one, and he also pretty much destroyed his hip. It will need a replacement. Otherwise he'll be spending the rest of his life on a walker or in a wheelchair no matter how much therapy he does.'

'Jeez,' I said. 'Does he know?'

'The doctor who set the break will have told him what he needs to know right now. You called the ambulance?'

'Yes, ma'am.'

'Well, you may have saved his life. Between the shock and possibly spending a night outdoors . . .' She shook her head.

'It was the dog. I heard his dog howling.'

'Did the dog call 911?'

I admitted that had been me.

'If you want to see him, you better go on down. I just gave him a shot for pain, and it will probably put him under before long. Broken leg and hip aside, he's severely underweight. Easy pickings for osteoporosis. You might get fifteen minutes before he's off to see the wizard.'

3

Mr Bowditch's leg was up in a pulley contraption that looked straight out of a 1930s comedy movie . . . only Mr Bowditch wasn't laughing. Neither was I. The lines on his face looked deeper, almost carved. The dark circles under his eyes were darker. His hair appeared lifeless and thin, the red streaks in it looking faded. I guess he had a roommate, but I never saw him because a green drape was drawn across the other half of 322. Mr Bowditch saw me and tried to straighten up in his bed, which made him grimace and hiss out a breath.

'Hello there. What's your name again? If you told me, I don't remember. Which, given the circumstances, might be forgivable.'

I couldn't remember if I had, either, so I gave it again (or for the first time), then asked how he was feeling.

'Extremely shitty. Just look at me.'

'I'm sorry.'

'Not as sorry as I am.' Then, with an effort to be civil: 'Thank you, young Mr Reade. They tell me you may have saved my life. It doesn't feel like it's worth much just now, but as the Buddha supposedly said, "It changes." Sometimes for the better, although in my experience that's rare.'

I told him – as I had my father, the EMTs, and Mrs Richland – that it was really the dog who had saved him; if I hadn't heard her howling, I would have biked on by.

'How is she?'

'Fine.' I took a chair by his bed and showed him the pictures I'd taken of Radar with her monkey. He went back and forth between them several times (I had to show him how to do that). The pics made him seem happier, if not necessarily any healthier. *Facing a long period of convalescence*, the nurse had said.

When he handed the phone back, the smile was gone. 'They haven't told me how long I'm going to be in this damn sickbay, but I'm not stupid. I know it's going to be awhile. I guess I need to think about putting her down. She's had a good life, but now her hips are—'

'Jeez, don't do that,' I said, alarmed. 'I'll take care of her. Happy to do it.'

He looked at me, and for the first time his expression wasn't one of irritation or resignation. 'You'd do that? Can I *trust* you to do that?'

'Yes. She's almost out of food, but my dad's getting a bag of that Orijen stuff today. Six morning, six evening. I'll be there. Count on it.'

He reached for me, maybe meaning to take my hand or at least give it a pat. I would have allowed it, but he pulled his hand back. 'That's . . . very good of you.'

'I like her. And she likes me.'

'Does she? Good. She's not a bad old pal.' His eyes were getting glassy, his voice a little slurry. Whatever the nurse had given him was starting to work. 'No harm in her, but she used to scare the shit out of the neighborhood kids. Which I appreciated. Nosy little brats, most of them. Nosy and noisy. As for burglars? Forget it. If they heard Radar they'd head for the hills. But now she's old.' He sighed, then coughed. It made him wince. 'And she's not the only one.'

'I'll take good care of her. Maybe walk her down the hill to my place.'

His eyes sharpened a little as he considered this possibility. 'She's never been in anyone else's since I got her as a pup. Just my house . . . the yard . . .'

'Mrs Richland said you took her on walks.'

'The nosy-parker across the street? Well, yes, she's right. We did go on walks. When Radar was able to go without getting tired. I'd be afraid to take her any distance now. What if I got her down Pine Street and she couldn't make it back?' He looked down at himself. 'Now *I'm* the one who couldn't make it back. Couldn't make it anywhere.'

'I won't push her. You know, overtax her.'

He relaxed. 'I'll pay you . . . for what she eats. And for your time, that too.'

'Don't worry about it.'

'She might be okay for awhile yet when I get home. *If* I get home.'

'You will, Mr Bowditch.'

'If you're going . . . feed her . . . better call me Howard.'

I didn't know if I could do that, but I agreed.

'Maybe bring me another picture?'

'Sure. I better go, Mr . . . Howard. You should rest up.'

'No choice.' His eyes slipped closed, then the lids slowly came up again. 'Whatever she gave me . . . whoo! High-tension stuff.'

His eyes closed again. I got up and headed for the door.

'Boy. What was your name again?'

'Charlie.'

'Thank you, Charlie. I thought maybe . . . give her another chance. Not for me . . . once was enough for me . . . life gets to be a burden . . . if you live long enough you'll find that out for yourself. But *her* . . . Radar . . . and then I got old and fell off the fucking ladder . . .'

'I'll bring you some more pictures.'

'You do that.'

I turned to go and then he spoke again, but I don't think it was to me. 'A brave man helps. A coward just gives presents.' He fell silent and began to snore.

Halfway down the hall, I saw the nurse I'd spoken to coming out of a room with what looked like a bag of cloudy pee. She saw me and put a towel over it. She asked if I'd had a nice visit.

'Yes, but he wasn't making much sense by the end.'

She smiled. 'Demerol will do that. Go on, now. You should be in school.'

4

By the time I got to Hillview, period two had been going on for ten minutes and the halls were empty. I went to the office to get an Excused Late slip from Mrs Silvius, a nice old lady with scary blue hair. She had to be at least seventy-five, long past the usual retirement age, but still plenty sharp and good-humored. I think good humor must be necessary when you're dealing with teenagers.

'I hear you saved a man's life yesterday,' she said as she signed the slip.

'Who told you that?'

'A little birdie. Tweet-tweet-tweet. Word gets around, Charlie.'

I took the slip. 'It really wasn't me, it was the guy's dog. I heard her howling.' I was getting tired of telling people this, because nobody believed me. Which was strange. I thought everyone liked stories about hero dogs. 'I just called 911.'

'Whatever you say. Now run along to class.'

'Can I show you something first?'

'Only if it's a speedy something.'

I took out my phone and showed her the picture I'd snapped of Mr Bowditch's TV. 'That's an antenna on top, right?'

'Rabbit ears, we called them,' Mrs Silvius said. Her smile was very similar to the one Mr Bowditch had worn when he was looking at the pictures of Radar with her monkey. 'We used to put tinfoil on the tips of ours because it was supposed to improve the reception. But look at the *television*, Charlie! My goodness! Does it actually work?'

'I don't know. I didn't try it.'

'The first TV we ever had looked like this. A table-model Zenith. It was so heavy my father strained his back carrying it up the steps to the apartment we lived in back then. We watched that thing by the hour! *Annie Oakley, Wild Bill Hickok, Captain Kangaroo, Crusader Rabbit* . . . gosh, until we got headaches! And once it wouldn't work, the picture just rolled and rolled, so my dad called a TV repairman who came with a suitcase full of tubes.'

'Tubes?'

'Vacuum tubes. They glowed orange, like old-fashioned lightbulbs. He replaced the one that had gone bad and it worked fine again.' She looked at the picture on my phone once more. 'Surely the tubes for this one would have burned out long ago.'

'Mr Bowditch probably bought more on eBay or Craigslist,' I said. 'You can buy anything on the Internet. If you can afford it, that is.' Only I didn't think Mr Bowditch *did* Internet.

Mrs Silvius handed my phone back. 'Go along, Charlie. Physics awaits you.'

5

Coach Harkness was on me that afternoon at practice like white on rice. Or, more accurately, like flies on shit. Because shit was how I played. During the three-cone footwork drill I kept moving the wrong way, and once I tried to move both ways at once and ended up on my ass, which caused much hilarity. During the double-play drill I got caught off my position at first and the ball from the second baseman went whizzing past where I should have been and ended up bouncing off the gym wall. When Coach hit me a dribbler up the line, I charged the ball okay, but didn't get my glove down and the ball – just a bunny, rolling at walking speed – went through my legs. But bunting was the final straw for Coach Harkness. I kept popping it up to the pitcher instead of laying one down along the third-base line.

Coach erupted from his lawn chair and stalked to the plate with his belly swinging and his whistle bouncing between his not inconsiderable breasts. 'Jesus *Christ*, Reade! You look like an old lady! Stop punching at the ball! Just get the bat down and let the ball hit it. How many times do I have to tell you?' He grabbed the bat, elbowed me aside, and faced Randy Morgan, that day's tryout pitcher. 'Throw! And put some goddam hair on it!'

Randy threw as hard as he could. Coach bent and laid down a perfect bunt. It trickled along the third-base line, just fair. Steve Dombrowski charged it, tried for a barehand pickup, and lost the handle.

Coach turned to me. 'There! That's how it's done! I don't know what's on your mind, but get rid of it!'

What was on my mind was Radar, back at Mr Bowditch's house, waiting for me to come. Twelve hours for me, maybe three and a half days for her. She wouldn't know why she had been left alone, and a dog couldn't play with the squeaky monkey if there was no one there to throw it. Was she trying not to make a mess in the house, or – with the dog door bolted – had she already done it somewhere? If so, she might not understand that it wasn't her fault. Plus that scraggy lawn and the sagging picket fence – those things were on my mind, too.

Coach Harkness handed me the bat. 'Now lay one down and do it right.'

Randy didn't try to drill it in there, just threw a batting-practice pitch to get me off the hook. I squared around . . . and popped it up. Randy didn't even have to get off the practice mound to glove it.

'That's it,' Coach said. 'Give me five.' Meaning five laps around the gym.

'No.'

All the chatter in the gym died. Both in our half and the girls' volleyball half. Everyone was watching. Randy put his glove over his mouth, maybe to hide a smile.

Coach put his hands on his meaty hips. 'What did you just say to me?'

I didn't drop the bat because I wasn't mad. I just held it out to him, and in his amazement he took it.

'I said no. I'm done.' I started for the door that led to the lockers.

'Get back here, Reade!'

I didn't even shake my head, just kept going.

'You come back now, not when you cool down! Because then it'll be too late!'

But I *was* cool. Cool and calm. Happy, even, like when you see the solution to a troubling math problem isn't half as hard as it looked at first.

'Goddammit, Reade!' He sounded a little panicked now. Maybe because I was his best hitter, or maybe because this rebellion was happening in front of the rest of the team. 'Get back here! Winners never quit and quitters never win!'

'Then call me a loser,' I said.

I went down the stairs to the locker room and changed up. That was the end of my baseball career at Hillview High, and did I regret it? No. Did I regret letting my teammates down? A little, but as Coach was fond of pointing out, there's no *i* in *team*. They would have to get along without me. I had other business to take care of.

6

I got the mail out of Mr Bowditch's box – nothing personal, just the usual dandruff – and let myself in through the back door. Radar couldn't quite jump up on me, I guess she was having a bad day, so I took her gently by the front paws, lifted her, and placed them on my waist so I could stroke her upturned head. I gave a few to her graying muzzle for good measure. She made her careful way down the porch steps, and did her business. Once again she gave that assessing look to the porch steps before climbing them. I told her she was a good girl and Coach Harkness would be proud.

I tossed the squeaky monkey for her a few times and took some pictures. There were other squeakies in her toy basket, but the monkey was clearly her go-to.

She followed me outside when I went to collect the fallen ladder. I carried it down to the shed, saw the heavy-duty padlock on the door, and just propped it under the eave. While I was doing it, Radar started to growl. She was crouched down twenty feet in front of the padlocked door, ears back and muzzle wrinkled.

'What is it, girl? If a skunk or a woodchuck got in there, I can't do anything abou—'

From behind the door came a scratching, followed by a weird chittering noise that stood up the hair on the back of my neck. Not an animal sound. I'd never heard anything exactly like it. Radar barked, then whined, then backed away with her belly still on the ground. I felt like backing away myself, but instead I whammed on the door with the side of my fist and waited. There was nothing. I could have chalked those sounds up to my imagination if not for Radar's reaction, but there was nothing I could do about it in any case. The door was locked and there were no windows.

I gave the door another wham, almost daring that weird sound to come again. It didn't, so I walked back to the house. Radar struggled to her feet and followed me. I looked back once, and saw that she was looking back, too.

7

I played monkey with Radar for awhile. When she lay down on the linoleum and gave me a look that said *all done*, I called my dad and told him I'd quit baseball.

'I know,' he said. 'Coach Harkness already called me. He said things got a little hot, but he was willing for you to come back on the condition that you apologize first to him and then to the whole team. Because you let them down, he said.'

That was irritating, but also funny. 'Dad, it wasn't the State Finals, just practice in the gym. And he was being a dick.' Although I was used to that; we all were. Coach H.'s picture could have been next to *dick* in the dictionary.

'So no apologizing, is that what I'm hearing?'

'I could apologize for not having my head on straight, because it wasn't. I was thinking about Mr Bowditch. And Radar. And this place. It's not falling down, but it's getting there. I could do a lot of stuff if I had time, and now I do.'

He took a few seconds to process that, then said, 'I'm not sure I understand why that feels necessary to you. Taking care of the dog, that I get, it's a mitzvah, but you don't know Bowditch from Adam.'

And what was I going to say to that? Was I going to tell my father that I'd made a deal with God? Even if he was kind enough not to laugh (he probably would be), he'd tell me that sort of thinking was best left to children, evangelicals, and cable-news-watching junkies who really believed some kind of magic pillow or diet would cure all their ills. Worst case scenario, he might think I was trying to lay claim to the sobriety he was working so hard to maintain.

There was something else, too: it was private. My thing.

'Charlie? Still there?'

'I'm here. All I can say is I want to do what I can until he's back on his feet again.'

Dad sighed. 'He's not a kid who fell out of an apple tree and broke his arm. He's old. He may *never* get on his feet again. Have you thought about that?'

I hadn't, and didn't see any reason to start. 'You know what they say in your program – one day at a time.'

He chuckled. 'We also say the past is history and the future's a mystery.'

'Good one, Dad. So are we okay with the baseball thing?'

'Yes, but making the All-State team at the end of the season would have looked good on your college apps. You know that, right?'

'I do.'

'What about football? Are you thinking of dumping that, too?'

'Not right now.' At least when it came to football I wouldn't have Coach Harkness to deal with. 'Mr Bowditch may be better by the time practice starts in August.'

'Or not.'

'Or not,' I agreed. 'The future's a mystery.'

'Indeed it is. When I think of that night your mother decided to walk down to the Zippy . . .'

He trailed off. I couldn't think of anything to say, either.

'Do one thing for me, Charlie. A reporter from *The Weekly Sun* came by and asked for your contact info. I didn't give it to him, but I got his. He wants to interview you about saving Bowditch. Human interest kind of deal. I think you should do it.'

'I didn't really save him, it was Radar—'

'You can tell him that. But if the colleges you apply to have questions about why you quit baseball, an article like that—'

'I got it. Give me his number.'

He did, and I put it in my contacts.

'You'll be home for dinner?'

'Soon as I give Radar hers.'

'Good. I love you, Charlie.'

I told him I loved him, too. Which was true. Good man, my dad. Had a hard time but got through it. Not everyone does.

8

After I fed Radar and told her I'd be back tomorrow, bright and early, I walked down to the shed. I didn't really want to, there was something very unpleasant about that windowless little building in the encroaching dark of a chilly April evening, but I made myself do it. I stood in front of the padlocked door, listening. No scratching. No weird chittering sound, like some alien creature in a science fiction movie. I didn't want to hit the door with my fist, so I made myself do it. Twice. Hard.

Nothing. Which was a relief.

I got on my bike, rode down Sycamore Street Hill, tossed my glove on the top shelf of my closet, then looked at it for awhile before closing the door. It's a good game, baseball. There's nothing like coming up in the top of the ninth and socking one right up the gap, and nothing like riding home on the bus from an away game after a big win, everybody laughing and rowdy and grab-assing around. So yeah – some regret, but really not a lot. I thought of that saying of the Buddha's: it changes. I decided there was a lot of truth in those two little words. A hell of a lot.

I called the reporter guy. *The Weekly Sun* was a freebie which contained a few local-interest news and sports stories buried in a shitload of ads. There was always a pile of them by the door of the Zippy with a sign saying TAKE ONE, to which some wit had added TAKE THEM ALL. The reporter's name was Bill Harriman. I answered his questions, once again giving Radar most of the credit. Mr Harriman asked if he could snap a picture of the two of us.

'Gee, I don't know. I'd have to have Mr Bowditch's permission, and he's in the hospital.'

'Ask him tomorrow or the next day, would you do that? I'll have to file the story soon if it's going to run in next week's issue.'

'I will if I can, but I think he was scheduled for another operation. They might not let me visit him, and I really can't do it without his permission.' The last thing I wanted was for Mr Bowditch to be mad at me, and he was the kind of guy who got mad easily. I looked up the word for people like that later on; it was *misanthrope*.

'Understood, understood. Let me know one way or the other soon as you can. Hey, aren't you the kid who scored the winning touchdown against Stanford Prep in the Turkey Bowl last November?'

'That was me, but it wasn't like a *SportsCenter* Top Ten play, or anything. We were on their two-yard line and I just punched it in.'

He laughed. 'Modest! I like that. Give me a call, Charlie.'

I said I would, hung up, and went downstairs to watch some TV with my dad before studying. I wondered how Radar was doing. Okay, I hoped. Getting used to a different routine. I thought of that saying of the Buddha's again. That was a good one to hold onto.

CHAPTER FOUR

Visiting Mr Bowditch. Andy Chen.
The Cellar. In Other News. A Hospital Meeting.

1

When I showed up the next morning at Number 1 Sycamore Street, Radar's greeting was exuberant but not as frenzied. That made me think she was getting used to the new order. She did the morning necessary, gobbled her breakfast (Dad had brought home a twenty-five-pound sack of her chow), then wanted to play with the monkey. I still had some time when she tired of that, so I went into the living room to see if the vintage television worked. I wasted some time looking for the zapper, but of course Mr Bowditch's idiot box was from the pre-zapper era of home entertainment. There were two big dials below the screen. The one on the right had numbers on it – channels, I presumed – so I turned the one on the left.

The hum from the TV wasn't as disturbing as the noises from the shed, but it was still a bit worrisome. I stepped back, hoping it wouldn't explode. After awhile, the *Today* show swam into view – Matt Lauer and Savannah Guthrie chatting it up with a couple of politicians. The picture wasn't 4K; it wasn't even 1K. But it was something, at least. I tried moving the antenna that Mrs Silvius had called rabbit ears. I turned it one way and the picture got better (*marginally* better). I turned it the other way and *Today* disappeared into a snowstorm. I looked behind the unit. The backing was full of small holes to let out the heat – which was considerable – and through them I saw the orange glow of tubes. I was pretty sure they were producing the humming sound.

I snapped it off, wondering how annoying it must have been to get up every time you wanted to change the channel. I told Radar I had to go to school, but I needed another picture first. I handed her the monkey.

'Do you mind holding that in your mouth? It's pretty cute.'

Radar was happy to oblige.

2

With no baseball practice I got to the hospital by mid-afternoon. At the desk I asked if Howard Bowditch was allowed to have visitors – a nurse had told me he was going to need another operation. The desk lady checked something on her monitor and told me I could go up and see. As I turned toward the elevators, she told me to wait up, she had a form for me to fill out. It was for my contact information 'in case of emergency.' The requesting patient was Howard Adrian Bowditch. My name had been filled in as Charles Reed.

'You are him, aren't you?' the desk lady said.

'Yes, but the last name is spelled wrong.' I scratched it out and printed *Reade*. 'He said for you to contact me? Doesn't he have anyone else? Like a brother or sister? Because I don't think I'm old enough to make any big decisions, like if . . .' I didn't want to finish, and she didn't need me to.

'He signed a DNR before he went up for surgery. A form like this is just if he needs you to bring him something.'

'What's a DNR?'

She told me. It was nothing I really wanted to hear. She never answered my question about relatives, because she probably didn't know – why would she? I filled out the form with my home address, email address, and cell number. Then I went upstairs, thinking there was a double shitload of things I didn't know about Howard Adrian Bowditch.

3

He was awake, and his leg was no longer suspended, but judging by his slow speech and the glassy look in his eyes, he was pretty stoned.

'You again,' he said, which wasn't exactly *mighty glad to see you, Charlie.*

'Me again,' I agreed.

Then he smiled. If I'd known him better, I would have told him he should use it more often. 'Drag up a chair and tell me how you like the look of this.'

There was a blanket up to his waist. He tossed it back, revealing a complex steel gadget that encased his leg from the shin to upper thigh. There were thin rods going into his flesh, the points of entry sealed off with little rubber gasket thingies that were dark with dried blood. His knee was bandaged and looked as big as a breadloaf. A fan of those thin rods went through the wrappings.

He saw the expression on my face and gave a chuckle. 'Looks like an implement of torture from the Inquisition, doesn't it? It's called an external fixator.'

'Does it hurt?' Thinking that was the stupidest question of the year. Those stainless steel rods had to go right into his legbones.

'I'm sure it would, but fortunately I have this.' He held up his left hand. In it was a gadget that looked like the sort of remote his old-school TV didn't have. 'Pain pump. Supposedly it allows me enough to damp down the pain, but not enough to get high. Only since I've never used anything stronger than Empirin, I believe I'm as high as a kite.'

'I think maybe you are,' I said, and this time he didn't just chuckle, he outright laughed. I laughed with him.

'It *will* hurt, I suppose.' He touched the fixator, which formed a series of metal rings around a leg so black with bruising it hurt just to look at it. 'I was told by the doctor who attached it early this morning that devices like this were invented by the Russians during the Battle of Stalingrad.' Now he touched one of the thin steel rods, just above the bloody gasket. 'The Russkies made these stabilizing rods out of bicycle spokes.'

'How long do you have to wear it?'

'Six weeks if I'm lucky and heal well. Three months if I'm not so lucky. They gave me some fancy hardware, I believe titanium was involved, but by the time the fixator comes off, my leg will have frozen solid. Physical therapy will supposedly thaw it, but I'm told said therapy "will involve considerable discomfort." As someone who knows who Nietzsche was, you might be able to translate that.'

'I think it means it'll hurt like hell.'

I was hoping for another laugh – a chuckle, at least – but he only produced a wan smile and gave the dope-delivering gadget a double click with his thumb. 'I believe you're exactly right. If I'd been fortunate enough to shuffle off this mortal coil during the operation, I could have spared myself that considerable discomfort.'

'You don't mean that.'

His eyebrows – gray and bushy – drew together. 'Don't tell me what I mean. It belittles me and makes you sound stupid. I know what I'm facing.' Then, almost grudgingly: 'I'm grateful to you for coming to see me. How is Radar?'

'Good.' I showed him the new pictures I'd taken. He lingered over the one of Radar sitting with her monkey in her mouth. At last he handed my phone back.

'Would you like me to print one out for you, since you don't have a phone I can send it to?'

'I would indeed like that. Thank you for feeding her. And for showing her affection. I'm sure she appreciates it. I do, too.'

'I like her. Mr Bowditch—'

'Howard.'

'Howard, right. I'd like to cut your grass, if that's okay. Is there a mower in that shed?'

His eyes turned wary and he put the pain controller down on the bed. 'No. There's nothing in that shed. Of use, that is.'

Then why is it locked? was a question I knew enough not to ask.

'Well, I'll bring ours up. We live just down the street.'

He sighed as if this was too much trouble for him to deal with. Given the day he'd put in, it probably was. 'Why would you do that? For pay? Are you looking for a job?'

'No.'

'Then why?'

'I don't exactly want to talk about it. I bet there are things you don't want to talk about, am I right?' The flour cannister for one. The shed for another.

He didn't chuckle, but his lips quirked. 'Too right. Is it the Chinese thing? Save a man's life and you're responsible for him thereafter?'

'No.' It was my father's life I was thinking about. 'Can we not go there? I'll cut your grass, and maybe I'll fix the fence out front, too. If you want.'

He looked at me a long time. Then, with an insight that startled me a little: 'If I say yes, will I be doing you a favor?'

I smiled. 'Actually you would be.'

'All right, fine. But a mower would take one chomp of that mess and die. There are a few tools in the cellar. Most of them are for shit, but there's a scythe that might cut it down to mow-able size if you took the rust off and sharpened the blade. There might even be a whetstone on the workbench. Don't let Radar go down the stairs. They're steep and she might fall.'

'Okay. What about the ladder? What should I do with that?'

'It goes under the back porch. I wish I'd left it there, then I wouldn't be here. Goddam doctors with their goddam bad news. Anything else?'

'Well . . . a reporter from *The Weekly Sun* wants to write a story about me.'

Mr Bowditch rolled his eyes. '*That* rag. Are you going to do it?'

'My dad wants me to. He said it might help with my college apps.'

'It might, at that. Although . . . hardly *The New York Crimes*, is it?'

'The guy asked about a picture of me with Radar. I said I'd ask you, but I figured you wouldn't want me to do that. Which is okay with me.'

'Hero dog, is that the angle he wants? Or the one you want?'

'I think she should get the credit, that's all, and she can't exactly bark for it.'

Mr Bowditch considered. 'All right, but I don't want him on the property. You stand with her on the walk. He can take his photo from the gate. *Outside* the gate.' He picked up the pain gadget and gave it a couple of pumps. Then – grudgingly, almost fearfully: 'There's a leash hanging on a hook by the front door. Haven't used it in a long time. She *might* like a walk down the hill . . . on the leash, mind. If she got hit by a car, I'd never forgive you.'

I said I understood that, and I sure did. Mr Bowditch had no brothers, no sisters, no ex-wife or one who'd passed on, either. Radar was what he had.

'And not too far. Once upon a time she could walk four miles, but those days are gone. You better go. I think I'll sleep until they bring me a plate of the slop this place calls supper.'

'Okay. Good to see you.' It actually was. I liked him, and I probably don't need to tell you why, but I will. I liked him because he loved Radar, and I already did, too.

I got up, thought about patting his hand, didn't, and headed for the door.

'Oh Christ, there's another thing,' he said. 'At least one that I can think of now. If I'm still here on Monday – and I will be – the groceries will come.'

'Delivery from Kroger's?'

He gave me that are-you-stupid look again. 'Tiller and Sons.'

I knew about Tiller, but we didn't shop there because it was what they call a 'gourmet market.' Meaning expensive. I had a vague memory of my mother getting me a birthday cake from there when I was five or six. It had lemon frosting and cream between the layers. I thought it was the best cake in the world.

'The man usually comes in the morning. Can you call them and tell them to postpone the delivery until the afternoon, when you'll be there? They have the order.'

'Okay.'

He put a hand on his forehead. I wasn't sure because I was in the doorway, but I thought it was shaking a little. 'And you'll have to pay. Can you also do that?'

'Sure.' I'd have Dad give me a blank check and fill in the amount.

'Tell them to cancel the weekly order after this one until they hear from me. Keep track of your expenses.' He ran his hand slowly down his face, as if to smooth out the lines – a lost cause if there ever was one. 'Goddam, I hate being dependent. Why did I ever get up on that ladder? I must have been taking stupid pills.'

'You'll be fine,' I said, but going down the hall to the elevators, I kept thinking of something he'd said when we were talking about the ladder: *Goddam doctors with their goddam bad news*. Probably he'd just been talking about how long it would take his goddam leg to goddam heal, and maybe having a goddam physical therapist (probably a goddam snoop in the bargain) in the house.

But I wondered.

4

I called Bill Harriman and told him he could take a picture of me and Radar if he still wanted to. I told him Mr Bowditch's conditions, and Harriman said that was fine.

'Kind of a recluse, isn't he? I can't find anything about him in our files, or in *The Beacon*.'

'I wouldn't know. Does Saturday morning work for you?'

It did, and we agreed on ten o'clock. I got on my bike and headed home, pedaling easy and thinking hard. First about Radar. Leash hanging in the front hall, deeper than I had yet penetrated the big old house. Now that I thought about it, there was no ID tag hanging on Radar's collar. Which probably meant no dog license certifying her free of rabies or anything else. Had Radar ever been to the vet? I was guessing not.

Mr Bowditch had his groceries delivered, which struck me as a high-class way to get your beer and skittles, and Tiller and Sons was certainly a high-class place where high-class people with a lot of folding green shopped. Which led me to wonder, as my father had, what Mr Bowditch had done for a living before he retired. He had an elegant way of talking, almost like a professor, but I didn't think retired teachers could afford to shop in a market that boasted of having a 'step-down wine cellar.' Old TV. No computer (I'd bet on that) and no cell phone. Also no car. I knew his middle name, but not how old he was.

When I got home I called Tiller and fixed the grocery delivery for three o'clock on Monday. I was thinking of taking my homework up to the Bowditch house when Andy Chen knocked on the back door for the first time in I didn't know how long. As little kids, Andy and I and Bertie Bird had been inseparable, even called ourselves the Three Musketeers, but Bertie's family had moved away to Dearborn (probably a good thing for me) and Andy was a brain who was taking a bunch of AP courses, including physics at the nearby branch of the University of Illinois. Of course he was also a jock, excelling in two sports I didn't play. Tennis was one. The other was basketball, coached by Harkness, and I could guess why Andy was here.

'Coach says you should come back and play baseball,' Andy said, after checking our fridge for any tasty bites. He settled on some left-over kung pao chicken. 'He says you're letting the team down.'

'Uh-oh, pack your bags, we're going on a guilt trip,' I said. 'I don't think so.'

'He says you don't have to apologize.'

'I wasn't planning on it.'

'His brain is basically fried,' Andy said. 'You know what he calls me? The Yellow Peril. As in "Get out there, Yellow Peril, and guard that big bastard."'

'You put up with that?' I was both curious and horrified.

'He thinks it's a compliment, which I find hilarious. Besides, two more seasons and I'll be out of Hillview and playing for Hofstra. Division 1, here I come. Full ride, baby. I will be the Yellow Peril no more. Did you really save that old guy's life? That's what I'm hearing at school.'

'The dog saved him. I just called 911.'

'It didn't rip your throat out?'

'No. She's a sweetie. And she's old.'

'She wasn't old the day *I* saw her. That day she was out for blood. Is it creepy inside? Stuffed animals? Kit-Cat Klock that follows you with its eyes? Chainsaw down cellar? Kids say he could be a serial killer.'

'He's not a serial killer and the house isn't creepy.' That was true. It was the shed that was creepy. That weird scuttering sound had been creepy. And Radar: *she* knew that sound had been creepy, too.

'Okay,' Andy said, 'I gave you the message. Got anything else to eat? Cookies?'

'Nope.' The cookies were at Mr Bowditch's house. Chocolate-marshmallow and pecan sandies that had surely come from Tiller and Sons.

'Okay. Later, dude.'

'Later, Yellow Peril.'

We looked at each other and broke up laughing. For a minute or two it was like we were eleven again.

5

On Saturday I got my picture taken with Radar. There was indeed a leash in the front hall, hanging next to a winter coat with a pair of old-fashioned galoshes beneath it. I thought about going through the pockets of the coat – just to see what I might see, you know – and told myself not to be a snoop. There was a spare collar attached to the leash, but no license tag; as far as town government knew, Mr Bowditch's dog was flying, ha-ha, under the radar. We went down the path out front and waited for Bill Harriman to show up. He did so on the dot, driving a beat-up old Mustang and looking like he maybe graduated from college the year before.

Radar gave a few token growls when he parked and got out. I told her he was okay and she quieted down, only sticking her nose through the rusty gate to give his pantsleg a sniff. She growled again when he stuck his hand over the gate for a shake with me.

'Protective,' he observed.

'I guess she is.'

I expected him to have a big camera – I probably got the idea from some Turner Classic Movie about crusading newspaper reporters – but he took our picture with his phone. After two or three, he asked if she'd sit. 'If she will, take a knee beside her. That would be a good one. Just a boy and his dog.'

'She's not mine,' I said, thinking she actually was. For the time being, anyway. I told Radar to sit, not knowing if she would. She did, right away, as if just waiting for the command. I got down beside her. I noticed Mrs Richland had come out to watch with her hand shading her eyes.

'Put your arm around her,' Harriman said.

When I did, Radar licked my cheek. It made me laugh. And that was the picture that appeared in the next issue of the *Sun*. And not just there, as it turned out.

'What's it like in the house?' Harriman asked, pointing to it.

I shrugged. 'Like any other house, I guess. Normal.' Not that I knew, having only seen the Hall of Old Reading Matter, the kitchen, the living room, and the front hall.

'Nothing out of the ordinary, then? Because it looks spooky.'

I opened my mouth to say the TV was from before the days of cable, let alone streaming, then closed it again. It occurred to me that Harriman had progressed from picture-taking to interviewing. Trying to, at least; as a newbie, he wasn't exactly subtle.

'Nope, it's just a house. I better get going.'

'Will you be taking care of the dog until Mr Bowditch gets out of the hospital?'

This time I was the one who stuck out my hand. Radar didn't growl but watched closely for any funny business. 'Hope the pictures are okay. Come on, Radar.'

I started toward the house. When I looked back, Harriman was crossing the street to talk to Mrs Richland. There was nothing I could do about that, so I went around back with Radar coming along at my heel. I noticed that after walking for a bit, she limbered up.

I put the ladder under the back porch, where there was also a snow shovel and a big old pair of gardening shears that looked as rusty as the bolt on the gate and would probably be just as hard to operate. Radar peered down at me from halfway up the steps, which was cute enough for me to take another picture. I was getting foolish about her. I knew it and didn't mind owning it.

There were cleaning products under the kitchen sink, and a neat pile of paper grocery bags with the Tiller logo on them. There were also rubber gloves. I put them on, took a bag, and went on poop patrol. Got plenty, too.

On Sunday I put Radar on her leash again and walked her down the hill to our house. She moved slowly at first, both because of her arthritic hips and because she clearly wasn't used to being away from home. She kept looking at me for reassurance, which touched my heart. After awhile, though, she began to make her way more easily and confidently, stopping to sniff telephone poles and to squat here and there, so other passing dogs would know that Radar of Bowditch had been there.

Dad was home. Radar initially shrank back from him, growling, but when Dad held out his hand, she came forward enough to sniff it. Half a slice of bologna sealed the deal. We stayed for an hour or so. Dad quizzed me about my photo shoot and laughed when I told him how Harriman had tried to interview me about the inside of the house, and how I'd shut him down.

'He'll get better if he sticks with the news business,' Dad said. '*The Weekly Sun* is just the place where he starts building his clipbook.'

By then Radar was snoozing beside the couch where Dad had once passed out drunk. He bent down and ruffled her fur. 'I bet she was an *engine* when she was in her prime.'

I thought of Andy's story about the terrifying beast he had encountered four or five years earlier and agreed.

'You should see if he has any dog meds for her arthritis. And probably she should have a tablet for heartworm.'

'I'll check around.' I had taken off her leash, but now I clipped it to her collar. She raised her head. 'We should go back.'

'Don't want to keep her here for the day? She looks pretty comfortable.'

'No, I should take her back.'

If he asked why, I'd tell him the truth: because I didn't think Howard Bowditch would like it. He didn't ask. 'Okay. Want a ride?'

'That's all right. I think she'll be fine if we go slow.'

And she was. On the way back up the hill, she seemed glad to be sniffing grass that wasn't her own.

6

On Monday afternoon a neat little green van with TILLER & SONS painted on the side (in gold, no less) pulled up. The driver asked me where Mr Bowditch was. I told him and he handed the bags to me over the gate as if that were the usual thing, so I guess it was. I filled in the amount on the blank check Dad had signed – pretty horrified at the idea of a hundred and five scoots for three bags of groceries – and handed it back. There were lamb chops and ground sirloin, which I put in the freezer. I wasn't going to eat his food (cookies excepted), but I wasn't going to let it go to waste, either.

With that taken care of I went down cellar, closing the door behind me so Radar wouldn't try to follow. It wasn't the least bit serial-killerish, only musty and dusty, as if nobody had been down there for a long time. The overhead lights were fluorescent bars, one of them flickery and half-dead. The floor was rough cement. There were tools on pegs, including the scythe, which looked like the kind of thing Old Man Death carries in the cartoons.

In the center of the room was a worktable covered by a dropcloth. I lifted it for a peek and saw a partially assembled jigsaw puzzle that appeared to have a zillion pieces. From what I could see (there was no box to check it against), it was meant to be a mountain meadow with the Rockies in the background. There was a folding chair set up at one end of the table, where most of the remaining pieces were spread out. The seat was dusty, from which I deduced that Mr Bowditch hadn't been working his puzzle for quite some time. Maybe he'd given up. I know I would have; a lot of what was left to be assembled was plain old blue sky without even a single cloud to break the monotony. I'm talking about this at more length than it deserves, maybe . . . but then again maybe not. There was something sad about it. I couldn't express the reason for that sadness then, but I'm older now and think I can. It was about the jigsaw, but it was also the antique TV and the Hall of Old Reading Matter. It was about an elderly man's solitary pursuits, and the dust – on the folding chair, on the books and magazines – suggested that even those were winding down. The only things in the cellar that looked like they were used regularly were the washer and dryer.

I fluffed the cover back over the puzzle and checked out a cabinet between the furnace and the water heater. It was old-fashioned, full of drawers. I found screws in one, pliers and wrenches in another, stacks of rubber-banded receipts in a third, chisels and what had to be a whetstone in the fourth. I put the whetstone in my pocket, grabbed the scythe, and went upstairs. Radar wanted to jump on me and I told her to stand clear so I didn't accidentally poke her with the blade.

We went out back, where I knew I could get four bars on my phone. I sat on the steps and Radar sat beside me. I opened Safari, typed *sharpening with a whetstone*, looked at a couple of videos, then went to work. It didn't take long to put a pretty keen edge on the scythe.

I took a picture to show Mr Bowditch, then biked to the hospital. Found him sleeping. Biked back in the late afternoon light and fed Radar. Missed baseball a little.

Well . . . maybe more than a little.

7

On Tuesday afternoon I started scything the tall grass, first in the front yard and then in the back. After an hour or so I looked at my red hands and knew that blisters would soon form there if I wasn't careful. I put Radar on her leash, walked her down to our house, and found a pair of Dad's work gloves in the garage. We walked back up the hill, going slowly in deference to Radar's sore hips. I whacked away at the grass on the side while Radar snoozed, then fed her and knocked off for the day. Dad cooked hamburgers on the backyard grill, and I ate three. Plus cherry cobbler for dessert.

Dad drove me to the hospital and waited downstairs reading reports while I went up to visit Mr Bowditch. I saw he'd also had a hamburger, plus mac and cheese on the side, but he hadn't eaten much of either. Of course he hadn't spent two hours swinging a scythe, and although he tried to be pleasant and looked at some new pictures of Radar (plus one of the scythe and another of his half-cut front lawn), it was clear to me he was in a lot of pain. He kept pushing the button that released the dope. The third time he did it, it made a low buzzing sound, like when a contestant on a game show gives the wrong answer.

'Fucking thing. I'm maxed out for an hour. Better go, Charlie, before I start barking at you just because I feel miserable. Come back Friday. No, Saturday. Maybe I'll feel better by then.'

'Any word on when they're going to let you out?'

'Sunday, maybe. A lady came and said she wanted to help me work on a . . .' He raised his big hands, bruised on the backs from IV needles, and made quotation marks. '. . . "recovery plan." I told her to fuck off. Not in those exact words. I'm trying to be a good patient, but it's hard. It's not just the pain, it's . . .' He made a weak circling gesture, then dropped his arms back to the coverlet.

'Too many people,' I said. 'You're not used to it.'

'You understand. Thank God somebody does. And too much *noise*.

Before she left, the woman – her name's something like Ravenhugger – asked me if I had a bed on the first floor of my house. I don't, but the couch pulls out. Although it hasn't been made up as a bed in a long time. I guess . . . maybe not ever. I only bought it because it was on sale.'

'I'll make it up if you tell me where the sheets are.'

'Do you know how to do that?'

As the son of a widower who had been a very active alcoholic, I did. Also how to wash clothes and buy groceries. I'd been a good little co-dependent. 'Yes.'

'Linen closet. Second floor. Have you been up there yet?'

I shook my head.

'Well, I guess now is your chance. It's across from my bedroom. Thank you.'

'No prob. And the next time that lady comes in, tell her I'm your recovery plan.' I got up. 'Better go and let you get some rest.'

I went to the door. He spoke my name and I turned back.

'You're the best thing that's happened to me in a long time.' Then, as if speaking as much to himself as to me: 'I'm going to trust you. I can't see any choice.'

I told Dad what he'd said about me being the best thing that had happened to him, but not about the trusting part. Some instinct made me hold that back. Dad gave me a strong one-armed hug and kissed my cheek and said he was proud of me.

That was a good day.

8

On Thursday I forced myself to knock on the shed door again. I really did not like that little building. No one knocked back. Or scratched. I tried to tell myself I'd imagined that weird skittering sound, but if I had, Radar had imagined it, too, and I didn't think dogs were much in the imagination department. Of course, she could have been reacting to my reaction. Or if I'm going to tell the truth, she could have sensed my fear and my almost instinctive revulsion.

On Friday I trundled our Lawn-Boy up the street and went to work on the half-tamed yard. I figured I could have it looking relatively spiff by the weekend. The following week was spring vacation, and I planned to spend a lot of it at Number 1 Sycamore. I'd clean the windows, then go to work on the picket fence – get it standing up straight again. I thought seeing those things would cheer Mr Bowditch up.

I was mowing along the Pine Street side of the house (Radar was inside, wanting nothing to do with the roaring Lawn-Boy) when my phone vibrated in my pocket. I killed the mower and saw ARCADIA HOSPITAL on the screen. I took the call with a sinking in my gut, sure someone was going to tell me Mr Bowditch had taken a turn for the worse. Or worse still, passed away.

It was about him, all right, but it wasn't anything bad. A lady named Mrs Ravensburger asked if I could come in tomorrow morning at nine to talk about Mr Bowditch's 'recovery and aftercare.' I said I could, and she then asked if I could bring along a parent or guardian. I said probably.

'I saw your picture in the paper. With that wonderful dog of his. Mr Bowditch owes you both a debt of gratitude.'

I assumed she was talking about the *Sun*, and I guess she could have been, but Radar and I turned up elsewhere, too. Or maybe I should say everywhere.

Dad came in late, as he usually did on Fridays, and he had a copy of the *Chicago Tribune*, opened to page two, where the *Trib* ran a little sidebar called 'In Other News.' It collated bite-sized items of a more cheerful nature than the stuff on the front page. The one featuring Radar and me was headlined HERO DOG, HERO TEEN. I wasn't exactly shocked to see myself in the *Trib*, but I was surprised. This is a pretty good world, all evidence to the contrary notwithstanding, and there are thousands of people doing thousands of good deeds every day (maybe millions). A kid helping out an old guy who fell off a ladder and broke his leg was nothing special, but the picture sold it. Radar was caught in mid-lick, me with my arm around her neck and my head thrown back in laughter. And looking, dare I say, rather handsome. Which made me wonder if Gina Pascarelli, my daydream girl, had come across it.

'See that?' Dad asked, tapping the caption. 'AP. Associated Press. That picture's probably in five or six hundred newspapers today, coast-to-coast. Not to mention all over the Internet. Andy Warhol said eventually everyone in America would be famous for fifteen minutes, and I guess you're having your quarter-hour. Want to go out to Bingo's to celebrate?'

I certainly did, and while I was eating my beef ribs (the double rack), I asked Dad if he'd come with me to the hospital tomorrow, to talk to a lady named Mrs Ravensburger. He said it would be his pleasure.

9

We met in Ravensburger's office. With her was a young woman named Melissa Wilcox – tall and toned, her blond hair worn in a stubby, no-nonsense ponytail. She was going to be Mr Bowditch's physical therapist. She did most of the talking, checking a little notebook from time to time so as not to forget anything. She said that after 'some discussion,' Mr Bowditch had agreed to allow her into his home twice a week to work on his range of motion and get him on his feet again, first with Canadian crutches – the kind with metal circlets for arm support – then with a walker. She would also take his vitals to make sure he was 'progressing nicely' and check on something called pin care. 'Which you will have to do, Charlie.'

I asked her what that meant, and she explained that the rods going into his leg had to be swabbed regularly with disinfectant. She said it was a painful procedure, but not as painful as an infection that could lead to gangrene.

'I wanted to come four days a week, but he wouldn't have it,' Melissa said. 'He's very clear on what he will and won't have.'

Tell me about it, I thought.

'He'll need a lot of help at first, Charlie, and he says you'll give it.'

'According to him,' Mrs Ravensburger put in, '*you're* his recovery plan.' She was talking to me but looking at my dad, as if inviting him to object.

He didn't.

Melissa flipped to a new page on her little notebook, which was bright purple with a snarling tiger on the front. 'He says there's a bathroom on the first floor?'

'Yes.' I didn't bother telling her it was really small. She'd find that out on her first home visit.

She nodded. 'That's a big deal, because he won't be capable of climbing stairs for some time.'

'But he will be able to eventually?'

'If he works hard, sure. He's elderly – claims he doesn't know exactly *how* old he is, as a matter of fact – but he's in good shape. Doesn't smoke, says he doesn't drink, isn't carrying any extra weight.'

'That's a biggie,' Dad said.

'You bet it is. Weight-bearing is a huge concern, especially in the elderly. The plan is for him to leave the hospital on Monday. There have to be safety bars installed on the sides of the toilet before then. Can you do that this weekend? If not, we'll push his release back to Tuesday.'

'I can do it.' I saw more YouTube videos in my immediate future.

'He'll need a urinal for nights and a bedpan for emergencies. You okay with that?'

I said yes, and I was. I had cleaned up vomit on more than one occasion; dumping poo from a bedpan into the toilet might actually be a step up.

Melissa closed her notebook. 'There are a thousand other things – little things, most of them. This will help. Check it out.'

She took a pamphlet from the back pocket of her jeans. The title wasn't *Home Care for Dummies*, but it could have been. I said I'd read it and put it in my back pocket.

'I'll know better what's needed when I see the place for myself,' Melissa said. 'I thought of taking a run up there this afternoon, but he's very insistent that I not go inside until he's back.'

Yes, Mr Bowditch could be very insistent. I had discovered that early.

'Are you sure you want to take this on, Charlie?' Mrs Ravensburger asked. This time she didn't face-check my father first.

'Yes.'

'Even if it means staying with him the first three or four nights?' Melissa asked. 'I tried to discuss the possibility of a rehab unit – there's a nice one called Riverview that has vacancies – but he wouldn't hear of it. Said he just wanted to go home.'

'I can stay with him.' Although the thought of maybe sleeping upstairs in a bedroom I'd so far not even seen was weird. 'No problem. It's school vacation.'

Mrs Ravensburger turned to my dad. 'Are *you* all right with this arrangement, Mr Reade?'

I waited, not sure what he'd say, but he came through.

'A little worried about it, which is probably natural, but Charlie's responsible, Mr Bowditch seems to have formed a bond with him, and he really has no one else.'

I said, 'Ms Wilcox, about the house—'

She smiled. 'Melissa, please. We're going to be colleagues, after all.'

It was easier to call her Melissa than it was to call Mr Bowditch Howard, because she was closer to my age. 'About the house – don't take it personally, like he's afraid you're going to steal stuff or something. He's just . . . well . . .' I didn't quite know how to finish, but Dad did.

'He's a private person.'

'That's right,' I said. 'And you have to make allowances for him being a little grouchy, too. Because—'

Melissa didn't wait for the *because*. 'Believe me, if I had an external fixator holding my broken leg together, I'd be grouchy, too.'

'What's his insurance situation?' Dad asked Mrs Ravensburger. 'Can you say?'

Mrs Ravensburger and Melissa Wilcox exchanged a glance. Mrs Ravensburger said, 'I'm not comfortable going into detail about a patient's financial arrangements, but I will say that according to the bursar, he intends to take care of his expenses personally.'

'Ah,' Dad said, as if that explained everything. His face said it explained nothing. He got up and shook hands with Mrs Ravensburger. So did I.

Melissa followed us out into the hall, seeming to glide in her blinding white sneakers.

'LSU?' I asked.

She looked surprised. 'How'd you know?'

'The notebook. Basketball?'

She smiled. 'And volleyball.'

Given her height, I bet she had a hell of a smash.

CHAPTER FIVE

Shopping. My Father's Pipe.

A Call from Mr Bowditch. The Flour Cannister.

1

We went to the hardware store to get a safety-bar installation kit, then to Pet Pantry, where there was also a walk-in veterinary. I got heartworm chewables and Carprofen for Radar's arthritis. That stuff is supposed to be by prescription only, but when I explained the situation, the lady gave it to me, only specifying that the meds had to be a cash deal. She said Mr Bowditch bought all of Radar's stuff there, paying extra for delivery. Dad used his credit card for the safety-bar kit. I used my own money for the pills. Our last stop was the drugstore, where I bought a urinal with a long neck, a bedpan, the disinfectant I was supposed to use for the pin care, and two spray bottles of heavy-duty window cleaner. I paid for that stuff, too, but not cash. I had a $250 limit on my Visa, but wasn't worried the card would be refused. I was never what you'd call a shop-'til-you-drop type.

On the ride home I kept expecting Dad to talk to me about this commitment I'd made . . . which was, after all, pretty big for a kid of seventeen. He didn't, though; just listened to classic rock on the radio and sometimes sang along. I found out soon enough that he was just deciding what he wanted to say.

I walked up to Mr Bowditch's house, where I was greeted by Radar. I put her meds on the counter, then peeked in the bathroom. I thought the tight quarters would actually be helpful when it came to installing the safety bars (and for him using them), but that was tomorrow's job. I'd seen a pile of clean rags on the shelf over the washing machine in the cellar. I went down and grabbed a double handful. It was a pretty spring day, and my initial idea had been to spend it outdoors putting the fence to rights, but I decided that the windows should come first, so the stink of the cleanser would be out of the house when Mr Bowditch came back. It also gave me an excuse to tour the place.

In addition to the kitchen, pantry, and living room – the places where he actually lived – there was a dining room with a long table covered with a dustcloth. There were no chairs, which made it look pretty empty. There was also a room meant to be a study, or a library, or a combination of the two. I saw with real dismay that the ceiling had leaked and some of the books had gotten wet. These were nice ones, too, expensive-looking and leatherbound, not like the careless stacks in the back hall. There was a set of Dickens, a set of Kipling, a set of Mark Twain, and a set of someone named Thackeray. I decided that when I had more time, I'd pull them from their shelves, spread them on the floor, and see if they could be saved. There were probably YouTube videos about how to do that. I pretty much lived by the Tube that spring.

There were three bedrooms on the second floor, plus the linen closet and another, bigger, bathroom. His bedroom was lined with more bookshelves, and there was a reading lamp on the side of the bed where he obviously slept. The books in here were mostly paperbacks – mysteries, science fiction, fantasy, and pulp horror going back to the 40s. Some looked really good, and I thought if things went okay I'd ask to borrow some. I guessed Thackeray would be heavy going, but *The Bride Wore Black* looked right up my street. The bodacious bride on the cover was wearing black, all right, but not much of it. There were two books on his bedtable, a paperback called *Something Wicked This Way Comes*, by Ray Bradbury, and a thick hardcover tome titled *The Origins of Fantasy and Its Place in the World*

Matrix: Jungian Perspectives. On the cover was a funnel filling up with stars.

One of the other bedrooms held a double bed that had been made up but was covered with a plastic sheet; the third was completely empty and smelled stale. If I'd been wearing hard shoes instead of sneaks, my footfalls would have made spooky hollow sounds in that one.

Narrow stairs (*Psycho* stairs, I thought) led up to the third floor. It wasn't an attic but was being used as one. There was plenty of furniture jumbled up in the three rooms, including six fancy chairs that were probably supposed to go with the dining room table, and the bed from the empty room, with its head laid lengthwise across it. There were a couple of bikes (one missing a wheel), dusty cartons of old magazines, and in the third and smallest room, a wooden box of what looked like carpentry tools from the time when talking pictures were new. On the side, faded, were the initials A.B. I picked out the drill, thinking it would help with the safety bar installation, but it was frozen solid. And no wonder. The roof had leaked in the corner where the tools had been left, and the whole works – drill, two hammers, saw, a leveling gadget with a bleary yellow bubble in the middle – had gone to Rust City. Something needed to be done about the leaky roof, I thought, and before the next winter arrived or there would be structural damage. If there hadn't been already.

I started with the windows on the third floor, because they were the dirtiest. Filthy, in fact. I could see I'd be changing the water in my bucket often, and of course the insides were only half the job. I knocked off for lunch, heating a can of chili on the elderly Hotpoint.

'Should I let you lick the bowl?' I asked Radar. She looked up at me with those big brown eyes of hers. 'I won't tell if you won't.'

I put it down and she went at it. Then I went back to the windows. By the time I finished, it was mid-afternoon. My fingers looked pruney and my arms were tired from all the rubbing, but Windex and vinegar (a YouTube tip) really did make a difference. The house was filled with light.

'I like it,' I said. 'Want to take a stroll down to my house? See what Dad's up to?'

She barked that she did.

2

Dad was waiting for me on the front porch. His pipe was on the rail, along with a pouch of tobacco. Which meant we would be having the talk after all. A serious one.

There was a time when my dad smoked cigarettes. I don't remember how old I was when Mom gave him the pipe for his birthday. It wasn't a fancy Sherlock Holmes job, but I think expensive. I do remember she'd been asking him to quit the cancer sticks and he kept promising (vaguely, the way addicts do) that he would get around to it. The pipe did the trick. First he cut down on the butts, then let them go entirely not long before Mom crossed the goddam bridge to get us a box of chicken.

I liked the smell of the Three Sails he got at the tobacconist downtown, but quite often there was nothing to smell because it kept going out. That might have been part of Mom's master plan, but I never got a chance to ask her. Eventually the pipe went into the pipe-rack on the mantle. At least until Mom died. Then it came out again. I never saw him with another cigarette during his drinking years, but the pipe was always with him at night while he watched those old movies, although he rarely lit it or even filled the bowl. He chewed hell out of the stem and the bit, though, and had to replace both. He took the pipe with him to AA meetings when he started going. There was no smoking there so he chewed on the stem, sometimes (Lindy Franklin told me this) with the bowl upside-down.

Around the time of his second anniversary, the pipe went back into the rack on the mantle. I asked him about it once and he said, 'I'm two years sober. I think it's time I stopped teething.'

But the pipe still came out once in awhile. Before some of the big agent meetings at the Chicago office if he had to make a presentation. Always on the anniversary of Mom's death. And it was out now. Complete with tobacco, which meant this was going to be a *very* serious talk.

Radar climbed to the porch old lady style, pausing to inspect each step. When she finally made it, Dad scratched behind her ears. 'Who's a good girl?'

Radar made a woofing noise and lay down beside Dad's rocker. I took the other one.

'Did you get her started on the meds?'

'Not yet. I'll sneak the heartworm and the arthritis pill into her supper.'

'You didn't take the safety-bar installation kit.'

'That's for tomorrow. I'll read the instructions tonight.' Also the home-care-for-dummies pamphlet. 'I'll need to borrow your drill, if it's okay. I found someone's toolbox – initials A.B. on it, maybe his father's or grandfather's – but everything in it's rusty. The roof leaks.'

'You're welcome to use it.' He reached for the pipe. The bowl was already loaded. He had some kitchen matches in his breast pocket and he scratched one alight with his thumbnail, a skill that had fascinated me as a little kid. Still did, actually. 'You know I'd be happy to go up there with you and help out.'

'No, that's okay. It's a pretty small bathroom and we'd just get in each other's way.'

'But that's not really it, is it, Chip?'

How long had it been since he'd called me that? Five years? He held the lit match – already halfway down the stick – over the bowl and began sucking away. Also waiting for me to reply, of course, but I had nothing. Radar raised her head, smelled the fragrant tobacco smoke, then put her snout back on the porch boards. She looked pretty contented.

He shook out the match. 'There's nothing up there you don't want me to see, is there?'

That made me think of Andy, asking if there were a lot of stuffed animals and a spooky Kit-Cat Klock that followed you with its eyes. I smiled. 'No, it's just a house, kinda rundown, with a leaky roof. Something will have to be done about that, eventually.'

He nodded and puffed his pipe. 'I talked to Lindy about this . . . this situation.'

I wasn't surprised. Lindy was his sponsor, and Dad was supposed to talk about the things that bothered him. 'He says that maybe you have a caretaker mentality. From when I was boozing. God knows there were times when you did caretake me, young as you were. Cleaned the house, did the dishes, got your own breakfast and sometimes your dinner.' He paused. 'Those days are hard for me to remember and even harder to talk about.'

'It's not that.'

'Then what is it?'

I still didn't want to tell him I'd made a deal with God and had to keep up my end of the bargain, but there was something else I *could* tell him. Something he'd understand, and fortunately it was true. 'You know how they talk in AA about maintaining an attitude of gratitude?'

He nodded. 'A grateful alcoholic doesn't get drunk. That's what they say.'

'And I'm grateful you don't drink anymore. Maybe I don't tell you all the time, but I am. So why don't we say I'm trying to pay it forward, and leave it at that?'

He took his pipe from his mouth and swiped a hand across his eyes. 'All right, we will. But I want to meet him eventually. Feel like it's my duty. Do you understand that?'

I said I did. 'Maybe when he's a little bit down the road from the accident?'

He nodded. 'That works. I love you, kiddo.'

'Love you, too.'

'As long as you understand you're biting off a lot. You know that, right?'

I did, and I was aware I didn't know just how much. I thought that was good. If I really knew, I might lose heart. 'There's that other thing they say in your program, about taking it a day at a time.'

He nodded. 'Okay, but spring vacation will be over fast. You have to keep up with your studies no matter how much time you feel you have to spend up there. I insist on that.'

'Okay.'

He looked at the pipe. 'This thing's gone out. It always does.' He put it on the porch rail, then leaned down and scratched the thick fur on the nape of Radar's neck. She raised her head, then lowered it again. 'This is a damn good dog.'

'She is.'

'Fell in love with her, didn't you?'

'Well . . . yeah. I guess so.'

'She's got a collar but no tag, which means Mr Bowditch hasn't paid the dog tax. My guess is she's never been to the vet.' Mine, too.

'Never been vaccinated for rabies. Among other things.' He paused, then said, 'Got a question, and I want you to think about it. Very seriously. Are we going to end up on the hook for this? The groceries, the dog meds, the safety bars?'

'Don't forget the urinal,' I said.

'Are we? Tell me what you think.'

'He told me to keep track and he'd take care of the expenses.' This was half an answer at best. I knew it and Dad probably did, too. On second thought, strike the *probably*.

'Not that we're exactly in a hole on his account. A couple of hundred dollars is all. But the hospital . . . do you know how much a week's stay in Arcadia costs? Plus the operations, of course, and all the aftercare?' I didn't, but as an insurance adjuster, Dad did.

'Eighty thousand. Minimum.'

'There's no way we could be on the hook for *that*, could we?'

'No, that's all him. I don't know what kind of insurance he has, or if he has any. I checked with Lindy and he has nothing with Overland. Medicare, probably. Beyond that, who knows?' He shifted in his seat. 'I checked him out a little bit. I hope that doesn't make you mad.'

It didn't, and didn't surprise me, because checking people out was what my father did for a living. And was I curious? Of course. 'What did you find?'

'Almost nothing, which I would have said was impossible in this day and age.'

'Well, he doesn't have a computer or even a cell phone. Which lets out Facebook and any other social media.' I had an idea that Mr Bowditch would have sneered at Facebook even if he did have a computer. Facebook was *snoopy*.

'You said there were initials on the toolbox you found. A.B., right?'

'Right.'

'That fits. The property at the top of the hill comprises an acre and a half, which is a hell of a good patch. It was purchased by someone named Adrian Bowditch in 1920.'

'His grandfather?'

'Maybe, but given how old he is, it could have been his father.' Dad plucked his pipe off the porch rail, gave the bit a chew or two, then put it back. 'How old *is* he, anyway? Does he really not know, I wonder?'

'I guess it's possible.'

'When I saw him back in the old days – this was before he more or less holed up – he looked about fifty. I'd give him a wave and sometimes he'd flip a hand back to me.'

'Never spoke to him?'

'Might have said hi, I guess, or passed a word about the weather if it was worth commenting on, but he wasn't the conversational type. Anyway, that would have made him roughly the right age for Vietnam, but I couldn't find any military record.'

'So he didn't serve.'

'*Probably* didn't serve. I probably could have found out more if I was still working for Overland, but I'm not and I didn't want to ask Lindy.'

'I get it.'

'I established that he's got at least some money, because property taxes are a matter of public record, and the tab on Number 1 Sycamore in 2012 was twenty-two thousand and change.'

'He pays that every *year*?'

'It varies. The important part is he's paying it, and he was here when your mom and I moved in – maybe I told you that. He would have been shelling out a lot less back in the day, property taxes have gone up like everything else, but you're still talking six figures in all. It's a big lot. What did he do before he retired?'

'I don't know. I really just met the guy, and he was messed up when I did. We haven't had what you'd call a real heart-to-heart.' Although that was coming. I just didn't know it yet.

'I don't know, either. I looked but didn't find. Which, it bears repeating, I would have said was impossible in this day and age. I've heard of people going off the grid, but usually in the wilds of Alaska with a cult that thinks the world's going to end, or in Montana, like the Unabomber.'

'Una-who?'

'A domestic terrorist. Real name, Ted Kaczynski. You didn't happen to see any bomb-making equipment lying around Bowditch's house, did you?' Dad said this with a humorous lift of his eyebrows, but I wasn't entirely sure he was joking.

'The most dangerous thing I've seen was the scythe. Oh, and a rusty hatchet in that toolbox on the third floor.'

'Any pictures? Like of his father and mother? Or him, when he was young?'

'Nope. The only one I saw was a photo of Radar. It's on the table beside his easy chair in the living room.'

'Huh.' Dad reached for his pipe, changed his mind. 'We don't know where his money comes from – assuming he still has some – and we don't know what he did for a living. Something from home, I assume, because he's an agoraphobe. That means—'

'I know what it means.'

'My guess is he always tended in that direction and it got worse as he got older. He pulled in.'

'The lady across the street told me he used to walk Radar at night.' She pricked up her ears at the sound of her name. 'It seemed a little weird to me, most people walk their dogs in the daytime, but—'

'Less people on the streets at night,' Dad said.

'Yeah. He sure doesn't seem like a hiya-neighbor kind of guy.'

'One other thing,' Dad said. 'Kind of weird . . . but *he's* kind of weird, wouldn't you say?'

I passed on the question and asked about the other thing.

'He's got a car. I don't know where it is, but he's got one. I found the registration online. It's a 1957 Studebaker. He gets a rate on the excise tax because it's registered as an antique. Like the property tax, he pays the excise every year, but that's a lot cheaper. Sixty bucks or so.'

'If he's got a car, you should be able to find his driver's license, Dad. That will say how old he is.'

He smiled and shook his head. 'Good try, but no Illinois license has ever been issued in the name of Howard Bowditch. And of course you don't have to have a driver's license to buy a car. It might not even run.'

'Why pay the yearly tax on a car that doesn't?'

'Here's a better one, Chip – why pay the tax when you can't drive?'

'What about Adrian Bowditch? The father or grandfather? Maybe he had a license.'

'Didn't think of that. I'll check.' He paused. 'Are you sure you want to do this?'

'I do.'

'Then ask him about some of this stuff. Because as far as I can find, he's almost not there.'

I said I would, and that seemed to close the discussion. I thought about mentioning the weird scuttering sound I'd heard in the shed – the shed with a heavy padlock on the door even though there was supposedly nothing in it – but I didn't. That sound had grown vague in my mind, and I already had enough to think about.

3

I was still thinking about those things as I took the plastic dustcover off the bed in the guestroom where I'd sleep during part of spring vacation, or maybe even all of it. That bed was made up, but the sheets had a stale and musty smell. I took them off and put on fresh from the linen closet. *How* fresh I didn't know, but they smelled better, and there was another set for the pull-out couch, along with a comforter.

I went downstairs. Radar was sitting at the foot, waiting for me. I dropped the bedclothes on Mr Bowditch's easy chair and saw that I'd have to move it and the little table beside it to pull the couch out. When I moved the table, the drawer came partway open. I saw a litter of change, a harmonica so old most of the chrome finish was worn away . . . and a bottle of Carprofen. That made me happy, because I hadn't liked to think of Mr Bowditch ignoring his aging dog's discomfort, and it certainly explained why the Pet Pantry lady had been so willing to sell me more. What made me less happy was realizing the medication wasn't working very well.

I fed her, sticking a pill from the new bottle in her food – reasoning the stuff I'd just bought was fresher and maybe more powerful – then went back upstairs to get a pillow for the roll-out. Radar was once more waiting at the foot of the stairs.

'Jesus, you gobbled that fast!'

Radar thumped her tail and moved just enough for me to get by her.

I plumped the pillow a bit, then dropped it on what was now a bed in the middle of the living room. He might grouse about it, probably would, but I thought it would be okay. Pin care for his fixator looked easy enough, but I hoped there was something in *Home Care for Dummies* about how to get him from the wheelchair, which I assumed he'd arrive in, to the bed and back again.

What else, what else?

Stick the old bedclothes from the guestroom in the washer, but that could wait until tomorrow or even Monday. A phone, that was what else. He'd need one close at hand. His landline was a white cordless that looked like it belonged in a TCM cops-and-robbers movie from the 1970s, the kind where all the guys have sideburns and the chicks have puffed-up hair. I checked to make sure it worked and got a dial tone. I was putting it back in its charging cradle when it rang in my hand. I yelped, startled, and dropped it. Radar barked.

'It's okay, girl,' I said, and picked it up. There was no button to accept the call. I was still looking for one when I heard Mr Bowditch, tinny and distant: 'Hello? Are you there? *Hello?*'

So, no accept button and no way to check who was calling. With a phone this old, you just had to take your chances.

'Hello,' I said. 'It's Charlie, Mr Bowditch.'

'Why is Radar barking?'

'Because I yelled and dropped the phone. I was holding it in my hand when it rang.'

'Startled you, did it?' He didn't wait for an answer. 'I hoped you'd be there because it's Radar's dinnertime. You fed her, right?'

'Right. She ate it in about three gulps.'

He gave a hoarse laugh. 'That's her, all right. She's gotten a little shaky on her pins, but her appetite's as good as ever.'

'How are you feeling?'

'My leg hurts like damn hell even with the dope they're giving me, but they got me out of bed today. Dragging that fixator around makes me feel like Jacob Marley.'

'"These are the chains I wore in life."'

He gave that hoarse laugh again. I was guessing he was pretty stoned. 'Read the book or seen the movie?'

'Movie. Every Christmas Eve, on TCM. We watch a lot of TCM at our house.'

'Don't know what that is.' He wouldn't, of course. No Turner

Classic Movies on a TV equipped with nothing but – what had Mrs Silvius called them? Rabbit's ears?

'I'm glad I got you. They're going to let me come home on Monday afternoon, and I need to talk to you first. Can you come to see me tomorrow? My roommate will be down in the lounge watching the baseball game, so we'll have some privacy.'

'Sure. I made up the pull-out couch for you, also the bed upstairs for me, and—'

'Stop a minute. Charlie . . .' A long pause. Then, 'Is keeping secrets in your repertoire as well as making beds and feeding my dog?'

I thought about my father's drinking years – his lost years. I'd needed to look after myself a lot of the time back then, and I'd been angry. Angry at my mother for dying the way she did, which was stupid because no way was it her fault, but you have to remember I was only seven when she got killed on the goddam bridge. I loved my father, but I was angry at him, too. Angry kids get in trouble, and I had a very able enabler in Bertie Bird. Bertie and I were okay when we were with Andy Chen, because Andy was kind of a Boy Scout, but when we were on our own, we got up to some fairly outrageous shit. It was stuff that could have gotten us in a lot of trouble if we'd been caught, some of it police-type trouble, but we never were. And my father never knew. Never would, if I had my way. Did I really want to tell my dad that Bertie and I smeared dogshit on the windshield of our least favorite teacher's car? Just writing that down here, where I promised to tell everything, makes me cringe with shame. And that wasn't the worst of it.

'Charlie? Are you still there?'

'I'm here. And yeah, I can keep a secret. As long as you're not going to tell me you killed someone and the body's in that shed.'

It was his turn to be silent, but I didn't have to ask if he was still there; I could hear his raspy breathing.

'Nothing like that, but these are big secrets. We'll talk tomorrow. You seem like a straight arrow. I hope to Christ I'm right about that. We'll see. Now how much am I in the bucket for with you and your father?'

'Do you mean how much have we spent? Not that much. The groceries were the most. Couple of hundred in all, I guess. I saved the receipts—'

'There's also your time. If you mean to help me, you need to be paid. How does five hundred a week sound?'

I was flabbergasted. 'Mr Bowditch . . . Howard . . . you don't have to pay me anything. I'm glad to—'

'The workman is worthy of his hire. Book of Luke. Five hundred a week, and if things work out, a year-end bonus. All right?'

Whatever he'd done in his working life, it hadn't been digging ditches. He was comfortable with what Donald Trump calls the art of the deal, which meant he was comfortable overriding objections. And my objections were pretty weak. I'd made a promise to God, but if Mr Bowditch wanted to pay me while I fulfilled that promise, I didn't see any conflict. Plus, as my father was always reminding me, I had college to think about.

'Charlie? Do we have a deal?'

'If it works out, I guess we do.' Although if he turned out to be a serial killer after all, I wasn't going to keep his secrets for five hundred dollars a week. For that it would take at least a thousand. (Joke.) 'Thank you. I wasn't expecting anyth—'

'I know that,' he interrupted. An ace interrupter was Mr Howard Bowditch. 'In some ways you're quite a charming young man. A straight arrow, as I said.'

I wondered if he'd still think so if he knew that one day while we were skipping school, the Bird Man and I had found a cell phone in Highland Park and called in a bomb threat to Stevens Elementary. His idea, but I went along with it.

'There's a flour cannister in the kitchen. You may have seen it.' Not only had I seen it, he'd mentioned it to me, although he might have forgotten; he'd been in a lot of pain at the time. There was money in it, he'd said, then said it was empty. Said he forgot.

'Sure.'

'Take seven hundred dollars out of it, five as your first week's wages and two for expenses to date.'

'Are you sure—'

'Yes. And if you think it's bribe money, maybe sweetening you up for some outrageous request . . . it's not. Services rendered, Charlie. Services rendered. About that you can be perfectly straight with your father. About anything we might discuss in the future, no. I'm aware it's a lot to ask.'

'As long as it's not a crime,' I said, then amended it. 'Not a *bad* crime.'

'Can you come to the hospital around three?'

'Yes.'

'Then I'll say good evening. Please give Radar a pat from the stupid old man who should have stayed off that ladder.'

He hung up. I gave Radar several pats on the head and a couple of long strokes, nape to tail. She rolled over to have her belly rubbed. I was happy to oblige. Then I went into the kitchen and took the top off the flour cannister.

It was stuffed with money. There was a jumble of bills on top, mostly tens and twenties, a few fives and ones. I pulled them out. They made a fair-sized heap on the counter. Below the loose bills were banded stacks of fifties and hundreds. The bands were stamped FIRST CITIZENS BANK in purple ink. I pulled them out, too, and it took some wiggling because they were really crammed in there. Six banded stacks of fifties, ten to each. Five banded stacks of hundreds, also ten to a stack.

Radar had come out into the kitchen and was sitting by her food dish, looking at me with her ears pricked. 'Holy shit, girl. This is eight thousand dollars, and that's not counting the stuff on top.'

I counted out seven hundred dollars from the loose bills, neatened them, folded them over, and put the wad in my pocket, where they made a bulge. It was at least ten times the amount of money I'd ever had on my person. I picked up the banded bundles, started to put them back in the cannister, then paused. There were three little pellets in the bottom, kind of reddish. I had seen one of those before, in the medicine cabinet. I tipped them out and held them in the palm of my hand. I thought they were too heavy to be BBs, and if I was right in what I was thinking, it might go a long way toward explaining the source of Mr Bowditch's income.

I thought they were gold.

4

I hadn't ridden my bike, and the walk down the hill to our house only took ten or twelve minutes, but that night I made it last. I had thinking to do and a decision to make. As I walked, I kept touching the bulge in my pocket, making sure it was still there.

I'd tell Dad about Mr Bowditch's call and his offer of employment. I'd show him the cash, two hundred for what we'd spent and five hundred for me. I'd tell him to put four hundred of it in my college account (which just happened to be at First Citizens) and promise to put in another four hundred every week that I was working for Mr Bowditch . . . which might last right through the summer, or at least until football practice started in August. The question was whether or not I should tell him about how much money had been in the flour cannister. And, of course, those gold BBs. If they *were* gold.

By the time I let myself into our house, I'd made my decision. I'd keep the fact of the eight thousand in the cannister to myself, and the BBs that weren't BBs. At least until I'd had my talk with Mr Bowditch the next day.

'Hey, Charlie,' my father called from the living room. 'Dog okay?'

'She's fine.'

'Good to know. Grab yourself a Sprite and grab a chair. *Rear Window*'s on TCM.'

I grabbed a Sprite, came in, and muted the TV. 'I've got something to tell you.'

'What could be more important than James Stewart and Grace Kelly?'

'How about this?' I took the wad of money from my pocket and dropped it on the coffee table.

I expected surprise, caution, and worry. What I got was interest and amusement. Dad thought Mr Bowditch hiding money in one of his kitchen cannisters fit right in with what he called the agoraphobe's hoarding mentality (I'd told him about the Hall of Old Reading Matter, not to mention the old TV and the elderly kitchen appliances). 'Was there more in there?'

'Some,' I said. Which wasn't a lie.

Dad nodded. 'Did you check the other cannisters? There might be a few hundred in with the sugar.' He was smiling.

'Nope.'

He took the two hundred. 'A little more than we actually spent, but he'll probably need other stuff. Want me to deposit four hundred of yours?'

'Sure.'

'Good call. In one way, he's getting you cheap, at least for the first week. I think a full-time home helper would get more. On the other hand, you'll be earning while you learn, and you'll only be spending nights up there during your spring vacation.' He turned to look at me squarely. 'Are we clear on that?'

'Totally,' I said.

'Okay, good. Bowditch ratholing money makes me a little uneasy only because we don't know where it came from, but I'm willing to give him the benefit of the doubt. I like that he trusts you, and I like that you're willing to take this on. You thought you'd be doing it for free, didn't you?'

'Yeah. I did.'

'You're a good kid, Charlie. Not sure what I did to deserve you.'

Considering what I was holding back – not just about Mr Bowditch but some of the shit I'd pulled with Bertie – that made me a little ashamed.

Lying in bed that night, I imagined Mr Bowditch having a goldmine in his locked shed, maybe with a bunch of dwarves to work it. Dwarves with names like Sleepy and Grumpy. That made me smile. I had an idea that whatever was in the shed might be the big secret he wanted to tell me about, but I was wrong. I didn't find out about the shed until later.

CHAPTER SIX

Hospital Visit. The Safe. Stantonville.

Gold-Greed. Mr Bowditch Comes Home.

1

Mr Bowditch and I had quite the chat while his roommate was in the third-floor lounge, watching the White Sox play the Tigers with a heart monitor strapped to his chest.

'He's got some sort of ticker problem they can't quite fix,' Mr Bowditch said. 'Thank Christ I don't have that to worry about. I've got enough problems.'

He showed me how he could walk to the bathroom, leaning on those arm-sleeve crutches for all he was worth. It obviously hurt him, and when he came back from taking a leak, his forehead was wet with sweat, but I was encouraged. He might need the urinal with its long and somehow baleful neck for night calls, but it looked good for avoiding the bedpan. As long as he didn't fall in the middle of the night and break his leg all over again, that was. I could see the muscles in his scrawny arms trembling with every lunging step. He sat down on the bed with a sigh of relief.

'Can you help me with the—' He gestured at the ironmongery encasing his leg.

I lifted the leg with the fixator, and when it was stretched out, he sighed again and asked for a couple of pills from the Dixie cup on his night table. I gave them to him, poured some water from his pitcher, and down they went, his Adam's apple bobbing in his wrinkled neck like a monkey on a stick.

'They switched me from the morphine pump to this,' he said. 'OxyContin. The doctor says I'll get hooked, if I'm not already, and I'll have to kick the habit. Right now that seems like a fair trade. Just walking to the bathroom feels like a fucking marathon.'

I could see that, and the bathroom at his house was further from the roll-out. He might be needing the bedpan after all, at least to begin with. I went into the bathroom, wet down a washcloth, and wrung it out. When I bent over him, he pulled back.

'Here, here! What do you think you're doing?'

'Getting the sweat off you. Hold still.'

We never know when the turning points come in our relationships with others, and it was only later that I realized that was one for us. He held back a moment longer, then relaxed (a little) and allowed me to wipe his brow and cheeks. 'Feel like a fucking baby.'

'You're paying me, let me earn my fucking money.'

That made him chuckle. A nurse peeked in the door and asked if he needed anything. He said he didn't, and when she was gone, he told me to close the door.

'This is where I ask you to stand up for me,' he said. 'At least until I can stand up for myself. And Radar, too. You ready to do that, Charlie?'

'I'll do my best.'

'Yeah, maybe you will. It's all I can ask. I wouldn't put you in this position if I didn't have to. A woman named Ravensburger came to see me. Have you met her?'

I said I had.

'Hell of a name, isn't it? I try to think of a burger made out of raven meat and my mind just boggles.'

I won't say he was stoned on the Oxy, but I won't say he wasn't. As gaunt as he was, six feet tall and surely no more than a hundred and fifty, those pink pills had to pack a wallop.

'She talked to me about what she called my "payment options." I asked her what the damage was so far and she gave me a printout. It's in the drawer there . . .' He pointed. '. . . but don't bother about that just now.

'I said that's mighty high and she said good care is mighty expensive, Mr Bowditch, and you have gotten the best. She said if I needed to consult a payment specialist – whatever *that* is when it's home and dry – she'd be happy to facilitate a meeting, either before I leave or after I'm home. I said I didn't think that would be necessary. I told her I could pay in full, but only if I got a discount. Then we got down to the dickering. We finally settled on twenty per cent off, which comes to about a nineteen-thousand-dollar discount.'

I whistled. Mr Bowditch grinned.

'I tried to get her down to twenty-five per cent, but she wouldn't budge off twenty. I think that's the industry standard – and hospitals *are* an industry, in case you wondered. Hospitals and prisons, not much difference in how they run their businesses, except with prisons it's the taxpayers who wind up footing the bill.' He wiped a hand across his eyes. 'I could have paid the whole thing, but I enjoyed the dickering. Been a long time since I've had a chance to do any. Yard sales in the old days; bought a lot of books and old magazines. I like old things. Am I rambling? I am. Here's the point: I can pay, but I need you to make it possible.'

'If you're thinking about what's in the flour cannister—'

He waved that away as if eight thousand dollars were petty cash. In terms of what he owed the hospital, it was. 'Here is what I want you to do.'

He told me. When he was done, he asked me if I needed him to write it down. 'It's okay if you do, as long as you destroy your notes when the job's done.'

'Maybe just the safe combination. I'll write it on my arm, then wash it off.'

'You'll do it?'

'Yes.' I couldn't imagine not doing it, if only to find out if what he was telling me was real.

'Good. Repeat the steps back to me.'

I did, then used his bedside pen to write a series of numbers and turns on my upper arm, where the sleeve of my T-shirt would cover it.

'Thank you,' he said. 'You'll have to wait until tomorrow to see Mr Heinrich, but you can get ready tonight. When you feed Radar.'

I said okay, said goodbye, and left. I was – my dad's word – gobsmacked. Halfway down the elevator, I thought of something and came back.

'Changed your mind already?' He was smiling, but his eyes looked worried.

'No. I just wanted to ask you about something you said.'

'What was it?'

'Something about presents. You said a brave man helps but a coward gives presents.'

'I don't remember saying that.'

'Well, you did. What does it mean?'

'I don't know. It must have been the pills talking.'

He was lying. I lived with a drunk for several years, and I knew a lie when I heard it.

2

I biked back to 1 Sycamore Street, and it wouldn't be an overstatement to say I was wild with curiosity. I unlocked the back door and accepted an exuberant greeting from Radar. She was able to get up on her back paws for strokes, which made me think that the newer pills might be packing a punch. I let her out in the backyard to do some business. I kept sending her mental messages to hurry up and pick a spot.

When she was back in, I went upstairs to Mr Bowditch's bedroom and opened his closet. He had a lot of clothes, mostly slop-around stuff like flannel shirts and khaki pants, but there were two suits. One was black, one was gray, and both of them looked like the kind of suits George Raft and Edward G. Robinson wore in movies like *Each Dawn I Die*, double-breasted and wide in the shoulders.

I pushed aside the clothes and revealed a Watchman safe, medium-sized, old-fashioned, about three feet high. I squatted, and as I reached for the combination dial, something cold nuzzled my back where my shirt had pulled out of my pants. I yelped and turned to see Radar, her tail wagging slowly back and forth. The cold thing had been her nose.

'Don't do that, girl,' I said. She sat down, grinning as if to say she'd do what she wanted. I turned back to the safe. I got the combo wrong the first time, but on my second try, the door swung open.

The first thing I saw was a gun resting on the safe's single shelf. It was bigger than the one my dad gave my mom for those times when he had to be away for a few days . . . or once for a week, on a company retreat. That one was a .32, a ladies' gun for sure, and I thought he might still have it but wasn't entirely sure. There were times, when his drinking was at its worst, I'd gone looking for it, but I never found it. This one was bigger, probably a .45 revolver. Like most of Mr Bowditch's stuff, it looked old-school. I picked it up – gingerly – and found the catch that swung the cylinder. It was loaded, all six chambers. I swung the cylinder back into place and returned it to the shelf. Considering what he'd told me, a gun made sense. A burglar alarm might have made even more, but he didn't want any police calls at Number 1 Sycamore. Besides, in her earlier days, Radar had been a perfectly good burglar alarm – Andy Chen being a case in point.

On the floor of the safe was what Mr Bowditch had told me I'd find: a big steel bucket with a knapsack laid over the top. I picked up the knapsack and saw the bucket was filled almost to the top with those BBs that weren't BBs but solid gold pellets.

The bucket had a double handle. I grabbed it and lifted. From my squatting position I could barely manage it. There had to be forty pounds of gold in there, maybe fifty. I sat down and turned to look at Radar. 'Jesus Christ. This is a fucking *fortune*.'

She thumped her tail.

3

That night, after I fed her, I went upstairs and looked at the bucket of gold again, just to make sure I hadn't imagined it. When I got home, Dad asked me if I was ready for Mr Bowditch's homecoming. I said I was, but I had stuff to do before he arrived. 'Still okay to borrow your drill? And that power screwdriver?'

'Of course. And I'd still be glad to come up and give you a hand if I could, but I've got a meeting at nine. It's that apartment house fire I told you about. Turns out it may have been arson.'

'I'll be fine.'

'I hope so. Are you okay?'

'Sure. Why?'

'You just seem a little off. Worried about tomorrow?'

'A little,' I said. Which wasn't a lie.

You may wonder if I had any urge to tell my father about what I'd found. I didn't. Mr Bowditch had sworn me to secrecy, that was one thing. He claimed the gold hadn't been stolen 'in the usual sense,' and that was another. I'd asked what that meant, but all he would say is that nobody in the whole world was looking for it. Until I knew more, I was willing to take him at his word.

There was another thing. I was seventeen years old, and this was the most exciting thing that had ever happened to me. By far. And I wanted to chase it.

4

On Monday morning I biked up to Mr Bowditch's house bright and early to feed Radar, and she did the heavy looking on while I installed the safety bars. The toilet was already a cozy fit in the tiny bathroom, and the safety bars would make a descent to the unloading position even cozier, but I thought that was good. I foresaw a certain amount of grumbling, but it would be hard for him to fall. He could even hold onto the bars while he urinated, which I thought was a plus. I tried wiggling them and they stayed solid.

'What do you think, Rades? Good to go?'

Radar thumped her tail.

'You can weigh the gold on my bathroom scale,' Mr Bowditch told me during our conversation. 'It won't be exact, but a kitchen scale takes forever – I know from experience. Use the knapsack to weigh and carry. Go a little on the heavy side. Heinrich will weigh it himself, on a scale that's more accurate. Dig-i-tal, you know.' He broke it into syllables like that, making it sound both silly and pretentious.

'How do you get it to him when you need a cash infusion?' Stantonville was seven miles away.

'I take a Yoober. Heinrich pays.'

For a minute I didn't understand, then I did.

'What are you grinning about, Charlie?'

'Nothing. Do you do these exchanges at night?'

He nodded. 'Usually around ten, when most of the people in the neighborhood are tucked in for the night. Especially Mrs Richland from across the street. That one's a nosy-parker.'

'So you said.'

'It bears repeating.'

I had gotten the same impression.

'I don't think mine's the only business Heinrich does at night, but he's agreed to close the shop tomorrow so you can come in the morning, between nine-thirty and ten. I've never done an exchange of this size with him. I'm sure it will be all right, he's never played anything but straight with me, but there's a gun in the safe, and if you want to take it – for protection – that would be fine.'

I had no intention of taking it. I know guns make some people feel powerful, but I'm not one of those guys. Just touching it made me feel creepy. If you had told me I would be carrying it not too far in the future, I would have called you crazy.

I found a scoop in the pantry and went upstairs. I had washed the numbers off my arm after putting them in a password-protected note on my phone, but I didn't even need to consult it. The safe opened on my first try. I took the knapsack off the bucket and just marveled at all that gold. Unable to resist the impulse, I plunged my hands in up to the wrists and let the gold pellets run through my fingers. I did it again. And a third time. There was something hypnotic about it. I shook my head as if to clear it and started scooping gold.

The first time I weighed the knapsack, the scale registered a little over three pounds. I added more and got it up to five. The last time, the needle stopped at seven, and I decided that was good. If Mr Heinrich's dig-i-tal scale showed more than the agreed-upon six pounds, I could bring back the extra. I still had stuff to do at the house before Mr Bowditch's arrival. I reminded myself to get a bell he could ring in the night if he needed something. *Home Care for Dummies* suggested an intercom or baby monitor, but I thought Mr Bowditch might like something a little more old-school.

I had asked him how much six pounds of gold was worth, both wanting and not wanting to know the amount I'd be carrying on my back as I biked the seven miles – mostly rural – to Stantonville. He told me that the last time he checked with the Gold Price Group in Texas, it was going for about $15,000 a pound.

'But he can have it for fourteen a pound – that's the price we agreed on. It comes to $84,000, but he'll give you a check for $74,000. That will take care of my hospital bill with a little left over for me and a nice profit for him.'

Nice was putting it mildly. I don't know when Mr Bowditch last checked with the Gold Price Group, but as of the end of April in 2013, he was way low. I had checked the price of gold on my laptop before going to bed on Sunday night, and it was selling at better than $1,200 an ounce, which came to about $20,000 per pound. Six pounds would have gone for around $115,000 on the gold exchange in Zurich, which meant this Heinrich dude would be $40,000 to the good. And the gold wasn't like hot diamonds, where the buyer would insist on discounting because of the risk. The pellets were unmarked, anonymous, and could easily be melted down into little ingots. Or made into jewelry.

I'd thought about calling Mr Bowditch in the hospital to tell him he was selling cheap, but didn't. For a very simple reason: I thought he wouldn't care. I could sort of understand that. Even with six pounds taken from Cap'n Kidd's Bucket o' Gold, there was plenty left. My job (although Mr Bowditch never said it) was just to do the deal and not get ripped off. It was a hell of a responsibility, and I was determined to live up to the trust he'd put in me.

I buckled the straps on the knapsack, checked the floor between the closet safe and the bathroom scale for any gold pellets that had gotten away, and found none. I gave Radar a good stroking (for luck) and headed out carrying $115,000 in a beat-up old knapsack.

My old friend Bertie Bird would have called it a lot of cheddar.

5

Stantonville's downtown was a single street of cheesy shops, a couple of bars, and the kind of diner that serves breakfast all day along with a bottomless cup of bad coffee. A number of the shops were closed and boarded up, with signs saying they were for sale or lease. My dad said that once Stantonville was a thriving little community, a great place to shop for people who didn't want to go to Elgin, Naperville, Joliet, or all the way to Chicago. Then, in the 1970s, the Stantonville Mall opened. Not just a mall, either, but a supermall with a twelve-screen cineplex, a kiddie amusement park, a climbing wall, a trampoline area called Fliers, an escape room, and guys wandering around dressed as talking animals. That glitterdome of commerce was to the north of Stantonville. It sucked most of the life out of the downtown area, and what the mall missed got sucked out by the Walmart and Sam's Club to the south, on the turnpike exit.

Being on my bicycle, I avoided the pike and took Route 74-A, a two-lane running past farms and cornfields. There were smells of manure and growing things. It was a pleasant spring morning and would have been a pleasant ride, if I hadn't been aware of the small fortune I was carrying on my back. I remember thinking about Jack, the boy who'd climbed the beanstalk.

I was on Stantonville's main drag by nine-fifteen, which was a little early, so I stopped in the diner, got a Coke, and sipped it sitting on a park bench in a dirty little plaza featuring a dry fountain filled with trash and a bird-beshitted statue of someone I'd never heard of. I thought about that plaza and dry fountain later, in a place even more deserted than Stantonville.

I can't swear that Christopher Polley was there that morning; I can't swear he wasn't. Polley was the kind of guy who could fade into the landscape until he was ready for you to see him. He could have been in the diner, chowing down on bacon and eggs. He could have been in the bus shelter or pretending to study the guitars and boomboxes in the Stantonville Pawn & Loan. Or he could have been nowhere. All I can say is that I don't remember anyone in a retro White Sox hat, the kind with the red circle on the front. Maybe he wasn't wearing it, but I never saw that son of a bitch without it.

At twenty to ten, I tossed my half-full go-cup into a nearby trash barrel and pedaled slowly down Main Street. The business section, such as it was, ran only four blocks. Near the end of the fourth, just a stone's throw from a sign reading THANKS FOR VISITING BEAUTIFUL STANTONVILLE, was Excellent Jewelers We Buy & Sell. It looked as shabby and dilapidated as the rest of this dying town's businesses. There was nothing in the dusty show window. The sign hanging in the door from a little plastic cup said CLOSED.

There was a bell. I pushed it. No response. I pushed it again, very conscious of the pack on my back. I put my nose against the glass and cupped my hands to the sides of my face to cut the glare. I saw a shabby rug and empty display cases. I was starting to think either I'd made a mistake or Mr Bowditch had when a little man in a tweed cap, button-up sweater, and baggy pants came limping up the center aisle. He looked like the gardener in a British detective show. He stared at me, then limped away and pressed a button by the old-fashioned cash register. The door buzzed. I pushed it open and stepped inside to a smell of dust and slow decay.

'Come in back, come in back,' he said.

I stayed where I was. 'You're Mr Heinrich, right?'

'Who else?'

'Could I, um, see your driver's license?'

He frowned at me, then laughed. 'The old man sends a careful boy, and good for him.'

He took a beat-up wallet from his back pocket and flopped it open so I could see his driver's license. Before he flopped it closed again, I saw that his first name was Wilhelm.

'Satisfied?'

'Yes. Thank you.'

'Come in back. *Schnell*.'

I followed him into the back room, which he unlocked with a keypad, carefully shielding it from me while he punched in the numbers. Inside was all the stuff that wasn't up front, shelves crammed with watches, lockets, brooches, rings, pendants, chains. Rubies and emeralds flashed fire. I saw a tiara loaded with diamonds and pointed. 'Are those real?'

'*Ja, ja*, real. But I don't think you came here to buy. You came here to sell. You maybe noticed I didn't ask to see *your* driver's license.'

'That's good, because I don't have one.'

'I already know who you are. I saw your picture in the paper.'

'The *Sun*?'

'*USA Today*. You are nationwide, young Mr Charles Reade. At least for this week. You saved old Bowditch's life.'

I didn't bother telling him it had been the dog, I was tired of that, I only wanted to do my business and get out. All the gold and jewels freaked me out a little, especially when compared to the barren shelves out front. I almost wished I'd brought the gun, because I was starting to feel not like Jack the Beanstalk Boy but Jim Hawkins in *Treasure Island*. Heinrich was small and dumpy and undangerous, but what if he had a Long John Silver associate lurking somewhere? It wasn't an entirely paranoid idea. I could tell myself that Mr Bowditch had been doing business with Heinrich for years, but Mr Bowditch himself had said he'd never done an exchange of this magnitude.

'Let's see what you have,' he said. In a boys' adventure novel he would have been a caricature of greed, rubbing his hands together and all but drooling, but he just sounded businesslike, maybe even a little bored. I didn't trust that, and I didn't trust him.

I set the backpack on the counter. There was a scale nearby, and it was indeed dig-i-tal. I unzipped the flap. I held it open and when he peered in I saw something change in his face: a tightening of the mouth and a momentary widening of the eyes.

'*Mein Gott*. Look at what you have been carrying on your bicycle.'

The scale had a Lucite trough hanging on chains. Heinrich put small handfuls of gold pellets into the trough until the scale read two pounds. He set them aside in a plastic container, then weighed another two. When he finished weighing the last two and adding them to the rest, there was still a small creek of gold in one of the folds at the bottom of the backpack. Mr Bowditch had told me to go a little heavy, and I had done so.

'I think another quarter-pound left over, *hein*?' he said, peering in. 'You sell it to me, I give you three thousand dollars, cash money. Bowditch doesn't need to know. Call it a gratuity.'

Call it something he could hold over my head, I thought. I said thanks anyway and zipped the flap closed. 'You have a check for me, right?'

'Yes.' The check was folded into the pocket of his old-guy sweater. It was from the PNC Bank of Chicago, Belmont Avenue branch, and made out to Howard Bowditch in the amount of seventy-four thousand dollars. The memo opposite Wilhelm Heinrich's signature read *Personal Services*. It looked okay to me. I put it in my wallet and put the wallet in my left front pocket.

'He is a stubborn old man who refuses to move with the times,' Heinrich said. 'Often in the past, when we have dealt with much smaller amounts, I have given him cash. On two occasions, checks. I told him, "Have you not heard of electronic deposit?" And do you know what he said?'

I shook my head, but I could guess.

'He said, "I haven't heard of it and don't want to hear of it." And now, for the first time, he sends a *zwischen gehen* – an emissary – because he has had an accident. I would have said he had no one in the world he could trust with such an errand. But here you are. A boy on a bicycle.'

'And here I go,' I said, and went to the door leading back to the as-yet empty store, where he might or might not stock the display cases later. I half-expected the door to be locked, but it wasn't. I felt better once I was back where I could see daylight. Even so, the smell of elderly dust was unpleasant. Crypt-like.

'Does he even know what a computer is?' Heinrich asked, following me and shutting the door to the back room behind him. 'I'm betting not.'

I had no plans to be drawn into a discussion of what Mr Bowditch did or didn't know, and just said it was nice to meet him. Which wasn't true. I was relieved to see that no one had stolen my bike – leaving my house that morning, I'd been too preoccupied with other things to remember my bike lock.

Heinrich took me by the elbow. I turned and now saw the inner Long John Silver after all. He only needed a parrot on his shoulder to make the picture complete. According to Silver, his parrot had seen as much wickedness as the devil himself. I guessed Wilhelm Heinrich had seen his share of wickedness . . . but you have to remember that I was seventeen, and waist-deep in matters I didn't understand. In other words, I was scared to death.

'How much gold does he have?' Heinrich said in a low, guttural voice. His occasional use of German words and phrases had felt like an affectation to me, but just then he really *did* sound German. And not a nice German. 'Tell me how much he has and where he gets it. I'll make it worth your while.'

'I'll be going now,' I said, and did.

Was Christopher Polley watching as I mounted my bike and rode away with the remaining gold pellets in my backpack? I wouldn't know, because I was looking back over my shoulder at Heinrich's pale, pudgy face suspended above the CLOSED sign in his dusty shop door. Maybe it was imagination – probably it was – but I thought I could still see the greed on his face. Furthermore, I understood it. I remembered plunging my hands into that bucket and letting the pellets run through my fingers. Not just greed, but gold-greed.

Like in a pirate story.

6

Around four o'clock that afternoon, a van with ARCADIA OUTPATIENT on the side pulled up to the curb. I was waiting on the walk with Radar on her leash. The gate – now rust-free and newly oiled – was standing open. An orderly got out of the van and opened the back doors. Melissa Wilcox was standing there behind Mr Bowditch, who was in a wheelchair with his fixator-encased leg outstretched. She unlocked the wheelchair, pushed it forward, and hit a button with the heel of her hand. As the platform and wheelchair started to descend, my stomach also sank. I'd remembered the phone, the urinal, even the call-bell. His check from Heinrich was safe in my wallet. All good, but there was no wheelchair ramp, not in front and not in back. I felt like an idiot, but at least I didn't have to feel that way for long. I had Radar to distract me. She saw Mr Bowditch and launched herself at him. No sign of arthritis in her hips just then. I managed to snub the leash in time to keep her from getting her paws squashed by the descending lift, but I felt the shock go all the way up my arm.

Yark! Yark! Yark!

These weren't the big-dog roars that had so frightened Andy back in the day but cries so plaintive and human that they wrung my heart. *You're back!* those yarks said. *Thank God, I thought you were gone forever!*

Mr Bowditch held out his arms to her and she jumped up, paws on his outstretched leg. He winced, then laughed and cradled her head. 'Yes, girl,' he crooned. It was hard for me to believe he could make a sound like that even when I was hearing it, but he did; that grouchy old man *crooned*. There were tears in his eyes. Radar was making little sounds of happiness, her big old tail swishing back and forth.

'Yes, girl, yes, I missed you, too. Now get down, you're killing me.'

Radar dropped back onto all fours and walked beside the wheelchair as Melissa rolled it up the walk, bumping and yawing.

'No ramp,' I said. 'Sorry, sorry, I can build one, I'll look up how to do it on the Net, everything's on the Net.' I was babbling and couldn't seem to stop. 'I think everything else is more or less ready—'

'We'll hire someone to put in a ramp, so quit fussing,' Mr Bowditch interrupted. 'You don't need to do everything. One of the perks of being an amanuensis is delegating tasks. And there's no hurry. I don't go out much, as you know. Did you take care of that business matter?'

'Yes. This morning.'

'Good.'

Melissa said, 'You two should be able to lift that chair up the steps, strong guys like you. What do you think, Herbie?'

'No problem,' the orderly said. 'Right, chum?'

I said sure and took one side. Radar scrambled halfway up the steps, paused once when her back legs betrayed her, then got it back in gear and made it the rest of the way. She looked down at us, tail thumping.

'And someone should fix that path, if he's going to use it,' Melissa said. 'It's worse than the dirt road I grew up on back in Tennessee.'

'Ready, hoss?' Herbie asked.

We lifted the wheelchair up to the porch. I fumbled through Mr Bowditch's keys and finally found the one that opened the front door.

'Hey,' the orderly said. 'Didn't I see your picture in the paper?'

I sighed. 'Probably. Me and Radar. Out there by the gate.'

'No, no, last year. You scored the winning touchdown in the Turkey Bowl. Five seconds before the clock ran out.'

He raised one hand over his head, holding an invisible football, as I had done in the photo. Hard to tell why him remembering that picture instead of the more recent one made me happy, but it did.

In the living room, I waited – more nervous than ever – while Melissa Wilcox inspected the roll-out couch.

'Good,' she said. 'This is good. A little low, maybe, but we make do with what we have. You'll want a bolster or something to give that leg of his a little extra support. Who made the bed up?'

'I did,' I said, and her look of surprise also made me happy.

'Did you read the pamphlet I gave you?'

'Yes. I got this antibacterial stuff for pin care . . .'

She shook her head. 'Simple saline is all you need. Warm salt water. Do you feel ready to transfer him?'

'Hello?' Mr Bowditch said. 'Perhaps I could be a part of this conversation? I'm right here.'

'Yes, but I'm not talking to you.' Melissa said it with a smile.

'Um, not sure,' I said.

'Mr Bowditch,' Melissa said, 'now I *am* talking to you. Do you mind if Charlie test-drives you?'

Mr Bowditch looked at Radar, who was sitting as close as she could. 'What do you think, girl? Trust this kid?'

Radar barked once.

'Radar says okay and I say okay. Don't drop me, young man. This leg is singing high C.'

I moved the chair close to the bed, put on the brake, and asked if he could stand on his good leg. He pushed himself up partway, allowing me to unlock and lower the leg rest that had been supporting his bad one. He grunted but made it the rest of the way – swaying a little, but vertical.

'Turn so your butt's facing the bed but don't try to sit until I tell you,' I said, and Melissa nodded approvingly.

Mr Bowditch did that. I moved the wheelchair out of the way.

'Can't stand this way for long without the crutches.' The sweat was popping on his cheeks and brow again.

I squatted and took hold of the fixator. 'Now you can sit.'

He didn't sit, he dropped. And with a sigh of relief. He lay back. I put his bad leg on the bed, and my first transfer was complete. I wasn't sweating as much as Mr Bowditch was, but I was sweating, mostly from nerves. This was a bigger deal than taking throws from the pitcher.

'Not bad,' Melissa said. 'When you get him up, you'll want to hug him. Lace your fingers together in the middle of his back, and lift. Use his armpits—'

'For support,' I said. 'It was in the pamphlet.'

'I like a boy who does his homework. Make sure his crutches are always close, especially when standing from the bed. How do you feel, Mr Bowditch?'

'Like ten pounds of shit in a nine-pound bag. Is it time for my pills?'

'You had them before we left the hospital. You can have more at six.'

'That seems like a long time from now. How about a Percocet to tide me over?'

'How about I don't have any.' Then, to me: 'You'll get better at this, and so will he, especially as he mends and his range of movement increases. Step outside with me a moment, will you?'

'Talking behind my back,' Bowditch called. 'Whatever it's about, that young man will *not* be administering any enemas.'

'Whoa,' Herbie said. He was bent over, hands on his knees, examining the television. 'This is the oldest idiot box I've ever seen, partner. Does it work?'

7

The late-day sun was brilliant, and there was some warmth to it, which felt wonderful after a long winter and a cold spring. Melissa led me down to the outpatient van, leaned in, and unlocked the wide center console. She brought out a plastic bag and set it on the seat. 'Crutches are in back. Here's his drugs, plus two tubes of arnica gel. There's a sheet in here with the exact dosages, okay?' She took the bottles out and showed them to me one by one. 'These are antibiotics. These are vitamins, four different kinds. This one's a prescription for Lynparza. Get refills at the CVS in Sentry Village. These are laxatives. There are no suppositories, but you should read up on how to administer them if he needs one. He won't like it.'

'Not much he does like,' I said. 'Mostly Radar.'

'And you,' she said. 'He likes you, Charlie. He says you're trustworthy. I hope he's not just saying that because you came along at the right time to save his life. Because there's these.'

The biggest bottle was filled with twenty-milligram OxyContin pills. Melissa looked at me solemnly. 'This is a bad drug, Charlie. Very addictive. It's also extremely effective against the kind of pain your friend is now suffering and may continue suffering for eight months to a year. Perhaps longer, depending on his other issues.'

'What other issues?'

She shook her head. 'Not for me to say. You just stick to the dosing schedule and turn a deaf ear to his demands for more. He can actually get more before our therapy sessions, and knowing that will become one of his primary motivations – maybe his biggest – to continue with the therapy even when it hurts. And it will hurt. You need to keep them where he can't get at them. Can you think of a place?'

'Yes.' It was the safe I was thinking of. 'It'll work at least until he can climb the stairs.'

'So three weeks, if he sticks with his therapy. Maybe a month. Once he can go up, you'll need to think of another one. And it isn't just him you have to worry about. To the addicted, these pills are worth their weight in gold.'

I laughed. I couldn't help it.

'What? What's so funny?'

'Nothing. I'll keep them safe, and I won't let him talk me into more.'

She was looking at me closely. 'What about you, Charlie? Because I have no business giving these to a minor; so far as the doctor who prescribed them knows, they'll be administered by an adult caregiver. I could get in trouble. Would you be tempted to try one or two, and get a little bit high?'

I thought of my father, and what the booze had done to him, and how I had once believed we might be sleeping under highway bridges, all our possessions in a stolen shopping cart.

I took the big bottle of Oxy tablets and dropped it back into the bag with the rest of the medicines. Then I took her by the hand and looked into her eyes. 'Not fucking likely,' I said.

8

There was a little more instruction, which I drew out because I was nervous to be alone with him – what if something happened and that stupid 1970s phone decided not to work?

Then you'll call 911 on your twenty-first-century phone, I thought. *Like you did when you found him on the back steps*. But if he had a heart attack? What I knew about CPR I'd learned on TV shows, and if his motor stopped, there wouldn't be time to check out a YouTube video on the subject. I saw more homework in my future.

I watched them drive away and went back inside. Mr Bowditch was lying with one arm over his eyes. Radar sat attentively by the bed. Now it was just the three of us.

'You okay?' I asked.

He dropped his arm and turned his head to look at me. His expression was desolate. 'I'm in a deep hole, Charlie. I don't know if I can climb out.'

'You will,' I said, hoping I sounded more confident than I felt on that subject. 'Want something to eat?'

'I want my pain pills.'

'I can't—'

He raised a hand. 'I know you can't, and I won't lower myself – or insult you – by begging for them. Ever. At least, I hope not.' He stroked Radar's head again and again. She sat perfectly still, her tail moving slowly from side to side, her eyes never leaving him. 'Give me the check and a pen.'

I did that, along with a hardcover book he could use for support. He printed *FOR DEPOSIT ONLY*, then scrawled his signature. 'Will you bank that for me tomorrow?'

'Sure. First Citizens, right?'

'Right. Once it's in the system, I can write a check to cover my hospital stay.' He handed me the check, which I put back in my wallet. He closed his eyes, opened them again, and stared at the ceiling. His hand never left Radar's head. 'I am so tired. And the pain never takes a vacation. Doesn't even take a fucking coffee break.'

'Food?'

'Don't want it, but they tell me I have to eat. Maybe some s-and-s – sardines and Saltines.'

That sounded terrible to me, but I got them, along with a glass of ice water. He drank half of that greedily. Before starting on the sardines (headless and gleaming with grease – urk), he asked me if I still meant to stay the night.

'Tonight and all week,' I said.

'Good. I never minded being alone before, but now it's different. Do you know what falling off that ladder taught me? Or rather re-taught me?'

I shook my head.

'Fear. I am an old man, and I'm broken.' He said this without self-pity, but as a man states a fact. 'I think you should go home long enough to reassure your father that all is well so far, don't you? Perhaps have a bite of supper. Then you can come back and feed Radar and give me my goddam pills. They said I would become addicted, and it hasn't taken long to prove them right.'

'That sounds like a plan.' I paused. 'Mr Bowditch . . . Howard . . . I'd like to bring my dad up to meet you. I know you're not exactly a people-person even when you aren't busted up, but—'

'I understand. He wants to reassure himself, which is perfectly reasonable. But not tonight, Charlie, and not tomorrow. Wednesday, perhaps. By then I might feel a little better.'

'Okay,' I said. 'One more thing.' I wrote my cell number on a Post-it and put it on the little table beside his bed – a table that would soon be covered with rubs and gauze pads and pills (but not the Oxy). 'The bell is for when I'm upstairs—'

'Very Victorian.'

'But any time I'm gone and you need me, call me on my cell. Whether I'm in school or not. I'll tell Mrs Silvius in the office what the situation is.'

'All right. Go on. Reassure your father. But don't be late coming back, or I'll try to get up and find those pills myself.' He closed his eyes.

'Bad idea,' I said.

Without opening them, he said, 'The universe is full of them.'

9

Mondays are catch-up days for my father, often he's not home until six-thirty or even seven, so I didn't expect to find him there, and he wasn't. He was outside Mr Bowditch's front gate, waiting for me.

'I left work early,' he said when I came out. 'Worried about you.'

'You didn't have to—'

He slung an arm around my shoulders and gave me a hug. 'So sue me. I saw you come out and talk to a young woman while I was halfway up the hill. I waved, but you didn't see me. You looked like you were concentrating hard on whatever she was telling you.'

'And you've been waiting out here since then?'

'I thought about knocking on the door, but I guess in this situation I'm like a vampire. I can't come in until I'm invited.'

'Wednesday,' I said. 'I talked to him about it.'

'Sounds good. In the evening?'

'Maybe around seven. He gets his pain pills at six.'

We started walking down the hill. His arm was still around my shoulders. I didn't mind. I told him I didn't want to leave Mr Bowditch alone for long, so I couldn't stay for supper. I said I'd put together a few things – my toothbrush came to mind – and find something to eat in his pantry (just not sardines).

'You don't need to do that,' Dad said. 'I brought subs from Jersey Mike's. Take it back with you.'

'Great!'

'How is he?'

'In a lot of pain. I hope the pills he takes will help him sleep. He gets more at midnight.'

'Oxys?'

'Yes.'

'Keep them safe. Don't let him know where they are.' This was advice I'd already had, but at least Dad didn't ask if I might be tempted to try one myself.

At home I stuffed a couple of days' worth of clothes in my backpack, along with my Nighthawk portable hotspot – my phone was good, but the Nighthawk provided kickass WiFi. I added my toothbrush and the razor I'd started using two years before. Some guys at school were sporting stubble that year – it was a thing – but I like a clean face. I did it fast, knowing I could come back tomorrow for anything I forgot. I was also thinking of Mr Bowditch alone in his big old leaky house with only his elderly dog for company.

When I was ready to go, my father gave me another hug, then held me by the shoulders. 'Look at you. Taking on a serious responsibility.

I'm proud of you, Charlie. I wish your mother could see you. She'd be proud, too.'

'I'm kind of scared.'

He nodded. 'I'd be worried if you weren't. Just remember that if anything happens, you can call me.'

'I will.'

'You know, I was looking forward to you going to college. Now, not so much. This house is going to feel empty without you.'

'I'm just a quarter-mile up the street, Dad.' But there was a lump in my throat.

'I know. I know. Go on and get out of here, Chip. Do your job.' He swallowed. Something clicked in his throat. 'And do it well.'

CHAPTER SEVEN

First Night. Now You Know Jack.

A Simple Woodcutter. Therapy. My Father's Visit.

Lynparza. Mr Bowditch Makes a Promise.

1

I asked Mr Bowditch if it was okay to sit in his chair and he said of course. I offered him half of my sandwich and was kind of relieved when he said no – Jersey Mike's subs are the best.

'I might try a cup of soup after pill o'clock. Chicken noodle. We'll see.'

I asked if he wanted to watch the news. He shook his head. 'Put it on if you want, but I rarely bother. The names change but the bullshit never does.'

'I'm amazed it works. Don't the tubes blow out?'

'Of course. Just as the C-cells in a flashlight wear out. Or the nine-volt in a transistor radio.' I didn't know what a transistor radio was but didn't say so. 'Then you put in new ones.'

'Where do you get the tubes?'

'I buy from a company called RetroFit in New Jersey, but they become more expensive each year as the supply diminishes.'

'Well, you can afford them, I guess.'

He sighed. 'The gold, you mean. You're curious, of course you are, anyone would be. Have you told anyone? Your father? Perhaps a trusted teacher at school?'

'I can keep secrets. I told you that.'

'All right, no need to sound pissy. I had to ask. And we'll talk about it. But not tonight. Tonight I don't feel capable of talking about anything.'

'It can wait. But about the TV tubes . . . how do you get them, if you don't have any Internet?'

He rolled his eyes. 'Did you think that mailbox is out there just for decoration? Something to hang holly on at Christmas, perhaps?'

He was talking about snail-mail. It came as a revelation to me that people still used it to do business. I thought about asking him why he didn't just buy a new TV set, but I thought I knew the answer. He liked old things.

As the hands on the living room clock crawled toward six, I realized I wanted to give him the pills almost as much as he wanted to take them. Finally the time came. I went upstairs, got two, and gave them to him with a glass of water. He almost snatched them out of my hand. The room was cool, but his forehead was beaded with sweat.

'I'll give Radar her chow,' I said.

'Then take her out in the backyard. She's quick about doing the necessary but stay outside for a bit. Hand me that urinal, Charlie. I don't want you to see me using this goddam thing, and at my age it takes awhile to get going.'

2

By the time I came back and emptied the urinal, the pills were doing their work. He asked for the chicken soup – Jewish penicillin, he called it. He drank the broth and ate the noodles with a spoon. When I came back from rinsing the mug, he'd gone to sleep. It didn't surprise me. He'd put in a hell of a day. I went upstairs to his room, found his copy of *The Bride Wore Black*, and was deep into it when he woke up at eight o'clock.

'Why don't you turn on the TV and see if you can find that singing show?' he asked. 'Radar and I like to watch that sometimes.'

I turned on the television, flipped through the few available channels, and found *The Voice*, barely visible through a blizzard of snow. I adjusted the rabbit ears until the picture was as clear as it was going to get, and we watched a number of contestants do their thing. Most of them were pretty damn good. I turned to Mr Bowditch to tell him I liked the country guy, and he was fast asleep.

3

I left the bell beside him on his little table and went upstairs. I looked back once and saw Radar sitting at the foot. When she saw me looking down, she turned and went back to Mr Bowditch, where she spent that night and every night. He slept on that roll-out couch even after he was able to use the stairs again, because by then they were hard for her.

My room was okay, although the single standing lamp cast spooky shadows on the ceiling and the house creaked in its joints, as I'd pretty much known it would. I guessed that when the wind blew, it would be a regular symphony. I plugged in my Nighthawk and went to the Net. I was thinking about carrying that weight of gold on my back, and how it made me remember my mother reading me an old story from a Little Golden Book. I told myself I was just passing the time, but now I wonder. I think sometimes we know where we're going even when we think we don't.

I found at least seven different versions of 'Jack and the Beanstalk,' reading them on my phone by the light of that single lamp. I reminded myself to bring my laptop the next day, but for tonight the phone would have to do. I knew the story, of course; like Goldilocks and Red Riding Hood, it's part of the cultural river that carries kids downstream. I think I saw the animated cartoon version at some point after Mom read me the story, but can't remember for sure. The original story, courtesy of Wikipedia, was a lot more bloodthirsty than the one I remembered. For one thing, Jack is living with just his mother because the giant has killed his father during one of the giant's many rampages.

You probably know the story, too. Jack and his mom are broke. All they have is a cow. Mom tells Jack to take it to market and sell it and get at least five gold coins for it (no pellets in this story). On the way to town, Jack meets a fast-talking peddler who persuades him to trade the cow for five magic beans. His mother is furious and throws the beans out the window. Overnight, they sprout a magic beanstalk that goes high into the clouds. Up there is a huge castle (how it floats on clouds is something none of the versions go into) where the giant lives with his wife.

Jack basically steals golden stuff – coins, a goose that lays golden eggs, the golden harp that warns the giant. But it's not stealing in the usual sense, because the giant has stolen all the golden stuff for himself. I found out that the giant's famous chant – *Fee, fi, fo, fum, I smell the blood of an Englishman* – was cribbed from *King Lear*, where a character named Edgar says, *Child Roland to the dark tower came, His word was still Fie, foh, and fum, I smell the blood of a British man.* And something else I don't remember from any animated cartoon or Little Golden Book: the giant's sleeping chamber is littered with the bones of children. The giant's name gave me a chill, deep and premonitory.

Gogmagog.

4

I turned off the standing lamp at eleven and dozed until my phone's alarm woke me at quarter to twelve. I hadn't bothered to put the Oxy pills in the safe yet; they were on the bureau where I'd stashed my few clothes. I took two of them downstairs. Radar growled at me in the dark and sat up.

'Hush, girl,' Mr Bowditch said, and she did. I turned on the lamp. He was lying on his back, staring up at the ceiling. 'Here you are, right on the dot. Good. I really didn't want to ring that bell.'

'Have you slept?'

'Some. After I get these damn things down my gullet, I might be able to get under again. Maybe until dawn.'

I gave him the pills. He got up on one elbow to swallow them, then handed me the glass and lay back down. 'Better already. That's the psychological effect, I suppose.'

'Can I get you anything else?'

'No. Go back to bed. Growing boys need their rest.'

'I think I've done most of my growing.' At least I hoped so. I was six-four and weighed two-twenty. If I grew any more, I'd be a—

'Gogmagog.' I said it without thinking.

I expected a laugh but didn't even get a smile. 'Been studying up on your fairy tales?'

I shrugged. 'Carrying the gold to Stantonville made me think of the magic beans and the beanstalk.'

'So now you know Jack.'

'I guess I do.'

'In the Bible, Gog and Magog are the warring nations of the world. Did you know that?'

'No.'

'Book of Revelations. Put them together and you'd have a real monster. One best to stay clear of. Turn out the light, Charlie. We both need some sleep. You'll get yours, I may get mine. A little vacation from the pain would be nice.'

I gave Radar a pat, then turned off the light. I headed for the stairs, then turned back. 'Mr Bowditch?'

'Howard,' he said. 'You need to practice that. You're not the fucking butler.'

I thought I sort of was but didn't want to argue the point so late at night. 'Howard, right. What did you do for a living before you retired?'

He chuckled. It was a rusty sound, but not unpleasant. 'I was a part-time surveyor and a part-time logger. A simple woodcutter, in other words. The fairy tales are full of them. Go to bed, Charlie.'

I went to bed and slept until six, when it was time for more pills – not just the painkillers this time but the whole works. Once more I found him awake and looking up at the ceiling. I asked him if he had slept. He said yes. I'm not sure I believed him.

5

We had eggs for breakfast, scrambled by *moi*. Mr Bowditch sat on the edge of the roll-out couch to eat, with his fixator-encased leg on the hassock that went with his easy chair. He asked me again to leave while he used the urinal. When I came back, he was actually up and on his crutches, looking out the front window.

'You should have waited for me to help you,' I said.

He made a *tcha* sound. 'You straightened that picket fence.'

'Radar helped.'

'I bet she did. It looks better. Help me back to bed, Charlie. You'll have to hold my leg like you did before.'

I got him into bed. I took Radar for a walk along Pine Street, and the newer, fresher meds seemed to be helping, because she walked quite a distance, marking telephone poles and a hydrant or two along the way: Radar of Bowditch. Later on I took Mr Bowditch's check to the bank. At home – Dad long gone by then – I grabbed some more clothes and my laptop. Lunch was more s-and-s for Mr Bowditch and hotdogs for me. A frozen dinner would have gone down well (I like the Stouffer's), but Mr Bowditch didn't have a microwave. I put some of the meat from Tiller and Sons out to thaw. I could see YouTube cooking videos in my future, if we weren't going to be living on canned soup and sardines. I gave Mr Bowditch his noon pills. I called Melissa Wilcox to check in, as she'd asked me to do. I was supposed to tell her how many times Mr Bowditch had been up, what he was eating, and if he'd had a bowel movement. That last was a big no, and she wasn't surprised. She said OxyContin was a hell of a constipator. After lunch, I took an envelope out to his mailbox and raised the flag. It contained his personal check made out to Arcadia Hospital. I could have taken it myself, but Mr Bowditch wanted to be sure Heinrich's check cleared first.

I tell you these things not because they are particularly interesting but because they established a routine, one that continued through the rest of that spring and most of the summer. In some ways those were good months. I felt useful, needed. I liked myself better than I had in a long time. Only the end was terrible.

6

On the Wednesday afternoon of my spring vacation week, Melissa arrived for Mr Bowditch's first PT session. She called it physical therapy; he called it pain and torture. He got an extra Oxy, which he liked, and a lot of stretching and lifting of the bad leg, which he didn't. I was in the kitchen during most of it. Among other bons mots, I heard *cocksucker, fuckstick, motherfucker*, and *stop*. He said *stop* a lot, sometimes adding *goddam you*. Melissa wasn't fazed.

When it was over – twenty minutes that probably seemed a lot longer to him – she called me in. I'd brought down a couple of extra chairs from the third floor (not the straight-backed ones that went with the dining room table, which looked to me like implements of torture). Mr Bowditch was sitting in one of them. Melissa had brought along a big foam cushion, and the ankle of his bad leg was resting on it. Because the cushion was lower than the hassock, his knee – still bandaged – was slightly bent.

'Look at that!' Melissa cried. 'Five degrees of bend already! I'm not just pleased, I'm amazed!'

'Hurts like fucking hell,' Mr Bowditch grumbled. 'I want to go back to bed.'

She laughed merrily, as if that was the funniest thing she'd ever heard. 'Five more minutes, then up on your crutches. Charlie will help.'

He made the five minutes, then struggled up and got his crutches braced. He turned toward the bed, but lost one of them. It clattered to the floor and Radar barked. I caught him in time and helped him finish the turn. For the few moments we were locked together, me with my arm around him and his around me, I could feel his heart beating hard and fast. *Fierce* was the word that came into my mind.

I got him onto the bed, but in the process his bad leg bent a lot more than five degrees, and he screamed with pain. Radar was up at once, barking with her ears laid back.

'I'm okay, girl,' Mr Bowditch said. He was out of breath. 'Get down.'

She went to her belly, her eyes never leaving him. Melissa gave him a glass of water. 'As a special treat for good work, you can have your evening pain pills at five tonight. I'll be back on Friday. I know this hurts, Howard; those ligaments don't want to stretch. But they will. If you stick with it.'

'Christ,' he said. Then, grudgingly: 'Okay.'

'Charlie, walk me out.'

I did, carrying her bulky duffel bag of equipment. Her little Honda Civic was parked outside the gate. As I raised the hatchback and put the duffel in, I saw Mrs Richland across the street, once again shading her eyes to get a better view of the festivities. She saw me looking and twiddled her fingers.

'Will he really get better?' I asked.

'Yes. Did you see the bend in his knee? That's extraordinary. I've seen it before, but usually in younger patients.' She considered, then nodded. 'He'll get better. At least for awhile.'

'What does that mean?'

She opened the driver's door. 'Grumpy old cuss, isn't he?'

'He doesn't exactly have people skills,' I said, perfectly aware she hadn't answered my question.

She gave that cheery laugh again. I loved how pretty she was in the spring sunshine. 'You can say that again, hoss. Put it in lights. I'll be back Friday. Different day, same routine.'

'What's Lynparza? I know the other ones he takes, but not that one. What's it do?'

Her smile faded. 'I can't tell you that, Charlie. Patient confidentiality.' She slid behind the wheel. 'But you could look it up on the Internet. Everything's on the Net.'

She drove away.

7

At seven o'clock that night, my father opened the front gate – which I hadn't bothered to bolt – and came up the walk to where I was sitting on the porch steps. After Mr Bowditch's round of PT, I'd asked him if he'd like to put off his visit with my dad. I almost wished he'd say yes, but after a moment's consideration, he'd shaken his head. 'Let's do this. Set his mind at rest. He probably wants to make sure that I'm not a child molester.'

I said nothing to that, although in his current condition Mr Bowditch wouldn't be able to molest a Cub Scout, let alone a six-four galoot who had lettered in two sports.

'Hey, Charlie.'

'Hey, Dad.' I gave him a hug.

He was carrying a sixpack of Coke. 'Think he'd have any use for this stuff? I broke my leg when I was twelve and couldn't swill enough of it.'

'Come on in and ask him.'

Mr Bowditch was sitting in one of the chairs I'd brought down. He'd asked me to bring him a button-up shirt, and a comb for his hair. Except for the pj bottoms bulking over the fixator, I thought he looked pretty squared away. I was nervous, hoping he wouldn't be too grouchy with my dad, but I needn't have worried. His meds were kicking in, but it wasn't just that; the man actually had social skills. Rusty, but there. I guess some things are like riding a bike.

'Mr Reade,' he said. 'I've seen you back in the old days, but it's good to meet you officially.' He held out one of his big veiny hands. 'Pardon me if I don't stand.'

Dad shook with him. 'No problem, and please call me George.'

'I will. And I'm Howard, although I've had a hell of a time convincing your son of that. I want to tell you how good he's been to me. A Boy Scout without the bullshit, if you don't mind me saying.'

'Not at all,' Dad said. 'I'm proud of him. How are you doing?'

'Mending . . . at least that's what the Torture Queen tells me.'

'Physical therapy?'

'So they call it.'

'And here's a good girl,' Dad said, bending down to Radar and giving her big strokes. 'She and I have met.'

'I've heard. Unless my eyes deceive me, that looks like Coca-Cola.'

'They don't. Want some over ice? I'm afraid they're warm.'

'Coke on ice would be welcome. There was a time when a belt of rum in there would have added some zing.'

I tensed a little, but Dad just laughed. 'I hear you.'

'Charlie? Want to grab three of those tall glasses off the top shelf and fill 'em with ice?'

'Sure.'

'You might want to rinse 'em first. They haven't been used for awhile.'

I took my time, listening to the conversation as I rinsed the glasses and cracked the ice out of Mr Bowditch's old-fashioned tray. Mr Bowditch offered Dad condolences on the loss of his wife, said he'd had a few conversations with her on Sycamore Street ('when I used to get out more'), and she seemed like a lovely woman.

'That goddam bridge should have been paved over right away,' Mr Bowditch said. 'Her death could have been avoided. I'm surprised you didn't sue the city.'

He was too busy drinking to think of things like that, I thought. My old resentments were mostly gone, but not entirely. Fright and loss leave a residue.

8

It was dark when I walked with Dad back down the path to the gate. Mr Bowditch was in bed, having made the transfer with only a little help from me while Dad watched.

'He's not what I expected,' Dad said when we reached the sidewalk. 'Not at all. I expected grumpy. Maybe even surly.'

'He can be that way. With you he was kind of . . . I don't know what to call it.'

My father did. 'He extended himself. He wanted me to like him because he likes you. I see the way he looks at you, kiddo. You mean a lot to him. Don't let him down.'

'As long as he doesn't *fall* down.'

Dad hugged me and kissed my cheek and walked back down the hill. I watched him appear in each pool of streetlight, then disappear again. Sometimes I did still resent him for his lost years, because they were my lost years, too. Mostly I was just glad he was back.

'That went all right, didn't it?' Mr Bowditch asked when I went back inside.

'It went fine.'

'And what shall we do with our evening, Charlie?'

'I had an idea about that. Wait one.'

I'd downloaded two episodes of *The Voice* to my laptop. I set it on the table beside his bed, where we both could see it.

'Holy jumping Jesus, look at that picture!' he exclaimed.

'I know. Not bad, right? And no commercials.'

We watched the first one. I was up for two, but he fell asleep five minutes in. I took my laptop upstairs and read about Lynparza.

9

On Friday, I carried Melissa's equipment duffel out to her Civic again. I closed the hatchback and turned to her. 'I looked up Lynparza.'

'Thought you would.'

'It treats four things. I know he's not taking it for breast cancer or ovarian cancer, so which is it? Prostate or the other one?' I hoped to God it wasn't pancreatic. My dad's dad had it and died less than six months after the diagnosis.

'Patient confidentiality, Charlie – I can't say.' But her face was telling me something else.

'Come on, Melissa. You're not a doctor. And someone told you.'

'Because I have to work with him. To do that I need to know the overall picture.'

'I can keep a secret. You know that already, right?' Meaning the high-power painkillers that I wasn't actually old enough to dispense.

She sighed. 'It's prostate cancer. Abrams – the orthopedist who worked on him – saw it on the X-rays. Well advanced but not metastasized. Lynparza slows the growth of tumors. Sometimes actually reverses it.'

'Shouldn't he be on more drugs? Like chemo? Or radiation treatments?'

Mrs Richland was out again. She twiddled and we twiddled back.

Melissa hesitated, then must have decided that, having gone this far, there was no point in stopping. 'He saw Dr Patterson, who's head of the Oncology Department at Arcadia. He laid out the options, and Bowditch refused all of them except the Lynparza.'

'Why?'

'You'd have to ask him that, Charlie, but if you do, don't tell him about this conversation. I probably wouldn't lose my job, but technically I could. And listen, there are doctors – plenty of them – who'd say he made the right call. Prostate cancer slows down in old men. With the Lynparza, he might have years.'

10

That night we watched another episode of *The Voice*. When it was over, Mr Bowditch struggled up on his crutches. 'This could be a big night, Charlie. I think I'm actually going to take a shit.'

'The fireworks are ready,' I said.

'Save it for your stand-up routine.' When I tried to follow him to the kitchen, he turned his head and snapped, 'Go back and watch your gadget, for God's sake. If I fall down, you can pick me up.'

I went back. I heard the door to the little bathroom close. I waited. Five minutes passed. Then ten. I tossed Radar her monkey until she wouldn't chase it anymore and curled up on her rug. At last I went to the kitchen doorway and asked if he was okay.

'Fine,' he called back. 'But I could use a stick of dynamite. Fucking OxyContin.'

The toilet finally flushed and when he came out, he was sweaty but smiling. 'The *Eagle* has landed. Thank Christ.'

I helped him back into bed and decided to take advantage of his good mood. I showed him the bottle of Lynparza. 'I read up on this stuff, and you could be doing a lot more.'

'Is that so, Dr Reade?' But there was a faint smile at the corners of his mouth, and that gave me enough courage to go on.

'Doctors have got a lot of weapons against cancer now. I just don't get why you wouldn't use them.'

'It's quite simple. You know I'm in pain. You know I can't sleep without those goddam constipating pills. You've heard me scream at Melissa, who is a very nice woman. So far I've managed to avoid calling her a cunt or a bitch, but those unpleasant words could pop out at any time. Why would I want to add nausea, vomiting, and cramps to the pain I'm already suffering?'

I started to reply, but he got up on one elbow and made a shushing sound.

'There's something else, young man. Something a person your age can't understand. I've almost had enough. Not quite, but almost. Life gets old. You might not believe that, I know I didn't when I . . .' He paused. '. . . when I was young, but it's true.' He lay back, groped for Radar, found her, stroked her. 'But I didn't want to leave her alone, right? We're pals, she and I. And now I don't have to worry. If she outlives me, you'd take her. Wouldn't you?'

'Yes, of course.'

'As for the therapy . . .' His smile broadened. 'Today I got ten degrees of bend, and I've started using that rubber band thing to flex my ankle. I'm going to work hard, because I don't want to die in bed. Especially not on this fucking roll-out couch.'

11

We hadn't discussed the source of the gold – that was the elephant in the room – but on Sunday I realized there was something we *had* to discuss. I could still give him his morning and evening pills, but what was he going to do about the midday ones once I went back to school?

'I guess Melissa could give them to you on Monday, Wednesday, and Friday when she comes in for PT, but they really wouldn't have much time to work before you start exercising. And what about Tuesdays and Thursdays?'

'I'll just ask Mrs Richland in to give them to me. She could look the place over while she's here. Maybe take some pictures and put them on her Facebook or Twitter.'

'Very funny.'

'It's not just the midday pills,' he said. 'There's the ones at midnight.'

'I'll be here to—'

'No, Charlie. It's time you went back home. I'm sure your father misses you.'

'I'm just up the street from him!'

'Yes, and your bedroom is empty. There's just one person at the supper table when he comes home. Men on their own can sometimes start thinking bad thoughts. I know all about that, believe me. You will leave my noon pills with me when you come in the morning to check on me and feed Radar, and you will leave my midnight pills when you go home at night.'

'I'm not supposed to do that!'

He nodded. 'In case I cheat. Which would be a temptation, because I'm addicted to the goddam things. But I give you my word.' He got up on both elbows and fixed me with his eyes. 'The first time I cheat I'll tell you, and give the pills up entirely. Switch to Tylenol. That's my promise, and I'll keep it. Can you live with that?'

I thought it over and said I could. He put out his hand. We shook. That night I showed him how to access the films and TV shows stored on my laptop. I put two twenty-milligram Oxy pills in a little dish on the table beside his bed. I shouldered my backpack and held up my phone.

'If you need me, call. Day or night.'

'Day or night,' he agreed.

Radar followed me to the door. I bent, stroked her, gave her a hug. She licked my cheek. Then I went home.

12

He never cheated. Not once.

CHAPTER EIGHT

Water Under the Bridge. The Fascination of Gold. An Old Dog. Newspaper News. An Arrest.

1

At first I gave Mr Bowditch sponge baths three times a week, because there was no shower in the cramped downstairs bathroom. He allowed it but insisted on doing his privates himself (fine with me). I washed his scrawny chest and even scrawnier back, and once, after an unfortunate accident as he made his slow way to that cramped little bathroom, I washed his scrawny ass. The swearing and profanity that time was occasioned as much by embarrassment (*bitter* embarrassment) as anger.

'Don't worry about it,' I said when he was back in his pajama bottoms. 'I clean up Radar's crap in the backyard all the time.'

He gave me his patented was-you-born-stupid look. 'That's different. Radar is a *dog*. She'd shit on the lawn in front of the Eiffel Tower, if you let her.'

I found this mildly interesting. '*Is* there a lawn in front of the Eiffel Tower?'

Now came the patented Bowditch eye-roll. 'I don't know. I was making a point. Can I have a Coke?'

'Sure.' Since my dad had brought that sixpack, I always kept Coke in the house for Mr Bowditch.

When I brought it back, he was out of bed and sitting in his old easy chair, Radar by his side. 'Charlie, let me ask you something. All this you're doing for me—'

'I get a very nice check for it every week, which I really appreciate even if I don't always feel I'm doing enough to earn it.'

'You would have done it for free. You told me that while I was in the hospital, and I believe you meant it. So are you bucking for sainthood, or are you perhaps atoning for something?'

That was pretty sharp. I thought of my prayer – my deal with God – but I also thought of phoning in that bogus bomb threat to Stevens Elementary. Bertie thought it was the funniest thing ever, but all I could think about that night, with my dad drunk-snoring in the other room, was how we had scared a whole bunch of people, most of them little kids.

Meanwhile, Mr Bowditch was watching me closely. 'Atoning,' he said. 'For what, I wonder?'

'You gave me a good job,' I said, 'and I'm grateful. I like you even when you're grouchy, although I admit that it's a little harder then. Anything else is water under the bridge.'

He thought about that, then said something I haven't forgotten. Maybe because my mother died on a bridge when I was going to Stevens Elementary myself, maybe just because it seemed important to me, and still does.

'Time is the water, Charlie. Life is just the bridge it flows under.'

2

The time passed. Mr Bowditch continued to curse and sometimes scream during his therapy sessions, upsetting Radar so much that Melissa had to make her go outside before the day's PT started. The flexes hurt, hurt plenty, but by May Mr Bowditch was getting eighteen degrees of bend in his knee, and by June he was almost up to fifty. Melissa started to teach him how to crutch his way upstairs (and more importantly, how to descend without taking a disastrous tumble), so I moved his Oxy pills up to the third floor. I stored them in a dusty old birdhouse with a carved crow on top that gave me the willies. Mr Bowditch found it easier to get around on his crutches and began giving himself his own sponge-downs (which he called 'whore's baths'). I never had another occasion to wipe his bottom, because there was never another accident on the way to the jakes. We watched old movies on my laptop, everything from *West Side Story* to *The Manchurian Candidate* (which we both loved). Mr Bowditch talked about getting a new TV, which seemed a sure sign to me that he was re-engaging with life, but changed his mind when I told him it meant having either cable installation or a satellite dish (so not re-engaging all that much). I came in at six every morning and with no baseball practice or games (Coach Harkness gave me the stinkeye every time we passed in the hall), I got back to 1 Sycamore most afternoons by three. I did chores, mostly housecleaning, which I didn't mind. The floors upstairs were fucking filthy, especially the third floor. When I suggested cleaning the gutters, Mr Bowditch stared at me as if I were insane and told me to hire someone to do it. So Sentry Home Repair came, and once the gutters were cleaned to Mr Bowditch's satisfaction (he watched from the back porch, hunched over his crutches with his pj bottoms flapping around the fixator), he told me to engage them to repair the roof. When Mr Bowditch saw the estimate on that, he ordered me to dicker with them ('Play the poor old man card,' he said). I dickered and got them down twenty per cent. The home repair guys also put in a front porch ramp (which neither Mr Bowditch nor Radar ever used – she was afraid of it) and offered to fix the crazily tilted paving stones leading from the gate to the porch. I refused that offer and did it myself. I also replaced the warped and splintered front and back porch steps (with the help of several DIY YouTube vids). That was a busy clean-up-fix-up spring and summer on top of Sycamore Street Hill. Mrs Richland had lots to watch, and watch she did. In early July, Mr Bowditch went back to the hospital to have the external fixator removed, weeks ahead of Melissa's most optimistic estimates. When she told him how proud of him she was, and hugged him, the old guy was for once at a loss for words. My father came up on Sunday afternoons – at Mr Bowditch's invitation, unprompted by me – and we played three-man gin rummy, which Mr Bowditch usually won. On weekdays I fixed him something to eat, went down the hill for dinner with my dad, then came back to Mr Bowditch's house to wash up his few dishes, walk Radar, and watch movies with him. Sometimes we had popcorn. Once the fixator was off, I no longer had to do pin care, but I had to keep the healing holes clean where the pins had gone in. I exercised his ankles with big red rubber bands and made him do leg-bends.

Those were good weeks, at least mostly. Not everything was good. There were shorter walks for Radar before she began to limp and turned for home. She had more and more trouble getting up the porch steps. Once Mr Bowditch saw me carrying her and told me not to. 'Not until she can't do it for herself,' he said. And sometimes there were dots of blood on the rim of the toilet bowl after Mr Bowditch urinated, which took him longer and longer to do.

'Come on, you useless thing, make some water,' I heard him once say through the closed door.

Whatever the Lynparza was supposed to do, it wasn't doing so well. I tried to talk to him about it, asked him why he was working so hard to get on his feet if he was going to give 'what was really wrong with him' (my euphemism) free rein, and he told me to mind my beeswax. In the end it wasn't cancer that got him. It was a heart attack. Except not really.

It was the goddam shed.

3

Once – I think in June – I brought up the subject of the gold again, although obliquely. I asked Mr Bowditch if he didn't worry about the little German with the limp, especially after the big delivery I'd made so Mr Bowditch could pay his hospital bill.

'He's harmless. He does a lot of business in that back room of his, and so far as I know he's never drawn any attention from law enforcement. Or from the IRS, which would seem to me more likely.'

'Aren't you afraid he'll talk to someone? I mean, maybe he does business with people who have hot diamonds to sell, burglars and such, and he probably keeps quiet about that, but I'd have to think six pounds of solid gold pellets is on an entirely different level.'

He made a scoffing sound. 'Risk the considerable profit he's making on my transactions with him? That would be stupid, and stupid's one thing Willy Heinrich ain't.'

We were in the kitchen, drinking Coke in tall glasses (with sprigs of the mint that grew along the Pine Street side of the house). Mr Bowditch gave me a shrewd look from his side of the table. 'I don't think it's Heinrich you want to talk about at all. I think it's the gold that's on your mind, and where it comes from.'

I didn't reply, but he wasn't wrong.

'Tell me something, Charlie – have you been up there betimes?' He pointed to the ceiling. 'Looking at it? Checking it out, so to speak? You have, haven't you?'

I flushed. 'Well . . .'

'Don't worry, I'm not going to scold you. To me what's up there is just a bucket of metal that might as well be nuts and bolts, but I'm old. That doesn't mean I don't understand the fascination. Tell me, have you had your hands in it?'

I thought of lying but there was no point. He would have known. 'Yes.'

He was still looking at me in that shrewd way, left eye squinted, bushy right eyebrow raised. But smiling, too. 'Plunged your hands into the bucket and let those pellets run through your fingers?'

'Yes.' Now the flush on my cheeks was burning. I hadn't just done that the first time; I'd done it several times since.

'The fascination of gold is something quite apart from its cash value. You know that, don't you?'

'Yes.'

'Let us say – just for the sake of discussion – that Mr Heinrich talked too much to the wrong person after having too much to drink at that disgusting little bar down the street from his store. I'd bet this house and the land it sits on that old limping Willy doesn't ever drink to excess, probably doesn't drink at all, but let us say. And suppose that the person he talked to, perhaps on his own, perhaps with cohorts, waited for you to leave one night, then invaded my home and demanded the gold. My gun is upstairs. My dog, once fearsome . . .' He stroked Radar, who was snoozing beside him. '. . . is now even older than I am. What would I do in such a case?'

'I guess . . . give it to them?'

'Exactly so. I wouldn't wish them well, but I would give it to them.'

So I asked it. 'Where does it come from, Howard?'

'I may tell you that in time. I haven't made up my mind. Because gold isn't just fascinating. It's dangerous. And the place it came from is dangerous. I believe I saw a lamb chop in the fridge. And is there coleslaw? Tiller makes the best coleslaw. You should have some.'

In other words, discussion over.

4

One evening in late July Radar was unable to make it up the back porch steps when we came back from our Pine Street walk. She tried twice, then just sat at the bottom, panting and looking at me.

'Go on, pick her up,' Mr Bowditch said. He'd come out, leaning on one crutch. The other had been pretty much retired. I looked at him to make sure, and he nodded. 'It's time.'

When I picked her up, she yipped and bared her teeth. I slid down the arm cradling her haunches, trying to get away from the sore spot, and carried her up. It was easy. Radar had grown thin, her muzzle almost pure white, her eyes starting to get rheumy. I put her gently down in the kitchen, and at first her back legs wouldn't hold her. She gathered her resolve – I could see her do it – and limped to her rug near the pantry door, very slowly, and more or less collapsed onto it with a tired *whuff* sound.

'She needs to go to the vet.'

Mr Bowditch shook his head. 'She'd be frightened. I won't put her through that to no purpose.'

'But—'

He spoke gently, which frightened *me*, because it was so unlike him. 'No vet can help her. Radar is almost done. For now she just needs to rest, and I need to think.'

'About what, for God's sake!'

'About what's best. You need to go home now. Eat some supper. Don't come back tonight. I'll see you in the morning.'

'What about *your* supper?'

'I'll have sardines and crackers. Go on, now.' Then he said it again: 'I need to think.'

I went home, but I didn't eat much. I wasn't hungry.

5

After that, Radar stopped finishing her morning and evening meals, and although I carried her up the back steps – she could still go down them by herself – there started to be the occasional mess in the house. I knew Mr Bowditch was right about no vet being able to help her . . . except maybe at the very end, because it was clear that she was in pain. She slept a lot, and sometimes yelped and snapped at her hind-quarters, as if trying to get rid of whatever was biting her and hurting her. Now I had two patients, one getting better and one getting worse.

On the fifth of August, a Monday, I got an email from Coach Montgomery, setting out the schedule for football practice. Before replying to it, I did my father the courtesy of telling him I'd decided not to play my final year. Although Dad was clearly disappointed (I was disappointed myself), he said he understood. He had been at Mr Bowditch's the day before, playing gin, and had seen the condition Radar was in.

'There's still a lot of work waiting up there,' I said. 'I want to do something about the mess on the third floor, and once I feel safe about letting Howard go down to the basement, there's a jigsaw puzzle that needs finishing. I think he's forgotten all about it. Oh, and I need to teach him how to use my laptop so he can surf the Net as well as watch movies, plus—'

'Quit it, Chip. It's about the dog. Right?'

I thought about carrying her up those back steps, and how ashamed she looked when she messed in the house, and I just couldn't answer.

'I had a Cocker when I was a kid,' Dad said. 'Penny, her name was. It's hard when a good dog gets old. And when they get to the end of it . . .' He shook his head. 'It tears your heart out.'

That was it. That was it exactly.

It wasn't my dad who was pissed at the idea of me quitting football my senior year, it was Mr Bowditch. And he was pissed like a bear.

'Are you crazy?' he almost shouted. Color was flaring in his seamed cheeks. 'I mean are you flat-out, balls-to-the-wall *crazy*? You'll be a star on that team! You can play college ball, maybe with a scholarship!'

'You've never seen me play in your life.'

'I read the sports pages in the *Sun*, as crappy as they are. You won the goddam Turkey Bowl game last year!'

'We scored four touchdowns in that game. I only punched in the last one.'

He lowered his voice. 'I'd come to see your games.'

That stunned me to silence. Coming from someone who'd been a voluntary shut-in even before his accident, it was an amazing offer.

'You can still go,' I said finally. 'I'll go with you. You buy the hotdogs and I'll buy the Cokes.'

'No. *No*. I'm your boss, goddammit, I pay your salary, and I forbid it. You're not going to lose your last high school football season on my account.'

I do have a temper, although I'd never shown it with him. That day I did. I think it would be fair to say I snapped.

'It's not about you, it's not all about you! What about *her*?' I pointed to Radar, who raised her head and whined uneasily. 'Are *you* going to carry her up and down the back porch steps so she can piss and shit? You can barely goddam walk yourself!'

He looked shocked. 'I'll . . . she can do it in the house . . . I'll put down papers . . .'

'She'd hate that, you know she would. Maybe she's just a dog, but she has her dignity. And if this is her last summer, her last fall . . .' I could feel tears rising, and you'll only think that's absurd if you never had a dog you loved. '. . . I don't want to be on the practice field hitting a fucking *tackling dummy* when she passes! I'll go to school, gotta do that, but the rest of the time I want to be here. And if that isn't good enough for you, fire me.'

He was quiet, hands folded. When he looked back at me his lips were pressed together so tightly they almost weren't there, and for a moment I thought he was going to do just that. Then he said, 'Do you think a vet would make a house call, and perhaps ignore the fact that my dog hasn't been registered? If I paid him enough?'

I let out a breath. 'Why don't I try to find out?'

6

It wasn't a vet I found but a veterinarian's assistant, a single mom with three kids. It was Andy Chen who knew her and made the introduction. She came, examined Radar, and gave Mr Bowditch some pills she said were experimental, but much better than Carprofen. Stronger.

'I want to be clear about these,' she told us. 'They'll improve her quality of life, but they will also probably shorten her life.' She paused. '*Certainly* shorten it. Don't come to me when she's dead and say I didn't tell you that.'

'How long will they help?' I asked.

'They may not help at all. I told you, they're experimental. I only have them because they were left over after Dr Petrie finished a clinical trial. For which he was well paid, I might add – not that I saw any. If they do help, Radar here might get a good month. Maybe two. Probably not three. She won't exactly feel like a puppy again, but she'll be better. Then one day . . .' She shrugged, squatted, and stroked Radar's skinny side. Rades thumped her tail. 'Then one day she'll be gone. If she's still around at Halloween, I'd be very surprised.'

I didn't know what to say, but Mr Bowditch did, and Radar was his dog. 'Good enough.' Then he added something I didn't understand then but do now: '*Long* enough. Maybe.'

When the woman was gone (two hundred dollars to the good), Mr Bowditch crutched over and stroked his dog. When he looked back at me, he was wearing a small, crooked smile. 'No one in authority's going to arrest us for trafficking in illegal dog medicine, are they?'

'Doubt it,' I said. There would be a lot more trouble about the gold, if anyone found out about it. 'Glad you made the call. I wouldn't have been able to decide.'

'Hobson's Choice.' He was still stroking Radar, long glides of his hand from nape to tail. 'In the end, it seems to me that one or two good months are better than six bad ones. If it works at all, that is.'

It did work. Radar began to eat all of her chow again, and she could make it up the porch steps (sometimes with a little help from me). Best of all, she was good for a few games of chase-the-monkey-and-make-him-squeak at night. Still, I never expected her to outlive Mr Bowditch, but she did.

7

Then came what the poets and musicians call a caesura. Radar continued to . . . well, not improve, I couldn't call it that, but to seem more like the dog I met on the day Mr Bowditch fell off the ladder (although in the mornings she still struggled to get up from her rug and go to her food dish). Mr Bowditch *did* improve. He cut back on the Oxy and swapped the single armlet crutch he'd been using since August for a cane he found in a corner of the basement. Down there he was once more working on his jigsaw puzzle. I went to school, I spent time with my dad, I spent even more at 1 Sycamore Street. The Hedgehogs football team started the season 0–3, and my former teammates quit speaking to me. This was a bummer, but I had too much on my mind to let it get me down. Oh, and on several occasions – usually while Mr Bowditch was napping on the roll-out couch, which he was still using to be close to Radar – I opened the safe and plunged my hands into that bucket of gold. Feeling the always surprising weight of it and letting the pellets run through my fingers in little streamlets. At those times I thought of Mr Bowditch talking about the fascination of gold. I meditated on it, you could say. Melissa Wilcox now only came twice a week, and she marveled at Mr Bowditch's progress. She told him Dr Patterson, the oncologist, wanted to see him and Mr Bowditch refused, saying he felt fine. I took him at his word, not because I believed him but because I wanted to. What I know now is that it isn't just patients who go into denial.

A quiet time. A caesura. Then everything happened almost at once, and none of it was good.

8

I had a free period before lunch and usually took it in the library, where I might do homework or read one of Mr Bowditch's gaudy paperbacks. On that late September day I was deep into *The Name of the Game Is Death*, by Dan J. Marlowe, which was splendidly bloody. At quarter to twelve I decided to save the climax for a binge-read that evening, and grabbed a newspaper at random. There are computers in the library, but all the papers are paywalled. Besides, I liked the idea of reading the news in an actual newspaper; it felt charmingly retro.

I might have picked the *New York Times* or the *Chicago Tribune* and missed the story entirely, but the paper on top of the stack was the Elgin *Daily Herald* and that was the one I took. The big stories on the front page were about Obama wanting to take military action in Syria and a mass shooting in D.C. that left thirteen dead. I scanned them, checked the clock – ten minutes to lunch – and riffled through the pages on my way to the comics. I never made it that far. A story on the second page of the Area News section stopped me. And I mean cold.

STANTONVILLE JEWELER HOMICIDE VICTIM

A longtime Stantonville resident and businessman was found dead in his shop, Excellent Jewelers, late last night. Police responded to a phone call saying the door to the shop was open even though the Closed sign was still hanging in it. Officer James Kotziwinkle found Wilhelm Heinrich in the back room, the door of which was also open. When asked if the motive was robbery, Stantonville Police Chief William Yardley said, 'Although this crime is still being investigated, that would appear to be a no-brainer.' When asked if anyone heard sounds of a struggle, or perhaps gunshots, neither Chief Yardley nor Detective Israel Butcher of the Illinois State Police would comment, except to say that most of the businesses at the west end of Stantonville's main street have been vacant since the advent of the mall outside of town. Excellent Jewelers was a notable exception. Yardley and Butcher have promised 'a swift resolution to the case.'

The lunch bell went, but I sat where I was and called Mr Bowditch. He answered as he always did: 'If this is a telemarketer, take me off your list.'

'It's me, Howard. Mr Heinrich has been murdered.'

Long pause. Then: 'How do you know?'

I looked around. The library was a no-lunch zone, and now empty except for me, so I read him the article. It didn't take long.

'Damn,' Mr Bowditch said when I finished. 'Where am I supposed to trade off the gold now? He's been my go-to for almost twenty-five years.' No sympathy whatsoever. Not even any surprise, at least that I could detect.

'I'll do some Internet searches—'

'Carefully! Discreetly!'

'Sure, I'll be discreet as all hell, but I think you're missing the point here. You did a big deal with him, a *huge* deal, and now he's dead. If someone got your name out of him . . . if he was tortured, or even promised that he wouldn't be killed . . .'

'You've been reading too many of my old paperbacks, Charlie. You traded those six pounds of gold for me last April.'

'Not exactly the Dark Ages,' I said.

He paid no attention. 'I don't like blaming the victim, but he simply wouldn't leave that shop of his in that saggy-ass little town. The last time I did a deal with him in person, this was probably four months before I fell off the ladder, I told him "Willy, if you don't shut this place up and move out to the mall, someone is going to rob you." Someone finally did, and killed him in the bargain. That's your simple explanation.'

'Just the same, I'd feel better if you brought your gun downstairs.'

'If it will make you feel better, fine. Are you coming after school?'

'No, I thought I'd go out to Stantonville and see if I could score some crack.'

'The humor of young people is crude and rarely funny,' Mr Bowditch said, and hung up.

By the time I got in the lunch line it was a mile long and whatever slop the caff was serving would probably be cold. I didn't mind. I was thinking about the gold. Mr Bowditch had said that at his age it was just a bucket of metal. Maybe so, but I thought he was either lying or being disingenuous.

Otherwise, why would he have so *much*?

9

That was on Wednesday. I paid for the Elgin newspaper so I could get it on my phone, and on Friday there was another story, this time on the front page of the Area News section: **STANTONVILLE**

MAN ARRESTED IN JEWELRY STORE ROBBERY-MURDER. The arrestee was identified as Benjamin Dwyer, 44, 'of no fixed address.' Which I assumed meant homeless. The proprietor of the Stantonville Pawn & Loan called the cops when Dwyer tried to pawn a diamond ring 'of considerable value.' At the police station he was also found to be in possession of a bracelet studded with emeralds. The police rightly considered these rather suspicious possessions for a man of no fixed address.

'There, you see?' Mr Bowditch said when I showed him the article. 'A stupid man committed a stupid crime and was arrested when he tried to convert his spoils to cash in a stupid way. It wouldn't make a very good mystery story, would it? Even of the paperback-quickie type.'

'I guess not.'

'You still look bothered.' We were in the kitchen, watching Radar eat her evening meal. 'A Coke might cure that.' He got up and went to the refrigerator, hardly limping at all.

I took the Coke, but it didn't cure what was bothering me. 'That back room of his was filled with jewelry. There was even a tiara with diamonds, like a princess would wear to a ball.'

Mr Bowditch shrugged. To him it was a closed case, a done deal. 'You're being paranoid, Charlie. The real problem is what to do with some of the gold I still have on hand. Concentrate on that. But—'

'Be discreet, I know.'

'Discretion is the better part of valor.' He nodded sagely.

'What's that got to do with anything?'

'Not a goddam thing.' Mr Bowditch grinned. 'I just felt like saying it.'

10

That night I went on Twitter and searched for Benjamin Dwyer. What I got was a bunch of tweets about an Irish composer, so I changed my search to *Dwyer murder suspect*. That netted me half a dozen hits. One was from the Stantonville Police Chief, William Yardley, basically congratulating himself for the quick arrest. Another was from someone who ID'd herself as Punkette 44, and like so many on Twitter, she was thoughtful and compassionate: **I grew up in Stantonville, it sux. That guy Dwyer could murder everybody in it & be doing the world a favor**.

But the one that interested me was from BullGuy19. He wrote: **Benjy Dwyer a murder suspect? Don't make me laugh. He's been around Shitsville 1000 years. Should have VILLAGE IDIOT tattooed on his forehead**.

I thought I'd show that one to Mr Bowditch the next day, and suggest that if BullGuy19 was right, that would make Benjy Dwyer the perfect patsy. As it happened, I never got the chance.

CHAPTER NINE

The Thing in the Shed. A Dangerous Place. 911. The Wallet. A Good Conversation.

1

I no longer had to show up at six A.M. to feed Radar; Mr Bowditch was able to do it himself. But I'd gotten used to rising early, and I usually rode my bike up the hill around quarter of seven so I could take her out to do her business. After that, because it was Saturday, I thought we might go for a little stroll along Pine Street, where she always enjoyed reading the messages left on telephone poles (and leaving a few of her own). That day there was no walk.

When I came in Mr Bowditch was at the kitchen table, eating oatmeal and reading a cinderblock-sized book by James Michener. I got myself a glass of orange juice and asked him how he slept.

'Made it through the night,' he said without taking his eyes from his book. Not much of a morning person was Howard Bowditch. Of course he wasn't much of an evening person, either. Or noon, for that matter. 'Rinse that glass when you're done.'

'I always do.'

He grunted and turned a page in his cinderblock, which was called *Texas*. I gulped the rest of my juice and called for Radar, who came into the kitchen hardly limping at all.

'Walkies?' I said. 'Radie want to go walkie-walk?'

'Jesus,' Mr Bowditch said. 'Enough with the baby talk. In human years she's ninety-eight.'

Radar was at the door. I opened it and she picked her way down the back steps. I started to follow her, then remembered I'd need her leash if we were going to walk on Pine Street. Nor had I rinsed my juice glass. I did the glass and was heading for the peg in the front hall where the leash hung when Radar started to bark, harsh and fast and very, very loud. It was the farthest thing from her *I see a squirrel* bark.

Mr Bowditch snapped his book shut. 'What the fuck is up with her? You better go see.'

I had a very good idea of what was up with her, because I'd heard that sound before. It was her Intruder Alert bark. She was once more crouched down in the backyard grass, which was now much shorter and mostly poop-free. She was facing the shed, her ears laid back and her muzzle wrinkled to show her teeth. Foam flew from her mouth with each bark. I ran to her and grabbed her collar and tried to pull her back. She didn't want to come, but it was clear she also didn't want to go closer to the locked shed. Even with the fusillade of barks, I could hear that weird scraping, scratching sound. This time it was louder, and I saw the door moving a little. It was like a visible heart-beat. Something was trying to get out.

'Radar!' Mr Bowditch called from the porch. 'Get back here, *now*!'

Radar paid no attention, just went on barking. Something inside the shed hit the door hard enough for me to hear the thud. And there was a weird mewling sound, sort of like a cat but higher in pitch. It was like listening to chalk scream on a blackboard, and my arms hucked up in gooseflesh.

I got in front of Radar to block her view of the shed and moved at her, making her back up a step or two. Her eyes were wild, showing rings of white, and for a moment I thought she was going to bite me.

She didn't. There came another of those thuds, more scratching sounds, then that horrible high-pitched mewling. Radar had had enough. She turned and fled back to the porch, showing not a single sign of a limp. She scrambled up the steps and huddled at Mr Bowditch's feet, still barking.

'Charlie! Get away from there!'

'Something's inside and trying to get out. It sounds big.'

'Get back here, boy! You need to get back here!'

Another thud. More scratching. I had a hand over my mouth, as if to stifle a cry. I don't remember putting it there.

'Charlie!'

Like Radar, I ran. Because as soon as I couldn't see the shed anymore, it was easy to imagine the door busting off its hinges and some nightmare coming after me, skittering and lurching and making those inhuman cries.

Mr Bowditch was wearing his awful Bermuda shorts and his old slippers, which he called scuffs. The healing wounds where the fixator rods had gone into his flesh were very red against his pale skin.

'Get inside! Get inside!'

'But what—'

'Nothing to worry about, that door'll hold, but I need to take care of this.'

I came up the steps and was in time to hear what he said next, although he lowered his voice as people do when talking to themselves. 'Son of a bitch moved the boards and blocks. Must be a big one.'

'I heard something like that before, when you were in the hospital, but not as loud.'

He pushed me into the kitchen and then followed, almost tripping over Radar, who was cowering at his feet, then catching himself on the doorjamb.

'Stay here. I'll take care of this.'

He slammed the door to the backyard, then went limping and scuffling and swaying into the living room. Radar followed, her tail drooping. I heard him muttering, then a pained curse followed by a grunt of effort. When he came back, he was carrying the gun I'd asked him to bring downstairs. But not *just* the gun. It was in a leather holster, and the holster was attached to a leather belt studded with silver conchos. It looked like something out of *Gunfight at the O.K. Corral*. He cinched it around his waist so the holstered revolver rested just below his right hip. Rawhide strings – tie-downs – dangled against his madras shorts. It should have looked ridiculous – *he* should have looked ridiculous – but it didn't and he didn't.

'Stay in here.'

'Mr Bowditch, what . . . you can't . . .'

'*Stay in here goddammit!*' He grasped my arm so hard it hurt. He was breathing in quick rasps. 'Stay with the dog. I mean it.'

He went out, slamming the door behind him, and sidesaddled down the steps. Radar bunted her head against my leg, whimpering. I stroked her distractedly, looking through the glass. Halfway to the shed, Mr Bowditch reached into his left pocket and brought out his ring of keys. He picked one out and went on. He put the key in the big padlock, then drew the .45. He turned the key and opened the door, pointing the gun at a slight downward angle. I expected something or someone to come bursting out at him, but that didn't happen. I did see movement – something black and thin. Then it was gone. Mr Bowditch stepped into the shed and pulled the door shut behind him. Nothing happened for a long, long time that actually couldn't have been more than five seconds. Then there were two gunshots. The shed walls had to be very thick, because the sounds, which must have been deafening in that enclosed space, came to me as a pair of flat, toneless thuds, like a sledgehammer with its head swaddled in felt.

There was nothing for a lot longer than five seconds; more like five minutes. The only thing that held me was the imperative tone of Mr Bowditch's voice and the utterly fierce look on his face when he told me to stay in here, goddammit. Finally, though, that couldn't hold me any longer. I was sure something had happened to him. I opened the kitchen door, and just as I stepped out onto the back porch, the door of the shed opened and Mr Bowditch came out. Radar bulleted past me, no sign of arthritis then, and cut across the yard to him as he shut the door and snapped the padlock into place. A good thing he did, because it was the only thing he had to hold onto when Radar jumped up on him.

'Down, Radar, get down!'

She went to her belly, tail wagging like mad. Mr Bowditch came back to the porch much more slowly than he'd gone down to the shed, limping noticeably on his bad leg. One of the scars had broken open and blood was oozing out in dark red beads. They reminded me of the rubies I'd seen in Mr Heinrich's back room. He had lost one of his scuffs.

'Little help, Charlie,' he said. 'Fucking leg's on fire.'

I slung his arm around my neck, grasped his bony wrist, and almost hauled him up the steps and into the house.

'Bed. Have to lie down. Can't catch my breath.'

I got him into the living room – he lost his other scuff on the way because his feet were dragging – and got him on the rollaway.

'Jesus Christ, Howard, what was that? What did you shoo—'

'Pantry,' he said. 'Top shelf. Behind those bottles of Wesson Oil. Whiskey. This much.' He held his thumb and forefinger a smidge apart. They were trembling. I had thought he was pale before, but now, with those red spots fading from his cheeks, he looked like a dead man with living eyes.

I went into the pantry and found the bottle of Jameson's where he said it would be. Tall as I am, I had to stand on tiptoe to reach it. The bottle was dusty and almost full. Even as wrought-up as I was – scared, almost panicked – the smell when I uncapped it brought back vile memories of my father lolling on the couch in a semi-stupor or hung over the toilet, retching. Whiskey doesn't smell the same as gin . . . yet it does. All alcohol smells the same to me, of sadness and loss.

I poured a small knock in a juice glass. Mr Bowditch tossed it down and coughed, but some of the color came back into his cheeks. He unbuckled the gaudy gunbelt. 'Get this fucking thing off me.'

I pulled the holster and the belt slithered free, Mr Bowditch giving a muttered *fuck* when the buckle must have scraped the small of his back.

'What do I do with it?'

'Put it under the bed.'

'Where did you get the belt?' I had certainly never seen it.

'At the gettin' place. Just do it, but before you do, reload it.'

There were bullet loops on the belt between the conchos. I rolled the big gun's cylinder, filled the two empty chambers, holstered the gun, and put it back under the bed. I felt like I was dreaming awake.

'What was it? What was in there?'

'I'll tell you,' he said, 'but not today. Nothing to worry about. Take this.' He gave me his keyring. 'Put it on that shelf there. Give me two of those Oxys and then I'm going to sleep.'

I got him the pills. I didn't like him taking high-tension dope after high-tension whiskey, but it had only been a small knock.

'Don't go in there,' he said. 'You may in time, but for now don't even think of it.'

'Is it where the gold comes from?'

'That's complicated, as they say on the afternoon soap operas. I can't talk about it now, Charlie, and you must not talk about it to anybody. *Anybody*. The consequences . . . I can't even imagine. Promise me.'

'I promise.'

'Good. Now go away and let an old man sleep.'

2

Radar was usually happy to go down the hill with me, but that Saturday she wouldn't leave Mr Bowditch's side. I went down solo and fixed myself a deviled ham sandwich on Wonder Bread – the snack of champions. My dad left a note saying he was going to a nine A.M. AA meeting and bowling with Lindy and a couple of his other sober friends afterward. I was glad. I would have kept my promise to Mr Bowditch no matter what – *the consequences, I can't even imagine*, he'd said – but I'm pretty sure Dad would have seen something on my face anyway. He was a hell of a lot more sensitive to things like that now that he was sober. Usually that's a good thing. That day it wouldn't have been.

When I got back to Number 1, Mr Bowditch was still asleep. He looked a little better, but his breathing had a raspy quality. It was the way he'd sounded when I found him halfway up the porch steps with his leg broken. I didn't like it.

By evening the rasp was gone. I made popcorn, shaking it up old-school on the Hotpoint stove. We ate it while watching *Hud* on my laptop. It was Mr Bowditch's pick, I'd never heard of it, but it was pretty good. I didn't even mind that it wasn't in color. At one point Mr Bowditch asked me to freeze the picture while the camera was close-up on Paul Newman. 'Was he the handsomest man that ever lived, Charlie? What do you think?'

I said he could be right.

I stayed Saturday night. On Sunday, Mr Bowditch seemed better still, so I went fishing with my dad off the South Elgin Dam. We didn't catch anything, but it was nice to be with him in the mellow September sunshine.

'You're awful quiet, Charlie,' he said on the way back. 'Anything on your mind?'

'Just the old dog,' I said. This was mostly – but not entirely – a lie.

'Bring her down this afternoon,' Dad said, and I tried, but Radar still wouldn't leave Mr Bowditch.

'Go sleep in your own bed tonight,' Mr Bowditch said. 'Me 'n the old girl will be fine.'

'You sound hoarse. Hope you're not coming down with something.'

'I'm not. Just been talking most of the goddam day.'

'To who?'

'*Whom*. To myself. Go on, Charlie.'

'Okay, but call if you need me.'

'Yes, yes.'

'Promise. I gave you mine yesterday, now you give me yours.'

'I promise, for Chrissake. Now put an egg in your shoe and beat it.'

3

On Sunday Radar was no longer able to climb the back porch steps after doing her morning business, and she only ate half of her food. That night she ate none of it.

'Probably she just needs to rest,' Mr Bowditch said, but he sounded doubtful. 'Double up on those new pills.'

'Are you sure?' I asked.

He gave me a bleak smile. 'What can it hurt at this point?'

I did sleep in my own bed that night, and on Monday, Radar seemed a little better. But Mr Bowditch had also paid a price for Saturday. He was using his crutches again to get back and forth from the bathroom. I wanted to ditch school and stay with him, but he forbade it. That night he seemed better, too. Said he was bouncing back. I believed him.

More fool me.

4

On Tuesday morning at ten o'clock I was in Advanced Chem. We were split into groups of four, dressed in rubber aprons and gloves, determining the boiling point of acetone. The room was quiet except for murmuring voices, so the sound of my cell phone when it rang in my back pocket was very loud. Mr Ackerley looked at me with disapproval. 'How many times have I told you kids to silence—'

I took it from my pocket and saw BOWDITCH. I dropped my gloves and took the call going out of the room, ignoring whatever Ackerley was saying. Mr Bowditch sounded strained but calm. 'I believe I'm having a heart attack, Charlie. Actually I have no doubt.'

'Did you call—'

'I called *you*, so be quiet and listen. There's a lawyer. Leon Braddock, in Elgin. There's a wallet. Under the bed. Everything else you need is also under the bed. Do you understand that? *Under the bed*. Take care of Radar, and when you know everything, decide . . .' He gasped. 'Fuck, how that *hurts*! Like pig iron in the forge! When you know everything, decide what you want to do about her.'

That was it. He clicked off.

The chem room door opened as I was calling 911. Mr Ackerley came out and asked me what the hell I thought I was doing. I waved him off. The 911 operator asked me what my emergency was. With Mr Ackerley standing there with his mouth ajar, I told her and gave her the address. I untied my apron and let it fall to the floor. Then I ran for the door.

5

That was probably the fastest bike ride of my life, standing on the pedals and slicing across streets without looking. A horn blared, tires screeched, and someone hollered, 'Watch where you're going, you dumb shit!'

Fast as I was, the ER guys beat me. When I swerved around the corner of Pine and Sycamore, putting one foot down and dragging it on the pavement to keep from wiping out, the ambulance was just pulling away with its lights flashing and its siren whooping. I went around back. Before I could open the kitchen door, Radar bulleted through the dog door and was all over me. I went to my knees to keep her from leaping up and stressing those fragile back hips. She whined and yipped and licked my face. Don't even try to tell me she didn't know something bad had happened.

We went inside. A cup of coffee was spilled on the kitchen table and the chair he always sat in (it's funny how we pick our spots and keep to them) was overturned. The stove was still on, the old-fashioned percolator too hot to touch and smelling charred. Smelling like a chemistry experiment, you could say. I turned off the burner and used an oven mitt to move the percolator to a cold burner. During all this Radar never left my side, leaning her shoulder against my leg and rubbing her head on my knee.

A calendar was lying on the floor beside the entry to the living room. It was easy to imagine what had happened. Mr Bowditch drinking coffee at the kitchen table, the percolator staying hot on the stove for a second cup. A hammer hits his chest. He spills his coffee. His landline is in the living room. He gets up and goes in there, knocking over his chair, staggering once and pulling the calendar off the wall as he braces himself.

The retro phone was on the bed. There was also a wrapper that said Papaverine, something they had injected before transporting him, I supposed. I sat on the rumpled rollaway, stroking Radar and scratching behind her ears, which always seemed to calm her.

'He'll be okay, girl. Wait and see, he'll be fine.'

But in case he wasn't, I looked under the bed. Where, according to Mr Bowditch, I'd find *everything I needed*. There was the holstered gun on its concho-studded belt. There was his keyring and a wallet I'd never seen before. And there was an old-fashioned cassette tape recorder that I *had* seen, perched atop one of the plastic milk-crates of rickrack on the third floor. I looked in the recorder's window and saw there was a Radio Shack cassette in the machine. Either he had been listening to something or recording something. My money was on recording.

I put the keyring in one pocket and the wallet in another. I would have put the wallet in my backpack, but it was still at school. I took the rest of the stuff upstairs and put it in the safe. Before closing the door and spinning the combination, I went to one knee and plunged my hands wrist-deep in those gold pellets. As I let them sift through my fingers, I wondered what would happen to them if Mr Bowditch died.

Radar was whining and barking from the foot of the stairs. I went down, sat on the rollaway, and called my dad. I told him what had happened. Dad asked how he was.

'I don't know. I didn't see him. I'm going to the hospital now.'

Halfway across the goddam bridge, my phone rang. I pulled into the Zip Mart parking lot and took the call. It was Melissa Wilcox. She was crying.

'He died on the way to the hospital, Charlie. They tried to revive him, they tried everything, but the infarction was too bad. I'm sorry, I'm so sorry.'

I said I was, too. I looked at the window of the Zip Mart. The sign there was the same: a heaped plate of fried chicken that was THE BEST IN THE LAND. The tears came and the words blurred. Mrs Zippy saw me and came out. 'Everything all right, Cholly?'

'No,' I said. 'Not really.'

There was no point in going to the hospital now. I pedaled back across the bridge and then walked my bike up Sycamore Street Hill. I was too pooped to ride, especially not up that steep grade. I stopped outside our house, but that house was empty and would be until my father got home. Meanwhile, there was a dog that needed me. I guessed she really was my dog now.

6

When I got back to Mr Bowditch's house, I spent some time petting Radar. I cried while I did it, partly from shock but also because it was sinking in: there was a hole where I'd had a friend. The stroking soothed her, and it did the same for me, I guess, because I began to think. I called Melissa back and asked if there would be an autopsy. She told me there wouldn't be, because he hadn't died unattended and the cause was clear.

'The coroner will write out a death certificate, but he'll need some ID. Do you have his wallet, by any chance?'

Well, I had *a* wallet. It wasn't the same as the one Mr Bowditch carried in his hip pocket, that one was brown and the one I'd found under the bed was black, but I didn't tell Melissa that. I just said I had it. She said there was no rush, we all knew who he was.

I was starting to wonder about that.

I Googled Leon Braddock's number and called him. The conversation was short. Braddock said that all of Mr Bowditch's affairs were in order, because he had not expected to live long.

'He said he didn't intend to buy any green bananas. I thought that was charming.'

The cancer, I thought. That was why he put his affairs in order, that was what he expected to get him, not a heart attack.

'Did he come to your office?' I asked.

'He did. Earlier this month.'

When I was in school, in other words. And he hadn't told me anything about it.

'I bet he took a Yoober.'

'Beg pardon?'

'Nothing. Melissa – his physical therapist – says someone, the coroner I guess, needs to see ID for the death certificate.'

'Yes, yes, just a formality. If you take it to the hospital's front desk, they'll make a photocopy. Driver's license if he still has one – even an expired one would do, I think. Something with a picture. Not a rush, they'll release the body to the funeral home without it. I don't suppose you have any idea which funeral home—'

'Crosland,' I said. It was the one my mother was buried out of. 'Right here in Sentry.'

'Very good, very good. I'll take care of the expenses. He left money in escrow for just such a sad eventuality. Please tell me what the arrangements are, perhaps your parents can take care of that. I'll want to see you afterward, Mr Reade.'

'Me? Why?'

'I'll tell you when I see you. It will be a good conversation, I think.'

7

I gathered up Radar's food, dish, and meds. There was no way I was going to leave her in that house, where she'd wait for her master to come back from wherever he'd gone. I clipped her leash to her collar and walked her down the hill. She went slowly but steadily and mounted our porch steps with no trouble. She knew the place now and went immediately to her water dish. Then she lay down on her rug and went to sleep.

Dad came home shortly after noon. I don't know what he saw on my face, but he took one look and pulled me into a strong hug. I started crying again, this time a real flood. He cupped the back of my head and rocked me as if I were still a little boy, and that made me cry even harder.

When the waterworks finally stopped, he asked if I was hungry. I said I was, and he scrambled half a dozen eggs, throwing in handfuls of onions and peppers. We ate, and I told him what had happened, but there was plenty I didn't tell him about – the pistol, the noises in the shed, the bucket of gold in the safe. I didn't show him the keyring, either. I thought I might come clean soon, and he'd probably give me hell for holding back, but I was going to keep the crazy stuff to myself until I listened to that cassette tape.

I did show him the wallet. In the billfold were five dollar bills of a sort I'd never seen before. Dad said they were silver certificates, not all that rare, but as retro as Mr Bowditch's TV and Hotpoint stove. There were also three items of identification: a Social Security card made out to Howard A. Bowditch, a laminated card declaring Howard A. Bowditch was a member of the American Woodsman's Association, and a driver's license.

I looked at the photo on the Woodsman's Association card with fascination. In it Mr Bowditch looked about thirty-five, surely no older than forty. He had a full head of blazing red hair, combed back from his unlined forehead in neat waves, and he was wearing a cocky grin I'd never seen. Smiles, yes, and even a grin or two, but nothing this carefree. He was wearing a plaid flannel shirt and he certainly looked like a woodsy-type guy.

A simple woodcutter, he'd said to me not all that long ago. *The fairy tales are full of them.*

'This is really, really good,' my dad said.

I looked up from the card I was holding. 'What is?'

'This.'

He passed me the driver's license, which showed Mr Bowditch at sixty or so. He still had plenty of red hair, but it was thinning and fighting a losing battle against the white. The license had been good until 1996, according to what was printed below his name, but we knew better. Dad had checked online. Mr Bowditch had a car (somewhere) but had never held a valid Illinois driver's license . . . which was what this purported to be. I guessed Mr Heinrich might have known someone who could create fake DLs.

'Why?' I asked. 'Why would he?'

'Maybe lots of reasons, but I think he must have known a valid death certificate couldn't be issued without at least some identification.' Dad shook his head, not with irritation but admiration. 'This, Charlie, was burial insurance.'

'What should we do about it?'

'Roll with it. He had secrets, I'm sure, but I don't think he ever robbed banks in Arkansas or shot up a bar in Nashville. He was good to you and good to his dog and that's good enough for me. I believe he should be buried with his little secrets, unless his lawyer knows them. Or do you think differently?'

'I don't.' What I was thinking was that he'd had secrets, all right, but not little. Unless you considered a fortune in gold little, that was. And there was something in his shed. Or had been, until he shot it.

8

Howard Adrian Bowditch was laid to rest just two days later, on Thursday the twenty-sixth of September, 2013. The service took place at the Crosland Funeral Home, and he was buried at Sentry's Rest Cemetery, my mother's final resting place. Reverend Alice Parker conducted a non-sectarian service at my father's request – she had also officiated at my mother's service. Reverend Alice kept it short, but even so, I had plenty of time to think. Some of it was about the gold, but more of it was about the shed. He had shot something in there, and the excitement killed him. It took a little while, but I was sure that had done it.

Present at the funeral parlor service, and at the cemetery, were George Reade, Charles Reade, Melissa Wilcox, Mrs Althea Richland, a lawyer named Leon Braddock, and Radar, who slept through the funeral service and spoke up just once, at graveside: a howl as the coffin was lowered into the ground. I'm sure that sounds both sentimental and unbelievable. All I can say is it happened.

Melissa gave me a hug and a kiss on the cheek. She told me to call her if I wanted to talk, and I said I would.

I returned to the parking lot with Dad and the lawyer. Radar walked slowly beside me. Braddock's Lincoln was parked next to our humble Chevy Caprice. There was a nearby bench in the shade of an oak whose leaves were going gold. 'Perhaps we could sit here for a few moments?' Braddock asked. 'I have something rather important to tell you.'

'Wait,' I said. 'Keep walking.' I had my eyes on Mrs Richland, who had turned to look just as she always had on Sycamore Street, with one hand raised to shade her eyes. When she saw we were going to the cars – or appearing to – she got into hers and drove away.

'*Now* we can sit down,' I said.

'I take it that lady is the curious type,' Braddock said. 'Did she know him?'

'No, but Mr Bowditch said she was a nosy-parker, and he was right.'

We sat on the bench. Mr Braddock hoisted his briefcase onto his lap and unlatched it. 'I said we'd have a good conversation, and I believe you'll agree when you hear what I have to tell you.' He took out a folder, and from the folder a small sheaf of papers held with a gold clip. At the head of the one on top were the words LAST WILL AND TESTAMENT.

My dad began to laugh. 'Oh my God, he left something to Charlie?'

'Not quite correct,' Braddock said. 'He left *everything* to Charlie.'

I said the first thing that came to mind, which wasn't exactly polite. 'You're shitting me!'

Braddock smiled and shook his head. 'This is *nullum cacas statum*, as we lawyers say – a no-shit situation. He left you the house and the land it stands upon. Quite a piece of land, as it happens, worth at least six figures. *High* six figures, given Sentry's Rest property values. Everything in the house is also yours, plus a car currently in storage in the town of Carpentersville. And the dog, of course.' He bent and stroked Radar. She looked up briefly, then put her head back on her paw.

'This is really true?' Dad asked.

'Lawyers never lie,' Braddock said, then rethought what he'd said. 'At least they don't in matters such as this.'

'And there are no relatives to contest it?'

'We'll find that out when the will goes through probate, but he claimed to have none.'

'Is it . . . is it still okay for me to go inside?' I asked. 'I mean, I have a bunch of stuff there. Mostly clothes, but also . . . um . . .' I couldn't think what else I had at Number 1. All I could think about was what Mr Bowditch had done one day earlier that month while I was in school. He might have changed my life while I was taking a history quiz, or shooting hoops in the gym. It wasn't the gold I was thinking about just then, or the shed, or the gun, or the cassette tape. I was only trying to get my head around the fact that I now owned (or soon would) the top of Sycamore Street Hill. And why? Just because I'd heard Radar howling in the backyard of what kids called the Psycho House one chilly April afternoon.

Meanwhile, the lawyer was talking. I had to ask him to rewind.

'I said of course you can go in. It's yours, after all – lock, stock, and barrel. At least it will be once the will is probated.'

He put the will back in the folder, put the folder back in his briefcase, snapped the catches, and stood. From his pocket he fished a business card and gave it to my father. Then, perhaps remembering that Dad wasn't the named legatee of a property worth six figures (*high* six figures), he gave another one to me.

'Call if you have questions, and of course I will be in touch. I'll ask that the probate process be expedited, but it still may take as long as six months. Congratulations, young man.'

Dad and I shook hands with him and watched him go to his Lincoln. My father isn't ordinarily a cussing man (unlike Mr Bowditch, who was apt to drop a *goddam* into *pass the salt*) but as we sat there on that bench, still too stunned to get up, he made an exception. 'Holy fuck.'

'Right,' I said.

9

When we got home, Dad brought two Cokes from the fridge. We clinked cans. 'How do you feel, Charlie?'

'I don't know. I can't get my head around it.'

'Do you think he has anything in the bank, or did the hospital stay clean him out?'

'I don't know.' But I did. Not much in Citizens, maybe a couple of thousand, but there was the bucket of gold upstairs and maybe more in the shed. Along with whatever else was in there.

'It doesn't really matter,' Dad said. 'That property is golden.'

'Golden, right.'

'If this proves out, your college expenses are taken care of.' He let out a long sigh, pursing his lips so it made a *hooo* sound. 'I feel like a ninety-pound weight just slid off my back.'

'Assuming we sell it,' I said.

He gave me an odd look. 'Are you telling me you want to keep it? Do a Norman Bates and live in the Psycho House?'

'It doesn't look like the Haunted Mansion anymore, Dad.'

'I know. I know. You really spiffed it up.'

'Got a ways to go. I was hoping to get the whole thing painted before winter.'

He was still giving me the odd look – head cocked, slight frown creasing his brow. 'It's the land that's valuable, Chip, not the house.'

I wanted to argue – the idea of demolishing Number 1 Sycamore gave me the horrors, not because of the secrets it contained but because so much of Mr Bowditch was still in there – but I didn't. There was no point, because there was no money for a full-on paintjob anyway, not with the will in probate and no way to convert the gold to cash. I finished my Coke. 'I want to go up there and get my clothes. Can Rades stay here with you?'

'Sure. Guess she'll be staying here from now on, won't she? At least until . . .' He didn't finish, just shrugged.

'Sure,' I said. 'Until.'

10

The first thing I noticed was that the gate was open. I thought I'd shut it, but couldn't remember for sure. I went around the house, started up the back steps, and stopped on the second one. The kitchen door was open and I *knew* I'd closed that one. Closed it and locked it. I went the rest of the way up and saw I'd locked it, all right; splinters were sticking out all around the lockplate, which had been partly torn from the jamb. I didn't consider that whoever had broken in might still be there; for the second time that day I was too stunned to consider very much. The only thing I remember thinking was being glad I'd left Radar at our house. She was too old and fragile for more excitement.

CHAPTER TEN

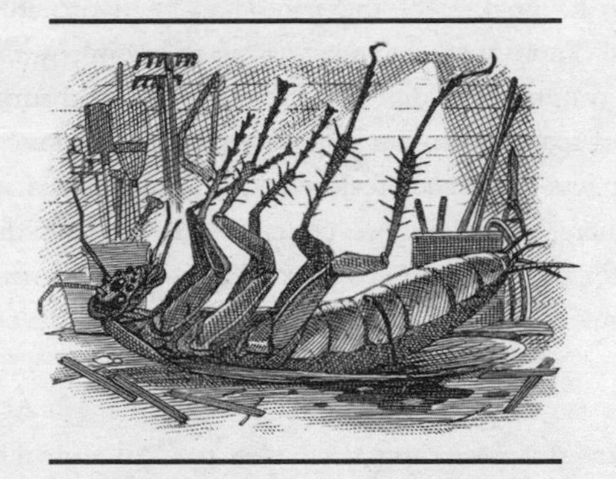

Wreckage. Mrs Richland. Obit Thieves.

The Tale of the Tape. Inside the Shed.

The Tale of the Tape, Continued.

1

All the kitchen cupboards had been opened and the pots and pans had been scattered across the linoleum, hell to breakfast. The Hotpoint had been pulled away from the wall and the oven door was open. The contents of the cannisters – SUGAR, FLOUR, COFFEE, COOKIES – had been spilled across the counter, but the one that had contained money no longer did, and the first coherent thought to cross my mind was *fucker didn't get it*. I'd put the cash (and the little gold pellets) in the safe months ago. In the living room the rollaway bed – now turned into a couch again, with Mr Bowditch no longer needing it – had been overturned and the cushions slashed. Same with Mr Bowditch's easy chair. The stuffing was everywhere.

Upstairs was worse. I wouldn't need to open my dresser to get my clothes, because they were scattered all over the room I'd been using. My pillows had been slashed, ditto mattress. It was the same in the master bedroom, only there the wallpaper had also been slashed and hung in great long strips. The closet door stood open and with the clothes heaped on the floor (the pockets of the pants had been turned out), the safe stood revealed. There were scratches along the seam by the handle, and more on the combination dial, but the safe had stood strong against the thief's attempts to break in. Just to be sure, I ran the combo and opened it. Everything was still there. I closed it, gave the dial a spin, and went downstairs. There, sitting on the couch where Mr Bowditch had slept, I called 911 for the third time that year. Then I called my father.

2

I realized there was one thing I needed to do before Dad came, and certainly before the police arrived. If I intended to lie, that was, and have the lie stand up. I took care of that, then went outside to wait. My father drove up the hill and parked at the curb. He hadn't brought Radar, and I was glad of that; the destruction of the house would have upset her more than she was already by the recent changes in her life.

Dad walked through the downstairs, surveying the destruction. I stayed in the kitchen, picking up the pots and pans and putting them away. When he came back, he helped me move the stove back against the wall. 'Holy crow, Charlie. What do you think?'

I told him I didn't know, but I thought I did. I just didn't know who. 'Will you wait here for the police, Dad? I'm going across the street for a minute. Mrs Richland's back, I saw her car. I want to talk to her.'

'The nosy-parker?'

'That's her.'

'Shouldn't you leave it for the cops?'

'If she's seen anything, I'll tell them to talk to her.'

'Doesn't seem likely, she was at the funeral with us.'

'I still want to talk to her. Maybe she saw something before.'

'Guys casing the joint?'

'Maybe.'

I didn't need to knock on her door; she was at her usual post at the end of the driveway. 'Hello, Charlie. Is everything all right? Your father was certainly in a hurry. And where is the dog?'

'At my house. Mrs Richland, someone broke into Mr Bowditch's while we were at the funeral and kind of trashed the place.'

'Oh my God, really?' She put her hand to her chest.

'Did you see anyone before? Like in the last couple of days? Someone who didn't belong on the street?'

She considered. 'Gee, I don't think so. Just the usual deliverymen – you know, Federal Express, UPS, the man who comes around to do things to the Houtons' lawn . . . *that* must cost a pretty penny . . . the postman in his little truck . . . how bad is the damage? Was anything stolen?'

'I really don't know much yet. The police might want to—'

'Talk to me? Of course! Happy to! But if it happened while we were at the funeral . . .'

'Yeah, I know. Thanks, anyway.' I turned to go.

'There *was* that funny little man selling magazine subscriptions,' she said. 'But that was before Mr Bowditch died.'

I turned back. 'Really?'

'Yes. You would have been in school. He had a satchel like the kind postmen used to carry in the old days. It had a sticker on it that said SUBSCRIPTION SERVICE OF AMERICA, I think that was it, and samples inside – *Time, Newsweek, Vogue*, some others. I told him I didn't want any magazines, that I read everything I want online. It's so much more convenient that way, isn't it? Also more ecological, without all that paper to dispose of in landfills.'

I wasn't interested in the environmental advantages of online reading. 'Did he go to other houses on the street?' Feeling that if anyone could answer that question it would be her.

'Quite a few. I believe he went to Mr Bowditch's house, but the old fellow didn't come to the door. Probably feeling too poorly. Or . . . I don't think he liked visitors much, did he? I'm so glad you made friends with him. So sad he's gone on. When it's animals, people say they've crossed the rainbow bridge. I like that, don't you?'

'Yes, that's pretty nice.' I hated it.

'I suppose his dog will be crossing the rainbow bridge soon, poor thing has gotten so thin and white around the muzzle. Will you keep him?'

'Radar? Sure.' I didn't bother telling her Radar was a female. 'What did the magazine salesman look like?'

'Oh, just a funny little man with a funny way of walking and talking. He walked with a kind of a *skip*, almost like a child, and when I told him I didn't want any magazines, he said *right-o*, like he was from England. But really he sounded as American as you or me. Do you think he was the one who broke in? He certainly didn't look dangerous. Just a funny little man with a funny way of talking. He said ha-ha a lot.'

'Ha-ha?'

'Yes. Not a real laugh, just ha-ha. "Seventy per cent off the newsstand price, ma'am, ha-ha." And he was little for a man. My height. Do you think he was the one?'

'Probably not,' I said.

'He was wearing a White Sox cap, I remember that, and corduroy pants. The cap had a red circle on the front.'

3

I was all for starting a global cleanup, but Dad said we should wait for the police. 'They'll probably want to document the scene.'

They showed up ten minutes or so later, in a squad car and an unmarked sedan. The guy driving the sedan had white hair and was carrying a considerable paunch. He introduced himself as Detective Gleason and the two uniformed cops as Officers Witmark and Cooper. Witmark had a camcorder; Cooper had a little case like a lunchbox, which I presumed contained evidence-collecting shit.

Detective Gleason surveyed the damage with a marked lack of interest, flapping back his checked sportcoat like wings every now and then to hitch up his pants. I guessed he couldn't be more than a year or two from getting a gold watch or a fishing rod at his retirement party. Meanwhile, he was serving out his time.

He directed Witmark to roll video of the living room and sent Cooper upstairs. He asked us a few questions (directing them at Dad, although I was the one who had discovered the break-in) and jotted our answers down in a little notebook. He snapped the notebook closed, stuffed it in the inside pocket of his sportcoat, and hitched up his pants. 'Obit thieves. Seen it a hundred times.'

'What are those?' I asked. Glancing at my dad, I could see he already knew. Maybe had from the moment he stepped in and looked around.

'When was his death notice in the paper?'

'Yesterday,' I said. 'His physical therapist got the form for the newspaper pretty soon after he died and I helped her fill in the blanks.'

Gleason nodded. 'Yup, yup, seen it a hundred times. These ghouls read the paper, find out when the services are going to be and the house'll be empty. They break in, grab anything that looks valuable. You'll want to look around, make a list of what's missing, and bring it to the station.'

'What about fingerprints?' Dad asked.

Gleason shrugged. 'They will have worn gloves. Everybody watches the cop shows these days, especially the perps. Cases like this, we usually don't—'

'Lieutenant!' That was Cooper, from upstairs. 'Got a safe up in the master bedroom.'

'Ah, well, now we're talking,' Gleason said.

We went upstairs with Gleason leading the way. He went slowly, sort of hauling himself along by the bannister, and at the top he was puffing and flushed. He hitched his pants and went into Mr Bowditch's bedroom. There he bent to look at the safe. 'Ah. Someone tried and failed.'

I could have told him that.

Witmark – the department's resident cinematographer, I guess – came in and started rolling video.

'Dust it, Loot?' Cooper asked. He was already opening his little lunchbox.

'We might get lucky here,' the detective (I use the word with hesitation) told us. 'The guy might have taken off his gloves to try the combo when he saw he couldn't force it.'

Cooper dusted black powder over the front of the safe. Some stuck; more drifted to the floor. Another mess for me to clean up. Cooper looked at his handiwork, then stood aside so Gleason could look.

'Wiped clean,' he said, straightening up and giving his pants a particularly violent hitch. Of course it was wiped clean – I had done it myself after calling 911. The robber might have left his fingerprints, but even if he did they still had to go, because mine were there, too.

'Don't suppose you know the combination, by any chance?' This was also directed to my father.

'I haven't even been in this room before today. Ask Charlie. He was the old guy's caretaker.'

Caretaker. The word was accurate enough, but it still struck me funny. I think because it was a word almost always applied to adults.

'No idea,' I said.

'Huh.' Gleason bent to the safe again, but briefly, as if it had ceased to interest him. 'Whoever inherits this pile will have to get a locksmith in here. If that doesn't work, a box-peeler who's good with nitro. I know of a couple in the jug at Stateville.' He laughed. 'Probably nothing much, old papers and maybe some cufflinks. Remember that big kerfuffle over Al Capone's safe? Geraldo Rivera sure got egg on his face with that one. Oh well. Come down to the station and make a full report, Mr Reade.'

Again talking to my dad. Sometimes I totally understood why women get pissed off.

4

I spent the night in our little guestroom on the ground floor. It was my mother's home office and sewing room when she was alive and that was how it stayed during my dad's drinking years, kind of like a museum. When he was sober six months or so, Dad turned it into a bedroom (with my help). Sometimes Lindy stayed over there, and a couple times newly sober guys Dad was working with, because that's what AAs are supposed to do. I used it the night of Mr Bowditch's funeral and the break-in at his house so Radar wouldn't have to try the stairs. I put down a blanket for her and she went to sleep at once, curled up nose to tail. I was awake longer, because the bed in there was too short for a guy six-feet-four, but also because I had a lot to think about.

Before I turned out the light I Googled Subscription Service of America. There was such a company, but it was *Services*, plural. Of course it was only one letter and Mrs Richland might have made a mistake about that, but the one I found was a consolidation outfit, strictly online. No door-to-door salesmen. I considered the idea that the guy was a real obit thief, casing the neighborhood . . . except that didn't work, because he had been carrying his sample bag around the neighborhood before Mr Bowditch died.

I believed the magazine salesman was the man who had killed Mr Heinrich. And by the way, just how had Heinrich been killed? The newspaper article didn't say. Wasn't it possible that the little man who said *right-o* and *ha-ha* had tortured him before killing him? To get the name of the man with the stash of gold goodies?

I turned from my right side to the left. My feet were sticking out and I fluffed the top sheet and the blanket back over them.

Or maybe torture hadn't been necessary. Maybe Mr Right-O just told Heinrich that if he gave up the name, he wouldn't be killed.

I went from my left side back to the right one. Fluffed the blankets again. Radar raised her head, made a whuffling sound, and went back to sleep.

Another question: had Detective Gleason spoken to Mrs Richland? If he had, would he deduce that Mr Bowditch had been targeted *before* he died? Or would he think the little guy was just casing the neighborhood for targets of opportunity? Maybe he'd think the little guy was just your ordinary garden-variety door-to-door salesman. If he even bothered to ask at all, that was.

Jackpot question: if Mr Right-O Ha-Ha was still after the gold, would he be back?

Right to left. Left to right. Fluff the blankets.

At some point I thought the sooner I listened to Mr Bowditch's tape the better, and after that I finally went to sleep. I dreamed that the little man with the skip in his walk was strangling me, and when I woke up the next morning, the sheet and blanket were all the way up around my neck.

5

I went to school on Friday, just so Mrs Silvius wouldn't forget what I looked like, but on Saturday I told my dad I was going up to Number 1 to start cleaning the place up. He offered to help.

'No, that's okay. Stay here with Radar. Kick back, enjoy your day off.'

'Are you sure? There have to be a lot of memories in that place for you.'

'I'm sure.'

'Okay, but call me if it starts to get you down. Or freak you out.'

'I will.'

'Shame he never told you the combination to that safe. We really will have to get somebody to crack it open so we can see what's inside. I'll ask around at work next week. Somebody will have a connection to a box-peeler. One not in prison.'

'Really?'

'Insurance investigators have connections to all sorts of sketchy people, Charlie. Gleason's probably right, nothing but old tax returns – assuming Bowditch ever filled any out, which I doubt – and some cufflinks, but maybe there's stuff in there that can explain just who the hell he was.'

'Well,' I said, thinking of the gun and the tape recorder, 'you hold that thought. And don't give Radar too many treats.'

'Bring her meds.'

'Already did,' I said. 'Kitchen counter.'

'Good on you, kiddo. Call if you need me. I'll come running.'

Good guy, my dad. Especially since he sobered up. Said it before, but it bears repeating.

6

There was yellow POLICE INVESTIGATION tape threaded in and out of the picket fence. The investigation (such as it was) had concluded when Gleason and the two unis left, but until Dad or I got someone to repair the lock on the back door, I thought I'd leave the tape up.

I went around back, but before I went inside the house, I walked down to the shed and stood in front of the door. No sounds came from within – no scratching, no thuds, no weird mewlings. *No, there wouldn't be*, I thought. *He killed whatever was making those noises. Two shots and boom-boom, out go the lights.* I took out his keyring and thought about trying them until one fit the lock, then put the keys back in my pocket. First I'd listen to the tape. And if it turned out to be nothing but Mr Bowditch warbling 'Home on the Range' or 'A Bicycle Built for Two' while high on OxyContin, the joke would be on me. Only I didn't believe that. *Everything else you need is also under the bed*, he'd told me, and the tape recorder had been under the bed.

I opened the safe and took it out – just an old black tape player, not as retro as the TV but far from new; the technology had marched on. I went down to the kitchen, put the recorder on the table, and pushed play. Nothing. Just the hiss of tape passing across the heads. I started to think it was a bust after all – something like that safe of Al Capone's Gleason had mentioned – then realized Mr Bowditch just hadn't rewound it. Very possibly because he'd been recording when the heart attack hit. The idea creeped me out a little. *How that hurts*, he'd said. *Like pig iron in the forge.*

I hit rewind. The tape spun backward for a long time. When it finally clicked to a stop, I pushed play again. There were a few seconds of silence, then a heavy clunk followed by raspy breathing I knew very well. Mr Bowditch began to speak.

I said I was sure I could tell this story, but I was also sure no one would believe it. This is where your disbelief begins.

7

Did your father investigate me, Charlie? I bet he did, I know I would have if I'd been in his shoes. And I bet that given his job, he had the resources to do it. If so, he will have found out that someone named Adrian Bowditch – maybe my father, he would have thought, more likely my grandfather – bought the land this house stands on in 1920. It wasn't either of them. It was me. I was born Adrian Howard Bowditch, in 1894. Which makes me just about a hundred and twenty years old. The house was finished in 1922. Or maybe it was 1923, I can't remember for sure. And the shed, of course, we mustn't forget the shed. That was built even before the house, and by my own hands.

The Howard Bowditch you know is a fellow who likes to keep himself and his dog . . . mustn't forget Radar . . . to himself. But Adrian Bowditch, my supposed father, was quite the rover. 1 Sycamore Street here in Sentry's Rest was his home base, but he was gone as much as he was here. I saw the changes in town every time I came back, like a series of snapshots. I found that fascinating, but also a bit disheartening. It seemed to me so much in America was going in the wrong direction, and still does, but I suppose that's neither here nor there.

I came back for the last time as Adrian Bowditch in 1969. In 1972, at the age of seventy-eight, I hired a caretaker named John McKeen – excellent older fellow, reliable, you'll find him in the town records if you choose to look – and went on my last trip, supposedly to Egypt. But that is not where I went, Charlie. Three years later, in 1975, I came back as my son, Howard Bowditch, age around forty. Howard supposedly lived most of his life up to then abroad with his mother, who was estranged from her husband. I always liked that detail. Estrangement is somehow more real than divorce or death. Also, it's a wonderful word, full of flavor. After Adrian Bowditch supposedly died in Egypt, I took up residence at the family manse and decided to stay. There was no doubt about ownership; I had willed it to myself. Rich, wouldn't you say?

Before I tell you the rest, I want you to stop the tape and go out to the shed. You can open it; you have my keys. At least I hope you do. There's nothing in there that can hurt you, the boards are back in place with the blocks on top of them. Christ, how heavy they were! But take my gun, if you like. And take the flashlight, too, the one in the kitchen cupboard. There are lights in the shed, but you'll still want the flashlight. You'll know why. See what there is to see. The one you first heard will be mostly gone, maybe entirely, but the remains of the one I shot will still be there. Most of it, anyway. When you've had a shufti, as the Brits used to say, come back and listen to the rest. Do it now. Trust me, Charlie. I'm depending on you.

8

I pushed stop and for a moment just sat there. He was crazy, had to be, although he had never *seemed* crazy. He'd been lucid even at the end, when he called me and said he was having a heart attack. There was something in that shed, all right – or had been – that much was undeniable. I'd heard it, Radar had heard it, and Mr Bowditch had gone out there and shot it. But a hundred and twenty years old? Hardly anyone lived that long, maybe one in ten million, and *nobody* came back at forty, impersonating his own son. Stuff like that only happened in stories of make-believe.

'Fairy tales,' I said, and I was so keyed up – so freaked out – that the sound of my own voice made me jump.

Trust me, Charlie. I'm depending on you.

I got up, feeling almost like I was outside myself. I don't know how to describe it any better than that. I went upstairs, opened the safe, and got Mr Bowditch's .45. It was still in the holster, and the holster was still on the concho belt. I strapped it on and knotted the tie-downs above my knee. Doing that made the inside me feel absurd, like a little kid playing cowboy. The outside me was glad to have the weight of it, and knowing it was fully loaded.

The flashlight was a good one, a long-barreled job holding six D-cells. I clicked it on once to make sure it worked, then went out and crossed the back lawn to the shed. *Have to mow this again soon*, I thought. My heart was beating hard and fast. It wasn't a particularly warm day, but I could feel sweat trickling down my cheeks and neck.

I got the keyring out of my pocket and dropped it. I bent down to get it and bumped my head on the shed door. I grabbed the ring and picked through the keys. One of them had a round head with the word *Studebaker* engraved on it in script. The ones that opened the front and back doors of the house I knew. Another was small, maybe for opening a lockbox, maybe even a bank safety deposit box. And there was a Yale key for the big silver Yale padlock on the shed door. I stuck it in the base of the lock, then pounded on the door with my fist.

'Hey!' I shouted . . . but a *low* shout. The last thing I wanted was for Mrs Richland to hear. 'Hey, if you're in there, get back! I'm armed!'

There was nothing, but I still stood there with the flashlight in my hand, paralyzed with fear. Of what? The unknown, which is the scariest thing there is.

Shit or git, Charlie, I imagined Mr Bowditch saying.

I made myself turn the key. The arm of the lock popped up. I took it out, swung the hasp, and hung the lock over it. A breeze ruffled my hair. I opened the door. The hinges squalled. It was black inside. The light of the outside world seemed to enter and just fall dead. On the tape he'd said there were lights, although there was certainly no power line going to the shed. I shone the flashlight on the right side of the door and saw a switch. I flipped it up and two battery-powered lights went on, one mounted high up on each side. Like emergency lights for when the power goes out in a school or movie theater. They made a low humming sound.

The floor was wooden planking. In the far lefthand corner, three boards were placed in a row with cinderblocks holding down the ends. I swung the flash to the right and saw something so horrible and unexpected that for a moment I couldn't comprehend it. I wanted to turn and run, but I couldn't move. Part of me was thinking (so far as *any* part of me could think in those first few seconds) that it was a macabre joke, a horror-movie creature made out of latex and wire. I could see a single coin of light where a bullet had gone through the wall after going through the thing I was looking at.

It was some kind of insect, but almost as big as a full-grown cat. It was dead, with its many legs sticking up. They were bent in the middle, like knees, and sprouted coarse hairs. A black eye peered sightlessly. One of Mr Bowditch's bullets had caught it in the abdomen, and its pale unknowable guts lay around its torn belly like weird pudding. A fine mist was drifting up from those innards, and as another gust of breeze slipped past me (still frozen in the doorway, my hand seemingly welded to the light switch), more mist began to rise from the thing's head and from spaces the armor plating on its back didn't cover. The staring eye fell in, leaving an empty socket that seemed to glare at me. I uttered a little cry, thinking it was coming back to life. But no. It was dead as dead could be. It was decomposing, and the fresh air was speeding the process.

I made myself step inside with the flashlight in my left hand, trained on the carcass of the dead bug. The gun was in my right. I didn't even remember drawing it.

When you've had a shufti, as the Brits used to say.

I guessed that meant when I'd had a look. I didn't like stepping away from the door, but I made myself do it. The outside me did it, because it meant to have a shufti. The inside me was basically gibbering with terror, amazement, and disbelief. I moved toward the boards with the blocks on top of them. On the way my foot struck something and when I shone the light on it, I gave a cry of disgust. It was an insect leg, or what remained of one; I could tell by the hairs on it and the knee-bend. I hadn't struck it hard, and I was wearing sneakers, but it broke in two. I thought it was part of the one I'd heard early on. It had died in here and this was all that was left.

Hey, Charlie, have a leg! I imagined my father saying, handing me a fried chicken drumstick. *It's the best in the land!*

I started to gag and put the heel of my hand over my mouth until the urge to throw up passed. If the dead bug had stunk badly, I'm sure I wouldn't have been able to hold back, but it seemed to have little smell, maybe because the decomp had progressed beyond that point.

The boards and cinderblocks were covering a hole in the floor, about five feet across. I first thought it was a well left over from the days before city water, but when I shone the light down between two of the boards, I saw short stone steps spiraling down the shaft. There were scuttering sounds and a low chittering deep in the dark. Half-glimpsed movement that froze me in place. More bugs . . . and not dead. They were retreating from my light, and suddenly I thought I knew what they were: cockroaches. They were giant economy-sized, but they were doing what cockroaches always did when you shone a light on them: running like hell.

Mr Bowditch had covered the hole, which led down to Christ only knew where (or *what*), but either he'd done a bad job – which wasn't like him – or the bugs had managed to shunt one or more of the boards aside over a long period of time. Like since 1920? My dad would have laughed, but my dad had never seen a dead roach the size of a tomcat.

I took a knee and shone the light between the boards. If there were more big roaches, they were gone. There were just those steps, spiraling down and down. A thought came to me then, at first odd and then not odd at all. I was looking at Mr Bowditch's version of Jack's beanstalk. It went down instead of up, but there was gold at the other end.

I was sure of it.

9

I backed out slowly, turned off the battery-powered lights, and shone my flash one last time on the horrid thing lying against the wall. More steam was rising from it now, and there *was* a smell, like sour peppermint. The fresh air was really doing a number on it.

I closed the door, snapped the lock, and went back to the house. I returned the flashlight to the cupboard and put the gun back in the safe. I looked at the bucket of gold pellets but felt no urge to put my hands in it, not today. What if I reached all the way to the bottom and felt a segment of hairy insect leg?

I got as far as the stairs before my legs gave out, and I had to grab the newel post to keep from taking a nasty tumble. I sat down at the top, shaking all over. After a minute or two I was able to get a grip on myself and go down, holding the bannister in a way that reminded me of Mr Bowditch. I sat down heavily at the kitchen table and looked at the tape player. Part of me wanted to eject the tape, yank it out in long brown ribbons, and dump it in the trash. But I didn't. Couldn't.

Trust me, Charlie. I'm depending on you.

I pushed play, and for a moment it was as if Mr Bowditch was in the room with me, seeing how terrified I was – how astounded – and wanting to soothe me. To bring me back from thinking about how that huge insect's eye had fallen in, leaving the empty socket to glare at me. And it worked, at least a little.

10

They're just cockroaches, and not dangerous. A bright light puts them to flight. Unless you ran screaming at the sight of the one I shot – and that's not like the boy I've come to know – then you looked through the boards and saw the well, and the steps going down. Sometimes a few of the roaches come up, but only when the weather starts to warm. I don't know why, because our air is lethal to them. They begin to decompose even when they're trapped below the boards, but they batter at them anyway. Some kind of instinctive death-wish? Who can say? In the last couple of years I've gotten careless about maintaining the barrier over the well, in the last few years I've gotten careless about a lot of things . . . and so a couple got up. It's been long years since that happened. The one you heard in the spring died on its own, nothing left now but a leg and one of its feelers. The other . . . well, you know. But they're not dangerous. They don't bite.

I call it the well of the worlds, a name I got from an old pulp horror story by a man named Henry Kuttner, and I didn't really find it at all. I fell into it.

I'll tell you as much as I can, Charlie.

As Adrian Bowditch, I was born in Rhode Island, and although I was good at math and loved to read . . . as you know . . . I didn't care for school, or for my stepfather, who beat me when things went wrong in his life. Which they often did, as he was a heavy drinker who couldn't hold a job for more than a few months at a go. I ran away when I was seventeen and went north to Maine. I was a strapping lad and caught on with a logging crew way to hell and gone up in Aroostook County. That would have been 1911, the year Amundsen made it to the South Pole. Do you remember me telling you I was a simple woodcutter? It was the truth.

Six years I did that job. Then, in 1917, there came a soldier to our camp, informing us that able-bodied men had to register for the draft at the Island Falls Post Office. Some of the younger lads piled into a truck, I among them, but I had no intention of feeding myself into the war machine somewhere in France. I reckoned that machine had enough blood to drink without adding mine, so I said so long to the boys as they lined up to register and hopped a freight headed west. I ended up in Janesville, not far from where we are now, and signed on with a cutting crew. When that played out I followed the cutting down to Sentry County, which is now Arcadia County. Our county.

There wasn't much cutting and I thought of moving on, maybe out to Wyoming or Montana. My life would have been very different if I'd done that, Charlie. I would have lived a normal span and we never would have met. But in Buffington – where the Forest Preserve is now – I saw a sign saying LAND SURVEYOR WANTED. And below that, something that looked made for me: MUST BE WISE IN THE WAYS OF MAPS AND THE WOODS.

I went into the county office, and after reading some maps – latitude, longitude, contours and such – I got the job. Son, I felt like the man who fell into a pile of shit and came up with a rose in his teeth. I got to spend every fucking day tramping the woods, blazing trees and making maps and charting old woods roads, of which there were many. Some nights I stayed with a family willing to take me in and some nights I camped under the stars. It was grand. There were times when I didn't see another living soul for days. That's not for everyone, but it was for me.

There came a day in the fall of 1919 when I was on Sycamore Hill, in what was known then as the Sentry Woods. The town of Sentry's Rest was here, but it was really just a village and Sycamore Street ended at the Little Rumple River. The bridge – the first *bridge – wasn't built for another fifteen years at least. The neighborhood you grew up in didn't come into existence until after World War II, when the GIs came home.*

I was walking in the woods where my backyard is now, pushing through the scrub timber and bushes, looking for a dirt road that was supposed to be somewhere up ahead, not thinking of a goddam thing except wondering where in the village a young man might get a drink, and down I went. One moment I was walking in the sunshine and the next I was in the well of the worlds.

If you shone the flashlight between the boards, you know I was lucky not to be killed. There's no handrail, and the steps wind around a nasty drop – just about a hundred and seventy-five feet. The walls are cut stone, did you notice? Very old. God knows how old. Some of the blocks have fallen out and tumbled to the bottom, where there's a pile of them. As I tilted toward the drop I threw my hand out and caught hold of a fissure in one of those empty sockets. Couldn't have been more than three inches wide, but it was enough to get my fingers into. I pulled myself back against the curve of the wall, looking up at daylight and bright blue sky, my heart beating what felt like two hundred licks to the minute, wondering what the hell I'd stumbled into. It surely wasn't any ordinary well, not with stone steps going down and cut stone blocks walling it around.

When I got my breath back . . . there's nothing like almost falling to your death down a black hole to make you lose your breath . . . when I got it back, I pulled my electric torch off my belt and shone it down. I couldn't see a goddam thing, but I heard rustling sounds, so something *was alive down there. I wasn't worried, I also carried a holstered side-piece on my belt in those days, because the woods weren't always safe. It wasn't animals you had to worry about so much . . . although there were bears back then, plenty of them . . . as it was men, especially shiners, but I didn't think there was any moonshine still down in that hole. I didn't know what might be, but I was a curious lad, and I was determined to see.*

I fixed my pack, which had come all crooked when I fell on the steps, and went down. Down and down, around and around. A hundred and seventy-five feet deep is the well of the worlds and a hundred and eighty-five stone steps of varying heights. At the end is a stone-sided tunnel . . . or it might be better to call it a corridor. It's high enough so you could walk it without ducking your head, Charlie, and have most of your height again to spare.

The floor was dirt at the foot of the steps, but after I went on a bit . . . I now know it measures out at a little more than a quarter-mile . . . it goes to stone flooring. That rustling sound kept getting louder and louder. Like paper or leaves blowing in a light breeze. Soon it was overhead. I raised up my torch and saw the ceiling was covered with the biggest damn bats you ever saw. Wingspans like on a turkey buzzard. They rustled more in the light and I lowered it back between my feet double-quick, not wanting to send them flying all around me. The idea of being smothered by their wings gave me what my mother would have called the fantods. Snakes and most insects are okay by me, but I've always had a horror of bats. Everyone has their own phobias, don't they?

I went on and on, a mile at least, and my torch was starting to fail. No Duracells back in those days, boy! Sometimes there was a colony of bats overhead and sometimes there wasn't. I made up my mind to go back before I was left in the dark and just then I thought I saw a spark of daylight up ahead. I snapped off my torch and sure enough, it was daylight.

I went toward it, curious as to where I might come out. My guess was the north bank of the Little Rumple, because it seemed to me I'd been heading south, although I couldn't be sure. I started for it, and just as I was nearing it, something happened to me. I can't describe it very well, but I need to try in case you decide to follow in my footsteps, so to speak. It was like being lightheaded, but it was more than that. I seemed to turn into a ghost, Charlie, like I could look down at my body and see right through it. I was insubstantial, *and I remember thinking that we all are, really, just ghosts on the face of the earth trying to believe we have weight and a place in the world.*

It lasted maybe five seconds. I kept walking even though I didn't really seem to be there. Then the feeling went away and I went to the opening at the end of the tunnel . . . maybe another eighth of a mile . . . and came out not on the bank of the Little Rumple but on the side of a hill. Below me was a field of gorgeous red flowers. Poppies, I think, but with a smell like cinnamon. I thought, 'Someone has rolled out the red carpet for me!' A path led through them to a road where I could see a small house . . . a cottage, really . . . with smoke coming from the chimney. Far away down the road, on the distant horizon, I could see the spires of a great city.

The path was very faint, as if no one had walked it in a very long time. A rabbit hopped across it as I started down, twice the size of an earthly rabbit. It disappeared into the grass and flowers. I—

There was a pause here, but I could hear Mr Bowditch breathing. It sounded raspier than ever. Labored. Then he resumed.

This is a ninety-minute tape, Charlie. I found a whole box of them amidst the rickrack on the third floor, from the days before cassettes became as obsolete as three-cent stamps. I could fill four of them, or five, maybe even the whole box. I have had many adventures in that other world, and would tell them if I had time. I don't believe I do. Since my little bit of target practice in the shed I haven't felt well at all. I'm having pain in the left side of my neck and down my left arm to the elbow. That sometimes fades a bit, but the heaviness in my chest doesn't. I know what such symptoms mean. There's a thunderstorm brewing inside me and I think it will break soon. I have regrets, many of them. Once I told you that a brave man helps but a coward only brings presents. Do you remember that? I brought presents, but only when I knew I wasn't brave enough to help when the terrible change came. I told myself I was too old, so I took gold and fled. Like Jack scurrying down the beanstalk. Only he was just a boy. I should have done better.

If you go to that other world, where two moons rise in the sky at night and there's no constellation the astronomers of earth have ever seen, you need to know certain things, so listen to me closely.

The air of our world is fatal to the creatures of theirs, except I guess for the bats. I once brought back a rabbit as an experiment. It died quickly. But the air of theirs is not fatal to us. It is invigorating, in fact.

The city was once a grand place but now it's perilous, especially at night. If you enter, go only by day and be very quiet once you pass through its gates. It may seem deserted, but it isn't. What rules there is dangerous and terrible, and what lies beneath is more terrible still. I have marked the way to a plaza behind the palace just as I used to mark the trees of the forest, with my original initials: AB. If you follow them . . . and if you are quiet . . . you'll be fine. If you don't, you may be lost in that terrible city until you die. I am speaking as one who knows. Without my blazes, I would be there still, dead or insane. What was once grand and beautiful is now gray and cursed and diseased.

There was another pause. The rasp in his breathing was louder now, and when he resumed, his voice was harsh, hardly like his own at all. I had an idea – almost a certainty – that while he was speaking these words I was in school, either on my way to chem class or already there, determining the boiling point of acetone.

Radar has been there with me, when she was young, hardly more than a puppy. She bounded down the steps of the well with no fear whatsoever. You know she goes to her belly when given the down *command; she also knows to be quiet when given the* hush *or* quiet *command. I gave it to her that day, and we passed beneath the colonies of bats without disturbing them. She went through what I've come to think of as* the border *with no appreciable discomfort. She was delighted with the field of red flowers, bounding through them and rolling in them. And she loved the old woman who lives in the cottage. Most people of our world would turn in disgust from such as she is now, but I believe dogs sense the inner nature and ignore the outer aspect. Is that overly romantic? Perhaps, but it seems that way to—*

Stop. Mustn't ramble. No time.

You may choose to take Radar with you, perhaps after you have a shufti on your own, but perhaps right away. Because time for her is growing short. With the new medicine, she may be able to negotiate those steps again. If she can, I'm sure the air of that place will enliven her. As sure as I can be, at least.

There were once games in the city, and the thousands of people who came to watch congregated in the plaza I spoke of as they waited for entry to the stadium which is part of the palace . . . or an adjunct to it, I suppose you'd say. Near this plaza is a huge sundial that must be a hundred feet in diameter. It turns, like the carousel in the novel. The Bradbury novel. I'm sure he . . . never mind, mind this instead: The sundial is the secret of my longevity, and I paid a price. You must not get on it yourself, but if you were to put Radar on it—

Oh Christ. I think it's happening. My God!

I sat with my hands clenched on the kitchen table, watching the spinning reels. Through the player's window I could see it was approaching the point I'd rewound it from.

Charlie, I hate to think of sending you into the source of so many of our earthly terrors, and I won't order you, but the sundial is there, and the gold is there, too. The blazes will lead you to it. AB, remember that.

I am willing you this house and the land, but it's not a gift. It's a burden. Every year it's worth more and every year the taxes go up. Worse than the taxman, far worse, I live in fear of . . . of that legal horror known as eminent domain, and I . . . you . . . we—

He was panting for breath now, and swallowing again and again, big hard glugs that registered clearly on the tape. I could feel my fingernails cutting into my palms. When he spoke again it was with terrible effort.

Listen, Charlie! Can you imagine what would happen if people found out there is another world within reach? One that can be accessed simply by descending a hundred and eighty-five stone steps and walking a corridor not much more than a mile in length? If the government realized that they had found a new world to exploit now that the resources on this one are nearly exhausted? Would they fear the Flight Killer, or waking the terrible god of that place from its long doze? Could they understand the terrible consequences of . . . but you . . . if you had the means . . . you—

There were rattles and clunks. Gasps for breath. When he spoke again, his voice was still audible but much fainter. He had put down the tape recorder with its little built-in mike.

I'm having a heart attack, Charlie . . . you know . . . I called you . . . there's a lawyer. Leon Braddock, in Elgin. There's a wallet. Under the bed. Everything else you need is also under the b—

There was a final clunk, followed by silence. He'd either turned it off on purpose or struck the little STOP button with a flailing hand. I was glad. I didn't need to listen to him suffer his final agonies.

I closed my eyes and sat there for . . . I don't know how long. Maybe a minute, maybe three. I remember reaching down once in my darkness, thinking I'd touch Radar and find some of the comfort stroking her always brought me. But Radar wasn't here. Radar was down the hill in a sane house where there was a sane backyard with no hole in it, no crazy well of the worlds.

What was I going to do? What in the name of God?

To start with, I took the cassette tape out of the machine and put it in my pocket. It was dangerous, maybe the most dangerous thing on earth . . . but only if people believed it was something other than the ravings of an old man having a heart attack. They wouldn't believe, of course. Unless they . . .

I got up on legs that felt undependable and went to the back door. I looked out at the shed Mr Bowditch – a much younger Mr Bowditch – had built over the well of the worlds. I looked at it for a long time. If someone went in there . . .

Dear God.

I went home.

CHAPTER ELEVEN

That Night. School Daze. Dad Leaves.

The Well of the Worlds. The Other.

The Old Woman. A Nasty Surprise.

1

'Are you all right, Charlie?'

I looked up from my book. I'd been deep into it. I would have said nothing could take my mind off the tape I'd listened to in Mr Bowditch's kitchen, the one that was now hidden on the top shelf of my closet under a stack of old T-shirts, but this one had. This one, which I'd taken from Mr Bowditch's bedroom, had conjured its own world. Radar was sleeping beside me, occasionally giving out with little snores.

'Huh?'

'I asked if you're all right. You hardly touched your dinner, and you've seemed off all evening. Thinking about Mr Bowditch?'

'Well, yeah.' It was the truth, although not exactly the way Dad thought.

'You miss him.'

'I do. A lot.' I reached down and stroked Radar's neck. My dog now. My dog, my responsibility.

'That's okay. The way it should be. Are you going to be okay next week?'

'Sure, why?'

He gave the sort of patient sigh that I think maybe only dads can give. 'The retreat. I told you about it. You had your mind on other things, I guess. I leave Tuesday morning for four wonderful days in the north woods. It's an Overland gig, but Lindy wangled me an invitation to come along. Plenty of seminars on liability, which will be merely okay, and some on vetting fraudulent claims, which is a big deal, especially for a firm just getting on its feet.'

'Like yours.'

'Like mine. Also, bonding exercises.' He rolled his eyes.

'Will there be drinking?'

'There will, a lot, but not by me. Are you going to be okay on your own?'

'Sure.' Assuming I didn't get lost in what Mr Bowditch claimed was a very dangerous city ruled over by a sleeping god.

Assuming I went at all.

'I'll be fine. If anything comes up, I'll call you.'

'You're smiling. Something funny?'

'Just that I'm not ten anymore, Dad.' Actually what made me smile was wondering if there was cell service in the well of the worlds. I was guessing Verizon hadn't opened that territory yet.

'Sure there's nothing I can help you with?'

Tell him, I thought.

'Nope. All good. What's a bonding exercise?'

'I'll show you. Get up.' He got up himself. 'Now stand behind me.'

I put my book on the chair and stood behind him.

'We're supposed to trust the team,' Dad said. 'Not that I actually have one, being a one-man show, but I can be a good sport. We climb trees with a—'

'*Trees?* You climb trees?'

'On many Overland retreats, sometimes not completely sober. With a spotter. We'll all do it, except for Willy Deegan, who has a pace-maker.'

'Jesus, Dad.'

'And we do this.' He fell backward with no warning, his hands loosely clasped at his waist. I wasn't playing sports anymore, but there was nothing wrong with my reflexes. I caught him easily, and looking at him upside-down, I saw his eyes were closed and he was smiling. I loved him for that smile. I gave him a heave and he went back on his feet. Radar was looking at us. She made a *rowf* sound and put her head back down.

'I'll have to trust whoever's behind me – it'll probably be Norm Richards – but I trust you more, Charlie. We're bonded.'

'That's great, Dad, but don't fall out of any trees. Taking care of one guy who took a fall is my limit. Now can I read my book?'

'Go for it.' He picked it up off the chair and looked at the cover. 'One of Mr Bowditch's?'

'Yes.'

'I read it when I was your age, maybe even younger. Crazy carnival comes to a little town right here in Illinois, as I remember.'

'Cooger and Dark's Pandemonium Shadow Show.'

'All I remember is that there was a blind fortune-teller. She was creepy.'

'Yeah, the Dust Witch is mondo-creepy, all right.'

'You read, I'll watch television and rot my brain. Just don't give yourself any nightmares.'

If I sleep at all, I thought.

2

Although Radar could probably make it up the stairs with the new medicine onboard, I went into the little guestroom and she padded after me, already perfectly at home in our place. I undressed to my shorts, propped the extra pillow under my head, and kept reading. On the tape, Mr Bowditch said there was a huge sundial in a plaza behind a palace, and it turned like the carousel in the Bradbury novel, and it was the secret of his longevity. The sundial had allowed him to come back to Sentry's Rest young enough to impersonate his own son. In *Something Wicked*, the carousel could make you older when it went forward, but younger when it was in reverse. And Mr Bowditch had said something else, or started to. *I'm sure he . . . never mind.*

Had he started to say that Ray Bradbury had gotten his idea for the carousel from the sundial in that other world? The idea of gaining or losing years on a merry-go-round was crazy, but the idea that a respected American author had visited that other place was even crazier. Wasn't it? Bradbury *had* spent his early childhood in Waukegan, which was less than seventy miles from Sentry's Rest. A brief visit to Bradbury's Wikipedia entry convinced me that that was just a coincidence, unless he had visited the other world as a little kid. If there was another world. Anyway, by the time he was my age he was living in Los Angeles.

I'm sure he . . . never mind.

I marked my place and put the book on the floor. I was pretty sure Will and Jim would survive their adventures, but I guessed they would never be so innocent again. Kids shouldn't have to face terrible things. I knew that from experience.

I got up and pulled on my pants. 'Come on, Rades. You need to go out and water the grass.'

She came willingly enough, not limping at all. She'd be lame again in the morning, but after a little exercise, her locomotion would smooth out. At least it had so far. That wouldn't last much longer, if the vet's assistant had been right. She'd said she'd be surprised if Radar made it to Halloween, and that was only five weeks away. A little less, actually.

Rades sniffed around on the lawn. I looked up at the stars, picking out Orion's Belt and the Big Dipper, that old standby. According to Mr Bowditch, there were two moons in that other world, and constellations the astronomers of earth had never seen.

Not possible, none of it.

Yet the well was there. And the steps. And that horrible fucking bug. I had seen those things.

Radar lowered her hindquarters in that delicate way of hers, then came to me, looking for a treat. I gave her half a Bonz and led her back inside. I'd read late, and my dad had gone to bed. It was time for me to do the same. Mr Bowditch's dog – my dog – plopped down with a sigh and a fart, no more than a tweet, really. I turned off the light and stared up into the dark.

Tell Dad everything. Take him out to the shed. The bug Mr Bowditch shot will still be there – some of it, anyway – and even if it was gone, the well will be there. This is heavy, so share the load.

Would my father keep the secret? Much as I loved him, I didn't trust that he would. Or could. There are a thousand slogans and mottos in AA, and one of them is *you're only as sick as your secrets*. Might he confide to Lindy? Or a trusted friend at work? His brother, my Uncle Bob?

Then I remembered something from school, way back in sixth or seventh grade. American History, Miss Greenfield. It was a quote from Benjamin Franklin: *Three may keep a secret, if two of them are dead.*

Can you imagine what would happen if people found out there is another world down there?

That had been Mr Bowditch's question, and I thought I knew the answer. It would be taken over. *Co-opted*, my hippy-dippy history teacher would have said. The house at 1 Sycamore Street would become a top-secret government installation. For all I knew the whole neighborhood would be cleared. And yes, then the exploitation would begin, and if Mr Bowditch was right, the consequences could be terrible.

I finally went to sleep, but dreamed I was awake and something was moving under the bed. I knew, in the way of dreams, what it was. A giant roach. One that bit. I awoke in a small hour of the morning, convinced it was true. But Radar would have barked and she was deeply asleep, whuffling her way through some unknowable dream of her own.

3

On Sunday I went up to Mr Bowditch's house to do what I had meant to do the day before: start cleaning the place up. There were some things I couldn't do, of course; the torn cushions and slashed wallpaper would have to wait. There was plenty of other stuff, but I had to take care of it in two separate shifts, because the first time I brought Radar, and that was a mistake.

She went from room to room downstairs, looking for Mr Bowditch. She didn't seem to be upset by the vandalism but barked furiously at the couch, only pausing to look at me every now and then as if to ask if I was stupid. Couldn't I see what was wrong? Her master's bed had disappeared.

I got her to follow me into the kitchen and told her to down, but she wouldn't, only kept looking toward the living room. I offered her a chicken chip, her favorite snack, but she dropped it onto the linoleum. I decided I'd have to take her back home and leave her with Dad, but when she saw the leash she ran (very limberly) through the living room and up the stairs. I found her in Mr Bowditch's bedroom curled up in front of the closet, on a makeshift bed of clothes that had been torn off their hangers. She seemed okay there, so I went back downstairs and made things as much better as I could.

Around eleven o'clock I heard the click of her nails on the stairs. Seeing her hurt my heart. She wasn't limping, but she moved slowly with her head down and her tail drooping. She looked at me with an expression as clear as words: *Where is he?*

'Come on, girl,' I said. 'Let's get you out of here.'

That time she didn't protest the leash.

4

In the afternoon I did what I could with the upstairs. The little man in the White Sox cap and corduroy pants (assuming it was him, which I did) hadn't done any damage on the third floor, at least that I could see. I thought he'd concentrated his attention on the second floor . . . and on the safe, once he found it. He'd have been keeping an eye on the time, too, knowing that funeral services only last so long.

I gathered up my clothes and put them in a little pile at the head of the stairs, meaning to take them home. Then I went to work on Mr Bowditch's bedroom, righting the bed (which had been turned over), re-hanging his clothes (tucking in pockets as I went), and picking up stuffing from the pillows. I was angry at Mr Right-O Ha-Ha for what seemed almost like a desecration of the dead, but I couldn't help thinking of some of the sorry crap I'd pulled with Bertie Bird – dogshit on windshields, firecrackers in mailboxes, full garbage cans overturned, JESUS JERKS OFF spraypainted on the signboard of Grace Methodist Church. We had never been caught, and yet I had. Looking at the mess Mr Ha-Ha had left behind and hating it, I realized I had caught myself. Back then I'd been as bad as the little man with the funny way of walking and talking. Worse, in some ways. The little man at least had a motive; he'd been looking for gold. The Bird Man and I had just been a couple of kids fucking off and fucking up.

Except, of course, the Bird Man and I had never killed anyone. If I was right, Mr Ha-Ha had.

One of the bedroom bookcases had been overturned. I set it upright and started re-shelving the books. At the bottom of the pile was that scholarly-looking tome I'd seen on his nightstand, along with the Bradbury novel I was currently reading. I picked it up and looked at the cover: a funnel filling with stars. *The Origins of Fantasy and Its Place in the World Matrix* – what a mouthful. And *Jungian Perspectives* to boot. I looked in the index to see if there was anything about the story of Jack and the Beanstalk. Turned out there was. I tried to read it, then just scanned it. It was everything I hated about what I thought of as 'hoity-toity' academic writing, full of five-dollar words and tortured syntax. Maybe that's intellectual laziness on my part, but maybe not.

So far as I could make out, the author of that particular chapter was saying there were actually *two* beanstalk stories: the bloodthirsty original and the sanitized version kids got in Mom-approved Little Golden Books and the feature-length cartoon. The bloodthirsty original bifurcated (there's one of your five-dollar words) into two mythic streams, one dark and one light. The dark one had to do with the joys of plunder and murder (as in Jack chopping down the beanstalk and the giant getting smooshed). The light one had to do with what the writer called 'the epistemology of Wittgensteinian Religious Belief,' and if you know what that one means even with its headlights on, you're a better man than I am.

I put the book on the shelf, left the room, then went back again to look at the cover. The inside was full of trudging prose, compound-complex sentences that allowed the eye no rest, but the cover was a little lyric, as perfect in its way as that William Carlos Williams poem about the red wheelbarrow: a funnel filling with stars.

5

On Monday I went to see my old pal Mrs Silvius in the office and asked her if I could take my once-a-semester community service day on Tuesday. She leaned over the desk toward me and spoke in a low, confidential voice. 'Do I smell a boy who wants to play hooky? I only ask because students are asked to give at least one week's notice before they take their in-service day. Not a requirement, Charlie, but a strong suggestion.'

'No, this is the real deal,' I said, making earnest eye contact. It was a useful technique when telling lies that I had learned from Bertie Bird. 'I'm going around to downtown merchants and pitching them on Adopt-A.'

'Adopt-A?' Mrs Silvius looked interested in spite of herself.

'Well, it's usually Adopt-A-Highway, I got into that with Key Club, but I want to go farther. Get store owners interested in Adopt-A-Park – we've actually got six of them, you know – and Adopt-An-Underpass – so many of them are messes, it's really a shame – maybe even Adopt-A-Vacant-Lot, if I can convince—'

'I get the drift.' She grabbed a form and scribbled on it. 'Take this around to your teachers, get a sign-off from all of them, bring it back to me.' And as I left: 'Charlie? I still smell hooky. I smell it all over you.'

I wasn't exactly lying about my community service project, but I was shading the truth about needing a day off from school to do it. During period five I went to the library, got a Jaycees booklet listing all the downtown merchants, and sent out an e-blast, just changing the salutations and the names of the various Adopt-A projects I'd thought up. It took half an hour, which left me with twenty minutes before the chime announcing the change of classes. I went back to the desk and asked Ms Norman if she had *Grimm's Fairy Tales*. The actual book wasn't in the library, so she handed me a Kindle with PROPERTY OF HILLVIEW HIGH Dymo-taped to the back and gave me the one-use-only code to download the book.

I didn't read any of the fairy tales, only ran down the contents and skimmed the introduction. I was interested (but not entirely surprised) to find that most of the ones I knew from childhood had darker versions. The original of 'Goldilocks and the Three Bears' was an oral tale that had been around since the 1500s, and there was no little girl named Goldilocks in it. The main character was a vile old woman who invaded the bears' home, basically broke all their shit, then jumped out a window and ran away into the woods, cackling. 'Rumpelstiltskin' was even worse. In the version I vaguely remembered, old Rumpel flew away in a huff when the girl tasked with spinning straw into gold guessed his name. In the 1857 version of *Grimm's*, he drove one foot into the ground, grasped the other, and tore himself apart. I thought that was a horror story worthy of the *Saw* franchise.

Period six was a single-semester course called America Today. I had no idea what Mr Masensik was saying; I was thinking about make-believe. How the carousel in *Something Wicked* was like the sundial in that land of Other, for instance. *The secret of my longevity*, Mr Bowditch had said. Jack had stolen gold from the giant; Mr Bowditch had also stolen gold from . . . who? Or what? A giant? Some pulp-fiction demon named Gogmagog?

Once my mind started down this path, I saw similarities everywhere. My mother had died on a bridge spanning the Little Rumple River. And what about the little man with the funny voice? Wasn't that how the story described Rumpelstiltskin? And then there was me. How many stories of make-believe featured a young hero (like Jack) on a quest in a fantastic land? Or take *The Wizard of Oz*, where a tornado lifted a little girl out of Kansas and into a world of witches and munchkins. I wasn't Dorothy and Radar wasn't Toto, but—

'Charles, have you fallen asleep back there? Or perhaps my mellifluous voice has hypnotized you? Entranced you?'

Laughter from the class, most of whom wouldn't have known *mellifluous* from a pisshole in the snow.

'No, I'm right here.'

'Then perhaps you'd give us your considered opinion concerning the blue-on-black shootings of Philando Castile and Alton Sterling.'

'Bad shit,' I said. I was still mostly in my own head and it just popped out of my mouth.

Mr Masensik favored me with his trademark thin smile, then said, 'Bad shit indeed. Please feel free to reenter your trance state, Mr Reade.'

He continued his lecture. I tried to pay attention, but then I thought of something Mrs Silvius had said, not *fee-fie-fo-fum, I smell the blood of an Englishman* but *I still smell hooky. I smell it all over you.*

Surely a coincidence – my father said if you bought a blue car, you saw blue cars everywhere – but after what I'd seen in the shed, I couldn't help wondering. And something else. In a fantasy story, the author would invent some way that the young hero or heroine could explore that world I was starting to think of as the Other. The author might, for instance, invent a retreat his parent or parents had to attend for several days, thus clearing the way for the young hero to visit the other world without provoking a bunch of questions he couldn't answer.

Coincidence, I thought as the class-ending chime went and kids bolted for the door. *Blue Car Syndrome.*

Except the giant roach was no blue car, and neither were those stone steps winding down into the dark.

I got Mr Masensik to sign my community service slip, and he gave me his thin smile. 'Bad shit, eh?'

'Sorry, sorry.'

'Actually you weren't wrong.'

I made my escape and headed for my locker.

'Charlie?'

It was Arnetta Freeman, looking relatively gorgeous in her skinny jeans and shell top. With blue eyes and blond hair down to her shoulders, Arnetta proved that white America ain't all bad. The year before – when I'd been more sporty and at least a little bit famous for my Turkey Bowl heroics – Arnetta and I had spent several study sessions in her basement family room. Some studying had been done, but a lot more making out.

'Hey, Arnie, what's up?'

'Do you want to come over tonight? We could study for the *Hamlet* test.' Those blue eyes looking deep into my brown ones.

'I'd love to, but my dad's leaving for most of the rest of the week tomorrow, some kind of business thing. I better stick around.'

'Oh. Poo. That's a shame.' She hugged two books tenderly to her breasts.

'I could Wednesday night. If you're not busy, that is.'

She brightened. 'That would be fantastic.' She took my hand and placed it on her waist. 'I'll quiz you on Polonius and maybe you can check out my Fortinbras.'

She gave me a peck on the cheek, then walked away, backside switching in a way that was, well, bewitching. For the first time since the library I wasn't thinking about real-world parallels to make-believe ones. My mind was on nothing but Arnetta Freeman.

6

My dad left bright and early on Tuesday morning, carrying his traveling bag and wearing his I'm-going-to-the-woods clothes: corduroy pants, flannel shirt, Bears hat. He carried a poncho slung over one shoulder. 'Rain in the forecast,' he said. 'That'll put the kibosh on any tree-climbing, for which I'm not sorry.'

'Club soda at cocktail hour, right?'

He grinned. 'Maybe with a slice of lime. Not to worry, kiddo. Lindy will be there and I'll stick with him. Take care of your dog. She's limping again.'

'I know.'

He gave me a quick one-armed squeeze and a kiss on the jaw. As he backed down the driveway, I held up my hand in a stop gesture and ran to the driver's side window. He lowered it. 'Did I forget something?'

'No, I did.' I leaned in, hugged him around the neck, and kissed his cheek.

He gave me a puzzled smile. 'What was that for?'

'I just love you. That's all.'

'Same here, Charlie.' He patted my cheek, backed into the street, and took off toward the goddam bridge. I watched him go until he was out of sight.

I guess that, down deep, I knew something.

7

I took Radar out back. Our yard wasn't much compared to Mr Bowditch's acre-plus, but it was big enough to give Rades some room to limber up. Which she eventually did, but I knew her time was getting short. If there was something I could do for her, it would have to be soon. We went back in and I gave her a few spoonfuls of the leftover meatloaf from last night, hiding an extra pill in it. She wolfed it down, then curled up on the living room rug, a place that she'd already staked out as her own. I rubbed her behind her ears, which always made her close her eyes and grin.

'I have to check something out,' I said. 'Be a good girl. I'll be back as soon as I can, okay? Try not to shit in the house, but if you have to, do it someplace where it'll be easy to clean up.'

She flapped her tail on the rug a couple of times. That was good enough for me. I rode my bike up to Number 1, keeping my eye out for a funny little man with a funny way of walking and talking. I saw no one, not even Mrs Richland.

I let myself in, went upstairs, opened the safe, and buckled the gunbelt around my waist. I didn't feel like a gunslinger in spite of the fancy conchos and the tie-downs; I felt like a scared kid. If I slipped on those spiral stairs and fell, how long would it be before someone found me? Maybe never. And if they did, what else would they find? On the tape, Mr Bowditch had said what he was leaving me wasn't a gift but a burden. I didn't fully understand that then, but as I took the flashlight from the kitchen cupboard and shoved the long barrel into the back pocket of my jeans, I sure did. I went out to the shed hoping that I'd get to the bottom of those steps and find not a corridor leading to some other world but only a pile of blocks and a scummy pool of groundwater.

And no big cockroaches. I don't care if they're harmless or not, no roaches.

I went into the shed, shone the light around, and saw that the roach Mr Bowditch had shot was subsiding into a dark gray puddle of goo. As I put the flashlight beam on it, one of the plates on what remained of its back slid off, making me jump.

I turned on the battery lights, went to the boards and blocks covering the well, and shone my light through one of the six-inch cracks. I saw nothing but the steps, winding down into darkness. Nothing moved. There were no scuttering sounds. This did not soothe me; I thought of a line from a dozen cheap horror movies, maybe a hundred: *I don't like it. It's too quiet.*

Be sensible, quiet is good, I told myself, but looking into that stone pit, the idea didn't have much force.

I understood that if I hesitated for long I'd back out, making it twice as hard to get even this far again. So I stuck the flashlight in my back pocket once more and lifted away the cement blocks. I slid the boards aside. Then I sat down on the lip of the well, my feet on the third step. I waited for my heart to slow down (a little), then stood on that step, telling myself there was plenty of room for my feet. This wasn't precisely true. I armed sweat from my forehead and told myself everything was going to be all right. This I didn't precisely believe.

But I started down.

8

A hundred and eighty-five stone steps of varying heights, Mr Bowditch said, and I counted them as I went down. I moved very slowly, with my back planted against the curving stone wall, facing the drop. The stones were rough and damp. I kept the flashlight trained on my feet. *Varying heights*. I didn't want to stumble. A stumble might be the end of me.

On number ninety, not quite halfway, I heard rustling beneath me. I debated shining my light toward the sound and almost decided not to. If I startled a colony of giant bats and they flew up all around me, I probably *would* fall.

That was good logic, but fear was stronger. I leaned out a bit from the wall, shone my light along the descending curve of the steps, and saw something black crouching two dozen steps below. When my light hit it, I had just enough time to see it was one of the jumbo roaches before it fled, scuttering into the black.

I took a few deep breaths, told myself I was all right, didn't believe it, and went on. It took nine or ten minutes to reach the bottom, because I was moving very slowly. It seemed even longer. Every now and then I looked up, and it wasn't particularly comforting to see the circle illuminated by the battery lights growing smaller and smaller. I was deep in the earth and going deeper.

I reached the bottom at the hundred and eighty-fifth step. The floor was packed earth, just as Mr Bowditch had said, and there were a few blocks that had fallen from the wall, probably from the very top, where frost and thaw would have first loosened them and then squeezed them out. Mr Bowditch had grabbed a crack in one of the spaces from which a block had fallen, and it had saved his life. The pile of fallen blocks was streaked with black stuff that I guessed was roach-shit.

The corridor was there. I stepped over the blocks and into it. Mr Bowditch had been right, it was so tall I didn't even think about ducking my head. Now I could hear more rustling up ahead and guessed they were the roosting bats Mr Bowditch had warned me about. I don't like the idea of bats – they carry germs, sometimes rabies – but they don't give me the horrors as they did Mr Bowditch. Going toward the sound of them, I was more curious than anything. Those short curving steps (*of varying heights*) ringing the drop had given me the fantods, but now I was on solid ground and that was a big improvement. Of course there were thousands of tons of rock and soil above me, but this corridor had been down here for a long time, and I didn't think it would pick this moment to collapse and bury me. Nor did I have to fear being buried alive; if the roof fell in, so to speak, I would be killed instantly.

Cheerful, I thought.

Cheerful I was not, but my fear was being replaced – overshadowed, at least – by excitement. If Mr Bowditch had been telling the truth, another world was waiting not far up ahead. Having come this far, I wanted to see it. Gold was the very least of it.

The dirt floor changed to stone. To cobblestones, in fact, like in old movies on TCM about London in the nineteenth century. Now the rustling was right over my head and I snapped off the light. Pitch darkness made me fearful all over again, but I did not want to find myself in a cloud of bats. For all I knew, they might be vampire bats. Unlikely in Illinois . . . except I wasn't really in Illinois anymore, was I?

I went on a mile at least, Mr Bowditch had said, so I counted steps until I lost count. At least there was no fear of my flashlight failing if I needed it again; the batteries in the long-barrel were fresh. I kept waiting to see daylight, always listening to the soft fluttering overhead. Were the bats really as big as turkey buzzards? I didn't want to know.

At last I saw light – a bright spark, just as Mr Bowditch had said.

I walked on and the spark turned into a circlet, bright enough to leave an afterimage on my eyes every time I blinked them shut. I had forgotten all about the lightheadedness Mr Bowditch had spoken of, but when it hit me, I knew exactly what he'd been talking about.

Once, when I was ten or so, Bertie Bird and I had hyperventilated our stupid selves and then hugged each other, good and tight, to see if we would pass out, as some friend of Bertie's had claimed. Neither of us did, but I went all swimmy and fell on my ass in what felt like slow motion. This was like that. I kept walking, but I felt like a helium balloon bobbing along above my own body, and if the string snapped I would just float away.

Then it passed, as Mr Bowditch had said it did for him. He said there was a border, and that had been it. I had left Sentry's Rest behind. And Illinois. And America. I was in the Other.

I reached the opening and saw the ceiling overhead was now earth, with fine tendrils of root dangling down. I ducked under some overhanging vines and stepped out onto a sloping hillside. The sky was gray but the field was bright red. Poppies spread in a gorgeous blanket stretching left and right as far as I could see. A path led through the flowers toward a road. On the far side of the road more poppies ran maybe a mile to thick woods, making me think of the forests that had once grown in my suburban town. The path was faint but the road wasn't. It was dirt but wide, not a track but a thoroughfare. Where the path joined the road there was a tidy little cottage with smoke rising from the stone chimney. There were clotheslines with things strung on them that weren't clothes. I couldn't make out what they were.

I looked to the far horizon and saw the skyline of a great city. Daylight reflected hazily from its highest towers, as if they were made of glass. *Green* glass. I had read *The Wizard of Oz* and seen the movie, and I knew an Emerald City when I saw one.

9

The path to the road and the cottage was about half a mile long. I stopped twice, once to look back at the hole in the hillside – it looked like the mouth of a small cave, with those vines dangling over the entrance – and once to look at my cell phone. I was expecting a NO SERVICE message, but I didn't even get that. My iPhone wouldn't come on at all. It was just a rectangle of black glass that over here would be useful as a paperweight but not for anything else.

I don't remember feeling dazed or amazed, not even by the sight of those glassy spires. I didn't doubt the evidence of my senses. I could see the gray sky above, a low ceiling that suggested rain not far off. I could hear the whicker of growing things against my pants as I walked the narrow path. As I descended the hill, most of the buildings of the city sank from sight; I could only see the highest three spires. I tried to guess how far away it was and couldn't. Thirty miles? Forty?

Best of all was the smell of the poppies, like cocoa and vanilla and cherries. Except for putting my face into my mom's hair to inhale her scent when I was small, it was the most delicious aroma that had ever graced my olfactories. Hands down. I hoped the rain would hold off, but not because I didn't want to get wet. I knew rain would increase that smell, and the beauty of it might kill me. (I'm exaggerating, but not as much as you might think.) I saw no rabbits, great or small, but I could hear them hopping around in the grass and flowers and once, for a few seconds, I saw tall ears. There was also the chirring sound of crickets, and I wondered if they were big, like the roaches and bats.

As I neared the back of the cottage – wooden sides, thatched roof – I stopped, bemused by what I could now make out. Hanging from the crisscrossing lines behind the cottage and on either side of it were shoes. Wooden ones, canvas ones, sandals, slippers. One line bowed under the weight of a suede boot with silver buckles. Was it a seven-league boot, like in the old fairy tales? It certainly looked like one to me. I came closer and reached out to touch it. It was as soft as butter and as smooth as satin. *Built for the road*, I thought. *Built for Puss in Boots. Where is the other?*

As if summoned by the thought, the cottage's back door opened and a woman came out with the other boot in her hand, the buckles gleaming in the mellow light of that white-sky day. I knew she was a woman because she was wearing a pink dress and red shoes, also because generous breasts plumped out the bodice of the dress, but her skin was slate gray and her face was cruelly deformed. It was as if her features had been drawn in charcoal and some bad-tempered deity had rubbed its hand across them, smearing and blurring them almost out of existence. Her eyes were slits, as were her nostrils. Her mouth was a lipless crescent. She spoke to me, but I couldn't tell what she was saying. I think her vocal cords were as blurred-out as her face. But the lipless crescent was unmistakably a smile, and there was a feeling – a *vibe*, if you like – that said I had absolutely nothing to fear from her.

'*Hizz, huzz! Azzie? Ern*?' She touched the boot hanging on the line.

'Yes, very nice,' I said. 'Do you understand me?'

She nodded and then made a gesture I knew well: a thumb-and-forefinger circle which means *okey-dokey* pretty much the world over. (Except, I guess, in certain rare cases where imbeciles flash it to mean *whites rule*.) She did some more *hizz* and *huzz*, then pointed at my tennis shoes.

'What?'

She snatched the boot from the line, where it had been held by two wooden clothespins, the old-fashioned kind that don't have springs. Holding the boots in one hand, she pointed at my tennies with the other. Then back to the boots.

Asking if I wanted to trade, maybe.

'I'm tempted, but they don't look my size.'

She shrugged and hung both boots up. Other shoes – and a single green satin slipper with a curled toe, like a caliph would wear – bobbed and turned in a hesitant breeze. Looking at that mostly erased face made me feel a little woozy. I kept trying to see her features as they had been. I almost could.

She walked closer to me and sniffed at my shirt with her slit of a nose. Then she raised her hands to her shoulders and pawed at the air.

'I don't get it.'

She bounced on her feet and made a sound that, when added to the way she had sniffed me, clarified things.

'Do you mean Radar?'

She nodded vigorously enough to make her thinning brown hair fly. She made a *wuzz-wuzz-wuzz* sound, which I guess was the closest she could come to *woof-woof-woof*.

'She's at my house.'

She nodded and put one hand on her chest above her heart.

'If you mean you love her, I do, too,' I said. 'When was the last time you saw her?'

The shoe-woman looked at the sky, seemed to calculate, then shrugged. 'Lon.'

'If you mean long, it must have been, because she's old now. Doesn't bounce too much these days. But Mr Bowditch . . . did you know him? If you know Rades, you must have known Mr Bowditch.'

She nodded with the same vigor and the remains of her mouth turned up in another smile. She only had a few teeth, but the ones I could see were a startling white against her gray skin. '*A'riyan*.'

'Adrian? Adrian Bowditch?'

She nodded hard enough to sprain her neck.

'But you don't know how long ago he was here?'

She looked at the sky, then shook her head.

'Was Radar young then?'

'*Hu-hee.*'

'Puppy?'

More nodding.

She took my arm and pulled me around the corner. (I had to duck under another line of dangling shoes to keep from being garroted.) Over here was a patch of earth that had been turned and raked, as if she was getting ready to plant something. There was also a ramshackle little cart leaning on a couple of long wooden handles. There were two burlap sacks inside with green things sticking out of the tops. She knelt down and motioned for me to do the same.

We faced each other that way. Her finger moved very slowly and hesitantly as she wrote in the dirt. She paused once or twice, remembering what came next, I think, then went on.

sh gud lif

And then, after a longer pause:

?

I puzzled over it and shook my head. The woman got on all fours and made her version of barking again. Then I got it.

'Yes,' I said. 'She's had a very good life. But now she's old, like I said. And she's not . . . not doing so well.'

It caught up with me, then. Not just Radar and not just Mr Bowditch, but everything. The gift that was a burden I was supposed to carry. The decomposing cockroaches and finding the house at Number 1 Sycamore torn apart, probably by the man who had murdered Mr Heinrich. By the pure craziness of being here, kneeling in the dirt with a mostly unfaced woman who collected shoes and hung them on crisscrossing clotheslines. But above all it was Rades. Thinking of how she sometimes struggled to get up in the morning or after a nap. Of how she sometimes didn't eat all her food and then gave me a look that said *I know I should want it but I don't*. I began to cry.

The shoe-woman put her arm around my shoulders and hugged me to her. '*O'ay*,' she said. Then, with an effort, she got it completely in the clear. 'Okay.'

I hugged her back. She had a smell, faint but nice. It was, I realized, the smell of the poppies. I cried it out in big wet sobs and she held me, patting my back. When I pulled away, she wasn't crying – maybe she couldn't – but the crescent of her mouth was turned down instead of up. I wiped my face with my sleeve and asked if Mr Bowditch had taught her to write, or if she already knew how.

She put her gray thumb near her first two fingers, which were kind of stuck together.

'He taught you a little?'

She nodded, then wrote in the dirt again.

frens

'He was my friend, too. He passed away.'

She cocked her head to one side, stringy clumps of hair falling to the shoulder of her dress.

'Died.'

She covered her slit eyes, as pure an expression of grief as I've ever seen. Then she gave me another hug. She let go, pointed to the shoes on the nearest line, and shook her head.

'No,' I agreed. 'He won't need shoes. Not anymore.'

She made a gesture toward her mouth and chewed, which was sort of awful. Then she pointed at the cottage.

'If you're asking if I want to eat, thanks, but I can't. I need to get back. Maybe another time. Soon. I'll bring Radar if I can. Before he died, Mr Bowditch said there was a way to make her young again. I know that sounds nuts, but he said it worked for him. It's a big sundial. There.' I pointed in the direction of the city.

Her slit eyes actually widened a little, and her mouth opened in what was almost an O. She put her hands to her gray cheeks, looking like that famous picture of the woman screaming. She bent to the dirt again and swept away what she had written. This time she wrote faster, and it might have been a word she'd used often, because the spelling was right.

danger

'I know. I'll be careful.'

She put her melted fingers to her half-erased mouth in a *shhh* gesture.

'Yes. Have to be quiet there. He told me that, too. Ma'am, what is your name? Can you tell me your name?'

She shook her head impatiently and pointed to her mouth.

'Hard for you to speak clearly.'

She nodded and wrote in the dirt.

Deerie. She looked at it, shook her head, brushed it away, tried again. *DORA*.

I asked if Deerie was a nickname. At least I tried, but *nickname* wouldn't come out of my mouth. It wasn't as if I'd forgotten it; I just couldn't seem to say it. I gave up and asked, 'Was Deerie Mr Bowditch's friendly name for you, Dora?'

She nodded and stood up, dusting her hands. I got up, too.

'It was very nice to meet you, Dora.' I didn't know her well enough to call her Deerie, but I understood why Mr Bowditch had. Her heart was kind.

She nodded, patted my chest, then patted her own. I think to show that we were simpatico. Frens. The crescent of her mouth once more turned up and she bounced on her red shoes, as I suppose Radar might have bounced before her joints got so painful.

'Yes, I'll bring her if I can. If she's able. And I'll take her to the sundial if I can.' Although I had no idea how.

She pointed at me, then gently patted her hands on the air, palms down. I'm not sure, but I think it meant *be careful*.

'I will. Thank you for your kindness, Dora.'

I turned toward the path, but she caught my shirt and tugged me toward the back door of her little domicile.

'I really can't—'

She nodded to say she understood I couldn't stay for a meal but kept tugging. At the back door, she pointed up. Something had been carved into the lintel, higher than Dora could reach. It was his initials: **AB**. His *original* initials.

I had an idea then, one that sprang from my inability to say the word *nickname*. I pointed to the initials and said, 'That's . . .' *Awesome sauce* was in my mind, the stupidest slang term I could think of, but a good test case.

I couldn't get it out of my mouth. It just wouldn't come.

Dora was looking at me.

'Amazing,' I said. 'That's amazing.'

10

I climbed the hill, ducked through the dangling vines, and started back along the passageway. The sense of faintness, *otherworldliness*, came and went. The bats were rustling overhead, but I was too preoccupied with what had just happened to pay the sound much mind, and I stupidly turned on the flashlight to see how much farther I had to go. They didn't all fly, but a couple did, and I saw them in the beam of the light. They were big, all right. *Huge*. I walked on in darkness, one hand outstretched to fend them off if they flapped my way, but they didn't. If there were big roaches, I didn't hear them.

I hadn't been able to say *nickname*. I hadn't been able to say *awesome sauce*. Would I be able to say *wisenheimer* or *knuckle sandwich* or *yo, you trippin', brah?* I didn't think so. I wasn't positive I knew what that inability meant, but I was pretty sure. I'd thought Dora understood me because she understood English . . . but what if she had understood me because I had been speaking *her* language? One where words like *nickname* and *awesome sauce* didn't exist?

When the cobblestones stopped and the dirt began, I felt it was safe to turn the light back on, although I kept it trained at the floor. It was a quarter of a mile between where the cobbles ended and the steps began, Mr Bowditch had said; even claimed to have measured it out. This time I didn't lose count of my paces, and I had just reached five hundred and fifty when I saw the steps. Far above, at the top of the well, I could see light from the battery-powered units he'd installed.

I climbed with more confidence than I'd felt when going down, but I still kept my right shoulder firmly planted against the wall. I emerged with no incident and was bending to slide the second board in place over the top of the well when something circular and very hard pressed into the back of my head. I froze.

'That's right, stay nice and still and we'll have no problem. I'll tell you when to move.' It was very easy to imagine that light sing-songy voice saying *What will you give me if I spin your straw into gold?*

'I don't want to shoot you, kiddo. And I won't, if I get what I came for.' And then he added, not as a laugh but like words in a book: 'Ha-ha.'

CHAPTER TWELVE

Christopher Polley. Spilled Gold. Not So Nice. Preparations.

1

I can't remember how I felt at that moment. I can remember what I thought, though: *Rumpelstiltskin is pointing a gun at the back of my head.*

'What's down there?'

'What?'

'You heard me. You were in that hole a long time, I was starting to think you *died*, so what's *down* there?'

Now another thought came: *He can't know. No one can.*

'Pumping machinery.' It was the first thing that came into my head.

'Pumping machinery? *Pumping* machinery? That's what it is, ha-ha?'

'Yes. Otherwise everything floods in the backyard when it rains. And it runs down the street.' Brains kicking into gear. 'It's old. I was checking to see if I've got to get someone from the city down here to look at it. You know, the Water Depar—'

'Bullshit. Ha-ha. What's *really* down there? Is there gold down there?'

'No. Just machinery.'

'Don't turn around, kiddo, wouldn't be smart. Not at all. You went down there with a great big gun, ha-ha, to check on a water pump?'

'Rats,' I said. My mouth was very dry. 'I thought there might be rats.'

'Bullshit story, total bullshit. What's that over there? More *pumping machinery*? Don't move, just look to your right.'

I looked and saw the moldering corpse of the big cockroach Mr Bowditch had shot. There wasn't much left.

Even such feeble invention as I'd managed so far failed me, so I said I didn't know, and the man I was thinking of as Rumpelstiltskin didn't really care. He had his eyes on the prize.

'Never mind. Right now let's check out the old guy's safe. Maybe we'll check out the *pumping machinery* later. In the house, kiddo. And if you make any noise on the way, I'm going to blow your head off. But first I want you to unbuckle the shootin' iron, partner, ha-ha, and drop it.'

I started to bend over, meaning to undo the knots holding the tie-downs. The gun went back against my head, and hard.

'Did I tell you to bend over? I didn't. Just unbuckle the belt.'

I unbuckled it. The holster hit my knee and turned over. The gun fell out on the shed floor.

'Now you can buckle up again. Nice belt, ha-ha.'

(At this point I'm going to stop most of the *ha-ha* shit, because he said it all the time, as a kind of verbal punctuation. Just let me add that it was *extremely* Rumpelstiltskin-ish. Which is to say, creepy.)

'Now turn around.'

I turned and he turned with me. We were like figures in a music box.

'Slow, chappie. Slow.'

I walked out of the shed. He walked with me. It had been overcast in the other world, but it was sunny here. I could see our shadows, his with one arm outstretched and a shadow gun in his shadow hand. My brains had managed to get from low gear into second, but I was a long way from third. I had been sandbagged, good and proper.

We climbed the back porch steps. I unlocked the door and we went into the kitchen. I remember thinking of all the times I'd been in here, never suspecting how soon I'd be entering for the last time. Because he was going to kill me.

Except he couldn't. I couldn't let him. I thought of people finding out about the well of the worlds and knew I couldn't let him. I thought about city cops or a State Police SWAT team or Army guys overrunning the shoe-woman's little yard, tearing down her crisscrossing lines and leaving her shoes in the dirt, scaring her, and knew I couldn't let him. I thought of those guys tromping into the abandoned city and awakening whatever slept there and knew I couldn't let him. Only I couldn't stop him. The joke was on me.

Ha-ha.

2

Up the stairs to the second floor we went, me in the lead and Rumpel-fucking-stiltskin behind me. I thought of suddenly lunging backward halfway up and knocking him the rest of the way down, but didn't try. It might work, but there was a good chance I'd be dead if it didn't. If Radar had been here, she'd have had a go at Rumpel, old or not, and would likely be dead already.

'Bedroom, chappie. The one with the safe.'

I went into Mr Bowditch's bedroom. 'You killed Mr Heinrich, didn't you?'

'*What?* That's the stupidest thing I ever heard. They caught the bloke who did that.'

I didn't pursue the subject. I knew, he knew, and he knew I knew. I knew other things, as well. Number one was that if I claimed I didn't know the combination to the safe and persisted in that lie, he would kill me. Number two was a variation of number one.

'Open the closet, kiddo.'

I opened the closet. The empty holster flapped against my thigh. Some gunslinger I turned out to be.

'Now open the safe.'

'If I do that, you'll kill me.'

There was a moment of silence as he digested this self-evident truth. Then he said, 'No I won't. I'll just tie you up, ha-ha.'

Ha-ha was exactly right, because how was he going to accomplish that? Mrs Richland had said he was a little man, her height, which meant about five-four. I was a foot taller, and had an athlete's build these days thanks to chores and bike riding. Tying me up without an accomplice to keep me covered would be impossible.

'You will? Really?' I made my voice tremble, which was, believe me, not a problem.

'Yes! Now open the safe!'

'You promise?'

'Right-o, old bean-o. Now open it, or I'll put a bullet in the back of your knee and you'll never dance the tango again, ha-ha.'

'Okay. Just as long as you really totally promise not to kill me.'

'Already asked and answered, as they say in court. Open the safe!'

Along with everything else I had to live for, I couldn't let that lilting voice be the last thing I heard. I just couldn't. 'Okay.'

I knelt in front of the safe. I thought *he's going to kill me* and *I can't let him kill me* and *I won't let him kill me.*

Because of Radar.

Because of the shoe-woman.

And because of Mr Bowditch, who had given me a burden to carry because there was simply no one else.

I grew calm.

'There's quite a bit of gold,' I said. 'I don't know where he got it, but it's awesome sauce. He paid his bills with it for years.'

'Stop talking and open the safe!' Then, as if he couldn't help himself: 'How much?'

'Man, I don't know. Maybe a million dollars' worth. It's in a bucket that's so heavy I can't even lift it.'

I had no clue how to turn the tables on the little fucker. If we had been face to face, maybe. Not with the muzzle of a gun less than an inch from the back of my head. But once I got to the varsity level in the sports I played, I'd learned to shut off my brains at game time and let my body take over. I had to do that now. There was no other option. Sometimes in football games when we were behind, especially at away games where hundreds of people were jeering at us, I'd focus on the opposing quarterback and tell myself he was a nasty son of a bitch and I was going to not just sack him but fucking *flatten* him. It didn't work very well unless the guy was a showboat who showed you his gloat-face after a big play, but it worked on this guy. He had a gloat-*voice*, and I had no problem hating him.

'Quit stalling, old bean old bean old beanbag. Open the safe or you'll never walk straight again.'

Never walk at all was more like it.

I turned the combination dial one way . . . then the other . . . then back the first way again. Three numbers down, one to go. I risked a look over my shoulder and saw a narrow face – a weasel's face, almost – under a retro White Sox ballcap with a high crown and a red circle where the O in *Sox* belonged. 'Can I have at least some?'

He gave a tittery little laugh. Nasty. 'Open it! Stop looking at me and open it!'

I turned the combination to the last number. I pulled the handle. I couldn't see him looking over my shoulder, but I could smell him: sour sweat, the kind that almost bakes into a person's skin after a long time without bathing.

The safe swung open. I didn't hesitate, because he who hesitates is lost. I grabbed the bucket by the rim and overturned it between my spread knees. Gold pellets flooded out and ran across the floor in all directions. At the same moment I dived into the closet. He fired, the sound not much louder than a medium-sized firecracker. I felt the bullet go between my shoulder and my ear. The hem of one of Mr Bowditch's old-fashioned suitcoats twitched as the bullet passed through it.

Mr Bowditch had plenty of shoes; Dora would have been envious. I grabbed a brogan, rolled over on my side, and threw it. He ducked. I threw the other one. He ducked again, but it hit him in the chest. He backed up onto the gold pellets, which were still rolling, and his feet went out from under him. He landed hard with his legs splayed but held onto his gun. It was a lot smaller than Mr Bowditch's .45 revolver, which probably accounted for the low-decibel bark.

I didn't try to get to my feet, just squatted and uncoiled from the thighs on down. I flew over the rolling gold like Superman and landed on top of him. I was big; he was small. The air went out of him with a *whuff* sound. His eyes were bulging. His lips were red and gleaming with spittle.

'Get . . . off . . . me!' A labored out-of-breath whisper.

As if. I grabbed for the hand holding the gun, missed my grip, and grabbed again before he could bring it around to my face. The gun went off a second time. I don't know where that bullet went and didn't care because it didn't go into me. His wrist was slippery with sweat, so I clamped down with all my strength and twisted. There was a snap. He uttered a high-pitched scream. The gun fell from his hand and hit the floor. I picked it up and pointed it at him.

He made that high-pitched scream again and put his good hand in front of his face, as if that would stop a bullet. The other one just flopped on his broken wrist, which was already beginning to swell. 'No, don't! Please don't shoot me! *Please!*'

Not one single fucking ha-ha.

3

You may have gotten a pretty good feeling about young Charlie Reade by this point, I'd guess – sort of like a hero in one of those YA adventure novels. I'm the kid who stuck with my father when he was drinking, cleaned up his vomit, prayed for his recovery (on his knees!), and actually got what he prayed for. I'm the kid who saved an old man when he fell off a ladder trying to clean the gutters. The kid who went to visit him in the hospital and then took care of him when he came home. Who fell in love with the old guy's faithful dog, and the faithful dog fell in love with him. I strapped on a .45 and braved a dark corridor (not to mention the giant wildlife therein) and came out in another world, where I made friends with an old lady with a damaged face who collected shoes. I'm the kid who overpowered Mr Heinrich's killer by cleverly dumping gold pellets all over the floor so he'd lose his balance and fall down. Gosh, I even played two varsity sports! Strong and tall, no acne! Perfect, right?

Only I was also the kid who put firecrackers in mailboxes, blowing up what might have been somebody's important mail. I was the kid who smeared dogshit on the windshield of Mr Dowdy's car and squeezed Elmer's Glue in the ignition slot of Mrs Kendrick's old Ford wagon when Bertie and I found it unlocked. I pushed over gravestones. I shoplifted. Bertie Bird was with me on all those expeditions, and it was the Bird Man who phoned in the bomb threat, but I didn't stop him. There were other things that I'm not going to tell you about because I'm too ashamed. All I'll say is that we scared some little kids so bad they cried and pissed themselves.

Not so nice, right?

And I was mad at this little man in his dirty corduroy pants and his Nike warm-up jacket and his clotted, greasy hair falling over the brow of his narrow weasel's face. I was mad (of course) because he would have killed me once he had the gold – he'd already killed once, so why not? I was mad because if he *had* killed me, the cops – possibly led by Detective Gleason and his intrepid sidekicks Officers Witmark and Cooper – would have entered the shed in the course of their investigations and found something that would have made the murder of Charles McGee Reade look piddling in comparison. I was maddest of all – you may not believe this, but I swear it's true – because the little man's intrusion made everything more difficult. Was I supposed to report him to the police? That would lead to the gold being discovered, and that would lead to about ten zillion questions. Even if I picked it all up and put it back in the safe, Mr Ha-Ha would tell them. Maybe to get some consideration from the district attorney; maybe just out of spite.

The solution to my problem was obvious. If he was dead, he couldn't tell anyone anything. Assuming Mrs Richland's ears weren't as sharp as her eyes (and the two gunshots really hadn't been very loud), the police wouldn't have to come. I even had a place to hide the body.

Didn't I?

4

Although his hand was still in front of his face, I could see his eyes between his splayed fingers. Blue, threaded with red, and starting to spill tears. He knew what I was thinking of doing; he could see it on *my* face.

'No. Please. Let me go. Or call the police if you have to. Just don't k-k-kill me!'

'Like you were going to kill me?'

'I wasn't! I swear to God, I swear on my mother's grave, *I swear I wasn't*!'

'What's your name?'

'Derek! Derek Shepherd!'

I hit him across the face with his gun. I could tell you I didn't mean to do it, or I didn't know I was going to do it until it was done, but those would be lies. I knew, all right, and it felt good. Blood burst from his nose. More trickled down from the side of his mouth.

'You think I've never seen *Grey's Anatomy*, asshole? What's your name?'

'Justin Townes.'

I hit him again. He tried to pull back, which did him no good. I'm not particularly fast on my feet, but there's nothing wrong with my reflexes. I'm pretty sure that one broke his nose instead of just bloodying it. He screamed . . . but in a high whisper.

'You must think I don't know Justin Townes Earle, either. I've even got one of his albums. You have one more chance, fuckwad. Then I put a bullet in your head.'

'Polley,' he said. His nose was swelling – the whole side of his face was swelling – and he sounded like he had a bad cold. 'Chris Polley.'

'Throw me your wallet.'

'I don't have a—'

He saw me draw back and put out the good hand again. I had plans for that hand, which will probably take me down even further in your estimation, but you have to remember I was in a fix. Also, I was thinking again of Rumpelstiltskin. Maybe I couldn't make this motherfucker stick his foot in the ground and tear himself in two, but I might be able to make him run away. Like the Gingerbread Man, ha-ha.

'Okay, okay!'

He got up and reached into the back pocket of his cords, which weren't just dirty; they were filthy. The warm-up jacket had a torn sleeve and ragged cuffs. Wherever this guy was staying, it wasn't the Hilton. The wallet was beat-up and scuffed. I flipped it open long enough to see a single ten in the billfold and a driver's license with the name Christopher Polley. It showed a picture of him as a younger man with an intact face. I flipped it closed and put it in my back pocket, with my own wallet. 'Looks like your license expired in 2008. You might want to renew it. If you live long enough, that is.'

'I can't—' His mouth snapped closed.

'Can't renew it? Had it jerked? OUI? Or prison? Have you been in prison? Is that why it took you so long to rob and kill Mr Heinrich? Because you were in Stateville?'

'Not there.'

'Where?'

He kept silent, and I decided I didn't care. As Mr Bowditch might have said, it wasn't germane.

'How did you know about the gold?'

'I saw some in the Kraut's store. Before I did my bit in County.' I could have asked how he found out who the gold came from, and how he set up the vagrant, Dwyer, but I was pretty sure I knew both of those things. 'Let me go, I'll never bother you again.'

'No, you won't. Because you'll be in jail, and not just county jail. I'm calling the cops on you, Polley. You're going away for murder, so let's hear you say ha-ha about that.'

'I'll tell! I'll tell about the gold! You won't get any!'

Well, I *would*, actually, according to the will it was mine, but he didn't know that.

'That's true,' I said. 'Thanks for pointing it out. I'll have to put you with the pumping machinery after all. Lucky for me you're a little shit. I won't strain my back.'

I raised the gun. I could tell you it was a bluff, but I'm not sure it was. I also hated him for tearing up Mr Bowditch's house, for *defiling* it. And as I believe I've said, killing him would simplify everything.

He didn't scream – I don't think he had air enough – but he moaned. The crotch of his pants darkened. I lowered the gun . . . a little.

'Suppose I told you you could live, Mr Polley. Not only live but go your own way, like the song says. Would that interest you?'

'Yes! *Yes!* Let me go and I'll never bother you again!'

Spoken like a true Rumpelstiltskin, I thought.

'How did you get here? Did you walk? Take the bus as far as Dearborn Avenue?' Given the single ten in his billfold, I doubted if he'd taken a Yoober. He could have cleaned out Mr Heinrich's back room – the stuff planted on Dwyer made that seem likely – but if so, he hadn't converted any of his stash into cash. Maybe he didn't know how. He might be crafty, but that wasn't necessarily the same thing as being smart. Or connected.

'I came through the woods.' He gestured with his good hand in the direction of the greenbelt behind Mr Bowditch's property, all that remained of the Sentry Woods that had covered this part of town a century ago.

I reappraised his filthy pants and torn jacket. Mrs Richland hadn't said the little man's corduroys were dirty, and she would have – her eyes were sharp – but she had seen him days ago. My guess was that he hadn't just *come* through the woods, he was living in them. Somewhere not far from the fence at the rear of Mr Bowditch's yard there was probably a piece of scavenged tarp serving as a shelter, with this man's few possessions inside. Any swag from Mr Heinrich's store would be buried close by, the way storybook pirates did it. Only storybook pirates buried their doubloons and pieces of eight in chests. Polley's was more likely in a satchel with a sticker on it saying SUBSCRIPTION SERVICE OF AMERICA.

If I was right, his camp would have been close enough to keep an eye out for one Charles Reade. He'd know who I was from Heinrich. He could have seen me on my trip to Stantonville. And after Polley's search of the house netted nothing but an unopenable safe, he had just waited for me, assuming I would come for the gold. Because it's what *he* would do.

'Get up. We're going downstairs. Watch out for the gold BBs unless you want to take another spill.'

'Can I have a few? Just a few? I'm broke, man!'

'And do what? Use one to pay for lunch at McDonald's?'

'I know a man in Chi. He won't give me what they're worth, but—'

'You can have three.'

'Five?' Trying to smile like he hadn't been planning to kill me once the safe was open.

'Four.'

He bent and picked them up quickly with his good hand and went to stuff them in his pants pocket.

'That's five. Drop one.'

He gave me a narrow angry look – a Rumpelstiltskin look – and dropped one. It rolled. 'You're a mean kid.'

'Coming from Saint Christopher of the Woods, that fills me with shame.'

He lifted his lip, showing yellowing teeth. 'Fuck you.'

I raised his gun, which I thought was a .22 automatic. 'You should never say fuck you to someone with a firearm. Not wise, ha-ha. Now go downstairs.'

He left the room, cradling his broken wrist to his chest and squeezing the gold pellets in his good hand. I followed. We went through the living room and into the kitchen. He stopped at the door.

'Keep going. Across the backyard.'

He turned to look at me, eyes wide and mouth trembling. 'You're going to kill me and put me down that hole!'

'I wouldn't have given you any of the gold if I was going to do that,' I said.

'You'll take it back!' He was starting to cry again. 'You'll take it back and put me down in the *h-h-hole*!'

I shook my head. 'There's a fence and you've got a broken wrist. You won't get over it without help.'

'I'll manage! I don't want your help!'

'Walk,' I said.

He walked, crying, sure he was going to be shot in the back of the head. Because again, it was what *he* would do. He only stopped blubbering when we passed the open door of the shed and he found himself still alive. We came to the fence, which was about five feet high – tall enough to keep Radar in when she had been younger.

'I don't want to see you again.'

'You won't.'

'Not ever.'

'You won't, I promise.'

'Shake on it, then.' I stuck out my hand.

He took it. Crafty, but not all that smart. Like I said. I twisted his hand and heard the crack of splintering bones. He shrieked and went to his knees with both hands held to his chest. I stuffed the .22 in the back of my pants like a bad guy in a movie, bent, grabbed him, and lifted. It was easy. He couldn't have weighed more than a hundred and forty, and at that point I was so jacked on adrenalin it was practically shooting out my ears. I threw him over the fence. He landed on his back in a pile of dead leaves and broken branches, gasping little cries of pain. His hands flopped uselessly. I leaned over the fence like a washerwoman in a story, eager for the latest village gossip.

'Go, Polley. Run away and never come back.'

'You broke my hands! *You broke my fucking—*'

'You're lucky I didn't kill you!' I shouted at him. 'I wanted to, I almost did, and if I ever see you again, I will! Now go! While you still have the chance!'

He gave me one more look, blue eyes wide, swelling face smeared with snot and tears. Then he turned and blundered into the poor-ass second growth that was all that remained of the Sentry Woods, broken hands held to his chest. I watched him go without the slightest regret for what I'd done.

Not very nice.

Would he come back? Not with two broken wrists, he wouldn't. Would he tell someone else, a friend or a partner in crime? I didn't think Polley had any partners or friends. Would he go to the cops? Given what I knew about Heinrich, the idea was ludicrous. All that aside, I simply couldn't bring myself to kill him in cold blood.

I went back inside and picked up the gold pellets. They were everywhere, and it took longer than the whole confrontation with Polley. I put them in the safe along with the empty concho belt and holster, then left. I made sure to untuck my shirt so it hung over the gun stuffed into my pants at the small of my back, but I was still glad Mrs Richland wasn't out at the end of the driveway, with her hand shielding her sharp eyes.

5

I walked back down the hill slowly, because my legs were trembling. Hell, my *mind* was trembling. I was climbing my own front porch steps before realizing that I was also hungry. Ravenous, in fact.

Radar was waiting to greet me, but not in the frantic way I expected; just a happy wag, a few bounces, and a head-rub against my thigh before heading back to her rug. I realized I'd expected frantic because it felt like I'd been gone a long time. In reality it had been less than three hours. A lot had happened in those hours – life-changing stuff. I thought of Scrooge in *A Christmas Carol* saying *The spirits have done it all in one night.*

There was leftover meatloaf in the fridge, and I made a couple of thick sandwiches, going heavy on the ketchup. I needed to fuel up, because my day was only beginning. I had a lot to do to prepare for tomorrow. I would not be going back to school, and my dad might – probably would – be coming home to an empty house. I was going to try to find the sundial Mr Bowditch had spoken of. I no longer doubted that it was there, and I no longer doubted it could turn back time for the elderly German Shepherd currently snoozing on her rug in the living room. I was less sure that I could get her down those winding steps, and I had no idea how I was supposed to get her forty (or fifty, or sixty) miles to the city. The one thing I *was* sure of: I couldn't afford to wait.

6

As I ate, I thought. If I was going to be gone, and with Radar, I had to lay a false trail that would lead in some direction other than to Mr Bowditch's house. An idea came to me while I was going out to the garage, and I thought it would serve. It would have to.

I got my dad's wheelbarrow, and a bonus. On one of the shelves was a bag of calcium hydroxide, more commonly known as quicklime. And why did Dad have that? You guessed it: roaches. Some in our basement, some in the garage. I put the bag in the wheelbarrow, then went into the house and showed Radar her leash.

'If I take you to the top of the hill, will you be good?'

She assured me with her eyes that she would, so I hooked her up and we walked to 1 Sycamore, me pushing the wheelbarrow and she walking beside it. Mrs Richland was back at her usual post, and I half-expected her to ask what all the rumpus had been about earlier. She didn't, just asked if I was planning to do some more work around the place. I said I was.

'You're very good to do it. I suppose his estate will be putting it up for sale, won't they? Maybe the estate will even pay you, but I wouldn't count on it. Lawyers are stingy. I hope the new owners don't tear it down, it looks so much nicer now. Do you know who inherited?'

I said I didn't.

'Well, if you happen to find out the asking price, let me know. We've been thinking about selling, ourselves.'

We suggested there was a Mr Richland. Who knew?

I said I would be sure to do that (in a pig's eye), and rolled the wheelbarrow around back with the end of Radar's leash looped over my wrist. The old girl was moving well, but it wasn't a particularly long walk up the hill. Miles to the abandoned city, though? She'd never make it.

Radar was calmer this time, but as soon as I unhooked her leash she went straight to the sofa bed in the living room, sniffed it over from end to end, and lay down beside it. I brought her a bowl of water, then went out to the shed with the bag of quicklime. I shook it over the remains of the cockroach and watched with some amazement as the decay sped up to a sprint. There was a hissing, bubbling sound. Vapor rose from the remains, which would soon be nothing but a puddle of lime-slime.

I picked up the revolver, took it back into the house, and put it in the safe. I saw a couple of pellets that had rolled away into a corner and dropped them into the bucket with the rest of the gold. When I went downstairs, Radar was fast asleep.

Good, I thought. *Get all the sleep you can, because tomorrow is going to be a busy day for you, girl.*

This was already a busy one for me, and that was also good. It didn't keep me from thinking about the other world – the red poppies flanking the path, the shoe-woman with almost no face, the glassy towers of the city – but staying busy probably kept me from having a delayed reaction to my close call with Christopher Polley. And it had been close. Very.

The little bastard hadn't bothered with the stacks of reading matter in the hall between the kitchen and the back door in his hunt for the gold. I didn't bother with the books, but I spent an hour wheelbarrowing stacks of magazines – conveniently done up in hayrope – out to the shed. I stacked some over the remains of the roach. I piled most of them near the well of the worlds. When I went down the next time – when *we* went down – I'd put the stacks on the boards and try to cover the opening entirely.

When I was done, I went back to the house and woke Radar. I gave her a treat from the pantry and walked her back home. I reminded myself to bring along her toy monkey tomorrow. She might want it once we got to where we were going. If, that was, she didn't fall off those stairs and pull me with her.

If she'd go down the stairs at all.

When I got back I put Polley's .22 auto, his wallet, and some other stuff into my pack – not much, I'd add more tomorrow from Mr Bowditch's pantry – and then sat down to write my father. I wanted to put it off and knew I couldn't afford to. That was a hard letter to write.

Dear Dad,

You are going to come back to an empty house, because I have gone to Chicago with Radar. I found someone on the Internet who has had amazing success with renewing the health and vitality of aging dogs. I've known about this guy for some time but didn't want to tell you because I know how you feel about 'quack cures.' Maybe that's what this is, but I can easily afford $750, thanks to my inheritance. I won't tell you not to worry because I know you will, even though there's nothing to worry about. What I WILL tell you is please don't try to fix your worry with a drink. If I came back and found you were boozing again, it would break my heart. Don't try to call me, because I'm turning off my phone. (On or off wouldn't matter where I was going.) I will be back, and if this works, I'll be back with a brand new dog!

Trust me, Dad. I know what I'm doing.

Love,

Charlie

Well, I hoped I knew.

I put the note in an envelope, wrote *DAD* on the front, and left it on the kitchen table. Then I opened my laptop and wrote an email to dsilvius@hillviewhigh.edu. It covered much the same territory. I thought if Mrs S. had been in the room while I was typing, she would have smelled hooky all over me. I set the email to arrive on her office computer Thursday afternoon. Two days of unexplained absence I could get away with, but probably not three. My purpose was to give Dad as much time at his retreat as I could. I could hope Mrs S. wouldn't call him when she got my email, but I knew she probably would, and he might be headed back then, anyway. The real purpose was to tell as many people as possible that I was going to Chicago.

To that end, I called the cop shop and asked if Detective Gleason was there. He was, and I asked him if they had any leads in the home invasion at 1 Sycamore Street. 'I wanted to ask today, because I'm taking Mr Bowditch's dog to Chicago tomorrow. I've found someone there who's done wonders with older dogs.'

Gleason told me there was nothing new, which was what I expected. I had taken care of the home invader myself . . . or so I hoped. Gleason wished me good luck with the old pooch. That was a wish I took to heart.

7

That evening I tucked three more of the new pills into Radar's chow. I would give her three more tomorrow. There weren't many more left in the bottle, but maybe that was okay. I didn't know for sure what they were, but I had an idea they were doggy speed. They were shortening her life at the same time they were pepping her up. I told myself I just had to get her down the steps, and after that . . . well, I didn't know after that.

My phone was working again (although I'd had to do a hard reset to get it to show the right time), and around seven o'clock it rang. DAD was in the window. I turned on the TV and jacked the volume a little before answering it.

'Hey, Charlie, everything okay?'

'It's fine. Climb any trees?'

He laughed. 'No trees, it's raining up here. A lot of rah-rah team spirit instead. Insurance Guys Gone Wild. What are you watching?'

'SportsCenter.'

'Dog okay?'

'Rades?' She looked up from her rug. 'She's good.'

'Still eating?'

'Every bite of her dinner and licked the bowl.'

'Glad to hear it.'

We talked a little more. He seemed unworried, so I guess I was putting on a good front. That made me glad and ashamed at the same time.

'I'll give you a call tomorrow night, if you want.'

'Nah, I might go out for burgers and mini-golf with a bunch of guys.'

'And girls?'

'Well . . . there might be girls present. I'll call you if something happens. Like the house catches on fire.'

'Sounds like a plan. Sleep well, Chip.'

'You too.' From where I was sitting, I could see the letter on the kitchen table. I didn't like lying to my dad but didn't see any other choice. It was an extraordinary situation.

I killed the TV and got ready to turn in at eight o'clock for the first time since forever. But I was planning on rising early. *Soonest begun, soonest done*, my mother used to say. Sometimes I couldn't exactly remember what she looked like without checking her picture, but I could remember all her little sayings. The mind is a weird machine.

I locked up, but not because I was afraid of Polley. He probably knew where I lived, but he had two broken hands and I had his gun. He was also without money and ID. My guess was that he was already hitching to what he called 'Chi,' where he'd try to turn those four gold pellets into cash. If he was able to sell them at all, I thought he'd get no more than twenty cents on the dollar, and that was all right with me. Awesome sauce. Every time I started to feel sorry for him, or guilty about what I'd done, I thought of him pressing the barrel of his little gun against the back of my head and telling me not to turn around, it wouldn't be smart. I was glad I didn't kill him, though. There was that.

I examined myself closely in the mirror as I brushed my teeth. I thought I looked the same as ever, which was sort of amazing after everything that had happened. I rinsed out my mouth, turned, and saw Radar sitting in the bathroom doorway. I bent and ruffled the fur at the sides of her face. 'You want to go on an adventure tomorrow, girl?'

She thumped her tail, then went into the guestroom and lay down at the foot of my bed. I double-checked my alarm to make sure it was set for five A.M., then turned off the light. I expected it would take me a long time to go to sleep after the day's rollercoaster ride, but I started to drift almost at once.

I asked myself if I was really going to risk my life and certainly get into a shitload of trouble, both with my dad and at school, for an old dog who'd already had – in canine years – a hell of a good run. The answer seemed to be yes, but that wasn't all. It was the wonder of the thing, the mystery of it. I had found another world, for Christ's sake. I wanted to see the city with the green towers and find out if it really *was* Oz, only with a terrible monster – Gogmagog – at its heart instead of a humbug projecting his voice from behind a curtain. I wanted to find the sundial and see if it actually did what Mr Bowditch said it did. And you have to remember I was seventeen, a prime age for both adventuring and foolish decisions.

But yeah, mostly it was the dog. I loved her, you see, and I didn't want to let her go.

I rolled over on my side and went to sleep.

CHAPTER THIRTEEN

Calling Andy. Radar Decides. Stew. Googir.

1

Rades seemed surprised that we were getting up in the dark, but she was willing to eat her breakfast (three more pills buried in it) and walk up the hill to Number 1. The Richland house was dark. I went upstairs to the safe, strapped on the .45, and tied it down. With Polley's .22 auto in my backpack, that made me a regular Two-Gun Sam. There were some empty spaghetti sauce jars in the pantry. I filled two with dry Orijen dog food, screwed the lids on tight, wrapped them in a dishtowel, and put them in my pack beneath a T-shirt and a pair of underwear (*Never leave on a trip without clean undershorts* was another of my mom's sayings). To this I added a dozen cans of King Oscar sardines (for which I'd gotten a taste), a sleeve of crackers, a few pecan sandies (only a few because I'd been nibbling on them), and a handful of Perky Jerky sticks. Also the two remaining Cokes from the fridge. I also tossed my wallet in my pack so I could put the long-barreled flashlight into my back pocket, as before.

You could say these were extremely thin supplies for what might be a round trip of as much as a hundred miles, and of course you'd be right, but my backpack was only so big and besides, the shoe-woman had offered to stand me a meal. Perhaps she could even add to my supplies. Otherwise I'd just have to forage, an idea that filled me with both anxiety and excitement.

The thing that troubled me the most was the padlock on the shed door. I thought if the shed was locked, nobody would bother about it. If it wasn't, somebody might check it out, and concealing the top of the well with piles of old magazines was mighty thin camouflage. I'd gone to sleep with this Agatha Christie-type problem unsolved but had woken up with what seemed to me to be a good answer. Not only would the shed be locked from the outside, there would be someone else to say I'd taken Radar to Chicago in hopes of a miracle cure.

Andy Chen was the solution.

I waited until seven o'clock to call him, thinking that by then he'd be up and getting ready for school, but after four rings I was pretty sure my call was going to voicemail. I was thinking out the message I'd leave when he answered, sounding impatient and a little out of breath.

'What do you want, Reade? I just got out of the fucking shower and I'm dripping all over the floor.'

'Ooo,' I said in a high falsetto, 'is the Yellow Peril naked?'

'Very funny, you racist fuck. What do you want?'

'Something important.'

'What's up?' Sounding serious now.

'Look, I'm at the Highball outside town. You know the Highball, right?'

Of course he did. It was a truck stop with the best assortment of video games in Sentry. We'd cram into some licensed driver's car – or take the bus, if no one with a license happened to be handy – and play until the money ran out. Or until we got kicked out.

'What are you doing there? It's a school day.'

'I've got the dog. The one that scared you so bad when we were kids? She's not doing so well, and there's someone in Chicago who's supposed to be able to help old dogs. Kind of rejuvenate them.'

'It's a scam,' Andy said flatly. 'Gotta be. Don't be stupid, Charles. When dogs get old, they get old, end of stor—'

'Will you shut up and listen? This guy's giving me and Rades a ride in his van for thirty bucks—'

'Thirty—'

'I have to go right now or he's gonna leave without us. I need you to lock up the house.'

'You forgot to lock your—'

'No, no, Mr Bowditch's! I forgot!'

'How did you get out to the Highba—'

'I'm going to lose my ride if you don't shut up! Lock the house, will you? I left the keys on the kitchen table.' Then, as if it were an afterthought: 'And lock the shed out back, too. The padlock's hanging on the door.'

'I'll have to ride my bike to school instead of taking the bus. How much will you pay me?'

'Andy, come on!'

'I'm kidding, Reade, I won't even ask you to blow me. But if anyone asks—'

'They won't. If they do, tell them the truth, I went to Chicago. I don't want you to get in trouble, just lock up the house for me. And the shed. I'll get the keys from you when we get back.'

'Yeah, I can do that. Are you staying overnight or—'

'Probably. Maybe even two nights. I gotta go. Thanks, Andy. I owe you one.'

I ended the call, shouldered my backpack, and grabbed the leash. I dropped Mr Bowditch's keyring on the table and hooked Radar up. At the foot of the back steps I stopped, looking across the grass to the shed. Did I really mean to get her down those narrow winding steps (*of varying heights*) on a leash? Bad idea. For both of us.

It wasn't too late to call it off. I could hit Andy back and tell him either I'd changed my mind at the last minute or the fictional van driver had left without me. I could walk Radar home, tear up the letter on the kitchen table, and trash the email that was waiting to go out to Mrs Silvius. Andy was right: when dogs got old, they got old, end of story. That didn't mean I couldn't still explore the other place; I'd just have to wait.

Until she died.

I unhooked her leash and started walking toward the shed. Halfway there I looked back. She was still sitting where I'd left her. I thought about calling her, the urge was strong, but I didn't. I kept walking. At the door to the shed I looked back again. She was still sitting at the foot of the back steps. I felt the sourness of disappointment that all my preparation – especially my inspiration about the padlock – had gone to waste, but there was no way I was going to leave her sitting there.

I was about to start back when Radar got to her feet and walked hesitantly across the backyard to where I stood in the open doorway. She hesitated, sniffing. I didn't turn on the battery lights because with her nose she didn't need them. She looked at the pile of magazines I'd stacked over whatever remained of the big cockroach, and I could see that educated nose of hers vibrating rapidly. Then she looked at the boards covering the well, and something amazing happened. She trotted to the well and started pawing at the boards, making little yipping sounds of excitement.

She remembers, I thought. *And the memories must be good, because she wants to go again.*

I hung the padlock over the latch and pulled the door partway closed, leaving enough light so I could see my way to the well. 'Radar, gotta be quiet now. *Hush*.'

The yipping stopped, but not the pawing at the boards. Her eagerness to go down there made me feel better about what was at the end of the underground corridor. And really, why would I feel bad about it? The poppies were beautiful and smelled even better. There was no harm in the shoe-woman; she had welcomed me, had comforted me when I broke down, and I wanted to see her again.

She wanted to see Radar again, too . . . and Radar wants to see her, I think.

'Down.'

Radar looked at me but stayed on her feet. She peered into the darkness between the boards, back at me, then back at the boards. Dogs find ways to get their points across, and to me this one seemed totally clear: *Hurry up, Charlie.*

'Radar, *down*.'

Very reluctantly she went on her belly, but the moment I moved the boards from parallel to a V shape, she was up and running down the steps, fleet as a puppy. There were patches of white on the back of her head and the base of her spine, near the tail. I saw those, and then she was gone.

I had been worried about getting her down the steps. That was pretty funny, wasn't it? As Mr Neville, my English teacher, was fond of saying: *Irony, it's good for your blood*.

2

I almost called for her to come back, then realized it was a terrible idea. She probably wouldn't pay any attention. If she did, and tried to turn around on those small steps, she'd almost certainly fall to her death. All I could do was hope she didn't miss her footing in the dark and fall to her death anyway. Or start barking. That would undoubtedly send any lurking jumbo cockroaches packing, but it would startle the bats – also jumbo-sized – into flight.

There was nothing I could do about it, anyway. All I could do was follow the plan. I descended the steps until I only stuck out from head to chest, with the boards once more in a V shape and close on either side of me. I began placing tied bundles of magazines on them, walling myself in. All the time I was doing it I listened for a thud and a final cry of pain. Or, if the fall didn't kill her, *many* cries as she lay on the packed dirt, dying by inches because of my bright ideas.

I was sweating like a pig as I pulled the boards close around me. I wriggled my arms up through the enclosing wall of magazines and grabbed one more bundle. I balanced it on my head like a tribal woman carrying a load of wash to the nearest river, then bent slowly. The last bundle came to rest on the hole I'd left. It landed slightly askew, but it would have to serve. If Andy just gave the shed a cursory look before locking it up, it would. Of course that left the question of how I was going to get out of the shed again, but that was a worry for another day.

I started down the steps, once again keeping my shoulder against the curve of the wall and the beam of the flashlight trained on my feet. The pack made it slow going. I counted steps again, and when I got to a hundred, I shone the light down the remainder of the shaft. Two eerie spots of light shone back up at me as the beam hit the reflective surface dogs have at the back of their eyes. She was down, she was okay, and she was waiting instead of running off down the corridor. The relief I felt was enormous. I got to the bottom as fast as I could, which wasn't very, because I didn't want to be the one lying there with a broken leg. Or two. I dropped to a knee and gave Radar a hug. She was perfectly willing to be hugged under ordinary circumstances, but this time she pulled away almost at once and turned toward the corridor.

'Okay, but don't scare the wildlife. *Hush*.'

She went ahead of me, not running but walking fast, and with no sign of a limp. At least yet. I wondered again exactly what the miracle pills were, and how much they were taking away while they were giving. One of my father's sayings was *There's no such thing as a free lunch*.

When we neared the place I thought of as the borderland, I risked disturbing the bats to raise the flashlight beam from the floor so I could watch her reaction. What I saw was nothing at all, and I was wondering if that effect wore off after one's initial exposure when that same lightheadedness swam through me – that sense of having an out-of-body experience. It passed as rapidly as it came, and shortly thereafter I saw the spark of light where the corridor opened onto the hillside.

I caught up with Radar. I brushed through the overhanging vines and looked down on the poppies. *Red carpet*, I thought. *Red carpet*.

We were in the other world.

3

For a moment Radar stood perfectly still, head forward, ears cocked, nose going. Then she started down the path at a trot, which was now the best speed she could make. Or so I thought. I was halfway down the hill when Dora came out of her little cottage with a pair of slippers in one hand. Rades was maybe ten feet in front of me. Dora saw us coming – more properly saw who was coming on four feet instead of two – and dropped the slippers. She fell to her knees and held out her arms. Radar broke into a full-out run, barking joyously. She pulled up a little at the end (or her aging rear legs did), but not enough to keep from slamming into Dora, who tumbled over on her back with her skirt flying up from her bright green stockings. Radar straddled her, barking and licking her face. Her tail wagged furiously.

I broke into a run myself, the loaded pack thumping up and down on my back. I ducked under a line of dangling shoes and grabbed Radar's collar. 'Quit it, girl! Get off her!'

But that wasn't going to happen right away, because Dora had her arms around Radar's neck and was hugging her head against her bosom . . . much as she had done for me. Her feet, clad in the same red shoes (with the green stockings her look was quite Christmassy), kicked up and down, doing a happy-dance. When she sat up, I saw there was the faintest touch of dull color in those gray cheeks, and gummy liquid – surely all she could manage for tears – was spilling from her narrow lashless eyes.

'*Rayyy!*' she cried, and hugged my dog again. Radar went to work licking her neck, tail whipping back and forth. *'Rayyy, Rayyy, RAYYY!'*

'I guess you guys know each other,' I said.

4

I didn't have to break into my supplies; she fed us and fed us well. The stew was the best I'd ever eaten, loaded with meat and potatoes, swimming in savory gravy. It crossed my mind – probably influenced by some horror movie or other – that we might be eating human flesh, but then I dismissed the idea as ridiculous. This woman was good. I didn't need to see a jolly expression or kindly eyes to know; it radiated from her. And if I didn't trust that, there was the way she had greeted Radar. And, of course, the way Radar had greeted her. I got my own hug when I helped her to her feet, but not like the one she'd given Rades.

I kissed her cheek, which seemed perfectly natural. Dora patted me on the back and pulled me inside. The cottage was a single large room, and toasty warm. There was no fire in the fireplace, but the stove was going full out, with the pot of stew simmering on a flat metal plate – what I believe is called a hob (although I could be wrong about that). There was a wooden table in the middle of the room with a vase of poppies in the center. Dora set out two white bowls that looked hand-made and two wooden spoons. She gestured for me to sit down.

Radar curled up as close to the stove as she could get without singeing her fur. Dora got another bowl from one of the cupboards and used the pump hanging over the kitchen sink to fill it with water. She set it down for Radar, who lapped eagerly. But, I noticed, without lifting her hindquarters from the floor. Which wasn't a good sign. I'd been careful to ration her exercise, but when she'd seen her old friend's house, nothing could have held her back. If she'd been on the leash (which was stowed in my pack), she would have jerked it out of my hand.

Dora put a teakettle on, served out the stew, then bustled back to the stove. She took mugs from the cupboard – like the bowls, they were rather lumpy – and a jar from which she spooned tea. *Ordinary* tea, I hoped, not something that would get me stoned. I felt stoned enough already. I kept thinking that this world was somehow below *my* world. It was a hard idea to shake because I'd gone down to get here. And yet there was sky above. I felt like Charlie in Wonderland, and if I'd looked out the cottage's round front window and seen the Mad Hatter bopping along the road out there (maybe with a grinning Cheshire cat on his shoulder), I wouldn't have been surprised. Or rather, *more* surprised.

The strangeness of the situation didn't change how hungry I was; I'd been too nervous to eat much breakfast. Still, I waited until she brought the mugs and sat down. This was ordinary politeness, of course, but I also thought she might want to say some sort of a prayer; a huzzy-buzzy version of *Bless this food we are about to eat*. She didn't, just picked up her spoon and gestured for me to dig in. As I said, it was delicious. I fished out a chunk of the meat and showed it to her, raising my eyebrows.

The crescent of her mouth turned up in her version of a smile. She put two fingers above her head and hopped a little in her seat.

'Rabbit?'

She nodded and made a grating, gurgling sound. I realized she was laughing, or trying to, and it made me sad, the same way I felt when I saw someone blind, or a person in a wheelchair who was never going to walk again. Most people like that don't want pity. They cope with their disabilities, help others, live good lives. They're brave. I get all that. Yet it seemed to me – maybe because everything in my personal system was working five-by-five – that there was something mean about having to deal with such things, out of whack and unfair. I thought of a girl I went to elementary school with: Georgina Womack. She had a huge strawberry birthmark on one cheek. Georgina was a cheerful little thing, smart as a whip, and most kids treated her decently. Bertie Bird used to trade lunchbox stuff with her. I thought she would make her way in life, but I was sorry she had to look at that mark on her face in the mirror every day. It wasn't her fault, and it wasn't Dora's fault that her laugh, which should have been beautiful and free, sounded like an ill-tempered growl.

She gave a final hop, as if for emphasis, then made a twirling gesture at me with her finger: *eat, eat.*

Radar struggled up, and when she finally got her back legs under her, she came to Dora. The woman slapped the heel of her gray hand against her gray forehead in a *what was I thinking* gesture. She found another bowl and put some meat and gravy in it. She looked at me, scant eyebrows lifted.

I nodded and smiled. 'Everybody eats at the House of Shoes.' Dora gave me her upturned crescent of a smile and set the bowl down. Radar got busy, tail wagging.

I scoped out the other half of the room while I ate. There was a neatly made bed, just the right size for a little shoe-woman, but most of that side was a workshop. Or maybe a rehab unit for wounded shoes. A lot of them had busted backs, or soles that were hanging down from the uppers like broken jaws, or holes in the soles or toes. There was a pair of leather workboots that had been slit down the backs, as if they had been inherited by someone whose feet were bigger than those of the original owner. A crooked wound in a silk bootee of royal purple had been stitched up with dark blue thread, probably the closest Dora had for a match. Some shoes were dirty and some – on a workbench – were in the process of being cleaned and polished with stuff in small metal pots. I wondered where they had all come from, but I wondered even more about the object that held pride of place in the workshop half of the cottage.

Meanwhile, I had emptied my bowl and Radar had emptied hers. Dora took them and raised her eyebrows in another question.

'Yes, please,' I said. 'Not too much more for Radar, or she'll sleep all day.'

Dora put her clasped hands to the side of her head and closed her eyes. She pointed at Radar. 'Nees.'

'Knees?'

Dora shook her head and did the pantomime again. *'Nees!'*

'She needs to sleep?'

The shoe-woman nodded and pointed to where Radar had been, by the stove.

'She slept there before? When Mr Bowditch brought her?'

Dora nodded again and dropped to one knee to pet Radar's head. Rades looked up at her with – I could be wrong, but I don't think so – adoration.

We finished our second bowls of stew. I said thank you. Radar said it with her eyes. While Dora cleared away our bowls, I got up to look at the object in the shoe hospital that had caught my attention. It was an old-fashioned sewing machine, the kind that runs by pumping a treadle. Written on its black casing in fading gold leaf was the word SINGER.

'Did Mr Bowditch bring you this?'

She nodded, patted her chest, lowered her head. When she looked up her eyes were wet.

'He was good to you.'

She nodded.

'And you were good to him. Also to Radar.'

She made an effort and produced a single understandable word: '*Yezz.*'

'You surely have a lot of shoes. Where do you get them? And what do you do with them?'

She didn't seem to know how to reply to that, and the gestures she made didn't help. Then she brightened and went to the workshop. There was a wardrobe which must have contained her clothes, and a great many more cupboards than in the kitchen half of the cottage. I assumed she stored her various shoe-repair equipment in them. She bent to one of the lower ones and brought out a little chalkboard, like the kind a child might have used in the old days of one-room schools and desks with inkwells. She rummaged further and came up with a stub of chalk. She pushed aside some of her works-in-progress on the workbench, wrote slowly, then held the chalkboard up for me to read: *yu see googir.*

'I don't understand.'

She sighed, rubbed it out, and beckoned me to the bench. I looked over her shoulder as she drew a little box and two parallel lines in front of it. She tapped the box, waved her arm around the cottage, and tapped the box again.

'This house?'

She nodded, pointed at the parallel lines, then pointed at the single round window to the left of the front door.

'The road.'

'Yezz.' She raised a finger to me – *attend this, young man* – and extended the parallel lines a bit. Then she drew another box. Above it she wrote *yu see googir* again.

'Googir.'

'Yezz.' She patted her mouth, then brought her fingers together rapidly in a snapping-crocodile gesture I understood perfectly.

'Talk!'

'Yezz.'

She tapped the non-word *googir*. Then she took me by the shoulders. Her hands were strong from her shoe-work, the gray fingertips hard with calluses. She turned me and walked me to the front door. When I got there, she pointed at me, made walking gestures with two fingers, and pointed to the right.

'You want me to go and see the googir?'

She nodded.

'My dog needs to rest. She's not in great shape.'

Dora pointed at Radar, made the sleeping gesture.

I thought to ask how far I was supposed to walk, but I doubted if she could answer that kind of question. This would have to be a yes-or-no-type operation.

'Is it far?'

Head-shake.

'The googir can talk?'

That seemed to amuse her, but she nodded.

'Googir? Does that mean good girl?'

The crescent smile. A shrug. A nod followed by a shake of the head.

'I'm kind of lost here. Will I be back before it gets dark?'

Strong nodding.

'And you'll keep Radar?'

'Yezz.'

I thought about it and decided to give it a try. If the googir could talk, I could get some answers. About Dora, and about the city. Googir might even know about the sundial that was supposed to make Radar young again. I decided I'd walk for an hour or so, and if I didn't find the googir's house, I'd turn around and come back.

I started to open the door (instead of a knob there was an old-fashioned iron latch). She held me by the elbow and raised a finger: *wait one*. She hurried back to Shoe Repair Central, pulled out a drawer in the workbench, got something, and hurried back to me. She had three small pieces of leather, less than palm-sized. They looked like shoe soles dyed green. She gestured for me to put them in my pocket.

'What are these for?'

She frowned, then smiled and turned her hands palms-up. Apparently that was too complicated. She touched the straps of my pack and gave me a questioning look. I decided what the hell and slipped it off. I put it beside the door, squatted, opened it, and jammed my wallet into my back pocket – like someone was going to ask me for ID, which was absurd. I looked at Radar as I did it, wondering how she'd take me leaving her with Dora. She raised her head when I stood up and opened the door, then laid it down again, perfectly content to stay where she was and snooze. Why not? Her belly was full of hot food and she was with a friend.

There was a walk leading to the wide dirt road – the thoroughfare – lined with poppies. There were other flowers as well, but they were either dying or dead. I turned for a look back. Over the door was a large wooden shoe, bright red, like the ones Dora wore. I thought it just about had to be a signboard. She was standing below it, smiling and pointing to the right, in case I'd forgotten which way to go in the last minute or so. It was such a mom thing to do that I had to grin.

'My name's Charlie Reade, ma'am. And if I didn't say so, thank you for feeding us. It's a pleasure to know you.'

She nodded, pointed at me, then patted above her heart. No translation needed for that.

'Can I ask one more thing?'

She nodded.

'Am I speaking your language? I am, aren't I?'

She laughed and shrugged – either she didn't understand or didn't know or felt it didn't matter.

'Okay. I guess.'

'O'ay.' She went in and shut the door.

There was a signboard at the head of the path, like the kind of menu board some restaurants put out on the sidewalk. The side on the right, in the direction I was supposed to go, was blank. A four-line verse was painted on the side facing left, in perfectly understandable English:

Give to me your broken shoes
For down the road you'll find ones new.
If you place your trust in me,
Lucky will your journey be.

I stood looking at this for much longer than it took to read it. It gave me an idea of where the shoes she was rehabbing came from, but that wasn't why. I *knew* that printing. I had seen it on shopping lists and on many envelopes I'd put in the mailbox at 1 Sycamore Street. Mr Bowditch had made that sign, God knew how many years ago.

5

Walking was easy without the pack, which was good. Looking around for Radar and not seeing her wasn't good, but I was sure she was safe with Dora. I couldn't keep track of the time very well with my phone out of commission, and with the constant overcast I couldn't even take a rough measure by the sun. It was up there, but only as a dull blob behind the clouds. I decided I'd use the old pioneer way of marking time and distance: I'd go three or four 'looks,' and if I still saw no sign of the googir, I'd turn around and go back.

As I walked, I thought about the signboard with the verse on it. A restaurant menu board would have stuff written on both sides, so people could see it both coming and going. This one only had the verse on one side, which suggested to me that traffic on the thoroughfare only went one way: toward the house I was supposed to find. I couldn't understand why that would be, but maybe the googir could tell me. If such a creature actually existed.

I had reached the end of my third look, where the road rose and went over a humped wooden bridge (the creekbed beneath it was dry), when I started to hear honking. Not cars but birds. When I got to the highest point of the bridge I saw a house on my right. On the left side of the road there were no more poppies; the woods had swooped right down to the edge. The house was much bigger than the shoe-woman's cottage, almost like a ranch house in a TCM Western, and there were outbuildings, two big and one small. The biggest one had to be a barn. This was a farmstead. Behind it was a large garden with neat rows of growing things. I didn't know what all of them were – no horticulturist was I – but I knew corn when I saw it. All the buildings were as old and gray as the shoe-woman's skin, but they looked sturdy enough.

The honking was coming from geese, at least a dozen of them. They surrounded a woman in a blue dress and a white apron. She held the apron up with one hand. With the other she was scattering handfuls of feed. The geese went after it greedily, with much flapping of wings. Nearby, eating from a tin trough, was a white horse that looked skinny and old. The word *spavined* came to mind, but since I didn't know exactly what *spavined* meant, I had no idea if it was right. There was a butterfly on its head – normal-sized, which was kind of a relief. As I approached, it flew off.

She must have seen me from the corner of her eye, because she looked up and went still, one hand deep in the pocket of her upheld apron as the geese jostled and flapped around her feet, honking for more.

I also went still, because now I understood what Dora had been trying to convey: goose girl. But that was only part of the reason I froze. Her hair was a rich dark blond with lighter streaks running through it. It fell to her shoulders. Her eyes were wide and blue, the farthest thing from Dora's constant half-erased squint. Her cheeks were rosy. She was young, and not just pretty; she was beautiful. Only one thing marred her storybook loveliness. Between her nose and chin there was nothing but a knotted white line, like the scar of a serious wound that had healed long since. At the right end of the scar was a dime-sized red blemish that looked like a tiny unopened rose.

The goose girl had no mouth.

6

As I came toward her, she took a step toward one of the outbuildings. It might have been a bunkhouse. Two gray-skinned men came out, one holding a pitchfork. I stopped, remembering that I was not only a stranger, I was armed. I raised my empty hands.

'I'm okay. Harmless. Dora sent me.'

The goose girl stood perfectly still for a few moments longer, deciding. Then the hand came out of her apron and she scattered more corn and grain. With the other hand she first motioned her farmhands to go back inside, then beckoned me to come ahead. I did, but slowly, still holding my hands up. A trio of geese came flapping and honking toward me, saw my empty hands, and hurried back to the girl. The horse looked around and went back to its lunch. Or maybe it was dinner, because the blob of sun was now moving toward the woods on the far side of the road.

The goose girl went on feeding her flock, seemingly unconcerned after her momentary startle. I stood at the edge of her yard, not knowing what to say. It occurred to me that Radar's new friend must have been having me on. I had asked if the googir could talk, and Dora had nodded, but she'd also been smiling. Big joke, send the kid to get answers from a young woman with no mouth.

'I'm a stranger here,' I said, which was stupid; I'm sure she could see that for herself. It was just that she was so beautiful. In a way, the scar that should have been a mouth and the blemish beside it made her even more beautiful. I'm sure that sounds weird, maybe even perverse, but it was true. 'I'm – *ouch*.' One of the geese had pecked my ankle.

That seemed to amuse her. She reached into her apron, brought out the last of the feed, made a tiny fist, and held it out to me. I opened my hand and she poured a little pile of what looked like wheat mixed with cracked corn into my palm. She used her other hand to hold mine steady, and the touch of her fingers felt like a low electric shock. I was smitten. Any young guy would have been, I think.

'I'm here because my dog is old, and my friend told me that in the city . . .' I pointed. '. . . there was a way to make her young again. I decided to give it a try. I've got about a thousand questions, but I see you're . . . not, you know . . . exactly *able* to . . .'

I stopped there, not wanting to dig the hole even deeper, and sprinkled my handful of feed for the geese. I could feel my cheeks burning.

This also seemed to amuse her. She dropped her apron and brushed it. The geese gathered around to get the last dusty bits, then headed off toward the barn, clacking and gossiping. The goose girl raised her arms over her head, pulling the fabric of her dress taut against admirable breasts. (Yes, I noticed – sue me.) She clapped twice.

The old white horse raised its head and ambled toward her. I saw its mane had been braided with bits of colored glass and ribbons. Such decoration suggested to me that it was a she. The next moment I became sure, because when the horse spoke, it was with a female's voice.

'I will answer some of your questions, because Dora sent you and because my mistress knows the belt with the pretty blue stones that you wear.'

The horse seemed to have no interest in the belt or the holstered .45; she was looking off at the road and the trees on the far side. It was the goose girl who was looking at the concho belt. Then she looked back up at me with those brilliant blue eyes.

'Have you come from Adrian?'

The voice came from the white horse – in the neighborhood, at least – but I could see the muscles moving in the girl's throat and around what had once been her mouth.

'You're a ventriloquist!' I blurted.

She smiled with her eyes and took my hand. It provoked another of those shocks.

'Come.'

The goose girl led me around the farmhouse.

CHAPTER FOURTEEN

Leah and Falada. Help Her.

A Meeting on the Road. Wolfies. Two Moons.

1

We only talked for an hour, and I ended up doing most of it, but it was long enough for me to be sure that she was no ordinary farmgirl. That probably sounds snobby, as if I don't believe farmgirls can be smart, or pretty, or even beautiful. I don't mean any of those things. I'm sure there are even farmgirls somewhere in this great round world of ours who are able to practice ventriloquism. There was something else, something more. She had a certain confidence, an *air*, as if she were used to having people – and not just farmhands – do her bidding. And after that first hesitation, probably caused by my sudden appearance, she showed absolutely no fear.

I probably don't need to tell you that it only took that hour for me to fall head over heels in love with her, either, because you probably already knew it. It's how these stories go, isn't it? Only for me it was no story, it was my life. It was also Charlie Reade luck: fall for a girl who was not only older, but whose mouth I could never kiss. I would have been glad to kiss the scar where it had been, though, which ought to tell you how bad I had it. One other thing I knew was that mouth or no mouth, she wasn't meant for the likes of me. She was more than just a girl feeding geese. A lot more.

Besides, how much romance can you make when the beautiful girl has to talk to the love-struck Romeo through a horse?

But that's what we did.

2

There was a gazebo near the garden. We sat inside, at a little round table. A couple of the hands came out of the corn headed for the barn with full baskets, so I guessed it was summer over here instead of early October. The horse cropped grass nearby. A gray girl with a badly deformed face brought a tray and set it down. On it were two cloth napkins, a glass, and two pitchers, one big and one the size of those teensy pitchers of half-and-half you get in diners. The big one held what looked like lemonade. The small one contained yellow gluck that might have been pureed squash. The goose girl motioned for me to pour from the big pitcher and drink. I did so, with some embarrassment. Because I had a mouth to drink with.

'Good,' I said, and it was – just the right mixture of sweet and tart.

The gray girl was still standing at the goose girl's shoulder. She pointed at the yellow gluck in the small pitcher.

The goose girl nodded, but her nostrils flared in a sigh and the scar that should have been a mouth pulled down a little. The serving girl took a glass tube from the pocket of a dress that was as gray as her skin. She bent, meaning to push it into the gluck, but the goose girl took the tube and laid it on the table instead. She looked up at the serving girl, nodded, and put her hands together, as if saying namaste. The girl returned the nod and left.

When she was gone, the goose girl clapped for the horse. She came and hung her head over the rail between us, still chewing her last mouthful.

'I am Falada,' the horse said, but her mouth didn't move the way the dummy's moves as it sits on the ventriloquist's knee; she just kept chewing. I had no idea why the girl was keeping up the voice-throwing charade. 'My mistress is Leah.'

I later knew the correct spelling thanks to Dora, but what I heard then was *Leia*, as in *Star Wars*. It seemed reasonable enough after everything else that had happened. I'd already met a version of Rumpelstiltskin, and an old woman who lived not in a shoe but below the sign of one; I myself was a version of Jack the Beanstalk Boy, and isn't *Star Wars* just another fairy tale, albeit one with excellent special effects?

'It's nice to meet you both,' I said. Of all the strange things that had happened to me that day (stranger things were ahead), that was in many ways the strangest – or maybe I mean the most surreal. I didn't know which one to look at and ended up swiveling back and forth, like someone watching a tennis match.

'Did Adrian send you?'

'Yes, but I knew him as Howard. He was Adrian . . . before. How long since you've seen him?'

Leah considered this, eyebrows drawn together. Even her frown was pretty (I will try to refrain from such observations from here on, but it will be hard). Then she looked up.

'I was much younger,' Falada said. 'Adrian was younger, too. He had a dog with him, not much more than a puppy. It danced everywhere. The puppy had a strange name.'

'Radar.'

'Yes.'

Leah nodded; the horse simply went on chewing, looking disinterested in the whole thing.

'Has Adrian passed on? I think if you are here and wearing his belt and weapon, that he has.'

'Yes.'

'He decided against another turn on the sundial, then? If so, he was wise.'

'Yes. He did.' I drank some of my lemonade, then put the glass down and leaned forward. 'I'm here for Radar. She's old now, and I want to take her to this sundial and see if I can . . .' I considered and thought of another science fiction fairy tale, one called *Logan's Run*. 'And see if I can renew her. I have questions—'

'Tell me your story,' Falada said. 'I may answer your questions afterward, if it seems good to me to do so.'

Let me stop here and say I got some information from Leah by way of Falada, but she got a hell of a lot more from me. She had a way about her, as if she were used to being obeyed . . . but it wasn't a mean or bullying way. There are people – well-bred people – who seem to realize they have an obligation to be pleasant and polite, and the obligation is double if they don't have to be. But pleasant or not, they usually get what they want.

Because I wanted to be back at Dora's house before dark (I had no idea what might come out of those woods after nightfall), I mostly stuck to my mission. I told her about how I had met Mr Bowditch, how I'd taken care of him, and how we had become friends. I told her about the gold and explained that I had enough for now, but in time I might need more in order to keep the well that led to this world secret from people in mine, who might misuse it. I didn't bother adding that I'd have to find a way to convert gold to cash now that Mr Heinrich was dead.

'Because later, years from now, there will still be taxes to pay, and they're quite high. Do you know what taxes are?'

'Oh yes,' Falada said.

'Right now, though, it's Radar I'm worried about. The sundial is in the city, right?'

'Yes. If you go there, you must be very quiet and follow Adrian's marks. And you must never, *never* go there at night. You are one of the whole people.'

'Whole people?'

She reached over the table to touch my forehead, one cheek, my nose, and my mouth. Her fingers were light, the touch fleeting, but more of those shocks went through me.

'Whole,' Falada said. 'Not gray. Not *spoiled*.'

'What happened?' I asked. 'Was it G—'

Her touch wasn't light this time; she slammed her palm against my mouth hard enough to drive my lips against my teeth. She shook her head.

'Never say his name lest you speed his waking.' She put a hand to her throat with her fingers touching her jaw on the right side.

'You're tired,' I said. 'What you're doing to make speech has got to be hard.'

She nodded.

'I'll go. Maybe we can talk more tomorrow.'

I started to get up, but she gestured for me to stay. There was no doubt about the command in that. She raised a finger in a gesture Radar would have understood: *Down*.

She put the glass tube in the yellow gluck, then raised the index finger of her right hand to the red blemish – the only flaw in her beautiful skin. I saw that all of her nails except for the one on that finger had been trimmed short. She pushed the nail into the blemish until the nail disappeared. She pulled. The flesh opened and a rill of blood ran down from it to her jawline. She inserted the straw in the small hole she'd made, and her cheeks hollowed as she sucked up whatever she took for nourishment. Half of the yellow stuff in the small pitcher disappeared, what would have been for me just a single swallow. Her throat flexed not just once but several times. It must have tasted as nasty as it looked, because she was choking it down. She pulled the straw out of what would have been a tracheotomy incision if it had been in her throat. The hole immediately disappeared, but the blemish looked angrier than ever. It shouted a curse against her beauty.

'Was that really enough?' I sounded appalled. I couldn't help it. 'You hardly drank any!'

She nodded in a weary way. 'The opening is painful and the taste is unpleasant after so many years of the same few things. Sometimes I think I'd rather starve, but that would bring too much pleasure in certain quarters.' She tilted her head to the left, in the direction I had come from and the direction in which the city lay.

'I'm sorry,' I said. 'If there was anything I could do . . .'

She nodded that she understood (of course people would want to do things for her, they'd fight each other to be first in line) and made the namaste gesture again. Then she picked up one of the napkins and blotted away the trickle of blood. I'd heard of curses – the storybooks are full of them – but this was the first time I'd seen one in action.

'Follow his marks,' Falada said. 'Don't get lost or the night soldiers will have you. And Radar.' That must have been a hard one for her, because it came out *Rayar*, making me think of Dora's ecstatic greeting to her. 'The sundial is in the stadium plaza, at the rear of the palace. You may accomplish your purpose there if you're quick and quiet.

As for the gold you speak of, that is inside. Getting it would be far more dangerous.'

'Leah, did you once live in that palace?'

'Long ago,' Falada said.

'Are you . . .' I had to force myself to say it, although the answer seemed obvious to me. 'Are you a princess?'

She bowed her head.

'She was.' Leah now referring to herself – through Falada – in the third person. 'The littlest princess of them all, for there were four sisters who were older, and two brothers – princes, if you like. Her sisters are dead – Drusilla, Elena, Joylene, and Falada, my namesake. Robert is dead, for she saw his poor crushed body. Elden, who was always good to her, is dead. Her mother and father are also dead. Few of her family are left.'

I was silent, trying to comprehend the enormity of such tragedy. I had lost my mother, and that was bad enough.

'You must see my mistress's uncle. He lives in the brick house near the Seafront Road. He will tell you more. Now my lady is very tired. She bids you good day and safe journey. You must stay the night with Dora.'

I got up. The blob of sun had almost reached the trees.

'My mistress wishes you good fortune. She says if you renew Adrian's dog as you hope, you must bring her here so my mistress can watch her dance and run as she once did.'

'I'll do that. Could I ask one more question?'

Leah nodded wearily and raised a hand – *say on, but be brief.*

I took the little leather shoes out of my pocket and showed them to Leah and then (feeling a bit foolish) to Falada, who showed absolutely zero interest. 'Dora gave me these, but I don't know what to do with them.'

Leah smiled with her eyes and stroked Falada's nose.

'You may see travelers on your way back to Dora's house. If they are barefooted, they have given broken or worn-out shoes for her to mend. You will see their bare feet and give them those tokens. Down the road *this* way . . .' She pointed away from the city. '. . . is a little store which is owned by Dora's younger brother. If travelers have those tokens, he will give them new shoes.'

I considered this. 'Dora repairs the broken ones.'

Leah nodded.

'Then the shoeless people go to her brother, the storekeeper.'

Leah nodded.

'When the broken shoes are renewed – like I hope to renew Radar – Dora takes them to her brother?'

Leah nodded.

'Does the brother sell them?'

Leah shook her head.

'Why not? Stores usually make a profit.'

'There is more to life than profit,' Falada said. 'My mistress is very tired and must rest now.'

Leah took my hand and squeezed it. I don't need to tell you how that made me feel.

She released it and clapped a single time. Falada ambled away. One of the gray farmhands came out of the barn and slapped the horse lightly on the flank. She walked toward the barn willingly enough, the gray man walking beside her.

When I looked around, the woman who'd brought the puree and the lemonade was there. She nodded to me and gestured toward the house and the road beyond. The audience – that's what it had been, I had no doubt – was over.

'Goodbye, and thank you,' I said.

Leah made the namaste gesture, then lowered her head and clasped her hands on her apron. The maid (or perhaps she was a lady-in-waiting) walked with me to the road, her long gray dress brushing the ground.

'Can you speak?' I asked her.

'Little.' It was a dusty croak. 'Hurts.'

We reached the thoroughfare. I pointed back the way I had come. 'How far to the brick house of her uncle? Do you know?'

She raised a misshapen gray finger.

'A day?'

She nodded – the most common form of communication here, I was learning. For those not able to practice ventriloquism, that was.

A day to get to the uncle. If it was twenty miles, it might be one day more to the city, more likely two. Or even three. Counting the return to the underground corridor leading to the well, maybe six days in all, and that was assuming all went okay. By then my father would be back and would have reported me missing.

He'd be scared, and he might drink. I'd be gambling my father's sobriety against the life of a dog . . . and even if the magic sundial existed, who knew if it would work on an elderly German Shepherd? I realized – you'll say I should have before – that what I was thinking of doing wasn't just crazy, it was selfish. If I went back now, no one would be the wiser. Of course I would have to break out of the shed if Andy had locked it, but I thought I was strong enough to do that. I'd been one of the few players on the Hillview squad who had been able to not just hit a tackling dummy and drive it back a foot or two but knock it over. And there was something else: I was homesick. I had only been gone a few hours, but with the day draining to an end in this sad, overcast land where the only real color was the great fields of poppies . . . yes, I was homesick.

I decided to take Radar and go back. Rethink my options. Try to make a better plan, one where I could be gone for a week or even two without anyone worrying. I had no idea what such a plan would be, and I think I knew deep down (in that dark little closet where we try to keep secrets from ourselves) that I would keep putting it off until Radar died, but that was what I meant to do.

Until, that was, the gray maid took me by the elbow. So far as I could tell from what remained of her face, she was scared to do that, but her grip was firm nonetheless. She pulled me toward her, stood on tiptoe, and whispered to me in her painful croak.

'Help her.'

3

I walked slowly back to Dora's House of Shoes, hardly aware of the declining daylight. I was thinking of how Leah (at that point still thinking of her as Leia) had opened the blemish beside what had been her mouth. How it had bled, how it must have hurt, but doing it because the pureed gluck was all she could take in to stay alive.

When had she last had an ear of corn, or a stalk of celery, or a bowl of Dora's tasty rabbit stew? Had she been mouthless when Radar was a puppy, gamboling around a much younger Falada? Was the beauty that existed in spite of what had to be extreme malnourishment a kind of cruel joke? Was she cursed to look well and healthy in spite of what must be constant hunger?

Help her.

Was there a way to do that? In a fairy tale there would be. I remembered my mother reading me the story of Rapunzel when I couldn't have been more than five. The memory was vivid because of the story's ending: terrible cruelty reversed by love. A wicked witch punished the prince who rescued Rapunzel by blinding him. I vividly remembered a picture of the poor guy wandering in the dark forest with his arms outstretched to feel for obstacles. Finally he was reunited with Rapunzel, and her tears restored his sight. Was there a way I could restore Leah's mouth? Probably not by crying on it, true, but maybe there was something I *could* do; in a world where riding a big sundial backward could peel away the years, anything might be possible.

Besides, show me a healthy teenage boy who doesn't want to be the hero of the story, one who helps the beautiful girl, and I'll show you no one at all. As for the possibility that my father might start drinking again, there was something Lindy told me once: 'You can't take credit for sobering him up, because he did that. And if he starts drinking again, you can't take the blame, because he'd do that, too.'

I was looking down at my shoes and deep in these thoughts when I heard the squeak of wheels. I looked up and saw a small, ramshackle cart coming my way, pulled by a horse so old he made Falada look like the picture of health and youth. There were a few bundles in it, with a chicken squatting on top of the biggest. Walking beside it – *trudging* beside it – were a young man and a young woman. They were gray, but not as gray as Leah's farmhands and maid. If that slate color was a sign of sickness, these people were still in the early stages . . . and, of course, Leah hadn't been gray at all, just mouthless. It was another mystery.

The young man pulled on the horse's reins and stopped him. The couple looked at me with a mixture of fear and hope. I could read their expressions easily enough, because their faces were mostly there. The woman's eyes had begun to draw up, but they were a long way from becoming the slits through which Dora observed the world. The man was worse; if not for the way his nose appeared to be melting, he might have been handsome.

'Ho,' he said. 'Are we well met? If not, have what you would take. You have a weapon, I have none, and I'm too tired and heartsore to fight you.'

'I'm no robber,' I said. 'Just a traveler, like you.'

The woman was wearing short lace-up boots that looked dusty but whole. The man's feet were bare. And dirty.

'Are you the one the lady with the dog told us we might meet?'

'That would be me, I guess.'

'Have you a token? She said you would, for I gave her the boots I was wearing. They were my father's, and falling to pieces.'

'You won't hurt us, will you?' the young woman asked. But her voice was that of an old woman. Not yet a growl like Dora's, but getting there.

These people are cursed, I thought. *All of them. And it's a* slow *curse. Which might be the worst kind.*

'I won't.' I took one of the small leather shoe-tokens from my pocket and gave it to the young man. He tucked it in his own pocket.

'He'll give my man shoes?' the woman asked in her growly voice.

I answered that question carefully, as befitted a boy whose father worked in the insurance biz. 'That was the deal as I understood it.'

'We must get on,' her husband – if that's what he was – said. His voice was a little better, but where I came from nobody would have given him a job as a TV announcer or audiobook reader. 'We thank you.'

From the woods on the far side of the road, a howl arose. It climbed until it was almost a shriek. It was a terrible sound, and the woman shrank against the man.

'Must get on,' he said again. 'Wolfies.'

'Where will you stay?'

'The lady with the dog showed us a picture-board and drew what we think was a house and barn. Have you seen it?'

'Yes, and I'm sure they'll take you in. But hurry, and I'll do the same. I don't think being on the road after dark would be . . .' *Would be cool* was what I thought, but I couldn't say it. 'It wouldn't be wise.'

No, because if wolfies came, these two had no house of straw or twigs to hide in, let alone one of bricks. They were strangers in the land. I at least had a friend. 'Go on, now. I think you'll get new shoes tomorrow. There's a store, or so I was told. The man will give you shoes if you show him your . . . you know . . . your token. I want to ask you a question, if I may.'

They waited.

'What is this land? What do you call it?'

They looked at me as if I had a screw loose – a phrase I probably wouldn't be able to say – and then the man replied. 'Tis Empis.'

'Thank you.'

They went their way. I went mine, picking up the pace until I was nearly jogging. I heard no more howls, but the gloom of twilight was thick by the time I saw the welcome window-glow of Dora's cottage. She had also placed a lamp at the foot of her steps.

A shadow moved toward me in the dark and I dropped my hand to the butt of Mr Bowditch's .45. The shadow solidified and became Radar. I dropped to one knee so she wouldn't stress those bad back legs of hers by trying to jump up. Which she was clearly preparing to do. I grabbed her around the neck and pulled her head against my chest.

'Hey, girl – how are you doing?'

Her tail was wagging so hard that her butt swung back and forth like a pendulum, and was I going to let her die if I could do something about it? Bullshit I was.

Help her, Leah's maid had said, and there on the darkening road, I made up my mind to help them both – the old dog and the goose girl princess.

If I could.

Radar broke away, went to the poppy-field side of the road, and squatted. 'Good idea,' I said, and unzipped my fly. I kept one hand on the butt of the revolver while I did my thing.

4

Dora had made up a bed for me near the fireplace. There was even a pillow with colorful butterflies on the case. I thanked her, and she dropped me a curtsey. I was amazed to see that her red shoes (like those worn by Dorothy in Oz) had been replaced by a pair of yellow Converse sneakers.

'Did Mr Bowditch give you those?'

She nodded and looked down at them with her version of a smile.

'Are they your for-best?' It seemed to me they must be, because they were spandy-clean, as if they'd just come out of the box.

She nodded, pointed at me, then pointed at the sneakers: *I wore them for you.*

'Thank you, Dora.'

Her eyebrows appeared to be melting into her forehead, but she raised what was left of them and pointed in the direction I'd come from. '*Zee*?'

'I don't get you.'

She turned to her workshop and got her little chalkboard. She erased the squares indicating the house and barn she must have showed the young man and woman, then printed in big capital letters: LEAH. She considered this, thinking, then added:?

'Yes,' I said. 'The goose girl. I saw her. Thank you for letting us stay the night. Tomorrow we'll be on our way.'

She patted her chest above her heart, pointed to Radar, pointed to me, then raised her hands in an encompassing gesture. *My house is your house.*

5

We had more stew, this time accompanied by chunks of rough bread. Rough, but delicious. We ate by candlelight, and Radar got her share. Before I let her have it, I took the bottle of pills from my backpack and sank two of them in the gravy. Then, thinking about how far we had to go, I put in a third one. I couldn't get over the idea that when I was giving them to her, I was robbing Peter to pay Paul.

Dora pointed to them and cocked her head.

'They're supposed to help her. We've got a long way to go, and she's not as strong as she used to be. She thinks she is, but she isn't. When they're gone, I guess—'

Another of those drawn-out howls came from the far side of the road. It was joined by another, then a third. They were incredibly loud, rising to screams that made me want to grit my teeth. Radar raised her head but didn't bark, just uttered a faint growl that came from deep in her chest.

'Wolfies,' I said.

Dora nodded, crossed her arms over her bosom, and gripped her shoulders. She gave an exaggerated shiver.

More wolves joined in. If they kept that up all night, I didn't think I'd be getting much rest before beginning my journey. I don't know if Dora read my mind or it just seemed that way. In either case, she rose and motioned me to come to the round window. She pointed skyward. She was short and didn't have to bend to look up, but I did. What I saw was another shock to my system in a day that had been a steady parade of them.

The clouds had parted in a long rift. In the river of sky that was revealed I could see two moons, one bigger than the other. They seemed to race through the void. The big one was *very* big. I didn't need a telescope to see the craters, valleys, and canyons on its ancient surface. It looked ready to fall on us. Then the rift closed. The wolves stopped howling, and I mean immediately. It was as if they had been broadcasting through a giant amplifier and someone had pulled the plug.

'Does that happen every night?'

She shook her head, spread her hands, then pointed to the clouds. She was good at communicating with her gestures and the few words she could write, but that one escaped me.

6

The only door in the cottage that didn't lead to the back or front was low and Dora-sized. After she had cleaned up our little supper (shooing me away when I tried to help), she went in this door and came out five minutes later wearing a nightgown that reached to her bare feet and a kerchief on what remained of her hair. The sneakers were in one hand. She put them carefully – reverently – on a shelf at the head of her bed. There was something else there, and when I asked for a closer look, she held it out to me, obviously reluctant to hand it over. It was a small framed photograph of Mr Bowditch, holding a puppy who was obviously Radar. Dora held it to her bosom, patted it, then put it back near the sneakers.

She pointed to the little door, then at me. I took my toothbrush and went in. I haven't seen many privies except in books and a few old movies, but I guessed that even if I'd seen a lot, this one would have been the neatest. There was a tin basin of fresh water and a toilet with a closed wooden lid. There were poppies in a wall vase, giving off their sweet smell of cherries. There was no smell of human waste. Zero.

I washed my hands and face and dried with a small towel embroidered with more butterflies. I dry-brushed my teeth. I was only in the privy for five minutes at most, maybe even not that long, but Dora was fast asleep in her little bed when I came out. Radar was sleeping beside her.

I lay on my own makeshift bed, which was a thickness of blankets and a neatly folded one to pull up over me. Which I didn't need right then, because the embers in the fireplace were still putting out good heat. Looking at them as they waxed and waned was hypnotic. The wolves were quiet with no moonlight to crazy them up, but a little wind was playing around the eaves, the sound sometimes rising to a low cry when it gusted, and it was impossible for me not to think of how far I was from my world. Oh, I could reach it again with just a short walk up the hill, a mile down the buried corridor, and a hundred and eighty-five spiral steps to the top of the well, but that wasn't the true measure. This was the other land. It was Empis, where not one but two moons raced across the sky. I thought of that book cover, the one showing a funnel filling up with stars.

Not stars, I thought. *Stories. An endless number of stories that pour into the funnel and come out in our world, barely changed.*

Then I thought of Mrs Wilcoxen, my third-grade teacher, who ended each day by saying, *What have we learned today, boys and girls?*

What had *I* learned? That this was a place of magic operating under a curse. That the people who lived here were suffering some sort of progressive sickness or disease. I thought I understood now why Dora's sign – the one Mr Bowditch had printed for her – only needed the shoe poem on the side that faced the abandoned city. It was because people came from that direction. How many I didn't know, but the blank side of the sign suggested that few if any came back. If I assumed the cloud-obscured blob of sun was setting in the west, then the young man and woman I'd met (plus all the rest of the people in the shoe-exchange program Dora and her brother were running) were coming from the north. *Evacuating* from the north? Was it a rolling curse, maybe even some kind of radiation originating in the city? I didn't have nearly enough information to be sure of that, or even half-sure, but it was an unpleasant thought just the same, because that was the way I was planning to go with Rades. Would my skin begin to turn gray? Would my voice begin dropping in register toward the growl of Dora, and Leah's lady-in-waiting? There had been nothing wrong with Mr Bowditch's skin and voice, but maybe this part of Empis had been okay, or mostly okay, when he was last here.

Maybe this, maybe that. I supposed if I started to see changes in myself, I could turn around and beat feet.

Help her.

That was what the gray maid had whispered to me. I thought I knew a way to help Radar, but how was I supposed to help a princess with no mouth? In a story, the prince would find a way to do that. It would probably be something unlikely, like Rapunzel's tears turning out to have magical sight-restoring properties, but palatable to readers who wanted a happy ending even if the teller had to pull one out of his hat. I wasn't a prince anyway, just a high school kid who had found his way into some other reality, and I had no ideas.

The embers were their own magic, waxing when the wind swirled down the chimney, waning when the gusts died. Looking at them, my eyelids seemed to gain weight. I slept, and at some point in the night, Radar crossed the room and lay down beside me. In the morning the fire was out, but the side of me she was lying against was warm.

CHAPTER FIFTEEN

Leaving Dora. Refugees.

Peterkin. Woody.

1

Breakfast was scrambled eggs – goose eggs, by their size – and chunks of bread toasted over a new fire. There was no butter, but there was wonderful strawberry jam. When the meal was finished, I cinched up my pack and put it on. I clipped Radar's leash to her collar. I didn't want her chasing any giant rabbits into the woods and meeting this world's version of a *Game of Thrones* direwolf.

'I'll come back,' I told Dora, with more confidence than I felt. I almost added *And Radar will be young again when I do*, but thought that might jinx the deal. Also, I still found the idea of magical regeneration easy to hope for but harder to believe, even in Empis.

'I think I can stay at Leah's uncle's house tonight – assuming he's not allergic to dogs, or something – but I'd like to be there before dark.' Thinking (it was hard not to) *wolfies*.

She nodded, but took my elbow and led me out the back door. The lines still crisscrossed the yard but the shoes, slippers, and boots had been taken in, presumably so they wouldn't get dampened by the morning dew (which I hoped wasn't radioactive). We went around the side of the cottage and there was the little cart I'd seen before. The sacks with the greenery poking out of the tops had been replaced by a package wrapped in burlap and tied with twine. Dora pointed at it, then at my mouth. She held a hand in front of her own mouth and opened and closed her partially melted fingers in a chewing gesture. It didn't take a rocket scientist to figure that one out.

'Jeez, no! I can't take your food and I can't take your cart! Isn't that how you take the shoes you mend to your brother's store?'

She pointed to Radar and made a number of limping steps, first toward the cart and then back to me. Then she pointed south (if I was right about my directions, that was) and walked her fingers in the air. The first part was easy. She was telling me that the cart was for Radar, once she started to limp. I thought she was also telling me someone – probably her brother – would come for the shoes.

Dora pointed to the cart, then made a little gray fist and hit me lightly in the chest three times: *You must.*

I saw her point; I had an elderly dog to care for and a long way to go. At the same time, I hated to take any more from her than I already had. 'Are you sure?'

She nodded. Then she held out her arms for a hug, which I was happy to give. She then dropped to her knees and hugged Radar. When she stood up again, she pointed first to the road, then to the crisscrossing lines, then to herself.

Get going. I have work to do.

I made my own gesture, two thumbs up, then went to the cart and tossed my knapsack in with the supplies she'd packed . . . which, based on what I'd eaten in the cottage so far, would probably be far more tasty than Mr Bowditch's sardines. I picked up the long handles and was delighted to find the cart weighed almost nothing, as if it had been made of this world's version of balsa wood. For all I knew, it was. Also, the wheels were well greased and didn't squeak, as the wheels of the young couple's cart had done. I thought pulling it would be hardly more difficult than pulling my little red wagon when I was seven.

I turned it around and walked to the road, ducking under more lines as I went. Radar padded along beside me. When I reached what I was then thinking of as the City Road (there wasn't a yellow brick in sight, so that name was out), I turned back. Dora was standing at the side of her cottage with her hands clasped between her breasts. When she saw me looking, she raised them to her mouth and then opened them toward me.

I dropped the handles of the cart long enough to copy her gesture, then set out on my way. Here is something I learned in Empis: good people shine brighter in dark times.

Help her, too, I thought. *Help Dora, too.*

2

We walked up hill and down dale, as one of those old stories might say. Crickets chirred and birds sang. The poppies on our left occasionally gave way to tilled fields where I saw gray men and women – not a lot – working. They saw me and stopped what they were doing until I went by. I waved, but only one of them, a woman wearing a big straw hat, waved back. There were other fields lying fallow and forgotten. Weeds sprouted among the growing vegetables, along with bright scarves of poppies, which I thought would eventually take over.

On the right, the woods continued. There were a few farmhouses, but most of them were deserted. Twice rabbits as big as small dogs hopped across the path. Radar looked at them with interest, but showed no inclination to chase them, so I unclipped her lead and tossed it in the cart. 'Don't disappoint me, girl.'

After an hour or so I stopped to untie the good-sized bundle of food Dora had packed for me. There were molasses cookies among the other goodies. No chocolate in those, so I gave one to Radar, who snarked it up. There were also three long glass jars wrapped in clean rags. Two were filled with water, and one contained what looked like tea. I drank some water and gave some to Radar in a pottery cup my friend had also packed. She lapped it up eagerly.

As I finished repacking, I saw three people trudging down the road toward me. The two men were just beginning to turn gray, but the woman walking between them was as dark as a summer thundercloud. One of her eyes was pulled up in a slit that stretched all the way to her temple, an awful thing to look at. Except for a single blue gleam of iris like a shard of sapphire, the other was buried in a lump of gray flesh. She was wearing a filthy dress that bulged out in what could only be a late-stage pregnancy. She held a bundle wrapped in a filthy blanket. One of the men was wearing a pair of boots with buckles on the sides – they reminded me of the one I'd seen hanging on a line in Dora's backyard when I made my first visit. The other man wore sandals. The woman's feet were bare.

They saw Radar sitting in the road and paused.

'Don't worry,' I called. 'She won't bite you.'

They came on slowly, then stopped again. It was the holstered gun they were looking at now, so I raised my hands, palms out. They began walking again, but shying way over to the left side of the road, looking at Radar, looking at me, then back to Radar again.

'We mean you no harm,' I said.

The men were skinny and tired-looking. The woman looked flat-out exhausted.

'Hold on a minute,' I said. In case they didn't understand me, I held up my hand in a policeman's stop gesture. 'Please.'

They stopped. It was a mighty sad-looking trio. Up close I could see that the men's mouths were beginning to turn up. Soon they would be crescents that hardly moved, like Dora's. They huddled next to the woman when I reached into my pocket and she pulled her bundle to her breasts. I got one of the little leather shoes and held it out to her.

'Take it. Please.'

She reached out hesitantly, then snatched it from my hand, as if she expected me to grab her. When she did, the blanket fell away from her bundle and I saw a dead baby, maybe a year or a year and a half old. It was as gray as the lid of my mother's coffin. Soon this poor woman would have another to replace it, and probably that one would die, too. If the woman didn't die first, that was, or during her labor.

'Do you understand me?'

'We understand,' said the man in the boots. His voice was grating but otherwise normal enough. 'What would you have with us, stranger, if not our lives? For we have nothing else.'

No, of course they didn't. If a person had done this – or caused it to be done – that person belonged in hell. The deepest pit thereof.

'I can't give you my cart or my food, for I have far to go and my dog is old. But if you walk another three . . .' I tried to say *miles*, but the word wouldn't come. I started again. 'If you walk until maybe midday, you'll see the sign of the red shoe. The lady who lives in that place will let you rest, and may give you food and drink.'

That wasn't exactly a promise (my dad was fond of pointing out what he called 'weasel words' in TV commercials for wonder drugs) and I knew Dora couldn't feed and water every group of refugees that passed her cottage. But I thought when she saw the state of the woman, and the horrific bundle she carried, that she would be moved to help these three. Meanwhile, the man in the sandals was examining the little leather shoe. He asked what it was for.

'Further on, past the woman I told you about, is a store where you can give that token for a pair of shoes.'

'Is there buryin'?' This was the man in boots. 'For my son needs a buryin'.'

'I don't know. I'm a stranger here. Ask at the sign of the red shoe, or at the farm of the goose girl farther on. Madam, I'm sorry for your loss.'

'He was a good boy,' she said, looking down at her dead child. 'My Tam was a good boy. He was fine when he was born, rosy as the dawn, but then the gray fell on him. Walk your way, sir, and we'll walk ours.'

'Wait a minute. Please.' I opened my pack, rummaged, and found two cans of King Oscar sardines. I held them out. They shied away from them. 'No, it's all right. It's food. Sardines. Little fish. You pull the ring in the top to get them, see?' I tapped it.

The two men looked at each other, then shook their heads. They wanted nothing to do with pull-top cans, it seemed, and the woman seemed to have disconnected from the conversation entirely.

'We need to get on,' said the one in the sandals. 'As for you, young man, you are going the wrong way.'

'It's the way I have to go,' I said.

He looked me straight in the eye and said, 'That way is death.'

They went on, trudging up dust from the City Road, the woman carrying her awful burden. Why did one of the men not take it from her? I was just a kid, but I thought I knew the answer to that. He was hers, her Tam, and his body was hers to carry for as long as she could carry it.

3

I felt stupid about not offering them the rest of the cookies, and selfish about keeping the cart. Until Radar fell behind, that was.

I was too deep in my own thoughts to notice when that happened, and you may be surprised (or not) to learn those thoughts had little to do with Sandal Man's doomish parting words. The idea that I could get killed going in the direction of the city came as no great surprise to me; Mr Bowditch, Dora, and Leah had all made that clear in their various ways. But when you're a kid it's easy to believe that you will be the exception, the one who wins through and gets the laurels. After all, who had scored the winning touchdown in the Turkey Bowl? Who had disarmed Christopher Polley? I was at an age when it's possible to believe that fast reflexes and reasonable care can surmount most obstacles.

I was thinking about the language we were speaking. What I heard wasn't exactly colloquial American English, but it wasn't archaic, either – there were no *thee*s and *thous* and *may't please yous*. Nor was it the *English* English of all those IMAX fantasy films, where all the hobbits and elves and wizards sound like Members of Parliament. It was the sort of English you'd expect to read in a slightly modernized fairy tale.

Then there was me.

I had said I couldn't give them my cart for I had far to go and my dog was old. If I'd been talking to someone in Sentry, I would have said *because I have a long way to go*. I had spoken of 'the sign of the red shoe' instead of saying *It's a little house with a shoe sign in front*. And I hadn't called the pregnant woman *ma'am*, as I would have in my hometown; I had called her *madam*, and it had come out of my mouth sounding perfectly okay. I thought again of the funnel filling with stars. I thought I was one of those stars now.

I thought I was becoming part of the story.

I looked for Radar and she wasn't there, which gave me a nasty jolt. I lowered the poles of the wagon to the road and looked behind me. She was twenty yards back, limping along as fast as she could with her tongue lolling from the side of her mouth.

'Jesus, girl, I'm sorry!'

I carried her to the cart, making sure to lace my hands under her belly and stay away from those painful back legs. I gave her another drink from her cup, tilting it so she could get as much as she wanted, then scratched behind her ears.

'Why didn't you say something?'

Well, duh. It wasn't that kind of fairy tale.

4

We walked on, hill and dale, dale and hill. We saw more refugees. Some shrank away, but two men walking together stopped and stood on their toes to peer into the cart and see what was there. Radar growled at them, but given her patchy fur and white muzzle, I doubt if she scared them much. The gun on my hip was different. They had shoes, so I didn't give out my last token. I don't think I would have suggested they stop at Dora's even if they'd been barefoot. I didn't give them any of my food, either. There were fields they could forage in if they were hungry enough.

'If it's Seafront you're going for, turn around, boy. The gray's come there, too.'

'Thanks for the . . .' *Info* wouldn't come out. 'Thanks for telling me.' I picked up the cart's poles but kept an eye on them to make sure they kept going.

Around noon we came to a marshy place that had overspread the road and turned it muddy. I bent my back and pulled the cart faster until we were through it, not wanting to get stuck. The cart wasn't much heavier with Radar onboard, which told me more than I really wanted to know.

Once we were back on dry ground again, I pulled over in the shade of what looked like one of the oaks in Cavanaugh Park. There was fried rabbit meat in one of the little bundles Dora had packed and I shared it even-Steven with Radar . . . or tried to. She ate two chunks but dropped the third between her front paws and looked at me apologetically. Even in the shade I could see that her eyes were growing rheumy again. It crossed my mind that she had caught whatever was going around – the gray – but I rejected the idea. It was age, pure and simple. It was hard to tell how much time she had left, but I didn't think it was a lot.

While we ate, more giant-sized rabbits went lolloping across the road. Then a couple of crickets that were about double the size of the ones I was used to, hopping nimbly along on their back legs. I was amazed at how much air they could get between jumps. A hawk – normal-sized – swooped down and tried to grab one of them, but the cricket took evasive action and was soon out of sight in the grass and weeds that bordered the forest. Radar watched this parade of wildlife with interest but without getting to her feet, let alone giving chase.

I drank some of the tea, which was sugary and delicious. I had to stop myself after a few swallows. God knew when there might be more.

'Come on, girl. Want to get to the uncle's. The idea of camping out near those woods doesn't thrill me.'

I picked her up, then paused. Written on the oak in fading red paint were two letters: **AB**. Knowing Mr Bowditch had been here before me made me feel better. It was as if he wasn't entirely gone.

5

Mid-afternoon. The day was warm enough for me to have worked up a good sweat. We hadn't seen any refugees for awhile, but as we reached the foot of a rise – long, but with a slope too mild to actually be called a hill – I heard scrambling from behind me. Radar had come to the front of the cart. She was sitting with her paws on the front and her ears up. I stopped and heard something ahead that might have been faint chuffing laughter. I started forward again but stopped short of the crest, listening.

'How do you like that, sweetie? Does it tickle?'

It was a high, fluting voice that cracked on *sweetie* and *tickle*. Otherwise it was weirdly familiar, and after a moment I realized why. It sounded like Christopher Polley. I knew it couldn't be, but it sure did.

I started forward again, stopping as soon as I could see into the dip on the other side of the rise. I had seen some strange things in this other world, but nothing so strange as a child sitting in the dust with a hand clamped around the back legs of a cricket. It was the biggest I'd seen so far, and red instead of black. In his other hand the child held what looked like a dagger with a short blade and a cracked haft held together with string.

He was too absorbed in what he was doing to see us. He stuck the cricket in its belly, producing a tiny spurt of blood. Until then I didn't know crickets *could* bleed. There were other droplets in the dirt, which suggested the kid had been at this nasty business for some time.

'Like that, honey?' The cricket lunged, but with its back legs hobbled, the kid pulled it back easily. 'How about a little in your—'

Radar barked. The kid looked around, not losing his hold on the big cricket's back legs, and I saw he wasn't a kid but a dwarf. And old. White hair straggled down his cheeks in clumps. His face was lined, the ones bracketing his mouth so deep that he looked like the kind of ventriloquist's dummy Leah could have used (if she wasn't pretending her horse could talk, that was). His face wasn't doing that melting thing, but his skin was the color of clay. And he still reminded me of Polley, partly because he was small but mostly because of the slyness in his face. Given that sly look added to what he was doing, I could easily imagine him capable of murdering a limping old jeweler.

'Who are you?' No fear, because I was at some distance and silhouetted against the sky. He hadn't seen the gun yet.

'What are you doing?'

'I caught this fella. It was quick, but old Peterkin was quicker. I'm trying to see if it feels pain. God knows I do.'

He prinked the cricket again, this time between two plates of its carapace. The red cricket bled and struggled. I started pulling the cart down the hill. Radar gave another bark. She was still standing with her legs braced on the board at its front.

'Curb your dog, sonny. I would, if I was you. If she comes a-near me, I'll cut her throat.'

I set down the poles and drew Mr Bowditch's .45 from the holster for the first time. 'You won't cut her or me. Stop doing that. Let it go.'

The dwarf – Peterkin – regarded the gun with puzzlement rather than fright. 'Now why would you want me to do that? I'm only having a little fun in a world where there's hardly any left.'

'You're torturing it.'

Peterkin looked amazed. 'Torture, you say? *Torture?* Oh you idiot, it's a damn *inseck*. You can't torture an inseck! And why would you care?'

I cared because watching him hold the thing's jumping legs, its only means of escape, while he poked it again and again, was ugly and cruel.

'I won't tell you twice.'

He laughed, and he even *sounded* a little like Polley, with his ha-ha interjections. 'Shoot me over an *inseck*? I don't think s—'

I aimed high and to the left and pulled the trigger. The report was much louder than it had been from inside Mr Bowditch's shed. Radar barked. The dwarf jerked in surprise and let go of the cricket. It hopped away into the grass, but crookedly. The damned little man had lamed it. Only an inseck, but that didn't make what this Peterkin had been doing right. And how many red crickets had I seen? Only this one. They were probably as rare as albino deer.

The dwarf got up and dusted off the seat of his bright green britches. He swept the ragged clumps of his white hair back like a concert pianist getting ready to play his big number. Leaden skin or no leaden skin, he seemed lively enough. Lively as a cricket, so to speak. And while he'd never sing on *American Idol*, he had a lot more voice than most people I'd met in the last twenty-four hours, and his face was all present and accounted for. Other than being a dwarf ('Never call them midgets, they hate it,' my dad told me once) and having a shitty complexion that could have used a shot of Otezla, he seemed pretty much okay.

'I see that you are an irritable boy,' he said, looking at me with disgust, and maybe (I hoped so) just a trace of fear. 'So why don't I go my way and you go yours.'

'That sounds good, but I want to ask you something before we part company. How come your face is more or less normal, and so many other folks seem to be getting uglier all the time?'

Not that he was any poster-boy himself, and I'm sure the question was on the rude side, but if you can't be rude to a guy you catch torturing a giant cricket, who can you be rude to?

'Maybe because the gods, if you believe in them, already played a trick on me. How would a big fellow like you know what it's like to be a little fellow like me, not even two dozen hands from ground to crown?' A whining note had come into his voice, the tone of someone who had – in AA lingo – a ring around his ass from sitting on the pity-pot.

I put my thumb and finger together and rubbed. 'See this? It's the world's smallest violin playing "My Heart Pumps Purple Piss for You."' *Piss* came out perfectly, I noted.

He frowned. 'Eh?'

'Never mind. My little joke. Trying to *tickle* you.'

'I'll go on now, if you don't mind.'

'Do that, but my dog and I would feel better if you'd put that knife away before you do.'

'You think just because you're one of the whole ones, you're better than me,' the little man said. 'You'll see what they do to ones like you if they catch you.'

'Who will?'

'The night soldiers.'

'Who are they, and what do they do to ones like me?'

He sneered. 'Never mind. I just hope you can battle, but I doubt it. You look strong on the outside, but I think you're soft on the inside. That's the way folks are when they don't have to struggle. Haven't missed many meals, have you, young sir?'

'You're still holding the knife, Mr Peterkin. Put it away or I might decide to make you throw it away.'

The dwarf jammed the knife into his waistband, and I sort of hoped he'd give himself a cut doing it – the nastier the better. Which was a mean thought. Then I had a meaner one: suppose I reached out and grabbed the hand that had held the red cricket's legs together and snapped it, as I had Polley's? As sort of an object lesson: *this is what it feels like*. I could tell you it wasn't a serious thought, but I think it was. It was too easy to see him using a chokehold on Radar while he used his dagger on her: prink, prink, prink. He never could have done it when she was in her prime, but her prime had been years ago.

But I let him pass. He looked back once before he went over the rise, and that look didn't say *Well met on the City Road, young stranger.* That look said *Don't let me catch you sleeping.*

No chance of that, he was on his way to wherever the rest of the refugees were going, but it wasn't until after he was gone that it occurred to me that I really should have made him drop the knife and leave it behind.

6

By late afternoon there were no more tilled fields and no more farms that looked like they were working at all. There were no more refugees, either, although at one deserted farm I saw handcarts filled with possessions in the overgrown front yard and thin smoke rising from the chimney. Probably a party that had decided to get under cover before the wolfies began to howl, I thought. If I didn't come to the house of Leah's uncle soon, it would be wise of me to do the same. I had Mr Bowditch's revolver and Polley's .22 popgun, but wolves tended to travel in packs, and they could be as big as moose, for all I knew. Also, my arms, shoulders, and back were getting tired. The cart was light, and at least there had been no more mudholes to power through, but I'd pulled it a long way since leaving Dora's.

I saw Mr Bowditch's initials – his original initials, **AB** – three more times, twice on trees overhanging the road and the last time on a huge rock outcropping. By then the blob of sun had dropped behind the trees and shadows were engulfing the land. I hadn't seen any dwellings for some time, and I was starting to worry that full dark might catch us still on the road. I really didn't want that. As sophomores we had been tasked to memorize at least sixteen lines of a poem. Ms Debbins had given us two dozen poems to choose from. I had picked something from 'The Rime of the Ancient Mariner,' and wished now I had chosen anything else, because the lines were just too apt: *Like one, that on a lonesome road doth walk in fear and dread, and having once turned round walks on, and turns no more his head . . .*

'Because he knows, a frightful fiend doth close behind him tread,' I finished aloud. I put down the poles of the cart and rolled my shoulders while I looked at **AB** on the rock. Mr Bowditch had really knocked himself out on that one; the letters were three feet high. 'Rades, you'd bark to alert me if you saw a frightful fiend behind us, right?'

She was fast asleep in the cart. No help from frightful fiends there.

I thought about getting a drink of water – I was pretty dry – and decided it could wait. I wanted to push on while there was still some daylight left. I picked up the poles and got walking, thinking that even a woodshed would look good at this point.

The road curved around the outcrop, then ran straight into the gathering twilight. And up ahead, surely no more than a mile, I could see the lighted windows of a house. As I drew closer I saw a lantern hanging from a post out front. I could just make out that the road forked sixty or seventy yards beyond the house, which was indeed made of brick . . . like that of the industrious little pig in the story.

A stone-flagged path led up to the front door, but before I used it I stopped to examine the lantern, which gave off a harsh white light that was hard to look at up close. I'd seen one like it before, in Mr Bowditch's basement, and didn't have to check the base to know it was a Coleman, available at any American hardware store. I guessed that the lantern, like Dora's sewing machine, had been a gift from Mr Bowditch. *A coward gives presents*, he'd said.

In the center of the door was a gilded knocker in the shape of a fist. I lowered the cart and heard a scrabbling as Radar made her way down its sloping floor to join me. I was reaching for the knocker when the door opened. Standing there was a man almost as tall as I was, but much thinner, almost gaunt. Because he was backlit by a blaze in the fireplace, I couldn't make out his features, just the cat on his shoulder and a fine gauze of white hair standing up around his otherwise bald head. When he spoke, it was again hard to believe that I hadn't stepped into a storybook and become one of the characters.

'Hello, young prince. I've been expecting you. You are welcome here. Come in.'

7

I realized I'd left Radar's leash in the cart. 'Um, I think I should probably get my dog's lead first, sir. I don't know how she does with cats.'

'She'll be fine,' the old man said, 'but if you have food, I suggest you bring it in. If you don't want to find it gone in the morning, that is.'

I went back and got Dora's care package and my pack. Plus the leash, just in case. The man of the house stepped aside and made a little bow.

'Come on, Rades, but be good. I'm counting on you.'

Radar followed me into a neat sitting room with a rag rug on a hardwood floor. There were two easy chairs close to the fire. A book had been laid open on the arm of one. There were a few others on a shelf nearby. The other side of the room was a narrow little kitchen like a ship's galley. On the table there was bread, cheese, cold chicken, and a bowl of what I was quite sure was cranberry jelly. Also a pottery pitcher. My stomach made a loud rumbling sound.

The man laughed. 'I heard that. There's an old saying, youth must be served. To which might be appended, "and often."'

There were two places set, and a bowl on the floor by one of the chairs, from which Radar was already drinking noisily.

'You knew I was coming, didn't you? *How* did you know?'

'Do you know the name we prefer not to speak?'

I nodded. In stories like the one I seemed to have entered, there's often a name that must not be spoken, lest evil awake.

'He hasn't taken everything from us. You saw that my niece was able to speak to you, yes?'

'Through her horse.'

'Falada, yes. Leah also speaks to me, young prince, although rarely. When she does, her communications aren't always clear and throwing her thoughts tires her even more than throwing her voice. We have many things to discuss, but first we'll eat. Come.'

He's talking about telepathy, I thought. *It must be, because she surely didn't phone him or shoot him a text.*

'Why do you call me young prince?'

He shrugged. The cat bobbed on his shoulder. 'A form of familiar address, that's all. Very old-fashioned. Someday perhaps a real prince will come, but from the sound of your voice it isn't you. You're *very* young.'

He smiled and turned toward the galley. The firelight shone fully on his face for the first time, but I think I knew already, simply by the way he held out one hand before him as he walked, testing the air for obstacles. He was blind.

8

When he sat, the cat jumped to the floor. Its fur was a luxuriant smoky brown. It approached Radar, and I got ready to grab her collar if she lunged at it. She didn't, just lowered her head and sniffed at the cat's nose. Then she lay down. The cat paced in front of her like an officer inspecting a soldier on parade (and finding her sloppy), then sashayed to the living room. She jumped into the chair with the book on its arm and curled up.

'My name is Charles Reade. Charlie. Did Leah tell you that?'

'No, it doesn't work that way. It's more like having an intuition. It's nice to meet you, Prince Charlie.' Now that the light was on his face, I could see his eyes were as gone as Leah's mouth, with only long-healed scars to mark where they had been. 'My name is Stephen Woodleigh. I once had a title – prince regent, as a matter of fact – but those days are gone. Call me Woody, if you like, for we live near the woods, don't we? I and Catriona.'

'That's your cat?'

'Yes. And I believe your dog is . . . Raymar? Something like that, surely. I can't remember.'

'Radar. She was Mr Bowditch's. He died.'

'Ah. I'm sorry to hear that.' And he looked sorry, but not really surprised.

'How well did you know him, sir?'

'Woody. Please. We passed the time. As you and I will, Charlie, I hope. But we should eat first, because it's a long way you've come today, I think.'

'Can I ask one question first?'

He smiled broadly, turning his face into a river of wrinkles. 'If you want to know how old I am, I really can't remember. Sometimes I think I was old when the world was young.'

'It's not that. I saw the book and wondered . . . if you're, you know . . .'

'How I read if I'm blind? Have a look. Meanwhile, would you like a leg or a breast?'

'Breast, please.'

He began serving out, and must have been used to doing it in the dark for a long time, because there was no hesitation in his movements. I got up and went to his chair. Catriona looked up at me with wise green eyes. The book was an old one, with a cover showing bats flying against a full moon: *The Black Angel*, by Cornell Woolrich. It could have come from one of the stacks in Mr Bowditch's bedroom. Except when I picked it up and looked at where Woody had left off, I saw no words, only little groups of dots. I put it back and returned to the table.

'You read braille,' I said. Thinking, *the language in books must change, too – get translated. How weird is that?*

'I do. Adrian brought me a lesson book and showed me the letters. Once I had those, I was able to teach myself. He brought me other books in braille from time to time. He was partial to fanciful stories, like the one I was reading while I waited for your arrival. Dangerous men and damsels in distress living in a world far different from this one.'

He shook his head and laughed, as if reading fiction were a frivolous pursuit, maybe even crazy. His cheeks were rosy from having sat close to the fire, and I saw no trace of gray in them. He was whole, yet he wasn't. Neither was his niece. He had no eyes to see with and she had no mouth to speak with, only a sore she opened with her fingernail to take whatever poor nourishment she could. Talk about a damsel in distress.

'Come. Sit.'

I came to the table. Outside a wolf howled, so the moon – *moons* – must have appeared. But we were safe in this house of bricks. If a wolfie came down the chimney, it would roast its furry assie in the fire.

'This whole world seems fanciful to me,' I said.

'Stay here long enough and it will be yours that seems like make-believe. Now eat, Charlie.'

9

The food was delicious. I asked for seconds, then thirds. I felt sort of guilty about it, but it had been a long day and I'd pulled that cart eighteen or twenty miles. Woody ate sparingly, nothing but a drumstick and a little of the cranberry jelly. I felt more guilty when I saw that. I remembered my mother delivering me to a sleepover at Andy Chen's house and Mom telling Andy's mom that I had a hollow leg and would eat them out of house and home if she let me. I asked Woody where he got his supplies.

'Seafront. There are some there who still remember such as we . . . or such as we were . . . and pay tribute. The gray has come there now. People are leaving. You probably met some on the road.'

'I did,' I said, and told him about Peterkin.

'A red cricket, you say? There are legends . . . but never mind. Glad you put a stop to it. Maybe you're a prince after all. Blond hair, blue eyes?' He was teasing.

'Nope. Both brown.'

'So. Not a prince and certainly not *the* prince.'

'Who is *the* prince?'

'Just another legend. This is a world of stories and legends, as is yours. As for food . . . I used to get more viands than I could eat from the people of Seafront, although usually fish rather than meat. As you might expect from the name. It was a long time before the gray came to that part of the world – how long I can't say, the days blend together when one is always in the dark.' He said that without self-pity, just stating a fact. 'I believe Seafront may have been spared for awhile because they are on a narrow peninsula, where the wind always blows, but no one knows for sure. Last year, Charlie, you would have met scores of people on the King's Road. Now the flood is ebbing.'

'The King's Road? That's what you call it?'

'Yes, but once it passes the fork, it's Kingdom Road. If you were to choose to go left at the fork, you would be on Seafront Road.'

'Where are they going? I mean, after Dora's house, and Leah's farm, and the store Dora's brother keeps.'

Woody looked surprised. 'Does he still keep it? I'm amazed. What does he have to sell, I wonder?'

'I don't know. I just know he gives them new shoes to replace their broken ones.'

Woody laughed, delighted. 'Dora and James! Up to their old tricks! The answer to your question is I don't know, and I'm sure they don't. Just away. Away, away, away.'

The wolves had been silent, but now they began howling again. It sounded like dozens of them, and I was very glad I'd reached Woody's house of bricks when I had. Radar whined. I stroked her head. 'The moons must be out.'

'According to Adrian, there's only one in your make-believe kingdom. As one of the characters in Mr Cornell Woolrich's book says, "You was robbed." Would you like a slice of cake, Charlie? I fear you may find it a trifle stale.'

'Cake would be wonderful. Do you want me to get it?'

'Not at all. After all these years here – it's quite the cozy den for an exile, don't you think – I know my way around very well. It's on a shelf in the pantry. Sit still. I'll be back in two ticks.'

While he got the cake, I helped myself to more lemonade from the pitcher. Lemonade seemed to be the go-to drink in Empis. He brought a big piece of chocolate cake for me and a sliver for himself. It made the cake we got in the high school caff look pretty lame. I didn't think it was stale at all, just a little stiff around the edges.

The wolves abruptly quit, again making me think of someone pulling a plug on an amp that had been turned up to eleven. It occurred to me that no one in this world would get that reference to *Spinal Tap*. Or any other movie.

'I guess the clouds are back,' I said. 'They go away, right?'

He shook his head slowly. 'Not since *he* came. It rains here, Prince Charlie, but it almost never shines.'

'Jesus,' I said.

'Another prince,' Woody replied, once again with the broad smile. 'Of peace, according to the braille Bible Adrian brought me. Are you replete? That means—'

'I know what it means, and I sure am.'

He stood. 'Then come sit by the fire. We need to talk.'

I followed him to the two chairs in his little parlor. Radar followed. Woody felt for Catriona, found her, and picked her up. She lay over his hands like a fur stole until he set her on the floor. There she spared a haughty glance for my dog, gave a dismissive flick of her tail, and strolled away. Radar lay down between the two chairs. I had given her a share of my chicken, but she ate only a little of it. Now she looked into the fire as if deciphering its secrets. I thought about asking

Woody what he'd do for supplies now that the town of Seafront had joined the evacuation, but decided not to. I was afraid he'd tell me he had no idea.

'I want to thank you for the meal.'

He waved this away.

'You're probably wondering what I'm doing here.'

'Not at all.' He reached down and stroked Radar's back. Then he turned the scars that had been his eyes to me. 'Your dog is dying, and there's no time to waste if you intend to accomplish what you came for.'

10

Full of food, safe in the house of bricks with the wolves silent for the time being and the fireplace warming me, I had been relaxing. Feeling content. But when he said Rades was dying, I sat up straight. 'Not necessarily. She's old, and she's got arthritis in her hips, but she's not . . .'

I thought of the vet's assistant saying she'd be surprised if Radar lived until Halloween, and fell silent.

'I'm blind, but my other senses work quite well for an old fellow.' His voice was kind, and that made it dreadful. 'In fact, my ears have grown more acute than ever. I had horses and dogs in the palace, as a boy and young man I was always out with them and loved them all well. I know how they sound when they're rounding the final turn for home. Listen! Close your eyes and listen!'

I did as he said. I could hear an occasional pop from the fireplace. Somewhere a clock was ticking. A breeze had picked up outside. And I could hear Radar: the wheeze each time she inhaled, the rattle each time she exhaled.

'You came to put her on the sundial.'

'Yes. And there's gold. Little gold pellets, kind of like birdshot. I don't need that now, but Mr Bowditch said later on I—'

'Never mind the gold. Just getting to the sundial . . . and using it . . . is a mission dangerous enough for such a young prince as yourself. It risks Hana. She wasn't there in Bowditch's time. You may find your way past her if you're careful . . . and lucky. Luck can't be discounted in such a business. As for the gold . . .' He shook his head. 'That's riskier yet. It's good you don't need it now.'

Hana. I filed the name away for later. There was something else I was immediately curious about.

'Why are *you* all right? Except for being blind, I mean.' I wished I could take it back as soon as the words were out of my mouth. 'Sorry. That didn't come out right.'

He smiled. 'No apology necessary. Given a choice between being blind and having the gray, I'd choose blindness every time. I have adjusted quite well. Thanks to Adrian, I even have make-believe stories to read. The gray is slow death. It becomes harder and harder to breathe. The face is swallowed up by useless flesh. The body closes up.' He raised one of his hands and made a fist. 'Like this.'

'Will that happen to Dora?'

He nodded, but he didn't have to. It was a child's question.

'How long does she have?'

Woody shook his head. 'Impossible to say. It's slow, and not the same for everyone, but it's relentless. That's the horror of it.'

'What if she left? Went to wherever the others are going?'

'I don't think she'd go and I don't think it matters. Once it comes, there's no outrunning it. Like the wasting disease. Is that what killed Adrian?'

I assumed he was talking about cancer. 'No, he had a heart attack.'

'Ah. A little pain, then gone. Better than the gray. As to your question, once upon a time . . . Adrian said that's how many stories start in the world he came from.'

'Yeah. It is. And things I've seen over here are like those stories.'

'As are things where you came from, I'm sure. It's all stories, Prince Charlie.'

The wolves began to howl. Woody fingered his braille book, then closed it and put it on a small table beside his chair. I wondered how he would find his place again. Catriona returned, jumped into his lap, and began to purr.

'Once upon a time, in the land of Empis and the city of Lilimar, where you are bound, there was a royal family going back thousands of years. Most – not all, but most – ruled wisely and well. But when the terrible time came, almost all of that family were killed. Slaughtered.'

'Leah told me some of that. You know, through Falada. She said her mother and father were dead. They were the king and queen, right? Because she said she was a princess. The littlest of them all.'

He smiled. 'Yes indeed, the littlest of them all. She told you her sisters were slain?'

'Yes.'

'What of her brothers?'

'That they were killed, too.'

He sighed and stroked his cat and looked at the fire. I'm sure he could feel its heat, and I wondered if he could see it a little, too – the way you can look at the sun with your eyes closed and see redness as your blood lights up. He opened his mouth as if to say something, then closed it again and gave his head a little shake. The wolves sounded really close . . . then they stopped. The way that happened all at once was eerie.

'It was a purge. You know what that means?'

'Yes.'

'But some few of us survived. We escaped the city and Hana won't leave it because she's an outcast from her own land, far to the north. There were eight of us who made it through the main gate. We would have been nine, but my nephew Aloysius . . .' Woody gave his head another shake. 'Eight of us escaped death in the city, and our blood protects us from the gray, but another curse followed us. Can you guess?'

I could. 'Each of you lost one of your senses?'

'Yes. Leah can eat, but it's painful for her to do so, as you may have seen.'

I nodded, although he couldn't see it.

'She can hardly taste what she eats, and as you saw, she can't speak except through Falada. She's convinced that *he* is fooled by that, if he listens. I don't know. Maybe she's right. Maybe he hears and it amuses him.'

'When you say *he* . . .' I stopped there.

Woody grasped my shirt and pulled. I leaned toward him. He put his lips to my ear and whispered. I expected Gogmagog, but that wasn't what he said. What he said was *Flight Killer*.

11

'He could send assassins against us, but he doesn't. He lets us live, those of us who remain, and living is punishment enough. Aloysius, as I said, never made it out of the city. Ellen, Warner, and Greta have taken their lives. I believe Yolande still lives, but she wanders, insane. Like me, she's blind, living for the most part on the kindness of strangers. I feed her when she comes and agree with the gibberish she speaks. These are nieces, nephews, and cousins, you understand – the close blood. Do you follow?'

'Yes.' I did, more or less.

'Burton has become an anchorite, living deep in the woods and constantly praying for Empis's deliverance with hands he can't feel when he presses them together. He can't feel wounds unless he sees blood. He eats, but he has no sense of whether his stomach is full or empty.'

'My God,' I said. I had thought being blind must be the worst, but it wasn't.

'The wolves leave Burton alone. At least they did. It's been two years or more since he came here. He may be dead, too. My little party left in a farrier's wagon, with me, not yet blind as you see me now, standing up and snapping a whip over a team of six horses that were crazed with fear. With me were my cousin Claudia, my nephew Aloysius, and my niece Leah. We flew like the wind, Charlie, the wagon's ironbound wheels striking up sparks from the cobblestones and actually flying in the air for ten feet or more from the top of the Rumpa Bridge. I thought the wagon might turn over or break apart when we came down, but it was sturdy-made and held together. We could hear Hana roaring from behind us, roaring like a storm, coming ever closer. I can still hear those roars. I lashed the horses and they ran as if hell was after them . . . as it was. Aloysius looked back just before we reached the gate, and Hana swatted his head from his shoulders. I didn't see that, all my attention was fixed ahead, but Claudia saw. Leah didn't, thank God. She was wrapped in a blanket. The next swipe of Hana's hand tore off the back of the wagon. I could smell her breath, can smell it still. Rotted fish and meat and the reek of her sweat. We got through the gate just in time. She roared when she saw we had escaped her. The hate and frustration in that sound! Yes, I hear it still.'

He stopped and wiped his mouth. His hand shook when he did it. I had never seen PTSD outside of movies like *The Hurt Locker*, but I was seeing it now. I don't know how long ago all that had happened, but the horror was still with him and still fresh. I didn't like being responsible for making him remember that time and speak of it, but I needed to know what I was getting into.

'Charlie, if you go into my pantry, you'll find a bottle of blackberry wine in the cold cupboard. I would like a small glass, if you don't mind. Have one yourself, if you'd like.'

I found the bottle and poured him a glass. The smell of fermented blackberries was strong enough to kill any desire I might have had to pour my own glass even without the healthy wariness I had for alcohol on account of my father, so I helped myself to some more lemonade instead.

He drank two big swallows, most of what was in the glass, and heaved a sigh. 'That's better. These memories are sad and painful. It's growing late and you must be tired, so it's time to talk about what you must do to save your friend. If you still intend to go ahead, that is.'

'I do.'

'You'd risk your life and sanity for the dog?'

'She's all I have left of Mr Bowditch.' I hesitated, then gave him the rest of it. 'And I love her.'

'Very well. I understand love. Here is what you must do. Listen carefully. Another day's walk will take you to the house of my cousin Claudia. If you move along briskly, that is. When you get there . . .'

I listened carefully. As if my life depended on it. The wolves howling outside suggested very strongly that it did.

12

Woody's toilet was an outhouse, connected to his bedroom by a short board passage. As I walked that passage, holding a lantern (the old-fashioned kind, not a Coleman), something hit the wall with a hard thump. Something hungry, I assumed. I dry-brushed my teeth and used the facility. I hoped Rades could hold her water until morning, because no way was I going to take her out until then.

I didn't have to sleep by the fire here, because there was a second bedroom. The small bed had a frilly coverlet embroidered with butterflies that just about had to be Dora's work, and the walls were painted pink. Woody told me that both Leah and Claudia had used it on occasion, Leah not for many years.

'Here they are as they were,' he said. He reached out carefully and took a small oval painting in a gilt frame from a shelf. I saw a teenage girl and a young woman. Both were gorgeous. They stood with their arms around each other in front of a fountain. They wore pretty dresses and bits of lace over their dressed hair. Leah had a mouth to smile with, and yes, they looked like royalty.

I pointed to the girl. 'This was Leah? Before . . .?'

'Yes.' Woody put the picture back in its place just as carefully. 'Before. What happened to us happened not too long after we fled the city. An act of pure, spiteful vengeance. They were beautiful, wouldn't you say?'

'I would.' I kept looking at the smiling younger girl and thought that Leah's curse was twice as terrible as Woody's blindness.

'Whose vengeance?'

He shook his head. 'I don't want to talk of it. I only wish I could see that picture again. But wishes are like beauty – vain things. Sleep well, Charlie. You must be on your way early if you are to reach Claudia's before sundown tomorrow. She may tell you more. And if you wake in the night – or if your dog wakes you – *don't go out*. Not for anything.'

'I totally understand that.'

'Good. I'm delighted to have made your acquaintance, young prince. Any friend of Adrian's is, as they say, a friend of mine.'

He left, walking confidently but with one hand held out before him, as must have been second nature to him after all the years he'd spent in darkness. How many had that been, I wondered. How long since the rise of Gogmagog and the purge that had decimated his family? Who or what was Flight Killer? How long since Leah had been a girl with a smiling mouth who took eating for granted? Were the years even the same here?

Stephen Woodleigh was Woody . . . like the cowboy in *Toy Story*. That was probably just a coincidence, but I didn't think the wolves and the house of bricks were. Then there was that thing he'd said about the Rumpa Bridge. My mother had died on the bridge over the Little Rumple, and a Rumpelstiltskin kind of guy had almost killed me. Was I supposed to believe *those* things coincidences?

Radar was sleeping beside my bed, and now that Woody had called my attention to the rattle and wheeze of her breathing, I couldn't unhear it. I thought either that or the sporadic howling of the wolves would keep me awake. But I had come a long way, and pulling a cart behind me. I didn't last long, I had no dreams, and didn't come to until early the next morning with Woody shaking my shoulder.

'Wake up, Charlie. I've made us breakfast, and you must be on your way as soon as you've eaten.'

13

There was a bowl heaped with scrambled eggs and a bowl similarly heaped with smoking sausages. Woody ate a little, Radar ate a little, and I took care of the rest myself.

'I've put your possessions in Dora's cart, and added something you'll want to show my cousin when you get to her house. So she knows you've come from me.'

'I guess she's not prone to intuitions, huh?'

He smiled. 'She is, actually, and I've done my best in that regard, but it's not wise to rely on such communications. It's something you may want later on, if your mission is successful and you're able to return to your own fairy-tale world.'

'What is it?'

'Look in your packsack and you'll see.' He smiled, reached out for me, and took me by my shoulders. 'You may not be *the* prince, Charlie, but you're a brave boy.'

'Someday my prince will come,' I half-sang.

He smiled; the wrinkles on his face flowed. 'Adrian knew that same song. He said it was from a moving picture that told a story.'

'Snow White and the Seven Dwarves.'

Woody nodded. 'He also said the real story was much darker.'

Aren't they all, I thought.

'Thank you for everything. Take care of yourself. And Catriona.'

'We take care of each other. Do you remember all I told you?'

'I think so, yes.'

'Most important?'

'Follow Mr Bowditch's marks, be quiet, and be out of the city before dark. Because of the night soldiers.'

'Do you believe what I told you about them, Charlie? You must, because otherwise you might be tempted to stay too long, if you haven't reached the sundial.'

'You told me Hana is a giant and the night soldiers are the undead.'

'Yes, but do you believe it?'

I thought of the big cockroaches and rabbits. I thought of a red cricket almost the size of Catriona. I thought of Dora with her disappearing face and Leah with a scar for a mouth.

'Yes,' I said. 'I believe it all.'

'Good. Remember to show Claudia what I put in your packsack.'

I hoisted Radar into the cart and opened my pack. On top, gleaming mellowly in the light of another cloudy day, was a gilt fist. I looked at the door to the brick house and saw the knocker was gone. I lifted it and was surprised by its weight.

'My God, Woody! Is this solid gold?'

'It is. In case you feel any temptation to push on past the sundial and into the treasury, remember you have this to add to whatever Adrian may have gleaned in the palace on his last visit. Fare you well, Prince Charlie. I hope you don't need to use Adrian's weapon, but if you have to, don't hesitate.'

CHAPTER SIXTEEN

Kingdom Road. Claudia. Instructions.

The Noisemaker. The Monarchs.

1

Radar and I approached the fork, which was marked by a signpost that pointed to Kingdom Road on the right. The one marking the Seafront Road had come loose and pointed straight down, as if Seafront resided underground. Radar gave a rusty bark, and I saw a man and a boy coming from the Seafront direction. The man was hopping along on a crutch, his left foot wrapped in a dirty bandage and barely touching the ground every few steps. I wondered how far he'd be able to go on just one good leg. The boy wasn't going to be much help; he was small and carrying their goods in a burlap sack which he switched from hand to hand and sometimes dragged along the road. They stopped at the fork and watched me as I bore right, past the signpost.

'Not that way, sir!' the boy called. 'That's the way to the haunted city!' He was gray, but not as gray as the man with him. They might have been father and son, but it was impossible to see a resemblance because the man's face had begun to blur and his eyes to pull up.

The man swatted him on the shoulder and would have gone sprawling if the boy hadn't steadied him.

'Leave him be, leave him be,' the man said. His voice was understandable but muffled, as if his vocal cords had been wrapped in Kleenex. I thought that before long he'd be huzzing and buzzing like Dora.

He shouted to me across the widening gap between the two roads, and it obviously hurt him. His grimace of pain made his dissolving features even more horrible, but he meant to have his say. 'Hello, whole man! Which of em did your mother flip her skirts for to leave you fair of face?'

I had no idea what he was talking about, so I said nothing. Radar gave another feeble bark.

'Is that a dog, Pa? Or a tame wolf?'

The man's answer was another whack on the boy's shoulder. Then he sneered at me and made a hand gesture I understood perfectly. Some things don't change, apparently, no matter what world you're in. I was tempted to give him back the American version but didn't. Dissing disabled people is crap behavior, even if the disabled person in question happens to be an asshole who whacks his son and casts aspersions on your mother.

'Walk well, whole man!' he screamed in his muffled voice. 'May today be your last!'

Always nice to meet pleasant people along the way, I thought, and walked on. Soon they were lost to sight.

2

I had Kingdom Road to myself, which gave me plenty of time to think . . . and to wonder.

The whole people, for example – what were they? *Who* were they? There was me, of course, but I thought if there was a whole-people record book, I'd be in it with an asterisk by my name, because I wasn't from Empis (at least this part of the world was called that; Woody had told me Hana the giant came from a place called Cratchy). It was nice to have Woody assure me – and he had – that I wouldn't start to turn gray and lose my face because, he said, whole people were immune to the gray. That had been this morning at breakfast, and he had refused to discuss it further because he said I had a long way to go and had to make a start. When I asked about Flight Killer, he only frowned and shook his head. He reiterated that his cousin Claudia could tell me more, and I had to be satisfied with that. Still, what the man on the crutch said was suggestive: *Which of em did your mother flip her skirts for to leave you fair of face?*

I also wondered about the constantly gray skies. At least in the daytime they were constantly gray, but at night the clouds sometimes parted to allow the moonlight to shine through. Which in turn seemed to activate the wolves. Not a single moon up there but two, one chasing the other, and that made me wonder exactly where I was. I'd read enough science fiction to know about the idea of parallel worlds and multiple earths, but I had an idea that when I passed through that place in the underground corridor where my mind and body seemed to separate, I might have arrived on a different plane of existence altogether. The possibility that I was on a planet in a galaxy far, far away made a degree of sense because of the two moons, but these weren't alien life forms; these were *people.*

I thought about that book on Mr Bowditch's bedtable, the one with a funnel filling up with stars on the cover. What if I'd found my way into the world matrix it was supposedly about? (I wished to God I'd put it in my pack along with food, Radar's pills, and Polley's gun.) The idea made me remember a movie I'd watched with my mom and dad when I was very young – *The NeverEnding Story*, it was called. Suppose Empis was like Fantasia in that movie, a world created out of collective imagination? Was that also a Jungian concept? How would I know, when I didn't even know if you pronounced the guy's name *Jung* or *Yung?*

I wondered about those things, but what I kept coming back to was more practical: my dad. Did he know I was gone yet? He might still be ignorant of the fact (and ignorance, so they say, is bliss), but like Woody, he might have had an *intuition* – parents, I'd heard, were prone to them. He would have tried to call, and when I didn't pick up, he'd text. He might just assume I was too busy with school shit to respond, but that wouldn't hold for long, because he knew I was pretty responsible about hitting him back as soon as I could.

I hated the idea of him worrying, but there wasn't anything I could do about it. I had made my decision. And besides – I have to say this if I'm going to tell the truth – I was glad to be here. I can't exactly say I was having fun, but yes, I was glad. I wanted answers to a thousand questions. I wanted to see what was over every next rise and turn. I wanted to see what the boy had called the haunted city. Of course I was scared – of Hana, of the night soldiers and something or someone called Flight Killer, most of all of Gogmagog – but I was also exhilarated. And there was Radar. If I could give her a second chance, I meant to do it.

Where I stopped to have lunch and rest for awhile, the woods had closed in on both sides. I saw no wildlife, but there was plenty of shade. 'Want some chow, Rades?'

I hoped she did, because I hadn't gotten any of the pills into her that morning. I opened my pack, got out a can of sardines, opened them, and tilted the can toward her so she could get a good smell. She lifted her nose but didn't get up. I could see more of that gummy stuff oozing out of her eyes.

'Come on, girl, you love these.'

She managed three or four steps down the slope of the cart, and then her rear legs gave out. She slid the rest of the way, sluing sideways and uttering a single high-pitched yelp of pain. She hit the hardpan on her side and lifted her head to look up at me, panting. The side of her face was smeared with dust. It hurt me to look at that. She tried to rise and couldn't.

I stopped wondering about the whole people, the gray people, even my dad. All of that was lost. I brushed away the dirt, picked her up, and carried her onto the narrow grass verge between the road and the bulking masses of trees. I laid her there, stroked her head, then examined her back legs. Neither appeared to be broken, but she yipped and bared her teeth – not to bite, but in pain – when I touched them high up. They felt okay to me, but I was pretty sure an X-ray would have shown badly swollen and inflamed joints.

She drank some water and ate a sardine or two . . . I think to please me. I had lost my own appetite but made myself eat some of the fried rabbit Dora had given me, plus a couple of cookies. I had to feed the engine. When I picked Rades up – carefully – and put her back in the cart, I could hear the rattle of her respiration and feel every rib. Woody had said she was dying, and he was right, but I hadn't come all this way to find my dog dead in the back of Dora's cart. I grabbed the poles and moved on, not running – I knew that would blow me out – but at a fast walk.

'Hang in. Things might be better tomorrow, so hang in for me, girl.'

I heard the thump of her tail against the cart as she wagged it.

3

The clouds darkened as I pulled the cart along Kingdom Road, but there was no rain. That was good. I didn't mind getting wet but getting soaked would make Radar's condition worse and I didn't have much to cover her with. Also, pulling the cart might be difficult or even impossible if a hard rain turned the road to muck.

Maybe four or five hours after Radar took her spill, I breasted a steep rise and stopped, partly to catch my breath but mostly just to look. The land fell away before me, and for the first time I could see the towers of the city clearly. In this dull light those towers had a sullen olive cast, like soapstone. A tall gray wall ran into the distance on both sides of the road, as far as I could see. I was still miles away and it was impossible to tell how high it was, but I thought I could make out a monstrous gate in the center. *If that's locked*, I thought, *I am truly fucked*.

The road between Woody's and where I stopped to rest and look had been curving, but it ran straight as a string to the city's gate. The woods began to draw back a few miles ahead, and I saw abandoned carts and what might have been hand plows in overgrown fields. I saw something else, too: a vehicle, or some sort of conveyance, coming in my direction. My eyes are good, but it was still miles away and I couldn't make out what it was. I touched the butt of Mr Bowditch's .45, not to confirm it was still there but for comfort.

'Rades? You okay?'

I looked over my shoulder and saw her looking back at me from the front of the cart. That was good. I grabbed the poles and began to walk again. My hands were raising a pretty decent crop of blisters, and I would have given a lot for a pair of work gloves. Hell, even a pair of mittens. At least it was downhill for awhile.

A mile or two further along (the towers sinking behind the high city wall as the road descended), I stopped again. I could now see the person coming my way appeared to be riding an oversized tricycle.

As we closed the distance between us, I saw the trike's rider was a woman, and making good speed. She was wearing a black dress that billowed all around her, and it was impossible not to think again of *The Wizard of Oz*. Specifically the black-and-white part at the beginning, when Almira Gulch rides her bicycle under threatening Kansas skies to get Dorothy's dog and have him put to sleep for biting her. There was even a wooden carry-basket on the back of the oncoming tricycle, although this one was much bigger than the Toto-sized one on the back of Miss Gulch's bike.

'Don't worry, Rades,' I said. 'She's not taking you anywhere.'

When she got really close, I stopped and flexed my stinging hands. I was ready to be friendly in case this was who I thought it was, but I was also ready to defend myself and my dog if she turned out to be the Empisarian version of the wicked witch.

The woman stopped by reversing the pedals of her tricycle and sending up a pretty good squelch of dust. Her dress quit billowing and fell limply against her body. She was wearing stout black leggings beneath the dress and big black boots. No need for any of Dora's replacement footwear for this lady. Her face was rosy with exercise and without the slightest trace of gray. If forced to guess, I would have said she was in her forties or fifties, but it would be just a guess. Time is strange in Empis, and so is the aging process.

'You're Claudia, aren't you?' I said. 'Wait, I have something to show you.'

I opened my pack and took out the gold door knocker. She barely gave it a glance, only nodded and leaned over her handlebars. Her hands were dressed in leather gloves that I bitterly envied.

'I'M CLAUDIA! DON'T REALLY NEED TO SEE THAT, I DREAMED YOU WERE COMING!' She tapped her temple and barked a laugh. 'DREAMS AREN'T TRUSTWORTHY, BUT THEN THIS MORNING I SAW THE SNAB! ALWAYS A SIGN OF RAIN OR COMPANY!' Her voice wasn't just loud, it was utterly toneless, like the voice of an evil computer in an old sci-fi movie. She added something I hardly needed: 'I'M DEAF!'

She turned her head. Her hair was done up in a high bun and I could have seen her ear if she'd had one. She didn't. As with Leah's mouth and Woody's eyes, there was just a scar.

4

She hitched up her skirts, dismounted her trike, and strode to the cart for a look at Radar. On the way, she tapped the butt of the holstered .45. 'BOWDITCH'S! I REMEMBER IT! AND I REMEMBER HER!'

Radar lifted her head when Claudia stroked her, then scratched behind her ears in the way Rades really liked. Claudia leaned close, apparently not the least bit afraid of being bitten, and sniffed. Radar licked her cheek.

Claudia turned back to me. 'SHE'S SICK AS HELL!'

I nodded. There was no point denying it.

'WE'LL KEEP HER GOING, THOUGH! WILL SHE EAT?'

I waggled my hand, meaning a little. 'Can you read lips?' I patted my own, then pointed to hers.

'NEVER LEARNED TO MUCH!' she blared. 'NO ONE TO PRACTICE ON! WE'LL GIVE HER BEEF BROTH! SHE'LL EAT THAT FOR GOD'S SAKE! BRING HER BACK A RIGHT SMART! DO YOU WANT TO PUT HER IN MY BASKET? WE MIGHT GO FASTER!'

I couldn't tell her that I was afraid of hurting Radar's sore back legs, so I just shook my head.

'ALL RIGHT, BUT COME ALONG SMART! THREE BELLS WON'T BE LONG! END O' DAY! THERE ARE GODDAMNED WOLVES, YOU KNOW!'

She pushed her big trike – the seat had to be at least five feet off the ground – in a circle, then clambered up. She pedaled slowly, and the road was wide enough for me to walk beside her, so Radar and I didn't have to eat her dust.

'FOUR MILES!' she shouted in her toneless voice. 'PULL LIVELY, YOUNG MAN! I'D GIVE YOU MY GLOVES BUT YOUR HANDS ARE TOO BIG! I'LL GIVE YOU SOME GOOD LINIMENT FOR THEM WHEN WE'RE UNDER COVER! MY OWN RECIPE AND IT'S DAMN GOOD! THEY LOOK MIGHTY SORE!'

5

By the time we neared Claudia's the day was darkening and I was all but done in. Two days of pulling Dora's cart made football practice seem like a breeze. Ahead of us, maybe a mile or two farther on, I could see the start of what might have been suburbs, although that word hardly fits – they were cottages like Dora's, but with broken roofs. They sat at a distance from one another at first, with little yards or garden plots, but shoulder to shoulder as they approached the city walls. There were chimneys, but no smoke came from any of them. Roads and streets began to sprout off here and there. Some kind of vehicle – I couldn't tell what – was stopped dead in the middle of the main road. At first I thought it was a long wagon for hauling freight. When we got closer, I thought it might be a bus. I pointed to it.

'TROLLEY!' Claudia boomed. 'BEEN THERE FOR A LONG LONG TIME! PULL ON, YOUNG MAN! STRAIN YOUR POOPER!' *That* one I'd never heard before; I'd save it for Andy Chen, assuming I ever saw him again. 'ALMOST THERE!'

From across the distance between the city and where we were there came the sound of three bells, spaced out and solemn: *DONG* and *DONG* and *DONG*. Claudia saw Radar perk up and turn toward the sound.

'THREE BELLS?'

I nodded.

'IN THE OLD DAYS THAT MEANT QUIT YOUR LABORS AND GO HOME TO SUPPER! NOW THERE'S NO LABOR AND NO ONE TO DO IT BUT THE BELLS RING ON! I CAN'T HEAR EM BUT I CAN FEEL EM IN MY TEETH, ESPECIALLY WHEN IT STORMS!'

Claudia's house stood on a weedy patch of ground in front of a scummy pond shrouded in bushes. The house was round and constructed of scavenged boards and pieces of tin. It looked mighty flimsy to me, making it hard not to think of the pigs and the wolf again. Woody's was a house of bricks, Claudia's a house of sticks. If there was another royal relative who'd been living in a house of straw, I guessed he or she had been gobbled up long ago.

When we reached it, I saw a number of dead wolves, three or four in front and another, paws sticking up out of the weeds, to one side. I couldn't see that one very well, but those in front were pretty decayed, with ribcages poking out through the remains of their fur. Their eyes were gone, probably plucked out by hungry crows, and the sockets seemed to stare at me as we turned onto the beaten path leading up to the door. I was relieved to see that they weren't gigantic, like the insect life . . . but they were plenty big. Or had been when still alive. Death had put them on a strict diet, as I suppose is the case with all living things.

'I SHOOT EM WHEN I CAN!' Claudia said, dismounting her trike. 'KEEPS THE OTHERS AWAY MOST OF THE TIME! WHEN THE SMELL WEARS THIN I SHOOT A FEW MORE OF THE FUCKERS!'

For royalty, I thought, *she's certainly got a foul mouth.*

I put down the cart poles, tapped her on the shoulder, and pulled Mr Bowditch's revolver out of the holster. I raised my eyebrows in a question. I wasn't sure she'd understand, but she did. Her grin showed several missing teeth.

'NAH, NAH, I DON'T HAVE ONE OF THOSE! CROSSBOW!' She mimed raising one. 'MADE IT MYSELF! AND THERE'S SOMETHING ELSE, EVEN BETTER! ADRIAN BROUGHT IT WHEN THAT ONE THERE WASN'T MUCH MORE THAN A PUP!'

She went up to the door and pushed it open with a brawny shoulder. I got Radar out of the cart and tried her on her feet. She was able to stand and walk, but at the stone step she paused and looked to me for help. I lifted her in. The house consisted of one large round room and what I assumed was a smaller one hidden by a blue velvet curtain enlivened with threads of scarlet and gold. There was a stove, a tiny kitchen, and a worktable scattered with tools. Also on the table were arrows in various stages of completion, and a wicker basket holding half a dozen finished ones. The tips glittered when she produced a long match and lit a couple of oil lamps. I picked one of the arrows up for a closer look at the tip. It was gold. And sharp. When I touched the pad of my index finger to one, a bead of blood immediately welled.

'HERE, HERE, DO YOU WANT TO GIVE YOURSELF AN AFFLICTION?'

She grabbed me by the shirt and pulled me to a tin-lined sink. There was a hand-pump hanging over it. Claudia gave the handle several hard plunges to get it going, then held my bleeding finger in the freezing water.

'It's just a little . . .' I began, then gave up and let her do her thing. She finished at last, and startled me by placing a kiss on the booboo.

'SIT! REST! WE'LL EAT SOON! NEED TO TEND THIS DOG OF YOURS, THEN YOUR MITTS!'

She put a kettle on the stove and when it was warm but not steaming, she produced a basin from under the sink and filled it. To this she added some foul-smelling stuff from a crock on one of the shelves. Those shelves were full of goods – some in cannisters, some in packages of what looked like cheesecloth tied with twine, most in glass jars. A crossbow hung on the wall to the right of the velvet curtain, and it looked like serious business. All in all, the place reminded me of a frontier home, and Claudia reminded me not of a royal relative but of a frontier woman, rough and ready.

She soaked a cloth in the stinking brew, wrung it out, then squatted over Radar, who looked suspicious. She began to press the cloth gently to those sore upper legs. While she did it, she made an odd crooning noise that I think was singing. It went up and down in pitch while her speaking voice was just a constant loud monotone, almost like announcements from my high school's PA system. I thought Radar might try to scramble away, or even bite her, but she didn't. She laid her head down on the rough boards and gave a sigh of contentment.

Claudia got her hands under Radar's body. 'ROLL OVER, HONEY! I NEED TO DO THE OTHER ONE!'

Radar didn't roll over, just sort of flopped. Claudia re-soaked the cloth and went to work on the other back leg. When she was finished, she tossed the cloth in the tin sink and got two more. She soaked them, wrung them out, and turned to me.

'HOLD EM FORTH, YOUNG PRINCE! THAT'S WHAT WOODY CALLED YOU IN THE DREAM I HAD!'

Telling her I was just plain old Charlie wasn't going to work, so I just held them out. She wrapped them in the warm wet cloths. The stink of her potion was unpleasant, but the relief was immediate. I couldn't tell her so with words, but she saw it on my face.

'GODDAMNED GOOD, ISN'T IT! MY NANA SHOWED ME HOW TO MAKE IT LONG AGO WHEN THAT TROLLEY STILL RAN ITS ROUTE TO ULLUM AND THERE WERE FOLKS TO HEAR THE BELLS! THERE'S WILLOW BARK IN IT, BUT THAT'S JUST THE START! JUST THE START, MY BOY! HOLD THEM ON THERE WHILE I GET US SOME GRUBBIT! YOU HAVE TO BE HUNGRY!'

6

It was steak and green beans, with something like apple-and-peach cobbler for dessert. I'd certainly had my share of free food – grubbit – since coming to Empis and Claudia just kept filling my plate. Radar had a dipper of beef broth with little globules of fat floating on top. She licked the bowl clean, licked her chops clean, and looked at Claudia for more.

'NAH, NAH, NAH!' Claudia bellowed, bending to scratch behind Radar's ears in the way she liked. 'YOU'D KACK IT RIGHT BACK UP, YOU SAD OLD BITCH, AND WHAT GOOD WOULD THAT DO? BUT THIS WON'T HURT YOU!'

There was a loaf of brown bread on the table. She plucked off a chunk with her strong, work-hardened fingers (*she* could have pulled that cart all day without raising a single blister), then grabbed an arrow out of the basket. She impaled the bread, opened the door of her stove, and stuck the bread in. It came out an even darker brown and flaming. She blew it out like a birthday candle, finger-smeared it with butter from the pottery crock on the table, then held it out. Radar got to her feet, picked it off the arrow-tip with her teeth, and took it into the corner. Her limp was better. I thought if Mr Bowditch had had some of Claudia's liniment, he maybe could have skipped the OxyContin.

Claudia pushed through the velvet curtain that concealed her boudoir and came back with a pad of paper and a pencil. She handed them to me. I looked at the stamped letters on the barrel of the pencil and felt a wave of unreality. What remained said COMPLIMENTS OF

SENTRY LUMB. There were only a few sheets left on the pad. I looked on the back and saw a faded price sticker: STAPLES $1.99.

'WRITE WHEN YOU HAVE TO BUT JUST NOD OR SHAKE YOUR HEAD IF YOU DON'T! SAVE THE FUCKING PAPER, ADRIAN BROUGHT IT WITH THE NOISEMAKER ON HIS LAST TRIP AND THAT'S ALL THAT'S LEFT! UNDERSTAND?'

I nodded.

'YOU CAME TO REFRESH ADE'S DOG, DIDN'T YOU?'

I nodded.

'CAN YOU FIND YOUR WAY TO THE SUNDIAL, YOUNG MAN?'

I wrote and held the pad out for her to see: *Mr Bowditch left his initials as a trail.* Which, I thought, would be better than breadcrumbs. Assuming rain hadn't washed them away, that was.

She nodded and bowed her head in thought. In the light of the lamps, I could see a clear resemblance to her cousin Woody, although he was much older. She had a kind of stern beauty under the years of work and target practice on marauding wolves. *Royalty in exile*, I thought. *She and Woody and Leah. Not the three little pigs but the three little bluebloods.*

At last she looked up and said, 'RISKY!'

I nodded.

'DID WOODY TELL YOU HOW YOU MUST GO AND WHAT YOU MUST DO?'

I shrugged and wrote, *I have to be quiet.*

She made a huffing sound, as if that were no help at all. 'I CAN'T KEEP CALLING YOU YOUNG MAN OR YOUNG PRINCE, ALTHOUGH YOU DO HAVE A BIT OF THE PRINCELY LOOK ABOUT YOU! WHAT'S YOUR NAME?'

I printed *CHARLIE READE* in capital letters.

'SHARLIE?'

It was close enough. I nodded.

She took a chunk of wood from the box by the stove, opened the stove door, rammed it in, slammed it shut. She resumed her seat, clasped her hands on the lap of her dress, and leaned forward over them. Her face was grave.

'YOU'LL BE TOO LATE TO TRY YOUR ERRAND

TOMORROW, SHARLIE, SO YOU'LL NEED TO OVERNIGHT IN A STORAGE SHED A BIT OF A WAY FROM THE MAIN GATE! IT HAS A RED WAGON WITH THE WHEELS GONE IN FRONT! WRITE IT DOWN!'

I wrote *storage shed, red wagon w/o wheels.*

'GOOD SO FAR! YOU'LL FIND IT OPEN BUT THERE'S A BOLT ON THE INSIDE! RUN IT IF YOU DON'T WANT A WOLF OR THREE FOR COMPANY! WRITE IT DOWN!'

Bolt door.

'KEEP YOUR PLACE UNTIL YOU HEAR THE MORNING BELL! ONE RING! YOU'LL FIND THE CITY GATE LOCKED BUT LEAH'S NAME WILL OPEN IT! ONLY HERS! LEAH OF THE GALLIEN! WRITE IT DOWN!'

I wrote down *Leah of the galleon.* She gestured for the pad to see what I had written, frowned, then gestured for the pencil. She scratched out *galleon* and changed it to *Gallien.*

'DID NO ONE TEACH YOU TO SPELL IN THAT LAND OF YOURS, BOY?'

I shrugged. Galleon or Gallien, they sounded the same. And if the city was deserted, who was going to hear me and let me in, anyway?

'YOU BE THERE AND THROUGH THE GATE GODDAMNED SOON AFTER THE MORNING BELL, BECAUSE YOU HAVE A GODDAMNED LONG TREK AHEAD OF YOU!'

She rubbed her forehead, and looked at me, troubled.

'IF YOU SEE ADE'S MARKS, ALL MAY BE WELL! IF YOU DON'T, LEAVE BEFORE YOU BECOME LOST! THE STREETS ARE A MAZE! YOU WOULD STILL BE WANDERING IN THAT HELLHOLE AT NIGHTFALL!'

I wrote *She'll die if I can't refresh her!*

She read it and thrust the pad back at me.

'DO YOU LOVE HER ENOUGH TO DIE WITH HER?'

I shook my head. Claudia surprised me with a laugh that was almost musical. I thought it was one small remnant of what her voice had been like before she had been cursed to a life of silence.

'NOT A NOBLE ANSWER, BUT THOSE WHO ANSWER NOBLY HAVE A WAY OF DYING YOUNG WITH THEIR PANTS FULL OF SHIT! WOULD YOU LIKE SOME ALE?'

I shook my head. She got up, rummaged in what I supposed was her cold pantry, and came back with a white bottle. She thumbed out a cork with a hole in it – to let the brew breathe, I guessed – and took a long drink. This was followed by a ringing belch. She sat down again, now clasping the bottle in her lap.

'IF THE MARKS ARE THERE, SHARLIE – ADRIAN'S MARKS – FOLLOW THEM AS BRISK AS YOU CAN AND QUIET! ALWAYS QUIET! PAY NO MIND TO VOICES YOU MAY HEAR, FOR THEY ARE THE VOICES OF THE DEAD . . . AND WORSE THAN THE DEAD!'

Worse than the dead? I didn't like the sound of that. And speaking of sound, there was the one the wooden wheels of Dora's cart were apt to make on paved streets. Maybe Radar could walk part of the way and I could carry her the rest?

'YOU MAY SEE STRANGE THINGS . . . CHANGES IN THE SHAPES OF THINGS . . . BUT PAY NO ATTENTION! EVENTUALLY YOU WILL COME TO A SQUARE WITH A DRY FOUNTAIN IN IT!'

I thought maybe I'd seen that fountain, in the picture of Claudia and Leah that Woody had shown me.

'NEARBY IS A HUGE YELLOW HOUSE WITH BROWN SHUTTERS! A PASSAGE RUNS THROUGH THE CENTER! THAT IS THE HOUSE OF HANA! ONE HALF OF THE HOUSE IS WHERE HANA LIVES! THE OTHER HALF IS THE KITCHEN WHERE HANA TAKES HER MEALS! WRITE IT DOWN!'

I did, and then she took the pad. She drew a passage with a curved top. Above it, she drew a butterfly with outstretched wings. For a quick sketch, it was very good.

'YOU MUST HIDE, SHARLIE! YOU AND YOUR DOG! WILL SHE BE QUIET?'

I nodded.

'QUIET, NO MATTER WHAT?'

I couldn't be sure of that, but I nodded again.

'WAIT FOR TWO BELLS! WRITE IT DOWN!'

2 bells, I wrote.

'YOU MAY SEE HANA OUTSIDE BEFORE TWO BELLS! YOU MAY NOT! BUT YOU WILL SEE HER WHEN SHE GOES

TO THE KITCHEN FOR HER MIDDAY MEAL! THAT IS WHEN YOU MUST GO THROUGH THE PASSAGE, QUICK AS EVER YOU CAN! WRITE IT DOWN!'

I didn't think I needed to – I wouldn't want to spend much time in Hana's vicinity if she was as fearsome as I'd heard – but it was clear Claudia was very worried about me.

'THE SUNDIAL ISN'T MUCH FURTHER ALONG! YOU'LL KNOW BECAUSE OF THE WIDE WALKWAYS! PUT HER ON THE SUNDIAL AND RUN IT BACKWARDS! USE YOUR HANDS! MIND ME, IF YOU RUN IT FORWARDS, YOU'LL KILL HER! AND STAY OFF IT YOURSELF! WRITE IT DOWN!'

I did, but only to please her. I'd read *Something Wicked This Way Comes* and knew the danger of turning the sundial the wrong way. The one thing Radar *didn't* need was to get older.

'COME BACK JUST AS YOU WENT IN! BUT BEWARE OF HANA! LISTEN FOR HER IN THE PASSAGE!'

I raised my hands and shook my head: *I don't understand.*

Claudia smiled grimly. 'THE GREAT BITCH ALWAYS TAKES A NAP AFTER SHE EATS! AND SHE SNORES! YOU'LL HEAR THAT, SHARLIE! IT'S LIKE THUNDER!'

I gave her two thumbs up.

'RETURN QUICKLY! IT'S FAR AND YOUR TIME WILL BE SHORT! YOU DON'T NEED TO BE THROUGH THE GATE WHEN THE THREE BELLS RING, BUT YOU MUST BE OUT OF LILIMAR SOON AFTER! BEFORE DARK!'

I printed *Night Soldiers*? on the pad and showed it to her. Claudia wetted her whistle with more ale. She looked grim. 'YES! THEY! NOW CROSS THAT OUT!'

I did, and showed her.

'GOOD! THE LESS SAID OR WRITTEN ABOUT THOSE BUGGERS THE BETTER! OVERNIGHT IN THE SHED WITH THE RED WAGON IN FRONT! LEAVE WHEN YOU HEAR THE MORNING BELL! COME BACK HERE! WRITE IT DOWN!'

I did.

'WE'RE FINISHED,' Claudia said. 'YOU SHOULD TURN IN NOW, FOR YOU MUST BE TIRED AND YOU HAVE FAR TO GO TOMORROW!'

I nodded and wrote on the pad. I held it up with one hand and took one of hers in the other. Written large on the pad was *THANK YOU.*

'NAH, NAH, NAH!' She squeezed my hand, then raised it to her cracked lips and kissed it. 'I LOVED ADE! NOT AS A WOMAN LOVES A MAN BUT AS A SISTER LOVES A BROTHER! I ONLY HOPE I'M NOT SENDING YOU TO YOUR DEATH . . . OR WORSE!'

I smiled and gave her two thumbs up, trying to convey that I'd be fine. Which I was not, of course.

7

Before I could ask any more questions – I had many – the wolves started in. A lot of them, howling their heads off. I saw moonlight shining between two boards that had shrunk apart from each other, and there came a slam against the side of the house so hard that it made the whole thing shiver. Radar barked and got to her feet, ears up. There was another slam, then a third, then two together. A bottle fell off one of Claudia's shelves and I smelled pickle brine.

I drew Mr Bowditch's gun, thinking *They'll huff and they'll puff til they beat her house down.*

'NAH, NAH, NAH,' Claudia boomed. She looked almost amused. 'FOLLOW ME, SHARLIE, AND SEE WHAT ADRIAN BROUGHT!'

She pushed back the velvet curtain and motioned me through. The big room was neat; her bedroom wasn't. I wouldn't go so far as to call Claudia a slob about her private quarters, but . . . you know what, actually I *would* go that far. Two quilts were rumpled and thrown back. Pants, shirts, and underwear that looked like cotton bloomers and chemises were scattered across the floor. She kicked garments out of her way as she led me to the far side of the room. I was less interested in what she meant to show me than I was in the wolf attack going on outside. And it *was* an attack, the battering at her flimsy wooden house now almost continuous. I was afraid that even if the clouds covered the moons, the assault wouldn't stop. They were cranked up and out for blood.

She opened a door, revealing a closet-sized room featuring a composting toilet that had certainly come from my world. 'SHITHOUSE!' she said. 'IN CASE YOU NEED IT IN THE NIGHT! DON'T WORRY ABOUT WAKING ME, I SLEEP LIKE A GODDAM STONE!'

I was sure of that, seeing as she was also as deaf as a stone, but I didn't think I'd be needing the bathroom if the wolves broke through. Not tonight, or ever. It sounded to me like dozens of them were out there, trying to get in while Claudia gave me the *House Beautiful* tour.

'NOW ATTEND YOU THIS!' Claudia said. She used the heel of her hand to slide back a panel next to the toilet. Inside was a car battery with ACDelco stamped on the side. Jumper clamps were attached to the terminals. The cables were attached to some sort of power converter. Another cable came out of the converter and connected to what looked like an ordinary light switch. Claudia was grinning broadly. 'ADRIAN BROUGHT IT AND THE FUCKING WOLVES HATE IT!'

Cowards bring presents, I thought.

She flipped the switch. The result was hammering blats of sound, like a bunch of car alarms magnified fifty or a hundred times. I put my hands over my ears, afraid that if I didn't I'd wind up as deaf as Claudia was. After ten or fifteen very long seconds, she flipped the switch down. I took my hands cautiously away from my ears. In the big room, Radar was barking like mad, but the wolves had stopped.

'SIX SPEAKERS! THOSE FUCKERS WILL BE RUNNING INTO THE WOODS LIKE THEIR TAILS ARE ON FIRE! HOW DO YOU LIKE IT, SHARLIE? WAS IT LOUD ENOUGH FOR YOU?'

I nodded and patted my ears. Nothing could withstand that sonic barrage for long.

'I ONLY WISH I COULD HEAR IT!' Claudia said. 'BUT I FEEL IT IN MY TEETH! HA!'

I still had the pad and pencil. I wrote on it and held it up. *What happens when the battery dies?*

She considered this, then smiled and patted my cheek with one hand. 'I GIVE YOU ROOM AND BOARD, YOU BRING ME ANOTHER! FAIR TRADE, YOUNG PRINCE? I SAY YES!'

8

I slept by the stove, as I had at Dora's. There was no lying awake and pondering my situation that night; Claudia gave me a pile of towels for a pillow and I was out as soon as my head landed on them. Two seconds later – that's what it felt like – she was shaking me awake. She was wearing a long coat with butterflies appliquéd on it, more of Dora's work.

'What?' I said. 'Let me sleep.'

'NAH, NAH, NAH!' She was deaf, but she knew perfectly well what I was saying. 'UP, SHARLIE! STILL FAR TO GO AHEAD OF YOU! TIME TO BE ABOUT YOUR BUSINESS! BESIDES, THERE'S SOMETHING I WANT TO SHOW YOU!'

I tried to lie back down, but she pulled me to a sitting position again.

'YOUR DOG'S WAITING! I'VE BEEN UP AN HOUR OR MORE! DOG, TOO! SHE'S HAD ANOTHER DOSE OF LINIMENT AND FEELING PERKY! LOOK AND SEE!'

Radar was standing beside her, wagging her tail. When she saw me looking, she nosed at my neck, then licked my cheek. I got up. My legs were sore, my arms and shoulders worse. I rotated them, then did a dozen forward shrugs, part of limbering up during preseason football practice.

'GO ON AND DO YOUR NECESSARY! I'LL HAVE SOMETHING WARM FOR YOU AFTER!'

I went into the little bathroom, where she'd left me a basin of warm water and a knuckle of hard yellow soap. I urinated, then washed my face and hands. There was a small square of mirror on the wall, no bigger than a car's rearview mirror. It was scratched and tarnished, but when I bent I could see myself. I straightened up, turned to go, then looked again, more closely. I thought my dark brown hair had lightened a bit. It did that in summer, after days in the sun, but there had been no sun here, only lowering clouds. Except at night, of course, when the clouds parted to let the moonlight shine through.

I dismissed it as nothing but the light of the single oil lamp and the cloudy scrap of mirror. When I went back out, she handed me a thick slice of bread wrapped around a double helping of scrambled eggs. I wolfed it down (not sure if that's a pun or not).

She handed me my pack. 'I PUT IN WATER AND COLD TEA! PAPER AND PENCIL, TOO! JUST IN CASE! THAT CART YOU'VE BEEN DRAGGING STAYS HERE!'

I shook my head and pantomimed picking up the poles.

'NAH, NAH, NAH! YOU'RE DONE WITH THAT UNTIL YOU RETURN WITH MY THREE-WHEELER!'

'I can't take your tricycle!'

She had turned away and didn't hear. 'COME OUT, SHARLIE! DAWN BREAKS SOON! YOU DON'T WANT TO MISS THIS!'

I followed her to the door, hoping she wouldn't be opening it to a pack of ravening wolves. There were none, and in the direction of what the boy had called the haunted city, the clouds had broken and I could see a scatter of stars. Sitting near Kingdom Road was Claudia's oversized trike. The big basket on the back had been lined with a soft white square of what looked like fleece, and I understood that was where Radar was supposed to ride. I realized the three-wheeler would be easier and faster than pulling the cart with Radar in it. But there was something else that was even better.

Claudia bent and held the lamp down to the oversized front wheel. 'ADE BROUGHT THESE TIRES, TOO! RUBBER! I'D HEARD OF IT BUT NEVER SEEN IT! MAGIC FROM YOUR WORLD, SHARLIE, AND *QUIET* MAGIC!'

That convinced me. No worries about hard wheels clattering on cobbles.

I pointed to the trike. I pointed to myself. I patted my chest above my heart. 'I'll bring it back, Claudia. I promise.'

'YOU'LL RETURN IT TO ME, YOUNG PRINCE SHARLIE! I'VE NO DOUBT!' She patted me on the back, then gave my bottom an unselfconscious whack that reminded me of Coach Harkness sending me in to play defense or pinch hit. 'NOW LOOK TO THE BRIGHT SKY!'

I did. As the stars paled, the sky over the city of Lilimar turned a beautiful peach shade. There may be such a color when days dawn in the tropics, but I'd never seen one exactly like it. Radar sat between us, head raised, scenting the air. Except for the gunk coming out of her eyes and how thin she was, I would have thought her perfectly okay.

'What are we looking for?'

Claudia didn't reply because she didn't see me speak. She was looking toward the city, where the towers and three tall spires rose, black against the brightening day. I didn't like the look of those glassy spires, even at a distance. Their configuration made them seem almost like faces that were looking at us. I told myself that was an illusion, no different than seeing a gasping mouth in the knothole of an old tree or a cloud that looked like a dragon, but it didn't work. Didn't come *close* to working. The idea – surely ridiculous – crept into my mind that the city itself was Gogmagog: sentient, watching, and evil. The idea of going any closer was frightening; the idea of using Leah's name to pass through its gate was terrifying.

Mr Bowditch did it and came back, I told myself. *You can, too*.

But I wondered.

Then the bell rang out its one long sonorous iron note: *DONG*.

Radar got to her feet and took a step toward the sound.

'FIRST BELL, SHARLIE?'

I raised one finger and nodded.

While the sound still lingered, something began to happen that was far more amazing than an oversized cockroach or a big red cricket: the sky over the crammed-together hovels and cottages outside the city began to darken, as if a shade were being rolled not down but *up*. I grabbed Claudia's arm, for a moment afraid I was seeing some strange eclipse not of the sun or moon but of the earth itself. Then, as the sound of the bell faded to nothing, the darkness broke apart in ten thousand cracks of daylight that pulsated and changed. I saw the colors – black and gold, white and orange, deepest royal purple.

They were monarch butterflies, each one the size of a sparrow, but so delicate and ephemeral that the morning light shone through them as well as around them.

'HAIL EMPIS!' Claudia cried, and raised both hands to the rising flood of life above us. That flood blocked the city skyline, blocked out the faces I thought I'd seen. 'HAIL THE GALLIEN! MAY THEY RULE AGAIN AND FOREVER!'

Loud as she was, I hardly heard. I was transfixed. Never in my life had I seen something so weirdly surreal and so beautiful. The butter-flies darkened the sky as they flew above us, traveling to God knew where, and as I felt the wind of their wings, I finally accepted – wholly and completely – the reality of this other world. Of Empis. I had come from a make-believe world.

This was reality.

CHAPTER SEVENTEEN

Leaving Claudia. Remembering Jenny.

A Night in the Storage Shed. The Gate.

The Haunted City.

1

Radar settled into the fleece-lined basket willingly enough, although she had a coughing fit I didn't like. Claudia and I waited until it eased and finally stopped. Claudia used the hem of her dress to wipe the rheum from Radar's eyes and the sides of her snout, then looked at me gravely.

'WASTE NO TIME IF YOU'D SAVE HER, SHARLIE!'

I nodded. She pulled me into an embrace, then let go and held me by my shoulders.

'HAVE A CARE! I'D BE SAD TO SEE YOU BACK WITHOUT HER BUT SADDER STILL NOT TO SEE YOU AT ALL! HAVE YOU GOT THE INSTRUCTIONS I GAVE YOU?'

I gave her two thumbs up and patted my back pocket.

'DON'T USE THAT GUN IN THE CITY OR EVEN APPROACHING IT!'

I nodded and put a finger to my lips: *Shhh.*

She reached up, tousled my hair, and smiled. 'FARE YOU WELL, YOUNG PRINCE SHARLIE!'

I mounted the trike and settled onto the seat. After my bike it felt like sitting on a tower. I had to put some muscle into the pedals to get going, but once the three-wheeler was rolling, it was easy. I looked around once and waved. Claudia waved back. And blew me a kiss.

I stopped briefly when I came to the abandoned trolley. One of the wheels had come off and it sat aslant. There were old claw marks on the wooden side nearest me, and a dried splash of ancient blood. *Wolfies*, I thought.

I didn't look inside.

2

The going was flat, and I moved along at a good pace. I thought I'd be at the storage shed she'd told me about well before dark. The sky had closed up again; the land was deserted and shadowless beneath low-hanging clouds. The monarchs had gone to wherever they went in the daytime. I wondered if I'd see them fly back to their roosting places outside the city. The wolves might steer clear of the houses and buildings outside the city wall after dark, but I wouldn't want to bet my life on that. Or Radar's.

At mid-morning I began to pass the first houses and cottages. A little further on, where the first byway intersected Kingdom Road, the hardpacked dirt gave way to a pavement of crushed stone. I would have preferred the hardpack, all in all, because that was for the most part smooth. There were potholes in the pavement I had to skirt. The tall trike's stability was fine as long as I could ride a straight course, but weaving was tricky. On several swerves I could feel one of the rear wheels leave the ground. I was able to compensate by leaning into the lift, as I did when turning corners on my bike, but I was pretty sure that even a moderately sharp turn would dump the thing on its side no matter how much I leaned. I could take a spill; I wasn't sure Radar could.

The houses were empty. The windows stared. Crows – not gigantic, but mighty big – strutted through run-to-seed front gardens, picking at seeds or any leftover bright thing. There were flowers, but they looked pallid and somehow wrong. Vines like clutching fingers crawled up the sides of slumped cottages. I passed a strangely askew building with crumbling limestone peering through what remained of the plaster facing. Swinging doors hung ajar, making the entrance look like a dead mouth. On the lintel above them was a stein, so faded that the painted beer inside looked like piss. Written above the stein in faded straggling maroon letters was the word BEWARE. Next to it was what had once probably been a store of some kind. A shatter of glass lay on the road in front. Mindful of the three-wheeler's rubber tires, I gave the broken glass a wide berth.

A bit further on – there were buildings on both sides now, standing almost shoulder to shoulder but with dark little passages between – we passed through a stink so strong and sewerish that it made me gag and hold my breath. Radar didn't like it either. She whined uneasily and stirred, making the three-wheeler rock a little. I'd been thinking about stopping for something to eat, but that stench changed my mind. It wasn't decaying flesh, but it was something that had spoiled in some wholly – and perhaps unholy – way.

An herbage rank and wild, I thought, and that line brought back memories of Jenny Schuster. Sitting with her under a tree, the two of us leaning against the trunk in the dappled shade, her wearing the tattered old vest that was her trademark and holding a paperback book in her lap. It was called *The Best of H.P. Lovecraft*, and she was reading me a poem called 'Fungi from Yuggoth.' I remembered how it began: *The place was dark and dusty and half-lost in tangles of old alleys near the quays*, and suddenly the reason why this place was freaking me out came into focus. I was still miles from Lilimar – what that refugee boy had called the haunted city – but even here things were wrong in ways I don't think I could have consciously understood if not for Jenny, who introduced me to Lovecraft when both of us were sixth graders, too young and impressionable for such horrors.

Jenny and I became book buddies during my father's last year of drinking and first year of sobriety. She was a girl friend, as opposed to *girlfriend*, which means something entirely different.

'I'll never understand why you want to hang with her,' Bertie said once. I think he was jealous, but I think he was also honestly perplexed. 'Do you, like, make out with her? Suck face? Swap spits?'

We did not and I told him so. I said she didn't interest me in that way. Bertie smirked and said, 'What other way is there?' I could have told him, but that would have perplexed him more than ever.

It was true that Jenny didn't have what the Bird Man would have called 'the kind of bod you want to explore.' At eleven or twelve most girls are showing the first faint curves, but Jenny was as flat as a board in front and straight all the way down. She had a rawboned face, mousy brown hair that was always in a tangle, and a storky way of walking. The other girls made fun of her, of course. She was never going to be a cheerleader or Homecoming Queen or star in a class play, and if she wanted such things – or the approval of the girls who mixed and matched and wore eyeshadow – she never showed it. I'm not sure she ever felt so much as an ounce of peer pressure. She didn't dress goth – wore jumpers with that funky vest on top and carried a Han Solo lunchbox to school – but she had a goth mentality. She worshipped a punk band called the Dead Kennedys, could quote lines from *Taxi Driver*, and loved the stories and poems of H.P. Lovecraft.

She and I and HPL connected toward the end of my dark period, when I was still getting up to stupid shit with Bertie Bird. One day in sixth-grade English class the discussion turned to the works of R.L. Stine. I had read one of his books – *Can You Keep a Secret?*, it was called – and thought it was mondo stupid. I said so, then said I'd like to read something that was really scary instead of fake scary.

Jenny caught up with me after class. 'Hey, Reade. Are you afraid of big words?'

I said I was not. I said if I couldn't figure a word out from the story, I looked it up on my phone. That seemed to please her.

'Read this,' she said, and handed me a battered paperback held together with Scotch tape. 'See if it scares you. Because it scared the living shit out of me.'

That book was *The Call of Cthulhu*, and the stories in it scared me plenty, especially one called 'The Rats in the Walls.' There were also lots of big words to look up, like *tenebrous* and *malodorous* (which was the perfect word for what I smelled near that bar). We bonded over horror, possibly because we were the only sixth graders who were willing to wade – and gladly – through the thickets of Lovecraft's prose. For over a year, until Jenny's parents broke up and she moved to Des Moines with her mother, we read the stories and poems to each other aloud. We also saw a couple of movies made out of his stories, but they sucked. None of them got how *big* that guy's imagination was. And how fucking dark.

As I pedaled my way toward the walled city of Lilimar, I realized this silent outer ring was too much like one of HPL's dark fairy tales of Arkham and Dunwich. Put in the context of that and other tales of otherworldly terror (we moved on to Clark Ashton Smith, Henry Kuttner, and August Derleth), I was able to understand what was so frightening and strangely disheartening about the empty streets and houses. To use one of Lovecraft's favorite words, they were *eldritch*.

A stone bridge took us over a dead canal. Large rats prowled through garbage so ancient there was no telling what it had been before it became garbage. The canal's slanting stone sides were streaked with blackish-brown crap – what Lovecraft would undoubtedly have called *ordure*. And the stink rising from the cracked black mud? He would have called it *mephitic*.

Those words came back to me. This place *brought* them back.

On the other side of the canal, the buildings crowded even closer together, the spaces between them not alleys or passages, but mere cracks a person would have to sidle through . . . and who knew what might be lurking in there, waiting for the sidler? These empty edifices overhung the street, seeming to bulge toward the trike and covering all but a zig-zag of white sky. I felt watched not just *from* those black and glassless windows, but *by* them, which was even worse. Something terrible had happened here, I was sure of it. Something monstrous and, yes, eldritch. The source of the gray might still be ahead, in the city, but it was strong even out here in these deserted environs.

Besides feeling watched, there was a crepitant sensation of being followed. Several times I snapped my head around, trying to catch someone or something (some *frightful fiend*) slipping along in our wake. I saw nothing but crows and the occasional rat, possibly headed back to its nesting place or colony in the shadows of that mud-floored canal.

Radar felt it, too. She growled several times, and once when I looked around, I saw her sitting up with her paws on the end of the wicker basket and looking back the way we had come.

Nothing, I thought. *These narrow streets and tumbledown houses are deserted. You've just got the heebie-jeebies. Radar, too.*

We came to another bridge over another desolate canal, and on one of its pillars I saw something that cheered me up – the initials **AB**, not quite covered by encrustations of sickly yellow-green moss. The crowded buildings had caused me to lose sight of the city wall for an hour or two, but on the bridge I could see it clearly, smooth and gray and at least forty feet high. In the center was a titanic gate crisscrossed with thick supports of what looked like cloudy green glass. The wall and gate were visible because most of the buildings between where I stood and the city wall had been reduced to rubble by what looked like a bombing attack. Some sort of cataclysm, anyway. A few charred chimneys stood up like pointing fingers, and a few buildings had been spared. One looked like a church. Another was a long building with wooden sides and a tin roof. In front of it was a wheelless red wagon engulfed in pale weeds.

I had heard the two bells signaling midday (*chow-time for Hana*, I thought) less than two hours ago, which meant I'd made much better time than Claudia had expected. There was plenty of daylight left, but I had no intention of approaching the gate today. I needed to rest and get my head on straight . . . if that were possible.

'I think we're here,' I told Radar. 'It's not the Holiday Inn, but it'll do.'

I pedaled past the abandoned wagon and up to the storage shed. There was a big roll-up door, its once jolly red faded to a sickly pink, and a smaller, man-sized door beside it. Chipped into the paint were the initials **AB**. Seeing them made me feel good, just as the ones on the bridge pillar had, but there was something else that made me feel even better: that sense of creeping doom had lifted. Maybe it was because the buildings were gone and I could feel space around me and see the sky again, but I don't think that was all. That sense of what Lovecraft might have called *ancient evil* was gone. Later, not too long after the three evening bells, I discovered why.

3

The man-sized door wouldn't open until I really put my shoulder into it, then burst open so suddenly I almost fell inside. Radar barked from her basket. The storage shed was gloomy and smelled stale, but not *mephitic* or *odorous*. Bulking in the gloom were two more trolleys, painted red and blue. They had undoubtedly been in the shed for years, but because they were out of the elements, the paint had stayed fresh and they looked almost cheerful. Poles jutted from their roofs, so I guessed at some time or other they must have run on overhead wires that provided current. If so, those wires were long gone. I had seen none on my journey. On the front of one, in old-fashioned letters, was the word SEAFRONT. Over the other, LILIMAR. There were stacks of ironbound wheels with thick wooden spokes and boxes of rusty tools. I also saw a line of torpedo-shaped lamps on a table that stood against the far wall.

Radar barked again. I went back and lifted her out of the basket. She staggered a little, then limped to the door. She sniffed and went inside without any further hesitation.

I tried the big roll-up door, the ones the trolleys must have used, but it wouldn't budge. I left the smaller one open for light and checked the lamps. It looked like it was going to be a dark night for Prince Sharlie and his faithful sidekick Radar, because the oil in their reservoirs was long gone. And Claudia's three-wheeler would have to spend the night outside, because the smaller door was too narrow for it.

The wooden spokes of the spare trolley wheels were dry and splintery. I knew I could break off enough wood for a fire, and I had brought the Zippo my dad used to light his pipe, but no way was I going to build a campfire inside. It was too easy to imagine sparks landing on the old trolleys and lighting them up, leaving us with no refuge but the church-type building. Which looked rickety.

I got out a couple of cans of sardines and some of the meat Dora had packed for me. I ate and drank a Coke. Radar refused the meat, tried a sardine, then dropped it on the dusty wooden floor. She had been happy with Dora's molasses cookies before, so I tried that. She sniffed, then turned her head away. Perky Jerky was also a no-go.

I stroked the sides of her face. 'What am I going to do with you, girl?'

Fix her, I thought. *If I can*.

I started for the door, wanting another look at the wall surrounding the city, then had an inspiration. I went back to my pack, rummaged, and found the last few pecan sandies in a Baggie underneath my useless iPhone. I offered her one. She sniffed it carefully, took it in her mouth, and ate it. Plus three more before turning away.

Better than nothing.

4

I watched the light through the open door and occasionally went out to look around. All was still. Even the rats and crows were avoiding this part of town. I tried tossing Rades her monkey. She caught it once and gave it a few token squeaks but didn't try bringing it back to me. She laid it between her paws and went to sleep with her nose touching it. Claudia's liniment had helped her, but the effects had worn off and she wouldn't take the last three pills the vet's assistant had given me. I thought she had used up her last real burst of energy running down the spiral steps and racing to meet Dora. If I didn't get her to the sundial soon, I'd find her not asleep but dead.

I would have played games on my phone to pass the time if it worked, but it was just a black glass rectangle. I tried restarting it, but didn't even get the apple. There was no fairy-tale magic in the world I had come from, and no magic from my world in this one. I put it back in my pack and watched the open doorway as the white overcast light began to weaken. The three evening bells donged and I almost closed the door then, but I didn't want to be in the dark, with nothing but Dad's lighter to knock it back, until I had to. I kept my eye on the church (if that was what it was) across the road, and thought when I could no longer see it, I'd shut the door. The absence of birds and rats didn't necessarily mean the absence of wolves or other predators. Claudia had told me to bolt myself in, and that was just what I intended to do.

When the church was just a dim shape in a darkening world, I decided to pull the door shut. Radar raised her head, perked her ears, and gave a low *woof*. I thought it was because I'd gotten up, but that wasn't it. Old or not, her ears were better than mine. I heard it a few seconds later: a low fluttering sound, like paper caught in a fan. It approached rapidly, growing in volume until it was the sound of a rising wind. I knew what it was, and as I stood in the doorway with one hand on the three-wheeler's seat, Radar joined me. We both watched the sky.

The monarchs came from the direction I had arbitrarily decided was the south – the direction I'd come from. They darkened the darkening sky in a cloud below the clouds. They settled on the church-type building across the way, on a few standing chimneys, on piles of rubble, and on the roof of the storage shed where Radar and I had taken shelter. The sound of them settling up there – there must have been thousands – was less a fluttering than a long drawn-out sigh.

Now I thought I understood why this part of the bombed-out wasteland seemed safe to me rather than desolate. It *was* safe. The monarchs had kept this one outpost in a world that had once been better, one that existed before the members of the royal family had been either assassinated or driven out.

In my world, I believed – and I wasn't alone – all that royalty business was so much bullshit, fodder for supermarket tabloids like the *National Enquirer* and *Inside View*. Kings and queens, princes and princesses, were just another family, but one that had lucked into all the right numbers in the genetic version of Mega Millions. They took down their britches when they had to shit, just like the lowliest peons.

But this wasn't that world. This was Empis, where the rules were different.

This really was the Other.

The cloud of monarch butterflies had finished their homecoming, leaving only the growing dark. The sigh of their wings faded away. I would bolt the door because Claudia had told me to, but I felt safe. Protected.

'Hail Empis,' I said softly. 'Hail the Gallien, and may they rule again and forever.'

And why not? Just why the fuck not? Anything would be better than this desolation.

I closed the door and bolted it.

5

In the dark there was nothing to do but go to sleep. I put my pack between the two trolleys, next to where Radar had curled up, laid my head on it, and was asleep almost at once. My last thought was that with no alarm to wake me up, I might oversleep and get a late start, which could be lethal. I needn't have worried; Radar woke me up, coughing and coughing. I gave her some water and that eased it a little.

I had no clock but my bladder, which was pretty full but not bursting. I thought about urinating in one of the corners, then decided that was no way to treat a safe haven. I unbolted the door, opened it a little way, and peered out. No stars or moonlight showed through the low-hanging clouds. The church across the road looked blurry to me. I rubbed my eyes to clarify my vision, but the blur remained. It wasn't in my eyes, it was the butterflies, still fast asleep. I didn't think they lived long in our world, only weeks or months. Over here, who knew?

Something shifted at the very edge of my vision. I looked, but either it had been my imagination or whatever had been there was gone. I pissed (looking over my shoulder as I did it), then went back inside. I bolted the door and made my way to Radar. There was no need to use Dad's lighter; her breathing was hoarse and loud. I drifted off to sleep again, maybe for an hour or so, maybe for two. I dreamed that I was in my own bed on Sycamore Street. I sat up, tried to yawn, and couldn't. My mouth was gone.

That snapped me awake to more canine coughing. One of Radar's eyes was open, but the other was stuck shut with that gooey stuff, giving her a sadly piratical look. I wiped it away and went to the door. The monarchs were still roosting, but a little light had come into the dull sky. It was time to eat something, then get going.

I held an open can of sardines under Radar's nose, but she turned her head away at once, as if the smell sickened her. There were two pecan sandies left. She ate one, tried to eat the other, and coughed it out. She looked at me.

I took her face in my hands and moved it gently from side to side in a way I knew she liked. I felt like crying. 'Hold on, girl. Okay? Please.'

I carried her out the door and set her carefully on her feet. She walked to the left of the door with the glassy care of the elderly, found the spot where I had pissed earlier, and added hers to mine. I bent to pick her up again but she circled around me and went to the righthand rear wheel of Claudia's trike – the one closest to the road. She sniffed at it, then dropped her haunches and pissed again. She gave a low growling sound as she did it.

I went to the rear wheel and bent down. There was nothing to see, but I felt sure that whatever I'd caught a glimpse of earlier had approached after I went back inside. Not only approached but pissed on my ride, as if to say *this is my territory*. I had my pack, but I decided there was something else I wanted. I went back inside. Rades sat, watching me. I hunted around until I found a moldering stack of blankets in the corner, perhaps meant – long ago – for trolley passengers to bundle around themselves in cold weather. If I hadn't decided to do my business outside, I might have pissed on them in the dark. I took one and shook it out. A number of dead moths fluttered down to the shed floor like big snowflakes. I folded it into a pad and carried it out to the three-wheeler.

'Okay, Rades, let's get this done. What do you say?'

I lifted her into the basket and then tucked the folded blanket down beside her. Claudia had instructed me to wait until the first bell before leaving, but with the monarchs roosting all around, I felt safe enough. I mounted up and started pedaling slowly toward the gate in the wall. After half an hour or so, the morning bell sounded. This close to the city it was very loud. The monarchs rose in a great wave of black and gold, heading south. I watched them go, wishing I were going that way myself – to Dora's, then to the tunnel entrance, then back into my own world of computers and magic steel birds that flew in the air. But just as the poem says, I had miles to go and promises to keep.

At least the night soldiers are gone, I thought. *Back to their crypts and mausoleums, because that's where things like them sleep*. There was no way I could know that for sure, but I did.

6

We reached the gate in less than an hour. I'd dismounted the trike. Overhead, the clouds were lower and darker than ever, and I didn't think the rain could hold off for much longer. My estimate that the gray wall was forty feet high turned out to be way wrong. It was seventy at least, and the gate was titanic. It was faced in gold – real gold, I was sure, not paint – and almost as long as a football field. The staves bracing it leaned this way and that, but not from age and decay; I was sure they had been placed that way, making strange angles. They made me think of Lovecraft again, and the mad, non-Euclidian universe of monsters that was always straining to overwhelm ours.

It wasn't just the angles that were disturbing. Those staves were of some cloudy green substance that looked like a kind of metallic glass. Something seemed to be moving in them, like black vapor. It made my stomach feel funny. I looked away and when I looked back, the black stuff was gone. When I turned my head and looked at the staves from the corner of my eye, the black stuff seemed to return. Vertigo swept through me.

Not wanting to lose what little breakfast I'd eaten, I looked down at my feet. And there, on one of the cobblestones, printed in paint that might once have been blue but had faded to gray, were the initials **AB**. My head cleared, and when I looked up I just saw the gate, crisscrossed by those green supports. But what a gate it was, like a CGI effect out of an epic movie. But this was no special effect. I rapped my knuckles on one of the cloudy green staves just to be sure.

I wondered what would happen if I tried Claudia's name on the gate, or Stephen Woodleigh's. They were both of the royal blood, weren't they? The answer was yes, but if I understood correctly (I wasn't sure I did, because I've never been good at untangling familial relationships), only Princess Leah was the heir-apparent to the throne of Empis. Or maybe it was the throne of the Galliens. It didn't matter to me, as long as I could get in. If the name didn't work, I was going to be stuck out here, and Radar would die.

Stupid Charlie actually looked for an intercom, the sort of thing you'd find beside the doorway of an apartment building. There was no such thing, of course, just those weird crisscrossing staves with impenetrable blackness between them.

I muttered, 'Leah of the Gallien.'

Nothing happened.

Not loud enough, maybe, I thought, but shouting seemed wrong in the silence outside the wall, almost like spitting on a church altar. *Do it anyway. Outside the city, it's probably safe enough. Do it for Radar.*

In the end I couldn't bring myself to shout, but I cleared my throat and raised my voice.

'Open in the name of Leah of the Gallien!'

I was answered by an inhuman scream that made me step back and almost fall over the front of the trike. You know that saying, my heart was in my mouth? Mine felt like it was ready to bolt out from between my lips, run away, and leave me dead on the ground. The screaming went on and on, and I realized it was the sound of some titanic machine starting up after years or decades. Perhaps not since Mr Bowditch had last used this world's version of *open sesame*.

The gate trembled. I saw those black tendrils writhing and rising in the off-kilter green staves. There was no doubt about them this time; it was like looking at sediment in a shaken bottle. The screech of the machinery changed to a rattling thunder, and the gate started to move to the left along what must have been a huge hidden track. I watched it slide by and the vertigo returned, worse than ever. I turned away, drunk-staggered four steps to the seat of Claudia's trike, and put my face down on it. My heart was slamming in my chest, my neck, even in the sides of my face. I couldn't look at those ever-changing angles as the gate opened. I thought I'd pass out if I did. Or see something so awful it would send me fleeing back the way I'd come, leaving my dying dog behind. I closed my eyes and reached out for a handful of her fur.

Hold on, I thought. *Hold on, hold on, hold on.*

7

At last the clattering rumble stopped. There was another of those protesting screeches, and silence returned. Returned? It fell like an anvil. I opened my eyes and saw Radar looking at me. I opened my hand and saw I'd pulled out a considerable swatch of her hair, but she hadn't complained. Maybe because she had greater pains to contend with, but I don't think that was it. I think she realized I needed her.

'Okay,' I said. 'Let's see what we've got.'

Ahead of me, inside the gate, was a vast tiled courtyard. It was lined with the remains of great stone butterflies on both sides, each on a pedestal and standing twenty feet high. Their wings had been broken and lay in piles on the courtyard floor. They made a kind of passageway. I wondered if, once upon a better time, each of those monarch butterflies (for of course that was what they were) had represented a king or queen in the line of Gallien.

The screaming started up again, and I realized the gate was preparing to roll shut. Leah's name might open it again; it might not. I had no intention of finding out. I mounted up and pedaled inside as the gate began to rumble shut.

The rubber wheels whispered on the tiles, which had once been colorful but were now faded. *Everything turning gray*, I thought. *Gray, or that sick shade of cloudy green.* The butterflies, perhaps once colorful but now as gray as everything else, loomed over us as we passed beneath and between. Their bodies were intact, but the faces as well as the wings had been battered off. It made me think of videos I'd seen of ISIS destroying ancient statues, artifacts, and temples they considered blasphemous.

We came to a double arch in the shape of butterfly wings. Something had been written above it, but that too had been battered. All that remained were the letters LI. My first thought was LILIMAR, the name of the city, but it could have been GALLIEN.

Before going through the arch, I looked back to check on Radar. We had to be quiet, each of the people I'd met made that point in his or her own way, and I didn't think that was going to be a problem with Rades. She was asleep again. Which was good in one way and worrisome in another.

The arch was damp and smelled of ancient decay. On the other side was a circular pool faced in lichen-encrusted stone. Perhaps once the water in that pool had been a cheerful blue. Perhaps once people had come here to sit on its stone coping, eating their midday meals while watching the Empisarian version of ducks or swans go gliding. Mothers might have held their children out so they could paddle their feet. Now there were no birds and no people. If there had been, they would have steered clear of that pool as if it were poison, because that's what it looked like. The water was an opaque viscous green that appeared almost solid. The vapor arising from it was indeed mephitic, what I imagined the stench of a tomb stuffed with decaying bodies would smell like. Surrounding it was a curving walkway just barely big enough for the three-wheeler. On one of the tiles to the right were Mr Bowditch's initials. I started that way, then stopped and looked back, certain I'd heard something. The shuffle of a footstep, or maybe the whisper of a voice.

Pay no mind to voices you may hear, Claudia had said. Now I heard nothing and nothing moved in the shadows of the arch I'd come through.

I pedaled slowly along the rightside curve of the stinking pool. On the far side was another butterfly arch. As I neared it, a drop of rain fell on the back of my neck, then another. They began to dot the pool, making brief craters on its surface. As I looked, something black emerged from it, just for a second or two. Then it disappeared. I didn't get a good look, but I'm pretty sure I saw the momentary gleam of teeth.

The rain began to come down harder. Soon it would be a torrent. Once in the shelter of the second arch, I dismounted and spread the blanket over my sleeping dog. Musty and moth-eaten or not, I was very glad I'd brought it.

8

Because I was ahead of schedule, I felt (hoped) that I could linger for awhile in the shelter of this arch, hoping the rain would let up. I didn't want to take Rades out in it, even with the blanket to cover her. Only how long was awhile? Fifteen minutes? Twenty? And just how was I supposed to tell? I had become used to checking my phone for the time and wished bitterly for Mr Bowditch's watch. It came to me as I stared at the rain sheeting down on what looked like a deserted business street crammed with green-fronted shops that I had become too used to my phone, period. My dad had a saying about computer-driven gear: Let a man get used to walking on a crutch and he can't walk without it.

The shops were on the far side of a dry channel. They looked to be the sort of places well-to-do people would visit, like an antique version of Rodeo Drive or the Oak Street District in Chicago. From where I was I could read one gold-plated (surely not *solid* gold) sign that read HIS MAJESTY'S BOOTERY. There were show windows from which the glass had been broken long ago. Many rains had driven the shards into the gutters. And in the middle of the street, curled like the body of a never-ending snake, was what had to be a trolley wire.

Something had been engraved on the paving just outside the arch where we were sheltering. I got on my knees for a close look. Most of it had been battered away, like the wings and faces of the butterflies, but when I ran my fingers over the beginning and the end, I thought I could make out GA and AD. The letters between might have been anything, but I thought maybe this main throughfare, which had been Kingdom Road outside the wall, became Gallien Road inside. Whatever it was, it led straight toward the high buildings and green towers of the central city. Three spires stood higher than the rest, their glassy pinnacles disappearing into the clouds. I didn't know it was the royal palace any more than I knew the remains of the letters had once spelled out Gallien Road, but I thought it was very likely.

Just when I began to think we'd have to push on and get drenched, the rain let up a little. I checked to make sure Radar was covered – nothing sticking out of the blanket but the end of her snout and her back paws – then mounted up and pedaled slowly across the dry channel. As we did, I wondered if I was crossing the Rumpa Bridge Woody had told me about.

9

The shops were fancy, but something was wrong about them. It wasn't just that they were deserted, or obvious that at some time in the distant past they had been looted, perhaps by Lilimar residents fleeing their city when the gray came. There was something else that was more subtle . . . and more awful, because it was still there. Still happening. The buildings seemed solid enough, vandalized or not, but they were *twisted* somehow, as if a gigantic force had pulled them out of shape and they hadn't been able to entirely snap back. When I looked directly at them – HIS MAJESTY'S BOOTERY, CULINARY DELIGHTS, CURIOUS TREASURES, TAILORS TO THE HOUSE OF (the rest of that one had been beaten away, as if what followed were profane), SPOKES AND WHEELS – they seemed okay. Normal enough, if anything could be said to be normal in the otherworldliness of the Other. But when I returned to minding my straight path down the wide street, something happened to them at the edge of my vision. Straight angles seemed to slither into curves. Glassless windows seemed to move, like eyes squinting for a better look at me. Letters became runes. I told myself this was nothing but my hopped-up imagination, but I couldn't be sure. One thing I *was* sure of: I didn't want to be here after dark.

At one cross-street, a huge stone gargoyle had tumbled into the street and stared at me upside-down with its lipless mouth stretched open to show a pair of reptilian fangs and a pitted gray tongue. I made a wide arc around it, relieved to get past its chilly upside-down gaze. As I moved on there was a low thud. I looked back and saw the gargoyle had fallen over. Maybe one of the back wheels of the trike had brushed it, upsetting the precarious balance it had maintained for years. Maybe not.

Either way, it was staring at me again.

10

The palace – assuming that was what it was – grew closer. The buildings on either side looked like townhouses, once no doubt luxurious but now falling to ruin. Balconies had collapsed. Carriage lamps marking fancy stone walks had either fallen over or been knocked down. The walks themselves were sprouting brownish-gray weeds that looked nasty. The spaces between these stone houses had been choked with nettles. Going through would tear your skin to ribbons.

The rain started to come down heavily again as we reached even fancier houses, these constructed of marble and glass with wide steps (intact) and fancy porticoes (mostly smashed). I told Radar to hang in there, we had to be getting close, but I did it in a low voice. In spite of the downpour my mouth was dry. I never even considered turning it up to catch some rain, because I didn't know what might be in it, or what it would do to me. This was a terrible place. An infection had run through it, and I didn't want to drink any of it down.

Yet it seemed to me there was one good thing. Claudia had told me I might get lost, but so far it had been a straight shot. If Hana's yellow house and the sundial were near the majestic agglomeration of buildings overlooked by the three spires, Gallien Road would take me directly there. Now I could see vast windows in that great pile. They weren't stained glass, like those in a cathedral, but a shimmering deep green that reminded me of the staves in the outer gate. And that nasty pool.

Looking at them, I almost missed Mr Bowditch's initials painted halfway up a stone post with a ringbolt on top, presumably for hitching horses. There was a row of these, like blunt teeth, standing in front of a gigantic gray building with almost a dozen doors at the top of its steep steps, but not a single window. The post bearing the initials **AB** was the last in line before a narrower street branching off to the left. The crossbar of the letter **A** had been turned into an arrow that pointed down this narrow way, which was lined with more faceless stone buildings hulking eight or ten stories high. I could imagine that once these had been filled with Empisarian bureaucrats, doing the work of the kingdom. I could almost see them scurrying in and out, wearing long black frock coats and shirts with high collars, like men (I guessed they would all be men) in the illustrations of a Dickens novel. I didn't know if any of the buildings housed His Majesty's Royal Prison, but in a way they all looked like prisons to me.

I stopped, staring at the **A** crossbar that had been turned into an arrow. The palace was dead ahead, but the arrow was pointing me away from it. The question was this: did I keep on going straight, or did I follow the arrow? From behind me, in the basket and under a blanket that was now wet and would soon be soaking, Radar had another coughing fit. I almost disregarded the arrow and went straight on, figuring I could always come back if I ran into a dead end or something, but then I remembered two things Claudia had told me. One was that if I followed Mr Bowditch's marks, all would be well (*might* be well is what she actually said, but why quibble). The other was that I had, according to her, a goddamned long trek ahead of me. But if I continued the way I was going, it would be a goddamned short trek.

In the end, I decided to trust Claudia and Mr Bowditch. I turned the trike in the direction the arrow pointed and pedaled on.

The streets are a maze, Claudia told me. She was right about that, and Mr Bowditch's initials – his marks – took me ever deeper into it. New York made sense; Chicago made a degree of sense; Lilimar made no sense at all. I imagined it was the way London must have been during the time of Sherlock Holmes and Jack the Ripper (for all I know, it's that way now). Some of the streets were wide and lined with leafless trees that gave no shelter from the rain. Some were narrow, one so skinny that the three-wheeler barely fit. On that one we got some relief from the pelting rain, at least, because double-decker buildings hung over the street, almost touching. Sometimes there were trolley wires, a few still hanging down in tensionless swags, most lying in the street.

In one window I saw a headless dressmaker's dummy with a jester's cap and bells on its neck and a knife planted between its breasts. If that was someone's idea of a joke, it wasn't funny. After the first hour I had no idea how many rights and lefts I'd taken. At one point I went through a dripping underpass where the sound of the trike's wheels splashing through standing water sent back echoes that sounded like whispered laughter: *hah . . . haah . . . haaah.*

Some of his marks, the ones out in the weather, were so faded they were hard to see. If I lost the trail they made, I'd have to retrace my course or try to take a bearing from the three spires of what I assumed was the palace, and I didn't know if I could do that. For long stretches, the buildings crowding in on me blotted it out entirely. It was all too easy to imagine myself blundering through this snarl of streets until the two bells . . . and then the evening three . . . and then having to worry about the night soldiers. Only in this rain, and with the steady coughing from behind me, I thought by nightfall Radar would be dead.

Twice I passed gaping holes that slanted down into darkness. From these there wafted drafts of ill-smelling air and what sounded like those whispering voices Claudia had warned me about. The smell from the second one was stronger, the whispering louder. I didn't want to imagine terrified city-dwellers taking refuge in vast underground bunkers and dying there, but it was hard not to. Impossible, really. Just as it was impossible to believe those whispering voices were anything but the voices of their ghosts.

I didn't want to be here. I wanted to be home in my sane world, where the only disembodied voices came out of my EarPods.

I came to a corner with what might have been Mr Bowditch's initials on a lamppost or just a swatch of old blood. I got off the three-wheeler for a closer look. Yes, it was his mark, but almost gone. I didn't dare wipe the water and grime from it for fear of erasing it entirely, so I bent until my nose was almost touching it. The crossbar of the A pointed right, I was sure of it (almost sure). As I went back to the trike, Radar poked her head out of the blanket and whined. One of her eyes was glued shut with ooze. The other was at half-mast but looking behind us. I looked that way and heard a footstep – for sure, this time. And caught a flash of movement that could have been a bit of clothing – a cloak, maybe – as its wearer stepped around another corner a few streets back.

'Who's there?' I called, then clapped my hands over my mouth. *Quiet, be quiet*, everyone I'd met had told me that. In a much lower voice, almost a shouted whisper, I added, 'Show yourself. If you're a friend, I can be a friend.'

No one showed himself. I hadn't really expected them to. I dropped my hand to the butt of Mr Bowditch's revolver.

'If you're not, I have a gun and I'll use it if I have to.' Pure bluff. I'd been warned about that, too. And strongly. 'Do you hear me? For your sake, stranger, I hope you do.'

I didn't exactly sound like myself, and not for the first time. I sounded more like a character in a book or a movie. I almost expected to hear myself say *My name is Inigo Montoya. You killed my father. Prepare to die.*

Radar was coughing again, and she had started to shiver. I got back on the trike and pedaled in the direction the latest arrow pointed. It led me onto a zig-zagging street paved with cobblestones and for some reason lined with barrels, many of them overturned.

11

I continued to follow the initials, a few almost as bright as the day he put them there in red paint, most faded to ghosts of their former selves. Left and right, right and left. I saw no bodies or skeletons of the long departed, but I smelled rot almost everywhere and occasionally there was that sense of the buildings slyly changing their shapes.

I rode through puddles in places. In others, the streets had flooded completely, and the trike's big wheels ran through the murk almost hubcap deep. The rain diminished to a drizzle, then stopped. I had no clue as to how far I was from Hana's yellow house; with no phone to consult and no sun in the sky, my sense of time was completely fucked. I kept expecting the two midday bells to ring out.

Lost, I thought. *I am lost, I have no GPS, and I'll never get there in time. I'll be lucky to get out of this crazy place before dark.*

Then I crossed a little square with a statue in the middle – it was of a woman with her head swatted off – and realized I could see the three spires again. Only now I was looking at them from the side. I had an idea then, and it came to me – absurd but true – in the voice of Coach Harkness, who coached basketball as well as baseball. Coach Harkness striding up and down the sidelines, red in the face and with big patches of sweat showing at the armpits of the white shirt he always wore on game nights, following the flow of his team and screaming '*Back door, back door, dammit!*'

Back door.

That was where Mr Bowditch's trail of initials was leading me. Not to the front of that enormous central building, where Gallien Road no doubt ended, but behind it. I crossed the square to the left, expecting to find his initials on one of the three streets leading away from it, and so I did, painted on the side of a shattered glass building that might once have been a greenhouse of some kind. Now the side of the palace was on my right, and yes – the marks led me further and further around. I began to see a high curving shoulder of stonework behind the sprawl of the main buildings.

I pedaled faster. The next mark pointed me to the right, along what must have been, in better days, a wide boulevard. Back then it might have been fancy-shmancy, but now the pavement was cracked and crumbled away to gravel in some places. An overgrown median ran down the center. Among the weeds were enormous flowers with yellow petals and deep green centers. I slowed long enough to look at one that overhung the street on its long stem, but when I reached toward it, the petals closed with a snap inches from my fingers. Some white sappy fluid drooled out. I could feel heat. I pulled my hand back in a hurry.

Further along, maybe a quarter of a mile, I saw three looming roof-peaks, one on either side of the boulevard I was now traveling and one that appeared to be right over it. They were the same yellow as the hungry flowers. Directly ahead of me, the boulevard debouched into another square with a dry fountain in the center of it. It was huge and green, with random obsidian cracks running through its bowl. *WRITE IT DOWN, PRINCE SHARLIE* had been Claudia's constant scripture, and I checked the notes I'd taken just to be sure. Dry fountain, check. Huge yellow house straddling the road, check. Hide, double-check. I stuffed the sheet of paper into the side pocket of my pack to keep it from getting wet. Didn't even think about it at the time, but later on I had reason to be grateful it was in there instead of my pocket. Ditto my phone.

I rode slowly to the square, then more quickly to the fountain. Its pedestal was easily eight feet high and as thick as a tree trunk. Good cover. I dismounted and peeked around the pedestal. Ahead of me, no more than fifty yards from the fountain, was Hana's house . . . or houses. They were connected by a yellow-painted corridor over the central passageway, sort of like the skyways you see all over Minneapolis. Quite the abode, all in all.

And Hana was outside.

CHAPTER EIGHTEEN

Hana. Pinwheel Paths. The Horror in the Pool. The Sundial at Last. An Unwelcome Encounter.

1

Hana must have come out when the rain stopped, perhaps to savor the brightening day. She was sitting on an enormous golden throne below a striped awning of red and blue. I didn't think the gold was just plating, and I very much doubted that the jewels crusting the throne's back and arms were paste. I thought the king and/or queen of Empis would have looked ridiculously small when perched upon it, but Hana not only filled it, her enormous bottom squeezed out on the sides between the golden arms and the royal purple cushions.

The woman on that stolen (I had no doubt of it) throne was nightmarishly ugly. From where I had taken cover behind the dry fountain, it was impossible to tell how big she really was, but I'm six-four and it looked to me as if she'd tower over me by another five feet even sitting down. If so, that meant Hana would be at least twenty feet tall when standing.

An authentic giant, in other words.

She was wearing a circus-tent of a dress the same royal purple as the cushions she was sitting on. It came down to her tree-trunk calves.

Her fingers (each looked nearly as big as my hand) were dressed in many rings. They glimmered in the subdued daylight; if the day brightened more, they'd flash fire. Dark brown hair fell to her shoulders and onto the tidal wave of her bosom in clumpy snarls.

The dress announced her as female, but otherwise it would have been hard to tell. Her face was a mass of lumps and large infected boils. A red-rimmed crack ran down the center of her forehead. One eye squinted, the other bulged. Her upper lip rose to her gnarled nose, revealing teeth that had been filed into fangs. Worst of all, the throne was surrounded by a semicircle of bones that were almost certainly human.

Radar began to cough. I turned to her, put my head down next to hers, and looked into her eyes. 'Hush, girl,' I whispered. 'Please be *quiet*.'

She coughed again, then fell silent. She was still shivering. I started to turn away and the coughing started again, louder than ever. I think we would have been discovered if Hana hadn't chosen that moment to break into song:

'Stick-a-sticker Joe my love,
Stick it where it goes my love,
Stick-a-sticker all night long
Stick me with your prong-de-dong.
Prong-de-dong, oh prong-de-dong,
Stick me with your prong-de-dong!'

I had an idea that probably wasn't from the Brothers Grimm.

She went on – it seemed to be one of those songs like 'One Hundred Bottles of Beer' that has a zillion verses – and that was perfectly fine with me, because Radar was still coughing. I stroked her chest and belly, trying to ease her as Hana bellowed something about Joe my dear and have no fear (I half-expected 'stick it in my rear'). I was still stroking and Hana was still bellowing when the midday bells rang. This close to the palace they were deafening.

The sound rolled away. I waited for Hana to get up and go into her kitchen. She didn't. Instead she pressed two of her fingers against a boil on her shovel-sized chin and squeezed. Out came a gusher of yellowish pus. She wiped it up with the heel of her hand, examined it, and flung it into the street. Then she settled back. I waited for Radar to start coughing again. She didn't, but she would. It was only a matter of time.

Sing, I thought. *Sing, you great ugly bitch, before my dog starts coughing again and our bones wind up with the ones you're too fucking lazy to pick u—*

But instead of singing, she got to her feet. It was like watching a mountain rise up. I had used a simple ratio I'd learned in math class to figure her standing height, but I'd underestimated the length of her legs. The passage between the two halves of her house had to be twenty feet high, but Hana would have to bend to go through it.

When she was on her feet she pulled her dress out of the crack of her ass and let loose with a resounding fart that went on and on. It reminded me of the trombone break in my dad's favorite instrumental, 'Midnight in Moscow.' I had to clap my hands over my mouth to keep from braying laughter. Not caring if it started a coughing fit or not, I buried my face in the wet fur on Radar's side and gave vent to a burst of low gasping: *huh-huh-huh*. I closed my eyes, waiting for Radar to start up again, or for one of Hana's enormous hands to close around my throat and twist my head right off my neck.

It didn't happen, so I peered around the other side of the fountain's pedestal in time to see Hana thump her way to the right side of her house. The size of her was hallucinatory. She could have looked in the upstairs windows with no trouble at all. She opened the oversized door, and the aroma of cooking meat came out. It smelled like roast pork, but I had a horrible feeling pork wasn't what it was. She bent down and went in.

'*Feed me, you cockless bastard!*' she thundered. '*I be hungry!*'

That's when you must move, Claudia had said. Something like that, anyway.

I mounted the three-wheeler and pedaled for the passageway, bent over the handlebars like a guy in the last kilometer of the Tour de France. Before I entered it, I took a quick glance to my left, where the throne was. The castoff bones were small, almost certainly the bones of children. There was gristle on some and hair on others. Looking was a mistake, one I would have taken back if I could, but sometimes – all too often – we can't help ourselves. Can we?

2

The passageway was about eighty feet long, cool and damp, lined with mossy blocks of stone. The light at the other end was brilliant, and I thought when I came out in the plaza I might actually see the sun.

But no. Just as I exited the passageway, bent over the handlebars, the clouds swallowed up the brave little patch of blue and shadeless gray returned. What I saw stopped me cold. My feet fell off the pedals and the three-wheeler coasted to a stop. I was on the edge of a great open plaza. Eight ways curved in from eight different directions. Once their paving had been brightly colored: green, blue, magenta, indigo, red, pink, yellow, orange. Now the colors were fading. I supposed they would eventually be as gray as everything else in Lilimar, and so much of Empis beyond. Looking at those curving ways was like looking at a gigantic, once jolly pinwheel. Bordering the curving pathways were poles bedecked with pennants. Years ago – how many? – they might have snapped and fluttered in breezes untainted by the scent of rot and decay. Now they hung limp and dribbling rainwater.

At the center of this enormous pinwheel was another butterfly statue with the wings and head destroyed. The shattered remnants were heaped around the pedestal on which it stood. Beyond, a wider way led toward the back of the palace with its three dark green spires. I could imagine the people – the Empisarians – who had once filled those curving ways merging their separate groups into one single throng. Laughing and shoving good-naturedly, anticipating an impending entertainment, some carrying lunches in hampers or baskets, some stopping to buy from food-sellers hawking their wares. Souvenirs for the little ones? Pennants? Of course! I tell you I could see this, as if I had been there myself. And why not? I had been a part of such crowds on special nights to see the White Sox, and on one never-to-be-forgotten Sunday, the Chicago Bears.

Bulking above the back of the palace (*this* part of the palace – it sprawled everywhere) I could see a curved rampart of red stone. It was lined with tall poles, each topped with long traylike devices. Games had been played here, eagerly observed by masses of people. I was sure of it. Crowds had roared. Now the curving walkways and the main entryway were empty and as haunted as the rest of this haunted city.

In our fifth-grade history mod, my class had built a castle from Lego blocks. It seemed like play rather than learning to us then, but in retrospect it was learning after all. I still remembered most of the various architectural elements, and I saw some of them as I approached: flying buttresses, turrets, battlements, parapets, even what might have been a postern gate. But like everything else in Lilimar, it was wrong. Staircases ran crazily (and pointlessly, so far as I could tell) into and around strange toadstool-shaped excrescences with slitted glassless windows. They might have been guard posts; they might have been God knows what. Some of the stairways crisscrossed, reminding me of those Escher drawings where your eyes keep fooling you. I blinked and the staircases looked upside-down. Blinked again and they were rightside-up.

Worse, the entire palace, which had absolutely no symmetry, seemed to be *moving*, like Howl's castle. I couldn't exactly see it happening, because it was hard to hold the entire thing in my eyes . . . or my mind. The stairs were in various colors, like the pinwheel paths, which probably sounds cheery, but the overall feeling was one of some unknowable sentience, as if it wasn't a palace at all but a thinking creature with an alien brain. I knew my imagination was running away with me (no, I *didn't* know that), but I was very glad Mr Bowditch's marks had brought me around to the stadium side, so those cathedral windows couldn't stare directly down at me. I'm not sure I could have borne their green gaze.

I pedaled slowly along the wide entryway path, the wheels of the trike sometimes thumping over blocks that had been pushed out of true. The back of the palace was mostly blind stone. There was a series of large red doors – eight or nine – and an ancient traffic jam of wagons, more than a few overturned and a couple smashed to pieces. It was easy to imagine Hana doing that, maybe out of anger, maybe just for sport. I thought this was a supply area the rich and royal saw seldom if ever. This was the way the common folk came.

I spied Mr Bowditch's faded initials on one of the stone blocks close to this loading-and-unloading area. I didn't like being that close to the palace, even on its blind side, because I could almost see it moving. Pulsing. The crossbar of the **A** pointed left, so I diverted from the main way to follow the arrow. Radar was coughing again, and hard.

When I'd put my face against her fur to stifle my laughter, it had been wet and cold and matted. Could dogs get pneumonia? I decided that was a stupid question. Probably any creature with lungs could get it.

More initials led me to a line of six or eight flying buttresses. I could have gone under them but chose not to. They were the same dark green as the tower windows, maybe not stone at all but some kind of glass. Hard to believe glass could provide the tremendous weight-bearing load such a huge, rearing edifice would require, but glass was what it looked like. And once again I saw black tendrils inside, lazily writhing around each other as they slowly rose and sank. Looking at the buttresses was like looking at a line of strange green and black lava lamps. Those writhing black tendrils made me think of several horror movies – *Alien* was one, *Piranha* was another – and I wished I had never watched them.

I was starting to think I was going to make a full circuit of the palace, which would mean falling under the triple gaze of those spires, when I came to an alcove. It was between two windowless wings that spread apart in a **V**. There were benches here surrounding a little pool that was shaded by palm trees – crazy but true. The palms obscured what lay deeper in this alcove, but rearing above them, at least a hundred feet high, was a pole topped by a stylized sun. It had a face, and the eyes moved back and forth, like the tick-tocking eyes of a Kit-Cat Klock. To the right of the pool, Mr Bowditch had painted his initials on a stone block. The crossbar of this **A** didn't have an arrow; this time the arrow jutted from the apex. I could almost hear Mr Bowditch saying *Straight ahead, Charlie, and don't waste time.*

'Hang on, Rades, almost there.'

I pedaled in the direction the arrow pointed. It took me to the right of the pretty little pool. There was no need to stop and peer into it from between two of the palms, not when what I'd come for was so close, but I did. And as terrible as what I saw there was, I'm glad. It changed everything, although it would be a long time before I fully understood the crucial importance of that moment. Sometimes we look because we have to remember. Sometimes the most horrible things are what give us strength. I know that now, but at the time all I could think was *Oh my dear God, it's Ariel.*

Lying in that pool, once perhaps a soothing blue but now turned silty and dim with decomposition, were the remains of a mermaid. But not Ariel, the Disney princess daughter of King Triton and Queen Athena. No, not her. Most certainly not her. There was no sparkly green tail, no blue eyes, no billow of red hair. No cute little purple bra top, either. I thought this mermaid had once been blond, but most of her hair had fallen out and floated on top of the pool. Her tail might once have been green, but now it was a stupid lifeless gray, like her skin. Her lips were gone, revealing a ring of small teeth. Her eyes were empty sockets.

Yet once she had been beautiful. I was as sure of that as I was of the happy throngs that had once come here to see games or entertainments. Beautiful and alive and full of happy, harmless magic. Once she had swum here. It had been her home, and the people who had taken time to come to this pocket oasis had seen her, she had seen them, and both had been refreshed. Now she was dead, with an iron shaft protruding from the place where her fish tail became a human torso, and a coil of gray guts bulged from the hole. Only a whisper of her beauty and grace remained. She was as dead as any fish that ever died in an aquarium and floated there with all its lively colors faded. She was an ugly corpse partially preserved by cold water. While a truly ugly creature – Hana – still lived and sang and farted and ate her noxious food.

Cursed, I thought. *All cursed. Evil has fallen on this unlucky land.* That was not a Charlie Reade thought, but it was a true thought.

I felt hate for Hana rise up in me, not because she had killed the little mermaid (I thought the giant would have simply torn her to shreds) but because she, Hana, was alive. And would be in my way going back.

Radar began coughing again, so hard I could hear the basket creak behind me. I broke the spell of that pathetic corpse and pedaled around the pool and toward the pole with the sun atop it.

3

The sundial filled the part of the alcove where the V of the two wings narrowed. Before it was a sign on an iron pole. Faded but still legible, it said ALL KEEP OUT. The disc looked to be twenty feet in diameter, which made it – if my math was right – about sixty feet in circumference. I saw Mr Bowditch's initials on the far side. I wanted a good look at them. They had guided me here; now that I was, those last ones might tell me the right direction to turn the sundial. It wasn't possible to ride Claudia's three-wheeler across, because the sundial's circle was rimmed with short black and white pickets about three feet high.

Radar coughed, choked, and coughed some more. She was panting and shivering, one eye gummed shut, the other looking at me. Her fur was matted against her body, letting me see – not that I wanted to – how pitifully thin she'd become, almost skeletal. I dismounted the trike and lifted her out of the basket. Her shivering against me was convulsive: shudder and relax, shudder and relax.

'Soon, girl, soon.'

Hoping I was right, because this was her only chance . . . and it had worked for Mr Bowditch, hadn't it? But even after the giant and the mermaid, I found it hard to believe.

I stepped over the pickets and walked across the sundial. It was stone and divided into fourteen pie-wedges. *Now I think I know how long the days are here*, I thought. A simple symbol, worn but still recognizable, was engraved in the center of each wedge: the two moons, the sun, a fish, a bird, a pig, an ox, a butterfly, a bee, a sheaf of wheat, a bundle of berries, a drop of water, a tree, a naked man, and a naked woman who was pregnant. Symbols of life, and as I passed beside the high pole in the center I could hear the *click-click-click-click* of the eyes in the sun's face as they went back and forth, ticking time away.

I stepped over the short pickets on the far side, still holding Radar against me. Her tongue hung limply from the side of her mouth as she coughed relentlessly. Her time had grown short indeed.

I faced the sundial and Mr Bowditch's initials. The crossbar of the **A** had been turned into a slightly curved arrow pointing to the right, which meant that when I turned the sundial – *if* I could – it would be moving counterclockwise. That seemed correct. I hoped so. If it was wrong, I would have come all this way just to kill my dog by making her even older.

I heard whispering voices and paid them no mind. Radar was all I was thinking about, just her, and I knew what had to be done. I bent and gently laid her on the wedge engraved with the sheaf of wheat. She tried to raise her head but couldn't. She laid it sideways on the stone between her paws, looking at me with her one good eye. Now she was too weak to cough and could only wheeze.

Let this be right and God, please let it work.

I knelt and grasped one of the short rods ringing the sundial's circumference. I pulled on it with one hand, then both. Nothing happened. Radar was now making choking sounds between gasps for air. Her side went up and down like a bellows. I pulled harder. Nothing. I thought of football practice, and how I'd been the only one on the team not just able to move the tackling dummy, but to knock it over.

Pull, you son of a bitch. Pull for her life!

I gave it everything I had – legs, back, arms, shoulders. I could feel blood rushing up my straining neck and into my head. I was supposed to be quiet in Lilimar, but I couldn't restrain a low, growling grunt of effort. Had Mr Bowditch been able to do this? I didn't see how.

Just when I thought I still wasn't going to be able to budge it, I felt the first minuscule shift to the right. I couldn't possibly pull harder, but somehow I did, every muscle in my arms, back, and neck standing out. The sundial began to move. Instead of being directly in front of me, my dog was now a little to my right. I shifted my weight the other way and started pushing for all I was worth. I thought of Claudia telling me to *strain my pooper*. I was straining it now for sure, probably on the verge of turning the poor thing inside out.

Once I had it started, the wheel turned more easily. The first picket was beyond me, so I grabbed another, shifted my weight again, and pulled on it as hard as I could. When that one slipped past, I grabbed yet another. It made me think of the play merry-go-round in Cavanaugh Park, and how Bertie and I used to spin it until the little kids riding on it were screaming in joy and terror and their mothers were yelling at us to stop before one of them flew off.

Radar was a third of the way around . . . then half . . . then on her way back to me. The sundial was spinning easily now. Perhaps some ancient grease-clog in the machinery beneath it had been broken, but I kept yanking on those pickets, now going hand over hand as if climbing a rope. I thought I was seeing a change in Radar but believed it might be only wishful thinking until the sundial brought her all the way back to me. Both of her eyes were open. She was coughing, but the horrible wheezing had stopped and her head was up.

The sundial moved faster and I quit pulling at the pickets. I watched Radar on her second circuit and saw her trying to rise on her front paws. Her ears were up instead of flopping dispiritedly. I squatted, breathing hard, my shirt damp against my chest and sides, trying to figure out how many turns would be enough. I realized I still didn't know how old she was. Fourteen? Maybe even fifteen? If each circuit equaled a year, four turns on the sundial would be good. Six would put her back in the prime of life.

When she passed me, I saw she wasn't just propping herself on her front legs; she was sitting up. And as she came around for the third time, I saw something I could hardly credit: Rades was filling out, putting on weight. She wasn't yet the dog who had scared the shit out of Andy Chen, but she was getting there.

Only one thing bothered me – even without me yanking on the short posts, the sundial was still picking up speed. The fourth time around, I thought Radar looked worried. The fifth time she looked scared, and the wind of her passage blew the sweat-soaked hair off my forehead. I had to get her off. If I didn't, I'd be treated to the sight of my dog becoming a puppy, and then . . . nothing. Overhead the *click-click-click-click* of the sunface's eyes had become *clickclickclickclick*, and I knew that if I looked up I'd see its eyes going left and right faster and faster, until they were just a blur.

Amazing things can go through your mind in times of extreme stress. I flashed on a Turner Classic Movies Western I'd seen with my dad back in his drinking days. *Pony Express*, it was called. What I remembered was Charlton Heston, galloping hell-for-leather toward a lonely outpost where a bag of mail hung on a hook. Charlton snatched it without ever slowing his horse from its all-out gallop, and I was going to have to snatch Radar the same way. I didn't want to shout, so I got into a crouch and held my arms out, hoping she'd understand.

When the sundial came around and she saw me, she got to her feet. The wind of the speeding disc rippled her fur like invisible stroking hands. If I missed her (Charlton Heston hadn't missed the mailbag, but that was a movie), I'd have to jump on myself, grab her, and jump off. I might lose one of my seventeen years in the process, but sometimes desperate measures are the only measures.

As it happened, I didn't have to grab her at all. When I put her on the sundial, Rades couldn't have even walked on her own. After five – going on six – turns on it, she was an entirely different dog. She dropped to her haunches, flexed newly powerful back legs, and leaped into my outstretched arms. It was like being hit with a flying bag of concrete. I fell over on my back with Radar over me, forepaws planted wide on either side of my shoulders, wagging her tail like crazy and licking my face.

'Stop it!' I whispered, but the command didn't have much force because I was laughing. She went on licking.

At last I sat up and took a good look at her. She had been down to sixty pounds, maybe less. Now she had to go eighty or ninety. The wheezing and coughing were gone. The rheum drying on her snout was also gone, as if it had never been there. The white had disappeared both from her snout and the black saddle of fur on her back. Her tail, which had been a tattered flag, was bushy and full as it swished back and forth. Best of all – the surest indicator of the change the sundial had wrought – were her eyes. They were no longer filmy and dazed, as if she didn't know exactly what was going on within her or in the outside world around her.

'Look at you,' I whispered. I had to wipe my eyes. 'Just look at you.'

4

I hugged her, then stood up. The thought of finding the gold pellets never crossed my mind. I'd tempted fate enough for one day. More than enough.

There was no way this new and improved version of Radar would fit in the basket on the back of the three-wheeler. One look was enough to convince me of that. Nor did I have her leash. That was back at Claudia's house, in Dora's cart. I think part of me must have believed I'd never need such a thing again.

I bent, put my hands on the sides of her face, and looked into her dark brown eyes. 'Stay with me. And be quiet. *Hush*, Rades.'

We went back the way we came, me pedaling, Radar padding along beside me. I made it a point not to look in the pool. As we neared the stone passageway, the rain began again. Halfway along the passage, I stopped and dismounted the trike. I told Radar to sit and stay. Moving slowly, keeping my back to the passageway's moss-coated side, I slid to the end. Radar watched but didn't move – good dog. I stopped when I could see the golden arm of that grotesquely over-decorated throne. I took another step, craned my neck, and saw it was empty. Rain pattered down on the striped canopy.

Where was Hana? Which side of the two-part house? And what was she doing?

Questions for which I had no answer. She might still be eating her midday meal of stuff that smelled like pork but probably wasn't, or she might have already gone back to her living quarters for her after-noon nap. I didn't think we'd been gone long enough for me to assume she'd finished eating, but that was only a guess. The last little while – first the mermaid, then the sundial – had been intense.

From where I stood, I could see the dry fountain dead ahead. It would give us good cover, but only if we were unobserved until we got there. Just fifty yards, but when I imagined the consequences of being caught out in the open, it seemed a lot further. I listened for Hana's bellowing voice, louder even than Claudia's, and didn't hear it. A few verses of the prong-de-dong song would have come in handy for pinpointing her location, but here's something I learned in the haunted city of Lilimar: giants never sing when you want them to.

Nevertheless, a choice had to be made, and mine was to try for the fountain. I went back to Radar and was about to mount up on the trike when there was a loud slam to the left of the passageway's end. Radar started and turned that way, a low snarl beginning deep in her chest. I grabbed her before it could morph into a volley of barks and bent down. 'Quiet, Radar, hush.'

I heard Hana muttering – something I couldn't make out – and there was another of those great ripping farts. This one didn't make me feel like laughing, because she was walking slowly across the entrance to the passageway. If she looked to her right, Radar and I could stand against the wall and maybe in the dimness go unobserved, but even if Hana were nearsighted, Claudia's three-wheeler was too big to miss.

I drew Mr Bowditch's revolver and held it by my side. If she turned our way, I was going to shoot her, and I knew exactly what I was going to aim for: that red-rimmed crack running down the center of her forehead. I'd never practiced with Mr Bowditch's gun (or any gun), but my eyes were good. I might miss the first time, but I'd have four more chances even if I did. As for the noise? I thought of those bones scattered around the throne and thought, *fuck the noise.*

She never looked our way or toward the fountain either, only stared at her feet and went on muttering in a way that reminded me of Dad before he had to make a speech at the Overland National Insurance annual dinner, when he won Regional Employee of the Year. There was something in her left hand, but her hip mostly blocked it until she raised it to her mouth. She was gone from sight before she could bite into it, which was fine by me. I'm pretty sure it was a foot, and that there was already a crescent-shaped bite in one side, below the ankle.

I was afraid she might settle back onto the throne to polish off her after-lunch treat, but apparently the rain, even with the canopy to shield her, discouraged that idea. Or maybe she just wanted her nap. Either way, there was the slam of another door, this one to our right, then silence. I holstered the gun and sat down next to my dog. Even in the dimness I could see how good Radar looked – how young and strong. I was glad. Maybe that seems like a tame word to you, but it doesn't to me. I think gladness is a big, big deal. I couldn't keep my hands off her fur and marveling at how dense it was.

5

I didn't want to wait; all I wanted was to get the hell out of Lilimar with my renewed dog and take her into that supply shed and watch her eat as much as she could. I was betting that would be a lot. I'd give her a whole jar of Orijen if she wanted, and a couple of Perky Jerky sticks to top it off. Then we could watch the monarchs return to their roosting places.

That was what I wanted, but I made myself wait and give Hana a chance to settle down. I counted to five hundred by tens, then fives, then twos. I didn't know if that was time enough for the oversized bitch to get into full snooze mode, but I couldn't wait any longer. Getting out of her vicinity was important, but I also had to be out of the city by dark, and not just because of the night soldiers. Some of Mr Bowditch's marks were very faded, and if I lost his trail, I'd be in bad trouble.

'Come on,' I told Radar. 'But hush, girl, hush.'

I pulled the trike, wanting to have it behind me if Hana suddenly emerged and attacked. While she was swiping it out of the way, I might have time to draw and fire. Plus there was Radar, who was back to her fighting weight. I had an idea that if Hana messed with Rades, she was going to lose some flesh. That, I thought, would be a pleasant sight to see. Seeing Hana break Radar's neck with one swipe of her enormous hand, however, wouldn't be pleasant at all.

I paused at the mouth of the passageway, then started for the fountain with Radar beside me. There were games (particularly against our chief rival, St John's) that never seemed to end, but the walk in the open between Hana's house and the dry fountain in the square were the longest fifty yards of my life. I kept expecting to hear some Empisarian version of *fee-fi-fo-fum* and hear the ground-shaking thud of her running feet as she came after us.

A bird squalled – maybe a crow, maybe a buzzard – but that was the only sound. We made it to the fountain and I leaned against it to wipe a mixture of sweat and rainwater from my face. Radar was looking up at me. No shaking or shivering now; no coughing, either. She was grinning. Having an adventure.

I took another look for Hana, then mounted up and started pedaling for the fancy divided boulevard where, once upon a time, the elite folks had no doubt met to eat tea sandwiches and discuss the latest court gossip. Maybe in the evenings there had been Empisarian barbecues or lamplit cotillions in big backyards that were now overgrown with weeds, thistles, and dangerous flowers.

I went at a pretty good clip, but Radar kept up easily, loping along with her tongue flying jauntily from one side of her mouth. The rain was coming down harder, but I barely noticed. All I wanted was to retrace my course and get out of the city. I'd worry about drying off then, and if I caught a cold, I'm sure Claudia would stuff me full of chicken soup before I headed back to Woody's . . . then Dora's . . .

then home. My father would give me a whole raft of shit, but when he saw Radar, he'd . . .

He'd what?

I decided not to worry about that now. The first job was to get out of this unpleasant city, which wasn't deserted at all. And which wouldn't quite stay still.

6

It should have been easy – simply follow Mr Bowditch's marks in reverse, going in the opposite direction of each pointing arrow until we got back to the main gate. But when I came to the point where we'd entered the wide boulevard, his initials were gone. I was sure they'd been on a cobblestone in front of a sprawling building with a dirty glass cupola on top, but there wasn't a sign of them. Could the rain have washed them away? It didn't seem likely, considering all the rain that must have fallen on them over the years, and this set had still been relatively bright. More likely I'd been wrong.

I pedaled further down the boulevard, looking for **AB**. After passing three more side streets with no sign of them, I turned around and went back to the bankish-looking building with the cupola.

'I *know* it was here,' I said, and pointed down the crooked street to where an earthen pot containing a dead treelet lay overturned in the street. 'I remember that. I guess the rain washed away the marks after all. Come on, Rades.'

I pedaled slowly along, eyes peeled for the next set of initials, feeling uneasy. Because they were a chain, weren't they? Sort of like the chain that had led from my mother's fatal accident on the goddam bridge to Mr Bowditch's shed. If one link was broken, there was a good chance I'd be lost. *You would still be wandering in that hellhole at nightfall*, Claudia had said.

Further down this narrow street we came to a lane of ancient deserted shops. I believed we'd come that way, but there were no initials here, either. I thought I recognized what could have been an apothecary on one side, but the slumped, vacant-eyed building on the other didn't look familiar at all. I looked around for the palace, hoping to nail down our location that way, but it was barely visible in the sheeting rain.

'Radar,' I said, and pointed at the corner. 'Do you smell anything?'

She went in the direction I'd pointed and sniffed at the crumbling sidewalk, then looked up at me, waiting for further instructions. I had none to give, and I certainly didn't blame her. We'd come on the three-wheeler, after all, and even if we'd been walking, the downpour would have washed away any remaining scent.

'Come on,' I said.

We went down the street because I thought I remembered the apothecary, but also because we had to go *somewhere*. I thought the best plan would be to keep sighting on the palace and try to work my way back to Gallien Road. Using the main thoroughfare might be dangerous – the way Mr Bowditch's signs had skirted around it suggested as much – but it would lead us out. As I said, it was a straight shot.

The problem was that the streets seemed to insist on taking us away from the palace rather than toward it. Even when the rain slacked off and I could see those three spires again, they always seemed farther away. The palace was on our left, and I found plenty of streets leading in that direction, but they always seemed to dead-end or bend back to the right again. The whispering was louder. I wanted to dismiss it as the wind and couldn't. There *was* no wind. A building with two stories seemed to grow a third in the corner of my eye, but when I looked back, there were only two. A square building seemed to bulge out toward me. A gargoyle – something like a gryphon – seemed to turn its head to watch us.

If Radar saw or sensed any of this, it didn't seem to bother her, maybe she was just reveling in her new strength, but it bothered me plenty. It was harder and harder not to think of Lilimar as a living entity, semi-sentient and determined not to let us go.

The street ahead of us ended in a steep-sided gulch full of rubble and standing water – another dead end. On impulse I turned down an alley so narrow that the trike's back wheels scraped rusty flakes from the brick sides. Radar walked ahead of me. Suddenly she stopped and began barking. They were loud and strong, powered by healthy lungs.

'What is it?'

She barked again and sat, ears cocked, looking down the alley into the rain. And then, from around the corner of the street to which the alley connected, came a high voice I recognized at once.

'Hello, savior of insecks! Are you still an irritable boy, or are you now a scared boy? One who wants to run home to mommy but can't find his way?'

This was followed by a squall of laughter.

'I cleaned away your marks with lye, didn't I? Let's see if you can find your way out of the Lily before the night soldiers come out to play! No problem for me, this little fellow knows these streets like the back of his hand!'

It was Peterkin, but in my mind's eye I saw Christopher Polley. Polley, at least, had a reason to want revenge; I'd broken his hands. What had I done to Peterkin besides making him stop torturing an oversized red cricket?

Embarrassed him, that was what. It was all I could think of. But I knew something he almost certainly didn't: the dying dog he'd seen on Kingdom Road wasn't the dog I was traveling with now. Radar was looking back at me. I pointed down the alley. '*GET HIM!*'

She didn't need to be told twice. Rades sprinted toward the sound of that unpleasant voice, splashing up brick-tinged water from her paws, and darted around the corner. There was a surprised shriek from Peterkin and a volley of barking – the kind that had scared the hell out of Andy Chen once upon a time – and then a howl of pain.

'*You'll be sorry!*' Peterkin screamed. '*You and your damn dog!*'

I'll get you, my pretty, I thought as I pedaled down the narrow alley. I wasn't able to go as fast as I wanted to because the hubs of the back wheels kept scraping the sides. *I'll get you, and your little dog, too.*

'Hold him!' I shouted. 'Hold him, Radar!' If she could do that, he could lead us out of here. I would persuade him, just as I'd persuaded Polley.

But as I was nearing the end of the alley, Radar came back around the corner. Dogs can look shamefaced – anyone who's ever lived with one knows that – and that's how she looked just then. Peterkin had gotten away, but not unscathed. In her jaws, Radar held a good-sized scrap of bright green cloth that could only have come from Peterkin's britches. Even better, I saw two spots of blood.

I reached the end of the alley, looked to my right, and saw him clinging to the second-story cornice of a stone building twenty or thirty yards down the street. He looked like a human fly. I could see the metal gutter he must have climbed to get out of Radar's reach (but not quite quickly enough, ha-ha), and as I watched he scrambled onto a ledge and squatted there. It looked crumbly, and I hoped it would give way beneath him, but no such luck. It might have done if he'd been of an ordinary size.

'You'll pay for that!' he screamed, shaking a fist at me. 'The night soldiers will start by killing your damn dog! I hope they don't kill you! I want to watch Red Molly rip your guts from your belly in the Fair One!'

I drew the .45, but before I could shoot at him (given the distance I would almost certainly have missed), he gave another of his ugly screams, tumbled backward into a window with his little arms clasping his little knees to his little chest, and was gone.

'Well,' I said to Radar, 'that was exciting, wasn't it? What do you say we get the hell out of here?'

Radar barked once.

'And drop that piece of his pants before it poisons you.'

Radar did, and we went on. As we passed the window through which Peterkin had disappeared, I kept an eye out for him, hoping he'd appear like a target in a shooting gallery, but no luck on that, either. I guess cowardly fucks like him don't give you a second chance . . . but sometimes (if the fates are kind) you get a third one. I could hope for that.

CHAPTER NINETEEN

The Trouble with Dogs. The Pedestal. The Graveyard. The Outer Gate.

1

The trouble with dogs (supposing you don't beat or kick them, of course) is they trust you. You're the food-giver and shelter-provider. You're the one that can fish the squeaky monkey out from beneath the couch with one of your clever five-fingered paws. You are also the love-giver. The problem with that kind of unquestioning trust is that it carries a weight of responsibility. Mostly that's okay. In our current situation it was anything but.

Radar was clearly having the time of her life, practically bouncing along beside me, and why not? She was no longer the old half-blind German Shepherd I'd had to haul, first in Dora's cart and then in the basket behind Claudia's oversized trike. She was young again, she was strong again, she'd even had the chance to rip out the seat of a nasty old dwarf's pants. She was easy in her body and easy in her mind as well. She was with the food-giver, the shelter-provider, the love-giver. All was awesome sauce in her world.

I, on the other hand, was struggling against panic. If you've ever been lost in a big city, you'll know. Except here there was no friendly stranger I could ask for directions. And here the city itself had turned against me. One street led to another, but each new street led only to dead ends where gargoyles leered down from great blind buildings I'd swear hadn't been there when I turned around to check for Peterkin slinking along in our wake. The rain slackened to a drizzle, but my view of the palace was often blocked by buildings that seemed to grow the moment I looked away, cutting off the view.

And there was something worse. When I *was* able to glimpse the palace, it always seemed to be in a different place than the one I was expecting. As if it were moving, too. That could have been a fear-driven illusion – I told myself so again and again – but I didn't completely believe it. The afternoon was passing, and every wrong turn reminded me that dark was approaching. The fact was simple and stark: thanks to Peterkin, I had entirely lost my bearings. I almost expected to come upon a candy house where a witch would invite me and my dog – me Hansel, her Gretel – inside.

Meanwhile, Radar kept pace with the three-wheeler, looking up at me with a doggy grin that almost shouted *Aren't we having fun?*

On we went. And on.

Every now and then I got a clear view of the sky ahead and I stepped up on the three-wheeler's seat in an effort to glimpse the city wall, which had to be the biggest thing in the landscape, except for the three spires of the palace. I couldn't see it. And those spires were now on my right, which seemed impossible. Surely if I'd crossed in front of the palace I would have cut the Gallien Road, and I hadn't. I felt like screaming. I felt like curling up in a ball with my hands around my head. I wanted to find a policeman, which is what my mother told me children were supposed to do if they got lost.

And all the time Radar was grinning up at me: *Isn't this great? Isn't it just the coolest ever?*

'We're in trouble, girl.'

I pedaled on. No patch of blue in the sky now, and certainly no sun to guide me. Only buildings crowding in, some smashed, some merely vacant, all somehow hungry. The only sound was that faint, dull whispering. If it had been constant I might have been able to get used to it, but it wasn't. It came in bursts, as if I were passing congregations of the unseen dead.

That terrible afternoon (I can never convey to you *how* terrible) seemed to go on forever, but at last I began to sense the first draining toward evening. I think I cried a little but can't remember for sure. If I did, I think it was as much for Radar as for myself. I had brought her all this way, and I'd accomplished what I'd come for, but in the end it was all going to be for nothing. Because of the goddamned dwarf. I wished Radar had ripped out his throat instead of the seat of his pants.

Worst of all was the trust I saw in Radar's eyes every time she looked up at me.

You trusted a fool, I thought. *Worse luck for you, honey.*

2

We came to an overgrown park surrounded on three sides by gray buildings stacked with empty balconies. They looked to me like a cross between the expensive condos lining Chicago's Gold Coast and prison cellblocks. In the center of it was a piece of huge statuary on a high pedestal. It appeared to be a man and a woman flanking an enormous butterfly, but like all the other works of art I'd encountered in Lilimar (not to mention the poor murdered mermaid), it had been mostly destroyed. The head and one wing of the butterfly had been pulverized. The other wing had survived, and based on the way it had been carved (all color was gone, if there had ever been any), I was sure it was a monarch. The man and woman might have been a king and queen in days of yore, but there was no way to tell because both of them were gone from the knees up.

As I sat looking at this vandalized tableau, three bells rang out across the haunted city, each peal spaced out and solemn. *You don't need to be through the gate when the three bells ring*, Claudia had said, *but you must be out of Lilimar soon after! Before dark!*

Dark would be soon.

I started to pedal on – knowing it would be fruitless, knowing I was caught in the spiderweb Peterkin had called the Lily, wondering what fresh horror the night soldiers would bring when they came for us – and then I stopped, struck by a sudden idea that was simultaneously wild and perfectly reasonable.

I did a U-turn and returned to the park. I started to dismount the trike, considered the height of the pedestal that ruined tableau stood on, and changed my mind. I pedaled into the high grass, hoping there were none of those nasty yellow flowers to give me a burn. I also hoped the three-wheeler wouldn't get bogged down, because the ground was mushy from all the rain. I put my back into it and kept pedaling. Radar stayed with me, not walking or even running but leaping along. Even in my current situation, that was wonderful to see.

The statuary tableau was surrounded by standing water. I parked in it, hung my pack over the handlebars, stood on the seat of the trike, and reached up. By rising on my toes, I could just get my fingers over the gritty edge of the pedestal. Thanking God that I was still in fairly good shape, I did a chin-up, got first one forearm and then the other on a surface that was littered with stone chips, and scrambled the rest of the way. I had one bad moment when I thought I was going to tip over backward, landing on the trike and probably breaking something, but I gave one final lunge and grabbed the stone woman's foot. I got a couple of good belly-scratches from the rubble as I pulled myself the rest of the way but sustained no real damage.

Radar was looking up at me and barking. I told her to hush and she did. She kept wagging her tail, though: *Isn't he wonderful? Look how high he is!*

I got up and grasped the remaining wing of the butterfly. Maybe there was a little magic left in it – the good kind – because I felt some of my fear subside. Holding it first with one hand and then the other, I did a slow three-hundred-and-sixty-degree turn. I saw the three spires of the palace against the darkening sky, and now they were roughly where what remained of my sense of direction told me they should be. I couldn't see the city wall and hadn't really expected to. The pedestal I stood on was high, but too many buildings were in the way. Purposely, I was almost sure.

'Wait, Radar,' I said. 'This won't take long.' I hoped I was right about that. I bent down and picked up a piece of stone with a sharp point and held it loosely in my fist.

Time ticked by. I counted to five hundred by tens, then by fives, then lost count. I was too concerned with the darkening day. I could almost feel it draining away, like blood from a bad cut. At last, just when I'd begun to believe I'd climbed up here for nothing, I saw a darkness arise in what I'd decided to call the south. It came toward me. The monarchs were returning for the night. I held my arm out, pointing it like a rifle toward the oncoming butterflies. I lost sight of the cloud when I knelt down again but continued to hold my arm out straight. I used the point of the shard I'd picked up to scratch a mark on the side of the pedestal, then sighted along my outstretched hand at a gap between two buildings on the far side of the park. It was a start. Assuming the gap didn't disappear, that was.

I pivoted on my knees and slid my legs over the edge. My plan was to hold on until I was dangling from the side of the pedestal, but my hands slipped and I fell. Radar gave a single bark of alarm. I knew enough to let my knees flex and to roll when I landed. The ground was soft from the rain, which was good. I got splashed from head to toe with mud and water, which wasn't. I got up (almost falling over my eager dog when I did), wiped my face, and looked for my mark. I pointed my hand along it and was relieved to see the gap between the two buildings was still there. The buildings – wood, not stone – were diagonally across the park. I saw standing water in places and knew the three-wheeler would get bogged down for sure if I tried to ride it. I was going to owe Claudia an apology for leaving it behind, but I'd worry about that when I saw her. If I did.

'Come on, girl.' I slung on my pack and began to run.

3

We splashed through the wide puddles of standing water. Some were shallow, but in places the water was almost up to my knees, and I could feel the mud trying to suck the sneakers from my feet. Radar kept pace easily, tongue flying, eyes bright. Her fur was soaked and matted to her newly muscular body, but she didn't seem to mind. We were having an adventure!

The buildings looked to me like warehouses. We reached them and I stopped long enough to re-settle and re-tie one of my sopping sneakers. I looked back at the pedestal. I could no longer make out my mark – the ruined tableau was at least a hundred yards behind us – but I knew where it was. I pointed with both arms, back and ahead, then ran between the buildings with Radar right beside me. They'd been warehouses, all right. I could smell the ancient ghost-aroma of the fish that had been stored in them long ago. My pack bounced and jounced. We came out on a narrow lane lined with more warehouses. They all looked as if they'd been broken into – probably looted – long ago. The pair directly across from us were too close together to slip between, so I went right, found an alley, and ran through it. On the far side was someone's overgrown garden. I jinked to the left, back to what I hoped was my former straight line, and ran on. I tried to tell myself it wasn't twilight – not yet, not yet – but it was. Of course it was.

Again and again I had to detour around buildings that were in our way, and again and again I tried to regain the straight course to where I'd seen the butterflies. I was no longer sure I was doing that, but I had to try. It was all I had.

We passed between two great stone houses, the gap so narrow I had to sidle (Radar had no such problem). I came out, and to my right, in a walkway between what might once have been a grand museum and a glass-sided conservatory, I saw the city wall. It reared above the buildings on the far side of the street, the clouds so low in the gathering gloom that the top was lost.

'Radar! Come on!'

That gloom made it impossible to know if real dark had come or not, but I was terribly afraid it had. We ran down the street we'd come out on. Not the right one, but close to the Gallien Road, I felt sure of it. Ahead of us the buildings gave way to a cemetery on the far side of the street. It was full of leaning gravestones, memorial tablets, and several buildings that had to be crypts. It was the last place I wanted to venture into after dark, but if I was right – *God, please let me be right*, I prayed – that was the way we had to go.

I sprinted through tall iron gates standing ajar, and for the first time Radar hesitated, front paws on a crumbling concrete slab, rear paws in the street. I stopped too, long enough to catch my breath.

'I don't like it, either, girl, but we have to, so come on!'

She came. We weaved our way around the leaning grave markers. An evening mist was beginning to rise from the overgrown grass and thistles. I could see a wrought iron fence forty yards ahead. It looked too high to climb even if I hadn't had my dog with me, but there was a gate.

I tripped over a gravestone and went sprawling. I started to get up, then froze, at first not believing what I was seeing. Radar was barking wildly. A desiccated hand with yellowing bone showing through torn skin emerged from the ground. It opened and closed, clutching and releasing little showers of wet earth. When I saw such things in horror movies, I just laughed and hooted along with my friends and grabbed more popcorn. I wasn't laughing now. I screamed . . . *and the hand heard me*. It turned toward me like a fucking radar dish, clutching at the darkening air.

I leaped to my feet and ran. Rades ran beside me, barking and snarling and looking back over her shoulder. I reached the cemetery gate. It was locked. I drew back, lowered one shoulder, and hit it the way I'd once hit opposing linemen. It rattled but didn't give. Radar's barks were climbing the ladder, no longer *ROWF-ROWF-ROWF* but *YARK-YARK-YARK*, almost as if she were also trying to scream.

I looked back and saw more hands emerging from the ground, like ghastly flowers with fingers instead of petals. First just a few, then dozens. Maybe hundreds. And something else, something worse: the squall of rusty hinges. The crypts were about to give up their dead. I remember thinking that punishing trespassers was one thing – understandable – but this was ridiculous.

I hit the gate again, giving it everything I had. The lock broke. The gate burst open and I went flailing forward, arms waving, trying to keep my balance. I almost made it, then tripped over something else, maybe a curbstone, and went to my knees.

I looked up and saw that I had fallen into the Gallien Road.

I got to my feet, knees stinging and pants ripped. I looked behind me into the graveyard. There was nothing coming after us, but those waving hands were quite bad enough. I thought about the strength it would take to burst open coffin lids and claw through the intervening earth. For all I knew, the Empisarians didn't bother with coffins, maybe they just wrapped their dead in shrouds and called it good. The groundmist had taken on a blue glow, as if electrified.

'*RUN!*' I shouted at Radar. '*RUN!*'

We ran for the gate. We ran for our lives.

4

We'd come out on the road much further up from where we'd turned off to follow Mr Bowditch's marks, but I could see the outer gate in the gathering gloom. It might have been half a mile ahead, maybe a little less. I was gasping, and my legs felt heavy. Some of that was because my pants had gotten soaked with mud and water when I fell from the pedestal, but mostly it was simple exhaustion. I'd played sports for my entire scholastic career but had skipped basketball – not just because I didn't really care for Coach Harkness but because, given my size and weight, running really wasn't my thing. There was a reason I played first during baseball season; it was the defensive position requiring the least speed. I had to slow to a jog. Even though the gate didn't seem to be getting any closer, it was the best I could do if I didn't want to cramp up and have to stop.

Then Radar looked over her shoulder and began giving those high, frightened barks again. I turned and saw a flock of brilliant blue lights coming toward us from the direction of the palace. It had to be the night soldiers. I didn't waste time trying to convince myself otherwise, just picked up my pace again.

My breath ran in and out of me, each gasp and blow hotter than the last. My heart was thundering. Bright spots began to pulse in front of my eyes, expanding and contracting. I looked back again and saw the blue lights were closer. And they had gained legs. They were men, each surrounded by a fierce blue aura. I couldn't see their faces yet and didn't want to.

I stumbled over my own stupid feet, caught my balance, ran on. Full dark had arrived, but the gate was a lighter shade of gray than the wall, and I could see it was closer. If I could keep running, I thought we had a chance.

A stitch started in my side, not bad at first, then sinking in. It ran up my ribcage and drilled into my armpit. My hair, wet and muddy, flopped up and down on my forehead. My pack thudded against my back, so much ballast. I slipped it off and slung it into a nest of brambles beside a turreted building flanked by posts striped red and white and topped with stone butterflies. Those monarchs were still whole, probably because they were too high to reach without ladders.

I stumbled again, this time over a snarl of downed trolley wires, caught myself again, and ran on. They were closing in. I thought about Mr Bowditch's .45, but even if it worked against those apparitions, there were too many of them.

Then a wonderful thing happened: all at once my lungs seemed deeper and the stitch in my side disappeared. I'd never done enough extended running to experience a second wind, but it had happened to me a few times on long bike rides. I knew it wouldn't last long, but it didn't have to. The gate was now only a hundred yards ahead. I risked one more glance over my shoulder and saw that the shining troop of night soldiers had stopped gaining. I faced forward and put on even more speed, head thrown back, hands clenched and pumping, breathing deeper than ever. For thirty yards or so I even pulled ahead of Radar. Then she caught up again and looked over at me. No big *isn't this fun* grin on her chops now; her ears were flat against her skull and white rings showed around her brown eyes. She looked terrified.

At last, the gate.

I pulled in one last deep breath and screamed, '*OPEN IN THE NAME OF LEAH OF THE GALLIEN!*'

The ancient machinery under the gate screeched into life, then smoothed out to a deep rumble. The gate trembled and began to slide open on its hidden track. But slowly. Too slowly, I was afraid. Could the night soldiers leave the city, if we slipped through? I had an idea they couldn't, that their fierce blue auras would wink out and they'd crumble away . . . or melt, like the Wicked Witch of the West.

An inch.

Two.

I could see a tiny sliver of the outside world, where there were wolves but no shining blue men and no rotted hands coming out of graveyard earth.

I looked back and really saw them for the first time: twenty or more men with maroon lips the color of dried blood and parchment pale faces. They were dressed in loose pants and shirts that looked weirdly like army fatigues. That blue light was gushing from their eyes, spilling downward, coating them. They had features like ordinary men, but they were gauzy. I could glimpse the skulls beneath.

They were sprinting at us, leaving little splashes of blue light behind them that dimmed and faded out, but I didn't think they were going to make it in time. It was going to be very close, but I thought we were going to escape.

Three inches.

Four.

Oh God it was so *slow*.

Then came the sound of an old-fashioned firebell – *CLANG-A-LANG-A-LANG* – and the cadre of blue skeleton-men parted, ten or a dozen to the left and the rest to the right. Speeding up the Gallien Road came an electric vehicle like a jumbo golf cart or a squat open-air bus. In front, moving some sort of steering stick to and fro, was a man (I use the word advisedly) with graying hair falling to either side of his hideous half-transparent face. He was gaunt and tall. Others were crammed in behind him, their blue auras overlapping and dripping down to the wet pavement like strange blood. The driver was aiming right at me, meaning to crush me against the gate. I wasn't going to make it after all . . . but my dog could.

'Radar! Go to Claudia!'

She didn't move, only looked up at me in terror.

'Go, Rades! For God's sake GO!'

I had dumped my pack because its sodden weight was slowing me down. Mr Bowditch's gun was different. I couldn't shoot enough night soldiers with it to keep them from getting to me, and I'd no intention of letting them have it. I unbuckled the holster belt with its decorative conchos and slung it into the darkness. If they wanted the .45 they'd have to leave the walled city to look for it. Then I slapped Radar's hindquarters, and hard. Blue light washed over me. I know you can resign yourself to death, because in that moment I did it.

'GO TO CLAUDIA, GO TO DORA, JUST GO!'

She gave me one final wounded look – I'll never forget it – and then slipped through the widening gap.

Something hit me hard enough to drive me against the still-moving gate, but not hard enough to smash me against it. I saw the gray-haired night soldier lunge over his steering stick. I saw his outstretched hands, the fingerbones visible through the tallow of his glowing skin. I saw the eternal grin of his teeth and jaw. I saw blue streams of some awful reanimating power gushing from his eyes.

The gate was open enough for me now. I dipped away from the thing's clutching fingers and rolled toward the opening. For a moment I saw Radar standing in the darkness at the end of Kingdom Road, looking back. Hoping. I lunged toward her, one hand outstretched. Then those terrible fingers closed around my throat.

'No, kiddie,' the undead night soldier whispered. 'No, whole one. You've come to the Lily uninvited, and here you will stay.'

It leaned close, a grinning skull beneath a stretched gauze of pale skin. A walking skeleton. The others began to close in. One shouted a word – I thought it was Elimar, a combination of Empis and Lilimar – but now I know better. The gate began to close. The dead hand tightened, cutting off my air.

Go, Radar, go and be safe, I thought, then knew no more.

CHAPTER TWENTY

Durance Vile. Hamey. Feeding Time.

The Lord High. Interrogation.

1

Radar fights the urge to turn back to the new master, to return to the gate and jump up, her front paws scratching for entry. She doesn't do it. She has her orders and runs. She feels like she can run all night, but she won't have to because there's a safe place, if she can get in.

Slap-slap.

She lopes on and on, body low to the ground. There's no moonlight, not yet, and no wolves howl, but she feels them near. If there's moonlight they will attack, and she senses moonlight coming. If it does and they do, she will fight. They may overwhelm her, but she will fight to the end.

Slap-slap.

'Wake up, kiddie!'

The moons slide out of an unraveling cloud, the smaller in its eternal chase of the larger, and the first wolf howls. But there ahead is the red wagon, and the shelter where she and Charlie spent the night when she was still sick, and if she can reach it she can slip inside if the door is still open. She thinks he didn't close it all the way but isn't sure. That was so long ago! If it is she can stand on her back legs and push it closed with her paws. If it isn't she will put her back against it and fight until she can fight no more.

Slap-slap.

'Do you want to miss another meal? Nah, nah!'

The door is ajar. Radar pushes through it and

SLAP!

2

That one finally shattered the dream I'd been having and I opened my eyes to a chancy, shadowy light and someone kneeling over me. His hair straggled down to his shoulders and he was so pale, for a moment I thought it was the night soldier who'd been driving the little electric bus. I sat up fast. A bolt of pain went through my head, followed by a wave of dizziness. I raised my fists. The man's eyes widened and he drew back. And he *was* a man, not a pallid thing surrounded by an envelope of blue light that spilled from its eyes. These eyes were hollow and bruised-looking, but they were human eyes, and his hair was a dark brown that was almost black, not gray.

'Let him die, Hamey!' someone shouted. 'He's goddam thirty-one! They'll never go for sixty-four, those days are gone! One more and we're for it!'

Hamey – if that was his name – looked toward the voice. He grinned, showing white teeth in a dirty face. He looked like a lonesome weasel. 'Just trying to berdeck my soul, Eye! Do good to another, you know! Too close to the end not to think about the ever-after!'

'Fuck yourself and fuck your ever-after,' said the one called Eye. 'There's this world, then the fireworks, and that's all.'

I was on cold, damp stone. Over Hamey's scrawny shoulder I could see a wall of blocks oozing water with a barred window high up. Nothing between the bars but black. I was in a cell. *Durance vile*, I thought. I didn't know where that phrase came from, wasn't even sure I knew what it meant. What I knew was that my head ached terribly and the man who'd been slapping me awake had breath so bad it was like some small animal had died in his mouth. Oh, and it seemed I had wet my pants.

Hamey leaned close to me. I tried to draw back, but there were more bars behind me.

'You look strong, kiddie.' Hamey's stubble-ringed mouth tickled against my ear. It was horrible and somehow pathetic. 'Will you berdeck me like I berdeckted you?'

I tried to ask where I was, but all that came out were cracked pieces of sound. I licked my lips. They were dry and swollen. 'Thirsty.'

'That I can fix.'

He scurried to a bucket in the corner of what I now had no doubt was a cell . . . and Hamey was my cellmate. He was wearing ragged pants that stopped at his shins, like a castaway in a magazine cartoon. His shirt was barely a singlet. His bare arms glimmered in the chancy light. They were pitifully thin, but they didn't look gray. In the bad light it was hard to tell for sure.

'You goddam idiot!' This was someone else, not the one Hamey had called Eye. 'Why make it worse? Did your nurse drop you on your head when you was a babbin? The kiddie was barely breathin! You could've sat on his chest and made an end to him! Back to thirty, slick as spit!'

Hamey paid no mind. He took a tin cup from a shelf over what I assumed was his pallet and dipped it in the bucket. He brought it to me with one finger – as dirty as the rest of him – pressed against the bottom. 'Hole in it,' he said.

I didn't care, because it wasn't going to get a chance to leak very much. I snatched it and gulped it down. There was grit in it, but I didn't care about that, either. It was heaven.

'Blow him while you're at it, why don't you?' another voice asked. 'Give him a good old sucking, Hames, that'll bring him around smart as a pony-whip!'

'Where am I?'

Hamey leaned forward again, wanting to be confidential. I abhorred his breath, it was making my head ache even worse, but I stood it because I had to know. Now that I was coming around a little and leaving my wishful dream of Radar behind, I was surprised I wasn't dead.

'Maleen,' he whispered. 'Deep Maleen. Ten . . .' Something, some word I didn't know. '. . . below the palace.'

'Twenty!' Eye shouted. 'And you'll never see the sun again, new boy! None of us will, so get used to it!'

I took the cup from Hamey and made my way across the cell, feeling like Radar at her oldest and weakest. I filled it, put my finger over the water trickling from the small hole in the bottom, and drank again. The boy who once watched Turner Classic Movies and ordered online from Amazon was in a dungeon. No way to mistake it for anything else. Cells ran along both sides of a dank corridor. Gas lamps protruded from the walls between a few of the cells, muttering bluish-yellow light. Water dripped down from the hewn rock ceiling. There were puddles in the central passage. Across from me, a big fellow wearing what looked like the remains of long underwear bottoms saw me looking at him and jumped up on the bars, shaking them and making monkey noises. His chest was bare, wide, and hairy. His face was broad, his forehead was low, he was ugly as fuck . . . but there was none of that creeping disfigurement I'd seen on my way to this charming abode, and his voice was all present and accounted for.

'Welcome, new boy!' It was Eye . . . which, I found out later, was short for Iota. 'Welcome to hell! When the Fair One comes . . . *if* it comes . . . I believe I'll rip your liver out and wear it for a hat. First round you, second round whoever they send against me! Until then, have a pleasant stay!'

Down the corridor, near an iron-banded wooden door at the end, another prisoner, this one female, yelled, 'You should have stayed in the Citadel, kiddie!' Then, lower: 'And so should I. Starving would have been better.'

Hamey walked to the corner of the cell opposite the water bucket, dropped his pants, and squatted over a hole in the floor. 'I got the bads. Might have been field mushrooms.'

'What, a year and more since you et any?' Eye asked. 'You got the bads, all right, but mushrooms got nothing to do with it.'

I closed my eyes.

3

Time passed. I don't know how much, but I began to feel a little more like myself. I could smell dirt and damp and gas from the jets that gave this place some semblance of light. I heard the plink of falling water and prisoners moving around, sometimes talking to each other, or maybe to themselves. My cellmate was sitting near the water bucket, staring morosely at his hands.

'Hamey?'

He looked up.

'What are whole ones?'

He snorted laughter, then grimaced and clutched his stomach. '*We* are. Are you foolish? Did you drop from the sky?'

'Pretend I did.'

'Sit over here next to me.' And when I hesitated: 'Nah, nah, never worry about me. I ain't gointer tickle your nuts, if that's what you think. Might have a flea or two hop over to you, is all. I ain't even been able to get stiff these last six months or so. Bad guts'll do that.'

I sat down next to him and he gave my knee a clap.

'That's better. I don't like to speak for all those ears. Not that it matters what they hear, we're all fish in the same bucket, but I keep myself to myself – it's how I was taught.' He sighed. 'Worryin' don't help my poor guts any, I can tell you that. Seeing the numbers go up and up and up? Nasty! Twenty-five . . . twenty-six . . . now thirty-one. And they'll never go to sixty-four, Eye's right about that. Once we whole ones was like a full sack of sugar, but now the sack's empty except for the last few crystals.'

Did he say *crystals*? Or something else? My headache was trying to come back, my legs ached from walking and pedaling and running, and I was tired. It was as if I'd been scooped out somehow.

Hamey gave out another sigh that turned into a coughing fit. He held his belly until it passed. 'Flight Killer and his . . .' Some strange word my mind couldn't translate, something like *ruggamunkas*. '. . . keep shaking the sack, though. Won't be content until he gets every last fucking one of us. But . . . sixty-four? Nah, nah. This'll be the last Fair One, and I'll be among the first to go. Maybe the very first. Ain't strong, you see. Got the bads and food don't stick to me.'

He seemed to remember I was there, the new cellmate.

'But *you* . . . Eye seen you was big. And might be fast, if you had your strength.'

I thought of telling him I wasn't particularly fast but decided not to. Let him think what he wanted.

'He ain't scairt of you, Iota ain't scairt of nobody – except maybe for Red Molly and her bitch ma – but he don't want to work any harder than he has to, either. What's your name?'

'Charlie.'

Lowering his voice even further: 'And you don't know where you are? For real and true?'

Durance vile, I thought. 'Well, it's a prison . . . a dungeon . . . and I guess it might be under the palace . . . but that's about all.'

I had no intention of telling him why I'd come, or who I'd met along the way. I was returning to myself now, tired or not, and starting to think straight. Hamey could be pumping me. Getting info he could trade for privileges. Deep Maleen didn't seem like a place where there *were* privileges – the end of the line, so to speak – but I didn't want to risk it. Maybe they wouldn't care about one escaped German Shepherd from Sentry, Illinois . . . but then again, they might.

'Not from the Citadel, are you?'

I shook my head.

'Don't even know where it is, do you?'

'No.'

'Green Isles? Deesk? One of the Tayvos, maybe?'

'None of those places.'

'Where *are* you from, Charlie?'

I said nothing.

'Don't tell,' Hamey whispered fiercely. 'That's good. Don't tell none of these others, and I won't, neither. If you berdeck me. You'd be wise to. There's worse fates than Deep Maleen, young one. You might not believe it, but I know. The Lord High is bad, but all I know about the Flight Killer is worse.'

'Who is the Flight Killer? And the Lord High, who's he?'

'Lord High's what we call Kellin, chief of the night soldiers. He brought you in himself. I stayed in the corner. Those eyes of his—'

A muffled bell began to ring behind the ironbound door at our end of the dungeon room.

'Pursey!' Iota yelled. He jumped on his bars and began to shake them again. 'Ain't it just about fuckin' time! Get in here, Pursey, my old pal, and let's see what's left of your face!'

There was the sound of bolts being thrown – I counted four – and the door opened. First came a cart, almost like the kind you push around a supermarket, but made of wood. Behind it was a gray man whose face seemed to have melted. Only one eye remained to him. His nose barely jutted from a burl of flesh. His mouth was sealed shut except for a teardrop-shaped opening on the left side. His fingers were so melted his hands looked like flippers. He wore baggy pants and a baggy blouse-like top. A bell was hung around his neck on a rawhide loop.

He stopped just inside the door, seized the bell, and shook it. At the same time he looked back and forth with his one eye. 'Hak! Hak! Hak, oo astards!' Compared to this guy, Dora sounded like Laurence Olivier spouting Shakespeare.

Hamey grabbed me by the shoulder and pulled me back. Across from us, Eye was also stepping back. All the prisoners were. Pursey kept ringing his bell until he was satisfied we were far enough from the bars to make grabbing him impossible, although I didn't see any reason why anyone would; he was like a trustee in a prison movie, and trustees don't carry keys.

The cell Hamey and I were in was closest to him. Pursey reached into his cart, took out two good-sized hunks of meat, and flung them through the bars. I caught mine on the fly. Hamey grabbed for his but missed and it splatted to the floor.

Now the prisoners were yelling at him. One – I later found out it was Fremmy – inquired if Pursey's asshole was skinned over yet, and if so did he have to shit out of his mouth. They sounded like lions in the zoo at feeding time. Only that's wrong. They sounded like hyenas. These weren't lions, with the possible exception of Iota.

Pursey rolled his cart slowly down the corridor between the cells, sandals splashing (his toes were also sealed together), throwing meat left and right. His aim was good, one eye or not; none of the meat hit the bars and fell into the standing water of the corridor.

I raised my chunk to my nose and smelled. I guess I was still in fairy-tale mode, because I expected something rotten and nasty, maybe even infested with maggots, but it was a piece of beefsteak that could have come from the Sentry Hy-Vee market, albeit without the sanitary plastic wrap. It had barely touched fire (I thought of my dad ordering steak in a restaurant and telling the waiter to just run it through a warm room), but the smell was enough to squirt saliva into my mouth and set my stomach to roaring. The last real meal I'd had was in Claudia's wooden house.

Across from me, Eye was sitting on his pallet cross-legged, gnawing on his steak. Red juice ran into the matting of his beard. He saw me looking at him and grinned. 'Go on, kiddie, eat while you got teeth to eat with. I'll knock em out t'rectly.'

I ate. The steak was tough. The steak was delicious. Every bite made me hungry for the next.

Pursey had reached the last pair of cells. He threw meat into them and began backing up the way he'd come, ringing his bell with one flipper, pulling the cart with the other, and yelling 'Hak! Hak!' Which I presumed was *back, back*. No one seemed interested in catcalling him now, let alone rushing him. From everywhere came the sound of smacking and chomping.

I ate everything but a ring of fat and gristle, then ate that, too. Hamey, meanwhile, had taken a few bites of his steak and then subsided to his pallet, holding it on one bony knee. He was staring at it with a puzzled expression, as if wondering why he didn't want it. He saw me looking and held it out. 'Do you want it? Food don't like me and I don't like food. I used to put it away with the best of them, back in my sawmill days. Must have been those mushrooms. Eat the wrong kind and they fry your guts. That's what happened to me.'

I wanted it, all right, my stomach was still roaring, but I had enough restraint left to ask if he was sure. He said he was. I took it fast, in case he changed his mind.

Pursey had stopped outside our cell. He pointed at me with one of his melted hands. 'Helli onts ooo eee ooo.'

'I don't understand,' I said through a mouthful of mostly raw steak, but Pursey just started backing up again, until he was out the door. He gave one more ring of his bell, then shot the bolts: one, two, three, and four.

'He said Kellin wants to see you,' Hamey said. 'I ain't surprised. You're whole, but you ain't like us. Even your accent ain't—' He stopped and his eyes widened as some idea struck him. 'Tell him you're from Ullum! That'll work! Way north of the Citadel!'

'What's Ullum?'

'Religiouses! They don't sound like nobody else! Tell them you ducked the poison!'

'I don't have the slightest idea what you're talking about.'

'Hamey, don't be saying what you shu'nt!' someone shouted. 'You a *voonatick*!'

'Shut up, Stooks!' Hamey cried. 'This kiddie's going to berdeck me!'

Across the corridor, Eye got up and grasped the bars with grease-shiny fingers. He was smiling. 'You may not be a lunatic, but nobody's going to protect you, Hamey. There's no protection for any of us.'

4

There was no pallet for me. I actually thought about taking Hamey's – there was no way he could have stopped me – and then wondered just what the fuck I was thinking . . . or becoming. I had already taken his meal, but at least that had been offered. Besides, a damp stone floor wasn't going to keep me awake, not the way I felt. I'd come to not all that long ago, and after being out for God knew how long, but a great weariness suffused me. I had a drink from the bucket, then lay down on what I supposed was my side of the cell.

In the next one were two men: Fremmy and Stooks. They were young and looked strong. Not big, like Iota, but strong.

Fremmy: 'Babby go nappie-nap?'

Stooks: 'All *tiii*-red out?'

The Abbott and Costello of Deep Maleen, I thought. *And in the very next cell, how fucking lucky can I get?*

'Don't mind em, Charlie,' Hamey said. 'You sleep. Everybody gets it took out of them after being handled by the nightwatch. They suck it out of you. They suck your . . . I dunno . . .'

'Life force?' I asked. I felt like my eyelids had been dipped in cement.

'That's it! That's just what it is and just how they do! And it was Kellin himself carried you in. You must be strong, or the bastard would have cooked you like an egg. I've seen it happen, oh yes I have!'

I tried to ask him how long he'd been here but could only mumble. I was going down. I thought of the spiral steps that had led me here, and it seemed that I was running down them again, chasing after Radar. *Watch out for the roaches*, I thought. *And the bats*.

'Ullum, north of the Citadel!' Hamey was kneeling over me, as he had been when I first woke up in this shithole of a place. 'Don't forget! And you promised to berdeck me, don't forget that, either!'

I couldn't remember promising him any such thing, but before I could say so, I was gone.

5

I woke up with Hamey shaking me. Which was better than slapping. My hangover was gone. That was what it had been, and how my father had taken those, morning after morning during his drinking days, was beyond me. My left shoulder throbbed; probably I'd strained it when I fell from the pedestal, but the other aches and pains were much less.

'What . . . how long was I—'

'On your feet! It's them! Mind the limber sticks!'

I stood up. The door at our end of the corridor opened and filled with blue light. Three night soldiers followed it in, tall and pale inside their auras, the skeletons inside their bodies appearing and disappearing like shuttering shadows on a day when the clouds are racing. They held long sticks that looked like old-timey car aerials.

'Up!' one of them shouted. 'Up, time to play!'

Two of them walked ahead of the third, their arms outstretched like preachers welcoming a congregation to worship. As they went down the corridor, the cell doors squalled open, dripping down showers of rust flakes. The third stopped and pointed at me. 'Not you.'

Thirty prisoners stepped out into the corridor. Hamey gave me a despairing grin as he went, shrinking away from the stationary night soldier's aura. Eye grinned, raised both of his hands, made circles with his thumbs and forefingers, then pointed his middle fingers at me. Not quite the same as an American bird, but I was pretty sure it meant the same. As the prisoners followed the first pair of night soldiers down the corridor, I saw that two were women and two were black. One of the black men was even bigger than Iota, with the broad shoulders and wide butt of a pro football tackle, but he walked slowly, with his head down, and before he passed through the door at the end of the cellblock, I saw him stagger. That was Dommy. The women were Jaya and Eris.

The waiting night soldier extended a pale finger to me and curled it. His face was stern, but beneath it, coming and going, his skull flashed its eternal grin. He gestured with his stick for me to walk ahead of him to the door. Before I could go through it, he said 'Hold,' and then, 'Fuck.'

I stopped. On our right, one of the gas-jet fixtures had fallen out of the wall. It hung askew from its metal hose below a hole like a gaping mouth, still flaming and blackening one of the stone blocks with soot. As he put it back in, his aura brushed me. I felt all my muscles weaken and understood why Hamey had taken such care to avoid that blue envelope. It was like getting a shock from a frayed lamp cord. I stepped away.

'Hold, damn you, hold I say!'

The night soldier grabbed the fixture, which looked to be made of brass. It must have been hotter than hell, but he didn't show any pain. He jammed it back into the hole. The fixture stayed put for a moment, then fell out again.

'Fuck!'

A wave of unreality washed over me. I had been imprisoned in a dungeon, I was being taken God knew where by an undead creature that looked quite a bit like the Skeletor action-figure I'd had when I was small . . . and the creature was doing what was essentially a house-keeping chore.

He grasped the fixture again and cupped one hand over the flame, choking it. He dropped the dead fixture against the wall, where it made a little clink sound. 'Go! Walk, damn you!'

He struck my bad shoulder with his limber stick. It hurt like fire. Being whipped was both humiliating and infuriating, but it was better than the debilitating weakness I'd felt when his aura brushed me.

I walked.

6

He followed me down a long stone-throated corridor, close but not close enough for his aura to touch me. We passed a Dutch door, the top half open to let out the smell of good things cooking. I saw a man and a woman pass, one carrying a pair of buckets, the other a steaming wooden tray. They were dressed in white, but their skin was gray and their faces were subsiding.

'Walk!' The limber stick came down again, this time on the other shoulder.

'You don't have to hit me, sir. I'm not a horse.'

'Yes you are.' His voice was strange. It was as if his vocal cords were full of insects. 'You're *my* horse. Be grateful I don't make you gallop!'

We passed a chamber filled with implements I wished I didn't know the names of, but did: the rack, the Iron Maiden, the spider, the stretcher. There were dark stains on the plank floor. A rat as big as a puppy stood on its hind legs beside the rack and sneered at me.

Christ, I thought. *Christ and dear God almighty*.

'Makes you glad to be a whole one, eh?' my warder asked. 'Let's see how grateful you are when the Fair One starts.'

'What is that?' I asked.

My answer was another slash of the limber stick, this time across the back of my neck. When I put my hand there, it came away smeared with blood.

'To your left, kiddie, left! Don't hesitate, it ain't locked.'

I opened the door on my left and started up a steep and narrow stairway that seemed to go on forever. I marked off four hundred steps before I lost count. My legs began to ache again, and the narrow cut the limber stick had opened on the nape of my neck burned.

'Slowing down, kiddie. Better keep up if you don't want to feel the cold fire.'

If he was talking about the aura that surrounded him, I most definitely did not want to feel it. I kept climbing, and just when I felt that my thighs were going to cramp up and refuse to carry me any further, we reached a door at the top. By then I was gasping for breath. Not the thing behind me, which wasn't a surprise. He was dead, after all.

This corridor was wider, hung with velvet tapestries of red, purple, and blue. The gas-jets were enclosed in fine glass chimneys. *It's a residence wing*, I thought. We passed little alcoves that were for the most part empty, and I wondered if they had once contained butterfly sculptures. A few contained marble figures of naked women and men, and one held an exceedingly horrible *thing* with a cloud of tentacles obscuring its head. That made me think of Jenny Schuster, who had introduced me to H.P. Lovecraft's favorite pet monster, Cthulhu, also known as He Who Waits Below.

We must have walked half a mile down this richly appointed passage. Near the end we passed gold-framed mirrors facing each other, which made my reflection endless. I saw that my face and hair were filthy from my last frantic hours trying to escape Lilimar. There was blood on my neck. And I appeared to be alone. My night soldier guardian cast no reflection. Where he should have been there was only a faint blue haze . . . and the limber stick, seeming to float by itself. I glanced around to make sure he was still there and the stick came down on me, finding that same spot on the back of my neck. The burn was immediate.

'Walk! Walk, damn you!'

I walked. The corridor came to an end at a stout door that looked like solid mahogany banded with gold. The night soldier tapped my hand with his hateful stick, then tapped the door. I took the hint and knocked. The limber stick came down, cutting through my shirt at the shoulder.

'Harder!'

I hammered with the side of my fist. Blood was trickling down my upper arm and the back of my neck. Sweat mixed with it, stinging. I thought to myself, *I don't know if you can die, you miserable blue fuck, but if you can, and if I get the chance, I am going to kill your ass.*

The door opened and there stood Kellin, also known as the Lord High. Wearing, of all things, a red velvet smoking jacket.

7

Unreality surged through me again. The thing that had grabbed me seconds before I would have made good my escape had looked like something from an old-school horror comic – part vampire, part skeleton, part *Walking Dead* zombie. Now the gray hair that had hung in clumps around his pallid cheeks was neatly combed back from the face of a man who was elderly but seemingly in the bloom of ruddy-cheeked health. His lips were full. His eyes, bracketed by benign smile lines, looked out beneath lushly unkempt gray eyebrows. He reminded me of someone, but I couldn't think who.

'Ah,' he said, and smiled. 'Our new guest. Come in, please. Aaron, you may leave.'

The night soldier who had brought me – Aaron – hesitated. Kellin flapped a good-natured hand at him. He gave a little bow, stepped back, and closed the door.

I looked around. We were in a wood-paneled foyer. Beyond was a living room that made me think of a gentleman's club in a Sherlock Holmes story: richly paneled walls, high-backed chairs, a long sofa upholstered in dark blue velvet. Half a dozen lamps cast soft pools of glow, and I didn't think they were gas-powered. In this part of the palace, at least, there seemed to be electricity. And, of course, there had been the bus that had cut a path between the squad of night soldiers. The one this thing had been driving.

'Come, guest.'

He turned his back to me, seemingly unafraid that I would attack him. He led me into the living room, so different from the dank cell in which I'd awakened that a third wave of unreality washed over and through me. Maybe he was unafraid because he had eyes in the back of his head, peering out from that carefully combed (and rather vain) collar-length gray hair. It wouldn't have surprised me. By that point, nothing would have.

Two of the gentleman's club chairs faced each other over a small table with a tiled surface featuring a prancing unicorn. Perched on the unicorn's butt was a small tray with a teapot, a vial-sized container of sugar (I hoped it was sugar and not white arsenic), tiny spoons, and two cups with roses around the rims.

'Sit, sit. Tea?'

'Yes, please.'

'Sugar? There is no cream, I'm afraid. It gives me indigestion. In fact, guest, *food* gives me indigestion.'

He poured first for me, then for himself. I tipped half of the tiny vial into my cup, restraining myself from dumping it all in; I was suddenly greedy for sweetness. I raised it to my mouth, then hesitated.

'Do you think of poison?' Kellin continued to smile. 'If that was my desire, I could have ordered it done below, in Maleen. Or rid myself of you in countless other ways.'

I'd thought of poison, it was true, but that wasn't what had made me hesitate. The flowers rimming the cup weren't roses after all. They were poppies, which made me remember Dora. I hoped with all my heart that Rades would find her way back to that kind-hearted woman. I knew the chances were slim, but you know what they say about hope: it's the thing with feathers. It can fly even for those who are imprisoned. Maybe especially for them.

I raised my cup to Kellin. 'Long days and pleasant nights.' I drank. It was sweet and good.

'What an interesting toast. I've never heard it before.'

'I learned it from my father.' This was true. I thought not much else I might say in this richly appointed room would be the truth, but that was. He'd read it in some book or other, but I didn't intend to say that. Maybe the sort of person I was supposed to be couldn't read.

'I can't keep calling you guest. What is your name?'

'Charlie.'

I thought he'd ask for my last name, but he didn't. 'Charlie? *Charlie.*' He seemed to taste it. 'I've never heard such a name.' He waited for me to explain my exotic name – which was common as dirt where I came from – and when I didn't, he asked where I was from. 'For your accent is strange to my ear.'

'Ullum,' I said.

'Ah! So far, then? So far as that?'

'If you say so.'

He frowned, and I realized two things. One was that he was actually as pale as ever. The color in his cheeks and on his lips was makeup. The other thing was that the person he reminded me of was Donald Sutherland, who I had watched grow magically older in any number of Turner Classic Movies, from *M*A*S*H* to *The Hunger Games*. And one other thing: the blue aura was still there, although faint. A thin, transparent swirl deep in each nostril; a barely visible tingle at the bottom arc of each eye.

'Is it polite to stare in Ullum, Charlie? Perhaps even a sign of respect? Tell me.'

'I'm sorry,' I said, and drank the rest of my tea. There was a little film of sugar left in the bottom of the cup. I had to restrain myself from sticking in one dirty finger and mopping it up. 'This is all strange to me. *You* are strange.'

'Of course, of course. More tea? Help yourself, and don't spare the sugar. I don't use that either, and I can see you want more. I see a great deal. Some learn that to their sorrow.'

I didn't know how long the pot had been on the table in advance of my arrival, but the tea was still hot and mildly steaming. More magic, maybe. I didn't care. I was tired of magic. I just wanted to get my dog and go home. Except . . . there was the mermaid. That was wrong. And hateful. Hateful to murder beauty.

'Why did you leave Ullum, Charlie?'

There was a snare in that question. Thanks to Hamey, I thought I could avoid it. 'Didn't want to die.'

'Ah?'

'Ducked the poison.'

'Very wise of you, I'd say. What was foolish was coming here. Wouldn't you say?'

'I almost got out,' I said, and thought of another of my dad's sayings: *Almost only counts in horseshoes*. Every one of Kellin's questions felt like another land mine I had to step around or be blown up.

'How many others "ducked the poison," as you say? And were they all whole ones?'

I shrugged. Kellin frowned and put down his cup (he'd barely touched his tea) with a bang. 'Don't be impertinent with me, Charlie. That would be unwise.'

'I don't know how many.' It was the safest answer I could give, considering the only thing I knew about whole ones was that they didn't turn gray, lose their voices, and presumably die when their innards melted and their breathing tubes closed up. Hell, I didn't even know that for sure.

'My Lord Flight Killer grows impatient for thirty-two, he's very wise but a bit of a child in that respect.' Kellin raised a finger. The nail was long and looked cruel. 'The thing is, Charlie, he doesn't yet know that I have thirty-one. That means I can make away with you if I desire. So be very careful and answer my questions truthfully.'

I nodded, hoping I looked chastened. I actually *was* chastened, and I intended to be very careful. As for answering this monster's questions truthfully . . . no.

'It was pretty confused at the end,' I said. I was thinking about the mass poisonings at Jonestown. I hoped it had been like that in Ullum. I suppose that sounds gross, but I was pretty sure my life was at stake in this pleasant well-lit room. In fact I knew it.

'I imagine it was. They tried to pray away the gray, and when that didn't work . . . what are you smiling about? Did you find that funny?'

I couldn't very well tell him that there were fundamentalist Christians in my world – which I was betting was a lot farther away than Ullum – who believed they could pray the *gay* away. 'It was stupid. I find stupidity funny.'

He actually grinned at that, and I saw blue fire lurking between his teeth. *What big teeth you have, Kellin*, I thought. 'That's hard. Hard, are you? We'll see about that.'

I said nothing.

'So you left before they could pour their nightshade cocktail down your throat.'

It wasn't *cocktail* he said . . . but my mind instantly recognized the sense of what he did say and made the substitution.

'Yes.'

'You and your dog.'

I said, 'They would have killed her, too.' And waited for him to say, *You're not from Ullum, there are no dogs there, you're making everything up as you go.*

Instead he nodded. 'Yes, they probably would have. I'm told they killed the horses, cows, and sheep.' He looked down into his teacup meditatively, then snapped his head up. His eyes had turned blue and brilliant. They dripped vanishing electric tears down his wrinkled cheeks, and for just a moment I saw bone glimmering beneath his skin. 'Why *here*? Why come here to the Lily? Answer me a true answer or I'll turn your fucking head around on your fucking neck! You'll die staring at the door you were unfortunate enough to come in through!'

I hoped the truth would serve to keep my head where it belonged at least a little longer. 'She was old, and there were stories about a stone circle that . . .' I spun one of my fingers in the air. 'That could make her young again.'

'And did it work?'

He knew it had. If he hadn't seen her run before he broke through the posse of night soldiers in his little electric tram, the others had.

'It did.'

'You were lucky. The sundial is dangerous. I thought the slaying of Elsa in her pool might end its power, but the old magic is stubborn.'

Elsa. So that was Ariel's name in this world.

'I could send some of the grays out to break it up with sledges, but the Flight Killer would have to approve and so far he hasn't. Petra's whispering in his ear, I suppose. She likes that old sundial. Do you know what magic does, Charlie?'

I thought it did all sorts of things – allowing hapless pilgrims such as myself to visit other worlds, for instance – but I shook my head.

'It gives people hope, and hope is dangerous. Wouldn't you say?'

I considered saying hope was the thing with feathers and decided to keep that to myself. 'I don't know, sir.'

He smiled and just for a wink I clearly saw his naked jaw glimmer below his lips. 'But *I* know. Indeed I do. What else was it but hope of some happy afterlife that caused those living in your unfortunate province to poison themselves and their animals, when their prayers did not suffice to turn back the gray? You, however, had earthly hopes, and so you fled. Now you are here, and this is the place where all hope for such as yourself dies. If you don't believe that now, you will. How did you get past Hana?'

'I waited, then took my chance.'

'Brave as well as hard! My!' He leaned forward and I could smell him: an aroma of old rot. 'It wasn't just the dog that you dared Lilimar for, was it?' He raised one hand, showing that long nail. 'Tell me the truth or I'll cut your throat.'

I blurted out, 'Gold.'

Kellin waved a hand in dismissal. 'There's gold everywhere in the Lily. The throne where Hana sits and farts and dozes is made of it.'

'I couldn't very well carry a throne, though, could I, sir?'

That made him laugh. It was a horrible sound, like dry bones clattering. He stopped as abruptly as he started.

'I heard . . . the stories may have been wrong . . . that there were little golden pellets . . .'

'The treasury, of course. But you've never seen it for yourself?'

'No.'

'Never came to the games and gawked at it through the glass?'

'No.' Dangerous ground here, because I had only a vague idea of what he might mean. Or if it was a trap.

'What about the Dark Well? Do they tell of that even in Ullum?'

'Well . . . yes.' I was sweating. If this interrogation went on much longer, I was going to step on one of those mines. I knew it.

'But you turned back after the sundial. Why was that, Charlie?'

'I wanted to get out before dark.' I straightened up and tried to put some defiance into my face and voice. 'I almost made it.'

He smiled again. Beneath the illusion of his skin, his skull grinned. Had he – and the others – ever been human? I was guessing they had been. 'There's pain in that word, wouldn't you agree? Such pain in every *almost*.' He tapped his colored lips with that hideously long nail, studying me. 'I don't care for you, Charlie, and I don't believe you. No, not at all. I'm tempted to send you to the Belts, only Flight Killer wouldn't approve. He wants thirty-two, and with you in Maleen, we're but one short. So back to Maleen you go.'

He raised his voice to a shout so unnaturally loud it made me want to cover my ears, and for a moment there was only a skull wrapped in blue fire above the affectation of the red velvet smoking jacket. '*AARON!*'

The door opened and Aaron came back in. 'Yes, my lord.'

'Take him back but show him the Belts on the way. I want Charlie to see that his lot in the Maleen isn't the worst lot in the palace where King Jan, may his name be soon forgotten, once ruled. And Charlie?'

'Yes?'

'I hope you enjoyed your visit, and your tea with sugar.' This time the illusion of his face grinned along with the skull that was the reality. 'Because you'll never have such a treat again. You think you're smart, but I see through you. You think you're hard, but you'll soften. Take him.'

Aaron raised his limber stick but stood aside so I didn't have to touch his debilitating aura. When I reached the door, just as escape from this terrible room was at hand, Kellin said, 'Oh dear, I almost forgot. Come back, please, Charlie.'

I had watched enough reruns of *Columbo* with my father on Sunday afternoons to know the 'Just one more question' trick, but I still felt a sinking dread.

I came back and stood beside the chair I'd been sitting in. Kellin opened a small drawer in the tea table and brought something out. It was a wallet . . . but not *my* wallet. Mine was a cordovan Lord Buxton, given to me by my dad as a birthday present when I turned fourteen. This one was limp and black and scuffed.

'What is this? I'm curious.'

'I don't know.'

But once my initial shock wore off, I realized I did. I remembered Dora giving me the leather shoe tokens, then gesturing for me to take off my pack so I didn't have to carry it to Leah's. I had opened the pack and put my wallet in my back pocket, just an automatic thing. Not thinking about it. Not looking, either. I had been looking at Radar, wondering if she would be okay if I left her with Dora, and instead of my wallet I'd been carrying Christopher Polley's all this time.

'I found it and picked it up. Thought it might be something valuable. Stuck it in my pocket and forgot about it.'

He opened the billfold and pulled out the only money Polley had been carrying – a ten-dollar bill. 'This could be money, but I've never seen anything like it.'

Alexander Hamilton looked like he could be one of the whole people from Empis, maybe even royalty, but there were no words on the bill, just tangled gibberish that almost hurt my eyes. And instead of the number 10 in the corners, there were symbols: ∠ ¬. 'Do you know what this is?'

I shook my head. The words and numbers on the bill were apparently not translatable into either English or Empisarian but had fallen into some linguistic wasteland.

Next he brought out Polley's expired driver's license. His name was readable; everything else was a mass of runes broken by an occasional recognizable letter.

'Who is this Polley, and what kind of picture is it? I've never seen one like it.'

'I don't know.' Something I did know: throwing away my backpack so I could run faster had been fantastic luck. My own wallet was in it, and my phone – I'm sure he would have been interested in that – and the directions I'd jotted down at Claudia's command. I doubted if the words on that sheet would have been runic gibberish, like those on the ten-dollar bill or Polley's DL. No, those would have been written in Empisarian.

'I don't believe you, Charlie.'

'It's the truth,' I croaked. 'I found it in the ditch beside the road.'

'And those?' He pointed to my filthy sneakers. 'In a *ditch*? Beside the *road*?'

'Yes. With that.' I pointed to the wallet, then waited for him to produce Mr Bowditch's revolver. *What about this, Charlie? We found it in the high grass outside the main gate.* I was almost sure that was going to happen.

But it didn't. Instead of producing the gun, like a magician pulling a rabbit out of a hat, Kellin threw the wallet across the room. 'Get him out!' he shrieked at Aaron. 'He's filthy! His filth is on my rug, on my chair, even on the cup he used! *Get this lying scum out of my quarters!*'

I was very glad to go.

CHAPTER TWENTY-ONE

The Belts. Innamin.

Not a Spotch of Gray. Dungeon Days.

1

Instead of going back the way we'd come, Aaron directed me down three different flights of stairs, walking behind me and occasionally giving me a tap with his limber stick. I felt like a cow being driven to a pen, which was ugly and humiliating, but at least I didn't feel that I was being driven to the slaughterhouse. I was number thirty-one, after all, and thus valuable. I didn't know why, but an idea had begun to glimmer. Thirty-one was a prime number, divisible only by one and itself. Thirty-two, though . . . that was divisible all the way down.

We passed many doors along the way, most closed, a few either open or standing ajar. I heard no one inside these rooms. The feeling I got on our journey was one of desertion and dilapidation. There were the night soldiers, but I had an idea that the palace was otherwise not very populated. I had no idea where we were going, but at last I began to hear the sound of loud clattering machinery and a steady thudding drum, like a heartbeat. By then I was pretty sure we were even deeper than Deep Maleen. The gas-jets on the walls were increasingly far apart, and many were guttering. By the time we reached the end of the third staircase – by then the drum was very loud and the machinery even louder – most of the light was being provided by Aaron's blue aura. I raised my fist to beat on the door at the foot of the stairs, and hard – I didn't want another slash on the back of my neck from the hateful stick.

'Nah, nah,' Aaron said in his strangely insectile voice. 'Just open it.'

I lifted the iron latch, pushed the door open, and was hit by a wall of sound and heat. Aaron prodded me inside. Sweat sprang out on my face and arms almost immediately. I found myself on a parapet surrounded by a waist-high iron railing. The circular area below me looked like an exercise club in hell. At least two dozen gray men and women were speed-walking on treadmills, each with a noose around his or her neck. Three night soldiers lounged against the stone walls, holding limber sticks and watching. Another was on a kind of podium, banging on a high wooden cylinder like a conga drum. Painted on the drum were bleeding monarch butterflies, which was probably inaccurate – I don't think butterflies bleed. Directly across from me, beyond the treadmills, was a clattering machine, all fanbelts and pistons. It shook on its platform. Above it was a single electric light, like the kind mechanics use to look under the hoods of the cars they are fixing.

What I was seeing reminded me of the war boats in one of my favorite TCM movies, *Ben-Hur*. The men and women on those treadmills were slaves, just as the men rowing the war boats had been. As I watched, one of the women stumbled, clawed at the rope sinking into her neck, and managed to lunge to her feet again. Two of the night soldiers watched her, then looked at each other and laughed.

'Wouldn't want to be down there, kiddie, would you?' Aaron asked from behind me.

'No.' I didn't know which was more horrible – the prisoners striding along at a brisk walk that was just short of a run, or the way two of the skeleton-men had laughed when the woman lost her footing and began to choke. 'No, I wouldn't.'

I wondered how much juice that treadmill-powered rattletrap of a generator could put out. I was guessing not much; there had been electricity in the Lord High's apartments, but I hadn't seen it anywhere else. Only the gas-jets, which didn't look in very good shape, either.

'How long do they have to—'

'The shift is twelve hours.' It wasn't *hours* he said, but my mind again made the translation. I was hearing Empisarian, I was speaking it, and I was getting better at both. I probably wouldn't have been able to utter a slang term analogous to *awesome sauce* yet, but even that might come eventually. 'Unless they choke out. We keep a few in reserve for when that happens. Come on, kiddie. You've had your look. Time to leave.'

I was glad to go, believe me. But before I turned away, the woman who had fallen glanced up at me. Her hair hung in sweaty clumps. Her face was being buried in knots and hills of gray flesh, but there was enough of her features left for me to see her despair.

Did the sight of that despair make me as angry as the sight of the slaughtered mermaid? I'm not sure, because it all made me angry. A fair land had been turned foul, and this was the result: whole people locked in a dungeon, sick people with nooses around their necks forced to run on treadmills to provide electric lights for the Lord High and perhaps a fortunate few others, one of whom was almost certainly the man or creature in charge: Flight Killer.

'Be glad you're whole,' Aaron said. 'At least for a little while. Then you may regret it.'

Just for emphasis he whipped me across the neck with his limber stick, re-opening the cut there.

2

Someone, most likely Pursey, our trustee/warder, had thrown a dirty blanket into the cell I shared with Hamey. I shook it out, dislodging a fair number of lice (ordinary size, as far as I could tell), and sat down on it. Hamey was lying on his back, staring up at the ceiling. There was a scrape on his forehead, a crust of blood under his nose, and both of his knees were cut up. One of the cuts had sent runnels of blood down his left shin.

'What happened to you?' I asked.

'Playtime,' he said hollowly.

'He ain't got the stuff,' said Fremmy from the next cell. He had a black eye.

'Never had it at all,' said Stooks. He had a bruise on his temple, but otherwise looked okay.

'Shut up, both of you!' Eye called from across the way. 'Do for him if you draw him, until then leave him alone.'

Fremmy and Stooks subsided. Eye sat down with his back against the wall of his cell, staring sullenly between his knees at the floor. He had a gouge over one eye. From the other cells I could hear groans and the occasional stifled grunt of pain. One of the women was crying quietly.

The door opened and Pursey came in with a bucket swinging in the crook of one elbow. He paused to look at the gas-jet that had fallen out of the wall. He set his bucket down and put the gas-jet back in its jagged hole. This time it stayed. He took a wooden match from the pocket of his smock, scratched it on a stone block, and held it to the jet's little brass nipple. It flumped alight. I expected Fremmy to offer a comment, but that fine fellow seemed all out of humorous remarks for the time being.

'Innamin,' Pursey said through the teardrop that had once been a mouth. 'Innamin, ooo unt innamin?'

'I'll take some,' Eye said. Pursey handed him a small disc from his bucket. To me it looked like a wooden nickel, as in the old saying about don't take any. 'And give some to the new boy. If he don't need it, Useless does.'

'Liniment?' I asked.

'What the fuck else?' Iota began to spread some on the back of his wide neck.

'Each,' Pursey said to me. 'Each, ooo oy.'

I assumed he was telling the new boy to reach, so I stuck my hand through the bars. He dropped one of the wooden nickels into my hand.

'Thank you, Pursey,' I said.

He looked back at me. His expression might have been amazement. Maybe he'd never been thanked before, at least not in Deep Maleen.

There was a thick smear of bad-smelling stuff on the wooden disc. I hunkered down next to Hamey and asked him where it hurt.

'Everywhere,' he said, and tried to smile.

'What's the worst?'

Meanwhile, Pursey was toting his bucket down the aisle between the cells, droning 'Innamin, innamin, ooo unt innamin?'

'Knees. Shoulders. Gut's the worst, accourse, but no liniment will help that.'

He gasped when I rubbed the liniment into the scrapes on his knees, but sighed with relief when I did their backs and then his shoulders. I had gotten (and given) after-game massages during football season and knew where to dig in.

'That's good,' he said. 'Thank you.'

He wasn't dirty – not *too* dirty, at least, not the way I still was. I couldn't help remembering Kellin shrieking *Get him out, he's filthy!* As I certainly was. My sojourn in Empis had been extremely active, including a sprawl in cemetery mud and my recent trip to the Belts, which had been as hot as a sauna.

'I don't suppose there are showers in this place, are there?'

'Nah, nah, there used to be running water in the team rooms – from when there was real games – but now there's just buckets. All cold water, but – *ow!*'

'Sorry. You're all knotted up here, on the back of your neck.'

'You can give yourself a whore's bath after next playtime – that's what we call it – but for now you'll have to live with it.'

'The way you look and the rest of them sound, it must be playing rough. Even Eye looks banged up.'

'You'll find out,' Stooks said.

'But you won't like it,' Fremmy added.

From down the corridor someone began to cough.

'Cover it!' one of the women yelled. 'No one wants what you got, Dommy!'

The coughing continued.

3

Some time later Pursey returned with a cart filled with pieces of half-cooked chicken, which he tossed into the cells. I ate mine and half of Hamey's. Across from our cell, Eye dumped his bones down his shithole and shouted, 'Shut up, the gang of ya! I want to sleep!'

There was a little more after-dinner talk between the cells in spite of this decree, then it died to murmurs and finally ceased. So I guess the chicken really had been dinner, and this was nighttime. Not that there was any way to tell; our barred window never showed anything but unmitigated darkness. Sometimes we got steak, sometimes chicken, once in awhile bony filets of fish. Usually, but not always, there were carrots. No sweets. Nothing that Pursey couldn't fling through the bars, in other words. The meat was good, not the maggoty remains I would have expected in a dungeon, and the carrots were crunchy. They wanted us healthy and we all were except for Dommy, who had some sort of lung ailment, and Hamey, who never ate much and complained of the bellyache when he did.

Whether it was morning, noon, or night the gas-jets flared, but there were so few of them that Deep Maleen existed in a kind of twilight that was disorienting and depressing. If I'd had a sense of time when I came in (I hadn't), I would have lost it after the first twenty-four or thirty-six hours.

The places where Aaron had hit me with his limber stick stung and throbbed. I used the last of the liniment on them and it helped a little. I wiped at my face and neck. Dirt came off in clumps. At some point I slept and dreamed of Radar. She was loping along, young and strong and surrounded by a cloud of orange and black butterflies. I don't know how long I was out, but when I woke up the long room of cells was still quiet except for snores, the occasional fart, and Dommy's coughing. I got up and had a drink from the bucket, being careful to place my finger over the hole in the bottom of the tin cup. When I turned back to my blanket, I saw Hamey staring at me. The puffy circles under his eyes looked like bruises.

'You don't have to berdeck me. I take that back. I'm for it no matter what. They toss me around like a bag of grain, and that's just playtime. What's it going to be like when the Fair One comes around?'

'I don't know.' I thought to ask him what the Fair One was, but I had an idea it might be a blood-sport tourney, like cage fighting. Thirty-two was, as I'd already realized, divisible all the way down. As for 'playtime'? Practice. A run-up to the main event. There was something else I was more curious about.

'I met a boy and a man on my way to Lilimar. They were, you know, gray people.'

'Ain't they most of em,' Hamey said. 'Ever since Flight Killer came back from the Dark Well.' He smiled bitterly.

There was a ton of backstory in that one sentence, and I wanted to know what it was, but for the time being I stuck with the gray man who'd been hopping along on his crutch. 'They were coming from Seafront—'

'Were they now?' Hamey whispered without much interest.

'And the man said something to me. First he called me whole man—'

'Well ain'tcha? Not a trace of gray to you. Plenty of dirt but no gray.'

'Then he said, "Which of em did your mother flip her skirts for to leave you fair of face?" Do you have any idea what that means?'

Hamey sat up and stared at me, wide-eyed. 'Where in the name of every orange butterfly that ever flew did you *come* from?'

Across from us, Eye grunted and shifted in his cell.

'Do you know what it means or not?'

He sighed. 'Galliens ruled Empis since time out of mind, you know that much, don'tcha?'

I flapped my hand for him to go on.

'Thousands and thousands of years.'

Again it was like having two languages in my brain, meshing so perfectly they were almost one.

'In a way they still do,' Hamey said. 'Flight Killer being who he is and all . . . if he *is* still a he, and not turned into some creature from the well . . . but . . . where the fuck was I?'

'The Galliens.'

'They're gone now, that fambly tree has been chopped down . . . although some say a few still live . . .'

I knew that a few still did, because I'd met three of them. I had no intention of telling Hamey that.

'But there was a time, even when my father's father still lived, when there was many of the Gallien. Fair they were, male and female. As fair as the monarchs Flight Killer's rooted out.'

Well, he hadn't rooted all of them out, but I had no intention of telling him that, either.

'And they were randy.' He grinned, showing his teeth, so strangely white and healthy in that haggard face. 'You know what that means, don'tcha?'

'Yes.'

'The menfolk planted their seeds everywhere, not just here in Lilimar or the Citadel but in Seafront . . . Deesk . . . Ullum . . . even the Green Isles beyond Ullum, they say.' He gave me a sly smile. 'And the womenfolk weren't above a little adventure behind the door either, 'tis told. Randy men, randy women, and precious little rapin, for many common folk are happy to lay with kingsblood royal. And you know what comes of that sort of sporting, don't you?'

'Babies,' I said.

'Babbies, just so. It's their blood, Charlie, that berdecks us from the gray. Who knows what brince or courtier or even the king hisself laid down with my grammy, or my great-grammy, or even my mammy? And here I am without a spotch of gray on me. There's Eye, that great ape of a man, without a spotch, Dommy and Black Tom without a spotch . . . Stooks and Fremmy . . . Jaya and Eris . . . Double . . . Bult . . . Doc Freed . . . all the rest . . . and *you*. You who don't know a shitting thing. It almost makes me wonder . . .'

'What?' I whispered. 'What is it you wonder?'

'Never mind,' he said. He lay down and put one of his thin arms over his bruised-looking eyes. 'Just you might think twice about warshin away the dirt.'

From down the corridor the one they called Gully bellowed, '*There's some here that wants to sleep!*'

Hamey closed his eyes.

4

I lay awake, thinking. The idea that the so-called whole people were protected from the gray at first struck me as racist, right up there with bigoted dimwits saying white people were just naturally smarter than black people. I believed – as I've already said – that those of so-called royal blood put on their pants one leg at a time just like the unfortunate creatures sweating on the Belts to keep the Lord High's lights burning.

Only there was genetics to consider, wasn't there? The people of

Empis might not know about it, but I did. There could be unfortunate results as bad genes spread, and royal families were good at spreading them. Hemophilia was one, a facial malformation called the Habsburg Jaw was another. I had learned about such things in eighth-grade Sex Ed, of all places. Couldn't there also be a genetic code that provided immunity to the deforming gray?

In a normal world, the person in charge would have wanted to save such people, I thought. In this one, the person in charge – Flight Killer, a name that didn't exactly inspire feelings of safety and security – wanted to kill them. And the gray people probably didn't live long, either. Call it a curse or a disease, it was progressive. In the end, who would be left? I guessed the night soldiers would be, but who else? Was the Flight Killer surrounded by a cadre of protected followers? If so, who would they rule once the whole people had been eradicated and the gray people had died off? What was the end game? *Was* there one?

Something else: Hamey said the Galliens had ruled Empis for time out of mind but *that fambly tree has been chopped down*. Yet he'd also seemed to contradict himself: *In a way they still do*. Did that mean Flight Killer was of . . . what? The House of Gallien, like in a royalty-centric George R. R. Martin *Game of Thrones* novel? That seemed wrong, because Leah had told me (through her horse, of course) that her four sisters and two brothers were dead. Also her mother and father, presumably the king and queen. So who did that leave? Some bastard, like Jon Snow in the *Thrones* books? The crazy hermit somewhere in the woods?

I got up and went to the bars of the cell. Down from me, Jaya was standing at the bars of hers. There was a piece of bandage tied crookedly around her forehead with a bloom of blood seeping through it above her left eye. I whispered, 'You okay?'

'Yes. We shouldn't talk, Charlie. This is sleeping time.'

'I know, but . . . when did the gray come? How long has this Flight Killer been in charge?'

She considered the question. At last she said, 'I don't know. I was a girl in the Citadel when all that happened.'

Not much help. *I was a girl* might have meant six, twelve, or even eighteen years of age. I was thinking the gray could have started and the Flight Killer might have come to power around twelve or fourteen years ago, because of something Mr Bowditch had said: *cowards bring presents*. Like he saw it happening, gave his faves some goodies, helped himself to a shitload of gold pellets, and ran away. Also because of something Dora had said: Radar was little more than a puppy when Mr Bowditch showed up the last time. The curse had been happening then. Maybe. Probably. Plus, just to add to the fun, I didn't even know if Empis years were the same as the ones I knew.

'Sleep, Charlie. It's the only escape we have.' She started to turn away.

'Jaya, wait!' Across from me, Iota grunted, snorted, and turned over. 'Who was he? Before he turned into Flight Killer, who was he? Do you know?'

'Elden,' she said. 'Elden of the Gallien.'

I went back to my blanket and lay down on it. *Elden*, I thought. I knew the name. Falada the horse, speaking for her mistress, had told me that Leah had had four sisters and two brothers. Leah had seen Robert's poor crushed body. The other brother was also dead, although she hadn't said how it had happened, or if she had seen his corpse. The other brother was the one who had always been good to her, Falada said. Falada, who was actually Leah herself.

The other brother was Elden.

5

Three days passed. I say three because Pursey came nine times with his cart of half-cooked meat, but it might have been longer; in the gas-jet twilight of Deep Maleen, it was impossible to tell. During that time I tried to put together a history I thought of as The Fall of Empis, or The Rise of Flight Killer, or The Coming of the Curse. This was idiotic, based on the tiny scraps of information I had, but it passed the time. Some of the time, anyway. And I did have those scraps, poor as they were.

One scrap: Mr Bowditch spoke of two moons *rising in the sky*, but I had never seen the moons rise. Had hardly seen them at all. He also spoke of constellations no astronomers of earth had ever seen, but I had caught only occasional glimpses of the stars. Save for that one ephemeral patch of blue when I had been approaching the sundial, I'd seen little but clouds. In Empis, sky was in short supply. At least now it was.

Another scrap: Mr Bowditch had never mentioned Hana, and I think he would've. I didn't hear the giant's name until I visited the 'googir.'

It was the third scrap that interested me the most, the one that *suggested* the most. Mr Bowditch had talked about what might happen if people from our world discovered the way to Empis, a world no doubt filled with untapped resources, gold being only one of them. Just before he realized he was having a heart attack he'd said, *Would they* (meaning the would-be plunderers from our world) *fear waking the terrible god of that place from its long doze?*

Based on the tape, things were already bad in Empis when Mr Bowditch made his last visit, although Hana might not yet have been at her post back then. The city of Lilimar was already deserted and *perilous, especially at night*. Did that mean he knew from personal experience, like a final expedition to get more gold, or only that he'd heard it from sources he trusted? Woody, perhaps? I thought he'd made a final trip for gold, and that Hana hadn't been there.

Based on this shaky matchstick foundation, I built a skyscraper of supposition. When Mr Bowditch made his last visit, the King of Gallien (whose name was probably Jan) and the Queen of Same (name unknown) had already been deposed. At least five of their seven children had been killed. Leah escaped, along with Auntie Claudia and her uncle or cousin (I couldn't remember which) Woody. Leah claimed her brother Elden was also dead, but it was clear that Leah had loved him best (that was straight from the horse's mouth, ha-ha). Wasn't it possible that Leah would prefer to believe Elden dead than to believe he had become the Flight Killer? Did any sister want to believe her adored brother had become a monster?

Wasn't it possible that Elden had also escaped the purge – if that was what it had been – and awakened *the terrible god of that place from its long doze*? I thought that was the most believable of my suppositions, because of something Hamey had said: *Ever since Flight Killer came back from the Dark Well.*

That might just be bullshit legend, but what if it wasn't? What if

Leah's brother had gone down into the Dark Well (just as I had gone down another dark well to get here) either to escape the purge or on purpose? What if he had gone down as Elden and come back as the Flight Killer? Possibly the god of the Dark Well was directing him. Or perhaps Elden had been possessed by that god, *was* that god. An awful thought, but it made a degree of sense, based on the way everyone – gray people and whole people – were being wiped out, most of them slowly and painfully.

There were things that didn't fit, but a lot of things did. And as I say, it passed the time.

There was one question to which I couldn't supposition an answer: what could be done about it?

6

I got to know my fellow prisoners a bit, but because we stayed locked in our cells, it wasn't possible to cultivate what you'd call meaningful relationships. Fremmy and Stooks were the comedy duo, although they were more amused by their wit (or what passed for it) than anyone else, including me. Dommy was big, but he had that graveyard cough, which got worse when he was lying down. The other black guy, Tom, was much smaller. He had a fantastic singing voice, but only Eris could sweet-talk him into using it. One of his ballads told a story I knew. It was about a little girl who went to visit her grandmother only to find a wolf wearing Nana's nightgown. The 'Little Red Riding Hood' I remembered had a happy ending, but Tom's version ended with a bleak rhyme: *She ran but was caught, all her struggles went for naught.*

In Deep Maleen, happy endings seemed to be in short supply.

By the third day I was beginning to understand the true meaning of stir crazy. My dungeon colleagues might have been whole ones, but they weren't exactly MENSA candidates. Jaya seemed bright enough, and there was a fellow named Jackah who knew a seemingly inexhaustible supply of riddles, but otherwise their talk was desultory prattle.

I did pushups to keep the blood flowing, and squat thrusts, and ran in place.

'Look at the little prince, showing off,' Eye said once. Iota was a shithead, but I'd developed a liking for him nevertheless. In some ways he reminded me of my long-gone pal Bertie Bird. Like the Bird Man, Iota was right out front with his shithead-edness, and besides, I've always had admiration for good trash-talkers. Iota wasn't the best I'd ever known, but he wasn't bad, and although I was still your basic short-timer, I enjoyed winding him up.

'Look at this, Eye,' I said, and raised my palms-down hands to my chest. My knees smacked them. 'Let's see you do that.'

'And strain something? Pull a muscle? Give myself a rupture? You'd like that, wouldn't you? Then you could run away from me when the Fair One comes.'

'Not going to be one,' I said. 'Thirty-one's all there's going to be. Flight Killer's all out of whole people. Let's see you do this!' I raised my hands almost to chin level and kept slapping them with my knees. My endorphins, although weary, rose to the challenge. A little, anyway.

'You keep doing that, you'll tear your ass in two,' Bernd said. He was the oldest of us, mostly bald. What little hair he had left was gray.

That made me laugh and I had to stop. Hamey was lying on his pallet and chuckling.

'There'll be thirty-two,' Eye said. 'If we don't get another one soon, they'll stick in Red Molly. *She'll* make thirty-two. Bitch'll come back from Cratchy soon enough, and Flight Killer won't want to wait much longer for his entertainment.'

'Not *her*!' Fremmy said.

'Don't *ever* say her!' Stooks cried. They wore identical looks of alarm.

'I *do* say it.' Eye jumped up on the bars of his cell again and began shaking them. It was his preferred mode of exercise. 'Whole, ain't she? Although that great galoopin' mother of hers fell out of the ugly tree and scraped her fuckin face all the way down.'

'Wait,' I said. A horrible idea had come to me. 'You're not going to tell me her mother is . . .'

'Hana,' Hamey said. 'Her who guards the sundial and the treasury. Although if you got to the sundial, she must be slacking off on the job. Flight Killer won't like that.'

I hardly paid attention. That Hana had a daughter was amazing to me, mostly because I couldn't begin to imagine who had lain with her to produce offspring.

'Is Red Molly a . . . you know, a giant?'

'Not like her mother,' Ammit said from down the corridor. 'But she big. She go Cratchy to see her kin. Land of the giants, you know. She come back and snap you like a piece of kindling if she get a hold on you. Not me. I fast. She slow. Here's one Jackah don't know: I'm tall when I'm young, short when I'm old. What am I?'

'A candle,' Jackah said. 'Everyone knows that one, dummy.'

I spoke without thinking. 'Here comes a candle to light you to bed. Here comes a chopper to chop off your head.'

Silence. Then Eye said, 'High gods, where did you ever hear that?'

'I don't know. I think my mother used to say it to me when I was small.'

'Then your mother was a weirdy woman. Never say it again, it's an ill rhyme.'

Down the dank and dripping corridor of Deep Maleen, Dommy began to cough. And cough. And cough.

7

Two or three days later – guessing here; dungeon-time was no-time – Pursey came in to serve us breakfast, and this time it really *was* breakfast: sausage links tossed through the bars in fat strings. Nine or ten to a string. I grabbed mine on the fly. Hamey let his lie on the dirty floor, then picked it up and listlessly brushed at the dirt on the links. He looked at it for awhile, then dropped it again. There was a terrible similarity to the way Radar had behaved when she was old and dying. He went back to his pallet, drew his knees up to his chest, and turned to the wall. Across from us, Eye was squatting by the bars of his cell, eating his string from the middle, going back and forth like he was gobbling an ear of corn. His beard gleamed with grease around his mouth.

'Come on, Hamey,' I said. 'Try to eat just one.'

'If he won't, fling it in here,' said Stooks.

'We'll take care of it double-quick,' said Fremmy.

Hamey rolled over, sat up, and pulled his string of sausages into his lap. He looked at me. 'Do I have to?'

'You better, Useless,' Eye said. He was already down to two sausages, the ones at either end. 'You know what it means when we get these.'

Any residual heat the sausages might have had was gone and the centers were raw. I thought of a story I'd read on the Internet about a guy who'd gone to the hospital complaining of belly pains. The X-ray showed he had a huge tapeworm in his intestines. From eating undercooked meat, the article said. I tried to forget that (not really possible) and started eating. I had a good idea what breakfast sausages meant: playtime, dead ahead.

Pursey reversed back up the corridor. I thanked him again. He stopped and beckoned me with one melted hand. I went to the bars. In a hoarse whisper from the teardrop that was now his mouth, he said, '*Ont* osher *air*!'

I shook my head. 'I don't underst—'

'*Ont* osher *air*!'

Then he backed out, pulling his empty cart after him. The door shut. The bolts slammed. I turned to Hamey. He'd managed one of the sausages, bit into a second, gagged, and spit it into his hand. He got up and tossed it into our waste hole.

'I don't know what he was trying to tell me,' I said.

Hamey got our tin drinking cup and rubbed it on the remains of his shirt like a man polishing an apple. Then he sat down on his pallet. 'Come over here.' He patted the blanket. I sat down next to him. 'Now hold still.'

He looked around. Fremmy and Stooks had retreated to the far side of their crappy little apartment. Iota was absorbed in his final sausage, making it last. From other cells came sounds of chewing, burping, and smacking. Apparently deciding we were unobserved, Hamey spread his fingers – which he could do, being a whole person with hands instead of flippers – and ran them into my hair. I recoiled.

'Nah, nah, Charlie. Hold still.'

He dug at my scalp and yanked at my hair. Clouds of dirt showered down. I wasn't embarrassed, exactly (spend a few days in a cell, shitting and pissing in a hole in the floor, and you kind of lose the finer feelings), but it was still appalling to realize how filthy I was. I felt like Charlie Brown's friend Pig-Pen.

Hamey held up the tin cup so I could look at a blurry reflection of myself. Like a barber showing you your new haircut, only the cup was dented as well as curved, so it was a little like looking into a funhouse mirror. One part of my face was big, the other small.

'Do you see?'

'See what?'

He tilted the cup and I realized that my hair in front, where Hamey had scrubbed away the dirt, was no longer brown. It had turned blond. Down here, even with no sun to bleach it, it had turned blond. I grabbed the cup and held it close to my face. It was hard to tell for sure, but it looked like my eyes had also changed. Instead of the deep brown they'd always been, they seemed to have gone hazel.

Hamey cupped the back of my neck and pulled me close to his mouth. 'Pursey said: "Don't wash your hair."'

I pulled back. Hamey stared at me, his own eyes – as brown as mine used to be – wide. Then he pulled me close again.

'Are you the true prince? The one come to save us?'

8

Before I could answer, the door bolts were thrown back. This time it wasn't Pursey. It was four night soldiers, armed with limber sticks. Two walked ahead, arms outstretched, the cell doors squalling open on either side. 'Time to play!' one of them yelled in its buzzing, insectile voice. 'All kiddies come out to play!'

We left the cells. Aaron, who was not present in this bunch of boogeymen, had taken me to the right. We went to the left, all thirty-one of us in a double line, like real kiddies going on a fieldtrip. I walked at the end, the only one without a partner. The other two night soldiers walked behind me. At first I thought the muted crackling I was hearing, like low voltage, was my imagination, based on the previous times I'd been touched by the enveloping force that was keeping these horrors alive, but it wasn't. The night soldiers were electric zombies. Which, I thought, would be a hell of a good name for a heavy metal group.

Hamey was walking with Iota, who kept shoulder-bumping my skinny cellmate and making him stumble. I meant to say *Quit it*, but what came out of my mouth was 'Cease that.'

Eye looked back at me, smiling. 'Who died and made you God?'

'Cease,' I said. 'Why would you tease someone who's your fellow in this vile place?'

That didn't sound like Charlie Reade at all. That kid was a lot more apt to say *Quit fucking around* than what had just come out of my mouth. Yet it *was* me, and Iota's smile was replaced by a look of puzzled speculation. He gave a British-style salute – back of one big hand to his low forehead – and said, 'Sir yes sir. Let's see how much you order me around with a mouthful of dirt.'

Then he faced forward again.

CHAPTER TWENTY-TWO

The Playing Field. Ammit.

Washing Up. Cake. The Gas-Jets.

1

We climbed stairs. Of course we did. When you were kept prisoner in Deep Maleen, stairs were a way of life. After ten minutes of them, Hamey was breathing raggedly. Eye grabbed his arm and hauled him along. 'Hump, hump, hump, Useless! Keep up or your daddy will scold you!'

We came to a wide landing and double doors. One of the two night soldiers leading this fucked-up parade brushed his hands upward and the doors popped open. On the other side was a different, cleaner world: a white-tiled corridor with gas-jets polished to a high-gloss shine. The corridor was an upward-tending ramp, and as we walked in this unusually bright light (it made me squint, and I wasn't alone), I began to smell something that I knew from dozens of locker rooms: chlorine, like the cakes in urinals and the stuff in disinfecting footbaths.

Did I know what 'playtime' meant by then? Yes, of course. Did I understand what the so-called Fair One was? Ditto. In the cells, eating, sleeping, and talking was all we had to do. I was careful with my questions, wanting to preserve the fiction that I was from the religious community of Ullum, and I did a lot more listening than talking. But I was still amazed by that upward-tending corridor, which looked – almost – like something in an up-to-date and well-maintained sports complex on one of those many campuses where sports are a big rah-rah deal. Lilimar had gone to rack and ruin – hell, all of Empis had – but this corridor looked great, and I had an idea what it was leading to would also be great. Maybe even greater. I wasn't wrong.

We began to pass doors, each with a hooded gaslight over it. The first three said TEAMS. The next said EQUIPMENT. The fifth said OFFICIALS. Only as I passed that one (still Tail-End Charlie, no pun intended), I looked at it out of the corner of my eye and OFFICIALS became something in the same tangle of runic symbols as those on Polley's driver's license when Kellin showed it to me. I turned my head to look back just long enough to see it said OFFICIALS again, and then a limber stick came down on my shoulder. Not too hard, but plenty hard enough to get my attention.

'Walk, kiddie.'

Up ahead the corridor ended in a splash of bright light. I followed the others onto a playing field . . . but what a playing field it was. I stared around like the rube from Ullum I was pretending to be. I'd had many shocks since emerging from the tunnel between my world and Empis, but never until that moment did the thought *I must be dreaming* come into my mind.

Jumbo gas-jets in those traylike holders I'd seen from outside rimmed the bowl of a stadium that would have done a Triple-A baseball team proud. They shot bright streams of blue-white fire into the sky, which were reflected back down off the omnipresent clouds.

The sky. We were outside.

Not only that, but it was night, even though for us the day was just beginning. That made sense if our skeletal captors weren't able to exist in daylight, but it was still strange to realize that my usual waking-and-sleeping rhythms had been turned upside-down.

We walked across a dirt track and onto green grass atop springy turf. I had been on many playing fields – baseball and football – that were similar to this, but never one that was perfectly round. What game had been played here? There was no way to tell, but it must have been awesomely popular, because the pinwheel pathways leading in and the tiers of seats surrounding the field and rising to the stadium's circular rim had to mean whatever it was had drawn thousands of Empisarian fans.

I saw the three green spires rising into the clouds dead ahead. There were stone turrets on my right and left. There were night soldiers in their burning blue shrouds on some of the parapets running between the turrets, looking down at us. I had only been able to see the top curve of the stadium on my walk to the sundial because it was sunken at the rear of the palace grounds.

Somewhere – probably at the base of those three green-and-glass spires – there was a throne room and royal apartments. Like the shops along the wide Gallien Road, those were places for the high mucky-mucks. I had an idea that this was the place that had been important to the common folk, and I could almost see them streaming up those brightly colored pinwheel paths on game days, coming in from Seafront and Deesk, maybe even from Ullum and the Green Isles, carrying baskets of food and singing their team songs or chanting their team names—

A limber stick came down on my arm, harder this time. I turned and saw a grinning skull inside a scowling semi-transparent envelope of face. 'Quit gawking around like the veriest idiot! Time to run, kiddie! Time to pick up your feet!'

Iota led our pack onto the circular track bordering the circular, crazy-green field. The others followed him in twos and threes. Hamey was last. No surprise there. Overhanging what I assumed was the front of the field was a kind of suite that looked like a big open-air living room; all it needed to complete the picture was a fancy-ass chandelier. Padded chairs, like the ones down front at Guaranteed Rate Field, flanked what was obviously the seat of honor. It wasn't as big as Hana's throne, where she guarded the back entrance to the palace (when she wasn't eating or sleeping, that was), but the seat was extra wide and the arms slanted outward, as if whoever got the privilege of sitting there was a steroid-enhanced widebody from the ass on up. This seat was empty, but there were half a dozen people in the padded chairs on either side, watching as we ran past them. They were whole people dressed in good clothes – which is to say, not the rags most of us were wearing. One was a woman, her face pale with what I assumed was makeup of some kind. She was wearing a long dress with a ruffled collar. Her fingers and hairclips flashed with gems. Everyone in this suite was drinking what could have been beer or ale from tall glasses. One of the men saw me looking and raised his glass to me, as if toasting. They all wore expressions I'd call a mixture of boredom lightly spiced with mild interest. I hated them at once, as only a prisoner who's been whipped with limber sticks can hate a bunch of well-dressed idlers who are just sitting on their fannies and passing the time.

This place wasn't built for the likes of those assholes, I thought. *I don't know how I can know that, but I do.*

A limber stick came down, this time across the seat of my increasingly filthy pants. It stung like fire. 'Don't you know it's not polite to stare at your betters?'

I was coming to hate those insectile, buzzing voices, too. It was like listening to not just one Darth Vader but a whole platoon of them. I picked up the pace and passed Stooks. He flipped me an Empisarian bird as I went by. I flipped it right back.

I weaved my way through my Deep Maleen colleagues, taking a friendly bump from Tom and a harder, less friendly one from a slightly bowlegged hulk named Ammit. 'Watch where you're going, Ully,' he said. 'Ain't no god to protect you here. You has left all that behind.'

I left *him* behind, and happy to do it. Life was lousy enough without bad-tempered cellblock mates to make it worse.

In the center of the field was stuff I recognized from various athletic practices going all the way back to Peewee football and hockey. There was a double line of what looked like wooden railroad ties. There were big cloth bags filled with round bulges that could only be balls. There was a line of poles wrapped in burlap. On top of each was a crudely painted scowling face. Empisarian tackling dummies, no doubt. There were ropes with rings on the ends hanging from a T-bar and a wide board on high sawhorses with a square of hay on one side. Also a wicker basket filled with what looked like axe-handles. I didn't care for the look of those. Coach Harkness had put us through drills some might consider sadistic, but whacking each other with sticks? No.

I got to the front of the crowd as we reached the part of the running track directly across the field from the VIP box. Here I pulled even with Iota, who was running with his head back, his chest puffed out, and his hands pumping at his sides. All he needed was a couple of hand weights to look like any middle-aged gettin'-in-shape guy from my neighborhood. Oh, and maybe a tracksuit.

'Want to race?' I asked.

'What? So that bitch Petra and the rest of em can bet on who wins?' He jerked a thumb at the well-dressed whole people relaxing with their refreshing drinks. They had been joined by a couple of new ones. It was almost a cocktail party, by God. The group was flanked by a pair of night soldiers. 'Ain't we got enough to worry about without that?'

'I guess so.'

'Where the fuck are you really from, Charlie? You're no Ully.'

I was spared answering by the sight of Hamey quitting the track. He plodded toward the various clumps of practice gear with his head lowered and his thin chest heaving. Between the wicker basket of fighting sticks (I didn't know what else they could be) and the tackling dummies with their scowling plate faces, there were some benches and a table covered with pottery cups – small, like demitasses. Hamey took one, drained it, put it back on the table, then sat with his forearms on his thighs and his head down. The table was guarded – or perhaps 'minded' – by a night soldier who looked at Hamey but made no move to hit him.

'Don't try that,' Eye puffed, 'or they'll whip you until you bleed.'

'How does *he* get away with it?'

'Because they know he can't do this shit, that's why. He's Mr Useless, ain't he? But he's whole, and without him we're back down to thirty.'

'I don't see how . . . I mean, once the Fair One starts, assuming it ever does . . . how they can expect him to . . . you know. Fight.'

'They don't,' Eye said, and I detected a strange note in his voice. It could have been sympathy. Or maybe I mean fellow-feeling. It wasn't that he liked Hamey; it was that he liked the situation we were in less.

'Don't you ever lose your breath, kiddie? One more time around and I'll be sitting on the bench with Useless and they can whack me with their sticks all they want.'

I thought of telling him I'd played a lot of sports, but then he might ask me what kind, and I didn't even know what sport had been played on this big green tiddlywink. 'I kept in shape. At least until I came here. And you can call me Charlie instead of kiddie, okay? Kiddie's what *they* call us.'

'Charlie it is.' Eye jerked his thumb at Hamey, a picture of dejection as he sat on the bench. 'That poor sucker's just a warm body. Cannon fodder.'

Only he didn't say *sucker* and he didn't say *cannon fodder*. That was just how my mind translated whatever idiom he had used. 'They like seeing one match decided fast.'

Like number one against number sixteen in the NCAA Big Dance, I thought.

We were coming around to the VIP box again, and this time it was my turn to jerk my thumb at the well-dressed whole people who were watching us. When they weren't talking to each other, that was, because you could tell whatever they were chatting about was more important to them than the ragged slobs puffing and running below. We were just an excuse for getting together, like the guys that used to watch football practice back home. Behind us, the others were strung out and a couple of guys – Double and a guy named Yanno – had joined Hamey on the benches.

'How many of them are there?'

'What?' Iota was now puffing, too. I still had my wind. 'Elden's subjects?' He gave *subjects* a little emphasis, as if putting it in quotation marks. 'Don't know. Twenty. Maybe thirty. Maybe a few more. The bitch queens it over em because she's Flight Killer's favorite.'

'Petra?'

'Yah, her.'

'And that's *it*?'

Before he could reply, my old frienemy Aaron strode out of a walkway under the VIP box, waving his limber stick like a conductor about to start an orchestra on its first number. '*In!*' he called. '*Everybody in!*'

Iota jogged toward the equipment in the center of the field and I joined him. Most of the prisoners were puffing and blowing. Jaya and Eris were bending over, hands on knees, getting their breath back.

Then they joined the others at the table with the little cups on it. I tossed one back. It was mostly water, but there was something sour in it that had a kick. I still had my breath, but after drinking that little cup I felt like I had more of it.

Counting Aaron, there were now five night soldiers on the field, standing in a semicircle in front of us. Two more were bodyguarding the VIPs. The ones watching from the parapets were easy to count because of their bright blue auras: twelve. That meant nineteen in all, which I thought was just about the number that had chased me and Radar as we ran for the outer gate. Twenty when I added in Kellin, who either wasn't here or was watching from one of the parapets. Was that all of them? If so, the prisoners actually outnumbered the guards. I didn't want to ask Eye, because Aaron appeared to be watching me.

'Good run!' said Stooks.

'Better than sex!' said Fremmy.

'Except for with you,' said Stooks.

'Yes,' Fremmy agreed, 'I do give good sex.'

I reached for another cup and one of our guards pointed his stick at me. 'Nah, nah, one to a customer, kiddie.'

Except *one to a customer*, of course, wasn't what he said.

2

Next came playtime, which was on the whole less brutal than football practice. Until the end, that was.

First came the balls. There were sixteen of them in three bags. They looked like beachballs, but were sheathed in a silvery substance that weighted them down. For all I knew, it *was* silver. I could see my distorted reflection in the side of mine: dirty face, dirty hair. I decided I wasn't going to wash my hair, no matter how grotty it felt. I didn't think I was the 'true prince, the one come to save us,' I couldn't even save myself, but I had no wish to be singled out. I had seen the palace's torture chamber and had no desire to be a guest there.

We formed two lines of fifteen. Hamey was the odd man out, and one of the guards used his limber stick to command him to toss the sixteenth ball up and down. Which Hamey did, in lackadaisical fashion.

He was still out of breath from his walk up the inclined corridor and his one partial turn around the track. He saw me looking at him and gave me a smile, but the eyes above it were desolate. He might as well have had I'LL BE THE FIRST ONE TO GO tattooed on his forehead.

The rest of us threw the weighted balls – five pounds or so – back and forth. There wasn't much to it, just an arms and upper body warm-up, but many of my fellow prisoners clearly hadn't been athletically inclined in their old lives, because there were a lot of fumbles. I found myself wondering if most had been the equivalent of white-collar workers in the place they called the Citadel before the overthrow of the Butterfly Monarchy (little unintended pun there). Some were in good shape and a few had moves – Eye was one, Eris was another, Tom and Ammit were two more – but the rest were pretty clumsy. Coach Harkness would have called them gluefoots (never gluefeet). Fremmy and Stooks were gluefoots; so were Jaya and Double. Dommy had size, but he also had that cough. Then there was Hamey, who was, as Iota said, useless.

I was partnered with Iota. He tossed a series of soft lobs, shotputting our ball off the heel of his hand, so I did the same. We were told to take a step back after each pair of throws. After ten minutes or so of this, we were ordered back to the track for another run. Hamey tried his best, but soon slowed to a walk. I was jogging this time, basically lazing along. Ammit caught up to me easily, although his bowlegged stride caused him to rock side to side like a tugboat in a moderate swell. As we passed the VIPs, he swerved and bumped me again, only this time it wasn't really a bump but a good old-fashioned shoulder-check. I wasn't expecting it and went sprawling. Jaya tripped over me and went to her knees with a grunt. The others swerved around us.

We had finally captured the full attention of the swells in the box. They were looking at Jaya and me, pointing and laughing the way Andy, Bertie, and I might have laughed at some slapstick comedy routine in a movie.

I helped Jaya up. One of her elbows was bleeding. I asked if she was okay. She said she was, then ran on as one of the night soldiers approached with his limber stick raised. 'No touching, kiddie! Nah,

nah, nah!' I raised a hand, partly to show I understood, mostly to ward off a blow of the limber stick if he decided to launch one at my face.

The night soldier retreated a step. I caught up with Ammit. 'Why did you do that?'

His answer was one I could have heard from any of the stonebrained, would-be Alpha dogs I'd played sports with over the years – and there are plenty of them. If you've played, especially in high school, you know. Those are the guys who end up hanging by the fence at practice in their twenties or thirties, building beer-guts and talking about their glory days. 'Felt like it.'

Which meant Ammit needed a lesson. If he didn't get one, the bumping and pushing and tripping would never stop.

After a single circuit of the track, we were sent to the rings and told to do pull-ups. Half of my fellows could do five; six or seven could do one or two; I did a dozen, then stupidly decided to show off. 'Watch this!' I told Eye and Hamey.

I pulled myself up again and skinned the cat, legs over my head, a perfect three-sixty revolution. I had barely landed when I was whipped across the small of the back, and hard. First came the pain, then the burn, sinking in.

'No tricks!' Aaron shouted at me. His anger made his aura brighter, and his human face – fragile to begin with – disappeared almost completely. Here's a little factoid: you might think you'd eventually get used to being held prisoner by the living dead, but you never do. *'No tricks!* Break your wrist or your leg and I'll *flay* you!'

I stared at him from a crouch, lips skinned back, the fingers of my left hand tented on the ground. Aaron took a step away, but not because he was afraid. He did it to give himself all the room he needed to swing his fucking stick. 'Do you want to come at me? Do! If you need a lesson, I'll teach you one!'

I shook my head, causing my filthy hair to flop against my brow, and stood up very slowly. I was bigger and outweighed him by well over a hundred pounds – he was essentially a bag of bones – but he was protected by his aura. Did I want to be electrified? I did not.

'I'm sorry,' I said, and I thought for just a moment he looked surprised, as Pursey had when I thanked him. He motioned me to rejoin the others.

'*Run!*' he shouted at us. '*Run, you monkeys!*'

Not monkeys, but another mental substitution. We circled the track (this time Hamey didn't even try), drank more power water, then were directed to the tackling dummies.

Aaron stood back. One of the other night soldiers replaced him. 'First one to kill his enemy gets cake! Cake for the first killer! Step forward and pick a pole!'

There were thirty-one of us and only twelve of the tackling dummy poles. Eye grabbed my wrist and growled, 'See how it's done first.'

I was surprised by this helpful hint but more than willing. With cake as a possible reward, twelve of my fellow prisoners quickly stepped forward and touched a burlap-wrapped pole. Among them were Eris, Fremmy and Stooks, Double, and Ammit.

'Now step *back*!'

They retreated all the way to the table.

'And *kill* your *enemy*!'

They rushed forward. Well over half of them pulled back a little from the impact – it wasn't obvious, but I saw it. Three collided with their poles full tilt. Eris hit hard, but she was skinny and the leering plate atop her pole only shivered. Same with the other guy who didn't flinch. His name was Murf. Ammit's hit was a no-doubter. His plate flew off the top of the pole and landed ten feet away.

'Cake for this one!' Aaron proclaimed. 'This one gets cake!'

The watchers in the VIP box, led by the white-faced woman, cheered. Ammit raised his fisted hands and bowed to them. I don't think he recognized the distinctly satiric quality of those cheers. He wasn't, as they say, the sharpest knife or the brightest bulb.

The first twelve were replaced by twelve more, but Eye grabbed my wrist again and I stood pat. Nobody knocked a plate off this time. Eye, Hamey, Jaya, and I were among the last to have a go.

'Step *back*!'

We did.

'And *kill* your *enemy*!'

I ran at my post, lowering my right shoulder – my strong-side shoulder – without even thinking about it. I was pretty sure I could have hit the post hard enough to send the scowling plate-head flying, even without padding, but I pulled back as I'd seen some of the others do. My plate hardly shivered at all, but Iota's came off and flew almost as far as Ammit's had. This time none of the VIPs bothered cheering; they were once more lost in their own conversations.

Aaron had retreated to the walkway beneath the VIP box, and there he was joined by Kellin. No smoking jacket today; the Lord High was wearing tight whipcord breeches and an open-throated white shirt beneath his aura. They walked toward us together, and I felt the same *déjà vu* I'd felt when I saw the practice gear and the table with the drinks on it. Kellin and Aaron could have been the head coach and his assistant. This wasn't just an exercise period for the prisoners, but serious business. There was going to be a Fair One, and I had an idea Kellin and Aaron were the ones responsible for making sure it was a good show.

'*Sticks!*' Aaron shouted. '*Now sticks!*'

At that the whole people in the box showed more interest. Even the watching night soldiers on the parapets seemed to come to attention.

We went to the wicker basket containing the fighting sticks. They were like bokken sticks, but without any hilts – about three feet long and tapered at both ends. The wood was white and smooth and hard. Ash, I thought. Like Major League Baseball bats.

Kellin pointed at Eris. She stepped forward and took one of the sticks. Then he pointed at Hamey, which made my heart sink a little. He took one and held it with one hand on each tapered end. Eris had hers only by one end. *Defense and offense*, I thought. Neither of them looked thrilled, but only Hamey looked scared. I thought he had reason to be.

'*Kill your enemy!*' Aaron shouted it, his voice buzzier than ever.

Eris swung her stick. Hamey parried. She came at him from the side and Hamey parried again, but weakly; if she had swung with real force (she didn't), she probably would have knocked him off his feet.

'*Take him down!*' Kellin shrieked. '*Take him down, you useless cunt, or I'll take* you *down!*'

Eris swung low. Hamey made no effort to parry this time, and she cut the legs out from under him. He landed on the grass with a gasp and a thump. The whole people in the box cheered more lustily. Eris bowed to them. I hoped they were far enough away not to see the look of disgust on her face.

Aaron whipped Hamey's butt and legs with his limber stick. 'Up! Up, you pile of dung! Up!'

Hamey struggled to his feet. Tears were rolling down his cheeks and snot hung in double runners from his nose. Aaron raised his limber stick for another slash, but Kellin stayed him with a single shake of his head. Hamey had to stay in one piece, at least until the contest commenced.

Eris was kept on for another opponent. There was a lot of parrying, but no hard hits. They stepped back and the next pair took their place. It went like that, with a lot of thrusting and swiping and parrying, but there were no more cries of *take him down* or *kill your enemy*. Stooks and Fremmy, however, got whippings from one of the other night soldiers for laziness. From the way they took it, I thought it wasn't the first time.

Eye went at it with Tom, Bernd went at it with Bult, and in the end there was just me and Ammit. My guess is Aaron had seen the shoulder-check Ammit had given me on the running track and wanted it that way. Or perhaps Kellin had seen it from wherever he'd been before coming out on the field.

'Sticks!' Aaron shouted. God, I hated that buzzy voice. 'You two now! Sticks! Let's see how you go!'

Ammit held his by the end: offense. He was smiling. I held mine by both ends, cross-body, to parry. At least to start with. Ammit had done this before and expected no trouble from the new kid on the block. Maybe he was right. Maybe he wasn't. We'd see.

'*Kill your enemy!*' This time it was Kellin who shouted it.

Ammit went at me with no hesitation, rocking from side to side on his bowlegs, hoping to pin me between the drinks table and the basket that held the fighting sticks, which the previous sparring partners had replaced after their contests. He raised his stick and brought it down. There was no holding back in that swing; he meant to give me a concussion or worse. Putting me away made a certain kind of sense. He might be punished, but the population of the dungeon would be back down to thirty, meaning the Fair One would be put off until two more whole people could be found. He might even have seen it as taking one for the team, but I didn't believe that. For whatever reason, Ammit had decided he didn't like me.

I dropped into a semi-crouch and raised my own fighting stick. He hit it instead of my head. I rose from my crouch, pushing his stick and driving him back. Dimly, I heard a spatter of applause from the VIP box. I stepped out from between the basket and the table, crowding him, forcing him back into the open where I could use what speed I had. That wasn't much, granted, but with those bowlegs, Ammit was no greyhound himself.

He swung his stick first at my left side, then at my right. I parried easily now that I was in the clear. And I was angry. Very. Angry the way I'd been at Christopher Polley when I broke one of his hands, beat him up, and then broke the other one. The way I'd been angry at my father when he retreated into booze after my mother died. I left him alone, didn't complain about Dad's drinking (much), but I expressed that anger in other ways. Some I've told you, some I'm too ashamed to tell.

We went around in a circle on the grass, stepping and bending and feinting. The prisoners watched silently. Kellin, Aaron, and the other night soldiers were also watching. In the VIP box, the cocktail-party chatter had ceased. Ammit was starting to breathe hard, and he was no longer as quick with the stick. He was no longer smiling, either, and that was good.

'Come on,' I said. 'Come at me, you useless fuck. Let's see what you've got.'

He rushed forward, raising his stick over his head. I slid one of my hands down my own stick and jammed the butt end into his belly, just above the groin. The blow he'd launched came down on my shoulder, numbing it. I didn't pull back. I dropped my stick, reached cross-body with my left hand, and snatched his away. I hit him with it in the thigh, drew back, and hit him in the hip, really putting my own hips into the swing, as if trying to hit a line drive straight up the right-field power alley.

Ammit screamed in pain. 'Cry off! I cry off!'

I didn't give a fuck what he cried. I swung again and hit him in the arm. He turned and began to run, but he was out of breath. Also, those bowlegs. I looked at Kellin, who shrugged and swept a hand at my erstwhile foe, as if to say *as you will*. I took it for that, anyway. I went after Ammit. I could tell you I was thinking about the shoulder-check, and how the whole people in the box had laughed when I went down. I could tell you I was thinking about how Jaya had tripped over me and gone sprawling. I could even tell you that I was making sure no one else would decide to mess with the new boy. None of that would have been true. None of the others had shown the slightest animus toward me, except maybe for Eye, and that was before he got to know me a little.

I just wanted to fuck the dude up.

I hit him twice in the ass, good hard blows. The second drove him to his knees. 'Cry off! Cry off! *I cry off!*'

I raised my fighting stick over my head, but before I could bring it down, the Lord High grasped my elbow. There was that horrible feeling of being touched by a live wire, and the sense that all my strength was being drained out of me. If he'd held on, I would have blacked out as I had at the outer gate, but he let go.

'Enough.'

My hands opened and I dropped the stick. Then I went to one knee. The VIPs were applauding and cheering. My vision was swimming, but I saw a tall guy with a scar on his cheek whispering to the white-faced woman, casually cupping one of her breasts as he did so.

'Get up, Charlie.'

I managed to do it. Kellin nodded at Aaron.

'Playtime is over,' Aaron said. 'Everyone take another drink.'

I don't know about the rest of them, but I needed it.

3

The guards took us to one of the team rooms. It was, by the standards I was used to, large and luxurious. There were electric lights overhead, but apparently they weren't wired to the ramshackle generator and had been replaced by more gas-jets. The floors and walls were white-tiled and spotless, at least until we tracked our dirt in . . . plus assorted splotches of blood from the stick-fighting. The place was probably kept clean by grayfolk, I thought, although none were in evidence now.

There was a gutter of running water to piss in, which several of the men did. At either end were porcelain seats with holes in the center. I guessed those were for the women, although neither Jaya nor Eris availed themselves of them. They did strip off their tops as the men did, and without any observable self-consciousness. Jaya had taken several fighting-stick blows, and her ribs were blooming with bruises.

On one side of the room were wooden cubbies where team members must once have stored their gear (we, of course, had none to stow). On the other side was a long shelf lined with buckets for washing. A rag floated in each. There was no soap.

I pulled off my shirt, wincing at various aches and pains – most from the blows of the limber sticks. The worst was at the small of my back. I couldn't see that one, but I could feel the blood, now drying and tacky.

Several people were already at the buckets, washing their upper bodies, and a few had dropped their drawers to wash the rest. I thought I might skip that part of my ablutions, but it was interesting to note that in Empis, as well as in France (at least according to the ditty), they don't wear underpants.

Ammit limped toward me. Our guardians hadn't come in with us, which meant there was no one to break it up if he wanted a rematch. That was okay with me. I bent, bare-chested and still caked with days of dirt (maybe weeks by then), and balled up my fists. Then an amazing thing happened. Eye, Fremmy, Stooks, and Hamey stood in front of me in a line, facing Ammit.

The bowlegged man shook his head and put the heel of his hand to his brow, as though he had a headache. 'Nah, nah. I didn't believe it, but now I do. *Maybe* I do. Are you really the—'

Iota stepped forward and put a hand over Ammit's mouth before he could finish. With the other hand he pointed to a grate that might have supplied heat in the days when this stadium – and the city it served – had been a going concern. Ammit followed his gaze and nodded. With what was obvious pain, he dropped to one knee before me and put his hand to his forehead again.

'I apologize, Charlie.'

I opened my mouth to say *no problem*, but what came out was 'I accept gladly. Take your feet, Ammit.'

They were all looking at me now, and some of the others (not Iota, not then) had also put their hands to their foreheads. They couldn't all have headaches, so it had to be a salute. They believed something that was completely ridiculous. And yet—

'Wash, Charlie,' Gully said. He extended a hand to one of the buckets. For reasons I didn't understand, Eris was duck-walking along the shelf and running her hands along its underside. 'Go ahead. Clean yourself up.'

'Hair, too,' Eye said. And when I hesitated: 'It's all right. They need to see. So do I.' Then he added: 'I apologize for saying that about feeding you a mouthful of dirt.'

I told him no offense had been taken, not bothering to add that I'd heard plenty of trash-talk in my life. It wasn't just a sports thing; it was a guy thing.

I went to one of the buckets and wrung out the rag floating in it. I washed my face, neck, pits, and belly. I was very aware, excruciatingly so, that I had an audience watching me clean myself. When I'd finished everything I could reach, Jaya told me to turn around. I did so, and she washed my back. She was gentle around the slash where Aaron had hit me for skinning the cat on the rings, but I still winced.

'Nah, nah,' she said. Her voice was gentle. 'Be still, Charlie. I need to get the dirt out of the woundy so it don't fester up.'

When she was done, she pointed at one of the buckets that hadn't been used. Then she brushed at my hair, but only for a second before pulling back, as if she'd touched something hot.

I looked at Iota to be positive. He nodded. With no further ado I grabbed the bucket and dumped it over my head. The water was cold enough to make me gasp, but it felt good. I ran my hands through my hair, getting out a load of old dirt and grit. The water that puddled around my feet was filthy. I finger-combed back as much as I could. *Getting long*, I thought. *Probably look like a hippie*.

They were staring at me, all thirty of them. Some were actually gaping. All were round-eyed. Eye put the heel of his hand to his forehead and dropped to his knee. The others followed suit. To say I was flabbergasted doesn't cover it.

'Get up,' I said. 'I'm not who you think I am.'

Only I wasn't sure that was true.

They got to their feet. Eye came to me and grabbed a hank of hair that had fallen over my ear. He yanked it out – ouch – and showed me his palm. The lock of hair, even wet, shone bright in the light of the gas-jets. Almost as bright as Mr Bowditch's gold pellets.

'What about my eyes?' I asked. 'What color are my eyes?'

Iota squinted, going almost nose to nose with me. 'Still hazel. But they may still be changing. You need to keep them cast down as much as you can.'

'The bastards like that, anyway,' said Stooks.

'*Love* it,' added Fremmy.

'They'll come for us anytime,' Eris said. 'Let me . . . sorry, Prince Charlie, but I have to—'

'Don't call him that!' Tom said. 'Not ever! Do you want to get him killed? Charlie, always damn Charlie!'

'I'm sorry,' she whispered, 'and sorry to do this, but I have to.'

She had collected a lot of black gluck from under the shelf – a mixture of old grease and dirt.

'Bend to me. You're very tall.'

Of course I am, I thought. *Tall, Caucasian, now blond, and maybe blue-eyed all too soon. A dashing prince right out of a Disney animated feature.* Not that I felt much like dashing anywhere, and the whole thing was absurd. What Disney prince had ever smeared shit on a windshield or blown up a mailbox with a cherry bomb?

I bent. Very gently, she ran her fingers through my hair, dirtying it up again, darkening it. But I won't say the feel of her fingers on my scalp didn't give me a small frisson. From the way the color bloomed in Eris's cheeks, I wasn't the only one.

A fist hammered on the door. One of the night soldiers shouted, 'Playtime's over! Get out! Hump, hump! Don't make me tell you twice, kiddies!'

Eris stepped back. She looked up at me, then at Eye, Jaya, and Hamey.

'I think he's all right,' Jaya said, low. I hoped I was. I had no desire to visit the Lord High's apartments again.

Or the torture chamber. If taken there, I would be urged to tell everything . . . and eventually, I would. Where I came from, to start with. Who had helped me on my way and where they lived. Then who my fellow prisoners thought I was. *What* I was.

Their fucking savior.

4

We returned to Deep Maleen. The cell doors slammed shut and locked at the outstretched arms of the night soldiers. It was a neat trick. I wondered what other ones they had. Besides administering electric jolts at will, that was.

Hamey was staring at me with big eyes from his side of the cell – as far away from me as he could get. I told him to quit staring at me, it was making me nervous. He said, 'I apologize, Pr— Charlie.'

'You have to do better than that,' I said. 'Promise me you'll try.'

'I promise.'

'And you should try doing a little better at keeping what you think you know to yourself.'

'I told no one what I suspected.'

I looked over my shoulder and saw Fremmy and Stooks side by side, staring at us from their cell, and understood how the word had gotten around. Some stories (as you probably know yourself) are just too good not to pass on.

I was still inventorying my various aches and pains when the four bolts were drawn. In came Pursey, with a large slab of cake on a metal plate. *Chocolate* cake, from the look of it. My stomach cried out. He took it down the corridor to the cell Ammit shared with Gully.

Ammit reached through the bars and pinched off a good-sized hunk. He popped it into his mouth, then said (with obvious regret), 'Give the rest to Charlie. He beat me with the stick. Beat me like a redheaded stepchild.'

Not what he said; what I heard. Something my mother used to say after gin rummy with her friend Hedda. Sometimes Hedda beat her like a redheaded stepchild, sometimes like a rented mule, sometimes a big bass drum. There are phrases you never forget.

Pursey returned the way he'd come, the cake still on the plate but with that good-sized chunk gone. Longing eyes followed it. The slice was so big that Pursey had to turn the plate sideways to get it between the cell bars. I held it against the plate with my hand to keep it from falling to the floor, then licked off the frosting. My God, it was so good – I can taste it still.

I started to take a bite (promising myself I'd give some to Hamey, maybe even a bit to the Comedy Twins next door), then hesitated. Pursey was still standing in front of the cell. When he saw me looking at him, he put the heel of his poor melted hand against his gray forehead.

And bent his knee.

5

I slept and dreamed of Radar.

She was trotting along Kingdom Road toward the supply shed where we'd spent the night before entering the city. Every now and then she stopped and looked for me, whining. Once she almost turned around to go back, but then went on. *Good dog*, I thought. *Get safe, if you can.*

The moons broke through the clouds. The wolves began to howl, right on cue. Radar stopped trotting and broke into a run. The howls got louder, closer. In the dream I could see low shadows slinking to either side of Kingdom Road. The shadows had red eyes. *This is where the dream turns into a nightmare*, I thought, and told myself to wake up. I didn't want to see a pack of wolves – *two* packs, one on each side – burst from the streets and alleys of the destroyed suburbs and attack my friend.

The dream thinned. I could hear Hamey groaning. Fremmy and Stooks were murmuring together in the next cell. Before I could get all the way back to reality, a wonderful thing happened. A cloud darker than the night rolled toward Radar. When it flew across the racing moons, the cloud turned to lace. It was the monarchs. They had no business flying at night, they should have been roosting, but that's dreams for you. The cloud reached my dog and hovered a few feet above her as she ran. Some actually fluttered down onto her head, back, and newly powerful haunches, their wings slowly opening and closing. The wolves stopped howling, and I woke up.

Hamey was crouched over the waste hole in the corner, the rags of his pants puddled around his feet. He was clutching his belly.

'Shut it, can't you?' Eye called from his side of the corridor. 'Some are trying to sleep.'

'You shut it,' I called back, low. I went to Hamey. 'How bad is it?'

'Nah, nah, not bad.' His sweaty face said differently. Suddenly there was an explosive fart and a plop. 'Ah, gods, better. That's better.'

The stink was atrocious, but I grabbed his arm so he wouldn't fall over while he yanked up what remained of his britches.

'Oh my, who died?' Fremmy asked.

'I think Hamey's asshole finally fell out,' Stooks added.

'Cease,' I said. 'Both of you. There's nothing funny about sickness.'

They shut up immediately. Stooks started to put his palm to his forehead.

'Nah, nah,' I said (you pick up the lingua franca fast when you're jailed). 'Don't do that. Not ever.'

I helped Hamey back to his pallet. His face was haggard and pale. The thought of him fighting anyone in a so-called Fair One, even Dommy with his weak lungs, was ridiculous.

No, wrong word. Horrible. Like asking a parakeet to fight a Rottweiler.

'Food don't take to me. Told you. I used to be strong, worked twelve hours a day in the Brookey Sawmill, sometimes fourteen, and never begged an extra rest period. Then . . . I don't know what happened. Mushrooms? Nah, prob'ly not. Swallowed a bad bug, most likely. Now food don't take to me. It wasn't bad at first. Now it is. Do you know what I hope?'

I shook my head.

'Hope there's a Fair One and I make it that far. Then I can die outside and not because my belly busts while I'm trying to take a shit in this rotten fucking cell!'

'Did you get sick in here?'

I thought he must have – poisonous mushrooms either would have killed him quick or he would have gotten better eventually. And Deep Maleen wasn't exactly an antiseptic environment. But Hamey shook his head. 'I think on the road from the Citadel. After the gray came. Sometimes I think the gray would have been better.'

'How long ago was that?'

He shook his head. 'Don't know. Years. Sometimes I think I can feel that bug buzzing around down here.' He rubbed his flabby belly. 'Buzzing around, eating me a little at a time. Taking it slow. *Sloo-ow.*'

He armed sweat from his face.

'There were only five when they brought me and Jackah here.' He pointed down the corridor toward the cell Jackah shared with Bernd. 'Jackah and me made seven. The number goes up . . . someone dies and it goes down . . . but it always goes up again. Now it's thirty-one. Bult was here before me, he might be the longest . . . who's still alive . . . and he said back then Flight Killer wanted sixty-four. More contests that way! More blood and brains on the grass! Kellin . . . must have been him . . . convinced him he'd never get that many whole ones, so it's to be thirty-two. Eye says if there's no thirty-two soon, Flight Killer'll bring in Red Molly instead of saving her for the end.'

This I knew. And although I'd never seen Red Molly, I dreaded her because I *had* seen her ma. But there was something I didn't know. I leaned close to Hamey. 'Elden is Flight Killer.'

'So they call him.'

'Does he have another name? Is he Gogmagog?'

That was when I discovered the great distance – the chasm, the abyss – between fairy-tale magic like sundials that turn back time and the supernatural. Because *something heard*.

The gas-jets, which had been guttering along as usual and casting only the dimmest light, suddenly shot up in bright blue arrows that turned Deep Maleen flashbulb-bright. There were cries of fear and surprise from some of the cells. I saw Iota at his barred door, one hand shading his eyes. It only lasted for a second or two, but I felt the stone floor beneath me rise and then thud back. Rock dust sifted down from the ceiling. The walls groaned. It was as if our prison had cried out at the sound of that name.

No.

Not *as if*.

It *did* cry out.

Then it was over.

Hamey wrapped one of this thin arms around my neck, almost tight enough to choke off my air. Into my ear he whispered, *'Don't ever say that name! Do you want to wake what sleeps in the Dark Well?'*

CHAPTER TWENTY-THREE

Tempus est Umbra in Mente.

Hazy History. Cla. A Note. Seedings.

1

When I was a freshman at Hillview, I took Latin I. I did it because learning a dead language seemed like a cool idea, and because my dad told me that my mom took it at the same school, from the same teacher, Miss Young. He said Mom thought she was cool. By the time my turn came around, Miss Young – who taught French as well as Latin – was no longer young, but she was still cool. There were only eight of us in the class, and there was no Latin II when I was a sophomore, because Miss Young retired and that part of the HHS language program was closed down.

On our first day in class, Miss Young asked if we knew any Latin phrases. Carla Johansson raised her hand and said *carpe diem*, which meant seize the day. No one else was offering, so I raised my hand and gave one I'd heard from my Uncle Bob, usually when he had to get going somewhere: *tempus fugit*, meaning time flies. Miss Young nodded, and when nobody else offered, she gave us some more, like *ad hoc, de facto*, and *bona fide*. When class ended, she called me back, said she remembered my mother well and was sorry I'd lost her so young. I thanked her. No tears, not after six years, but I got a lump in my throat.

'*Tempus fugit* is a good one,' she said, 'but time doesn't always fly, as everyone who's ever had to wait around for something knows. I think *tempus est umbra in mente* is a better one. Roughly translated, it means time is a shadow in the mind.'

I thought of that often in Deep Maleen. Because we were entombed, the only way to tell night from day was that in daylight – daylight *somewhere*, not in our durance vile – the night soldiers came less frequently, their blue auras were reduced when they did, and their human faces became more apparent. For the most part they were unhappy faces. Tired. Haggard. I wondered if these creatures had, when still human, made some sort of devil's bargain which they regretted now that it was too late to cry it off. Maybe not Aaron and a few of the others, certainly not the Lord High, but the rest? Maybe. Or maybe I was just seeing what I wanted to see.

I thought I kept a rough hold on time during my first week in the dungeon, but after that I lost track. I believe we were taken up to the stadium for playtime every five or six days, but for the most part they were just practices and not bloody. The one exception was when Yanno (I'm sorry to keep throwing these names at you, but you have to remember there were thirty prisoners besides me) swung his fighting stick too hard at Eris. She ducked. He missed by a mile and dislocated his shoulder. This did not surprise me. Yanno, like the majority of my fellows, had never been what you'd call a Dwayne Johnson type to begin with, and being locked in a cell for the majority of the time hadn't exactly built him up. I exercised in my cell; few of the others did.

Another prisoner, Freed, fixed Yanno's shoulder when we were returned to the team room. He told Yan to hold still, grabbed him by the elbow, and yanked. I heard the clunk as Yanno's shoulder went back into place.

'That was good,' I said as we were escorted back to Maleen.

Freed shrugged. 'I used to be a doctor. In the Citadel. Many years ago.'

Only *years* wasn't the word he used. I know I've said that before, *you* know I've said it before, but I need to explain – try, at least –

why nothing ever quite fit in my mind. I always heard *years*, but when I asked questions about Empis and that word was used, it seemed to mean different things to different people. I got a picture of Empisarian history as the weeks (used advisedly) passed, but never a coherent timeline.

In Dad's AA meetings, beginners were advised to take the cotton out of their ears and stick it in their mouths; learn to listen so you can listen to learn, they say. I sometimes asked questions, but mostly I kept my ears open and my mouth shut. They talked (because there was little else to do), they argued about when thus-and-such had happened (or if it had happened at all), they told stories their parents and grandparents had told them. A picture began to form, hazy but better than no picture at all.

Once upon a time, long ago, the monarchy had been a *real* monarchy with a real army, for all I know even a navy. Sort of like England was, I suppose, in the days of James, Charles, and the Henry with all the wives. These Empis kings of yore – I can't say if there was ever a queen in charge, that's one of many things I don't know – were supposedly chosen by the high gods. Their rule was unquestioned. They were almost considered to be gods themselves, and for all I knew, they were. Is it so hard to believe that kings (and maybe members of their family) could levitate, strike enemies dead with a cross look, or heal sickness by touching, in a land where there were mermaids and giants?

At some point, the Galliens became the ruling family. According to my fellow prisoners, that was – you guessed it – *many years ago*. But as time passed, I'm guessing maybe five or six generations, the Galliens began to loosen the royal grip. In the time leading up to the gray, Empis was a monarchy in name only: the royal family still a big deal, but no longer the be-all and end-all. Take the Citadel. Doc Freed told me it was run by a Council of Seven, and the councilors were elected. He spoke of the Citadel as if it were this big important city, but the picture I got was of a small and wealthy town that prospered on trade between Seafront and Lilimar. Maybe other towns or principalities, like Deesk and Ullum (at least before Ullum went all gaga religious), were about the same, each with its own specialty, the inhabitants of each just going about their business.

The prisoners, most of whom became my friends – complicated by their belief that I was, or might be, some magical prince – knew only a little of Lilimar and the palace, not because it was a big secret but because they had their own lives and towns to take care of. They paid tribute to King Jan (Double actually thought he was King Jam, like something you'd spread on bread), because the amounts demanded were reasonable, and because the army – much reduced by then and renamed the King's Guard – kept up the roads and bridges. Tribute also paid for some fellows Tom called the riding sheriffs and Ammit called the possemen (these were the words I heard). The people of Empis also paid tribute because Jan was – *ta-da!* – the king and because folks tend to do what tradition demands. They probably bitched a little, the way people always do about paying taxes, then forgot all about it until the Empisarian equivalent of April 15th came around again.

What about the magic, you ask? The sundial? The night soldiers? The buildings that sometimes seemed to change their shapes? They took it for granted. If you find that strange, imagine a time-traveler from 1910 being transported to 2010 and finding a world where people flew through the sky in giant metal birds and rode in cars capable of going ninety miles an hour. A world where everyone went bopping around with powerful computers in their pockets. Or imagine a guy who's only seen a few silent black-and-white films plunked down in the front row of an IMAX theater and watching *Avatar* in 3-D.

You get used to the amazing, that's all. Mermaids and IMAX, giants and cell phones. If it's in your world, you go with it. It's wonderful, right? Only look at it another way, and it's sort of awful. Think Gogmagog is scary? Our world is sitting on a potentially world-ending supply of nuclear weapons, and if that's not black magic, I don't know what is.

2

In Empis kings came and went. For all I knew, the preserved bodies of the Galliens were kept in one of the huge gray buildings Radar and I had passed as we followed Mr Bowditch's initials to the sundial. King Jan was anointed with the usual rituals. Bult claimed a sacred cup made of gold was involved.

Jackah insisted that Jan's wife was Queen Clara, or maybe Kara, but most of the others insisted she had been Cora, and that she and Jan were third cousins or something. None of my fellows seemed to know how many children they'd had; some said four, some said eight, and Ammit swore there were ten. 'Those two must have fucked like royal rabbits,' he said. According to what I knew from a certain princess's horse, they were all wrong – there had been seven. Five girls and two boys. And this is where the story got interesting to me, you could even say relevant, although it remained maddeningly hazy.

King Jan fell ill. His son Robert, who'd always been the favored one as well as the older of the two boys, waited in the wings, ready to drink from the sacred cup. (I imagined engraved butterflies around the rim.) Elden, the younger brother, was pretty well forgotten . . . except by Leah, that was, who idolized him.

'By all accounts he was an ugly limping fuck,' Dommy said one night. 'Not one clubfoot but both of them.'

'Warty, too, I heard,' Ocka said.

'Hump on his back,' Fremmy said.

'Heard it was a lump on his neck,' Stooks said.

It was interesting to me, even illuminating, that they talked about Elden – the ugly, limping, nearly forgotten prince – and the Flight Killer as two different people. Or like a caterpillar that morphs into a butterfly. At least part of the King's Guard had also morphed, I believed. Into the night soldiers.

Elden was jealous of his brother and jealousy grew into hatred. All of them seemed to agree on this point, and why not? It was a classic story of sibling rivalry that would have been at home in any fairy tale. I knew good stories are not always true stories, or not completely true, but this one was plausible enough, human nature being what it is. Elden decided to take the kingship, either by force or by guile, and be revenged on his family. If Empis as a whole also suffered, so be it.

Did the gray come before or after Elden became the Flight Killer? Some of my fellows said before, but I think it was after. I think he brought it somehow. One thing I'm sure of is how he got his new name.

'The butterflies were everywhere in Empis,' Doc Freed said. 'They darkened the skies.'

This was after the practice when he yanked Yanno's shoulder back in place. We were returning to our dungeon keep, walking side by side. Doc was speaking low, almost whispering. It was easier to talk going down the stairs, and the pace was slow because we were tired out. What he said made me think of how passenger pigeons had once darkened the skies of the Midwest. Until they were hunted out of existence, that was. Only who would hunt monarch butterflies?

'Were they good to eat?' I asked. That was, after all, why the passenger pigeons went bye-bye; they were cheap food on the wing.

He snorted. 'Monarchs are poisonous, Charlie. Eat one, you might only get an upset stomach. Eat a handful and you could die. They were everywhere, as I say, but they were especially thick in Lilimar and the suburbs that surround it.'

Did he say *suburbs* or *smallies*? It came to the same thing.

'People grew milkweed in their gardens for the larvae to eat, and flowers for the butterflies to drink nectar from when they emerged. They were considered the luck of the kingdom.'

I thought of all the defaced statues I'd seen – spread wings hammered to rubble.

'The story goes that once Elden's family was killed and only he was left, he walked through the streets in a red robe with a snowy ermine collar, the golden crown of the Galliens on his head. The skies were dark with monarchs, as was typical. But each time Elden raised his hands, thousands fell dead from the skies. When the people fled the city – a few stayed, paid homage, swore allegiance – they ran through drifts of dead butterflies. It's said that inside the city wall, those drifts were ten feet deep. Millions of dead monarchs with their bright colors fading to gray.'

'That's awful,' I said. We were almost back by then. 'Do you believe it?'

'I know they also died in the Citadel. I saw them dropping out of the skies myself. Others will tell you the same.' He brushed at his eyes, then looked up at me. 'I'd give a deal to see a butterfly while we're out on that playing field. Just one. But I suppose they're all gone.'

'No,' I said. 'I've seen them. A lot of them.'

He took my arm, his grip surprisingly strong for a little man – although if the Fair One came, I didn't think the doc would last much longer than Hamey. 'Is that the truth? Do you swear it?'

'Yes.'

'On your mother's name, now!'

One of our guards looked back, frowning, and made a threatening gesture with his limber stick before facing forward again.

'On my mother's name,' I said, keeping it low.

The monarchs weren't gone, and neither were the Galliens – not all, at least. They had been cursed by whatever power now lived in Elden – the same power that had reduced the closer suburbs to rubble, I assumed – but they were alive. I didn't tell Freed that, though. It might have been dangerous for both of us.

I thought of Woody's story about Hana chasing the remains of his family to the city gates, and how she had swatted off the head of Woody's nephew Aloysius. 'When did Hana come? *Why* did she come, if the giants live in the north?'

He shook his head. 'I don't know.'

I thought that perhaps Hana had been on a visit to the home folks in Cratchy when Mr Bowditch made his last gold-getting expedition, but there was no way to tell. He was dead, and as I say, Empisarian history was hazy.

That night I lay awake a long time. I wasn't thinking about Empis, or the butterflies, or the Flight Killer; I was thinking about my father. Missing him and worrying about him. For all I knew, he might think I was as dead as my mother.

3

Time slipped away unmarked and uncounted. I gathered my little crumbs of information, although for what purpose I wasn't sure. Then one day we came back from a practice slightly more arduous than the others had been lately, to find a bearded man a lot bigger than either me, Dommy, or Iota, in Iota's cell. He was dressed in muddy short pants and an equally muddy striped shirt, the sleeves cut off to show slabs of muscle. He was squatting on his hunkers in the corner, knees up around his ears, as far from the blue presence also occupying the cell as he could get – the blue presence being the Lord High.

Kellin held up one hand. The gesture was almost lackadaisical, but the pair of night soldiers leading us stopped at once and stood at attention. We all stopped. Jaya was beside me that day, and her hand crept into mine. It was very cold.

Kellin stepped out of Eye's cell and looked us over. 'My dear friends, I would like you to meet your new compatriot. His name is Cla. He was found on the shore of Lake Remla after his little boat sprang a leak. He nearly drowned, didn't you, Cla?'

Cla said nothing, only looked at Kellin.

'Answer me!'

'Yes. I almost drowned.'

'Try again. Address me as Lord High.'

'Yes, Lord High. I almost drowned.'

Kellin turned back to us. 'But he was rescued, my dear friends, and as I'm sure you can see, there is not a bloom of gray anywhere on him. Just dirt.' Kellin tittered. It was an awful sound. Jaya's hand tightened on mine. 'Introductions aren't common in Deep Maleen, as you no doubt know, but I felt my new dear friend Cla warranted one, because he is our thirty-second guest. Isn't that wonderful?'

No one said anything.

Kellin pointed at one of the night soldiers at the head of our unlucky procession, then at Bernd, who was in front beside Ammit. The night soldier hit Bernd in the neck with his stick. Bernd screamed, went to his knees, and clapped his hand over an ooze of blood. Kellin bent toward him.

'What is your name? I won't apologize for having forgotten. There are so many of you.'

'Bernd,' he choked. 'Bernd of the Cita—'

'No such place as the Citadel,' Kellin said. 'Not now and not ever again. Just Bernd will do. So tell me, Bernd of Nowhere At All, is it wonderful that King Elden, the Flight Killer, now has thirty-two? Answer up loud and proud!'

'Yes,' Bernd said. Blood dripped between his clutching fingers.

'Yes *what*?' And then, as if teaching a small child to read, 'Won . . . won . . . won . . .? Loud and proud, now!'

'Wonderful,' Bernd said, looking down at the wet stones of the corridor.

'Woman!' Kellin said. 'You, Erin! Is it Erin?'

'Yes, Lord High,' Eris said. No way was she going to correct him.

'Is it wonderful that Cla has joined us?'

'Yes, Lord High.'

'How wonderful?'

'Very wonderful, Lord High.'

'Is it your cunt that stinks or your asshole, Erin?'

Eris's face was a blank, but her eyes were on fire. She lowered them, which was wise. 'Probably both, Lord High.'

'Yes, I think both. You, now – Iota. Step to me.'

Eye stepped forward, almost to the protective blaze of blue surrounding Kellin.

'Are you happy to have a cellmate?'

'Yes, Lord High.'

'Is it won . . . won . . .?' Kellin flapped one white hand, and I realized he was happy. No, not just happy, over the moon. Or, considering where we were, *moons*. And why not? He had been set a gathering task, and it was now complete. I also realized how much I hated him. I also hated the Flight Killer, sight unseen.

'Wonderful.'

Kellin slowly reached toward Iota, who tried to stand his ground but flinched back when the hand was less than an inch from his face. I heard the air crackle and saw Eye's hair stir in response to whatever force was keeping Kellin alive.

'Wonderful what, Iota?'

'Wonderful, Lord High.'

Kellin had had his fun. He strode through us impatiently. We tried to get away, but some weren't fast enough and got walloped by his aura. They went to their knees, some silent, some whimpering in pain. I pushed Jaya out of his way, but my arm entered the blue envelope around him and scalding pain ran up to my shoulder, locking all of the muscles. It was two long minutes before they loosened.

They should let the gray slaves go free and run their old generator on that power, I thought.

At the door, Kellin spun to face us, finishing with a stamp of his foot like a Prussian drill instructor. 'Listen to me, dear friends. Barring a few exiles who don't matter and a few fugitive whole people who may have scarpered in the early days of Flight Killer's reign, you are the last of the royal blood, the watered-down spawn of rakes, rascals, and rapists. You will serve at Flight Killer's pleasure, and you will serve soon. Playtime is over. The next time you step on the Field of Elden, formerly the Field of the Monarchs, it will be for the first round of the Fair One.'

'What about him, Lord High?' I asked, pointing at Cla with the arm that still worked. 'Doesn't he get a chance to practice?'

Kellin gazed at me with a thin smile. Behind his eyes I could see the empty sockets of his skull. '*You* will be his practice, kiddie. He survived Lake Remla, and he'll survive you. Look at the size of him! Nah, nah, when it's the second round, you'll not be taking part, my insolent friend, and I for one will be glad to be rid of you.'

With those comforting words, he left.

4

It was steak for dinner that night. It almost always was after 'playtime.' Pursey rolled his cart up the corridor, tossing the half-cooked meat into our cells – sixteen cells, each now occupied by two prisoners. Pursey once more raised his malformed hand to his brow as he tossed me mine. It was a quick and furtive gesture, but there was no mistaking it. Cla caught his chunk on the fly and sat in the corner, holding the half-raw meat in his hands and snaffling it down in big tearing bites. *What big teeth you have, Cla*, I thought.

Hamey ate a few token bites of his, then tried to give it to me. I wouldn't take it. 'You can manage more than that.'

'For what reason?' he asked. 'Why eat, suffer the cramps, then die anyway?'

I fell back on my father's acquired wisdom. 'One day at a time.' As if there were days in Maleen, but he ate a few more bites to please me. I was the promised prince, after all, the fabled PP. Although the only magic in me had to do with mysterious changes in hair and eye color, and that was magic I had no control over and no use for.

Eye asked Cla about his near drowning. Cla did not reply. Fremmy and Stooks wanted to know where he'd come from and where he had been going – was there a safe haven somewhere? Cla did not reply. Gully wanted to know how long he'd been on the dodge. Cla did not reply. He ate his meat and wiped greasy fingers on his striped shirt.

'Don't talk much without the Lord High in front of you, do you?' Double asked. He was standing at the bars of the cell he shared with Bernd, a few down from mine. He was holding his last bit of steak – which, I knew, he would save for later if he woke up in the night. The routines of prison are sad but simple.

Cla replied from his corner, without getting up or looking up. 'Why would I talk to those who will soon be dead? I understand there's to be a contest. Very well. I'll win it. If there's a prize, I'll take it and be on my way.'

We greeted this in thunderstruck silence.

Finally Fremmy said, 'He don't understand.'

'Got bad information,' Stooks said. 'Or maybe there was still water in his ears and he didn't hear so good.'

Iota dipped from their bucket, drank, then jumped up on the bars of the cell that had been a single until today, stretching his muscles and shaking the bars as was his wont, then let go and turned to face the oversized galoot hunkered in the corner.

'Let me explain something to you, Cla,' he said. '*Clarify*, as it's said. The Fair One is a tournament. Such tourneys were often held on the Field of the Monarchs during the days of the Galliens, and people came in their thousands to watch. From everywhere they came, even giant-fellows from Cratchy, tis said. The contestants were usually members of the King's Guard, although ordinary folk could participate if they wanted to test the hardness of their skulls. There was blood, and combatants were often carried unconscious from the field, but this is to be the old version, from long before the Galliens, when Lilimar was only a village not much bigger than Deesk.'

I knew some of this, but even after long days and weeks, not all. I listened intently. So did the rest, because we in durance vile rarely discussed the Fair One. It was a taboo subject, as I imagine the electric chair was in the old days and lethal injection is now.

'Sixteen of us will fight the other sixteen. To the death. No quarter, no crying off. Anyone who refuses to fight will find himself – or herself – on the rack, or in the Maiden, or pulled like taffy candy on the strappado. Do you understand?'

Cla sat in his corner, seeming to consider. At last he said, 'I can fight.'

Eye nodded. 'Yes, you look like you can, when you're not facing the Lord High or spitting up lakewater. The sixteen fight again, leaving eight. The eight fight again, leaving four. Four becomes two.'

Cla nodded. 'I'll be one of those. And when the other man lies dead at my feet, I'll claim my prize.'

'Yes you will,' Hamey said. He had come to stand beside me. 'In the old days the prize was a bag of gold and, tis said, a life's freedom from the king's levy. But that was the old days. *Your* prize will be to fight Red Molly. She's a giant, and too big for the special box where Flight Killer's lickspittles sit, but I've seen her many times standing below it. You're big, almost seven feet I judge, but the red bitch is bigger.'

'She not catch me,' Dash said. 'She slow. I fast. They en't call me Dash for no reason.'

No one said the obvious: fast or not, scrawny Dash would be long gone before anyone had to face Red Molly.

Cla sat, thinking this over. At last he got up, big knees cracking like knots in a fire, and approached the drinking bucket. He said, 'I'll beat her, too. Hit her until her brains come out of her mouth.'

'Let's say you do,' I said.

He turned to me.

'You still won't be done. Kill the daughter – you probably won't but say you do – and you won't stand a chance against the mother. I've seen her. She's fucking Godzilla.'

That wasn't, of course, the word that came out of my mouth, but whatever I said, there were murmurs of agreement from the other cells.

'You've all been beaten down until you're scared of your own shadows,' Cla said, perhaps forgetting that when Kellin had told Cla to address him as Lord High, he had done so at once. Of course Kellin and the rest of the night soldiers were different. They had those auras. I thought of how my muscles had locked up when Kellin touched me.

Cla picked up the bucket of drinking water. Iota seized his slab of an arm. 'Nah, nah! Use the cup, dummy! Pursey won't bring the watercart again until—'

I never saw a man as big as Cla move so fast, not even in ESPN

Classic highlights of Shaquille O'Neal when he played college hoops for LSU – and even at seven feet and three hundred and twenty pounds, Shaq had had sublime moves.

The bucket was at Cla's mouth and tilting. A second later, or so it seemed, it was clattering across the stone floor, the water spilling. Cla turned to look at it. Eye was on the cell floor, propped on one hand. The other was at his throat. His eyes bulged. He was gagging. Cla bent for the bucket and picked it up.

'If you killed him, you'll pay a high price,' Yanno said. Then added, with unmistakable relief: 'There won't be no Fair One.'

'There will be,' Hamey said dolefully. 'Flight Killer won't wait. Red Molly'll take Eye's place.'

But Eye wasn't killed. He eventually got to his feet, staggered to his pallet, and lay down on it. For the next two days he couldn't speak above a whisper. Until Cla came, he was the biggest of us, the strongest, the one you would have expected to still be standing when the blood sport known as the Fair One came to an end, yet I had never even seen the throat-punch that took him down.

Who was supposed to stand against a man who could do that in the first round of the competition?

According to Kellin, that honor would go to me.

5

I often dreamed of Radar, but on the night after Cla took Iota down, I dreamed of Princess Leah. She wore a red dress with an empire waist and a tightly fitted bodice. Peeping from beneath the hem were matching red shoes, their buckles encrusted with diamonds. Her hair was tied back with a complicated rope of pearls. She wore a golden locket in the shape of a butterfly on the swell of her bosom. I was sitting beside her, not dressed in the rags of the clothes I'd been wearing when I came to Empis with my sick and dying dog but in a dark suit and a white shirt. The suit was velvet. The shirt was silk. On my feet were suede boots with folded tops – the sort of boots a Dumas musketeer might wear in a Howard Pyle illustration. From Dora's collection, no doubt. Falada was grazing contentedly nearby while Leah's gray-skinned handmaid groomed her with a brush.

Leah and I were holding hands and looking at our reflections in a still pool of water. My hair was long and golden. My few spots of acne were gone. I was handsome and Leah was beautiful, especially so because her mouth had returned. Her lips were curved in a small smile. There were dimples at the corners of her mouth, but no sign of a sore. Soon, if the dream held, I would kiss those red lips. Even in this dream I recognized it for what it was: the final sequence of an animated Disney film. At any moment a petal would fall into the pool, rippling the water and making our reflections waver as the lips of the reunited prince and princess met and the music soared. No darkness would be allowed to mar the perfect storybook ending.

Only one thing was out of place. In the lap of her red dress, Princess Leah was holding a purple hairdryer. I knew it well, even though I'd only been seven when my mother died. All of her useful things, including that, had gone to the Goodwill Store because my father said every time he looked at what he called her 'woman stuff,' his heart broke again. I had no problem with him giving most of it away, only asked if I could keep her pine sachet and her hand mirror. Dad had no problem with that, either. They were still on my dresser at home.

Mom had called her hairdryer the Purple Raygun of Death.

I opened my mouth to ask Leah why she had my mom's hairdryer, but before I could, her maid spoke: '*Help her.*'

'I don't know how,' I said.

Leah smiled with her new and perfect mouth. She stroked my cheek. 'You're faster than you think, Prince Charlie.'

I started to tell her I wasn't fast at all, which was why I'd played on the line in football and first base in baseball. It was true I'd shown some speed in the Turkey Bowl game against Stanford, but that had been a short and adrenalin-fueled exception. Before I could say anything, though, something hit me in the face and I jerked awake.

It was another piece of steak – a small one, hardly more than a scrap. Pursey shuffled down the corridor, tossing a few more small pieces into other cells, saying 'Wef'ovas, wef'ovas.' Which I assumed was the best he could do with *leftovers*.

Hamey was snoring away, exhausted by 'playtime' and his usual post-dinner struggle to empty his bowels. I took my little bit of steak, sat with my back against the cell wall, and bit into it. Something crackled under my front teeth. I looked and saw a piece of paper, hardly bigger than a fortune cookie fortune, tucked into a slice in the meat. I took it out. Written in neat and tiny cursive, the handwriting of an educated man, was this:

I will help you if I can, my prince. There is a way out of here from the Officials' Room. It is dangerous. Destroy this if you value my life. Yours in Service, PERCIVAL

Percival, I thought. *Not Pursey but Percival. Not a gray slavey but a real man with a real name.*

I ate the paper.

6

The next day we had sausages for breakfast. We all knew what that meant. Hamey looked at me with desolate eyes and a smile. 'At least I'm done with the belly cramps. No more straining to shit, either. Do you want these?'

I didn't but took his four links, hoping they'd give me a little extra energy. They sat in my stomach like lead. From the cell on the other side of the corridor, Cla was looking at me. No, that's wrong. He was eye-fucking me. Iota gave me a shrug that said *What are you gonna do*. I gave it back to him. What indeed.

There was waiting. We had no way to keep time, but it slowed anyway. Fremmy and Stooks sat side by side in their cell. Fremmy said, 'As long as they don't put us against each other, old pal, that's all.'

I thought they probably would. Because it was cruel. That, at least, turned out to be wrong.

Just when I began to believe it wouldn't be today after all, four night soldiers appeared, Aaron in charge. He was always on the field during 'playtime,' waving his limber stick like a conductor's baton, but this was the first time he'd come to Deep Maleen since taking me to see the Lord High. And to check out the torture chamber, of course.

The cell doors rattled open on their rusty tracks. 'Out! Out, kiddies! A good day for half of you, a bad one for the rest!'

We stepped out of the cells . . . all but a slight, balding man named Hatcha. 'I don't want to,' he said. 'I'm sick.'

One of thc night soldiers approached him, but Aaron waved him off. He stood in the door of the cell Hatcha shared with a much bigger man named Quilly, who hailed from Deesk. Quilly shrank back, but Aaron's aura brushed him. Quilly gave a soft cry and clutched his arm.

'You are Hatcha of what was once called the Citadel, is that right?'

Hatcha nodded miserably.

'And you feel ill. The sausages, perhaps?'

'Maybe,' Hatcha said, not looking up from the trembling knot of his hands. 'Probably.'

'Yet I see you ate all but the strings.'

Hatcha said nothing.

'Listen to me, kiddie. It's the Fair One or the Maiden. I'd see to your time visiting that lady myself, and it would be long time. I'd close the door slow. You'd feel the spikes touch your eyelids . . . just gentle, you know . . . before they punched through. And your stomach! Not as soft as your eyes, but soft enough. What's left of those sausages will come dribbling out while you scream. Now does that sound like a treat?'

Hatcha groaned and stumbled from the cell.

'Excellent! And here we all are!' Aaron cried. 'Off to the games we go! Hump, kiddies! Hump, hump, hump! Such fun awaits!'

We humped.

As we made the climb we'd made many times before – but never until then knowing only half of us would come back – I thought of my dream. Of Leah saying *you're faster than you think, Prince Charlie.*

I didn't feel fast.

7

Instead of going directly to the field, we were marched into the team room we'd been using after practices. Only this time the Lord High was there, resplendent in a full-dress uniform which looked blue-black inside his aura. He was fully charged up for the occasion. I wondered where the energy that powered those auras came from, but such questions weren't much of a priority that day.

On the shelf where there had been thirty-one buckets for washing after 'playtime,' there were now just sixteen, because only sixteen would need to clean up after the day's festivities. In front of the shelf, propped on an easel, was a large poster board with **FAIR ONE FIRST ROUND** printed at the top. Below it were the matchings. I remember them perfectly; I think in such a terrible situation, a person would either remember everything . . . or nothing at all. I apologize for throwing out even more new names, but I must, if for no other reason than those with whom I was imprisoned deserve to be remembered, if only briefly.

'Here you see the order of battle,' Kellin said. 'I expect you all to put up a good show for His Majesty Elden. Do you understand?'

No one replied.

'You may find yourself pitted against one you consider a friend, but friendship no longer matters. Each contest is to the death. *To the death.* Bringing your opponent low but not killing him will only earn both of you far more painful deaths. Do you understand?'

It was Cla who replied. 'Yus.' He looked at me as he said it and drew a thumb across his enormous neck. And smiled.

'The first set comes soon. Be ready.'

He left. The other night soldiers followed him. We examined the poster board in silence.

FAIR ONE FIRST ROUND

First Set

Fremmy to Murf
Jaya to Hamey
Ammit to Wale

Second Set

Yanno to Freed
Jackah to lota
Mesel to Sam

Third Set

Tom to Bult
Dommy to Cammit
Bendo to Dash

NOONS

Fourth Set

Double to Evah
Stooks to Hatcha
Pag to Quilly

Fifth Set

Bernd to Gully
Hilt to Ocka
Eris to Viz

Sixth Set

Cla to Charlie

I had seen similar seedings not just on TV, during the NCAA's Selection Sunday, but in person, when the matchups for the Arcadia Babe Ruth tournament were announced each spring on posters at every participating field. That was strange enough, but the most surreal element was that single word in the middle: NOONS. Flight Killer and his retinue would watch nine prisoners killed in battle . . . then enjoy a spot of lunch.

'What would happen if we all refused?' Ammit asked in a ruminative tone of voice I wouldn't have expected from a fellow who looked as if he had once earned his bread and cheese shoeing horses. And knocking them flat if they didn't cooperate. 'Just asking, mind you.'

Ocka, a big fellow with a nearsighted squint, laughed. 'Do you mean a strike? Like the millers in my father's time? And deprive the

Flight Killer of his day's entertainment? I think I'd rather live until tomorrow than spend this one screaming in agony, thank you very much.'

And I thought Ocka probably would live until tomorrow, considering he'd be fighting skinny little Hilt, who had a lame hip. Ocka might go down in the second round, but if he won today, he would still be alive to wash up afterward and eat dinner tonight. I looked around and saw the same simple calculation on many faces. Not, however, on Hamey's. After one look at the board, he had gone to a bench and now sat there, head hanging. I hated to see him that way, but I hated the ones who had put us in this terrible position even more.

I looked at the board again. I had expected to see Fremmy against Stooks and the two women, Jaya and Eris, against each other – a girlfight, what could be more amusing? But no. There didn't appear to have been any thought about the seedings. They might have been drawn out of a hat. Except for the last one, that was. Just the two of us on the field, the day's finale.

Cla to Charlie.

CHAPTER TWENTY-FOUR

First Round. The Last Set. My Prince.

'What Do *You* Think?'

1

Jaya sat down next to Hamey on the bench and took his hand. It lay limply in hers. 'I don't want this.'

'I know,' Hamey said without looking at her. 'It's all right.'

'Maybe you'll beat me. I'm not strong, you know – not like Eris.'

'Maybe.'

The door opened and two night soldiers came in. They looked as excited as living corpses can, their auras pulsing as if within them dead hearts were still beating.

'First set! Hump, hump! Don't keep His Majesty waiting, kiddies! He's taken his place!'

At first none of them moved, and for a wild moment I almost believed Ammit's strike was going to happen . . . until I thought of the consequences for the strikers, that was. After looking at the board again to be sure some miracle hadn't changed the listings, the first half-dozen got up: Fremmy and Murf, Ammit and a short, tubby fellow named Wale, Hamey and Jaya. She was holding his hand as they went out, shrinking to avoid the aura of the night soldier standing closest to her.

In the days of Gallien rule, the rest of us would have heard the anticipatory cheers of a packed stadium as the combatants emerged. I strained my ears and thought I heard a faint spatter of applause, but it could have been my imagination. Probably was. Because the stands of the Field of Elden (formerly the Field of the Monarchs) were almost entirely empty. The boy I'd met on my journey here had been right: Lilimar was a haunted city, a place where only the dead, the living dead, and a few ass-kissers still remained.

No butterflies here.

If not for the night soldiers, escape might be possible, I thought. Then I remembered there were also a couple of female giants to consider . . . and Flight Killer himself. I didn't know what he was now, what transformation he might have undergone, but one thing seemed sure: he was no longer Leah's clubfooted little brother, with a hump on his back or a lump on his neck.

Time passed. Hard to tell how long. Several of us visited the pissing-gutter, me included. Nothing brings on the need to piss like the fear of dying. At last the door opened and Ammit entered. He had a small cut across the back of his hairy left hand. Otherwise he was unmarked.

Mesel hurried to him as soon as Ammit's undead escort stepped back. 'What was it like? Is Wale really—'

Ammit pushed him so hard that Mesel went sprawling on the tiles. 'I'm back and he's not. That's all I've got to say and all you need to hear. Leave me alone.'

He went to the end of the bench, sat down, and put his hands to the sides of his bent head. It was a posture I'd seen many times on baseball fields, most often when a pitcher gave up a key hit and got pulled. It was the posture of a loser, not a winner. But of course we would all be losers, unless something happened.

Save her, Leah's gray maid had whispered to me. And was I now supposed to save them all, just because my hair was blond under repeated applications of dirt? It was absurd. Cla continued to eye-fuck me. He intended to still be around at dinnertime.

Come the last death match of the day, I wouldn't even be able to save myself.

The next one to return was Murf. One of his eyes was swollen shut and the right shoulder of his shirt was damp with blood. Stooks saw, understood that his comedy partner was no more, gave a soft cry, and covered his eyes.

We waited, watching the door. At last it opened and Jaya came in. She was as pale as windowglass, but seemingly unmarked. Tears streamed down her cheeks.

'I had to,' she said. Not just to me, to all of us. 'I had to, or they would have killed us both.'

2

The second set was called – Yanno to fight Doc Freed, Iota to fight Jackah, Mesel to fight Sam. When they were gone, I sat down next to Jaya. She wouldn't look at me, but the words spilled out of her, as if keeping them in would burst something inside her.

'He couldn't really fight, you know how he is, how he *was*, but he put up a show of it. For me, I think. They were crying for blood, you'll hear it when your turn comes, crying for him to put the bitch down, crying for me to get behind him and stab him in the neck—'

'There are *knives*?' I asked.

'No, spears with short handles. Also gloves with spikes on the knuckles. They're laid out on the table where the drinks were when we practiced. They want you in close, you know, they want to see as much stabbing and punching as they can before someone goes down, but I took one of the poles, you know, the . . .' She mimed a swing.

'The fighting sticks.'

'Yes. We went around and around. Fremmy was dead, his throat cut, and Hamey almost slipped in the blood. Wale was lying on the track.'

'Yuh,' Ammit said without looking up. 'Stupid git tried to run.'

'We were the last. That was when Aaron said five minutes more or we'd both be put down. He could see we weren't really trying. Hamey ran at me, waving his little spear off to one side, so stupid, and I hit him in the stomach with the butt of my stick. He screamed. He dropped the spear on the grass and kept screaming.'

Hamey's stomach, I thought. His endlessly sick stomach.

'I couldn't stand the sound. They were applauding and laughing and saying things like *good hit* and *the kitty brought him low with that*, and Hamey kept screaming. I picked up the spear. I never killed anybody but I couldn't stand him screaming, so I . . . I . . .'

'You can stop there,' I said.

She looked at me, eyes full, cheeks wet. 'You have to do something, Charlie. If you're the prince that was promised, you have to do something.'

I could have told her that Prince Charlie's first job would be not getting killed by Cla, but I thought she felt badly enough without that, so I just gave her a brief hug.

'Is he there? The Flight Killer?'

She shuddered and nodded.

'What does he look like?' I was thinking of that seat of honor with the armrests slanting outward, as if whoever it was meant for was extremely fat or at least extremely bulky.

'Awful. *Awful*. His face is green, as if there's something wrong with him inside. Long white hair falling down his cheeks from under the crown he wears. His eyes are as big as soft-boiled eggs. It's a *broad* face, so wide it's hardly human. His lips are fat and red, like he was eating strawberries. That was all of him I could see. He's swaddled in a huge purple robe from the chin down, but I could see it *moving*. Like he was holding a pet underneath. He's awful. Monstrous. And he laughs. The others applauded when I . . . when Hamey died, but he just laughed. Drool came out of his mouth on both sides, I saw it in the gaslights. There was a woman beside him, tall and beautiful, with a little beauty mark beside her mouth . . .'

'Petra,' I said. 'A man grabbed her by the boob and kissed her neck after I knocked Ammit down.'

'She . . . she . . .' Jaya shuddered again. 'She kissed him where his spit ran down. She *licked it off his green face*.'

Iota came in, escorted by a night soldier. He saw me and gave a nod. So Jackah was gone.

3

When the door closed, I went over to Iota. He didn't have a mark on him.

'The bitch is there,' he said. 'Red Molly. Watching from the track, below the box where the swells sit. Her hair ain't really red but orange. The color of carrots. Sticks up all around her head in quills. Fifteen feet from toes to top. Wearing a leather skirt. Tits like boulders. Each of em must weigh as much as a five-year-old kiddie. Got a knife in a scabbard on her hip, looks almost as long as the little spears they give us to fight with. I think she watches to see what moves the winners make. For later, you know.'

That made me think of Coach Harkness, and practices on Thursdays before Friday night games. On those afternoons we knocked off twenty minutes early and sat in a team room less fancy than this one but otherwise about the same. Coach would roll in a TV and we'd watch our upcoming opponents – their moves and plays. Especially the quarterback. He'd show us the enemy QB twenty or thirty times on isolated camera – every fake, jink, and stutter-step. I told Uncle Bob about that once, and he laughed and nodded. 'Coach is right, Charlie. Cut off your enemy's head, the body dies.'

'I didn't like her watching like that,' Eye said. 'I was hoping she'd take me for granted, and when we got down to it maybe I could find a way to stick her or brain her. Instead, she's going to get four chances to watch how I do and I ain't going to get a chance to see how *she* does at all.'

I didn't remark on his unspoken assumption that I'd be gone by then, promised prince or no promised prince. 'Cla thinks it's going to be him.'

Eye laughed as if he hadn't just killed one of his longtime mates in Maleen. 'It'll be Cla against me when it's down to two, no doubt – I've come to like you, Charlie, but I don't think you'll even put a touch on him – but I know his weakness.'

'Which would be what?'

'He did me down that once, poked me so hard in my throat it's a damn wonder I can still talk, but I learned from it.' Which didn't answer the question.

Mesel came in next, so Sam was finished. A few minutes later the door opened again and I was surprised to see Doc Freed come in, although not entirely under his own power. Pursey was with him, one of his flipper hands hooked into Freed's armpit, helping him along. Doc's right thigh was bleeding heavily through a makeshift bandage and his face was grotesquely battered, but he was alive and Yanno was not.

I was sitting with Double and Eris. 'He won't be able to fight again,' I said. 'Not unless the second round's six months from now and maybe not even then.'

'It won't be six months,' Eris said. 'It won't even be six days. And he'll fight or he'll die.'

It sure wasn't high school football.

4

Bult and Bendo survived the third set. So did Cammit. He was cut in several places when he came back and said he'd been sure he was done for. Then poor Dommy had one of his coughing fits, bad enough to double him over. Cammit saw his opportunity and ran his short spear into the back of Dommy's neck.

Doc was lying on the floor, either asleep – unlikely, given his injuries – or passed out. While the rest of us were waiting for the third set to be over, Cla continued staring at me with that endless grin. The only time I could get away from it was when I went to one of the buckets to scoop out a handful of water. But when I turned back, there he was, eye-fucking me.

I know his weakness, Iota had said. *He did me down that once but I learned from it.*

What had he learned?

I replayed the fight (if you could call it that) in Eye's cell: the brilliant speed of Cla's rabbit-punch to Eye's throat, the rolling bucket, Cla turning to see it, Yanno – now the late Yanno – saying *if you killed him, you'll pay a high price*, Eye picking himself up and going to his pallet while Cla bent to pick up the bucket. Maybe thinking to brain Eye with it if he tried again.

If there was something there, I didn't see it.

When the third set was done, Pursey came in pushing a cart. Aaron accompanied him. There was the smell of roast chicken, which I would have found enticing under other circumstances, but not when it was apt to be my last meal.

'Eat hearty, kiddies!' Aaron cried. 'You can't say we don't feed you well!'

Most who'd won their battles for the day eagerly grabbed meat from the cart. Those who had yet to fight declined . . . with one exception. Cla grabbed a half-chicken from Pursey's cart and chomped into it, his eyes never leaving me.

The blow.

Iota on the stones of his cell.

The rolling bucket.

Eye crawls to his pallet, hand at his throat.

Cla looks for the bucket, picks it up.

What was there that Iota had seen and I was missing?

The cart came to me. Aaron was watching Pursey, so there was no salute. Then Doc Freed groaned, rolled on his side, and vomited across the floor. Aaron turned and pointed at Cammit and Bendo, sitting side by side on a nearby bench. 'You and you! Clean that mess up!'

I took this momentary distraction to raise my hand with my thumb and finger pinched together. I wiggled my hand in a writing gesture. Pursey gave a hardly perceptible shrug, maybe because he understood or maybe to make me stop before Aaron saw. When Aaron turned back, I was selecting a drumstick from the rolling buffet and thinking that Pursey's understanding or lack of it wouldn't matter if Cla killed me in the day's final match.

'Last meal, kiddie,' that jumbo gentleman said to me. 'Enjoy it.'

He's trying to psych me out, I thought.

Of course I'd already known that, but the actual words for what he was doing brought it into focus, made it concrete. Words have that power. And they opened something inside me. A hole. Maybe even a well. It was the same thing that had opened during my nasty outings with Bertie Bird, and during my confrontations with Christopher Polley, and Peterkin the dwarf. If I was a prince, it certainly wasn't of the kind where the movie ended with the vapidly pretty blond guy embracing the vapidly pretty girl. There was nothing pretty about my dirt-caked blond hair, and my battle with Cla wouldn't be pretty, either. It might be short, but it wouldn't be pretty.

I thought, *I don't want to be a Disney prince. To hell with that. If I have to be a prince, I want to be a dark one.*

'Stop looking at me, fuckface,' I said.

His smile was replaced with a look of surprised puzzlement, and I realized why even before I threw my drumstick at him. It was because that word, *fuckface*, came from the well, came out in *English*, and he hadn't understood it. I missed him by a mile – the drumstick clanged on one of the buckets and fell to the floor – but he jerked in surprise anyway and turned toward the sound. Eris laughed. He swiveled toward her and got to his feet. The constant grin became a snarl.

'Nah, nah, *nah*!' Aaron shouted. 'Save it for the field, kiddie, or I'll shock you so badly you won't be able to go out and Charlie will be declared winner by default. Flight Killer won't like that, and I'll make you like it less!'

Disgruntled and fuming, clearly off his game for the moment, Cla resumed his seat, glowering at me. It was my turn to grin. It felt dark and it felt good. I pointed at him.

'I'm going to fuck you up, honey.'

Bold words. I might regret them, but when they came out, they felt just fine.

5

Some time after 'noons,' the fourth set was called. Again there was the waiting, and one by one they came back: Double first, then Stooks, Quilly last. Stooks was bleeding from a cheek so badly cut I could see the gleam of his teeth, but he was walking under his own power. Jaya gave him a towel to stanch the worst of the bleeding and he sat on a bench near the buckets, the white towel quickly turning red. Freed was propped in the corner close by. Stooks asked if there was anything Doc could do for his slashed face. Freed shook his head without looking up. The idea that the wounded were supposed to fight another round, and soon, was crazy – beyond sadistic – but I had no doubt it was true. Murf had killed one half of the comedy team; if he drew Stooks in the second round, Murf would put him down easily, stabbed shoulder or no stabbed shoulder.

Cla was still looking at me, but the grin was gone. I thought his appraisal of me as an easy kill might have changed, which meant I couldn't count on him to be careless.

He'll move fast, I thought. *The way he moved on Eye*. In my dream, Leah had said *You're faster than you think, Prince Charlie . . .* only I really wasn't. Unless, that was, I was able to find some hate-powered overdrive gear.

The fifth set was called: Bernd and Gully, little Hilt and big Ocka, Eris and a short but muscular fellow named Viz. Before Eris left, Jaya embraced her.

'Nah, nah, none of that!' one of the night guards said in his unpleasant locust-like buzz. 'Hump, hump!'

Eris left last, but she was the first to return, bleeding from one ear but otherwise unhurt. Jaya flew to her, and this time there was no one to stop their embrace. We'd been left alone. Ocka came back next. For a long time after that, no one. Finally Gully was carried in by a gray man – not Pursey – and laid on the floor. He was unconscious, barely breathing. One side of his head looked caved in above the temple.

'I want him next,' Bult said.

'I hope I get *you* next,' Ammit growled. 'Shut up.'

More time passed. Gully stirred but didn't wake. I went to the pisstrough. I needed to go but couldn't. I sat back down, hands clasped between my knees, as I always did at baseball and football games before the National Anthem was played. I didn't look up at Cla but I could feel him looking at me, as if his stare had weight.

The door opened. Two night soldiers flanked it. Aaron and the Lord High passed between them. 'Last match of the day,' Aaron said. 'Cla and Charlie. Come on, kiddies, hump it.'

Cla got up at once and walked past me, turning his head to give me one final grin as he did. I followed. Iota was looking at me. He raised one hand and gave me an odd salute, not to his forehead but at the side of his face.

I know his weakness.

As I passed the Lord High, Kellin said, 'I'll be glad to be rid of you, Charlie. If I hadn't needed thirty-two, I would have done it already.'

Two night soldiers ahead of us, Cla ahead of me, walking with his head slightly lowered and his hands swinging at his sides, already made into loose fists. Behind us walked the Lord High and Aaron, his lieutenant. My heart was beating slow and hard in my chest.

He did me down that once but I learned from it.

Up the corridor we walked, toward the brilliant rows of gaslight rimming the stadium. We passed the other team rooms. We passed the Equipment Room.

The blow, Iota goes down, the bucket rolls, Iota crawls for his pallet, Cla turns to look for the bucket.

We passed the Officials' Room, from which there was a way out, at least according to Pursey's note.

I throw the drumstick. It hits a bucket. Cla turns to look.

I started to get it then, and sped up a little as we came out of the corridor onto the dirt track surrounding the playing field. I didn't draw even with Cla, but almost. He didn't look at me. His attention was on the center of the field, where the weapons were placed in a line. The rings and ropes were gone. Two leather gloves with stabbing spikes on the knuckles were on the table where there had been drinks during our practices. There were the fighting sticks in their wicker basket, and two short stabbing spears in another.

Iota hadn't answered my question when I asked, but maybe when I was leaving, he did. Maybe that odd salute he gave me wasn't a salute. Maybe it was a message.

There was some applause as we followed the night soldiers toward the VIP box, but I barely heard it. Nor did I pay attention at first to the spectators flanking the box, or even to Elden Flight Killer. I was paying attention to Cla, who had turned to follow the rolling bucket on the floor of the cell he shared with Iota, and the drumstick I'd hucked at him in the team room. Cla who didn't seem to realize I had pulled almost even with him, and why?

I know his weakness, Iota had said, and now I thought I did, too. Eye hadn't given me a salute; he'd mimicked the sort of blinker a horse might wear.

Cla had either little peripheral vision or none at all.

6

We were led – no, *herded* – to the part of the track in front of the royal viewing box. I stood beside Cla, who didn't just shift his eyes to look at me but turned his whole head. Immediately Kellin whapped him across the back of the neck with his limber stick, drawing a thin line of blood.

'Never mind looking at the make-believe prince, you great idiot. Pay heed to the real king, instead.'

So Kellin knew what the other prisoners believed, and was I surprised? Not much. Dirt could only conceal the striking change in the color of my hair for so long, and my eyes were no longer even hazel; they were gray going on blue. If Elden hadn't insisted on the full complement of contestants, I would have been killed weeks ago.

'Kneel!' Aaron shouted in his nasty buzz of a voice. 'Kneel, you of the old blood! Kneel before the new blood! Kneel before your king!'

Petra – tall, dark-haired, beauty mark beside her mouth, green silk dress, complexion as white as cottage cheese – shouted, *'Kneel, old blood! Kneel, old blood!'*

The others – there couldn't have been more than sixty, seventy at most – took up the cry. *'Kneel, old blood! Kneel, old blood! Kneel, old blood!'*

Had this happened with the other contestants? I didn't think so. This was special to us, because we were the last match of the day, the star attraction. We knelt, neither of us wanting to be whipped with limber sticks, or worse, shocked by the auras of our captors.

Elden Flight Killer looked like a man at death's door – *one foot in the grave and the other on a banana peel*, Uncle Bob would have said. That was my first thought. The second, close on its heels, was that he wasn't a man at all. He might have been once, but no more. His skin was the color of an unripe Anjou pear. His eyes – blue, huge, wet, each as big as one of my palms – bulged from wrinkled, sagging sockets. His lips were red, somehow feminine, and so loose they sagged. A crown sat askew, with a horrid jauntiness, on his thin white hair. His purple robe, shot with fine windings of gold, was like a gigantic caftan that covered him all the way down from his bloated neck. And yes, it was moving. *Like he was holding a pet underneath*, Jaya had said. Except it was rising up and subsiding in several different places at once.

To my left, on the track, stood Red Molly in a short leather skirt like a kilt. Her thighs were muscular and enormous. Her long knife hung in a scabbard on her right hip. Her orange hair stood up in short spikes, a kind of punk-rock do. Wide suspenders held up her skirt and covered part of her otherwise naked breasts. She saw me looking at her and puckered her lips in a kiss.

Flight Killer spoke in a clotted voice that sounded nothing like the insectile buzz of the night soldiers. It was as if he were speaking through a throat filled with some viscous liquid. No, none of the others had been subjected to anything like this; they would have said. The horror of that inhuman voice was indelible.

'Who is King of the Gray World, formerly Eis?'

Those in the box and the rest of the spectators responded smartly, shouting it out. '*Elden!*'

Flight Killer was looking down at us with those huge egglike eyes. Limber sticks came down on my neck and Cla's. 'Say it,' Kellin buzzed.

'Elden,' we said.

'Who brought down both the monarchs of earth and the monarchs of the air?'

'*Elden!*' Petra shouted it with the rest, and louder. Her hand was caressing one of Elden's hanging green jowls. The purple robe rose and fell, rose and fell, in half a dozen different places.

'Elden,' Cla and I said, not wanting to be swatted again.

'Let the match begin!'

This was a call that seemed to require no response except applause and a few cheers.

Kellin was between the two of us, just far enough away to keep his aura from touching us. 'Stand and face the field,' he said.

We did so. I could see Cla from the corner of my eye, on my right; he turned his head to take a quick glance at me, then faced forward. Seventy or so yards dead ahead were the weapons of combat. There was something surreal about their careful spacing, like prizes to be won in some homicidal game show.

I could see at once that someone (maybe Flight Killer himself, but my money was on the Lord High) had tilted the game in Cla's favor, if not outright rigged it. The wicker basket of stabbing spears, obviously the weapons of choice, was on the right, which was Cla's side. Twenty yards to the left was the table with the spike-studded leather gloves. Twenty yards further to the left, more or less facing me, was a basket of fighting sticks, useful to clobber with, not so useful when it came to killing. No one told us what came next; no one had to. We were going to sprint to the weapons, and if I wanted a stabber instead of a glove or a bando stick, I'd have to get ahead of Cla, then cross in front of him.

You're faster than you think, Leah had told me, only that had been in a dream and this was real life.

You might ask yourself if I was terrified. I was, but I was also drawing from that dark well I'd discovered as a child, when my father seemed bent on honoring the memory of his wife, my mother, by crashing and burning and leaving us homeless. I had hated him for awhile and hated myself for hating. Bad behavior had resulted. Now I had other things to hate, and no reason to feel bad about it. So yes, I was terrified. But part of me was also eager.

Part of me wanted this.

Flight Killer called out in his bubbling, inhuman voice – something else to hate: '*NOW!*'

7

We ran. Cla had moved with blinding speed when he attacked Eye, but that had been a quick burst in an enclosed space. It was seventy yards to the weapons. There was a lot of weight for him to carry, over three hundred pounds, and I thought that sprinting full out, I could draw even with him halfway to the spread-out fighting gear. Dream Leah had been right – I was faster than I thought. But I'd still have to cut in front of him, and when I did, I'd be squarely in his slightly reduced field of vision. More dangerous still, my back would be to him.

I veered left instead, leaving him an uncontested path to the spears. I hardly glanced at the spiked gloves; lethal they might be, but to use one I'd have to get in Cla's stabbing zone, and I'd seen how quick he was when he had an opponent up close. It was the fighting sticks I went for. Over several 'playtimes' I'd gotten quite handy with them.

I grabbed one out of the basket, turned, and saw Cla already charging, the spear held low at his right hip. He swept it up, hoping to open me from balls to belly and end it fast. I stepped back and brought my stick down on his arms, hoping to jolt the spear loose. He cried out in pain and anger but held on. The audience pattered applause and I heard a woman, almost certainly Petra, scream, '*Cut off his pizzle and bring it to me!*'

Cla charged again, this time with the spear raised high over his shoulder. There was no finesse to him; like Mike Tyson in the old boxing vids I'd watched with Andy Chen and my father, he was your basic brawler, used to putting his opponents down with a brutal frontal attack. It had always worked for Cla before; it would work now against a much younger opponent. He had the advantage in both weight and reach.

According to the dream Leah, I was faster than I thought. I was certainly faster than Cla thought. I stepped aside like a toreador avoiding the charge of a bull and whistled the fighting stick down on his arm, just above the elbow. The spear flew from his hands and landed on the grass. The audience gave an *aaahhh* sound. Petra shrieked her displeasure.

Cla bent to snatch up his weapon. I brought the fighting stick down on his head two-handed, using all my strength. The stick shattered in half. Blood jumped from Cla's scalp and began running down his cheeks and neck in freshets. The blow would have laid out any other man – Eye and Ammit included – but Cla only shook his head, picked up the stabbing spear, and faced me. No grin now; he was snarling and red-eyed.

'Come for me, you bitch's child!'

'Fuck that. Let me see what you've got. You're as dumb as you are ugly.'

I held out what remained of my fighting stick. Now the end facing Cla was a rat's nest of splinters. It was hard wood, and if he ran on those splinters, they wouldn't buckle. They'd punch into his gut, and he knew it. I feinted at him, and when he drew back, circled to his right. He had to turn his head to keep me out of his blind spot. He lunged and I stuck him in the meat of one forearm, tearing open a flap of skin and sending a stream of blood to the green grass.

'*Finish him!*' Petra screamed. I knew her voice now, and hated it. Hated her, hated them all. '*Finish him, you great ugly hulk!*'

Cla charged. I moved to the left this time, backpedaling behind the table with the fighting gloves on it. Cla never slowed. He was breathing in quick dry rasps. I threw myself to the side, the point of his spear barely missing my neck. Cla hit the table, overturned it, and landed on it, snapping off one of its legs. He held onto the stabbing spear, but that was all right with me. I moved in on his blind spot, jumped on his back, and squeezed his midsection with my thighs as he reared up. I put the remains of my fighting stick against his throat as he lunged to his feet. He clawed at me from behind, whacking my shoulders with his big hands.

What followed was an insane piggyback ride. I had my legs locked around his thick waist and my shattered three feet of fighting stick digging into his throat. I could feel each attempt he made to swallow. He began making a gurgling sound. At last, with no other option but unconsciousness followed by death, he threw himself on his back with me beneath him.

I was expecting it – what other move did he have left? – but it still blew the breath out of me. Three hundred-plus pounds will do that. He rocked from side to side, trying to break my grip. I held on even as black spots began to dance in front of my eyes and the sounds of the cheering spectators began to sound echoey and far away. The only one that came through clearly was the voice of Flight Killer's consort, like a sharp needle stabbing into my head: *'Get up! Break his grip, you great brute! GET UP!'*

I might be crushed to death under the great brute, but I was damned if he was going to break my grip. I'd done a lot of pushups in my cell, and a lot of pull-ups on the rope-rings. I put those muscles to good use even as my consciousness began to wane. I pulled . . . pulled . . . and at last his struggles began to weaken. With the very last of my strength I shoved his top half off me and wriggled from beneath his bulk. I crawled across the grass, hair hanging in my eyes, taking in great whooping gusts of air. It seemed I couldn't get enough, or get it down to the bottom of my abused lungs. My first attempt to find my feet failed and I crawled on, gasping and coughing, sure that fucking Cla, *mother*fucking Cla, was getting up behind me and I'd feel the spear going in between my shoulderblades.

On my second try I made it upright, staggered around in a drunken circle, and beheld my opponent. He was also crawling . . . or trying to. Most of his face was obscured with blood from the head-hit I'd given him. What I could see was purple from strangulation.

'*Finish!*' Petra screamed. Red spots flushed through her white makeup. She seemed to have changed sides. Not that I wanted her support. '*Finish! Finish!*'

The others took it up: '*FINISH! FINISH! FINISH!*'

Cla rolled over and looked up at me. If it was mercy he wanted, it wasn't mine to give.

'*FINISH! FINISH! FINISH!*'

I picked up his spear . . .

He raised one hand and touched the heel of his palm to his forehead. 'My prince.'

. . . and brought it down.

I'd like to tell you that I came back to my better self at the very end. To say I felt regret. It wouldn't be true. There's a dark well in everyone, I think, and it never goes dry. But you drink from it at your peril. That water is poison.

8

I was made to kneel before Elden, his bitch, and the other important members of his retinue.

'Well-fought, well-fought,' Elden said, but in an absent kind of way. He was indeed drooling from the sides of that slack mouth. Some pus-y liquid – not tears – oozed from the corners of his huge eyes. 'Bearers! I want my bearers! I'm tired and must rest until dinner!'

A quartet of gray men – deformed but brawny – came hurrying down one of the steep aisles bearing a palanquin with gold trim and purple velvet curtains.

I didn't see him get into it, because I was gripped by the hair and pulled to my feet. I'm tall, but Red Molly towered over me. Looking up at her reminded me of looking up at the statue I'd climbed to watch for the monarchs coming home to roost. Her face was pasty and round and flat, like a great pie-plate dusted with flour. Her eyes were black.

'Today you fought an enemy,' she said. Her voice was a basso rumble, far from comforting but better than the locust-buzz of the night soldiers or the liquidity of Elden's voice. 'Next time you fight a friend. Should you survive, *I'll* cut off your pizzle.' She lowered her voice. 'And give it to Petra. To add to her collection.'

I'm sure that the hero of an action movie would have managed a smart comeback, but I looked into that wide face and those black eyes and couldn't think of a fucking thing.

9

It was the Lord High himself who escorted me to the team room. I looked back once before stepping into the corridor, just in time to see the palanquin, curtains drawn, swaying up the steep aisle. I presumed Petra, she of the beauty mark, was inside with Flight Killer.

'You surprised me, Charlie,' Kellin said. Now that the pressure of his duties as the day's master of ceremonies was over, he sounded relaxed, maybe even amused. 'I thought Cla would have your head quicky-quick. Next time you'll fight one of your friends. Not Iota, I think – we'll save him. Perhaps little Jaya. How would you enjoy stopping her heart as you did Cla's?'

I didn't answer, just walked ahead of him down the sloping corridor, keeping as far from his high-voltage aura as possible. When we reached the door Kellin didn't follow, only closed it behind me. Thirty-two of us had gone to the field. Now there were only fifteen to register surprise that it wasn't Cla stepping in but Charlie, banged up but otherwise unhurt. No, make that only fourteen. Gully was unconscious.

For a moment they only looked at me. Then thirteen of them fell to their knees and put their palms to their foreheads. Doc Freed couldn't kneel, but he gave the salute from where he sat against the wall.

'My prince,' Jaya said.

'*My prince*,' the others echoed.

I had never been so glad in my life that Empis was a land without closed-circuit TV.

10

We washed off the dirt and the blood. The horror of the day stayed. Eris got Freed's pants down and cleansed the deep wound in his thigh as well as she could. Every now and then she'd pause in her labor to look at me. They were all looking at me. Finally, because it was creeping me out, I told them to stop. Then they made a business of *not* looking at me, which was as bad, maybe worse.

After ten or fifteen minutes, four night soldiers came in. The leader gestured with his limber stick for us to come. There were no grays, so Gully had to be carried. I moved to take his top half, but Ammit shouldered me aside. Gently. 'Nah, nah. Me 'n the big boy will do it.' Presumably meaning Iota, since the other big boy was now so much cooling meat. 'Help the doctor, if you would.'

But I wasn't allowed to do that, either. I was, after all, the promised prince. Or so they thought. Hair and eye color aside. I thought maybe I was just a seventeen-year-old kid who happened to be in good shape, had gotten lucky drawing an opponent without much side-vision, and had been able to harness his worst impulses long enough to survive. Besides, did I want to be the prince in this dark fairy tale? I did not. What I wanted was to get my dog and go home. And home never seemed so distant.

We made our slow way back to our cells in Deep Maleen: Murf with his shoulder wound, Jaya and Eris, Ammit, Iota, Doc Freed, Bult, Bendo, Mesel, Cammit, Double, Stooks with his badly slashed face, Quilly, Ocka, unconscious Gully . . . and me. Sixteen. Except neither Doc Freed nor Gully would be able to fight the next round. Not that they would be excepted; I knew better. They would be placed against opponents who'd slaughter them quicky-quick for the pleasure of Elden, Petra, and Flight Killer's smattering of subjects. Those who drew Freed and Gully in the next round would, in effect, be given a bye. Nor were Murf and Stooks likely to survive to what would be called, in March Madness, the Elite Eight.

The door at the end of the cellblock was opened. Eye and Ammit carried Gully through. Quilly and Freed came next, Quilly basically holding the doc up so he wouldn't have to try walking on his bad leg. Not that Freed was up to much walking; he was in and out of consciousness, chin bouncing on his chest. As we entered Maleen, he said something so terrible, so lost, that I will never forget it: 'I want my mama.'

The gas-jet inside the door had fallen out of its hole again and dangled on its metal hose. It had gone out. One of our guards slammed it back into the hole where it belonged and looked at it for a moment, as if daring it to fall out. It didn't.

'Special dinners tonight, kiddies!' one of the others proclaimed. 'Big food and dessert to follow!'

We entered our cells. Eye, Stooks, and I were now enjoying – if that is the word – singles. Quilly carried Freed into his cell, laid him gently on his pallet, then went into the one he shared with Cammit. We waited for the night soldiers to exit with their arms outstretched, causing the cell doors to slam, but they just left, locking the door to the outer world behind them: one bolt, two bolt, three bolt, four. Apparently as well as 'big food,' we were to be allowed to mingle, at least for a little while.

Eris was in Gully's cell, examining his head wound, which was (no need to go into details) horrific. His breath came in irregular rasps. Eris looked up at me with tired eyes. 'He'll not last the night, Charlie.' Then she laughed bitterly. 'But then, none of us will, for it's always night here!'

I patted her shoulder and walked back to Iota's cell, which he had elected not to leave. He sat against the wall, wrists on his knees, hands dangling. I sat down beside him.

'What the devil do you want?' he asked. 'I'd just as soon be alone. If it please you, that is, your royal fucking majesty.'

Speaking low, I said, 'If there was a way out of here – a way to escape – would you try it with me?'

He raised his head slowly. He looked at me. And began to smile. 'You just show me the way, my love. Only show me.'

'What about the others? Those who are able?'

The smile widened. 'Does royal blood make you stupid, Princey? What do *you* think?'

CHAPTER TWENTY-FIVE

A Banquet. I Receive a Visitor.

Inspiration Doesn't Knock.

'Who Wants to Live Forever?'

1

It wasn't just chunks of half-raw meat for the survivors that night; it was a regular banquet. Pursey and two other grayfolk, a man and a woman dressed in stained white tunics, rolled in not one cart but three. They were flanked fore and aft by night soldiers, limber sticks at the ready. The first cart contained a huge pot that made me think of the wicked witch's kitchen in 'Hansel and Gretel'. Stacked around it were bowls. In the second was a tall ceramic cannister and small cups. In the third were half a dozen pies with golden brown crusts. The mingled smells were heavenly. We were killers now, killers who had murdered our fellows, but we were also hungry, and if not for the pair of watching Skeletors, I think we would have charged those carts. As it was, we retreated to the open doors of our cells and watched. Double kept wiping his mouth with his arm.

We were each given a bowl and a wooden spoon. Pursey dipped stew to the rim of each bowl from the pot. It was thick and creamy (real cream, I think), loaded with big chunks of chicken, plus peas, carrots, and corn. I had wondered before where the food was coming from, but right then I only wanted to eat.

'Puh ih in your cell,' Pursey said in his rough, dying voice. 'There's more.'

From the cannister there came a fresh fruit salad – peaches, blueberries, strawberries. Unable to wait – the sight and smell of real fruit made me desperate – I tilted the ceramic cup to my mouth and ate it all, wiping the juice from my chin and licking my fingers. I could feel my whole body welcome it after a steady diet of meat and carrots, meat and carrots, and more meat and carrots. The pies were divided up fifteen ways – none for Gully, whose eating days were done. There were no plates for the pie, so we used our hands. Iota's slice was gone even before the last portions had been handed out. 'Apple!' he said, and crumbs flew from his lips. 'And damn good!'

'Eat well, kiddies!' one of the night soldiers proclaimed, then laughed.

For tomorrow we die, I thought, hoping it wouldn't be tomorrow. Or the next day. Or the day after that. I still had no idea how we were going to get out of here even if Pursey did know a way from the Officials' Room. What I knew was that I wanted it to be before the second round of the Fair One, where I might – very likely – be pitted against Jaya. There wouldn't be anything fair about that.

The guards and kitchen crew left, but for the time being the cell doors remained open. I dug into the chicken stew. It was delicious. Oh my God, so delicious. *Yummy fo' my tummy*, the Bird Man would have said in days of yore when we were sitting on our bikes outside the Zip Mart and eating Twinkies or Slim Jims. I looked next door and saw Stooks gobbling, holding his hand to the side of his face to keep the chicken gravy from oozing out of his cheek. There are images that will always stay with me from my time in Deep Maleen. That's one of them.

When my bowl was empty (I'm not ashamed to say I licked it clean, just like Jack Sprat and his wife), I picked up my slice of pie and bit into it. Mine was custard rather than apple. My teeth struck something hard. I looked and saw a stub of pencil poking out of the custard. Wrapped around it was a small scrap of notepaper.

No one was looking at me; they were all concentrating on their meals, so different from our usual fare. I slipped the paper and pencil under Hamey's pallet. He wouldn't mind.

With the cells open, we were free to congregate for post-banquet chats. Iota crossed to my cell. Ammit joined him. One on each side, but I wasn't afraid of them. I felt my princely status rendered me immune from bullying.

'How do you reckon to get past the night soldiers, Charlie?' Iota asked. *Reckon* wasn't what he said; it was what I heard.

'I don't know,' I admitted.

Ammit growled.

'At least not yet. How many are there, do you think? Counting Kellin?'

Iota, who had been in Deep Maleen for a long time, considered. 'Twenty, maybe twenty-five at most. Not many of the King's Guard stood with Elden when he came back as the Flight Killer. Those who didn't are all dead.'

'*Them* are dead,' Ammit said, meaning the night soldiers. He wasn't wrong.

'Yuh, but when it's day – day in the world above – they're weaker,' Iota said. 'Blue glows around em are less. You must have seen that, Charlie.'

I had, but touching one, even trying, would result in a disabling shock. Iota knew that. The others would, as well. And the odds were against us. Before the first round, we outnumbered them. Now we didn't. If we waited until after the second round, there would only be eight of us left. Less, if some were wounded as badly as Freed and Gully.

'Ah, you ain't got no fucking idea,' Ammit said and waited – hopefully, I think – for me to contradict him.

I couldn't, but I knew something they didn't. 'Listen to me, you two, and spread the word. There *is* a way out.' At least there was if Pursey was telling the truth. 'If we can get past the night soldiers, we'll use it.'

'What way?' Iota asked.

'Never mind that for now.'

'Say there is. How are we going to get past the blues?' Back to that.

'I'm working on it.'

Ammit swatted a hand dangerously close to my nose. 'You don't have nothing.'

I didn't want to play my trump card, but I saw no choice. I ran my hands into my hair and lifted it, showing the blond roots. 'Am I the prince that was promised, or not?'

For that they had no answer. Iota even put his palm to his brow. Of course, being full of food as he was, he might just have been being generous.

2

Pursey and his two-man kitchen crew came back shortly thereafter, accompanied by a pair of night soldiers. Their blue envelopes were noticeably weaker – pastel instead of almost indigo – so somewhere above us the sun was up, although probably hidden under the usual bank of clouds. Given a choice between another bowl of chicken stew and seeing daylight, I would have picked daylight.

Easy to say when your belly's full, I thought.

We put our bowls and cups in the cart. All of them shone, making me think of how Radar had licked her bowl clean in better days. Our cell doors slammed shut. Day above, but another night for us.

Maleen settled down with rather more burps and farts than usual, but eventually those were joined by snores. Killing is a tiring and dispiriting job. The wait to see if one will live or die is even more tiring and dispiriting. I thought of adding Hamey's pallet to my own to pad the stone floor we slept on, but I couldn't bring myself to do it. I lay looking up at the always-black barred window. I was exhausted, but every time I closed my eyes I saw either Cla's in that last moment when they were the eyes of a living man, or Stooks with his hand held to his cheek to keep his stew from dribbling out.

At last I slept. And dreamed of Princess Leah by the pool, holding my mother's funky hairdryer – the Purple Raygun of Death. There was a purpose for that dream, either Empisarian magic or the more ordinary magic of my subconscious trying to tell me something, but before I could get hold of it, something woke me. A rattling sound and something scraping on stone.

I sat up and looked around. The dead gas-jet was moving in its hole. First clockwise, then counterclock.

'What—'

That was Iota, in the cell across from me. I put my finger to my lips. 'Shhh!'

That was just instinct. Everyone else was asleep, a couple moaning with what were undoubtedly bad dreams, and there were certainly no listening devices, not in Empis.

We watched the gas-jet rock back and forth. At last it fell out and hung by its metal hose. Something was inside. At first I thought it was a big old rat, but the shadowy shape looked too *angular* to be a rat. Then it squeezed through and scuttered quickly down the wall to the puddly stone floor.

'What the *fuck*!' Iota whispered.

I stared, dumbfounded, as a red cricket as large as a tomcat hopped its way toward me on its muscular back legs. It was still limping, but only a little. It came to the bars of my cell and looked up at me with its black eyes. The long feelers rising from its head reminded me of the rabbit ears on Mr Bowditch's old-school TV. There was an armored plate between its eyes and a mouth that looked frozen in a fiendish grin. And there was something on its underbelly that looked like a scrap of paper.

I dropped to one knee and said, 'I remember you. How's the leg? Looks better.'

The cricket hopped into the cell. That would have been easy for a cricket in the world I'd come from, but this one was so big it had to squeeze through. It looked at me. It *remembered* me. I reached out, slowly, and stroked the top of its chitinous head. As if it had been waiting for my touch, it fell on its side. There was indeed a bit of folded paper on its armored belly, stuck there with some kind of glue. Gently, I pulled it free, trying not to rip it. The cricket regained its six legs – four for walking, it looked like to me, and the two big ones in back for jumping – and leaped to Hamey's pallet. Where it resumed looking at me.

More magic. I was getting used to it.

I unfolded the paper. The note was written in letters so tiny I had to hold it close to my face to read it, but there was something else that seemed far more important to me just then. It was a little bunch of hair, held to the note with that same gluey substance. I lifted it to my nose and smelled. The aroma was faint but unmistakable.

Radar.

The note read: *Are you alive? Can we help you? PLEASE REPLY IF YOU CAN. Dog is safe. C.*

'What is it?' Eye whispered. 'What did it bring you?'

I had paper – one small sheet – from Pursey, and the stub of pencil. I could reply, but to say what?

'Charlie! What did it—'

'Shut up!' I whispered back. 'I need to think!'

Can we help you, the note asked.

The big question had to do with that pronoun. The note was from Claudia, of course. Somehow, probably because of Radar's sense of smell and innate direction finder, my dog had found her way to Claudia's house of sticks. That was good, that was wonderful. But Claudia lived alone. She was an *I*, not a *we*. Had Woody joined her? Perhaps even Leah, mounted on the faithful Falada? They would not be enough, royal blood or no royal blood. But if they had mustered others, the grayfolk . . . was that too much to hope for? Probably it was. Except, if they really believed I was the promised prince, then maybe . . .

Think, Charlie, think.

What I thought of was the stadium, once the Field of the Monarchs, now the field of Elden. There was no electricity to light it – not from the rickety, slave-powered generator Aaron had shown me – but lit it was, at least when the Fair One was happening, by banks of jumbo gas-jets mounted all around the stadium's circular rim.

I had a thousand questions and only one scrap of paper. Not an ideal situation, especially since getting any of them answered was extremely unlikely. But I also had one idea, which was better than none. The problem was it wouldn't even come close to working unless I could think of a way to neutralize the night soldiers.

If I could . . . and if this providential red cricket, to whom I'd once done a good turn, would return a message to Claudia . . .

I folded over my one precious scrap of paper and tore it carefully in two. Then, very small, I printed this: *Alive. Watch for next night Field of Monarchs lights up. Come if you are many. Not if you are few.* I thought about signing the note as she had, *C*, then thought better of it. At the bottom of my half-scrap, smaller than ever, I printed (not without embarrassment) *Prince Sharlie.*

'Come here,' I whispered to the cricket.

It sat on Hamey's pallet without moving, the joints of its oversized back legs sticking up like bent elbows. I snapped my fingers and it took a leap, landing in front of me. It was a hell of a lot spryer than the last time I'd seen it. I gave it a gentle push with my tented fingers and it fell obligingly on its side. The glue-stuff on its belly was still plenty sticky. I attached the note and told it, 'Go on. Take it back.'

The cricket got up but didn't move. Iota was staring at it, his eyes so big they looked in danger of falling out of their sockets.

'Go,' I whispered, and pointed at the hole above the dangling gas-jet. 'Go back to Claudia.' It occurred to me that I was giving instructions to a cricket. It further occurred to me that I had lost my mind.

It looked at me with its solemn black eyes for a moment or two longer, then turned and squeezed back through the bars. It hopped to the wall, felt the stone with its front legs as if testing it, then scampered up as neat as you please.

'*What* the *fuck* is *that*?' Stooks said from the cell next door.

I didn't bother answering him. It was red, and it was big, but if he couldn't tell it was a cricket, he was blind.

The hole was a tighter squeeze than the space between my cell bars, but it got through with my note still attached. Considering who might have read the message if it had fallen to the floor, that was also excellent. Of course there was no way of telling if it would stay on while the red cricket made its way back through whatever twists and turns had brought it here. Assuming it did, there was no way of knowing if it would still be stuck on when the cricket reached Claudia. Or if it would go to her at all. But what other option did I – *we* – have?

'Stooks. Eye. Listen to me and pass it on. We have to wait until the second round, but before it happens, we're getting the fuck out of here.'

Stooks's eyes lit up. 'How?'

'I'm still working that out. Now leave me alone.'

I wanted to think. I also wanted to stroke the little bundle of hair Claudia had sent me, and wish I could stroke the dog it had come from. Yet just knowing Radar was safe had rolled a weight from my shoulders I hadn't even been aware I was carrying.

'I don't understand why that red bug came to you,' Eye said. 'Is it because you're the prince?'

I shook my head. 'Do you know the story about the mouse that pulled the thorn out of the lion's paw?'

'No.'

'I'll tell you sometime. After we're out of here.'

3

There was no 'playtime' the next day, and no banquet, either. There was breakfast, however, and because Pursey was on his own, I was able to pass him a note on the other half of the paper he'd given me. There were only five words on it: *How go from Officials' Room?* He didn't read it, just tucked it away somewhere beneath the baggy blouse-like shirt he wore and kept rolling his cart down the corridor.

The word spread: *Prince Charlie has an escape plan.*

I hoped that if any night soldiers came to check on us – unlikely in the daytime, but it had happened – they wouldn't sense the new energy and alertness in their captive gladiators. I didn't think they would; most of them were pretty dull, it seemed to me. But Aaron wasn't dull, and neither was the Lord High.

In any case, the die was cast – always assuming Jiminy Cricket brought my note back to Claudia. When the second round came, the last heirs of the Gallien might show up at the gate of the haunted city with a posse of grayfolk. If we could get out of here and join them, there was a chance of freedom, maybe even overthrow of the creature who had taken power and cursed the once pleasant land of Empis.

I thought I'd settle for freedom. I didn't want to die in this damp cell, or on the killing field for the pleasure of Elden and his sycophants, and I didn't want any more of my fellow prisoners to die, either. There were only fifteen of us left. Gully passed the night of the banquet – while the banquet was still going on, for all I knew. Two gray men carried him off after breakfast the next morning, supervised by a night soldier whose name might have been Lemmil, or Lammel, or maybe even Lemuel. It made no difference to me. I wanted to kill him.

I wanted to kill them all.

'If there's a way to deal with the night soldiers, you better figure it out quick, Princey,' Ammit said after Gully was taken away. 'I don't know about Flight Killer, but that bitch who's with him, that Petra, won't want to wait long for some more killing. She was getting off on it.'

Getting off on it wasn't exactly what he said, but it wasn't wrong.

Dinner the night after the banquet was chunks of half-raw pork. Just looking at mine made my stomach turn over, and I almost tossed it down the waste hole. It was good that I didn't, because there was another note from Pursey tucked inside it, written in that same educated script: *Move tall cabinet. Door. May be locked. Destroy this. Yours in service, Percival.*

I could have used more, but that was what I had to settle for, and it would only matter if we could get to the Officials' Room in the first place. We could deal with the limber sticks, but only if we could do something about the high voltage that surrounded our captors. But say we did.

Could we kill them when they were dead already?

4

I dreaded breakfast the next day, knowing if Pursey brought sausages, the second round was going to happen before I had any idea of what to do with the blue boys. But it was big flapjacks coated with some kind of berry syrup. I caught mine, ate it, then used the cup with the hole in the bottom to wash the syrup off my hands. Iota was looking at me through the bars of his cell and licking his fingers, waiting for Pursey to be gone.

When he was, he said, 'We've got another day for the hurt ones to heal up a little, but if it isn't tomorrow it'll probably be the next day. Three at most.'

He was right, and they were all depending on me. Absurd for them to put their trust in a high school kid, but they needed a rainmaker, and I was elected.

In my head I heard Coach Harkness say, *Drop down and give me twenty, you waste of space.*

Because I had no better idea, and felt like a waste of space, I did. Hands wide apart. Down slow, chin touching the stone floor, then up slow.

'Why you do that?' Stooks asked, hanging over the bars and watching me.

'It's soothing.'

After you get past the initial stiffness (and the body's predictable protest at being asked to do actual work), it always is. While I went down and up, I thought about the dream: Leah holding my mother's purple hairdryer. Believing the answer to my problem – *our* problem – lay in a dream was undoubtedly magical thinking, but I had come to a magical place, so why not?

Here's a little side-note that isn't a side-note at all – just wait for it. I read *Dracula* in the summer before seventh grade. This was also at the urging of Jenny Schuster, not long before she and her family moved to Iowa. I was going to read *Frankenstein* – I had it from the library – but she said it was boring, a shit-ton of bad writing combined with a lot of bullshit philosophy. *Dracula*, she said, was a hundred times better, the coolest vampire story ever written.

I don't know if she was right about that – it's hard to take the literary judgments of a twelve-year-old too seriously, even if she is a horror maven – but *Drac* was good. Yet long after all the bloodsucking, the stakes pounded into hearts, and the dead mouths stuffed with garlic had pretty much left my mind, I remembered something Van Helsing said about laughter, which he called King Laugh. He said that King Laugh didn't knock but only barged in. You know that's true if you ever saw something funny and couldn't help laughing, not just in the moment but every time you remembered it. I think true inspiration is like that. There's no link you can put your finger on, saying *oh sure, I was thinking about* this *and it led me to* that. Inspiration doesn't knock.

I passed twenty pushups, then thirty, and just as I was about to quit, lightning struck. At one moment the idea wasn't there; at the next it was, and full-blown. I got up and went to the bars.

'I know what we're going to do. I don't know if it will work, but there's nothing else.'

'Tell me,' Iota said, so I told him about my mother's hairdryer, which he didn't understand at all; where he came from, a woman with long hair let it dry in the sun after washing. The rest of it, though, he got just fine. So did Stooks, who was listening from the cell next to mine.

'Spread the word,' I said. 'Both of you.'

Stooks put his palm to his forehead and bowed. The bowing stuff still gave me the creeps, but if it held them together, I'd take it until I could go back to being an ordinary kid. Except I didn't really think that was going to happen, even if I lived through this. Some changes are permanent.

5

It was sausages the next morning.

Pursey was usually silent as he served us, but that morning he had something to say. It was brief. 'Eee, eee.' Which I took to mean *eat, eat.*

The rest of them got three links. I got four, and not just because I was the Prince of Deep Maleen. Tucked into each one was a wooden match with a sloppy sulphur head. I slipped two into one of my dirty socks and two in the other. I had an idea what they were for. I hoped I was right.

6

There was another agonizing wait. At last the door opened. Aaron appeared along with Lemmil – or whatever his name was – and two others. 'Out, kiddies!' Aaron called, spreading his arms to open the doors. 'A good day for eight, a bad day for the rest! Hump, hump!'

We stepped out. There was no Hatcha crying sick today; Stooks had taken care of him, although poor old Stooksie's face would never be the same. Iota looked at me with a half-smile. One eyelid flicked in what could have been a wink. I took some courage from that. Also from knowing that whether we were able to escape or not, Elden Flight Killer, Petra, and his crew of suck-asses were going to be cheated of their Fair One.

As I started to pass Aaron, he held me back with the point of his limber stick against the ragged remains of my shirt. The semi-transparent human face on top of his skull was smiling. 'You think you're special, don't you? You bay'nt. The others think you're special, don't they? They'll learn better.'

'Traitor,' I said. 'Traitor to all you swore.'

The smile disappeared from what was left of his humanity; beneath it, the skull grinned its eternal grin. He raised his limber stick, meaning to bring it down on my face, splitting it from hairline to chin. I stood waiting for it, even turning my face up a little to receive the blow. Something else had spoken through me, and it had spoken true words.

Aaron lowered his stick. 'Nah, nah, I'll not mark you. I'll leave that for whoever puts paid to you. Hump, now. Before I decide to hug you and make you shit in your britches.'

He wouldn't, though. I knew it, and Aaron did, too. The second round matches had been set, and he couldn't afford to mess up the seedings by giving me a shock that might render me unconscious or even kill me.

I followed the others and he brought his switch down on my thigh, cutting into my pants. The initial sting was followed by burning pain and a flow of blood. I didn't make a sound. Wouldn't give the dead son of a bitch the satisfaction.

7

We were taken to the same team room, two doors down from the Officials' Room that might – *might* – be a way out. The poster board was set up in the middle of the room, as it had been before, only this time with fewer matches.

FAIR ONE SECOND ROUND

First Set

Ocka to Gully (d)
Charlie to Jaya
Murf to Freed

Second Set

Bendo to Bult
Cammit to Stooks
Eris to Quilly
Double to Mesel

Third Set

Ammit to`lota

So this time the big boys were scheduled for the final match. I thought it would have been a good one, too, but no matter how the next few minutes turned out it wasn't going to happen.

The Lord High was waiting for us as he had before the first round, decked out in his fancy uniform. To me it looked like something that might have been worn by the dictator of a poor Central American country on a state occasion.

'Here we are again,' he buzzed. 'Some of you a little banged up, but no doubt ready and eager for battle. What do you say?'

'Yes, Lord High,' I said.

'Yes, Lord High,' the others echoed.

He looked at my bleeding thigh. 'You look a trifle banged up already, Prince Charlie.'

I said nothing.

He surveyed the others. 'Isn't that what you call him? Prince Charlie?'

'No, Lord High,' Ammit said. 'He's just a little whoreson who likes to put on airs.'

Kellin liked that. His human lips smiled a little; beneath it the frozen grin just went on and on. He returned his attention to me. 'Tis said the true prince can float, and change his shape. Can you float?'

'No, Lord High,' I said.

'Change your shape?'

'No.'

He raised his limber stick, which was thicker and longer than those held by his troops. 'No *what?*'

'No, Lord High.'

'Better. I'll give you kiddies a bit of time to ready yourselves,' Kellin said. 'Cleanse yourself for your betters, please do, and consider today's order of battle as you wash. Wet your hair and pull it back, they'll want to see your faces. I expect you to put on a good show for His Majesty, as you did in the first round. Understood?'

'Yes, Lord High,' we said, just like a good little first-grade class should.

He – *it* – swept those bottomless eyes over us again, as if he suspected something was up. Maybe he did. Then he left, followed by the others.

'Look at this,' Ocka gloated. 'Me against a dead man! I should be able to win that one, all right.'

'Today all of us are going to win or none of us are,' I said. I looked at the shelf where sixteen washing buckets were lined up – yes, they had even put one out for Gully.

'Fucking true,' Eye growled.

'Jaya and Eris, either side of the door. Those two buckets have to be full to the top if they're not already. The rest of you, take buckets but get down. On your hands and knees.'

'Why do that?' Bendo asked.

I thought of an old grammar school joke then: Adam and Eve on the verge of having sex for the first time. 'Stand back, honey,' Adam says, 'I don't know how big this thing gets.'

'Because I don't know what's going to happen.'

And because, I thought, *you never use a hairdryer when you're taking a bath. My mother told me that.*

Out loud I said, 'We're going to cleanse, all right, but not ourselves. This is going to work.'

It sounded good, but I wasn't sure. The only thing I was sure of was that when it happened, it was going to happen fast.

8

'I hear footsteps,' Eris whispered. 'They're coming.'

'Wait until they get inside,' I said. 'They won't see you, they'll be looking straight ahead.'

I hoped.

The two women raised their buckets to their chests. The rest of us were crouched on our hands and knees, each with a full bucket of wash-water close at hand. Ammit and Iota hulked protectively over me on either side. The door opened. It was the same pair of night soldiers who days ago had escorted the first set out for the first round. I'd been hoping for Kellin or Aaron but wasn't surprised. Those two would be out on the field, ready to manage the festivities.

The night soldiers stopped, looking at the line of us crouched on the floor. One said, 'What are you do—'

I shouted, '*NOW!*'

Jaya and Eris doused them.

As I've said, I didn't know what might happen, but I never imagined what actually did: they exploded. There was a pair of brilliant flashes that whited out my vision for a moment. I heard something – no, several somethings – whoosh over my head, and a burn like a bee sting drilled into my upper arm. I heard a high-pitched scream, a war-cry from either Jaya or Eris. My head was down and I didn't see which one. It was followed by several yells of startled pain from either side of me.

'Up!' I shouted.

At that point I wasn't clear on what had happened, but we had to get out of there, that much I totally understood. The detonations of the night soldiers hadn't been loud, more like the thuds heavy furniture would make when dropped on a rug, but the woman's war-cry had been *plenty* loud. Plus there was a rattle of shrapnel. As I got to my feet, I saw there was something sticking out of Iota's forehead above his left eye. Blood was dribbling down the side of his nose. It was a shard of bone. There was another one in my arm. I plucked it out and dropped it.

Several others had sustained injuries, but no one looked incapacitated except for Freed, and he pretty much was already. Murf, who was supposed to be his opponent in the first set, was supporting him.

Iota picked the piece of bone out of his forehead and stared around, unbelieving. Shards of bone were everywhere. They looked like broken crockery. All that remained of the night soldiers were their uniforms, which were shredded, as if they had sustained close-range blasts from shotguns loaded with birdshot.

A hand curled around my neck and Ammit, unwounded, pulled me into a rough hug. 'If you hadn't told us to get down, we would have been cut to pieces.' And he put a kiss on my cheek. 'How did you know?'

'I didn't.' The only thing I'd been thinking was that I wanted us crouched and ready to charge, like the front line of a football team. 'Everybody out. Bring your buckets. Eye and Ammit, you lead. We're going to the Officials' Room two doors up. If more night soldiers come, you two douse them and then drop to the floor. *Everyone* drops to the floor, but try not to spill your buckets. Now we know what happens.'

As we went out with our buckets (Eris kicked aside one of the shredded uniforms, then spit on it), I took one look behind me. The team room where we were supposed to wait until it came our turn to fight was now a boneyard.

Good.

9

Ammit and Iota led the way. Eris had grabbed the late Gully's bucket to replace hers. Jaya, her bucket now empty, brought up the rear. Just as we reached the door of the Officials' Room, two more night soldiers came humping down the corridor from the brightly lit field.

'Oi!' one of them cried. (I'm pretty sure it was *oi*.) 'What are you lot doing out? It's just supposed to be the first set!'

Ammit and Iota stopped. We all stopped. Ammit, sounding beautifully confused: 'En't it supposed to be all of us this time? To salute His Majesty?'

They came closer. 'First set only, you dummocks!' the other said. 'The rest of you back in—'

Ammit and Iota looked at each other. Eye nodded. They took a step forward in perfect tandem, as if it had been planned, threw their buckets of water, and dropped. The rest of us were already down, this time not merely crouching, but on our bellies. We had been immensely lucky the first time; we might not be again.

These two also exploded. In addition to the flashes and the thudding sounds, I heard a kind of electrical crackling, like a small transformer just before an excessive power-load fries it, and I caught a whiff of ozone. Clouds of bone flew over us, rattling off the walls and bouncing along the floor.

Ammit got up and turned to me, all his teeth showing in a grin that was beyond fierce – it was fiendish. 'Let's all of us run out there, Charlie! We got almost a dozen more buckets! Let's blow up as many of those fucks as we can!'

'Not at all. We'd get some and then they'd massacre us. We're escaping, not fighting.'

Ammit's blood was up, and all the way. I didn't think he was going to listen to me, but Eye grabbed his neck and gave him a shake. 'Who's the prince, asshole? You or him?'

'Him.'

'That's right, and we do what he says.'

'Come on,' I said. 'Bendo? Bult? Buckets full?'

'Half,' Bult said. 'I regret to say I spilled some, my prin—'

'Get ahead of us, facing the mouth of the runway. Double, you and Cammit, too. If more come—'

'We'll give em a bath, right so,' Cammit said.

I led the rest of them, swinging my own bucket. I'd also lost some water – my pantslegs were wet – but the bucket was still three-quarters full. The door to the Officials' Room was locked. 'Ammit. Eye. See what you can do.'

They hit the door together. It burst open. It was dim inside, and the afterimage of the explosions hanging in front of my eyes didn't help. 'Who can see?' I shouted. 'There's a tall cabinet, who can s—'

One of our rearguard shouted then. A moment later there was a brilliant flash. By its light I saw the cabinet standing against the far wall, flanked by half a dozen wooden chairs. There was a howl of pain, then a second brilliant flash.

Bendo, Double, and Cammit came in, Cammit bleeding heavily from his face and arm. There were bone fragments sticking out of both wounds like yellowish-white quills. 'Got two more,' Bendo panted, 'but the second one did for Bult before I got 'im. Pulled him into a hug . . . he started *shaking* . . .'

So we'd lost one, but if Bendo was right, the night soldiers had lost six. Not a bad score, but there were still plenty of others.

'Eye, help me move this cabinet.'

I didn't get a chance to help. Eye strode to the cabinet, which looked like my nana's Welsh dresser. He put his shoulder to it and gave a mighty push. It slid four feet, tottered, and fell over with a crash. There was a door behind it, just as Pursey's note had promised.

There were shouts – *buzzy* shouts – from somewhere. Still distant but alarmed. I didn't know if the Lord High had guessed his prisoners were trying to escape, but he and his cadre of night soldiers had to know *something* was up.

Stooks lifted the latch of the door and pulled it open. That surprised me, but also gave me hope. *Door may be locked*, Pursey's note had said. Not *maybe* but *may be*. I hoped I was right about what he meant.

'Go,' I said. 'All of you.'

They crowded in, Murf still supporting Freed. My vision was clearing a little now, and I saw a torpedo-shaped lantern sitting on one of the wooden chairs. I mentally blessed Pursey – *Percival* – with many blessings. If they discovered he'd helped us it would go badly for him if the escape failed. Maybe if it didn't.

Iota backed out. 'It's fucking dark in there, Charlie. I . . .' He saw the lantern. 'Oh! If we only had owt to light it with.'

I put down my bucket, reached into my sock, and produced a sulphur match. Eye stared at it, then at me, with amazement. 'You really *are* the prince.'

I handed him the match. 'Maybe, but I don't know how this works. You do it.'

While he was lighting the lamp – its glass reservoir was filled with either kerosene or something similar – running steps came toward us from the field.

'Oi, oi! What's going on in there?' I knew that voice, insect-buzz or not. 'Why is that door open?'

Iota looked at me and raised his hands: lit lamp in one, the other empty. No bucket.

'Get in there,' I said. 'Pull the door shut. I think it locks on the inside.'

'I don't want to leave y—'

'GO!'

He went.

Aaron appeared in the door, his blue aura pulsing so bright it was hard to look at. And there I was, with a bucket dangling from one hand. He stopped, momentarily too startled by what he was seeing to move.

Should have kept coming, I thought. I took a step forward and threw the bucket of water at him.

I saw it in the air as if in slow motion: a big amorphous crystal.

The skull under Aaron's skin continued to grin, but on what remained of his human face I saw shocked surprise. I had just time to think of the Wicked Witch of the West screeching *I'm melting! I'm melting!* He dropped his damned limber stick and raised one arm, as if to block what was coming. I went flat just before the brilliant detonation sent Aaron into what I sincerely hoped was a hellish afterlife.

Bones flew above me . . . but not all of them passed harmlessly. This time it wasn't a bee sting in the arm but lines of pain along my scalp and across my left shoulder. I got to my feet, staggered, and turned to the door. I could hear others coming now. I wished for more water, and there was a sink on the far side of the room, but there was no time.

I lifted the latch and pulled, expecting the door to be locked. It wasn't. I went in, closed it, and grabbed the lantern by its wooden handle. I lowered it and saw two bolts. They looked sturdy. I hoped to God they were. Just as I shot the second one, I saw the inner latch lift and the door began to rattle in its frame. I stepped back. The door was wood, not metal, but I still didn't want to risk getting shocked.

'Open! Open in the name of Elden Flight Killer!'

'Kiss my asshole in the name of Elden Flight Killer,' somebody said from behind me.

I turned. By the lantern's paltry glow I could see all thirteen of them. We were in a square corridor lined with white tiles. It made me think of a subway tunnel. There were unlit gas-jets at head-height, marching away into the gloom. My fellow prisoners – *ex*-prisoners, at least for the time being – were all looking at me, eyes wide, and except for Ammit and Iota, they all looked scared. They were waiting, God help me, for Prince Charlie to lead them.

Hammering on the door. Through the cracks at the sides and bottom, bright blue light.

Leading was easy enough, at least for the moment, because there was only one way to go. I pushed through them, holding up the lantern, feeling absurdly like Lady Liberty with her torch. Something occurred to me then, a line from a war movie I'd seen on TCM. It was out of my mouth before I knew I was going to say it. I suppose I was either hysterical or inspired.

'Come on, you sons of bitches! Do you want to live forever?'

Ammit laughed and clapped me on the back so hard I almost dropped the lantern, which would have left us in what the old-timey horror novels liked to call 'the living dark.'

I started walking. They followed. The hammering on the door faded, then was left behind. Kellin's night soldiers would have a hell of a hard job breaking it down, too, because it opened outward and because, inside their auras, there really wasn't much to them . . . as we now knew.

God bless Percival, whose note hadn't been timid, as I had first thought. It had been an invitation: the door may be locked. As in, *behind you.*

'Who wants to live forever?' Iota roared, and a flat echo came back from the tiles.

'I do,' Jaya piped up . . . and you may not believe it, but we laughed.

All of us.

CHAPTER TWENTY-SIX

The Tunnel and the Station. Scratching.

The Trolley House. Red Molly.

The Welcoming Party. A Mother's Grief.

1

I think the tunnel was a little over a mile and a half long from the Officials' Room to where we finally emerged, but at the time, with only a single lantern to lead us, it seemed to go on forever. It tended always upward, broken every now and again by short flights of stairs – six in one, eight in another, four in a third. Then it took a square turn to the right and there were more steps, this time a longer flight. By then Murf could no longer support Freed, so Ammit was carrying him. When I made it to the top, I paused to get my wind back and Ammit caught up to me. Not breathing hard at all either, curse him.

'Freed says he knows where this comes out,' Ammit said. 'Tell him.'

Freed looked up at me. In the pale glow of the lantern, his face was a horror of lumps, bruises, and cuts. Those he might recover from, but the leg wound was infected. I could smell it.

'I sometimes came with the officials in the old days,' Freed said. 'The judges and boundarymen. To doctor the cuts and breaks and broken heads, you understand. It wasn't like the Fair One, murder for the sake of murder, but [*a word I couldn't translate*] was plenty rough.'

The rest of our merry band was bunched below us on the stairs. We couldn't afford to stop, but we needed (*I* needed) to know what was ahead, so I cranked my fist at the doc, telling him to go on but to make it fast.

'We didn't use the tunnel to come to the Field of the Monarchs, but we often used it when we left. Always, if Empis lost because of calls that enraged the crowd.'

'Kill the ump,' I said.

'Eh?'

'Never mind. Where does it come out?'

'The Trolley House, of course.' Freed managed a feeble smile. 'Because, you must understand, when Empis lost a match, it was wise to leave the city as soon as possible.'

'How close is this Trolley House to the main gate?'

Freed said what I wanted to hear and feared I would not. 'Quite close.'

'Let's go,' I said. I almost added *hump, hump*, but didn't. That was the language of our captors, and I wanted none of their belittling talk. We'd done for seven of them. No matter how it went at the end of the tunnel, there was that.

'Who still has buckets with water in them?' I called back.

Six did, but none were full. I asked them to come up behind me. We'd use what we had, then do what we could.

2

We came to another flight of steps and Ammit, out of breath at last by the time we got to the top of them, shifted Freed to Iota. Freed said, 'Leave me. I'm just dead weight.'

'Save your breath to cool your porridge,' Eye growled. It might have been *porridge* – as in the story of Goldilocks and the Three Bears; it might have been *soup*.

The corridor now tended up more steeply, like the one leading to the field. I hoped we'd reach the end soon, because the reservoir of fuel in the lantern was almost gone and the light was dimming. Then, on our right, I began to hear a scratching and scrabbling beyond the tile wall. Quite close. I remembered my doomed run for the outer gate, tripping over the gravestones, and the hackles on my neck rose.

'What's that?' Quilly asked. 'It sounds like . . .'

He didn't finish, but we all knew what it sounded like: fingers. Fingers in the earth, clawing toward the sound of our passage.

'I don't know what it is,' I said. Which was probably a lie.

Eris said, 'When his mind is not at rest – Elden, I mean – the dead grow restless. So I've heard. It might only be a story to scare children. Even if it's true, I don't . . . I don't think they can get in here.'

I wasn't so sure about that. I'd seen hands rising from the ground, the dead reaching into the living world, and I'd also heard the squall of rusty hinges, as though *something* were emerging from the crypts and tombs. Maybe several somethings.

'Rats is all.' That was Mesel. He was trying to sound authoritative. 'Maybe voles. Or ferrets. Anything else, just stories to frighten children. Like she says.'

I didn't really think they could get through the tile wall between us and them, but I was still grateful when we left the scratching behind. If it *had* been the graveyard, I had at least a rough idea of where we were, and if I was right, we were indeed close to the gate.

As we reached another flight of stairs, steep and long, the lantern began to gutter.

'Leave me, leave me,' Freed moaned. 'I'm done.'

'Shut up or I'll do you m'sel',' Eye panted, and started up the stairs with Freed in his arms. I followed and the rest followed me. At the top was a little room with benches on either side and a door. It was locked, and this time not on the inside. That would have been too easy. The handle was a rusty lever. Ammit seized it, turned it, and pulled with all his might. It broke off.

'*Fuck!*' He dropped it and examined his bleeding hand. 'Eye, get with me! Right beside me and hump it!'

Eye passed Doc Freed to Cammit and Quilly, then crowded in beside Ammit, shoulder to shoulder. The flame inside the lantern gave a final jump, like a dying man's last gasp. For a moment I could see our shadows on the white tiles, and then we were plunged into utter darkness. Jaya moaned.

'With me!' Ammit snarled. 'On three, hit it as dammit hard as you ever hit anything in your dammit life! One . . . two . . . *THREE!*'

For a moment there was a bit of light as the door shuddered in its frame, then we were in the dark again.

'Oh, you can hit harder than that, you fucking—' *Pussy? Cunt?* I heard both, overlapping. 'On three! One . . . two . . . *THREE!*'

The door's bolts must have been sturdy, because they held. It was the hinges that gave way, sending the door flying back. Iota and Ammit stumbled out. Eye went to his knees and Ammit hauled him to his feet. The rest of us followed.

'Thank the high gods!' Ocka cried. His voice echoed back from some vast space: *ank-ank* and *odds-odds*. A moment later we were enveloped in a cloud of leathery wings.

3

Eris and Jaya shrieked in perfect harmony. They weren't the only ones to cry out; I think most of us yelled or screamed in terror. I know I did. I dropped the lantern to cover my head and heard it shatter on the stone floor.

'Bats,' Freed wheezed. 'Just bats. They roost . . .' He began to cough and couldn't finish, but pointed up into the deep shadows.

Ammit heard him and bellowed it. '*Bats! They won't hurt ye! Stand your ground and swat em away!*'

We swung our arms, me hoping they weren't *vampire* bats, because they were huge, like the ones in the tunnel between Illinois and Empis. I could glimpse them as they swooped and turned, because faint light – I think cloud-shrouded moonlight – was coming through a line of small high windows. I could see most of the others, all waving their arms madly. Cammit and Quilly were carrying Freed, so they couldn't swat, but Doc himself was waving his arms feebly and coughing up a storm.

The colony swooped away, back to the heights of the enormous room in which we found ourselves. This part of Trolley House appeared to be a garage. There were at least twenty trolleys in neat rows. Painted on their blunt snouts were their destinations: SEAFRONT, DEESK, ULLUM, TAYVO NORTH, TAYVO SOUTH, GREEN ISLES. The posts on their roofs, meant to draw power from the overhead wires (most of those now down in the streets), hung limp and dispirited. On the sides of the ones I could see, in gold flake, were words decidedly out of vogue in Empis these days: FRIENDSHIP, AMITY, KINDNESS, and LOVE.

'How do we get out?' Stooks asked.

Eris said, 'Did you never learn to read?'

'As well as any plowboy, I guess,' Stooks said, sounding grumpy. Of course I'd be grumpy, too, if I had to hold my cheek with my hand to keep the food from squirting out.

'Read that, then,' Eris said, pointing above a high central arch on the far side of the garage.

Printed above it was WAY OUT.

We went through the arch, thirteen would-be escapees falling in behind their clueless prince. We came out in a room almost as big as the garage, with a row of what had to be ticketing stations on one side and a number of smaller arches with destinations painted over them on the other. The glass of the ticket windows had been shattered, a giant butterfly centerpiece had been broken to bits, and a mural of monarchs had been splashed with paint, but the vandals hadn't been able to deface all the butterflies: high above, running all around the room, were bright yellow tiles with a monarch on each one. Seeing what Elden's cronies hadn't been able to destroy brought me comfort, and if I was right, there might be something I could use nearby.

'Come on,' I said, and pointed to a bank of doors. I broke into a run.

4

We burst into the outside world, a few still swinging buckets. We huddled at the top of the steps leading down to the Gallien Road, Cammit and Quilly grunting as they carried Freed between them. I heard the clang of the Lord High's squat bus and saw a dozen or so night soldiers running in front of it, spread out across the wide thoroughfare. I had thought Kellin's little vehicle might be the only motorized transport left in Lilimar, but I was wrong. There was one ahead of the night soldiers, leading the pack, and unlike the bus, it wasn't powered by electricity. It blatted and backfired as it came toward us. Enormous handlebars jutted from the front of a board wagon. Four ironbound wheels struck sparks from the cobbles.

At the front, adding to whatever power the wagon's motor was supplying, was Red Molly, sitting on a high seat and pedaling for all she was worth. Her huge knees flashed up and down. She was bent over the handlebars like a daredevil motorcycle rider. We might have been able to beat the rest to the gate, but she was coming fast.

I saw red-and-white-striped posts, I saw the downed snarl of trolley wires I had almost tripped over, and I saw the nest of brambles into which I'd thrown my pack so I could run a little faster. I hadn't made it that time and I wasn't going to make it this time, either. None of us were unless that pack was still there.

'That bitch, I'll take er on!' Iota growled, balling his fists.

'I'll stand with you,' Ammit said. 'I will or dammit.'

'No,' I said. I was thinking of Woody's nephew Aloysius, and how Red Molly's mother had swatted his head from his shoulders. 'Eye, wait.'

'But I can—'

I grabbed his shoulder. 'She hasn't seen us yet. She's looking straight ahead. I've got something. Trust me.' I looked at the others. 'Stay here, all of you.'

Hunching low, I ran down the steps. The blatting, burping motor-wagon was now close enough for me to see Red Molly's features . . . but she was still looking straight ahead, squinting – maybe nearsighted – and expecting to see the crowd of us running for the gate.

I could have caught her by surprise, maybe, but then a small figure dressed in green britches – green britches with the seat torn out – ran into the street, waving its arms. '*He's there!*' Peterkin screeched, pointing directly at me. How had he seen us? Had he been waiting? I never knew, and I never gave a shit, either. That pipsqueak fuck had a way of turning up at the worst possible moment.

'*He's there, right there!*' Pointing. Leaping up and down in his excitement. '*Do you not see him, you great half-blind bitch, HE'S RIGHT TH—*'

She never slowed, simply leaned down and swatted him. Peterkin rose into the air. I caught one glimpse of his face, stamped with a terminal expression of shocked surprise, and then he separated at the middle. Red Molly's blow had been strong enough to literally rip him in two. He must have risen twenty feet in the air, intestines uncoiling as he went. I thought of Rumpelstiltskin again, was powerless not to.

Red Molly was grinning, and the grin revealed teeth filed to points.

They hadn't found my backpack, thank God. It was still in the brambles. Thorns scrawled cuts up my bare arms as I pulled it out. I didn't feel them. One of the straps holding the pack closed slid out easily; the other bound up. I tore it away and pulled out cans of sardines, a jar of Jif, a spaghetti sauce jar filled with dog food, a shirt, my toothbrush, a pair of undershorts—

Iota grabbed my shoulder. My little band of water-warriors had followed him down the steps against my orders, but that was for the best after all.

'Eye, take them and run! Carry Freed yourself. The ones who still have water, they're your rearguard! At the gate, shout *open in the name of Leah of the Gallien!* Can you remember?'

'Yuh.'

'*YOUUU DIE NOW!*' Red Molly screamed. Her voice was a deep baritone powered by mighty lungs.

'Then go!'

Eye waved one meaty arm at the others. 'Come on, you lot! Hump it for your lives!' Most did. Ammit didn't. He had apparently appointed himself my guardian.

There was no time to argue with him. I found Polley's .22 and yanked it free, along with a few more cans of sardines and a package of Nabisco Honey Grahams that I didn't even remember packing. Red Molly stopped thirty feet from the Trolley House steps and scrambled down from her high seat, one arm sodden to the elbow with Peterkin's blood. Ammit placed himself in front of me, which was a problem unless I intended to shoot him in the head. I shoved him aside.

'Get out of here, Ammit!'

He paid no attention, only threw himself at Red Molly with a bellow of rage. He was a big man, but next to the giant he looked not much larger than Peterkin, now lying dead in two pieces up the street. For a moment she was too surprised by this unexpected attack to move. Ammit took advantage while he could. He grabbed one of her wide suspenders and pulled himself up one-handed. He opened his mouth and buried his teeth in her arm just above the elbow.

She screeched in pain, grabbed him by his greasy mop of hair, and pulled his head away. She balled up a fist and drove it not into his face but through it. His eyes bulged in two different directions, as if not wanting to see the red hole that had been his nose and mouth. She lifted him, still with only one hand, and shook that big man to and fro like a marionette. Then she threw him in the direction of the graveyard, blood fanning up from her bitten arm. Ammit was brawny and fearless, but she had disposed of him as if he had been no more than a child.

Next she turned to me.

I was sitting on the cobbled pavement of the Gallien Road, legs splayed, Polley's .22 automatic held out in both hands. I remembered how it had felt to have that gun pressed into the back of my head. I thought again of Rumpelstiltskin, and how much Polley had reminded me of that fairy-tale dwarf: *What will you give me if I spin your straw into gold?* Polley would have killed me once he got Mr Bowditch's treasure and tumbled me down the magic well hidden in Mr Bowditch's shed.

Mostly I remember hoping that the little gun would stop a giant, just as David's little stone had stopped Goliath. It might, if it was mostly loaded. It had been fired twice already, back in a less magical world.

She came toward me, grinning. Her wounded arm was pouring blood. She didn't seem to mind. Maybe Ammit's final bite would start an infection that would kill her if I couldn't.

'You're no prince,' she said in that rumbling baritone. 'You're a bug. Nothing but a *bug*. I'll just step on you and—'

I fired. The gun gave a polite bang, not much louder than the Daisy air rifle I'd had when I was six years old. A small black hole appeared over Red Molly's right eye. She reared back and I shot her again. This time the hole appeared in her throat, and when she gave a howl of pain, blood jetted from the hole. It came out under so much pressure that it looked solid, like the shaft of a red arrow. I fired again and this time the black hole, not much bigger than the period you put at the end of a sentence, appeared at the top of her nose. None of it stopped her.

'*YOUUU—!*' she screamed, and reached for me.

I didn't pull back or even try to dodge; that would have fucked up my aim and it was far too late to run. She would have caught me in a pair of *mother may I* giant steps. Just before she could grab my head as she'd grabbed Ammit's, I fired five more times in rapid succession. Each shot went into her open, screaming mouth. The first two – maybe the first three – took most of her teeth with them. In *The War of the Worlds*, our most sophisticated weapons didn't do much to stop the rampaging Martians; it was earthly germs that killed them. I don't think any single bullet from Polley's little gun did for Red Molly, nor even all eight, which was every cartridge left in the clip.

I think she pulled her broken teeth down her throat . . . and choked on them.

5

If she had fallen on me, her weight might have held me pinned until Kellin and his night soldiers arrived, or killed me outright. She had to go five hundred pounds, minimum. But she went to her knees first, gasping and choking and holding her bleeding throat. Her eyes bulged sightlessly. I scrambled back on my ass, tipped over on my side and rolled. The night soldiers were closing in, I'd never beat them to the gate, and the gun was used up – slide back, chamber empty.

She made one final effort to reach me, waving her wounded arm and stippling my cheeks and forehead with her blood. Then she fell on her face. I stood up. I could run, but what was the point? Better to face them head-on and die as best I could.

What I thought of then was my father, who would still be hoping I'd come home. He and Lindy Franklin and my Uncle Bob would have papered every town between Sentry and Chi with pictures of me and Radar – HAVE YOU SEEN THIS BOY OR THIS DOG? The passage to Empis would be left unguarded, and maybe that was more important than one bereft father, but as the night soldiers neared, it was Dad I was thinking of. He'd gotten sober, and for what? Wife gone, son lost without a trace.

But if Iota could lead the others through the gate, where I didn't believe the night soldiers could go, they'd be free. There was that.

'*Come on, you sons of bitches!*' I screamed.

I tossed the useless gun away and spread my arms wide. Behind the line of blue shapes, Kellin had stopped his little bus. Content just to watch me killed, I thought at first, but it wasn't me he was looking at. It was the sky. The night soldiers stopped, still seventy or eighty yards away. They were looking up, too, with identical expressions of amazement on the gauzy human faces that overlaid their skulls.

There was enough light to see by even though the two ever-racing moons were hidden. A cloud below the clouds was coming over the outside wall. It was unrolling toward the Gallien Road, the fancy shops and arches, and the palace beyond, where the three glass-green spires shone in the lights ringing the field.

It was a cloud of monarchs, the sort of group known as a kaleidoscope. They flew above me without stopping. It was the night soldiers they wanted. They halted, circled, and then dive-bombed *en masse*. The soldiers raised their arms, as the Flight Killer was said to have done after his coup, but they didn't have his power and the butterflies didn't die. Except, that is, for the ones that struck those high-voltage auras first. There were brilliant flashes when they hit the blue envelopes. It was as if a crowd of invisible children were waving Fourth of July sparklers. Hundreds burned up, but thousands more followed, either smothering the deadly auras or shorting them out. The cloud seemed to solidify as it engulfed the night soldiers.

But not Lord High Kellin. His little electric bus made a tight U-turn and headed back to the palace, making good speed. Some of the monarchs broke off and chased it, but it was too fast for them, and the roof would have protected the son of a bitch anyway. The night soldiers that had been chasing us were finished. All of them. The only movement where they had been was the flutter of delicate wings. I saw one bony hand rise . . . and then sink back into the orange-red mass on top of it.

I ran for the outer gate. It was open. My party of prisoners had gone outside, but something else came in at a dead run. Something black, low to the ground, and barking like hell. I had thought the only thing I wanted was to get the hell out of the haunted city of Lilimar, but now I realized there was something else I wanted more. I thought of Dora, when she'd caught sight of my dog, how she had called to her as best she could in her broken voice. My voice was also broken, not by some degenerative curse but by sobs. I fell to my knees and held out my arms.

'Radar! Radar! RADES!'

She collided with me and knocked me over, whining and licking my face from top to bottom. I hugged her with all my strength. And I cried. I couldn't stop crying. Not very princely, I suppose, but as you may have guessed already, this isn't that kind of a fairy tale.

6

A bellowing voice that I knew very well broke up our happy reunion. 'SHARLIE! PRINCE SHARLIE! GET THE FUCK OUT OF THERE SO WE CAN SHUT THE GATE! COME TO US, SHARLIE!'

Right, I thought, getting to my feet. *And strain your pooper, Prince Sharlie.*

Radar danced around me, barking. I ran toward the gate. Claudia was standing just outside of it, and she wasn't alone. Woody was with her, and between them, astride Falada, was Leah. Behind them were the remaining escapees from Deep Maleen, and behind those were others – a crowd of people I couldn't make out.

Claudia wouldn't cross into Lilimar, but she grabbed me as soon as I came through the gate and pulled me into a hug so strong I felt my spine creak.

'Where is he?' Woody asked. 'I hear the dog, but where—'

'Here,' I said. 'Right here.' This time it was my turn to hug.

When I let him go, Woody put his palm to his forehead and dropped to one knee. 'My prince. It was you all along, and you've come just as the old stories said you would.'

'Get up,' I said. With tears still pouring from my eyes (plus snot from my nose that I wiped away with the back of my hand) and blood all over me, I never felt less princely in my life. 'Please, Woody, get up. Rise.'

He did. I looked at my group, watching with awe. Eris and Jaya were hugging each other. Eye had Freed in his arms. It was clear that some of my friends, maybe all, knew exactly who these three people were: not just whole people but whole people of the true blood. They were the exiled royalty of Empis, and except perhaps for insane Yolande and Burton the anchorite, they were the last of the Gallien line.

Behind the dungeon refugees were sixty or seventy gray people, some carrying torches and some with torpedo lanterns similar to the one Pursey had left for me. Among them I saw someone I knew. Radar had run to her already. I went to her, barely aware that the deformed people who had been cursed by Elden – or by the being that had used him as its puppet – were falling to their knees all around me, their palms to their foreheads. Dora also tried to go to her knees. I wouldn't let her. I embraced her, kissed both of her gray cheeks and the corner of her crescent mouth.

I brought her back to Woody, Claudia, and Leah.

'CLOSE IN THE NAME OF LEAH OF THE GALLIEN!' Claudia bellowed.

The gate began to trundle slowly shut, its machinery groaning like a thing in pain. As it did, I saw an enormous figure loping in long strides down the central thoroughfare. Clouds of monarchs swirled above and around it, some even lit on the broad shoulders and blocky head, but this was no night soldier and the figure simply ignored them. As the gate passed the halfway mark on its hidden track, she gave a wail of grief so loud and so awful that everyone except Claudia covered their ears.

'*MOLLY!*' Hana screamed. '*OH MY MOLLY! OH MY DEAR, HOW CAN YOU LIE SO STILL?*'

She bent over her dead daughter, then stood. There were many of us gathered before the closing gate, but it was me she was looking at.

'*COME BACK!*' She raised fists like boulders and shook them. '*COME BACK, YOU COWARD, SO I CAN KILL YOU FOR WHAT YOU'VE DONE TO MY DEAR ONE!*'

Then the gate crashed closed, cutting off the sight of Red Molly's bereft mother.

7

I looked up at Leah. No blue dress this night. No white apron. She was dressed in dark pants tucked into high leather boots and a quilted blue vest with a monarch butterfly, the royal crest of the Gallien, on the left side, above her heart. Around her waist was a wide belt. Hanging from one hip was a dagger. On the other was a scabbard holding a short sword with a golden hilt.

'Hello, Leah,' I said, feeling suddenly shy. 'I'm very glad to see you.'

She turned away from me with no sign that she'd heard – she might have been as deaf as Claudia. Her mouthless face was a stone.

CHAPTER TWENTY-SEVEN

A Conference. The Snab. No Disney Prince. Prince and Princess. The Pact.

1

I remember two things with great clarity about our conference. No one mentioned the name Gogmagog, and Leah never looked at me. Not once.

2

There were six people and two animals in the storage shed later that night – the shed where Radar and I had sheltered before entering Lilimar. Woody, Claudia, and I sat together on the floor. Radar lay beside me with her muzzle firmly planted on my leg, as if wanting to be sure I would not escape her again. Leah sat apart from us, on the steps at the front of the Seafront trolley. In the far corner was Franna, the gray woman who had whispered *help her* to me just before I left the farm of the 'googir.' Franna was stroking Falada's head, which was deep in a sack of grain Iota was holding for her. Outside were the rest of the Deep Maleen escapees, and a growing number of grayfolk. There was no howling; wolfies apparently didn't care for crowds.

Mr Bowditch's .45 was once more on my hip. Claudia might be

deaf, but her eyes were keen. She had seen the gleam of the blue stones in the concho belt as it lay deep in the weeds growing hard by the outside wall near the gate. The gun needed to be oiled and cleaned before I could be sure it worked, and I'd have to take care of that later. I thought I might be able to find what I needed on one of the littered worktables at the back of the shed. This had pretty clearly been a repair shop, once upon a better time.

Woody said, 'The snake has been wounded, but still lives. We have to cut off its head before it can renew its poison. And you must lead, Charlie.'

He took a pad and a fancy nib pen from the pocket of his coat and wrote on it, as quickly and surely as any sighted person, as he spoke. He held it up to Claudia. She read and nodded vigorously. 'YOU MUST LEAD, SHARLIE! YOU ARE THE PRINCE THAT WAS PROMISED! ADRIAN'S HEIR FROM THE MAGIC WORLD!'

Leah briefly looked up at Claudia, then down again, a sheaf of hair screening her face. Her fingers played along the knurled grip of her sword.

I certainly hadn't promised anything to anyone. I was tired and afraid, but there was something more important than those things. 'Let's say you're right, Woody. Let's say allowing Flight Killer to renew his poison is dangerous for us and all of Empis.'

'It would be,' he said quietly. 'It is.'

'Even so, I won't lead a crowd of mostly unarmed people into the city, if that's what you're thinking. Half of the night soldiers might be dead, there weren't all that many to begin with—'

'No,' Woody agreed. 'Most died the true death rather than go on half-alive, in the service of a monster.'

I was looking at Leah – in truth I could hardly take my eyes from her – and I saw her flinch, as if Woody had struck at her.

'We killed seven and the monarchs killed even more. But that leaves the rest.'

'No more than a dozen,' Eye growled from the corner. 'Maybe not that many. The monarchs killed ten that I counted, and Kellin's bunch weren't even thirty to start with.'

'Are you sure?'

He shrugged. 'Stuck in that place for what felt like forever, there was nothing to do but count. When I wasn't counting night soldiers, I was counting drips from the ceiling or the blocks in my cell floor.'

There had been forty-three blocks in the floor of mine.

'Even a dozen is too many when they can shock you unconscious by touching or kill you by hugging,' I said. 'And there's Kellin to command those who are left.'

Woody scrawled KELLIN on his pad and held it up for Claudia. Being blind, he held it up in the wrong place. I moved it so she could see.

'KELLIN! YES!' Claudia shouted. 'AND DON'T FORGET HANA!'

No, it wouldn't do to forget Hana, who would be out for blood.

Woody sighed and rubbed his face. 'Kellin was the leader of the King's Guard when my brother reigned. Smart and brave. Back then I would have added loyal. I would never have believed he'd turn against Jan. But then, I never would have believed Elden would do what he did.'

He couldn't see Leah turn away from him as she had from me when I looked up at her to say hello. But I saw.

'Here's how I see it,' I said. 'We have to stop the Flight Killer before he does something else. Something worse. I mean, look what he's done already. He's turned the whole goddam kingdom gray. He's turned the *people* gray, except for a few who are . . .' I almost said *by-blows*, a term I'd heard my dad use about Scooter MacLean, a grammar school classmate of mine with unfortunate jug-ears. 'Who are whole,' I finished lamely. 'And he's been rooting those out. I just don't know how to deal with him. Or when.'

'When's easy,' Iota said. He had finished feeding Falada and was tucking the depleted sack into one of the panniers strapped across her flanks. 'Daylight. The blue boys are weaker then, and they can't go out in the sun at all. Or *poof*. Nothing but bones.' He looked at Woody. 'At least that's what I heard.'

'I've heard that, too,' Woody said, 'but I wouldn't trust it for a fact.' He was scribbling on his pad and held it up to Claudia. I couldn't see what he had written there, but she shook her head and smiled.

'NAH, NAH, HE CAN'T DO MORE THAN HE HAS ALREADY WITHOUT GOING TO *IT*, AND HE CAN'T DO THAT UNTIL

THE MOONS KISS! THAT'S THE LEGEND, AND I BELIEVE IT'S TRUE LORE!'

Leah looked up, and for the first time she seemed engaged. She turned to Falada. When the horse began to speak, Iota's reaction was amusing, to say the least.

'My mistress saw them tonight when the clouds broke for a few moments, and Bella has almost caught up to Arabella!'

Woody reached out to Claudia and tapped her arm to get her attention. He pointed in Leah's direction, pointed skyward, and moved two fingers in front of Claudia's face, one barely trailing the other. Claudia's eyes widened and her smile disappeared. She looked at Leah. 'YOU SAW THIS?'

Leah nodded.

Claudia turned back to me with an expression on her face I hadn't seen before. It was fear. 'THEN IT MUST BE TOMORROW! YOU MUST STOP HIM, SHARLIE! YOU'RE THE ONLY ONE WHO CAN! HE MUST BE KILLED BEFORE ARABELLA KISSES HER SISTER! HE CAN'T BE ALLOWED TO OPEN THE DARK WELL AGAIN!'

Leah jumped to her feet, grabbed Falada's bridle, and started to lead her toward the door. Radar raised her head and whined. Franna followed Leah and touched her shoulder. Leah shrugged her away. I got up.

'LEAVE HER, LEAVE HER, HER HEART IS BROKEN AND NEEDS TIME TO MEND,' Claudia said. She no doubt meant well, but her blaring voice robbed her words of any intended compassion. Leah shrank from them.

I went to her anyway. 'Leah, please. Come ba—'

She pushed me so hard I almost fell down.

And left, leading the horse that was her voice.

3

There was no need for her to open the door, because with no wolves in the vicinity there was no reason to pull it closed. The crowd of grayfolk was still growing, and when Leah emerged, leading her horse, those standing fell to their knees. They all put their palms to their foreheads. There was no doubt in my mind that if ordered by her or the other two surviving royals to re-take the city, or at least try, they would do it.

It was my coming that had led to this. Any effort to deny it broke down when met by one simple fact: they really thought I was the prince that had been promised. I didn't know about Leah, but Woody and Claudia believed the same thing. That made the crowd of would-be rebels, Dora among them, my responsibility.

I started after Leah, but Claudia caught my arm. 'NAH, STAY! FRANNA WILL WATCH OVER HER.'

Woody said, 'Be at your ease for now, Charlie. Rest if you can. You must be exhausted.'

I explained that we escapees might become sleepy once the sun was up, but for now we were wide awake. It didn't hurt to be jacked up on adrenalin and the hard-to-believe joy of being out of the dungeon and away from the killing field.

Woody listened, nodded, and wrote a note for Claudia. I was fascinated at how neat and even his writing was, even though he couldn't see. The note said, *Charlie and his band are used to waking night, sleeping day*. Claudia nodded that she understood.

'She's angry because she loved him, isn't that right? When I met her she said – through Falada – that Elden was always good to her.'

Woody wrote on his pad and held it up to Claudia: *He wants to know about L and E.* Beneath this he had drawn a question mark.

'TELL HIM WHAT YOU WILL,' Claudia boomed. 'WE HAVE A LONG NIGHT AND LONG NIGHTS ARE GOOD FOR STORIES. HE DESERVES TO KNOW.'

'All right,' Woody said. 'Know then, Charlie, that Leah chooses to believe Elden dead because she will not believe, *cannot*, that he has become the Flight Killer. As children they were like this.' He put his hands together and interlaced the fingers. 'Some of it was just the circumstances of birth. They were the two youngest, and when they weren't ignored, they were picked on. The older sisters – Dru, Ellie, Joy, and Fala – hated Leah because she was her mother and father's youngest, their pet, but also because they were plain and she was pretty—'

'WHAT'S HE TELLING YOU?' Claudia blared. I decided she

could read lips a little after all. 'IS HE BEING DIPLOMATIC, AS WAS HIS JOB IN THE DAYS WHEN JAN SAT THE THRONE? NAH, NAH, TELL THE TRUTH, STEPHEN WOODLEIGH! LEAH WAS AS BEAUTIFUL AS A SUMMER MORNING AND THE OTHER FOUR WERE AS UGLY AS STONE BOATS! THOSE FOUR TOOK AFTER THEIR FATHER, BUT LEAH WAS HER MOTHER'S IMAGE!'

Again, *ugly as stone boats* wasn't exactly what she said but what I heard. I think I don't have to tell you that what I was hearing was another fairy tale. All it lacked was a glass slipper.

'The girls sharpened their already sharp tongues on Elden,' Woody said. 'Called him Stumpy and Deadfoot and Mr Squint and Grayface—'

'Grayface? Really?'

Woody gave a thin-lipped smile. 'You begin to see a bit of his revenge, do you not? Since Elden Flight Killer came to rule, Empis is populated almost solely by grayfaced people. He's rooting out the few who are immune to the curse, and he would kill every monarch butterfly if he could. He wants no flowers in his garden, only weeds.'

He leaned forward, clasping his knees, his pad of paper in one hand.

'But girls use only words. His brother terrorized Elden with punches and kicks when there was no one around to see but his loyal cadre of lickspittles. There was no need for it; Robert was as fair of face as Elden was ugly, he was petted and cosseted by his parents while Elden was largely ignored by them, and Robert had no cause for jealousy on account of the throne, since he was the older and bound to take it when Jan died or stepped down. He just hated and loathed his younger brother. I think . . .' He paused, frowning. 'I think there's always a reason for love, but sometimes hate just *is*. A kind of free-floating evil.'

I didn't reply, but thought of my two Rumpelstiltskins: Christopher Polley and Peterkin. Why had the dwarf gone to all the trouble of erasing the trail of initials that would have taken me out of the city long before dark? Why had he risked his life – and lost it – to point me out to Red Molly? Because I'd crossed him in the matter of the red cricket? Because I was tall and he was short? I didn't believe that for a minute. He'd done it because he could. And because he wanted to cause trouble.

Franna came back in and whispered in Woody's ear. He nodded.

'She says there's a church nearby that hasn't been destroyed. Leah has gone in there with Dora – the lady who mends the shoes – and a few others to sleep.'

I remembered seeing the church. 'Maybe that's good. She must be tired.' For Claudia's benefit I pointed to Franna at the door, then put my hands together and laid my head against them.

'TIRED? LEAH AND ALL OF US! WE'VE HAD A LONG TRIP, SOME OF THESE FOR MANY DAYS!'

'Go on, please,' I said to Woody. 'You were saying the girls hated Leah and Robert hated Elden—'

'They all hated Elden,' Woody said. 'All but Leah. There was a feeling at court that he wouldn't survive to twenty.'

I thought of the flabby, drooling thing in the VIP spectators' box, his complexion gone past gray to an even more unhealthy green, and wondered how old Elden was now. I also wondered what had been shifting around beneath that purple caftan-cum-robe . . . but wasn't sure I really wanted to know.

'The two youngest were driven together by the hate and dislike of the others, also because they genuinely loved each other, and . . . I think . . . because they were smarter. They explored almost every nook and cranny of the palace, from the tips of the spires where they were forbidden to go, but where they went anyway, to the lower levels.'

'Deep Maleen?'

'Likely, and deeper still. There are many ancient ways beneath the city where few have been for long years. I don't know if Leah was with him when he stumbled on the way to the Deep Well – she refuses to talk about the years when they began to grow out of their childhood – but they did go almost everywhere together, except perhaps for the palace library. Smart as she was, Leah was never a one for books; Elden was the reader of the two.'

'Bet his brother made fun of him for that, too,' Eye put in.

Woody turned to him and smiled. 'Truly said, you friend of Charlie. Robert and the sisters as well.'

'WHAT ARE YOU TELLING HIM NOW?' Claudia asked. Woody scribbled a brief recap on his pad. She read it, then said: 'TELL HIM ABOUT ELSA!'

I straightened up. 'The mermaid?'

'Yes,' Woody agreed. 'The palace mermaid. Did you by chance see her?'

I nodded. I wasn't going to say I'd seen what was left of her.

'She lived in a little hidden alcove,' Woody said. 'A grotto, almost. I'd like to believe she lives there still, but I very much doubt it. She's probably died of neglect or starvation. And, possibly, sadness.'

She had died, all right, but it hadn't been neglect, starvation, or sadness that had killed her.

'Elden and Leah fed her, and she sang to them. Strange songs, but beautiful. Leah used to sing some herself.' He paused. 'When she still had a mouth to sing with.'

I stroked Radar's head. She looked up at me sleepily. Our trip had been hard for her as well as for me, but for Rades things had turned out well. She had a new lease on life and was with people who loved her. Thinking about her escape made me think of how I had gotten the news of her survival.

'Tell me about the cricket,' I said to Claudia. 'The red cricket. Big as this.' I held my hands apart. 'I don't understand how it got to you. Did it come with Radar? And why—'

She gave me an exasperated look. 'DID YOU FORGET I CAN'T HEAR YOU, SHARLIE?'

I had, actually. I could tell you it was because her hair was down tonight, covering the sides of her head where her ears had been, but that wouldn't be true. I just forgot. So I told Woody about how I'd saved the red cricket from Peterkin, and how I'd later seen it coming out of a hole in the dungeon wall with a note stuck to its belly. One with a little bundle of Radar's fur folded inside. How I had attached my own note to it and sent it on its way, following my father's dictum: *expect nothing but never lose hope.*

'Good advice,' Woody said, and began to scratch on his pad. He wrote fast, every line amazingly straight. Outside the door, the gray-folk were settling in for the night, those who had brought blankets sharing them. Across the way I could see Falada tied to a hitching post outside the church and cropping grass.

Woody passed the pad to Claudia, and as she read what was written there, she began to smile. It made her beautiful. When she spoke it wasn't in her usual booming voice but in a much lower one, as if talking to herself.

She said, 'In spite of Elden's best efforts on behalf of the entity he serves – he may not believe he is that thing's tool, but he surely is – the magic survives. Because magic is hard to destroy. You've seen that for yourself, haven't you?'

I nodded and stroked Radar, who had been dying and was now young and strong again after her six turns on the sundial.

'Yes, the magic survives. He calls himself Flight Killer now, but you've seen for yourself that thousands, no, MILLIONS, of the monarchs still live. And while Elsa may be dead, the Snab still lives. Thanks to you, Sharlie.'

'The Snab?' Iota asked, sitting up straight. He smacked his forehead with the palm of one big hand. 'High gods, why didn't I know when I saw it?'

'When he came to me . . . oh, Sharlie . . . when he came . . .'

To my alarm, she began to weep.

'To HEAR again, Sharlie! Oh to HEAR again, even though not a human voice, was so WONDERFUL—'

Radar got up and padded across to her. Claudia put her head close to Radar's for a few moments, at the same time stroking her sides from neck to tail. Taking comfort. Woody put an arm around her. I thought about doing the same but didn't. Prince or not, I was too shy.

She raised her head and wiped the tears from her cheeks with the heels of her hands. When she resumed, it was at her usual volume.

'ELSA THE MERMAID SANG TO THE CHILDREN, DID STEPHEN TELL YOU THAT?'

'Yes,' I said, then remembered she was deaf and nodded.

'SHE WOULD SING TO ANY WHO STOPPED TO LISTEN, BUT ONLY IF THEY WOULD CLEAR THEIR MINDS OF OTHER THOUGHTS SO THEY COULD HEAR. ROBERT AND LEAH'S SISTERS HAD NO TIME FOR SUCH SILLINESS, BUT ELDEN AND LEAH WERE DIFFERENT. THEY WERE BEAUTIFUL SONGS, WEREN'T THEY, WOODY?'

'They were,' he said, although from the expression on his face I doubted if he'd had much time for Elsa's songs, either.

I tapped my forehead, then leaned forward and tapped hers. I raised my hands in a questioning gesture.

'YES, SHARLIE. NOT SONGS THAT COULD BE HEARD WITH EARS, FOR MERMAIDS CAN'T SPEAK.'

'But the cricket?' I made jumping gestures with a hand. 'The . . . what did you call it? A snab?'

I'll spare you Claudia's booming voice for a bit, shall I? The red cricket wasn't *a* snab, but *the* Snab. Claudia called him the king of the small world. I assumed then that she meant insects (*It's just a damn inseck*, Peterkin had said), but later I came to believe that the Snab might be the ruler of many of the creatures I'd seen. And like Elsa the mermaid, the Snab could speak to humans, and it had spoken to Claudia after accompanying Radar to her house. According to Claudia, the Snab made most of the trip riding on Radar's back. That was hard for me to picture, but I could understand why; the cricket was still recovering from an injured back leg, after all.

The Snab told her the dog's master had been either killed or taken prisoner in Lilimar. It had asked Claudia if there was anything it could do, beyond shepherding the dog safely back to her. Because, it said, the young man had saved its life and that sort of debt had to be repaid. It told her that if the young man were still alive, he would have been imprisoned in Deep Maleen, and it knew a way in.

'The Snab,' Iota said in a wondering voice. 'I saw the Snab and didn't even know. I'll be poked.'

'It didn't speak to *me*,' I said.

Woody smiled at that. 'Were you listening?'

Of course I hadn't been; my mind had been filled with my own thoughts . . . just as the minds of many who passed Elsa didn't hear her songs because they were too busy to listen. That much is true about songs (and many stories) even in my own world. They speak mind to mind, but only if you listen.

It occurred to me that I had not only been saved by a dream of my mother's hairdryer, but also by a cricket king to whom I had done a good turn. Remember when I said at the outset that no one would believe my story?

4

Woody and Claudia were tired, I could see that, even Radar was now snoozing, but there was more I needed to know. 'What did Leah mean about the moons kissing?'

Woody said, 'Perhaps your friend can tell you.'

Iota was eager to do so. He had been told the story of the sky-sisters as a child, and as you probably know for yourself, dear reader, it's the stories of our childhood that make the deepest impressions and last the longest.

'They chase each other, as everyone has seen. Or did, before the clouds came so thick and constant.' He glanced at Woody's scars. 'Those with eyes, anyway. Sometimes it's Bella in the lead, sometimes Arabella. Most of the time one leads the other by a lot, but then the distance begins to close.'

I had seen that for myself on the occasions when the clouds rifted apart.

'Eventually one passes the other, and on that night they merge and appear to kiss.'

'In the old days it was told by men of wisdom that someday they'll actually collide,' Woody said, 'and both will be smashed to bits. They might not even need to collide for them to be destroyed; their mutual attraction might pull them to pieces. As sometimes happens in human lives.'

Iota had no interest in such philosophical postulates. He said, 'Tis also told that on the night when the sky-sisters kiss, every evil thing is set free to work wickedness on the world.' He paused. 'When I was a youngster we were forbidden to go out on nights when the sisters kissed. The wolves howled, the wind howled, but not just the wolves and the wind.' He looked at me somberly. 'Charlie, the *world* howled. As if it was in pain.'

'And Elden can open this Deep Well when it happens? That's the legend?'

No answer from Woody or Eye, but the looks on their faces was enough to tell me that, as far as they were concerned, it was no legend.

'And a creature lives in this Deep Well? The thing that turned Elden into the Flight Killer?'

'Yes,' Woody said. 'You know its name. And if you do, you know that even saying that name is dangerous.'

I *did* know.

'LISTEN TO ME, SHARLIE!' At Claudia's bellowing, toneless voice Radar opened her eyes and lifted her head, then lowered it again. 'TOMORROW WE GO INTO THE CITY AND RE-TAKE IT WHILE THE NIGHT SOLDIERS ARE AT THEIR WEAKEST! LEAH WILL LEAD US, AS IS HER RIGHT, BUT YOU MUST FIND ELDEN AND SLAY HIM BEFORE HE CAN OPEN THE WELL! IT SHOULD BE LEAH, SHE IS THE RIGHTFUL HEIR TO THE THRONE AND AS SUCH IT SHOULD BE HER TASK . . . HER BURDEN . . . BUT . . .'

She didn't want to say the rest any more than she wanted to speak the name of Gogmagog, the lurker in the Deep Well. And she didn't have to. Leah was firm in her belief that her beloved brother, with whom she had listened to the songs of the mermaid, couldn't be the Flight Killer. In spite of all she must have heard and all she herself was suffering, it was easier for her to believe Elden was dead, that the monster who ruled over the ruins of Lilimar and its few remaining inhabitants was an imposter who had taken his name. If she discovered it was indeed Elden, and found him somewhere deep in the maze of tunnels and catacombs far below, she might hesitate.

And be murdered, as so many of her relatives had been.

'YOU ARE THE PRINCE WHO HAS BEEN PROMISED,' Claudia said. 'YOU HAVE ALL THE SENSES OF WHICH WE HAVE BEEN ROBBED. YOU ARE ADRIAN'S HEIR, HE WHO CAME FROM THE MAGIC WORLD. YOU ARE THE ONE WHO MUST KILL ELDEN BEFORE HE CAN OPEN THAT HELLPIT!'

Iota was listening with wide eyes and a dropped jaw. It was Woody who broke the silence. He spoke quietly, but each word hit me like a blow.

'Here is the worst thing, the worst possibility: what went back into the Deep Well once may not go back again. By opening it, Elden risks not just the graying of our world, but its total destruction. And then? Who knows where that thing might go?'

He leaned forward until his eyeless face was inches from mine.

'Empis . . . Bella . . . Arabella . . . there are other worlds than these, Charlie.'

Indeed there were. Hadn't I come from one of them?

I think that's when the coldness started to come over me, the one I remembered from the worst of my outings with Bertie Bird. And from Polley, when I'd broken first one of his hands and then the other. And from Cla. I had thrown the drumstick at him and said *I'm going to fuck you up, honey*. Which I did, and without regret. I was no Disney prince, and maybe that was good. A Disney prince wasn't what the people of Empis needed.

5

Claudia and Woody were asleep. So were the grayfolk who had come with them. They'd had an arduous trip, and more work for them lay ahead in the day – or days – to follow. I, on the other hand, had never felt more awake, and not just because my waking and sleeping hours had been turned upside-down. I had a thousand unanswered questions. The most terrible was what Gogmagog might do if it got out of its well. I was haunted by the idea that it might come to our world, just as the oversized cockroach had done.

The roach that started it all, I thought, and almost laughed.

I went outside. The sounds of the sleepers – grunts, moans, the occasional fart – reminded me of my nights in Deep Maleen. I sat against the wall of the shed and looked up at the sky, hoping for a break in the clouds, just enough to see a single star or two, possibly even Bella and Arabella, but there was only blankness. Which in daytime would be more gray. Across Kingdom Road, Falada continued to graze outside of the church. A few dying campfires illuminated more sleepers over there. There had to be a hundred people now, at least. Not yet an army, but getting there.

Shadows moved beside me. I turned and saw Eye and Radar. Eye squatted on his hunkers. Rades sat beside him, her nose moving delicately as she took in the scents of the night.

'Can't sleep?' I asked.

'Nah, nah. The clock inside my head's all wrong.'

Join the club, I thought.

'How often do the moons pass overhead?'

He considered. 'Three times a night at least, sometimes ten.'

This made no sense to me, because I lived in a world where the clock of the universe always ran on time. Moonrise and moonset could be predicted to a nicety ten, fifty, a hundred years in advance. This was not that world. This was a world where mermaids and a red cricket called the Snab could project songs and thoughts into the heads of those who listened.

'I wish I could see them. See how close together they really are.'

'Well, you can't, but you may see their glow through the clouds when they pass. The brighter the glow, the closer they be. But why bother? Unless you think the princess was lying about what she saw?'

I shook my head. There had been no mistaking the look of alarm on Leah's face.

'Is it true you come from another world?' Iota asked abruptly. 'A magic world? I think it must be so, because I've never seen a weapon like the one you wear on your hip.' He paused. 'I've never seen a one like you, either. I thank the high gods I didn't have to stand against you in the first round of the Fair One. I wouldn't be here.'

'You'd have laid me out, Eye.'

'Nah, nah. You're a prince, all right. I never would have thought it at first, but you are. There's something in you that's as hard as old paint.'

And dark, I thought. *My own dark well, of which I'd do well to beware.*

'Could you find him?' he asked, stroking Radar's head with one big scarred hand. 'We can take care of the rest, I've no doubt – with the night soldiers in their daylight weakness and not able to protect them, Elden's little crew of asslickers will run like the rabbits they are, and we'll slaughter them like rabbits – but Flight Killer! Can you find him, if he's gone deep? Do you have, I dunno . . . some . . .'

Spidey sense was what I thought, but not what came out of my mouth. 'Some princey sense?'

He laughed at that but said yes, he supposed that was what he meant.

'I don't.'

'What about Pursey? The one who helped us? Could he find his way to the Dark Well?'

I considered the idea, then shook my head. I hoped like hell that

Pursey was still alive, but knew the chances were small. Kellin would know we hadn't escaped on our own. He might give me credit for the lethal trick with the buckets of water, but knowing about the door with the cabinet in front of it? That had to have come from an insider. And even if Pursey had so far escaped death and the torture chamber's inducements to talk, the chances of him knowing the way to the Dark Well were small.

We were in deep shadow where not even the flickering light of the last dying campfires could reach, so I took another sulphur match from my sock and scratched it on the side of the building. I brushed back my hair and held it in front of my eyes. 'What do you see? Still hazel?'

Iota leaned close. 'Nah. Blue. Bright blue, my prince.'

I wasn't surprised. 'Call me Charlie,' I said, and shook out the match. 'As for the world I came from . . . I think all worlds are magic. We just get used to it.'

'What now?'

'For me? I'm going to wait. You can wait with me or go back inside and try to sleep.'

'I'll stay.'

'We will, too,' someone said. I turned and saw the two women, Eris and Jaya. It was Eris who had spoken. 'What are we waiting for, my prince?'

'Call him Charlie,' Eye said. 'He likes it better. Modest, you know. Like a prince in a story.'

'We'll see what I'm waiting for, or we won't. Now be quiet.'

We were quiet. Crickets – presumably not red ones – sang in the weeds and in the rubble of the ruined suburb that sprawled outside the city. We breathed free air. It was good. Time passed. Falada cropped, then merely stood with her head down, presumably dozing. Radar was fast asleep. After awhile Jaya pointed at the sky. Behind the massed clouds, two bright lights were passing, traveling at high speed. The lights weren't touching – kissing – but even with the cloud cover we could see they were very, very close. They passed behind the triple spires of the palace and were gone. The circle of gas-jets ringing the stadium had gone out. The city was dark, but inside the wall, the remaining night soldiers would be patrolling.

An hour passed, then two. My interior clock was as wrong as Iota's, but it had to be closing on first light when what I had been expecting – what the dark part of my nature had been hoping for – happened. Princess Leah emerged from the church. With the pants and boots and short sword, it could be no one else. Eye sat up straight and opened his mouth. I put a hand on his chest and raised a finger to my lips. We watched as she untied Falada and led her toward the city gate, keeping her clear of the cobbled surface of the road, where the clop of her hooves might alert some light sleeper. The princess was little more than a darker shape in the darkness when she mounted up.

I stood. 'No one needs to go with me,' I said, 'but after all we've been through, I won't stop you if you decide to come.'

'Right beside you,' Eye said.

'I'll go,' Eris said.

Jaya merely nodded.

'Not you, Radar,' I said. 'Stay with Claudia.'

Her ears drooped. Her tail stopped wagging. There was no mistaking the hope and pleading in those eyes.

'No,' I said. 'One trip to the Lily is all you get.'

'Woman's getting ahead of us, Charlie,' Eye said. 'And the main gate is close. If we're going to catch up with her—'

'Walk, but slowly. We've got plenty of time. She won't try entering until daylight. She wants to see with her own eyes that the Flight Killer isn't her brother, and I imagine she'd like to save Elden if he still lives, but she's not stupid. We'll catch up to her before she goes in and I'll persuade her to join us.'

'How will you do that?' Eris asked.

'By any means necessary.' No one said anything to that. 'Elden may be at the Dark Well already, waiting for the moons to kiss. We have to get there and stop him before it happens.'

'By any means necessary,' Eris said, low.

'What if Leah don't know the way?' Iota asked.

'Then,' I said, 'we're hung.'

'My prince,' Jaya said. 'Charlie, I mean.' She turned and pointed.

Radar was padding along behind us. She saw me looking and raced to catch up. I knelt and took her head in my hands. 'Disobedient dog! Will you go back?'

She only looked at me.

I sighed and stood up. 'All right. Come along.'

She walked at my heel, and that was how we four – five, counting Radar – advanced on the haunted city.

6

The gate was close – looming – when something jumped out at us from a ruined building on the left side of the road. I drew Mr Bowditch's .45, but before I could bring it up, let alone aim, the shape took a large (but still slightly crooked) leap and landed on Radar's back. It was the Snab. We were astonished; Radar wasn't. She had carried this passenger before and seemed perfectly willing to do it again. The Snab settled on her neck, like a lookout.

I saw no sign of Leah and Falada camped outside the gate. I didn't like that. I stopped, trying to decide what to do next. The Snab jumped down from its mount, went almost to the gate, then turned right. Radar followed, nosed at the cricket (who didn't seem to mind), then looked back at us to see if we were coming.

A paved path, perhaps meant for maintenance in the old days, led through the rubble near the outside of the wall, which here was covered with shags of ivy. The Snab led the way, jumping through weeds and nimbly hurdling spilled bricks. After no more than a hundred steps I saw a white shape in the dark ahead of us. It let out a whicker. Sitting beside Falada, cross-legged and waiting for dawn, was Princess Leah. She saw the cricket first, then the rest of us. She got to her feet and stood facing us with her hand on the hilt of her sword and her feet apart, as if ready for combat.

Falada spoke, but dispensed with the third person. 'So. Sir Snab has led you to me. And now that you've found me, you must go back.'

'Who keeps your geese, my lady, while you are away?'

Not what I expected to say and not the way Charlie Reade of Sentry, Illinois, would have said anything.

Her eyes widened, then crinkled a bit at the corners. With no mouth it was hard to be sure, but I think she was amused as well as surprised. Falada said, 'My mistress's men, Whit and Dickon, keep them very well.'

As in Dick Whittington, I thought.

Jaya: 'Does that horse—'

Leah waved her to silence. Jaya shrank back and dropped her eyes. 'Now that your foolish question has been answered, leave us. I have serious business.'

I looked into her upturned face, beautiful except for the scar where her mouth should have been and the ugly sore beside it.

'Have you eaten?' I asked. 'Because you have to be strong for what's ahead, my lady.'

'I've taken what I need,' Falada said. I could see Leah's throat working with the effort it took to throw her voice. 'Now go – I command you.'

I took her hands. They were small in mine, and cold. She was putting up a good front – the haughty princess in total control – but I thought she was scared to death. She tried to pull her hands back. I held on.

'No, Leah. It's I who commands you. I'm the promised prince. I think you know that.'

'Not the prince of this world,' Falada said, and now I could hear the clicks and mumbles in Leah's throat. Her polite speech was of necessity rather than desire. If she hadn't been forced – and with great effort – to speak through the mare, she would have torn me a new one. There was no amusement in her eyes now, just fury. This woman who fed the geese from her apron was used to being obeyed without question.

'No,' I agreed. 'Not the prince of this world, and not a prince in mine, but I have spent long days in a dungeon, I've been forced to kill, and I've seen my companions die. Do you understand me, Princess? Do you understand my *right* to command you?'

Falada said nothing. One tear fell from Leah's left eye and made a slow path down her smooth cheek.

'Walk with me a little way, please.'

She shook her head violently enough to make her hair fly around her face. Again she tried to pull her hands away and again I held them.

'There's time, at least an hour before first light, and your whole world may depend on what we say one to the other. Even mine may be at risk. So *please*.'

I let go of her hands. I took one of the remaining sulphur matches from my sock. I pushed some of the ivy aside, struck the match on the rough stone, and held it in front of my face as I'd done with Iota. She stood on tiptoe to peer at me, close enough that I could have kissed her upturned brow.

'Blue,' Falada said.

'It *does* talk,' Eris murmured.

'Nah, nah, it's her,' Iota said in the same low voice. They were awestruck. I was, too, and why not? There was magic here, and now I was part of it. That terrified me, because I was no longer entirely myself, but it also exalted me.

'Come, lady. We need to talk. Please come.'

She did.

7

We went a little way down the path from the others, the ivy-covered city wall on our left, the rubble of the destroyed suburb on our right, the dark sky above us.

'We need to stop him,' I said. 'Before he brings some terrible cataclysm.'

Radar was walking between us with the Snab perched on her neck, and it was the Snab who answered. This voice was much clearer than the one Leah used when she was speaking through Falada. 'It is not my brother. Flight Killer is *not* Elden. He would never do such terrible things. He was gentle and loving.'

People change, I thought. *My father did, and I did when I was with Bertie. I remember wondering why a good person like me was doing such shitty things.*

'If he lives,' the Snab said, 'he's a prisoner. But I don't believe that. I believe he's dead, like so many of my family.'

'I believe that, too,' I said. It was no lie, because surely the Elden she had known – the one who held her hand as they explored the secret ways of the palace, the one who listened to the songs the mermaid sang – that Elden *was* dead. All that remained was Gogmagog's puppet.

We stopped. Her throat worked and the Snab spoke. So much ventriloquism had to be hurting her, even though the Snab was her most ideal conduit, but she had to say what she'd held in her heart for so long.

'If he's a prisoner, I'll set him free. If he's dead, I will avenge him, that the curse on this sad land might be lifted. This is my job and not yours, you son of Adrian Bowditch.'

I wasn't his son, only his heir, but this didn't seem to be the time to tell her that.

'Flight Killer has almost certainly gone to the Dark Well, Princess. There he'll wait until the moons kiss and the way is opened. Can you find it?'

She nodded but looked uncertain.

'Will you lead us there? Because there's no way we can find it by ourselves. Would you, if I promise to leave Flight Killer's fate to you when we face him?'

For a long time there was no answer. She wasn't sure I'd keep my promise, and she was right to be unsure. If she recognized Elden and couldn't bring herself to kill him – even the way he was now – would I honor her wish and let him live? I thought of Dora's ruined face and honest heart. I thought of Pursey's bravery, for which he had most likely already paid a high price. I thought of the gray refugees I'd seen making their way from Seafront to some place of refuge that probably didn't exist. Put those wounded and becursed people on one side of a scale and a princess's tender heart on the other, and there was no way they would balance.

Would you really give Leah of the Gallien such a promise?

I didn't think that was a return to the third person; I think the Snab might have been speaking for itself that time, but I had no doubt that Leah wanted to know the same thing.

'I would.'

She said, 'Do you promise on the soul of your mother, that she might burn in the fires of hell if you break your word?'

'I do,' I said without hesitation, and that was a promise I meant to keep. When Leah saw what her brother had become, she might kill him herself. I could hope for that. If not, I'd give Mr Bowditch's gun to Iota. He had never fired one before, but I didn't expect any trouble on that account; guns are like cheap cameras, all you have to do is point and shoot.

You and your friends will follow Leah, and obey her?

'We will.'

She probably knew she couldn't stop me from following her. The others might obey a command from Empis's queen-in-waiting, but I wouldn't. As she had already said, through Falada, I was not a prince of this world, and not bound by her commands.

Overhead, the sky brightened. We humans looked up. So did Radar. Even the Snab did. Bright orbs lit the clouds. The moons were now so close together they looked like a figure-eight lying on its side. Or the eternity symbol. In mere seconds they passed behind the palace spires and the sky was dark again.

'All right,' the Snab said. 'I agree to your terms. No more talk, please. It hurts.'

'I know,' I said. 'And I'm sorry.'

Radar whined and licked Leah's hand. Leah bent and stroked her. The pact was made.

CHAPTER TWENTY-EIGHT

Into the City. The Sound of Mourning. Hana. She Who Once Sang. Gold. The Kitchen. The Receiving Chamber. We Must Go Up to Go Down.

1

Leah led us back to where the others waited. She sat down again without a word from Falada or the Snab. Iota looked at me. I nodded – done deal. We sat down with her and waited for dawn. It started to rain again, not hard but steadily. Leah took a poncho from the single saddlebag Falada carried and slipped it over her shoulders. She beckoned to Radar, who looked at me for permission, then went to Leah. She flapped the poncho over her. The Snab went, too. They were dry. The rest of us, dressed in the rags we'd escaped wearing, got wet. Jaya began to shiver. Eris hugged her. I told them they could go back. Both women shook their heads. Iota didn't bother, just sat with his head bowed and his hands clasped.

Time passed. There came a moment when I looked up and realized I could see Leah. I raised a hand to her in question. She only shook her head. At last, when the day had brightened to a watery dawn, she got to her feet and tied Falada to a piece of iron that jutted from the remains of a brick wall rising from the rubble. She started down the path without looking to see if we were following. The Snab was on Radar's back again. Leah walked slowly, occasionally brushing aside the thick growth of ivy, looking, then moving on. After five minutes or so, she stopped and began to tear at the vines. I moved to help her, but she shook her head. We had an agreement – a pact – but it was clear she wasn't happy about it.

She pulled away more of the ivy and I saw the small door that had been hiding behind it. There was no latch, no knob. She beckoned to me and pointed at it. For a moment I didn't know what was expected of me. Then I did.

'Open in the name of Leah of the Gallien,' I said, and the door swung open.

2

We entered a long barnlike building filled with ancient maintenance equipment. The shovels, hoes, and wheelbarrows were all covered in a thick pall of dust. The floor was also dusty, and there were no tracks except for the ones we left behind us. I spotted another of those bus/cart hybrids. I looked into it and saw a battery so corroded it was just a green lump. I wondered where these little vehicles – two at least, one still operative – had come from. Had Mr Bowditch brought in equipment from our world piecemeal and assembled it here? I didn't know. All I knew for sure was that the present regime cared little about keeping Lilimar neat and tidy. What it cared about were blood sports.

Leah led us out a door on the far side. We found ourselves in a kind of junkyard filled with disassembled trolleys, piles of power poles, and great snarls of trolley wires. We weaved our way through this useless equipment, up a set of wooden steps, and into a room I and the other escapees recognized: the trolley storage area.

We were crossing the main terminal when the morning bell rang its one reverberating *BONG*. Leah stopped until the sound faded away, then went on. She still didn't look back to see if we were following.

Our footfalls echoed. Overhead a dark cloud of giant bats fluttered their wings but didn't stir otherwise.

'Last time we were going,' Eris said in a low voice. 'This time we're coming. I've got a score of my own to settle with that bitch.'

I didn't reply. I wasn't interested. My mind was fixed.

We went out into the rain. Radar suddenly bolted down the Trolley House steps and past one of the red and white posts with its stone butterfly on top. She nosed into the brambles. I saw one strap of my discarded backpack, then heard the last thing I would have expected but one I recognized at once. Radar came trotting back with her squeaky monkey. She dropped it at my feet and looked up at me, wagging her tail.

'Good girl,' I said, and gave it to Eye. He had pockets. I didn't. The broad way leading to the palace was deserted but not empty. Red Molly's body was gone, but the bones of the night soldiers who'd come after us were scattered for forty yards, most buried under heaps of dead monarch butterflies.

Leah had stopped at the foot of the steps, head cocked, listening. We joined her. I could hear it, too: a kind of high moaning, like wind gusting around the eaves on a winter night. It rose and fell, rose and fell, climbed to a shriek, then subsided to moaning again.

'High gods, what is it?' Jaya whispered.

'The sound of mourning,' I said.

'Where's the Snab?' Iota asked.

I shook my head. 'Didn't like the rain, maybe.'

Leah started up the Gallien Road toward the palace. I put a hand on her shoulder and stopped her. 'We should go in from behind and come out near the games field. I can't find the way, a little shit named Peterkin wiped away Mr Bowditch's marks, but I bet you know how to get there.'

Leah put her hands on her slim hips and stared at me with exasperation. She pointed toward the sound of Hana grieving her daughter. Then, in case I was too thick to understand, she raised her hands high above her head.

'The princess is right, Charlie,' Iota said. 'Why go that way if we can avoid the big bitch by going in the front door?'

I took his point, but there were other points that seemed more important to me. 'Because she eats human flesh. I'm pretty sure it's why she was kicked out of giantland, whatever you call it around here. Do you understand that? *She eats human flesh*. And she serves *him*.'

Leah looked up into my eyes. Very slowly, she nodded and pointed to the gun I wore.

'Yes,' I said. 'And there's another reason, my lady. Something I need you to see.'

3

We went a little way further up the Gallien Road, then Leah turned left into a byway so narrow it wasn't much more than an alley. She led us through a maze of streets, never hesitating. I hoped she knew what she was doing; it had been many years since she'd been here. On the other hand, we had Hana's howls of grief to guide us.

Jaya and Eris caught up to me. Eris looked grim, set. Jaya looked freaked out. She said, 'The buildings don't stay steady. I know that's crazy, but they don't. Every time I look away, I see them change out of the corner of my eye.'

'And I keep thinking I hear voices,' Eye said. 'This place feels . . . I dunno . . . haunted.'

'Because it is,' I said. 'We're going to exorcise it, or die trying.'

'Exercise?' Eris asked. Hana's howling grew steadily louder.

'Never mind,' I said. 'One thing at a time.'

Leah led us down an alley where the buildings were so close together it felt like we were slipping through a crevasse. I could see the bricks of one building and the stone of the other moving slowly in and out, as if they were breathing.

We emerged on a street I recognized. It was the boulevard with the weedy median running down the middle and what might once have been high-end shops catering to royals and royal hangers-on lining the sides. Iota reached out to touch (or maybe pick) one of the enormous yellow flowers and I grabbed his wrist. 'You don't want to do that, Eye. They bite.'

He looked at me. 'Truly?'

'Truly.'

Now I could see the roofpeaks of Hana's enormous street-straddling house. Leah moved to her right and began sidling along the broken shopfronts, looking through the rain at the deserted square with its dry fountain. Hana's cries of grief were now just short of unbearable each time her sobs rose and became shrieks. Leah looked back at last. She beckoned me forward, but patted the air with one hand: *softly, softly*.

I bent down to Radar and whispered for her to hush. Then I joined the princess.

Hana was on her bejeweled throne. Across her lap was the body of her daughter. Red Molly's head lolled on one side of the throne, her legs hung down on the other. There were no songs about Joe my love this morning. Hana stroked Molly's orange bristles, then raised her lumpy face into the rain and let out another howl. She put one meaty arm beneath the fallen woman's neck, raised her head, and covered Molly's forehead and the remains of her blood-spattered mouth with kisses.

Leah pointed to her, then raised her hands to me, palms out: *What next?*

This, I thought, and began walking across the square toward where Hana sat. One hand was on the butt of Mr Bowditch's gun. I didn't realize Radar was with me until she began to bark. They came full-throated, from deep in her chest, with a snarl each time she drew breath. Hana looked up and saw us coming.

'Steady, girl,' I said. 'With me.'

Hana cast the body aside and rose. One of Red Molly's hands landed in a litter of small bones. '*YOU!*' she screamed, her bosom rising in a groundswell. '*YOUUUU!*'

'That's right,' I said. 'Me. I am the prince that was promised, so kneel before me and accept your fate.'

I didn't expect her to obey, and I wasn't wrong. She came at me in leaping strides. Five would bring her to me. I allowed her three, because I didn't want to miss. I wasn't afraid. That darkness had come over me. It was cold, but clear. I suppose that's a paradox, but I stand by it. I could see that red-rimmed crack running down the center of her forehead, and as she blotted out the sky above me, screaming something – I don't know what – I put two bullets into it. The .45

revolver was to Polley's .22 what a shotgun is to a kid's popgun. Her boil-infested forehead caved in like a snow-crust when someone stamps on it with a heavy boot. The brown snaggles of her hair flew out in back, along with a fan of blood. Her mouth fell open, revealing filed teeth that would no more rend and chew the flesh of children.

Her arms flew up into the gray sky. Rain ran down her fingers. I could smell gunsmoke, strong and acrid. She blundered in a half-circle, as if for one more look at her dear one. Then she collapsed. I felt the thud run through the stones under my feet when she landed.

Thus fell Hana the giantess, who guarded the sundial, the pool, and the entrance to the Field of the Monarchs behind Lilimar Palace.

4

Iota was standing in front of the right wing of Hana's house – the kitchen wing. With him was a gray man with almost no face left; it was as if the flesh had come loose from his skull and slid downward, engulfing one eye and all of his nose. He was dressed in a bloodstained white blouse and white pants. I assumed he was – had been – Hana's cook, the one she'd called a cockless bastard. I had no problem with him. My business was in the palace.

But Leah's business with Hana wasn't done, it seemed. She walked toward the fallen giantess, drawing her sword. Blood was pooling around Hana's head and running between the stones.

Eris stepped forward and took Leah's arm. Leah turned, and her expression needed no words: *How dare you touch me?*

'Nah, my Lady of Gallien, I mean no disrespect, but stay just a moment. Please. For me.'

Leah seemed to consider, then stepped back.

Eris went to the giant and spread her feet in order to walk up one of those enormous splayed legs. She hiked up her filthy skirt and pissed on the slack white flesh of Hana's thigh. When she stepped away, tears were rolling down her cheeks. She turned to face us.

'I came south from the village of Wayva, a place no one has heard of nor ever will, because this devil-cunt laid waste to it, killing dozens. One was my grandda'. The other was my mother. Now do what you will, my lady.' And Eris actually dropped a curtsey.

I went over to stand with Iota and the cook, who was trembling all over. Eye brought his palm to his forehead as he looked at me and the cook did the same. 'You brought down not one giant but two,' Iota said. 'If I live long – I know the chances are small – I'll never forget it. Or Eris pissing on her. Surprised your dog don't want to have a go.'

Leah stepped to the giant's side, raised her sword high above her head, and brought it down. She was a princess and the heir to the throne, but she had been doing the work of a farmwoman in exile, and she was strong. Still, it took her three swipes of the blade to sever Hana's head.

She knelt, wiped her blade on a swatch of the giant's purple dress, and re-sheathed it. She stepped to Iota, who bent and saluted her. When he straightened, she pointed to the twenty feet of dead giant, then to the dry fountain.

'At your command, my lady, and more than willing.'

He went to the body. Strong as he was, big as he was, he still had to use both hands to lift the head. It swung back and forth as he carried it to the fountain. Eris didn't see; she was weeping in Jaya's arms.

Iota gave a loud grunt – '*HUT!*' – and his shirt split up the sides as he heaved the head. It landed in the fountain, staring up open-eyed into the rain. Like the gargoyle I'd passed on my way in.

5

We went along one of the pinwheel paths, this time with me leading. The back of the palace loomed over us, and again I knew it as a living thing. Dozing, perhaps, but with one eye open. I could swear some of the turrets had moved to new locations. The same was true of the crisscrossing stairways and the parapets, which looked like stone at one eyeblink and deep green glass filled with writhing black shapes at the next. I thought about Edgar Allan Poe's poem about the haunted palace, where a hideous throng rushed out forever, to laugh but smile no more.

Here Mr Bowditch's initials remained. Looking at them was like meeting a friend in a bad place. We came to the red loading doors with their traffic jam of wrecked wagons, then to the dark green flying buttresses. I led my party around them, and although it took a little longer, I heard no objections.

'More voices,' Iota said, low. 'Hear em?'

'Yes,' I said.

'What are they? Demons? The dead?'

'I don't think they can hurt us. But there's power here, no doubt, and not good power.'

I looked at Leah, who made a rapid circling gesture with her right hand: *Hurry*. I understood that. We couldn't waste this precious daylight, but I had to show her. She had to see, because seeing is the start of understanding. Of accepting a long-denied truth.

6

Our curving walkway brought us close to the pool surrounded by its ring of palms, their fronds now lying limp in the rain. I could see the high pole in the center of the sundial, but it was no longer topped with the sun. Because of Radar's trip on it, the sun had ended up facing the other way. It was now showing the two moons of Empis. They also had faces and the eyes also moved . . . toward each other, as if estimating the distance left between them. I could see Mr Bowditch's final mark, **AB**, with an arrow from the top of the **A** pointing straight ahead toward the sundial.

And the pool.

I turned to my little party. 'Princess Leah, please come with me. The rest of you stay until I call.' I bent to Radar. 'You too, girl. Stay.'

There were no questions or protests.

Leah walked beside me. I led her to the pool and gestured for her to look. She saw what remained of the mermaid lying below water now fouled with decomposition. She saw the shaft of the spear protruding from Elsa's midriff, and the coil of intestines floating up from it.

Leah gave a muffled groan that would have been a scream if it had been able to escape her. She put her hands over her eyes and collapsed on one of the benches where Empisarians who had made the trek from their towns and villages might once have sat to marvel at the beautiful creature swimming in the pool, and perhaps to listen to a song. She bent over her thighs, still making those muffled groaning sounds, which to me were more terrible – more bereft – than actual sobs would have been. I put my hand on her back, suddenly afraid that her inability to fully voice her grief might kill her, the way an unlucky person could choke to death on a lodgment of food in the throat.

At last she lifted her head, looked at the dull gray remains of Elsa again, then raised her face to the sky. Rain and tears ran down her smooth cheeks, across the scar of her mouth, over the red sore she had to massage open to eat despite the pain that had to entail. She raised her fists to the gray sky and shook them.

I took her hands gently in my own. It was like holding rocks. At last they loosened and clasped mine. I waited until she looked at me.

'Flight Killer murdered her. If he didn't do it himself, he ordered it done. Because she was beautiful, and the force that governs him hates all beauty – the monarchs, good people like Dora who were once whole people, the very land you are meant to rule over. What *he* loves is violence and pain and murder. He loves *gray*. When we find him – *if* we find him – will you kill him if I should fall?'

She looked at me doubtfully, her eyes swimming with tears. At last she nodded.

'Even if it's Elden?'

She shook her head as violently as before and pulled her hands free of mine. And from the pool where the dead mermaid lay came Leah's thrown voice, mournful and trembling: 'He would never kill Elsa. He loved her.'

Well, I thought, *that's not exactly a no.*

Time was passing. Hours of daylight still remained, but I didn't know if the moons needed to kiss above Empis for the Dark Well to open; for all I knew they could pass on the other side of the world with the same terrible result. The eyes of Bella and Arabella on the sundial's high centerpost tick-tocked back and forth as if to underline this idea.

I turned and called for the others.

7

We walked around the sundial, but with an exception: Radar walked across it, stopping just long enough to piss beside the centerpost, which made me think of Eris and the fallen giant.

The pinwheel paths merged into the broad central path. It ended at seven doors. I tried the one in the middle and found it locked. I told it to open in the name of Leah of the Gallien, the Empisarian version of *open sesame*, and it did. That I had expected, but something else happened that I had not. The building seemed to recoil at the sound of the princess's name. I didn't see it so much as I felt it, as I had felt the thud in my feet when Hana's six or seven hundred pounds of newly dead weight crashed to the ground.

The tangle of whispering voices, heard not so much with ears as in the center of the head, suddenly stopped. I wasn't foolish enough to believe the entire palace had been cleansed – *exorcised* was the word I'd used to Iota – but it was clear to me that not only the Flight Killer had power. *It would be stronger if she could speak herself*, I thought, but of course she couldn't.

Inside the doors was a vast lobby. Once, like the Trolley House, it had been decorated with a circular mural, but it had been splashed with black paint so that nothing remained but a few high-flying monarchs near the ceiling. I thought again of ISIS zealots destroying the cultural artifacts of civilizations that had gone before them.

In the center of the lobby were a number of red-painted kiosks, not much different from the ones my dad and I had passed through many times at Guaranteed Rate Field when we went to Chicago to see the White Sox play. 'I know where we are,' Iota muttered. He pointed. 'Wait, Charlie. One minute.'

He pounded up one of the ramps, looked, and ran back.

'The seats are empty. So is the field. They've all gone. Bodies, as well.'

Leah gave him an impatient look that seemed to ask what else had he expected, then led us to the left. We traveled a circular hallway past a number of shuttered booths that almost had to be concessions. Radar padded beside me. If there was trouble, I expected she'd sense it first, but so far she seemed alert but calm. Just past the last of the booths, I stopped, staring. The others did, as well. Only Leah displayed no interest in what so amazed me. She went on a little way before she realized we weren't following. She made that circular *hurry* gesture again, but for the moment we were frozen.

Here the stone sidewall had been replaced by a panel of curving glass at least thirty feet long. It was dusty – everything in the palace was dusty – but we could still see what was inside, lit by a line of overhead gas-jets, hooded so they acted as spotlights. I was looking into a vault heaped with drifts of gold pellets like the ones I'd found in Mr Bowditch's safe. They had to be worth billions of American dollars. Among them, scattered carelessly, were gems: opals, pearls, emeralds, diamonds, rubies, sapphires. Mr Heinrich, the old limping jeweler, would have had a heart attack.

'My God,' I whispered.

Eris, Jaya, and Iota seemed interested but not even close to gobsmacked.

'I've heard of this,' Iota said. 'It's the treasury, ain't it, my lady? The treasury of Empis.'

Leah nodded impatiently and gestured for us to come. She was right, we had to move on, but I stayed a few moments longer, drinking in that enormous cache of wealth. I thought of my many trips to see the White Sox, and that one special Sunday to see the Bears play at Soldier Field. Both stadiums had glassed-in displays of memorabilia, and I thought this might be something similar: on their way to whatever game or games they'd come to see, the common ruck could stop to gape at the riches of the kingdom, no doubt protected by the King's Guard during the reign of the Galliens, more recently by Hana. I didn't know how Mr Bowditch had gained access to it, but what he'd taken, with permission or without it, was no more than a drop in the bucket. So to speak.

Leah gestured more strongly – both hands tossed back over her shoulders. We followed her. I took one look back, thinking that if I jumped into one of those drifts, I'd be in gold up to my neck. Then I thought of King Midas, who died of starvation – according to the fairy tale – because everything he tried to eat turned to gold when he touched it.

8

Further down the corridor I began to catch a faint aroma that brought back unpleasant memories of Deep Maleen: sausages. We came to open double doors on the left. Beyond was a huge kitchen with a line of ovens set in brick, three stoves, spits for turning meat, and sinks big enough to bathe in. This was where the food was prepared for the crowds that came on game days. The oven doors were open, the stove-burners dark, and there was nothing turning on the spits, but the ghostly aroma of sausages lingered. *I'll never eat another one as long as I live*, I thought. *Maybe not steak, either.*

Four gray men cringed against the far wall. They were wearing baggy pants and blouses similar to the ones Pursey had worn, but none of them were Pursey. At the sight of us, one of these unfortunates raised his apron and covered what remained of his face. The others only stared, their half-erased features showing varying degrees of dismay and fright. I went in, shrugging off Leah's attempt to pull me on down the passage. One by one the members of the kitchen crew fell to their knees and raised their palms to their foreheads.

'Nah, nah, stand up,' I said, and was a little dismayed by the alacrity with which they obeyed. 'I mean you no harm, but where is Pursey? Percival? I know he was one of you.'

They looked at each other, then at me, then at my dog, then at Iota hulking beside me . . . and of course they shied glances at the princess, who had come once more to the castle she'd called home. Finally the one who had covered his face dropped his apron and stepped forward. He was trembling. I'll spare you his slurred speech. He was understandable enough.

'The night soldiers came for him and took him in their grip. He shook, and then he swooned. They carried him away. I think he may be dead, great sir, for their touch kills.'

That I knew, but it didn't always kill, or I would have been dead weeks ago. 'Where did they take him?'

They shook their heads, but I had a good idea, and if the Lord High wanted to interrogate Pursey – *Percival* – he might still be alive.

Leah, meanwhile, had seen something. She bolted across the room to the big food-preparation island in the center. On it was a sheaf of papers tied with string and a quill pen, its feathers dark with grease and the nib dark with ink. She grabbed both, then made that impatient twirling gesture that said we had to go. She was right, of course, but she would have to put up with a little side-trip to the apartment I had already visited. I owed Percival. We all did. And I owed Kellin, the Lord High, as well.

I owed him a payback, and as we all know, payback's a bitch.

9

Not far past the kitchen, the corridor ended at a tall door crisscrossed with formidable iron bands. On it was a sign in letters three feet high. Looked at dead-on, I could read the words NO ENTRY. When I turned my head to glimpse it from the peripheral vision Cla had sadly lacked, the words became a tangle of runic symbols . . . which, I'm sure, my cohorts could read perfectly well.

Leah pointed at me. I approached the door and spoke the magic words. Bolts crashed back on the far side and the door creaked ajar.

'Should have tried that in Maleen,' Eris said. 'You could have saved us a lot of grief.'

I could have said I'd never thought of it, which was true, but that wasn't all of it. 'I wasn't the prince then. I was still . . .'

'Still what?' Jaya asked.

Still changing, I thought. *Deep Maleen was my cocoon.*

I was saved having to finish. Leah beckoned with one hand and pulled at what remained of my shirt with the other. She was right, of course. We had an apocalypse to stop.

The hallway beyond the door was much wider and hung with tapestries depicting everything from fancy-dress royal weddings and balls to hunting scenes and landscapes of mountains and lakes. An especially memorable one showed a sailing ship caught in the protruding claws of some giant subsurface crustacean. We walked at least half a mile before coming to double doors ten feet high. On one was a banner showing an old man dressed in a neck-to-toe red robe. On his head was the crown I'd seen on Flight Killer's head – there was no mistaking it. On the other door was a much younger woman, also wearing a crown on her blond curls.

'King Jan and Queen Cova,' Jaya said. Her voice was soft and awestruck. 'My mother had a pillow with their faces on it. We weren't allowed to touch it, let alone lay our heads on it.'

There was no need for me to speak Leah's name here; the doors opened inward at her touch. We stepped onto a wide balcony. The room below had a feeling of vastness, but it was hard to tell for sure because it was very dark. Leah sidled to her left, slipping into the shadows until she was almost gone. I heard a faint squeaking noise, followed by the smell of gas and a low hissing from the darkness above and around us. Then, first by ones, then twos and threes, gas-jets bloomed. There had to be over a hundred, ringing an enormous room. More lit up in a huge, many-spoked chandelier. I know you're reading a lot of *huge* and *great* and *enormous*. Better get used to it, because *everything* was . . . at least until we got to the claustrophobe's nightmare I will tell of soon.

Leah was turning a small valve-wheel. The gas-jets brightened. The balcony was actually a gallery, lined with high-backed chairs. Below us was a circular room with a bright red flagstone floor. In the center, on a kind of dais, were two thrones, one slightly bigger than the other. Scattered about were chairs (much plusher than those on the balcony) and small divans like love-seats.

And it stank. The aroma was so thick and foul it was almost visible. I could see heaps of rotted food here and there, some of it squirming with maggots, but that wasn't all. There were also piles of shit on the flagstones, and especially big piles on the two thrones. Blood, now dried to maroon, splashed the walls. Two headless bodies lay below the chandelier. Hanging from it on either side, as if to keep it in balance, were two more, the twisted faces bunched – almost mummified – with age. Their necks were stretched grotesquely long but hadn't yet torn free of the heads they were supposed to support. It was like looking at the aftermath of some awful murder-party.

'What happened here?' Iota asked in a hoarse whisper. 'My high gods, *what*?'

The princess tapped me on the arm. Her mouthless face looked both exhausted and sad. She was holding out one of the papers she'd taken from the kitchen. On one side, someone had written a complicated recipe in crabbed cursive. On the other Leah had printed, and in a fair hand: *This was my father and mother's reception hall*. She pointed to one of the hanging mummies and wrote: *I think Luddum. My father's chancellor.*

I put an arm around her shoulders. She laid her head all too briefly against my arm, then pulled away.

'It wasn't enough to kill them, was it?' I asked. 'They had to defile this place.'

She nodded wearily, then pointed past me to a flight of stairs. We went down them, and she led us toward another set of double doors, these stretching at least thirty feet high. Hana could have walked through them without ducking.

Leah motioned to Iota. He placed his palms against the doors, leaned forward, and pushed them open along hidden tracks. While he did that, Leah faced the beshitted thrones where her mother and father had once listened to the requests of their subjects. She dropped to one knee and put her palm to her forehead. Her tears fell on the dirty red flagstones.

Silent, silent.

10

The room beyond the reception hall would have put the nave of Notre Dame cathedral to shame. The echoes turned the footsteps of we five into the march of a battalion. And the voices had returned, all those entwined whispers full of malice.

Above us were the three spires, like great vertical tunnels full of shadowy green gleams that deepened to purest ebony. The floor we walked across was hundreds of thousands of small tiles. Once they had made an enormous monarch butterfly, and in spite of the vandalism that had chipped away at it, the shape remained. Below the central spire was a golden platform. From its center, a silver cable rose into the darkness. There was a pedestal beside it with a large wheel protruding from its side. Leah motioned to Iota. Then she pointed at the wheel and made cranking motions.

Eye stepped up, spat on his hands, and began to crank. He was a strong man and he kept at it for quite awhile without flagging. When he finally stepped back, I took over. The wheel turned steadily, but it was hard work; after ten minutes or so, I felt like I was turning the damn thing through some kind of glue. There was a tap on my shoulder. Eris took over. She managed a single revolution, then Jaya took a turn. Hers was little more than a token effort, but she wanted to be part of the team. Nothing wrong with that.

'What are we doing?' I asked Leah. The golden platform was pretty clearly a lift that went up the central spire, but it hadn't moved. 'And why are we doing it, if the Flight Killer has gone below?'

There was a croak from thin air, almost a word. *Must*, I think it was. Leah put her hands to her throat and shook her head, as if to say ventriloquism was now too difficult. Then she wrote on another of the recipe papers, using Jaya's back as a support. The ink on the nib of her quill pen was very faint by the time she finished, but I could read it.

We must go up to go down. Trust me.

What choice?

CHAPTER TWENTY-NINE

The Lift. The Spiral Staircase.

Jeff. The Lord High.

'The Queen of Empis Will Do Her Duty.'

1

Iota returned to the wheel, and now the resistance was so great that he grunted with each quarter-turn. He moved it half a dozen times, the last only a few inches. Then, from somewhere overhead, a soft chime sounded. It echoed and died away. Leah motioned Eye to step back. She pointed to the platform. She pointed to us, then raised her arms and made an air-hug.

'All of us?' I asked. 'Is that what you mean? Close together?'

She nodded, then managed a final act of ventriloquism, clutching her throat as she did it. Tears of pain spilled down her cheeks. I didn't want to imagine her throat lined with barbwire but couldn't help it.

'Dog. Middle. Now.'

We humans stepped on. Radar held back, crouching and looking worried. As soon as our weight hit the platform, it began to rise.

'Radar!' I shouted. 'Jump, jump!'

For a second I thought she was going to be left behind. Then her hindquarters bunched and she leaped. Her leash was long gone, but she was still wearing her collar. Iota grabbed it and hauled her onboard. We shuffled around, making room for her in the middle. She sat, looked up at me, and whined. I knew how she felt. There was hardly room for all of us, even crammed together backs to bellies.

The floor fell away. At six feet we might have been able to jump without being hurt. At twelve we might have been able to jump without being killed. Then it was eighteen feet, and forget about it.

Eye was on one side with his toes over the edge. I was on the other, also with at least a quarter of my feet in open air. Eris, Jaya, and Leah were grouped around Radar, Leah actually straddling her. Now the floor had to be seventy feet below us. The air was dusty, and I thought if I started sneezing I might tumble off, which would be an ignominious end for the promised prince.

The voices whispered and twined. One I heard clearly said *Your father's brain is eating itself.*

Jaya began to sway and closed her eyes. 'I don't like the high,' she said. 'I never liked the high, even the barn loft. Oh, I can't do this, let me off.'

She began to struggle, raising her arms to push Eris, who bumped into Iota, almost sending him off the edge. Radar gave a bark. If *she* panicked and started to move around, Leah would fall. And me.

'Hold that woman, Eris,' Iota growled. 'Keep her still before she kills us all.'

Eris reached across Radar – and over Leah, who bent her knees in a half-crouch. Eris got her arms around Jaya. 'Close your eyes, dear. Close your eyes and pretend this is all a dream.'

Jaya closed her eyes and seized Eris around the neck.

The air was colder up here, and I was slimy with sweat. I began to shiver. *Sick*, whispered a voice that wafted past me like a diaphanous scarf. *Sick and slip, slip and fall.*

Below me, the stone floor was now just a small square in the gloom. The wind was blowing and the sometimes-stone, sometimes-glass sides of the spire creaked.

Sick, the voices whispered. *Sick and slip, slip and fall. Fall for sure.*

We went on rising, which seemed insane to me with Flight Killer somewhere below us, but it was too late to change course now. I could only hope that Leah knew what she was doing.

We passed among thick struts of dressed stone topped with inches of dust, and now there was green glass on either side of us. Black shapes twined sinuously through it. The sides were narrowing in.

And then, suddenly, the platform stopped.

Above us, the spire narrowed into darkness. I could make out something up there, maybe a landing, but it was at least forty feet above the stopped platform where we stood crowded around my dog, who was ready to bolt at any second. Below us were leagues of empty air.

'What's happening?' Eris asked. 'Why did we stop?' Her voice was thin with terror. Jaya jerked in her arms and bumped Iota again. He waved his arms wildly to keep his balance.

'How the fuck we're supposed to get down is a better question,' he growled. 'This is what you call a pre-dicky-dicament.'

Leah was looking up anxiously, tracing the silver cable with her eyes.

'This ain't half a way to end the story,' Eye said, and actually laughed. 'Four hundred feet up and crammed together like cattle.'

I thought of shouting *Rise, in the name of Leah of the Gallien*, knew it was absurd, and was about to try it anyway when the platform jerked back to life. This time I was the one waving my arms to keep from plunging over the side. I think I would have gone anyway if Leah hadn't grabbed me around the neck. Her grip was strong enough to choke my air off for a few seconds, but under the circumstances it would have been churlish to complain.

Radar scrambled to her feet and we all swayed in unison. The platform actually seemed to be shrinking around us. The curved walls of the spire were now almost close enough to touch. I looked at the approaching landing and prayed for it to come in reach before the lift stopped again, or started to plunge.

Neither happened. The platform stopped at the landing with a gentle bump, there was another chime – louder up here – and Radar scrambled off, thumping Leah a good one with her rear end and sending her into Eris and Jaya. They teetered over the blackness. I shoved Leah with one hand and Jaya with the other. Iota pushed Eris and we tumbled onto the landing on top of one another, like clowns out of the little car at the circus. Iota began to laugh. I joined him. Eris and Jaya also began to laugh, although Jaya was weeping, too. There was a fair amount of hugging.

Leah put her face down on Radar's back and reached out with one hand. I took it and squeezed it. She squeezed back.

'I'd like to know something,' Iota said. 'I'd like to know where in fuck we are and why in fuck we came here.'

I pointed to Leah and shrugged. *Her deal, not mine.*

2

The landing was small and there was no railing, but we were able to stand in a line, which was safer than being crammed together on a six-by-six platform of solid gold. And that platform now began to sink back down to the floor, leaving us stranded up here.

Leah pointed to her right. Iota was first in line, and he began to sidle that way, looking down at the blackness of the drop and the descending lift platform. The rest of us followed, Jaya looking resolutely across to the far side of the spire. We were holding hands like a bunch of paper dolls. Probably not wise, since if one of us lost their balance, we might all go over the edge, but that didn't stop us.

At the end of the landing was a low arch. Iota bent, let go of Eris's hand, and duck-walked through. Radar went next, then Jaya and Leah. I came last, sparing one final look down at the descending platform, which was now almost out of sight.

There was another curved catwalk on the other side of the arch, and another chasm beyond it. We had ascended almost to the top of the central spire; we were now at the top of the one on the right. Leah made her way to the head of our little parade, each of us holding her around the waist as she passed. I could hear the rapid chuff of breath in and out of her nose. I wondered how much strength it had taken her to vocalize as much as she had, and when she'd last eaten. By now she had to be going on sheer guts . . . but then, that was true of all of us.

'Aren't you glad you came?' I whispered to Jaya as we began to move again, now shuffle-stepping around the top of this second spire.

'Shut up, my prince,' she whispered back.

The catwalk ended at another arch on the far side of the spire, this one blocked by a wooden door no more than five feet high. Magic words weren't needed. Leah ran a bolt at the top and used both hands to lift a double latch. There was no doubt she'd been up here before. I could imagine her and Elden as children, the runts of the litter and largely forgotten, exploring a palace that had to sprawl over seventy or a hundred acres, finding its ancient secrets, daring death on that platform (how had they ever been able to turn the wheel that powered it?) and God knew how many other dangerous places. It was a wonder they hadn't been killed on one of their safaris. The corollary to that thought was that it would have been better for all of us if Elden had been.

Once the door was open, we could hear the sound of the wind outside. Its constant low moan made me think of the sounds Hana had made as she held the body of her slain daughter. The landing beyond the door was only big enough for one person at a time (or perhaps, I thought, for two small, curious children standing close together).

Leah went first. I followed and saw we were at the top of a narrow barrel that seemed to drop all the way to ground level. On our left was a wall of stone blocks. On the right was curving green glass with those capillaries of black floating lazily upward. The glass was thick and dark, but enough daylight strained through for me to see the way down: a narrow stairway turning on itself in a tight spiral. There was no railing. I reached out and touched the glass with my fingers. The result was startling. Those black tendrils drew together in a cloud and flocked toward my touch. I pulled my hand back in a hurry and the black threads resumed their lazy perambulations.

But those things see us or sense us, I thought. *And they're hungry*.

'Don't touch the glass wall,' I said to the others. 'I don't think they can get through, but there's no sense riling them up.'

'What is *riling*?' Jaya asked.

'Never mind, just don't touch the glass wall.'

Leah, now half a dozen steps below me, made that twirling gesture again, like an ump signaling a home run.

We began our descent.

3

The stairs were better than the elevator platform – less scary – but still dangerous. They were steep, and the constant circling made us all (with the possible exception of Radar) dizzy. Looking down the center of the spiral was a bad idea; it made the vertigo worse. After Leah and me came Radar, Iota, then Jaya. Eris brought up the rear.

After a descent of a hundred steps or so, we came to another of those low doors. Leah passed it, but I was curious. I peered into a long room, musty and dusty, filled with dim shapes, some covered with sheets. The idea that I was looking into an enormous attic bemused me at first, but then I realized that every palace must have one. They just don't bother to put it in the storybooks.

After descending further – the glass wall thicker, the light dimmer – we came to another door. I opened it and saw a corridor lit with a few guttering gas-jets. Many more were out. A crumpled and dusty tapestry lay abandoned on the floor.

'Leah, hold up.'

She turned to me and raised her hands, palms out.

'Are there more doors as we go down? Opening on different parts of the palace? Living quarters, perhaps?'

She nodded, then made the twirling gesture again, the one that said we had to push on.

'Not yet. Do you know of an apartment that's lit by electricity rather than gaslight?' What I actually said – I think – was *do you know of chambers*. But that wasn't why she looked puzzled. She didn't know *electricity* any more than Jaya had known *riling*, as in *riling them up*.

'Magic lights,' I said.

That she understood. She raised three fingers, considered, then raised four.

'Why are we stopping?' Jaya asked. 'I want to get *down*.'

'Hold your water,' Iota said. 'I know what he's about. Or at least I think I do.'

I thought of asking Leah if Mr Bowditch had installed the magic lights and the generator to power them, but I already knew. *Cowards bring presents*. But based on what I'd seen of the old-fashioned genny, he'd done it long ago, probably when he'd still been Adrian instead of Howard.

One of the suites graced with slave-driven electricity was almost certainly the private quarters of the late king and queen, but that wasn't the one I was interested in.

Leah didn't just point down the tight spiral of the stairway; she jabbed her finger repeatedly. She had only two things in mind: finding Flight Killer before he could open the Dark Well, and assuring herself that the usurper wasn't her brother. I cared about those things as much as she did, but I cared about something else, too. I had been in the particular hell of Deep Maleen, after all, as had Iota and the two women who had elected to come with us.

'Not yet, Leah. Hear me, now. Do you remember a suite of rooms, one equipped with the magic lights, that had a long blue velvet sofa?' She made no sign that she did, but I remembered something else. 'What about a table with a tiled surface? The tiles make a picture of a unicorn that looks almost as if it's dancing. Do you remember that?'

Her eyes widened and she nodded.

'Is there a door from these stairs that opens on that part of the residences?'

She put her hands on her hips – sword on one, dagger on the other – and looked at me with exasperation. She jabbed her finger downward.

I fell into the vernacular I'd learned in Maleen. 'Nah, nah, my lady. Say if we can enterwise that part from here. Tell me!'

Reluctantly, she nodded.

'Then take us there. We've still got lots of daylight . . .' I might actually have said a *moit* of daylight. '. . . and there's other business than yours.'

'What business?' Jaya asked from behind me.

'I think that's where we'll find the Lord High.'

'Then we must go there,' Eris said. 'He has much to answer for.'

Fucking right, I thought.

4

We passed three more doors on our continuing descent, and I began to think Leah meant to bypass Kellin's cozy nest. His *electrified* cozy nest. Then she stopped at another door, opened it, and took a startled step backward. I steadied her with one hand and drew Mr Bowditch's .45 with the other. Before I could look through the door, Radar hurried past me, wagging her tail. Leah put her palm to her forehead, not in salute but in the distracted gesture of a woman who feels her troubles will never end.

Crouching in the corridor, just past the point where the swinging door would have knocked it over, was the Snab. Radar nosed it between its antennae, tail wagging. Then she dropped on her belly and the Snab hopped aboard.

Iota was looking over my shoulder, fascinated. 'You do get around, Sir Snab, don't you? How did you find us?'

I had an idea about that. Claudia had been able to hear the Snab in her head, and maybe that ability was a two-way street. If so, the Snab might have been tracking us with a kind of telepathic GPS. It was a crazy idea, but any crazier than a mermaid with a similar ability? Or a youth-renewing sundial?

As for how El Snabbo had shown up here, my guess was that Leah wasn't the only one who knew the palace's secret ways, and a cricket, even a big one, could go places a human couldn't. That I'd observed for myself, in Deep Maleen.

'Why is it here?' Eris asked. 'To guide us?'

If so, it had made a wasted trip, because I knew where we were, although Aaron had brought me a different way. Same wide corridor, with the gas-jets enclosed in fancy glass chimneys. Same tapestries, same marble statues, although the one that had reminded me of Cthulhu had fallen to the floor and broken in two . . . which in my opinion was no great loss.

I put my hands on my knees and lowered my face until it was almost touching the Snab's. It looked back at me fearlessly from its place on the nape of Radar's neck. 'Why are you here? Were you waiting for us? What's your deal?'

Claudia had said something about having to clear her mind. I tried to clear mine, and I think I did a pretty good job of it, given the circumstances and the time-pressure we were laboring under, but if the Snab was sending telepathic messages, they weren't on my wave-length.

They were on someone's, however.

Jaya said, 'Prince Charlie, the Snab wishes you well and hopes for our success.'

I didn't think she was making it up, exactly, but guessed it might be wish fulfillment. Then she said something that changed my mind.

Iota listened and began to grin, revealing significant holes in his dental equipment. 'Really?' he said. 'I'll be dipped in shit!' (Not what he said; what I heard.) 'Let me take care of this, Charlie. May I? As a favor to the one who spent much longer in Deep Maleen than you did?'

I gave him permission. I'd take it back if I could and use the .45, but I didn't know. The Snab didn't, either, or it surely would have told Jaya. Thinking of that helps, but not enough. In the whole history of the world – *all* the worlds – not knowing never changed a single mistake.

5

There was a good-sized hole in the wainscoting behind the pedestal where the statue of the tentacled horror had stood, which made me remember the defective gas-jet in Deep Maleen. A draft moaned in the hollow spaces behind the wall, and bad-smelling air puffed out.

'That's where the little lord came from, sure as cream makes butter,' Iota said. He had taken the lead in our procession, Leah close behind him. I tried to walk beside her, but she pulled ahead without giving me a glance. Rades took her place, the Snab still mounted on her back. Jaya and Eris brought up the rear. We passed the gold-framed mirrors I remembered and came at last to the mahogany door that gave on the Lord High's apartment. Because it was one of the few with electric power, I guessed the chambers might once have belonged to Luddum, King Jan's chancellor, but I never knew for sure.

Leah drew her dagger and I drew the .45, but we both stayed behind Iota. He looked at Jaya and mouthed, *Behind the door?*

She nodded. Iota rapped with his big dirty knuckles. 'Anyone at home? May we come in?'

Without waiting for an answer, he turned the knob (gold, of course) and drove his shoulder into the door. It flew back and there was a grunt from behind it. Iota pulled the knob toward him, then slammed the door back again. Another grunt. A third time . . . a fourth . . . the grunts stopped . . . a fifth. Radar was barking. When Eye pulled the door toward him again, the man who had been standing behind it fell out in a heap on the thick red rug that covered the floor of the foyer. His forehead, nose, and mouth were bleeding. In one hand he held a long knife. When he turned his face up to look at us, I recognized one of the men from the VIP box – the one with the scar on his cheek who had been whispering to Petra. He raised the knife and flailed out with it, laying a shallow cut across Iota's hairy shin.

'Nah, nah, none of that, kiddie,' Eye said, and stepped on the scarred man's wrist, bearing down until the man's hand opened and the knife dropped to the rug. I picked it up and tucked it into Mr Bowditch's concho belt, opposite the holster.

Leah dropped to her knees beside the scarred man. He recognized her and smiled. Blood oozed from his split lips. 'Princess Leah! I am Jeff. Once I put a bandage on your arm when you cut it – do you remember?'

She nodded.

'And once I pushed your little pony-trap out of a mudhole. There were three of us, but my love for you was strong and I pushed the hardest. Do you remember that, as well?'

She nodded again.

'I never wanted to be a part of this, I swear to you, Princess. Will you let me go, in memory of the old days, when you were a child and Lilimar was fair?'

She nodded that she would indeed let him go, and plunged her dagger up to the hilt into one of his upstaring eyes.

6

There was no electricity in the apartment today, but the scarred man – Jeff, or maybe he spelled it Geoff – had turned the gaslights partway up so he could see to do his dirty work. My guess is he hadn't expected five of us, or for us to know where he was lying in wait. Not to mention the Snab, a cricket buckaroo riding on my dog's back.

Eris found the little brass lever that controlled the gas and turned the jets up to full. We found Kellin in the next room, lying on an enormous canopied bed. The chamber was dark. His hands were clasped on his chest. His hair was combed back and he was wearing the same red velvet smoking jacket he'd had on when he interrogated me. A faint blue haze hung around him. It looked like eyeshadow on his closed lids. He didn't stir as we approached and stood around his stolen bed. Never had an old man looked so dead, and he soon would be. I didn't know if there was running water in the toilet cubicle I saw to the left of the room, but there was surely a pump. I thought my old friend the Lord High could use a good bath.

Jaya and Eris spoke at the same time. Jaya: 'Where's the Snab?' Eris: 'What's that sound?'

It was a mix of chattering and squeaking, punctuated by quick, sharp hisses. As the sound approached, Radar began to bark. Did I notice how pale Iota had become when I turned toward the living room to see what was coming? I think so, but I'm not sure. Most of my attention was on the bedroom doorway. The Snab entered in two springy leaps, then jumped aside. What followed were the hidden denizens of the palace's walls and dark places: a flood of enormous gray rats. Jaya and Eris both screamed. Leah couldn't, but she backed away against the wall, eyes wide and hands raised to the scar of her mouth.

I had no doubt the Snab had summoned them. It was, after all, the lord of small things. Although most of the rats were bigger than it was.

I stepped back from the bed. Iota stumbled and I grabbed him. He was breathing rapidly and I should have known then that something was wrong with him, but I was watching the rats. They swarmed up the dangling bedclothes and onto the body of the Lord High. His eyes flashed open. They were almost too bright to look at. The aura around him changed from pale blue to a deeper, purer shade. The first wave of rats were fried when they entered it. The stink of cooking meat and burning fur was atrocious, but they didn't stop. Fresh troops squirmed over the bodies of their dead comrades, chittering and biting. Kellin struggled to throw them off. An arm rose from the boiling rat-pile and began to beat at them. One was clinging to his thumb, swinging back and forth like a pendulum, its tail wrapped around his bony wrist. There was no blood, for Kellin had none to give. I could see blue light giving occasional blinks through the rats covering him. He screamed, and a rat the size of a full-grown tomcat tore off his upper lip, exposing his gnashing teeth. And still the rats came, pouring through the bedroom doorway and surging up the bed until the Lord High was buried beneath a living, biting blanket of fur and tails and teeth.

There was a thud beside me as Iota collapsed in the corner of the room, across from where the three women cowered and Radar barked. Leah was holding Rades's collar with both hands. White foam was coming from the corners of Iota's mouth and dripping down his chin. He looked up at me and tried to smile.

'Poi . . .'

For just a moment I thought he was talking about the Hawaiian delicacy. Then I understood the word he couldn't finish.

There was a muffled explosion and a flash of light. Rats – some on fire, some only smoldering – flew in all directions. One hit me in the chest and slid down my tattered shirt, leaving a trail of guts behind. The women who could vocalize screamed again. I heard the Snab's wings start making that distinctive cricket sound. The rats obeyed at once, reversing direction and flowing back the way they'd come, leaving hundreds of bodies behind. Kellin's bed was littered with guts and soaked with rat blood. Kellin himself was a disassembled skeleton below a grinning skull lying askew on a silk pillow.

I tried to pick Iota up, but he was far too heavy for me. 'Eris!' I shouted. 'Eye's down! Help me! It's bad!'

She made her way through the diminishing tide of rats, hopping and crying out when they ran over her feet . . . but not a single one bit her, or any of us. Leah followed. Jaya hung back, then she came, too.

I got Iota under the arms. Eris took one leg, Leah the other. We carried him, trying not to trip over the last few rats, including one with no back legs but still pulling itself gamely along after its fellows.

'Sorry,' Iota said. His voice was guttural, coming from a throat that was rapidly closing up. Foam flew. 'Sorry, wanted to see it through . . .'

'Shut up and save your breath.'

We laid him on the long blue sofa. He began to cough, spewing more curds of foam into Leah's face as she knelt to brush his hair back from his sweating forehead. Jaya grabbed a doily or some such thing from the unicorn table and wiped away some of the mess. Leah didn't seem to notice. Her eyes were fixed on Iota's. What I saw in hers was kindness and pity and mercy.

He tried to smile at her, then looked at me. 'It was on the blade of his knife. An old . . . trick.'

I nodded, thinking of how carelessly I'd shoved that knife into the concho belt. If I'd even nicked myself, Eye wouldn't be the only one foaming at the mouth.

He looked back at Leah. He raised his arm very slowly, as if it weighed a hundred pounds, and touched the heel of his palm to his forehead. 'My . . . Queen. When the time comes . . . do your duty.' His hand dropped.

So Iota – whom I'd first seen clinging to the bars of his cell like a monkey – passed away. After all he'd been through, and big man though he was, it took but one tiny cut on the shin to do for him.

His eyes were open. Leah closed them, bent, and pressed the scar of her mouth to one stubbly cheek. It was the best she could do for a kiss. Then she got up and pointed to the door. We followed, stepping around the corpses of a few rats that had died on the way out. She stopped before going into the corridor, looked back, and put her hands to her throat.

Iota spoke one last time, as Falada had spoken, and the Snab.

'The Queen of Empis will do her duty. This I swear.'

CHAPTER THIRTY

One More Stop. The Dungeon. Resolute. Impossible Stars. The Dark Well. Gogmagog. The Bite.

1

We followed a trail of dead and wounded rats to the hole in the wainscoting; Eris actually helped one three-legged bruiser get inside, then grimaced and wiped her hands on her shirt (which couldn't have done much good, covered in dirt and blood as it was). We came to the door giving on the spiral stairs, which I guessed might be some sort of emergency exit for the royalty, in case of fire. I tapped Leah on the shoulder.

'One more stop before we go after Flight Killer,' I said. 'On the level of Deep Maleen and the torture chamber. Will you do that?'

She made no protest, only gave a weary nod. There was still a curd of bloody foam on her cheek. I reached out to wipe it away and this time she didn't shrink back.

'Thank you. There may be someone there who helped us—'

She turned away before I could finish. Outside the palace, Woody and Claudia and their followers – by now they might be swelled to the size of a real army – had probably entered the city. If there was a barracks where the remaining night soldiers slept, the grayfolk could be slaughtering them even now, and hooray for that, but in here time was fleeting and there was no magic sundial to turn it back.

We went down the staircase – down and down, around and around. None of us spoke. The death of Iota sat on us like a weight. Even Radar felt it. She couldn't stay beside me, the barrel we were descending was too narrow for that, but she walked with her nose touching my calf, ears down and tail drooping. The air got chillier. Water oozed from the lichen growing on stone blocks that had been placed here hundreds of years before. *No*, I thought, *longer than that. Thousands, maybe*.

Then I started to smell something, very faintly. 'High gods,' Eris said, and laughed. There was nothing cheerful about it. 'The wheel turns and here we are, back where we came from.'

We had passed several more doors on our way down, some large, some smaller. Leah stopped at a small one, pointed, then went down several more steps to give me room. I tried the door. It opened. I had to bend almost double to go through. I found myself in another kitchen, this one little more than a closet compared to the one we'd passed on our way in. Here there was only one stove, no oven, and a long low grill, probably powered by gas but now out. On it was a row of sausages, burned black.

Jaya made a sound between a cough and a retch. I suppose she was thinking of all the meals we'd taken in our cells, especially the ones before 'playtime' and the first round of the Fair One. I had read about PTSD, but reading about something and understanding it are very different things.

On a shelf beside the grill was a tin cup like the ones we'd had in our cells, only this one had no hole in the bottom you had to put your finger over. It was filled with sulphur matches like the kind Pursey had given me. I grabbed it, and since I had no pockets, I relocated the .45 in the concho belt and poked the cup of matches into the holster.

Leah led us to the door, peeked out, then gestured for us to follow, twirling her fingers as before – *quickly, quickly*. I wondered how much time had passed. It was still daylight, surely, but what would that matter if Bella and Arabella kissed on the other side of the world? I guessed that the Flight Killer was already at the Dark Well. Waiting for it to open so he could try to make another bargain with the thing that lived there, either blind to the terrible events that might result or not caring. I thought the latter more likely. Elden of the Gallien, Elden the Flight Killer, a flabby, greedy, green-faced goblin waiting to call something from another world into this one . . . and then, perhaps, into mine. I considered telling Leah to forget about taking us to the torture chamber. Pursey – *Percival* – might not even be there, or he might be dead. Surely stopping Flight Killer was more important.

Eris touched my shoulder. 'Prince Charlie . . . are you sure about this? Is it wise?'

No. It wasn't. Except without Percival – a man with the gray disease so advanced in him he could barely talk – none of us would be here.

'We go,' I said curtly.

Eris touched her palm to her forehead and said no more.

2

I recognized the passage where Leah was waiting for us, shifting from foot to foot, clasping and unclasping the hilt of her sword. To the right of the auxiliary kitchen was the way to the dungeon. To the left, and not far, was the torture chamber.

I ran, leaving the others behind. Except for Radar, who loped beside me, tongue flying from the side of her mouth. It was farther than I remembered. When I reached the open door of the chamber, I paused long enough to think something that wasn't quite a prayer – just *please, please*. Then I went in.

At first I thought it was empty . . . unless, that was, Percival had been enclosed in the Iron Maiden. But if he had been, blood would surely have been oozing out, and there wasn't any. Then a pile of rags in the far corner stirred. It raised its head, saw me, and tried to smile with what remained of its mouth.

'Pursey!' I shouted, and ran to him. 'Percival!'

He struggled to salute me.

'Nah, nah, it's I who should salute you. Can you stand?'

With my help, he was able to get to his feet. I thought he'd wrapped one of his hands in a dirty piece of the blouse he wore, but when I looked at it more closely, I saw it had been wrapped around his wrist instead and knotted tightly to stop the bleeding. I could see a dark, crusty patch on the stones where he'd been lying. His hand was gone. Some bastard had chopped it off.

The others arrived. Jaya and Eris stood in the doorway, but Leah came in. Percival saw her and raised his remaining hand to his brow. He began to cry. '*Hinceh.*' It was the closest he could get to *princess*.

He tried to bend a leg to her and would have fallen if I hadn't held him up. He was filthy, bloody, and disfigured, but Leah put her arms around his neck and hugged him. I loved her for that, if for nothing else.

'Can you walk?' I asked him. 'If you take it slow and rest every-while, can you? Because we're in a hurry. *Desperate* hurry.'

He nodded.

'And you can find the way out?'

He nodded again.

'Jaya!' I said. 'This is where you part company with us. Percival will guide you out. Walk with him, let him rest as he needs.'

'But I want to—'

'I don't care what you want, this is what I need from you. Take him out of this . . . this *pit*. There will be others by now.' *There better be*, I thought. 'Get him to Claudia or Woody and get him medical attention.' *Medical attention* isn't what I said, but Jaya nodded.

I hugged Percival as Leah had. 'Thank you, my friend. If this works out, they should put up a statue of you.' *Maybe with butterflies perched on your outstretched arms*, I thought, and headed for the door. Leah was already there, waiting.

Jaya put an arm around him. 'I'll be with you every step, Pursey. Only guide me.'

'*H'rince!*' Percival said, and I turned back. He made every effort to speak clearly. '*H'light Iller!*' He pointed to the door. '*Hor ovvers! An itch! Hee itch!*' Now he pointed at Leah. '*Hee ows a'way!*' Now he pointed upward. '*Ella an Ara'ella! Oon! Oon!*'

I looked at Leah. 'Did you understand him?'

She nodded. Her face was dead pale. The sore through which she took nourishment stood out like a birthmark.

I turned to Eris. 'Did you?'

'Flight Killer,' she said. 'Four others. And the bitch. Or maybe it was the witch. Either way I think he must mean Petra, the cunt with the mole on her face who was next to him in the box. He said the princess knows the way. And something about Bella and Arabella.'

'They kiss soon,' Jaya said, and Percival nodded.

'Take care of him, Jaya. Get him out of here.'

'I will if he really knows the way. And make sure I see you again. All of you.' She bent and gave Radar's head a quick goodbye stroke.

3

Leah led us away from the circular stairway and into a different corridor. She paused at a door, opened it, shook her head, and went on.

'Does she really know where she's going?' Eris whispered.

'I think so.'

'You *hope* so.'

'It's been a long time since she was here.'

We came to another door. No. Then another. Leah peered into this room and beckoned. It was dark. She pointed to the cup of matches I'd taken from the kitchen. I tried to scratch one on the seat of my pants, a cool trick I'd seen some old-time cowboy do in a TCM movie. When that didn't work, I scraped it alight on the rough stone beside the door and held it up. The room was paneled in wood rather than faced with stone, and filled with clothes: uniforms, cooks' whites, overalls, and woolen shirts. A heap of moth-eaten brown dresses lay below a line of wooden dowels. In the corner was a box of white gloves, going yellow with age.

Leah was already crossing the room, Radar trailing her but looking back at me. I lit another match and followed. Leah stood on her toes, grabbed two of the dowels, and pulled. Nothing happened. She stepped back and pointed at me.

I handed the cup of matches to Eris, grabbed the dowels, and yanked. Nothing happened, but I felt some give. I pulled harder and the entire wall swung outward, bringing with it a gust of ancient air. Hidden hinges squalled. Eris lit another match and I saw cobwebs, not whole but hanging in gray tatters. Added to the heap of dresses pulled down from the dowels, the message was clear: someone had been through this door before us. I lit another match and bent down. In the dust were overlapping tracks. If I'd been a brilliant detective like Sherlock Holmes, I might have been able to deduce how many had gone through this hidden door, maybe even how far ahead of us they were, but I was no Sherlock. I did think they might have been carrying something heavy, based on how the tracks were blurred. As if they'd been shuffling rather than walking. I thought of Flight Killer's fancy palanquin.

More steps led down, curving to the left. More tracks in the dust. Far below was dim light, but not from gas-jets. It was greenish. I didn't like it much. I liked the voice that whispered from the air in front of me even less. *Your father is dying in his own filth*, it said.

Eris drew in a sharp breath. 'The voices are back.'

'Don't listen,' I said.

'Why don't you tell me not to *breathe*, Prince Charlie?'

Leah beckoned us. We started down the stairs. Radar whined uneasily, and I guessed she might be hearing voices, too.

4

Down we went. The green light grew stronger. It was coming from the walls. *Oozing* from the walls. The voices grew stronger, too. They were saying unpleasant things. Many about my dismal exploits with Bertie Bird. Eris was crying behind me, very softly, and once she murmured, 'Won't you stop? I never meant to. Won't you please stop?'

I almost wished I could face Hana or Red Molly again. They had been horrible, but they had substance. You could strike out against them.

If Leah heard the voices, she gave no sign. She descended the stairs at a steady pace, back straight, her tied-back hair brushing between her shoulderblades. I hated her stubborn refusal to acknowledge that Flight Killer was her brother – hadn't we heard his cronies shouting his name at the Fair One? – but I loved her courage.

I loved *her*.

By the time the steps ended in an arch overgrown with moss and torn cobwebs, we had to be at least five hundred feet deeper than Deep Maleen. Maybe more. The voices faded. What replaced them was a dark humming that seemed to come from either the damp stone walls or from the green light, which was much brighter now. It was a *living* light, and that humming sound was its voice. We were approaching some great power, and if I had ever doubted the existence of evil as a real force, something separate from that which lived in the hearts and minds of mortal men and women, I didn't now. We were only on the rim of the thing generating that force but getting closer to it with every step we took.

I reached out to touch Leah's shoulder. She jerked, then relaxed when she realized it was just me. Her eyes were wide and dark. Looking into her face instead of at her resolute back, I realized she was as terrified as we were. Maybe more, because she knew more.

'You came here?' I whispered. 'You and Elden came here as *children*?'

She nodded. She held out her hand and gripped thin air.

'You held hands.'

She nodded. *Yes*.

I could see them, hand in hand, running everywhere . . . but no, that was wrong, they wouldn't have been running after all. Leah could run, but Elden had clubbed feet. She would walk with him even if she wanted to sprint ahead to the next thing, the next surprise, the next secret place, because she loved him.

'Did he have a cane?'

She raised her hand and showed me a V. So, two canes.

Everywhere together except for one place. *Leah was never a one for books*, Woody had said. *Elden was the reader of the two*.

'He knew about that secret door in the room where the clothes were stored, didn't he? He read about it in the library. Probably he knew about other places, too.'

Yes.

Old books. Perhaps forbidden books like the *Necronomicon*, the made-up one Lovecraft liked to write about. I could see Elden poring over just such a book, the ugly boy with the clubbed feet, the boy with lumps on his face and a hump on his back, the one who was forgotten except when there was a cruel practical joke to be played

(I knew all about those, Bertie and I had played our share during my dark period), the one who was ignored by everyone except his little sister. Why wouldn't he be ignored when his handsome elder brother would eventually take the throne? And by the time Robert ascended, sickly limping Elden, bookworm Elden, would probably be dead anyway. Such as he didn't live long. They caught a bug, coughed, took fever, and died.

Elden reading the old dusty books, either from high shelves or from a locked cabinet he pried open. Maybe at first just looking for power to use against his bullying brother and sharp-tongued sisters. Thoughts of vengeance would come later.

'It wasn't your idea to come here, was it? Other parts of the castle, maybe, but not here.'

Yes.

'You didn't like it here, did you? The secret rooms and the rising platform, they were okay, fun, but this was bad and you knew it. Didn't you?'

Her eyes were dark and troubled. She made no sign, yes or no . . . but her eyes were wet.

'Elden, though – he was fascinated by it. Wasn't he?'

Leah only turned and began walking again, making that twirling *come on* gesture with one hand. Back straight.

Resolute.

5

Radar had gone ahead of us a little way, and now she was nosing at something on the floor of the passage – a scrap of green silk. I picked it up, looked at it, tucked it into the holster with the tin cup of matches, thought no more about it.

The way was wide and high, more tunnel than passage. We came to a place where it split in three, each bore lit with that pulsating green light. Over each entrance was a keystone carved in the shape of the thing I'd last seen in two pieces on the floor of the residence wing: a squidlike creature with a nest of tentacles obscuring the horror of its face. The monarchs were a blessing; that thing was a blasphemy.

Here's another fairy tale, I thought. *One meant for adults instead of children. No big bad wolf, no giant, no Rumpelstiltskin. That's a version of Cthulhu over those arches, and is that what Gogmagog is? High priest of the Elder Gods, dreaming his malevolent dreams in the ruins of R'lyeh? Is* that *what Elden wants to ask another favor of?*

Leah paused, started toward the lefthand passage, stopped, started toward the center passage, and hesitated again. She was looking ahead. I was looking down at the floor, where I could see tracks in the dust going into the righthand bore. That was the way Flight Killer and his entourage had gone, but I waited to see if she'd remember. She did. She entered the righthand passage and started walking again. We followed. The smell – the stench, the *mephitic odor* – was worse now, the hum not louder but more pervasive. Flabby, misshapen mushrooms, as white as a dead man's fingers, were growing out of the cracks in the walls. They turned to watch us pass. At first I thought that was my imagination. It wasn't.

'This is terrible,' Eris said. Her voice was low and desolate. 'I thought Maleen was bad . . . and the field where we had to fight . . . but they were nothing to this.'

And there was nothing to say to that because she was right.

We walked on and on, the way always trending downward. The smell was worse, and the hum got steadily louder. It was no longer just in the walls. I could feel it in the center of my brain, where it seemed not to be a sound but a black light. I had no idea where we were in the world above, but surely we'd passed beyond the palace grounds. Far beyond. The tracks thinned and disappeared. No dust had fallen this far down, and there were no dangling cobwebs. Even the spiders had deserted this godforsaken place.

The walls were changing. In places the stones had been replaced by great dark green blocks of glass. Within their depths, fat black tendrils swirled and swarmed. One rushed at us and its headless front folded open, becoming a mouth. Eris gave a weak scream. Radar was now walking so close beside me that my leg brushed her side at every step.

We finally emerged in a great vaulted room of dark green glass. The black tendrils were everywhere in the walls, darting in and out of strange carved shapes that changed when you looked at them. They curved and twisted, made shapes . . . faces . . .

'Don't look at those things,' I told Eris. I guessed Leah already knew; if she had remembered how to get here, she would surely remember those weird, changing shapes. 'I think they'll hypnotize you.'

Leah was standing in the center of this gruesome nave, looking around, bewildered. It was ringed with passages, each pulsing with green light. There had to be at least a dozen of them.

'I don't think I can,' Eris said. Her voice was a trembling whisper. 'Charlie, I'm sorry, but I don't think I can.'

'You don't have to.' The sound of my voice was flat and strange, I think because of the humming. It sounded like the voice of the Charlie Reade who'd gone along with every dirty trick the Bird Man thought up . . . and then added some of his own. 'Go back, if you can find your way. Stay here and wait for us if you can't.'

Leah turned a complete circle, doing it slowly and looking at each passage in turn. Then she looked at me, raised her hands, and shook her head.

I don't know.

'This is as far as you went, isn't it? Elden went on from here without you.'

Yes.

'But eventually he came back.'

Yes.

I thought of her waiting here in this strange green chamber with the weird carvings and the black things dancing in the walls. A little girl holding steady – holding resolute – in spite of that insidious hum. Waiting here alone.

'Did you come with him other times?'

Yes. Then pointed up, which I didn't understand.

'After that, did he come without you?'

A long pause . . . then: *Yes*.

'And there came a time when he didn't come back.'

Yes.

'You didn't go after him, did you? Maybe this far but no further. You didn't dare.'

She covered her face. It was answer enough.

'I'm going,' Eris blurted. 'I'm sorry, Charlie, but I . . . *I can't*.'

She fled. Radar went after her to the entrance we'd emerged from, and if she'd gone with Eris, I wouldn't have called her back. The hum was invading my bones now. I had a strong premonition that neither Princess Leah nor I were ever going to see the world outside again.

Radar returned to me. I knelt and put an arm around her, taking what comfort I could.

'You assumed your brother was dead.'

Yes. Then she clasped her throat and guttural words emerged in front of her. 'Is dead. *Is*.'

The self I had become – was still becoming – was older and wiser than the high school kid who had emerged in that field of poppies. This Charlie – *Prince* Charlie – understood that Leah had to believe that. Otherwise the guilt of not trying to rescue him would have been too great to bear.

Yet I think by then she knew better.

6

The floor was polished green glass that seemed to go down to endless depths. The black things swarmed beneath us, and there was no way to doubt that they were hungry. No dust here and not a single track. If they had left any, a member of Flight Killer's coterie had wiped them away just in case someone – us, for instance – tried to follow. With Leah unable to remember, there was no way to tell which of the twelve passages they'd taken.

Or maybe there was.

I remembered the woman with the beauty mark beside her mouth shouting *Kneel, old blood! Kneel, old blood!* Petra was her name, and she had been wearing a green silk dress.

I retrieved the scrap I'd found and held it out to Radar, who sniffed it without much interest – the hum and the black shapes in the glass blocks were affecting her, too. But she was what I had. What *we* had.

'Which one?' I said, and pointed to the tunnels. She didn't move, only looked up at me, and I realized the terrible atmosphere of this place had made me stupid. There were commands she understood, but *which one* wasn't among them. I held the scrap of dress to her nose again. 'Find, Radar, find!'

This time she lowered her nose to the floor. One of those black shapes seemed to leap at her and she danced back, but then she put her nose down again – my good dog, my brave dog. She went toward one of the tunnels, backtracked, and went to the next one on the right. Then she turned to me and barked.

Leah didn't hesitate. She sprinted into the tunnel. I followed. The green glass floor in this passage tilted down more steeply. If the incline had been even a bit more severe, I think we would have lost our footing. Leah increased her lead. She was fleet of foot; I was the galoot who could only be allowed to play first base.

'Leah, wait!'

But she didn't. I ran as fast as the inclined floor would allow. Radar, lower to the ground and with four legs instead of two, did better. The hum began to fade, as if somewhere a hand was turning down the volume on a gigantic amplifier. That was a relief. The green glow from the walls also faded. What replaced it was a fainter light that brightened – slightly – as we came to the mouth of the passage.

What I saw there, even after everything I'd experienced, was all but impossible to believe. The mind rebelled against what the eyes reported. The room of many passages had been enormous, but this underground chamber was far bigger. And how could it be a chamber when above me was a night sky littered with pulsing yellowish stars? That was where the light was coming from.

This can't be, I thought, then realized that yes, it could. Hadn't I already come out into another world, after descending another set of stairs? I had come out in the world of Empis. Now here was a third.

More stairs circled a colossal shaft that had been driven into solid rock. Leah was descending them, running full-out. At the bottom, five hundred or more feet below, I could see the Flight Killer's palanquin, the gold-threaded purple curtains closed. The four men who had carried it were cringing against the curved wall and looking up at those alien stars. They had to be strong men to have carried Flight Killer all this way, and brave, but from where I stood with Radar beside me, they looked small and terrified.

In the center of the stone floor was a huge derrick easily a hundred yards high. It was not unlike those I'd seen at construction sites in my hometown, but this one appeared to have been constructed of wood, and looked weirdly like a gibbet. The jointed mast and supporting boom formed a perfect triangle. The load hook was attached not to the well-cap I'd imagined when I imagined the Dark Well but to a gigantic hinged hatch that pulsed with a sickly green light.

Standing near it in his purple caftan-like robe, the golden crown of the Galliens absurdly askew on his straggling white hair, was the Flight Killer.

'*Leah!*' I screamed. '*Wait!*'

She gave no sign that she heard – she might have been as deaf as Claudia. Down this final circle of stairs she ran under the dim light of nightmarish stars shining from another universe. I ran after her, drawing Mr Bowditch's gun as I went.

7

The men who had carried the palanquin started up the stairs to meet her. She stood with her legs apart in fighting stance, and drew her sword. Radar was barking hysterically, either in terror of this awful place I was sure we'd never leave, or because she understood the men were threatening Leah. Maybe both. Flight Killer peered up and the crown tumbled from his head. He picked it up, but what came from under the purple robe wasn't an arm. I didn't see what it was (or didn't want to), and at that moment I didn't care. I had to get to Leah if I could, but I already recognized that I wouldn't be in time to save her from Flight Killer's bearers. They were too close, the range was too long for the revolver, and she was in the way.

She braced the hilt of the sword against her stomach. I heard the one in the lead shout something. He was waving his arms as he climbed, the other three behind him. I caught *Nah, nah!* but not any of the rest. She didn't have to smite him; in his panic he ran on her sword without slowing. It went in to the hilt and came out on the other side in a spray of blood. He tilted toward the drop. She tried to yank her sword free, but it wouldn't come. Her choice was simple and stark: let go and live or hold on and follow the man over the side. She let go. The impaled man fell a hundred or more feet from where Leah had skewered him and crashed down not far from the palanquin he'd helped to carry. He might have been promised gold, or women, an estate in the countryside, or all three. What he'd gotten was death.

The other three came on. I ran faster, disregarding the very real possibility of stumbling – maybe over my dog – and taking a mortal fall. I saw I was still not going to be in time. They were going to get to her first and now she had only the dagger to defend herself with. She drew it and put her back to the wall, ready to fight to the death.

Only there was no fight and no death. Even the man she'd killed probably had no intention of engaging her – *Nah, nah* was what he'd been shouting just before the impalement. These fellows had had enough. All they wanted was to get the hell out. They ran past her without a look.

'*Come back!*' Elden cried. '*Come back, you cowards! Your king commands you!*'

They paid no heed, leaping up the stone steps two and three at a time. I grabbed Radar's collar and pulled her tight against me. The first two palanquin-bearers got past us, but the third stumbled against Radar, who'd had enough. She thrust her head forward and chomped deep into his thigh. He waved his arms in an effort to regain his balance, then fell into the shaft, his final diminishing shriek cut short when he struck bottom.

I started forward and down again. Leah hadn't moved. She was peering at the grotesque figure in the flapping purple robe, trying to make out his features in the dim light of the stars glowing in that insane abyss over our heads. I had almost reached her when the light began to brighten. But not from the stars. The hum returned, only now it was deeper, not *mmmmmmmm* but *AAAAAAA*, the sound of some alien being, colossal and unknowable, scenting a meal it knows will be delicious.

I looked up. Leah looked up. Radar looked up. What we saw swimming out of that dark star-shot sky was terrible, but the real horror was this: it was also beautiful.

If my time-sense wasn't entirely shot, it was still daylight somewhere above us. Bella and Arabella had to be on the far side of the world of which Empis was a part, but here those two moons were just the same, projected out of a black void that had no business existing, washing this hellhole in their pallid and eldritch light.

The larger was closing in on the smaller, and it wasn't going to pass behind or in front. After the high gods only knew how many thousands of years, the two moons – these, and the real ones somewhere around the curve of the planet – were on a collision course.

They came together in a crash that was soundless (it really *was* a projection, then) and accompanied by a brilliant flash of light. Pieces flew in every direction, filling that dark sky like smashed chunks of glowing crockery. That toneless bray – AAAAAAAA – grew even louder. Deafening. The boom of the derrick began to rise, narrowing the triangle between it and the supporting mast. There was no sound of machinery, but I wouldn't have heard it anyway.

The fierce glare of the disintegrating moons blotted out the stars and bathed the floor below in brilliance. The hatch over the Dark Well began to rise, pulled by the derrick's hook. The grotesque creature in the purple robe was also looking up, and when Leah looked down, their eyes met. His were deep in sagging sockets of greenish flesh; hers were wide and blue.

In spite of all the years and all the changes, she recognized him. Her dismay and horror were unmistakable. I tried to hold her back, but she pulled free with a convulsive jerk that almost sent her over the edge. And I was in shock, numbed by what I had seen – the collision of two moons in a sky that had no right to exist. The pieces were spreading and starting to dim.

A crescent of darkness appeared at the edge of the Dark Well hatch and quickly widened into a black grin. That long, hoarse cry of satisfaction grew louder. The Flight Killer stumbled toward the well. His purple robe rose in several different directions. For a moment that horrible flabby head was obscured, and then the robe fell to one side and lay on the stone floor. The man beneath it was only half a man, as Elsa had only been half a woman. His legs had been replaced by a gnarl of black tentacles that hurried him along, teetering from side to side. Others protruded from the hanging sac of his belly, rising toward the rising hatch like obscene erections. His arms had been replaced by snakelike horrors that wavered around his face like seaweed in a strong current, and I realized that whatever the thing in the well might be, it wasn't Cthulhu. *Elden* was this world's Cthulhu, as surely as Dora was the old woman who lived in a shoe and Leah was the goose girl. He had traded deformed feet and a hunched back – kyphosis – for something far worse. Did he consider the trade fair? Had revenge and the slow destruction of the kingdom been enough to balance the scales?

Leah reached the bottom of the stairs. Overhead, the fragments of Bella and Arabella continued to expand.

'*Leah!*' I shouted. '*Leah, for God's sake stop!*'

Just past the palanquin with its limply hanging drapes, she did stop – but not because I'd called to her. I don't think she even heard me. All her attention was fixed on the flabby thing that had been her brother. Now he was bending eagerly over the rising hatch, the loose flesh of his face hanging down like dough. The crown fell off his head again. More of those black tentacles emerged from his neck, his back, and the cleft of his buttocks. He was turning into Cthulhu before my eyes, lord of the old gods, a nightmare fairy tale come to life.

But the real monster was below. Soon it would emerge.

Gogmagog.

8

I remember what happened next with heartbreaking clarity. I saw it all from where I was standing, maybe a dozen steps above the abandoned palanquin, and still see it in my dreams.

Radar was barking but I could barely hear her over the constant maddening drone from the Dark Well. Leah raised her dagger and with no hesitation plunged it deep into the feeding-sore beside what had been her mouth. Then, using both hands, she raked it across the scar, right to left.

'*ELDEN!*' she screamed. Blood flew from her re-opened mouth in a fine spray. Her voice was hoarse – from her feats of ventriloquism, I supposed – but the first word she'd spoken without having to project it from deep in her throat was loud enough for her wretched brother to hear, even over the hum. He turned. He saw her, really *saw* her, for the first time.

'ELDEN, STOP WHILE THERE'S STILL TIME!'

He hesitated, that forest of tentacles – more of them now, many more – waving. Did I see love in those bleary eyes? Regret? Sorrow, maybe shame that he'd cursed the only one who had loved him along with all those who had not? Or only the need to preserve what was slipping away after a reign that had been all too short (but doesn't it seem that way to all of us, when the end comes)?

I didn't know. I was running down the last steps, past the palanquin. I had no plan in mind, just a need to get her away before the thing down there could emerge. I thought of the giant cockroach that had escaped into Mr Bowditch's shed, and how Mr Bowditch had shot it, and that reminded me – finally – that I still had his gun.

Leah walked into that waving glut of tentacles, seemingly unaware of the danger they posed. One of them caressed her cheek. Elden was still looking at her, and was he crying?

'Go back,' he croaked. 'Go back while you can. I can't . . .'

One of those tentacles wrapped around her blood-streaked neck. It was clear what he couldn't do: stop the part of him that had been possessed by the thing below. All those books he'd read in the palace library – had none contained the most basic story of all cultures, the one that says when you deal with the devil you make a devil's bargain?

I grabbed the tentacle – one that might have been part of an arm when Elden first made his bargain – and yanked it free of her throat. It was tough and coated with some kind of slime. Once it was no longer choking Leah, I let it slither out of my grip. Another wrapped around my wrist, a second one around my thigh. They began to pull me toward Elden. And the opening well.

I raised Mr Bowditch's gun to shoot him. Before I could, a tentacle curled around the barrel, jerked it away, and sent it spinning across the rough stone floor in the direction of the abandoned palanquin. Radar was now standing between Elden and the well, all her hackles up, barking so hard that foam flew from her jaws. She lunged to bite him. A tentacle – one that had been part of Elden's left leg – snapped out like a whip and sent her sprawling. I was being dragged forward. The monster might have been weeping for his sister, but it was also grinning in anticipation of some awful victory, real or imagined. Two more tentacles, small ones, emerged from that grin to taste the air. The derrick was still pulling the hatch, but something else – something beneath – was pushing it as well, widening the gap.

Another world down there, I thought. *A black one I never want to see.*

'You were all part of it!' the flabby, green-faced creature shrieked at Leah. '*You were all part of it or you would have come with me! You would have been my queen!*'

More of Flight Killer's tentacles seized her – legs, waist, once more around the neck – and dragged her forward. Something was coming out of the well, an oily black substance stippled with long white thorns. It hit the floor with a wet slap. It was a wing.

'*I AM the queen!*' Leah cried. '*You aren't my brother! He was kind! You're an assassin and a pretender! You are an imposter!*'

She plunged the dagger, still dripping with her blood, into her brother's eye. The tentacles fell away from her. He staggered back. The wing rose and gave a flap that sent a nauseating gust of air into my face. It wrapped around Elden. The thorns impaled him. He was dragged to the lip of the well. He gave a final shriek before the thing plunged its hooked thorns into his chest and dragged him in.

But having its puppet wasn't enough to satisfy it. A bubble of alien flesh rose from the well. Huge golden eyes stared at us from what was otherwise no face at all. There was a scraping, grinding sound, and a second thorn-covered wing emerged. It gave an exploratory flap and another gust of putrescent air struck me.

'*Go back!*' Leah shouted. Blood sprayed from her ragged liberated mouth. Droplets struck the emerging thing and sizzled. '*I, the Queen of Empis, command you!*'

It continued to emerge, now flapping both of its thorny wings. Strings of some noisome fluid sprayed from it. The light from the shattered moons had continued to fade and I could barely see the humped, twisted thing that was rising, its sides bulging in and out like a bellows. Elden's head was disappearing into its strange flesh. His dead face, stamped with his final expression of horror, looked out at us like the face of a man disappearing into quicksand.

Radar's barks were now more like screams.

I think it might have been some kind of dragon, but not of the sort seen in any book of fairy tales. It was from beyond my world. Leah's, too. The Dark Well opened into some other universe beyond all human comprehension. And Leah's command did nothing to stop it.

It came out.

It came out.

The moons had kissed and soon it would be free.

9

Leah didn't command it again. She must have decided it was useless. She only craned her neck to watch that thing as it grew from the well. Now there was only Radar, barking and barking, but somehow – miraculously, heroically – holding her ground.

I realized that I was going to die, and it would be a mercy. Assuming, that was, life didn't continue in some terrible hellish drone (*AAAAAAA*) once I – and Leah, and Radar – were taken into the thing's alien being.

I had read that at such moments one's whole life flashes before one's eyes. What flashed before me, like illustrations in a book whose pages are quickly fanned, were all the fairy tales I had encountered in Empis, from the shoe woman and the goose girl to the houses of the Three Little Exiles to the mean sisters who never would have taken their beautiful little sister (or deformed little brother) to the ball.

It was growing, growing. Thorny wings flapping. Elden's face had disappeared into its unknowable guts.

Then I thought of another fairy tale.

Once upon a time there had been a mean little man named Christopher Polley who had come to steal Mr Bowditch's gold.

Once upon a time there had been a mean little man named Peterkin who had been torturing the Snab with a dagger.

Once upon a time my mother was struck by a plumber's truck on the Sycamore Street Bridge, and killed when it drove her into one of the bridge stanchions. Most of her stayed on the bridge, but her head and shoulders had gone into the Little Rumple River.

Always Rumpelstiltskin. From the very beginning. The Original Fairy Tale, you might say. And how did the queen's daughter get rid of that troublesome elf?

'*I KNOW YOUR NAME!*' I shouted. The voice was not my own, no more than many of the thoughts and insights in this story belonged to the seventeen-year-old boy who first came to Empis. It was the voice of a prince. Not of this world and not of mine. I had begun by calling Empis 'the Other,' but *I* was the other. Still Charlie Reade, sure, but I was someone else as well, and the idea that I had been sent here – that my clock had been wound and set years ago, when my mother walked across that bridge, munching a chicken wing – for just this moment was impossible to doubt. Later, when the person I was in that underground world began to ebb away, I *would* doubt it, but then? No.

'I KNOW YOUR NAME, GOGMAGOG, AND I COMMAND YOU TO RETURN TO YOUR LAIR!'

It screamed. The stone floor shook and cracks ran across it. Far above us, graves were once more giving up their dead and a great crevasse was zig-zagging its way across the Field of the Monarchs. Those huge wings flapped, raining down stinking drops that burned like acid. But you know what? I *liked* that scream, because I was a dark prince and that was a scream of pain.

'GOGMAGOG, GOGMAGOG, YOUR NAME IS GOGMAGOG!'

It screamed each time I spoke its name. Those screams were in the world; they were also deep in my head, as the hum had been, threatening to burst my skull. The wings beat frantically. Great eyes glared at me.

'*RETURN TO YOUR LAIR, GOGMAGOG! YOU MAY COME AGAIN, GOGMAGOG, IN TEN YEARS OR A THOUSAND, GOGMAGOG, BUT NOT THIS DAY, GOGMAGOG!*' I spread my arms. '*IF YOU TAKE ME IN, GOGMAGOG, I'LL BURST YOUR GUTS WITH YOUR NAME BEFORE I DIE!*'

It began to retreat, folding its wings over those hideous staring eyes. The sound of its descent was a liquid *shloooop* that made me want to vomit. I wondered how the hell we were supposed to make that gigantic derrick lower the lid, but Leah had that one. Her voice was hoarse and broken . . . but couldn't I see lips emerging from the mangled wreck of her mouth? I'm not sure, but having been force-fed so much make-believe, I gladly swallowed that one.

'Close in the name of Leah of the Gallien.'

Slowly – far too slowly for my taste – the derrick's boom began to lower the hatch. The tautness came out of the cable and at last the hook swung free. I let out my breath.

Leah threw herself into my arms, hugging for all she was worth.

The blood from her newly opened mouth was warm on my neck. Something thudded into me from behind. It was Radar, rear paws on the floor, front ones propped on my ass, tail wagging like mad.

'How did you know?' Leah asked in her broken voice.

'A story my mother told me,' I said. Which was, in a way, true. She had told me now by dying then. 'We have to go, Leah, or we're going to have to find our way in the dark. And you need to stop talking. I can see how much it hurts.'

'Yes, but the hurt is wonderful.'

Leah pointed to the palanquin. 'They must have brought at least one lantern. Do you still have matches?'

For a wonder, I did. We walked hand in hand to the abandoned palanquin, Radar between us. Leah bent down once along the way, but I hardly noticed. I was concentrating on getting something to light our way before the light from the shattered moons faded entirely.

I brushed back one of the palanquin's curtains, and there, cringing against its far side, was the one member of Elden's party I'd forgotten about. *Flight Killer*, Percival had said. *Four others. And the bitch*. Or maybe he'd said *the witch*.

Petra's hair had come loose from the crisscross strings of pearls that had bound it. Her white makeup had cracked and run. She stared at me with horror and loathing. 'You ruined everything, you hateful brat!'

Brat made me smile. 'Nah, nah, sweetheart. Sticks and stones will break my bones, but words will never hurt me.'

Hanging from a little brass hook at the front of the palanquin was just what I was hoping for – one of those torpedo-shaped lanterns.

'I was his consort, do you hear? His chosen one! I let him touch me with those loathsome snakes that used to be his arms! I licked his drool! He didn't have long to live, any fool could see that, and I would have ruled!'

Not worthy of a response, in my humble opinion.

'I would have been Queen of Empis!'

I reached for the lantern. Her lips peeled back from teeth that had been filed to points, like Hana's. Perhaps that had been the coming fashion in the Flight Killer's hellish court. She lunged forward and buried those fangs in my arm. The pain was immediate and excruciating.

Blood seeped out from her clamped lips. Her eyes bulged from their sockets. I tried to pull free. My flesh tore but her teeth stayed clamped.

'Petra,' Leah said. Her voice was down to a hoarse growl. 'Have this, you stinking crone.'

The roar of Mr Bowditch's .45, which Leah had stooped to pick up, was deafening. A hole appeared in the caked white makeup just above Petra's right eye. Her head fell back, and before she crashed to the floor of the palanquin I saw something I could have done without: a doorknob-sized gobbet of my forearm hanging from those filed teeth.

Leah didn't hesitate. She tore down one of the palanquin's hanging side-drapes, ripped a long piece from the bottom, and tied it around the wound. Now it was almost completely dark. I reached into the gloom with my good arm to get the lantern (the idea that Petra might come to life and batten on that one, too, was ridiculous but strong). I almost dropped it. Prince or no prince, I was shaking with shock. My arm felt as if Petra hadn't just bitten it but poured gasoline into the wound and set it on fire.

'You light it,' I said. 'The matches are in the holster.'

I felt her fumble at my hip, then heard her scratch one of the sulphur matches on the side of the palanquin. I tipped back the lantern's glass chimney. She turned a little knob on the side to advance the wick and lit it. Then she took it from me, which was good. I would have dropped it.

I started for the spiral staircase (I thought I'd be happy never to see another of those), but she held me back and pulled me down. I felt her tattered mouth move against my ear as she whispered.

'She was my great-aunt.'

She was far too young to be your great anything, I thought. Then I remembered Mr Bowditch, who had gone on a trip and come back as his own son.

'Let's get out of here and never come back,' I said.

10

We climbed out of the pit very slowly. I had to stop and rest every fifty steps or so. My arm was throbbing with each beat of my heart, and I could feel the makeshift bandage Leah had put on soaking with blood. I kept seeing Petra as she fell back dead with a chunk of my flesh in her mouth.

When we got to the top of the steps I had to sit down. My head was throbbing now as well as my arm. I remembered reading somewhere that when it comes to starting a dangerous, perhaps even lethal infection, nothing but the bite of a rabid animal beats one from a supposedly healthy human . . . and how was I to know how healthy Petra had been after years of commerce (my mind balked at the idea of actual congress) with Elden? I imagined I could feel her poison coursing up my arm to the shoulder, and from there to my heart. Telling myself I was full of shit didn't help much.

Leah gave me a few moments to sit with Radar anxiously nuzzling the side of my face, then pointed to the reservoir of the lantern. It was almost empty, and the glow from the walls had gone with the death of Elden and the retreat of Gogmagog. Her point was clear – if we didn't want to have to stumble our way out in the dark, we had to move.

We were about halfway up the steep incline leading to the huge chamber with its ring of twelve passages when the lantern guttered and went out. Leah sighed, then gripped my good hand. We walked slowly on. The dark was unpleasant, but with the hum and the whispering voices gone, it wasn't so bad. The pain in my arm was. The bite hadn't clotted; I could feel warm blood in my palm and between my fingers. Radar sniffed it and whined. I thought of Iota dying from the nick of a poisoned knife. Like the memory of my flesh hanging from Petra's pointed teeth, it wasn't anything I wanted to think about, but was helpless not to.

Leah stopped and pointed. I realized I could see her point because now there was light in the passage again. Not the sick green light from those strange half-glass, half-stone walls but a warm yellow glow, waxing and waning. As it brightened Radar ran toward it, barking her head off.

'No!' I shouted. That made my headache worse. 'Stay, girl!'

She paid no attention, and those weren't the furious, terrified barks she'd voiced in the dark universe we'd left behind (but not far enough, it would never be far enough). These were excited barks. And something was coming out of the growing glow. *Jumping* out of it.

Radar went flat, tail and rump wagging, and the Snab leaped onto her back. Following it was a swarm of fireflies.

'The lord of small things,' I said. 'I'll be damned.'

The fireflies – there had to have been at least a thousand – formed an incandescent cloud over my dog and the big red cricket on her back, and the two of them were beautiful in their low and shifting light. Radar rose, I think at some command from her rider that wasn't meant for human ears. She started up the inclined floor. The fireflies headed back that way, swirling over them.

Leah squeezed my hand. We followed the fireflies.

11

Eris was waiting in the cathedral-sized room with the twelve passages. The Snab had brought a battalion of fireflies to us, but had left a platoon to keep Eris from being in total darkness. When we emerged, she ran to me and hugged me. When I stiffened in pain, she drew back and looked at the makeshift bandage, soaked with blood and still dripping.

'High gods, what happened to you?' Then she looked at Leah, and gasped. 'Oh, my lady!'

'Too much to tell.' Thinking it might be too much to tell ever. 'Why are you here? Why did you come back?'

'The Snab led me. And brought light. As you see. You need medical attention, both of you, and Freed is far too ill.'

It will have to be Claudia, then, I thought. *Claudia will know what to do. If anything can be done.*

'We need to get out of here,' I said. 'I am so sick of being underground.'

I looked at the red cricket on Radar's back. It looked back at me, those small black eyes giving it a singularly solemn aspect. 'Lead on, Sir Snab, if you would be so kind.'

And so it did.

12

Several people were crowded into the clothes storage room when we finally came out. The fireflies streamed away over their heads in a banner of light. Jaya was there, and Percival, and several others from my time of incarceration in Deep Maleen, but I don't remember which ones. By then I was growing increasingly woozy, and my headache was so bad that it seemed to have materialized into a pulsing white ball of pain hanging about three inches in front of my eyes. The only two things I remember clearly are that the Snab was no longer on Radar's back, and Percival looked better. It was impossible to say how, given that white ball of pain in front of me and the bone-deep throb in my torn arm, but he did. I was sure of it. Our greeters knelt at the sight of the princess, and raised their hands to their lowered brows.

'Up,' she croaked. Her voice was almost gone, but I thought that was from overuse, and would come back in time. The idea that her vocal cords had been permanently ruptured was too horrible even to consider.

They rose. With Leah supporting me on one side and Eris on the other, we left the overcrowded storage room. I made it most of the way to the first staircase, then my legs gave out. I was carried, maybe by my friends from Deep Maleen, maybe by grayfolk, maybe both. I can't remember. I do remember being carried through the reception hall and seeing at least three dozen grayfaced men and women cleaning the mess that had been left there by those of King Jan's court who had elected to give their allegiance to the Flight Killer. It seemed to me that one of the cleaners was Dora, wearing a red cloth wrapped around her hair and her splendidly yellow canvas shoes on her feet. She raised her hands to her mouth and blew me a kiss with fingers that were beginning to look like fingers again, rather than flippers.

She isn't there, I thought. *You're delirious, Prince Charlie. And even if she is, her fingers can't be regenerating. Stuff like that only happens in—*

In what? Well . . . in stories like this.

I craned my neck for another look at her as I was carried out into the next room, some kind of antechamber, and saw the bright head-rag and the brighter sneakers, but I couldn't be sure it was Dora. She was back to me and on her knees, scrubbing away filth.

We passed through more rooms, and down a long hallway, but by then I was fading toward unconsciousness, and would be glad to go if it took me to a place where my head didn't feel like it was bursting and my arm didn't feel like a blazing Yule log. But I held on. If I was dying – and it certainly felt like I was – I wanted to do it outside, breathing free air.

Bright light struck me. It made my headache worse but it was still wonderful because it wasn't the sick light of the underground world beneath Lilimar. It wasn't even the far friendlier glow of the fireflies. This was daylight, but it was more.

It was *sunlight*.

I was carried into it, half-sitting, half-lying down. The clouds were unraveling and I could see blue sky above the great plaza in front of the palace. Not just enough blue to make a pair of overalls, but acres of blue. No, *miles* of it. And my God, what sunshine! I looked down and saw my shadow. Seeing it made me feel like Peter Pan, that Prince of the Lost Boys.

A vast cheer went up. The city gate was open and the plaza was filled with the grayfolk of Empis. They saw Leah and went to their knees with a great rustle that gave me gooseflesh.

She was looking at me. I think that look said *I could use a little help here.*

'Put me down,' I said.

My bearers did, and I found I could stand. All the pain was still there, but something else was there, as well. It had been there when I cried Gogmagog's name in a voice that wasn't my own and it was here now. I raised my arms, the good right and the left that was still dripping blood, turning to scarlet the new bandage Jaya had at some point put on. Like the poppies on the hill behind Dora's trim little house.

The people below were silent, waiting, on their knees. And in spite of the power I felt rushing through me just then, I remembered they were not kneeling for me. This wasn't my world. My world was the other, but I had one more job to do here.

'Listen to me, people of Empis! The Flight Killer is dead!'

They roared approval and thanks.

'The Dark Well is shut and the creature that lives there is pent inside!'

Another roar greeted this.

Now I felt that power, that *otherness*, leaving me, taking the strength I had borrowed with it. Soon I'd be plain old Charlie Reade again . . . if Petra's bite didn't kill me, that was.

'Hail Leah, people of Empis! Hail Leah of the Gallien! HAIL YOUR QUEEN!'

I think it was a boffo line to go out on, as my dad might have said, but I'll never know for sure, because that's when the hinges fell out of my knees and I lost consciousness.

CHAPTER THIRTY-ONE

Visitors. The Queen in White. Mercy.

Woody and Claudia. Leaving Empis.

1

I spent a long time in a beautiful room with billowing white curtains. The windows behind them were open, letting in not just a breeze but a reservoir of fresh air. Did I spend three weeks in that room? Four? I don't know, because they didn't keep weeks in Empis. Not our weeks, anyway. The sun came up and went down. Sometimes at night those curtains were illuminated by the light of the shattered moons. The remains of Bella and Arabella had formed a kind of necklace in the sky. I never saw it then, just the shifting light through billowing curtains of finest gauze. There were times when one of my nurses (Dora was the best, Our Lady of the Shoes) would want to close the windows behind the curtains lest 'night vapors' make my already parlous condition worse, but I wouldn't allow it because the air was so sweet. They obeyed because I was the prince, and my word was law. I didn't tell any of them that I was reverting back to plain old Charlie Reade. They wouldn't have believed me anyway.

Many people came to visit with me in the room of billowing curtains. Some of them were dead.

Iota came one day – I remember his visit clearly. He dropped to one knee, put his palm to his forehead, then took the low chair beside my bed where my gray nurses sat to scrape off the old poultices (which hurt), clean the wound (which hurt more), and then put on fresh poultices. That greenish muck – Claudia's creation – stank to high heaven, but it was soothing. That's not to say I wouldn't have preferred a couple of Advils. A couple of Percocets would have been even better.

'You look fucking terrible,' Eye said.

'Thank you. Very kind.'

'It was wasp venom that did for me,' Eye said. 'On the knife. You remember the knife, and the man behind the door?'

I did. Jeff, a good old American name. Or Geoff, a good old British one. 'I had an idea Petra had him tapped for her consort once Elden died and she became queen of the realm.'

'He probably had one of the gray men stick that knife into a nest long enough to get a good coating. Poor fellow was likely stung to death.'

I thought that more than likely, if the wasps in Empis were as big as the roaches.

'But would that bastard care?' Iota continued. 'Nah, nah, not that bitch's son. Wasps weren't so dangerous in the old days, but . . .' He shrugged.

'Things changed once Flight Killer was in charge. For the worse.'

'For the worse, yuh.' He looked quite amusing, sitting in that low chair with his knees up around his ears. 'We needed someone to save us. We got you. Better than nothing, I suppose.'

I raised my good hand and poked up the ring finger and pinky, my old friend Bertie's way of shooting someone the bird.

Iota said, 'Petra's poison may not be as bad as what was slathered on that bastard's knife, but from the look of you it was bad enough.'

Of course it was bad. She had licked off the Elden-thing's drool, and that residue had been in her mouth when she bit me. Thinking of it made me shudder.

'Fight it,' he said, getting up. 'Fight it, Prince Charlie.'

I didn't see him come in, but I saw him leave. He passed through the billowing curtains and was gone.

One of the gray nurses came in, looking concerned. It was possible to discern expressions on the faces of the afflicted now; the worst of the deformities might remain, but the steady progression of the disease – the *curse* – had been arrested. More, there was slow but steady improvement. I saw the first tinge of color in many gray faces, and the webbing that had turned hands and feet into flippers was dissolving. But I didn't believe there would be permanent recovery for any of them. Claudia could hear again – a little – but I thought Woody would always be blind.

The nurse said she'd heard me speaking and thought I might be lapsing back into delirium.

'I was talking to myself,' I said, and maybe I was. Radar had never so much as raised her head, after all.

Cla dropped by for a visit. He didn't bother with the palm-to-brow salute, nor did he sit down, just hulked over the bed. 'You cheated. If you'd played straight, I would have laid you out, prince or no prince.'

'What did you expect?' I asked. 'You had at least a hundred pounds on me, and you were fast. Tell me you wouldn't have done the same in my shoes.'

He laughed. 'You got me there, I give it to you, but I think your days of breaking a fighting stick over anybody's neck are over. Are you going to get better?'

'Fucked if I know.'

He laughed some more and walked to the billowing curtains. 'You've got some hard bark on you, I'll say that much.' And he was gone. If he was there at all, that is; *you've got some hard bark on you* was a line from an old TCM movie my dad and I watched during his drinking days. Can't remember the name of the film, only that Paul Newman was in it, playing an Indian. You think some of the things in my story are hard to believe? Try imagining Paul Newman as an Indian. That's a real credibility-strainer.

That night – or some other, I can't be sure – I woke to the sound of Radar growling and saw Kellin, the Lord High himself, sitting at my bedside in his fancy red smoking jacket.

'You're getting worse, Charlie,' he said. 'They tell you the bite looks better and maybe it does, but that infection's gone deep. Soon you'll boil with it. Your heart will swell up and burst, and I'll be waiting for you. I and my troop of night soldiers.'

'Don't hold your breath,' I said, but that was silly. He couldn't draw it, hold it, or let it out. He'd been dead even before the rats got to him. 'Get out, traitor.'

He did, but Radar continued to growl. I followed her gaze and saw Petra in the shadows, grinning at me with her filed teeth.

Dora often slept in the antechamber, and she came running on her bowed legs when she heard my scream. She didn't raise the gaslights, but held one of those torpedo-shaped lanterns. She asked if I was all right and if my heart was beating regular, because all the nurses had been told to watch out for any changes in its rhythm. I said I was, but she took my pulse anyway, and checked the latest poultice.

'Was it ghosties, maybe?'

I pointed to the corner.

Dora padded over there in her splendid canvas shoes and raised the lantern. No one was there, but I really didn't need her to show me that, because Radar had gone back to sleep. Dora bent and kissed my cheek as well as her bent mouth would allow. 'A' right, a' right, everything a' right. Sleep now, Charlie. Sleep and heal.'

2

I also had visits from the living. Cammit and Quilly; then Stooks, swaggering in as if he owned the place. His slashed cheek had been sewn up in a dozen looping black stitches that made me think of a Frankenstein movie I'd watched on TCM with my dad.

'Gointer leave one hell of a scar,' he said, rubbing at the stitches. 'I'll never be pretty again.'

'Stooks, you were never pretty.'

Claudia came often, and then one day – around the time I thought that yes, I'd probably live – Doc Freed came with her. One of the nurses was pushing him in a wheelchair that must have belonged to some king or other, because the wheel-spokes looked like solid gold. My old nemesis Christopher Polley would have shit himself with envy.

Freed's mangled and infected leg had been amputated, and he was clearly in great pain, but he had the look of a man who would live.

I was delighted to see him. Claudia gently scraped away my current poultice and washed the wound. Then they bent over it with their heads almost touching.

'Healing,' Freed pronounced. 'Wouldn't you say?'

'YES!' Claudia shouted. She really could hear again – a little, anyway – but I thought she might end up speaking in that toneless blare for the rest of her life. 'PINK FLESH! NO SMELL EXCEPT FROM THE WIDOW'S MOSS IN THE POULTICE!'

'Maybe the infection's still there,' I said. 'Maybe it's gone deep.'

Claudia and Freed exchanged an astonished glance. The doc was in too much pain to laugh, so Claudia did it for him. 'WHAT GAVE YOU A STUPID IDEA LIKE THAT?'

'No, huh?'

'Disease may hide, Prince Charlie,' Doc Freed said, 'but infection is a show-off. It stinks and pustulates.' He turned to Claudia. 'How much of the surrounding flesh did you have to take?'

'UP TO THE ELBOW AND ALMOST DOWN TO THE WRIST! A HATEFUL FUCKING GORE SHE GAVE HIM, AND IT WILL LEAVE A HOLLOW WHERE THE MUSCLE WON'T EVER COME BACK. YOUR DAYS OF PLAYING GAMES ARE PROBABLY OVER, SHARLIE.'

'But you'll be able to pick your nose with both hands,' Freed said, which made me laugh. It felt good to laugh. I'd had plenty of nightmares since coming back from the Dark Well, but laughter had been in short supply.

'You should lie down and let someone give you some of that pain stuff they have,' I told the doc. 'Little leaves you chew up. You look worse than I do.'

'I'm mending,' he said. 'And Charlie . . . we owe you our lives.'

There was truth in that, but not the whole truth. They also owed the Snab, for instance. It had gone to wherever Snabs go, although it might turn up in time (it had a way of doing that). Percival, however, was a different matter. He didn't come to see me on his own, so I asked that he be brought. He came into the room of the billowing curtains shyly, dressed in cooks' whites and crushing a beret type of hat to his chest. I suppose it was an Empisarian chef's toque.

His bow was deep, his hand salute trembly. He was afraid to look at me until I offered him a chair and a glass of cold tea to drink. I thanked him for all he'd done and told him how happy I was to see him. That loosened his tongue, first a little and then a lot. He gave me news of Lilimar no one else had bothered to pass on. I think because he saw it from a workingman's point of view.

The streets were being cleaned, the rubbish and rubble were being picked up. Hundreds of people who had come to the city to help overthrow Elden's rotten reign had left for their towns and farms, but hundreds more had replaced them, come to do their duty for Queen Leah before returning to their homes in places like Seafront and Deesk. To me it sounded like the WPA projects I'd read about in school. Windows were being washed, gardens were being replanted, and someone wise in the ways of plumbing had gotten the fountains started, one by one. The dead, no longer restless, had been reburied. Some of the shops had been re-opened. More would follow. Percival's voice was still slurred and garbled, sometimes hard to understand, but I'll spare you that.

'The glass in the three spires is changing by the day, Prince Charlie! From that ugly dark green to the blue that it was in the old days! Wise folk, those who remember how things worked in the old days, are putting the trolley wires back up. It will be a long time before the cars are running again, and the damn things were always breaking down even in the best of times, but it will be nice to have them.'

'I don't understand how they *can* run,' I said. 'There's no electricity except for that little generator on one of the lower levels of the palace, that I guess my friend Mr Bowditch brought.'

Percival looked puzzled. He didn't understand *electricity*, which I think must have come out in English rather than Empisarian.

'Power,' I said. 'Where do the trolleys get their power?'

'Oh!' His face, lumpy, but improving, cleared. 'Well, the stations give the power, of course. It's—'

And now it was a word that *I* didn't understand. He saw that and made a waving gesture with one hand.

'The stations on the river, Prince Charlie. On the streams, if they're big ones. And from the sea, oh, there's a whopping station at Seafront.'

I think he was talking about some form of hydroelectric power. If so, I never found out how it was stored. There were many things about Empis that remained mysterious to me. Compared to how it could exist at all – and *where* – made the question of power storage seem picayune. Almost pointless.

3

The sun came up, the sun went down. People came, people went. Some dead and some alive. The one I wanted most to see – the one who had gone to the well with me – didn't come.

Until one day she did. The goose girl who was now a queen.

I was sitting on the balcony beyond the curtains, looking down at the palace's central plaza and remembering unpleasant things, when the white curtains billowed out instead of into the room, and she stepped between them. She was wearing a white dress belted at her slim (still too slim) waist with a fine gold chain. There was no crown on her head, but on one finger was a ring with a jeweled butterfly on its face. I guessed it was the signet of the realm, and served her when toting around a golden headpiece would have been too much trouble.

I got up and bowed, but before I could put my hand to my forehead, she took it and squeezed it and placed it between her breasts. 'Nah, nah, none of that,' she said in such a perfect workingman's accent that it made me laugh. Her voice was still husky, but no longer hoarse. A lovely voice, really. I guessed it wasn't how she had sounded before the curse, but it was fine. 'Hug me, rather, if your hurt arm allows.'

It did. I hugged her tight. There was a faint smell of perfume, something like honeysuckle. I felt as if I could have hugged her forever.

'I thought you wouldn't come,' I said. 'I thought you'd cast me aside.'

'I've been very busy,' she said, but her eyes shifted away from mine. 'Sit with me, my dear. I need to look at you, and we need to talk.'

4

The half a dozen or so nurses who had been tending to me had been let go to perform other duties, there was no shortage of work in the weeks after the fall of the Flight Killer, but Dora remained. She brought us a large pitcher of Empisarian tea.

'I'll drink a lot,' Leah said. 'It doesn't hurt me to talk now . . . well, very little . . . but my throat is always dry. And my mouth is as you see.'

It was no longer sealed, but it was still badly scarred and always would be. Her lips were healing wounds lined with dark red scabs. The ugly sore she'd used to feed herself was almost entirely gone, but her mouth would never be completely mobile again, no more than Woody would regain his sight or Claudia the full use of her ears. I thought of Stooks saying *I'll never be pretty again*. Queen Leah of the Gallien never would be, either, but that didn't matter. Because she was beautiful.

'I didn't want you to see me like this,' she said. 'When I'm with people – which is all day, it seems – I have to keep myself from covering it. When I look in a mirror . . .' She raised her hand. I took it before she could put it over her mouth and set it firmly in her lap.

'I'd be happy to kiss it, if it didn't hurt you.'

She smiled at that. It was lopsided but charming. Maybe *because* it was lopsided. 'You're a bit young for love-kisses.'

I love you anyway, I thought.

'How old are you?' This was an impertinent question to ask a queen, surely, but I needed to know what kind of love I'd have to settle for.

'Twice your age, anyway. Perhaps more.'

I thought of Mr Bowditch then. 'You haven't been on the sundial, have you? You're not, like, a hundred years old, or anything?'

She managed to look amused and horrified at the same time. 'Never. No one goes on the sundial, because it's very dangerous. When games and contests were played on the Field of the Monarchs – that will happen again, although there's much repair work to be done first – the sundial was locked in place, motionless, and guarded for good measure. Lest someone from the thousands who came on those days be tempted. It's very old. Elden told me once that it was here before Lilimar was built, or even thought of.'

Hearing that made me uneasy. I bent down and stroked my dog, who was curled up between my feet. '*Radar's* been on it. That's most of the reason I came, because Rades was dying. As you must know, from Claudia.'

'Yes,' Leah said, and bent to pet Radar herself. Rades looked up sleepily. 'But your dog is an animal, innocent of the bad strain that lives in the hearts of every man and woman. The strain that destroyed my brother. I'd guess that strain lives in your world, too.'

I couldn't argue that.

'No royal would go around on that even once, Charlie. It changes the mind and the heart. Nor is that all it does.'

'My friend Mr Bowditch rode on it, and he wasn't a bad guy. In fact, he was a good guy.'

This was true, but as I looked back, I realized it wasn't *completely* true. Getting through Mr Bowditch's anger and solitary nature had been difficult. No, almost impossible. I would have given up if I hadn't made a promise to God (*the God of my understanding*, people in my dad's AA group always say). And I never would have known him at all if he hadn't fallen and broken his leg. He had no wife, no kids, no friends. He was a loner and a hoarder, a guy who kept a bucket of gold pellets in his safe and liked his old things: furniture, magazines, TV, vintage Studebaker in storage. He was, in his own words, a coward who had brought presents instead of taking a stand. If you wanted to be cruel – I didn't, but if you did – he'd been a bit like Christopher Polley. Which is to say, like Rumpelstiltskin. That wasn't a comparison I wanted to make but was helpless not to. If I hadn't come, and if he hadn't loved his dog, Mr Bowditch would have died unremarked and unremembered in his house at the top of the hill. And with no one to guard it, the passage between the two worlds would certainly have been discovered. Had he never thought of that?

Leah was looking at me, twirling her signet ring on her finger, and smiling her lopsided little smile. 'Was he good on his own? Or did you make him good, Prince Charlie?'

'Don't call me that,' I said. If I couldn't be her prince, I didn't want to be anyone's. Nor was that even a choice. My hair was darkening again, and my eyes were changing back to their original color.

She put her hand to her mouth, then forced herself to lower it to her lap again. 'Good on his own, Charlie? Or were you his mercy from the high gods?'

I didn't know how to answer her. I had felt older during much of my time in Empis, and sometimes stronger, but now I felt weak and uncertain again. Seeing Mr Bowditch without the softening filter of memory was a shock. I remembered how that old house at 1 Sycamore Street had smelled until I aired it out: sour and dusty. *Pent.*

She said, and not without alarm, '*You* didn't ride on it, did you?'

'No, just pulled Radar off. And she jumped, too. But I felt its power. Can I ask you a question?'

'Yes, of course.'

'The golden platform. We went up to go down. Down those spiral stairs.'

She smiled a little, all she could manage. 'We did. It was risky, but we managed.'

'Did the staircase between the walls go all the way to that underground chamber?'

'Yes. Elden knew two ways. That, and the one from the little room full of clothes. There may be others, but if there were, he never showed me.'

'So why did we go the long way?' *And almost fall*, I didn't say.

'Because it was said the Flight Killer couldn't walk more than a few steps. That made the stairs between the walls safer. And I didn't want to chance coming onto his party, but in the end there was no choice.'

'If we hadn't stopped at the Lord High's apartment . . . Iota might still be alive!'

'We did what had to be done, Charlie. You were right about that. I was wrong. Wrong about many things. I need you to know that, and I need you to know something else. I'm ugly now from the nose down—'

'You're not—'

She held up a hand. 'Hush! You see me as a friend, I love you for it and always will. Others don't and won't. Yet as queen I'll have to marry before I grow much older. Ugly or not, there will be many willing to embrace me, at least with the lights out, and there's no need for kisses to produce an heir. But men who ride the sundial, even a single turn, are sterile. And women are barren. The sundial gives life, but it also takes it away.'

Which explained why there were no little Bowditches, I supposed. 'But Petra—'

'*Petra!*' She laughed scornfully. 'All Petra wanted was to be queen of the ruin my brother created. And she was barren, anyway.' She sighed and drank, emptying her glass and pouring another. 'She was mad, and she was cruel. If Lilimar and Empis had been given into her grip, she would have ridden the sundial again and again and again. You saw how she was for yourself.'

I had. And felt it. I was still feeling it, although her poison was out of my wound and the pain had been replaced by a deep itch Dora swore would go away in time.

'Elden was the other reason I was so slow in coming to see you, Charlie, although thoughts of you have never left my mind and I suppose they never will.'

I almost asked if she was *sure* I was too young for her, but didn't. For one thing, I wasn't meant to be a queen's consort, let alone a king. For another, I had a father who would be desperate to know I was still alive. There was a third reason for going back, too. The threat Gogmagog posed to our world might be over (at least for the time being), but there was also the threat our world would pose to Empis. If, that was, our world found out it was here, with all its untold wealth accessible from a certain shed in Illinois.

'You were there when I killed my brother. I loved him as he once was, I tried to see him as he once was, but you forced me to see the monster he became. Every time I look at you, I remember him, and what I did. I remember what it cost me. Do you understand that?'

'It wasn't a bad thing, Leah. It was a good thing. You saved the kingdom, and not so you could be queen. You saved it because it needed to be saved.'

'That's true, and there is no need for false modesty between the two of us who have been through so much, but you still don't understand. I *knew*, you see. That the Flight Killer was my brother. Claudia told me years ago and I called her a liar. When I'm with you, I'll always know I should have done it sooner. What held me back was the selfish need to love his memory. While the kingdom suffered, I fed my geese and tended my garden and felt sorry for myself. You . . . I'm sorry, Charlie, but when I see you, I see my shame. That I chose to be a mute farmgirl while my land and my people died slowly all around me. *And all along I knew*.'

She was crying. I reached out to her. She shook her head and turned away, as if she couldn't stand for me to see her tears.

I said, 'Just now when you came, Leah, I was thinking of a bad thing I did. A shameful thing. May I tell you?'

'If you like.' Still not looking at me.

'I had a friend, Bertie Bird. A good friend but not a *good* friend, if you see what I mean. I went through a hard time after my mother died. My father did, too, but I didn't think very much about his hard time, because I was just a kid. All I knew was I needed him and he wasn't there. I think you must understand that.'

'You know I do,' Leah said, and drank more tea. She had almost emptied the pitcher, and it was a big one.

'We did some bad things, Bertie and I. But the one I was thinking of . . . there was a park we used to cut through on our way home from school. Cavanaugh Park. And one day we saw a crippled man there, feeding the pigeons. He was wearing shorts and had big braces on his legs. Bertie and I thought he looked stupid. Robo-Dude, Bertie called him.'

'I don't know what that m—'

'Never mind. It doesn't matter. He was a crippled man on a bench, enjoying the sun, and Bertie and I looked at each other, and Bertie said, "Let's swipe his crutches." I guess it was that strain you talked about. The evil. We swooped down and took them and he yelled at us to bring them back, but we didn't. We took them to the edge of the park and threw them in the duck pond. Bertie threw one and I threw the other. Laughing the whole time. We threw the crippled man's crutches in the water and how he ever got home I don't know. They splashed, and we laughed.'

I poured the rest of the tea. It only filled half the glass, which was good because my hand was shaking and my eyes were streaming. I hadn't cried since I cried for my father in Deep Maleen.

'Why do you tell me this, Charlie?'

I didn't know when I started – I thought that was one story I'd never tell anybody – but I knew now. 'I stole your crutches. All I can say in my defense is that I had to.'

'Ah, Charlie.' She touched the side of my face. 'You couldn't be content here, anyway. You're not of this world, you're other, and if you don't go back soon, you'll find yourself unable to live in either.' She stood. 'I must go. There's much to do.'

I walked her to the door. In eighth grade, we studied haiku in English class, and one of them came back to me then. Very gently, I touched one finger to her scabbed mouth. 'When there is love, scars are as pretty as dimples. I love you, Leah.'

She touched my lips as I had touched hers. 'I love you, too.'

She slipped out the door and was gone.

5

The next day Eris and Jaya came to visit, both wearing coveralls and big straw hats. All who worked outside were now wearing hats, because the sun shone every day, as if to make up for the years of clouds, and everyone's skin – not just those of us who had spent a long time in durance vile – was fishbelly white.

We had a pleasant visit. The women chattered away about the work they were doing, and I told them about my recovery, which was almost complete. None of us wanted to talk about Deep Maleen, or the Fair One, or the escape, or the night soldiers. Certainly not about the dead we'd left behind. They laughed when I told them how Stooks had swaggered in. I forbore telling them about my midnight visits from Kellin and Petra – nothing funny about those. I learned that a party of giants had come from Cratchy, to pledge fealty to the new queen.

Jaya spied my pack and knelt before it, gliding her palms over its red nylon body and black nylon straps. Eris was kneeling beside Radar and gliding her hands through her fur.

'Ooo,' Jaya said, 'this is *fine*, Charlie. Was it made where you came from?'

'Yes.' In Vietnam, most likely.

'I'd give a dear lot to have one like.' She lifted it by the straps. 'And so heavy! Can you carry it?'

'I'll manage,' I said, and had to smile. Damn right it was heavy; along with my clothes and Radar's monkey, it contained a solid gold door knocker. Claudia and Woody had insisted I take it.

'When do you leave?' Eris asked.

'Dora tells me that if I can walk to the city gate and back without fainting tomorrow, I can go the day after.'

'So soon?' Jaya asked. 'Too bad! There are parties at night, you know, when the day's work is done.'

'I guess you'll have to party hearty for both of us,' I said.

That night Eris returned. She was alone, her hair was down, she was wearing a pretty dress instead of her working clothes, and she didn't waste time. Or words. 'Will you lie with me, Charlie?'

I said I would be happy to lie with her, if she would excuse any clumsiness, on account of me not having had the pleasure so far in my life.

'Lovely,' she said, and began to unbutton her dress. 'You can pass on what I teach you.'

As to what followed . . . if it was a thank-you fuck, I didn't want to know. And if it was a mercy fuck, all I can say is hooray for mercy.

6

I had two more visitors before I left Lilimar. Claudia came in, leading Woody by the elbow of a black alpaca coat. The scars on Woody's eyes had loosened and pulled apart, but what I could see in the gaps was nothing but white.

'WE CAME TO WISH YOU WELL AND TO THANK YOU!' Claudia boomed. She was close to Woody's left ear, and he pulled back with a little wince. 'WE CAN NEVER THANK YOU ENOUGH, SHARLIE. THERE WILL BE A STATUE OF YOU, NEAR ELSA'S POOL. I HAVE SEEN THE DRAWINGS, AND THEY ARE QUITE—'

'Elsa's dead with a spear in her guts.' I didn't realize I was angry with them until I heard my voice. 'Lots of people are dead. Thousands, tens of thousands for all I know. While you two sat on your hands. Leah I understand. She was blinded by love. She couldn't bring herself to believe her brother was the one who did all this . . . this *shit*. But you two believed, you *knew*, and still you sat on your hands.'

They said nothing. Claudia wouldn't look at me and Woody couldn't.

'You were the royals, the only ones left other than Leah. The only ones that mattered, at least. They would have followed you.'

'No,' Woody said. 'You're wrong, Charlie. Only Leah could rally them. Your coming caused her to do what a queen must do – lead.'

'You never went to her? Told her what her duty was, no matter how much doing it might hurt? You were older, presumably wiser, and you never gave her counsel?'

More silence. They were whole people and thus not cursed with the gray, but they had suffered their own afflictions. I could understand how that had weakened them and made them fearful. But I was still angry.

'She needed you!'

Claudia reached out and took my hands. I almost pulled them away, then didn't. In a soft voice she probably couldn't hear herself, she said, 'No, Sharlie, you were the one she needed. You were the promised prince, and now the promise has been fulfilled. What you say is true – we were weak, we lost our courage. But please don't leave us in anger. Please.'

Did I know before then that a person can choose not to be angry? I don't think I did. What I knew was that I didn't want to leave that way, either.

'All right.' I spoke loud enough for her to hear. 'But only because I lost your three-wheeler.'

She sat back with a smile. Radar had put her nose on Woody's shoe. He bent over to stroke her. 'We can never repay your courage, Charlie, but if there's anything we have that you want, it's yours.'

Well, I had the door knocker, which felt like it weighed about four pounds, and if the price of gold now was roughly the same as it had been when I left Sentry, it was worth about $84,000. Added to the pellets in the bucket, I was pretty well set. Living large in the hood, as they say. But there *was* one thing I could use.

'How about a sledgehammer?'

Not exactly what I said, but they got the idea.

7

I'll never forget the terrible winged thing that tried to emerge from the Dark Well. That's a bad memory. A good one to balance it out was leaving Lilimar the following day. No, *good* isn't good enough.

It's a fine memory, the sort you take out when no one has a kind word for you and life seems as tasteless as a slice of stale bread. It wasn't fine because I was leaving (although I'd be a flat liar if I didn't say how much I was looking forward to seeing my dad); it was fine because I was given a send-off that was fit for . . . I was going to say *fit for a king*, but I guess what I mean is fit for a departing prince who was reverting back to a suburban kid from Illinois.

I was riding shotgun in a cart pulled by a pair of white mules. Dora, wearing her red headscarf and her fine canvas shoes, held the reins. Radar sat behind us, ears up, tail swishing slowly back and forth. Both sides of the Gallien Road were lined with grayfolk. They knelt with their palms to their foreheads as we approached, then stood and cheered as we passed. My surviving mates from Deep Maleen trotted beside us, Eris pushing Doc Freed in his gold-accented wheelchair. She looked up once and tipped me a wink. I tipped her one right back. Above us flew a cloud of monarch butterflies so thick they darkened the sky. Several lit on my shoulders, wings flexing slowly, and one touched down on Radar's head.

Standing at the open gate, wearing a dress the same deep blue as the triple spires had become, the crown of the Galliens on her head, was Leah. Her legs were planted apart in a way that reminded me of how she had stood on the stone stairs above the Dark Well, sword drawn. Resolute.

Dora gigged the mules to a stop. The crowd that had followed us fell silent. In her hands, Leah held a garland of blood-red poppies, the only flowers that had continued to grow during the gray years, and it did not surprise me – nor will it you, I think – to know that the people of Empis called those flowers Red Hope.

Leah raised her voice to be heard by those crowding the street behind us. '*This is Prince Charlie, who now goes to his home! He carries our thanks with him, and my enduring gratitude! Speed him with love, people of Empis! This is my command!*'

They cheered. I bent my head to receive the garland . . . and to hide my tears. Because, you know, in the fairy tales, the prince never cries. Queen Leah kissed me, and although her mouth was broken, that was the best kiss I've ever had, at least since my mother died.

I feel it still.

CHAPTER THIRTY-TWO

Here's Your Happy Ending.

1

On my last night in Empis I stayed where I had on my first, in Dora's little house near the well of the worlds. We ate stew, then went outside to watch the vast wedding band of gold in the sky that had been Bella and Arabella. It was very beautiful, as broken things sometimes are. I wondered again just where this world was, and decided it didn't matter; that it *was*, was enough.

I slept again beside Dora's fireplace, with my head on the pillow with the butterfly appliquéd on it. I slept without night visitors and without bad dreams of Elden or Gogmagog. It was mid-morning when I finally woke up. Dora was hard at work on the sewing machine Mr Bowditch had brought her, a pile of broken shoes to her left and mended ones to her right. I wondered how much longer that trade would last.

We had one final meal together: bacon, thick slices of homemade bread, and an omelet made from goose eggs. When the meal was done, I buckled on Mr Bowditch's gunbelt one last time. Then I dropped to one knee and put my palm to my forehead.

'Nah, nah, Charlie, stand.' Her voice was still choked and furry but improving every day. Every hour, it seemed. I got to my feet. She held out her arms. I didn't just hug her, I picked her up and swung her around, making her laugh. Then she knelt and fed my dog two scraps of bacon from her apron.

'Rayy,' she said, and hugged her. 'I love you, Rayy.'

She walked halfway up the hill with me, toward the hanging vines that covered the entrance to the tunnel. Those vines were greening up now. My pack was heavy on my back, and the sledgehammer I swung from my right hand was heavier, but the sun on my face felt fine.

Dora gave me one final hug, and Radar one final pat. Tears stood in her eyes, but she was smiling. She *could* smile now. I walked the rest of the way on my own and saw another old friend was waiting for us, red against the growing green of the vines. Radar immediately went on her belly. The Snab leaped nimbly onto her back and looked up at me, antennae twitching.

I sat down next to them, slipped off my pack, and unbuckled the flap. 'How are you doing, Sir Snab? Leg all healed up?'

Radar barked once.

'Good, that's good. But this is as far as you go, right? The air of my world might not agree with you.'

Lying on top of the door knocker, wrapped in a Hillview High T-shirt, was what Dora had called an *ay-ye-yi*, which I took to mean *baby light*. She was still having problems with consonants, but I thought that might improve in time. The baby light was a stub of candle inside a round of glass. I put my pack back on, tilted the glass sleeve, and lit the candle with a sulphur match.

'Come on, Rades. It's time.'

She got to her feet. The Snab jumped down. It paused, took one more look at us with its solemn black eyes, then hopped off into the grass. I saw it for a moment longer because it was moving in the still air, and the poppies weren't. Then it was gone.

I took a final look down the hill at Dora's house, which seemed ever so much better – cozier – in the sunshine. Radar looked back, too. Dora waved from beneath her lines of hanging shoes. I waved back. Then I grabbed the sledgehammer and brushed aside the hanging vines, revealing the darkness beyond.

'Want to go home, girl?'

My dog led the way inside.

2

We reached the border between the worlds, and I felt the disorientation I remembered from my other trips. I staggered a little and the baby light went out, even though there was no draft. I told Radar to wait and took another match from one of the empty bullet-loops in Mr Bowditch's concho belt. I struck a light on rough stone and re-lit the candle. The giant bats fluttered and cheeped overhead, then settled. We went on.

When we came to the well with its spiral encirclement of narrow steps, I shielded the candle and looked up, hoping I wouldn't see light filtering down from above. Light would mean someone had moved the boards and bundles of magazines I'd used as camouflage. That would not be good. I thought I did see very faint light, but that was probably okay. The camouflage hadn't been perfect, after all.

Radar went up four or five steps, then looked back at me to see if I was coming. 'Nah, nah, doggie, me first. I don't want you in front of me when we get to the top.'

She obeyed, but very reluctantly. Dogs' noses are at least forty times keener than those of humans. Maybe she could smell her old world up there, waiting. If so, it must have been an aggravating trip for her, because I had to keep stopping to rest. I was better, but not *all* better. Freed had told me to take it easy, and I was trying to follow the doctor's orders.

When we made it to the top, I was relieved to see the final bundle of magazines, the one I'd balanced on my head like a load of wash, still in place. I stayed below it for at least a minute, probably more like two or three. Not just to rest this time. I had been eager to get home and still was, but now I was also scared. And a tiny bit homesick for what I'd left behind. In that world there had been a palace and a beautiful princess and deeds of derring-do. Maybe somewhere – off the coast of Seafront, perhaps – there were still mermaids, singing each to each. In the world below, I'd been a prince. In the one above, I'd have to write college applications and take out the trash.

Radar bumped her muzzle into the back of my knee and gave two sharp barks. Who says dogs can't talk?

'Okay, okay.'

I head-lifted the bundle, stepped up, and shoved it aside. I pushed away the bundles on either side, having to work slowly because my left arm wasn't up to much (it's better now but will never be what it was in my football and baseball days – thanks, Petra, you bitch). Radar gave a few more barks, just to hurry me along. I had no problem slipping between the boards I'd laid over the well's mouth – I had lost a lot of weight during my time in Empis, most of it in Deep Maleen – but I had to wriggle out of the pack first and push it across the floor. By the time I got out, my left arm was singing. Radar popped out after me with disgusting ease. I checked the deep divot Petra's bite had left, afraid the healing wound might have broken open, but it looked okay. What surprised me was how cold it was in the shed. I could see my breath.

The shed was just as I'd left it. The light I'd seen from below was filtering through the cracks in the sides. I tried the door and found it padlocked shut on the outside. Andy Chen had come through for me. I hadn't really believed anyone would check on the abandoned backyard shed for me (or my dead body), but it was still a relief. It meant, however, that I would have to use the sledgehammer. Which I did. One-handed.

Luckily, the boards were old and dry. One cracked on the first blow and broke out on the second, letting in a flood of Illinois daylight . . . and a fine swirl of snow. With Radar barking encouragement I broke through two more. Rades leaped through the gap and immediately squatted to pee. I swung the sledge one more time and knocked out another long piece of board. I tossed my pack through, turned sideways, and stepped out into sunshine. Also into four inches of snow.

3

Radar bounded across the yard, pausing every now and then to bury her snout and fling snow into the air. It was puppy behavior and made me laugh. I was overheated from my climb up the spiral stairs and my work with the sledge, so by the time I got to the back porch I was shivering. It couldn't have been more than twenty-five degrees. Add the strong breeze blowing, and the real temperature was probably half that.

I got the spare key from its spot under the mat (which Mr Bowditch had called the unwelcome mat) and let myself in. The place smelled musty, and it was chilly, but someone – almost certainly my dad – had turned the heat up a little, to keep the pipes from freezing. I remembered seeing an old barncoat in the front closet, and it was still there. Also a pair of galoshes with red woolen socks flopping from the tops. The galoshes were tight on my feet, but I wouldn't be wearing them long. Just down the hill. The gunbelt and revolver went on the closet shelf. I'd put them back in the safe later . . . always assuming the safe with its secret stash was still there.

We went out the back, around the house, and through the gate I'd had to climb over that first time, in response to Radar's howls and Mr Bowditch's weak cries for help. That now seemed like at least a century ago. I started to turn toward Sycamore Street Hill, but something caught my eye. In fact *I* caught my eye. Because it was my face on the phone pole at the intersection of Sycamore and Pine. My Junior Class Photo, it so happened, and the first thing that struck me about it was how young I looked. *There's a kiddie who didn't know nothing about nothing*, I thought. *Maybe he believed he did, but nah, nah.*

In big red letters above the picture: **HAVE YOU SEEN THIS BOY?**

In bright red letters below them: **CHARLES MCGEE READE, AGE 17.**

And below that: **Charles 'Charlie' Reade disappeared in October of 2013. He is 6'4" and weighs 235 pounds. He was last seen . . .**

Et cetera. I got stuck on two things: how weatherbeaten the poster looked, and how wrong it was about my current weight. I looked around, almost expecting to see Mrs Richland staring at me with her hand shading her eyes, but it was just Radar and me standing on the salted sidewalk.

Halfway to the house I stopped, caught by a sudden impulse – wild but strong – to turn around. To go back through the gate at 1 Sycamore, around the house, into the shed, down the winding stairs, and finally into Empis, where I would learn a trade and make a life. Apprentice myself to Freed, perhaps, who would teach me to be a sawbones.

Then I thought of that poster and all the others like it, everywhere in town and all over the county, put up by my father and my Uncle

Bob and my dad's sponsor, Lindy. Maybe all his other AA friends, too. If, that was, he hadn't resumed drinking.

Please God, no.

I started walking again, the buckles of a dead man's galoshes jingling, and the dead man's rejuvenated dog at my heel. Trudging up the hill toward me was a little boy in a quilted red jacket and snowpants. He was dragging a sled by a piece of clothesrope. Probably bound for the sliding hill at Cavanaugh Park.

'Hold up, kiddie.'

He looked at me distrustfully but stopped.

'What day is it?' The words came out smoothly enough, but they seemed to have corners. I suppose that doesn't make any sense, but it's how they felt, and I knew why. I was speaking English again.

He gave me a look that asked if I was born stupid or just grew that way. 'Saturday.'

So my father would be at home, unless he was at an AA meeting.

'What month?'

Now the look said *duh*. 'February.'

'2014?'

'Yuh. Gotta go.'

He went on his way to the top of the hill, sparing my dog and me one distrustful glance back over his shoulder. Probably to make sure we weren't following with ill intent.

February. I'd been gone four months. Strange to think about, but not as strange as the things I'd seen and done.

4

I stood in front of the house for a minute or so, steeling myself to go inside, hoping I wouldn't find my father passed out on the couch with *My Darling Clementine* or *Kiss of Death* playing on TCM. The driveway had been plowed and the walk was shoveled. I told myself that was a good sign.

Radar got tired of waiting for me and ran up the steps, where she sat and waited to be let in. Once upon a time I'd had a key to the door, but it had been lost somewhere along the way. *Like Claudia's trike*, I thought. *Not to mention my virginity*. Turned out it didn't matter.

The door was unlocked. I let myself in, registered the sound of the TV – a news channel, not TCM – and then Radar was running down the hall, barking hello.

When I entered the living room she was on her back paws, the front ones planted on the newspaper my father had been reading. He looked at her and then he looked at me. For a moment he didn't seem to register who was standing in the doorway. When he did, shock loosened the muscles in his face. I'll never forget how that moment of recognition made him look both older – the man he would be in his sixties and seventies – and younger, like the kid he'd been at my age. It was as if some interior sundial turned both ways at once.

'Charlie?'

He started to stand up, but at first his legs wouldn't hold him and he plumped back down again. Radar sat beside his chair, thumping her tail.

'Charlie? Is it really you?'

'It's me, Dad.'

This time he made it to his feet. He was crying. I started to cry, too. He ran for me, stumbled on an endtable, and would have fallen if I hadn't caught him.

'Charlie, Charlie, thank God, I thought you were dead, we all thought that you were . . .'

He couldn't talk anymore. I had a lot to tell him, but right then I couldn't talk, either. We embraced each other over Radar, who got between us, wagging her tail and barking. I think I know what you want, and now you have it.

Here's your happy ending.

EPILOGUE

Questions Asked and Answered (Some, at Least). A Final Trip to Empis.

1

If you think that there are places in this story where it doesn't sound like a young man of seventeen wrote them, you would be right. I returned from Empis nine years ago. Since then I've done a lot of reading and writing. I graduated from NYU *cum laude* (missed *summa* by a hair) with a degree in English. I'm now teaching at the College of Liberal Arts in Chicago, where I hold a well-attended seminar called Myth and Fairy Tales. I am considered quite the bright spark, mostly because of an expanded version of an essay I wrote as a grad student. It was published in *The International Journal of Jungian Studies*. The pay was bupkes, but the critical cred? Priceless. And you want to believe that I cited a certain book whose cover showed a funnel filling up with stars.

Good to know, you might say, *but I have questions.*

You're not the only one. I'd like to know how the reign of Good Queen Leah is going. I'd like to know if the grayfolk are still gray. I'd like to know if Claudia of the Gallien is still blaring. I'd like to know if the way to that horrible underground world – the lair of Gogmagog – has been blocked up. I'd like to know who took care of the remaining night soldiers, and if any of my fellow prisoners from Deep Maleen were in at their finish (probably not, but a man can dream). I'd even like to know how the night soldiers opened our cells the way they did, by just extending their arms.

You'd like to know how Radar's doing, I suppose. The answer is very well, thanks, although she's slowed down a bit; after all, it's been nine years for her, too, which makes her pretty dang old for a German Shepherd, especially if you add her old life and her new one together.

You'd like to know if I told my father where I'd been for those four months. The answer – if I may borrow from the facial expression of a certain small, sled-pulling kiddie – is *duh*. How could I not? Was I supposed to tell him that some miracle drug obtained in Chicago had changed Radar from an elderly arthritic dog at death's door into a hale and hearty German Shep who looked and acted about four?

I didn't tell him everything right away, there was far too much, but I was straight with him about the basics. There was a connection, I said, between our world and another. (I didn't call it Empis, just the Other, which was what I called it when I first came.) I told him I'd gotten there from Mr Bowditch's shed. He listened carefully, then asked me – as you have surely guessed – where I'd *really* been.

I showed him my arm, and the deep divot above my wrist that will remain there for the rest of my life. That didn't convince him. I opened my pack and showed him the gold door knocker. He examined it, hefted it, and suggested – tentatively – that it must be a gilt-coated yardsale item actually made of lead.

'Break it open and see for yourself. Might as well, it'll have to be melted down eventually and sold. There's a bucket of gold pellets in Mr Bowditch's safe from the same place. I'll show you that when you're ready to look. It's what he was living on. I sold some myself to a jeweler in Stantonville. Mr Heinrich. He's dead now, so eventually I guess I'll have to find someone else to do business with.'

That got him a little farther down the road to belief, but what finally convinced him was Radar. She knew her way around our house to all her favorite spots, but the real convincer was the stippling of small scars on her snout from an unfortunate encounter with a porcupine when she was young. (Some dogs never learn about those, but once was enough for Rades.) My dad had noticed them when we were keeping her after Mr Bowditch broke his leg, and after he died – when she was on the verge of stepping out. The same scars remained on the younger version, probably because I'd hauled her off the sundial before she reached and passed the age when she got a noseful of quills. Dad looked at them for a long time, then looked at me with wide eyes.

'This is impossible.'

'I know it seems that way,' I said.

'There's really a bucket of gold in Bowditch's safe?'

'I'll show you,' I repeated. 'When you're ready. I know it's a lot to take in.'

He sat cross-legged on the floor, petting Radar and thinking. After awhile he said, 'This world you claimed to have visited is magic? Like Xanth in those Piers Anthony books you used to read in junior high? Goblins and basilisks and centaurs and all that?'

'Not quite like that,' I said. I'd never seen a centaur in Empis, but if there were mermaids . . . and giants . . .

'Can I go there?'

'I think you have to,' I said. 'At least once.' Because Empis really wasn't much like Xanth. There was no Deep Maleen or Gogmagog in the Piers Anthony books.

We went a week later – the prince who was a prince no longer and Mr George Reade of Reade Insurance. I spent that week at home eating good old American food and sleeping in a good old American bed and answering questions from good old American cops. Not to mention questions from Uncle Bob, Lindy Franklin, Andy Chen, various school administrators, and even Mrs Richland, the neighborhood nosy-parker. By then my father had seen the bucket of gold. I also showed him the baby light, which he examined with great interest.

Do you want to know the story I whomped up with the help of my dad . . . who just happened to be a crack insurance investigator, remember, a guy who knew a lot of the pitfalls liars fall into and thus how to avoid them? Probably you do, but let's just say that amnesia played a part, and add in how Mr Bowditch's dog died in Chicago before I ran into trouble I can't remember (although I *do* seem to remember being conked on the head). The dog my dad and I have now is Radar II. I bet Mr Bowditch, who came back to Sentry as his own son, would have liked that one. Bill Harriman, the reporter from *The Weekly Sun*, asked me for an interview (he must have had an in with one of the cops). I declined. Publicity was the last thing I needed.

Do you wonder what happened to Christopher Polley, the nasty little Rumpelstiltskin who meant to kill me and steal Mr Bowditch's treasure? I did, and a Google search turned up the answer.

If you think back to the beginning of my story, you may remember me being afraid that my father and I would end up homeless, sleeping under an overpass with all our possessions piled in a shopping cart. That didn't happen to us, but it did to Polley (although I don't know about the shopping cart). The police found his body beneath a Tri-State Tollway overpass in Skokie. He had been stabbed repeatedly. Although he carried no wallet or identification, his fingerprints were on file, part of a long arrest record going back to his teens. The news article quoted Skokie Police Captain Brian Baker as saying the victim had been unable to defend himself because he had two broken wrists.

I can tell myself that Polley might not have survived his assailant's attack in any case – there wasn't much to him and I'd taken his gun – but I can't be sure. Nor can I be sure that the motive of the killing was the swag from the jewelry store robbery. Did he talk about it to the wrong person in an attempt to sell it, and pay with his life? I don't know, can't know, but in my heart I'm sure. I'm less sure that he died at the same time Red Molly was batting Peterkin out of her way with enough power to tear that unpleasant dwarf in half, but I think that may have been the way of it.

I can tell myself Polley brought it on himself, and that is true, but when I think of him raising his useless hands to ward off the knife-strokes of whoever was kneeling over him in that trash-littered underpass, I can't help feeling sorry and ashamed. You may say I have no reason to feel shame, that I did what I had to do to save my life and the shed's secret, but shame is like laughter. And inspiration. It doesn't knock.

2

On the Saturday after I came home, a big snowstorm swept in from the Rockies. My father and I tramped up to Mr Bowditch's house – me wearing boots that didn't cramp my feet – and went around to the back. Dad regarded the busted-out side of the shed with disapproval.

'That will have to be repaired.'

'I know, but it was the only way I could get out, once Andy padlocked the door.'

There was no need of the baby light, because we had two flashlights. We had left Radar at home. Once we came out of the tunnel, she would have made straight for the House of Shoes, and I didn't want to see Dora. I didn't want to see anyone from my time there. I just wanted to convince my dad the other world was real and then get out. There was something else, too – strange and probably selfish: I didn't want to hear my father speaking Empisarian. That was mine.

We went down the spiral stairs, me leading. My dad kept saying he couldn't believe it, just couldn't believe it. I hoped to God I wasn't pushing him toward a mental breakdown, but given the stakes, I felt I had no choice.

I still feel that way.

In the tunnel, I told him to shine his light at the stone floor. 'Because there are bats. Big ones. I don't want them flying around us. Also, we're going to come to a place where you may feel dizzy, almost like an out-of-body experience. That's the crossover point.'

'Who made this?' he asked softly. 'Jesus Christ, Charlie, *who made this*?'

'You might as well ask who made the world.'

Ours, and others. I'm sure there are others, maybe as many as there are stars in the sky. We sense them. They funnel down to us in all the old stories.

We came to the crossover, and he would have fallen, but I was ready and put my arm around his waist.

'Maybe we should go back,' he said. 'I feel sick to my stomach.'

'Just a little further. There's light up ahead, see?'

We came to the vines. I brushed them aside and we stepped out into Empis, with a cloudless blue sky above us and Dora's house down the hill. There were no shoes hanging on her crisscrossing lines, but there was a horse grazing near King's Road. The distance was too great to be positive, but I'm pretty sure I knew that horse, and why not? The queen no longer needed Falada to speak for her, and a city is no place for a horse.

My father was looking around, wide-eyed and slack-jawed. Crickets – not red ones – jumped in the grass.

'My God, they're so *big*!'

'You should see the rabbits,' I said. 'Sit down, Dad.' *Before you fall down*, I didn't add.

We sat. I gave him some time to take it in. He asked how there could be *sky* under the *ground*. I said I didn't know. He asked why there were so many butterflies, all of them monarchs, and I told him again that I didn't know.

He pointed at Dora's house. 'Who lives down there?'

'That's Dora's house. I don't know her last name.'

'Is she home? Can we see her?'

'I didn't bring you here for a meet-and-greet, Dad, I brought you so you'd know it's real, and we're never coming here again. No one from our world can know about this one. It would be a disaster.'

'Judging by what we did to a good many indigenous peoples, not to mention our own climate, I'd have to agree with you.' He was starting to take hold, and that was good. I'd been afraid of denial, or a terminal freakout. 'What are you thinking about doing, Charlie?'

'What Mr Bowditch should have done years ago.'

And why hadn't he? I think because of the sundial. *The bad strain that lives in the hearts of every man and woman*, Leah had said.

'Come on, Dad. Let's go back.'

He stood up, but paused for another look when I held aside the vines. 'It's beautiful, isn't it?'

'It is now. And it's going to stay that way.'

We would protect Empis from our world, and also protect our world – at least try – from Empis. Because below Empis is a world of darkness where Gogmagog still lives and rules. It might never escape now that Bella and Arabella have shared a final shattering kiss, but when it comes to such unknowable creatures it's best to be careful. As careful as one can be, at least.

That spring, my dad and I repaired the hole I'd made in the side of the shed. That summer I worked for Cramer Construction – mostly in the office, because of my arm, but I spent a fair number of hardhat hours as well, learning all I could about concrete. A lot of stuff was on good old YouTube, but when you've got an important job to do, there's nothing like practical experience.

Two weeks before I left for my first semester at NYU, Dad and I placed pieces of sheet steel over the mouth of the well. One week before I left, we poured concrete over them and the entire floor of the shed. While it was still wet, I encouraged Radar to put her pawprints in it.

I'm going to tell you the truth: sealing that well under steel and seven inches of concrete hurt my heart. Somewhere down below it is a world full of magic and people I loved. One person in particular. As the concrete flowed sluggishly out of the mixer I'd borrowed from Cramer to do the job, I kept thinking of Leah standing on the stairs, sword drawn, legs braced in a fighting stance. And of how she had cut open her sealed mouth to cry out her brother's name.

I lied just now, okay? My heart didn't just hurt, it cried out *no* and *no* and *no*. It asked how I could leave wonder behind and turn my back on magic. It asked if I really meant to plug the funnel the stars fall through.

I did it because I had to. Dad understood that.

3

Do I dream, you ask? Of course. Some of them are of the thing that came out of the well, and I wake from those with my hands over my mouth to stifle my screams. But as the years pass, those nightmares come less. More often these days I dream of a field blanketed in poppies. I dream of Red Hope.

We did the right thing, I know that. The only thing. And still my dad keeps an eye on the house at 1 Sycamore Street. I come back often and do the same, and eventually I will come back to Sentry for good. I may marry, and if I have children, the house on the hill will go to them. And when they are small, and wonder is all they know, I will read them the old stories, the ones that start *once upon a time*.

November 25th, 2020–February 7th, 2022

ACKNOWLEDGMENTS

I don't think I could have written this book without the help of Robin Furth, my research assistant. She knows more about Empis (and Charlie Reade) than I do. So thanks to her, and thanks also to my wife, Tabby, who gives me time to do this crazy job and dream my crazy dreams. Thanks to Chuck Verrill and Liz Darhansoff, my agents. Thanks are also due to Gabriel Rodríguez and Nicolas Delort, who dressed up my story with wonderful illustrations and made it look like the classic novels of mystery and adventure in days of old, from *Treasure Island* to *Dracula*. Their prodigious talents are on view at the head of each chapter. And I also want to thank you, Constant Reader, for investing your time and imagination in my tale. I hope you enjoyed your visit to that other world.

One other thing: I have a Google Alert on my name, and over the last year I've seen many obituaries of those lost to COVID who have enjoyed my books. *Too* many. I mourn the passing of each one and send condolences to the surviving friends and family members.

Don't miss HOLLY by Stephen King, available from Hodder & Stoughton from September 2023

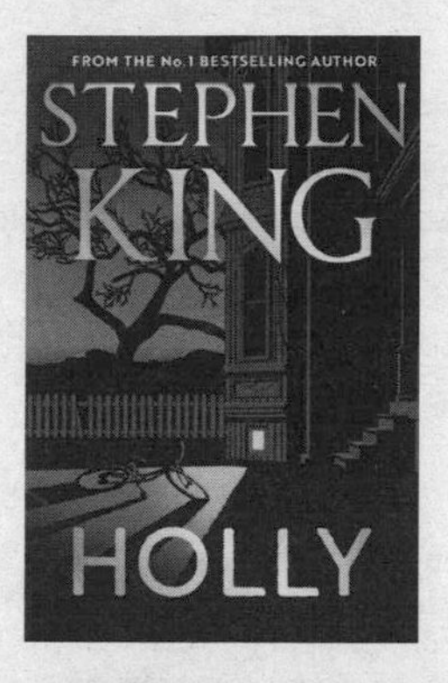

Holly Gibney, one of Stephen King's most compelling and ingeniously resourceful characters, returns in this thrilling novel to solve the gruesome truth behind multiple disappearances in a Midwestern town.

Bonnie Dahl is missing.

Mere blocks from where Bonnie Dahl disappeared live Professors Rodney and Emily Harris. They are the picture of bourgeois respectability: married octogenarians, devoted to each other, and semi-retired lifelong academics. But they are harbouring an unholy secret in the basement of their well-kept, book-lined home, one that may be related to Bonnie's disappearance.

Holly must summon all her formidable talents to outthink and outmanoeuvre the shockingly twisted professors.

'I could never let Holly Gibney go. She was supposed to be a walk-on character in *Mr Mercedes* and she just kind of stole the book and stole my heart. *Holly* is all her' – STEPHEN KING

Turn over to read the opening pages . . .

First published in Great Britain in in 2023 by Hodder & Stoughton
An Hachette UK company

A CIP catalogue record for this title is available from the British Library

Hardback ISBN 978 1 399 71291 0
Trade Paperback ISBN 978 1 399 71292 7
eBook ISBN 978 1 444 73172 9

Typeset in Bembo by Palimpsest Book Production Ltd,
Falkirk, Stirlingshire

Printed and bound in Great Britain by
Clays Ltd, Elcograf S.p.A.

Hodder & Stoughton policy is to use papers that are natural, renewable and recyclable products and made from wood grown in sustainable forests. The logging and manufacturing processes are expected to conform to the environmental regulations of the country of origin.

Hodder & Stoughton Ltd
Carmelite House
50 Victoria Embankment
London EC4Y 0DZ

www.hodder.co.uk

October 17, 2012

1

It's an old city, and no longer in very good shape, nor is the lake beside which it has been built, but there are parts of it that are still pretty nice. Longtime residents would probably agree that the nicest section is Sugar Heights, and the nicest street running through it is Ridge Road, which makes a gentle downhill curve from Bell College of Arts and Sciences to Deerfield Park, two miles below. On its way, Ridge Road passes many fine houses, some of which belong to college faculty and some to the city's more successful businesspeople – doctors, lawyers, bankers, and top-of-the-pyramid business executives. Most of these homes are Victorians, with impeccable paintjobs, bow windows, and lots of gingerbread trim.

The park where Ridge Road terminates isn't as big as the one that sits splat in the middle of Manhattan, but close. Deerfield is the city's pride, and a platoon of gardeners keep it looking fabulous. Oh, there's the unkempt west side near Red Bank Avenue, known as the Thickets, where those seeking or selling drugs can sometimes be found after dark, and where there's the occasional mugging, but the Thickets is only three acres of 740. The rest are grassy, flowery, and threaded with paths where lovers stroll and benches where old men read newspapers (more and more often on electronic devices these days) and women chat, sometimes while rocking their babies back and forth in expensive prams. There are two ponds, and sometimes you'll see men or boys sailing remote-controlled boats on one of them. In the other, swans and ducks glide back and forth. There's a playground for the kiddies, too. Everything, in fact, except a public pool; every now and then the city council discusses the idea, but it keeps getting tabled. The expense, you know.

This night in October is warm for the time of year, but a fine drizzle has kept all but a single dedicated runner inside. That would be Jorge Castro, who has a gig teaching creative writing and Latin American Lit at the college. Despite his specialty, he's American born and bred; Jorge likes to tell people he's as American as *pie de manzana*.

He turned forty in July and can no longer kid himself that he is still the young lion who had momentary bestseller success with his first novel. Forty is when you have to stop kidding yourself that you're still a young anything. If you don't – if you subscribe to such self-actualizing bullshit as 'forty is the new twenty-five' – you're going to find yourself starting to slide. Just a little at first, but then a little more, and all at once you're fifty with a belly poking out your belt buckle and cholesterol-busters in the medicine cabinet. At twenty, the body forgives. At forty, forgiveness is provisional at best. Jorge Castro doesn't want to turn fifty and discover he's become just another American manslob.

You have to start taking care of yourself when you're forty. You have to maintain the machinery, because there's no trade-in option. So Jorge drinks orange juice in the morning (potassium) followed most days by oatmeal (antioxidants), and keeps red meat to once a week. When he wants a snack, he's apt to open a can of sardines. They're rich in Omega 3s. (Also tasty!) He does simple exercises in the morning and runs in the evening, not overdoing it but aerating those forty-year-old lungs and giving his forty-year-old heart a chance to strut its stuff (resting heart rate: 63). Jorge wants to look and feel forty when he gets to fifty, but fate is a joker. Jorge Castro isn't even going to see forty-one.

2

His routine, which holds even on a night of fine drizzle, is to run from the house he shares with Freddy (theirs, at least, for as long as the writer-in-residence gig lasts), half a mile down from the college, to the park. There he'll stretch his back, drink some of the Vitaminwater stored in his fanny pack, and jog back home. The drizzle is actually invigorating, and there are no other runners, walkers, or bicyclists to weave his way through. The bicyclists are the worst, with their insistence that they have every right to ride on the sidewalk instead of in the street, even though there's a bike lane. This evening he has the sidewalk all to himself. He doesn't even have to wave to people who might be taking the night air on their grand old shaded porches; the weather has kept them inside.

All but one: the old poet. She's bundled up in a parka even though it's still in the mid-fifties at eight o'clock, because she's down to a hundred and ten pounds (her doctor routinely scolds her about her weight) and she feels the cold. Even more than the cold, she feels the damp. Yet she stays, because there's a poem to be had tonight, if she can just get her fingers under its lid and open it up. She hasn't written one since midsummer and she needs to get something going before the rust sets in. She needs to *represent*, as her students sometimes say. More importantly, this could be a *good* poem. Maybe even a *necessary* poem.

It needs to begin with the way the mist revolves around the streetlights across from her and then progress to what she thinks of as *the mystery*. Which is everything. The mist makes slowly moving halos, silvery and beautiful. She doesn't want to use *halos*, because that's the expected word, the lazy word. Almost a cliché. *Silvery*, though . . . or maybe just silver . . .

Her train of thought derails long enough to observe a young man (at eighty-nine, forty seems very young) go slap-slapping by on the other side of the road. She knows who he is; the resident writer who thinks Gabriel García Márquez hung the moon. With his long dark hair and little pussy-tickler of a mustache, he reminds the old poet of a charming character in *The Princess Bride*: 'My name is Inigo Montoya, you killed my father, prepare to die.' He's wearing a yellow jacket with a reflective stripe running down the back and ridiculously tight running pants. He's going like a house afire, the old poet's mother might have said. Or like the clappers.

Clappers makes her think of bells, and her gaze returns to the streetlight directly across from her. She thinks, *The runner doesn't hear silver above him / These bells don't ring.*

It's wrong because it's prosy, but it's a start. She has managed to get her fingers under the lid of the poem. She needs to go inside, get her notebook, and start scratching. She sits a few moments longer, though, watching the silver circles revolve around the streetlights. *Halos*, she thinks. *I can't use that word, but that's what they look like, goddammit.*

There is a final glimpse of the runner's yellow jacket, then he's gone into the dark. The old poet struggles to her feet, wincing at the pain in her hips, and shuffles into her house.

3

Jorge Castro kicks it up a bit. He's got his second wind now, lungs taking in more air, endorphins lit up. Just ahead is the park, scattered with old-fashioned lamps that give off a mystic yellow glow. There's a small parking lot in front of the deserted playground, now empty except for a passenger van with its side door open and a ramp sticking out onto the wet asphalt. Near its foot is an elderly man in a wheelchair and an elderly woman down on one knee, fussing with it.

Jorge pulls up for a moment, bending over, hands grasping his legs just above the knees, getting his breath back and checking out the van. The blue and white license plate on the back has a wheelchair logo on it.

The woman, who is wearing a quilted coat and a kerchief, looks over at him. At first Jorge isn't sure he knows her – the light in this small auxiliary parking lot isn't that good. 'Hello! Got a problem?'

She stands up. The old guy in the wheelchair, dressed in a button-up sweater and flat cap, gives a feeble wave.

'The battery died,' the woman says. 'It's Mr Castro, isn't it? Jorge?'

Now he recognizes her. It's Professor Emily Harris, who teaches English literature . . . or did; she might now be emerita. And that's her husband, also a teacher. He didn't realize Harris was disabled, hasn't seen him around campus much, different department in a different building, but believes the last time he did, the old guy was walking. Jorge sees her quite often at various faculty get-togethers and culture-vulture events. Jorge has an idea he's not one of her favorite people, especially after the departmental meeting about the now-defunct Poetry Workshop. That one got a little contentious.

'Yes, it's me,' he says. 'I'm assuming you two would like to get home and dry off.'

'That would be nice,' Mr Harris says. Or maybe he's also a professor. His sweater is thin and he's shivering a little. 'Think you could push me up that ramp, kiddo?' He coughs, clears his throat, coughs again. His wife, so crisp and authoritative in department meetings, looks a bit lost and bedraggled. Forlorn. Jorge wonders how long they've been out here, and why she didn't call someone for help. *Maybe she doesn't have a phone*, he thinks. *Or left it at home. Old people can be forgetful about such things*. Although she can't be much more than seventy. Her husband in the wheelchair looks older.

'I think I can help with that. Brake off?'

'Yes, certainly,' Emily Harris says, and stands back when Jorge grabs the handles and swings the wheelchair around so it faces the ramp. He rolls it back ten feet, wanting to get a running start. Motorized wheelchairs can be heavy. The last thing he wants is to get it halfway up only to lose momentum and have it roll back. Or, God forbid, tip over the side and spill the old guy on the pavement.

'Here we go, Mr Harris. Hang on, there may be a bump.'

Harris grasps the side-rails, and Jorge notices how broad his shoulders are. They look muscular beneath the sweater. He guesses that people who lose the use of their legs compensate in other ways. Jorge speeds at the ramp.

'Hi-yo Silver!' Mr Harris cries cheerfully.

The first half of the ramp is easy, but then the chair starts to lose momentum. Jorge bends, puts his back into it, and keeps it rolling. As he does this neighborly chore, an odd thought comes to him: this state's license plates are red and white, and although the Harrises live on Ridge Road just like he does (he often sees Emily Harris out in her garden), the plates on their van are *blue* and white, like those of the neighboring state to the west. Something else that's strange: he can't remember ever seeing this van on the street before, although he's seen Emily sitting ramrod straight behind the wheel of a trim little Subaru with an Obama sticker on the back bum—

As he reaches the top of the ramp, bent almost horizontal now, arms outstretched and running shoes flexed, a bug stings the back of his neck. Feels like a big one from the way heat is spreading out from the source, maybe a wasp, and he's having a reaction. Never had one before but there's a first time for everything and all at once his vision is blurring and the strength is going out of his arms. His shoes slip on the wet ramp and he goes to one knee.

Wheelchair's going to backroll right on top of me—

But it doesn't. Rodney Harris flips a switch and the wheelchair rolls inside with a contented hum. Harris hops out, steps spryly around it, and looks down at the man kneeling on the ramp with his hair plastered to his forehead and drizzle wetting his cheeks like sweat. Then Jorge collapses on his face.

'Look at that!' Emily cries softly. 'Perfect!'

'Help me,' Rodney says.

His wife, wearing her own running shoes, takes Jorge's ankles. Her husband takes his arms. They haul him inside. The ramp retracts. Rodney (who really is also Professor Harris, as it happens) slides into the leftside captain's chair. Emily kneels and zip-ties Jorge's wrists together, although this is probably a needless precaution. Jorge is out like a light (a simile of which the old poet would surely disapprove) and snoring heavily.

'All good?' asks Rodney Harris, he of the Bell College Life Sciences Department.

'All good!' Emily's voice is cracking with excitement. 'We did it, Roddy! We caught the son of a bitch!'

'Language, dear,' Rodney says. Then he smiles. 'But yes. Indeed we did.' He pulls out of the parking lot and starts up the hill.

The old poet looks up from her work notebook, which has a picture of a tiny red wheelbarrow on the front, sees the van pass, and bends back to her poem.

The van turns in at 93 Ridge Road, home of the Harrises for almost twenty-five years. It belongs to them, not the college. One of the two garage doors goes up; the van enters the bay on the left; the garage door closes; all is once more still on Ridge Road. Mist revolves around the streetlights.

Like halos.

Stephen King

Iconic Stories

STEPHEN KING
THRILLING SUSPENSE

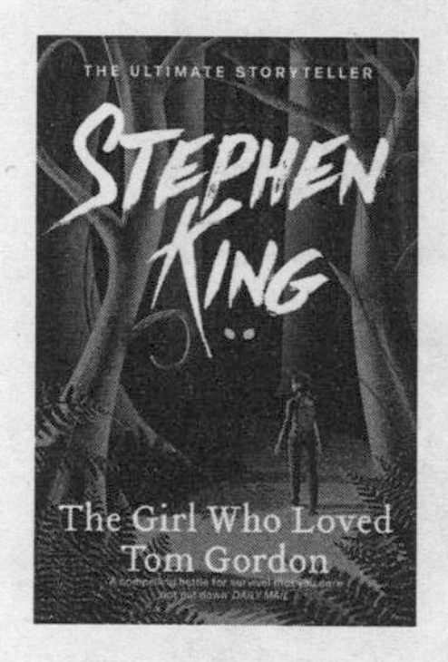

H
HODDER

STEPHEN KING

SCIENCE FICTION, ADVENTURE AND FANTASY

ACCLAIMED NON-FICTION